ADVANCE PRAISE

✦

"*Gods, Heroes, and Monsters: A Sourcebook of Greek, Roman, and Near Eastern Myths* successfully reflects the current trend in Classical Studies toward viewing the ancient Mediterranean as an interconnected world, one in which people and texts circulated widely. By bringing such a rich variety of texts and mythological traditions together in translation, this collection will make it possible to offer the introductory student a rich and complicated view of the ways in which the different cultures of the ancient Mediterranean interacted and influenced each other over time."

CAROL DOUGHERTY
William R. Kenan, Jr. Professor of Classical Studies, Wellesley College

"López-Ruiz has created an outstanding resource for the study of Classical mythology in a wider historical and geographical framework. With authoritative introductions placing each document in context, solid translations, and helpful annotations, this volume at last provides a convenient way to introduce students to the Mediterranean and Near Eastern antecedents of ancient Greek and Roman myths."

DEBORAH LYONS
Miami University (Ohio)

"In 1984, Walter Burkert argued that Greek myths ought to be viewed in a broad Near Eastern perspective. In this important new volume, Carolina López-Ruiz presents a unique compendium of Egyptian, Hittite, Ugaritic, Biblical, Greek, and Roman sources that enable us to study the connections further. It includes many rarely or never before published texts in English enhanced by authoritative introductions and organized in novel ways that strike a good balance between student accessibility and high-level scholarship."

NANNO MARINATOS
University of Illinois, Chicago

GODS,
HEROES,
AND
MONSTERS

A SOURCEBOOK of

GREEK,

ROMAN, and

NEAR EASTERN

MYTHS

✦ in Translation ✦

Edited by
CAROLINA LÓPEZ-RUIZ
The Ohio State University

GODS,
HEROES,
AND
MONSTERS

NEW YORK   OXFORD
OXFORD UNIVERSITY PRESS

Oxford University Press is a department of the University of Oxford.
It furthers the University's objective of excellence in research,
scholarship, and education by publishing worldwide.

Oxford   New York
Auckland   Cape Town   Dar es Salaam   Hong Kong   Karachi
Kuala Lumpur   Madrid   Melbourne   Mexico City   Nairobi
New Delhi   Shanghai   Taipei   Toronto

With offices in
Argentina   Austria   Brazil   Chile   Czech Republic   France   Greece
Guatemala   Hungary   Italy   Japan   Poland   Portugal   Singapore
South Korea   Switzerland   Thailand   Turkey   Ukraine   Vietnam

For titles covered by Section 112 of the US Higher Education Opportunity
Act, please visit www.oup.com/us/he for the latest information about
pricing and alternate formats.

Published by Oxford University Press
198 Madison Avenue, New York, New York 10016
http://www.oup.com

Library of Congress Cataloging-in-Publication Data

Lopez-Ruiz, Carolina.
  Gods, heroes, and monsters : a sourcebook of Greek, Roman, and Near
Eastern myths in translation / edited by Carolina Lopez-Ruiz.
      pages cm
  Includes bibliographical references and index.
  ISBN 978-0-19-979735-6
1. Mythology, Greek. 2. Mythology, Roman. 3. Mythology, Egyptian.
4. Mythology, Assyro-Babylonian. I. Title.
  BL312.L66 2014
  201'.3–dc23   2013016588

Printing number: 9 8 7 6 5 4 3 2 1
Printed in the United States of America on acid-free paper

Cover Image: Shroud showing the deceased between Osiris and Anubis. Painting on linen. Ptolemaic Egypt,
180 BCE. *Aegyptisches Museum, Staatliche Museen, Berlin, Germany. Photo Credit: Erich Lessing / Art Resource, NY*
Inside Front Cover Map: The Near East and the Mediterranean in the Late Bronze Age
Inside Back Cover Map: The Mediterranean in the Archaic Period, eighth–sixth centuries BCE

✦ To my children, Alfonso and Sarah ✦

CONTENTS

✦

✦

PART SEVEN   PLATO'S MYTHS   535

✦

✦

LIST OF MAPS

✦

LIST OF FIGURES

✦

INTRODUCTION

✦

UNLIKE other introductions to classical mythology, this volume sets itself apart by systematically including, alongside more familiar Greek and Roman texts, comparable narratives from the ancient Near East, specifically from Mesopotamia, Egypt, the Hittite kingdom, Ugarit, Phoenicia, and from Israel. These sources amount to about one third of the volume you are holding. This more comprehensive approach requires some explanation, especially for readers who might intuitively associate the term "classical" or even "ancient" with the literatures of Greece and Rome.

The premise of this anthology reflects our increased knowledge of the interconnected cultures of the ancient world and the growing realization that the mythological narratives of Greece and Rome evolved from and were in dialogue with their counterparts in the ancient Near East. Moreover, in the critical and most creative period, reaching from the mid-second to the late first millennium BCE, Greece and Rome participated in a world whose center of gravity lay to their east, in the arc from the Nile to Mesopotamia. This volume, therefore, proposes a reconsideration of the "classical." The *Epic of Gilgamesh*, from Mesopotamia, was, after all, a true "classic" in its time, required reading for all who claimed to be educated. It was translated into a host of languages and used in schools throughout the Near East and beyond, and it is now becoming clear that it also directly influenced Greek heroic motifs. Many mythological stories were shaped in response to each other, not only within the region where they originated but across languages and peoples and down through the centuries. Even with the dramatic changes that Christianity and Islam brought, so-called pagan myths and even religious practices adapted to the new religions and survived.

Why have the Near Eastern masterpieces, then, not been considered "classical"? The fates of these literatures were shaped by historical developments. First, the more ancient languages of the Near East had more time in which to change, to be overridden, and even lost, as happened to Sumerian and Akkadian, whereas more recent ones, such as Greek and Latin, were encoded as the official languages of the two halves of the Roman Empire, and so their literatures survived. The Hebrew Bible obviously has its own remarkable history of transmission and preservation, but that also required a continuous investment of effort by later generations. Greek and

Latin texts were copied and used for educational purposes in the Greek-speaking eastern Roman Empire (Byzantium) and in the medieval Latin West. It was this part of the world in which the modern nations of Europe developed, and it is from them that our traditions of scholarship derive, including our notion of the "classical."

By contrast, Mesopotamian, Egyptian, and other non–Greco-Roman texts were excluded from this canon, at least in their original languages. By the time of Thucydides and Herodotos, composers of the first histories, some early civilizations of the ancient Near East, such as those of Ugarit and the Hittites, had long since disappeared, both destroyed in wars and unknown to Greeks of the "classical" period, though the legacies of these lost cultures partly survived in Anatolia and Syro-Palestine. Later Near Eastern cultures, such as neo-Assyrian, neo-Babylonian, Phoenician, and Egyptian, were eventually subsumed into the Hellenistic and Roman empires. Their texts, at least those that survived inscribed on papyri, stone monuments, or clay tablets, were buried and had to wait for millennia before they could be uncovered and deciphered. (Paradoxically, tablets from these lost cultures were often preserved by the very same fires that destroyed them, since the fires "cooked" the sun-dried clay.) Thus, as the great literary traditions of the Near East fell into oblivion, the Greek and Latin "classics" were codified and partially preserved for posterity. Their uninterrupted transmission in manuscript form, thanks in large part to the efforts of Arab scholars during the ninth and tenth centuries CE, ensured that they would be studied and commented upon. In the process, they exerted powerful influence on philosophy, literature, and the arts, inspiring such movements as the Renaissance, the Enlightenment, and Romanticism.

During this long period of time, stretching over a thousand years, little was known about ancient Near Eastern cultures. In the Western view of history, ideas about the ancient Near East were principally represented by whatever classical historians (mostly Herodotos) and the Hebrew Bible had to say about them. This changed dramatically with the beginning of archaeological exploration in the nineteenth century, enabled first by Napoleon's campaign in Ottoman Egypt (1798–1801) and the excavation of Mesopotamian sites in the nineteenth century by European diplomats and explorers, who thus became the first archaeologists. The decipherment of Egyptian hieroglyphs by Jean-François Champollion in 1822 and of cuneiform tablets from Mesopotamia in the 1850s opened up a whole new phase in our knowledge of these languages and cultures. Additional sites, cultures, and languages, including Hittite and Ugaritic, were discovered in the twentieth century. Tablets and even archives continue to appear today, enriching our **corpus** of Near Eastern literatures and filling in the blanks of the mosaic of ancient cultures, forcing us to reconsider their legacy and mutual interrelations.

But by the time this amazing process of discovery began to peak in the nineteenth century, the concept of Greco-Roman literature as "classical" was too entrenched to readily make room for the "oriental" newcomers. Ancient literature was perceived as a fundamentally "Western" inheritance. Preconceived dichotomies between East and West, rooted entirely in the political and religious developments of the Middle Ages (especially the conflict with Islam) and the advent of "modernity" (especially the "Eastern Question" regarding the dissolution of the Ottoman Empire), greatly impacted the classification of cultures and literatures. In recent decades, however, increasing collaboration and dialogue between the fields of Classics and Near Eastern studies is bringing us closer to a more accurate and comprehensive view of the ancient world and the different ways in which its inhabitants, their literatures, and intellectual traditions interacted.

Independent developments within the field of Classical Studies have encouraged such collaboration, though more always remains to be done. Specifically, for the past half-century classical Greece has gradually ceased to be regarded as a singular exemplar of virtuous qualities such as freedom, democracy, purity, and reason. Historical scholarship has broken down this notion, and at the same time it has removed some of the barriers that had been erected around classical culture to keep it free of contamination by the "Other," such as the Semitic cultures of the Near East. One of these barriers was the theory that Greece should be classified among the Indo-European cultures, together with Celtic, Nordic, and Aryan-Indian. While it is true that the Greek language is part of the Indo-European language family, a genetic model cannot be so easily transferred to its culture as a whole. The selection of texts in this volume is premised on scholarship that finds that Greek mythology developed within its contemporary Near Eastern context and borrowed extensively from it.

This immediately raises the problematic concept of "influence." There are, of course, cases of direct influence or simple diffusion, but we are mostly dealing with texts that are far apart in time and space: narrative themes and elements would normally have passed through many stages of adaptation, usually oral, before they acquired their final form (i.e., the written version that we have). And adaptation means that they would have been thoroughly formatted to fit their new host culture and the narrative goals of each poet, bard, or writer. Sometimes the direction of transmission can be ascertained: for example, the Mesopotamian flood story was adopted in ancient Israel and Greece, the Greek myths were taken up and reworked by the Romans, and so on. Still, it is in the variations and adaptations themselves that we can appreciate the uniqueness of each act of reception. Every instance, every text, is a unique literary artifact, and many of them have generated whole disciplines of study. With their fascinating similarities and sharp contrasts, the texts gathered here represent some of the most famous stories that have fueled the imaginations of generations across the Mediterranean and the lands of the Fertile Crescent for millennia.

✦

THE stories we call "myths" were much more than entertaining tales. The Greek word *mythos*, which was eventually attached to fictional or legendary stories, was in earlier times used for any speech, utterance, or narrative. For the ancients, what we call "myths" were stories *about gods and heroes,* stories valued and preserved as part of the tradition of particular communities, for whom these stories were inseparable from all central aspects of culture. Gods were real (worshipped, prayed to, feared) in a world organized to a great degree around religious festivals and daily rituals. Heroes, on the other hand, were central in ancient people's perception of their remote past and their recent history as well (stories about city founders, lawgivers, beginnings of institutions, etc.). In Near Eastern cultures, with Mesopotamia as the greatest example, king lists, rituals, law codes, and historical events were written down at the same time as epic stories and cosmogonies. But in Greece before the eighth century BCE no written records preserved information (except for Linear B texts, which apparently were for purely administrative purposes). Hence "myths" alone carried the torch of community memory for centuries, preserving and reshaping genealogies and ideas of origins of whole cities and peoples (whether true or invented) and explaining the current religious order. Myths did more than reinforce abstract theological beliefs; they explained the role of festivals and ritual practices and provided narratives to which people pinned their beliefs in the afterlife. However, while myths were the prime carrier for narratives and beliefs about the gods, we should be cautious about reading them as ancient "doctrine": these narratives were malleable, and there was no Scripture or official Church. Not everyone even believed that Homer and Hesiod had accurately represented the gods (especially the philosophers, such as Xenophanes and Plato).

Even as mythical narrative gradually became distinct from other historical, scientific, philosophical discourse, myths still had a place in the new literary and intellectual modes, as shown by the self-conscious use of myths in Herodotos, as well as Livy's histories and in Plato's philosophical dialogues. Far from being discarded in the light of "reason," narratives called myths could be used to express higher truths, and in turn myths have continued to be studied as containing "hidden" and deeper messages for centuries, whether through allegorical interpretations in antiquity and the Middle Ages or through psychoanalytical, anthropological, and structuralist approaches (among others) today. These multi-faceted and porous narratives were in continuous dialogue with the realities of people's lives and beliefs: myths helped to create the mindscapes of ancient peoples, offered some stability to the universe's ungraspable nature, while, in turn, the changing world continuously reshaped the myths as needed. The subject of the use and meaning of myths is vast, and the reader will find suggested readings in the Bibliography at the back of this volume.

How This Book Is Organized

SELECTIONS are always difficult to make, and choice requires exclusion. My guiding principle was to represent major themes and myths around which Near Eastern, Greek, and Roman texts coalesce. Another goal was to include at least some entire books or self-contained sections in them, tablets, or poems when possible, while avoiding the complete texts of accessible classical works that can easily be assigned separately to complement the present selection, such as the poems of Homer, the Greek tragedies, and Hellenistic and Roman epics. Hence, the Trojan War is represented here by one book of the *Iliad* only, and some important mythical clusters have been omitted, among them the Theban saga, including the Seven Against Thebes and the Oedipus story (best represented in the tragedies by Aeschylus and Sophocles). Likewise, the Argonauts' myth (best treated in Apollonios Rhodios' epic poem *Argonautika*) is here only briefly quoted in Part One and alluded to by Jason and Medea in Euripides' *Medea* (in Part Five). Within each thematic section or part, the texts are arranged by cultures (Mesopotamian, Egyptian, other Near Eastern texts, then Greek, then Roman) and in a roughly (not always strict) chronological order (archaic Greek before classical, and so on).

The introductions to each of the seven thematic sections and the headnotes that accompany each document are addressed to nonspecialists, especially undergraduate students and the general public. I avoid entering into detailed discussions and theoretical interpretations. The goal is to offer guidance for the major motifs and facilitate comprehension, contextualization, and cross-textual comparison. Rather more detail has been allowed for texts that are less well known outside specialized circles, such as the Ugaritic, Phoenician, Egyptian, and Hittite sources. Footnotes are also minimal and intended to clarify obscure references and occasionally provide background as well as cross-references to other sections in the book. Beyond that, each instructor can decide how much general historical, archaeological, and theoretical background to include in his or her lectures. The independent reader will find an essential list of readings for all authors and texts in the Bibliography, which can serve as a point of departure for a more profound exploration. I have privileged monographs over articles or collections of essays when possible, and English and recent books where available. Other aids, such as maps (including two historical maps) and a timeline, will help the reader situate the texts in their historical context. Because the book covers a wide range of cultures, genealogical charts of the Greek gods are not included. Greek myths represent just one genealogical tradition, and so to represent all of the divine family trees included in this volume would have been extremely complicated and not especially helpful. Instead, I hope the reader will benefit from a Glossary at the back of the volume that explains technical terms used in scholarship (terms are highlighted in bold the first time they appear in the text) as well as an Index of Place Names and Characters.

The seven parts in the book are not mutually exclusive, as stories normally touch on many themes that resist strict classification. The intention was to group together those stories that have a core theme in common, so as to facilitate and stimulate comparison across traditions. Plato's myths, on the other hand, have been included in a separate section, even though each one corresponds to one of the thematic sections of the book. It seemed appropriate to group Plato's stories together in this way so that they could be approached holistically, via a single introduction. In any event, the broad thematic organization of *Gods, Heroes, and Monsters* does not preclude reading the stories in a different order or in combination with other texts not included here.

In principle, I have chosen texts that are literary elaborations of a myth, avoiding as much as possible ancient "encyclopedic entries" such as we find in Apollodorus, which I have used very selectively. For instance, I have generally privileged Ovid's poetic retelling of a Greek myth over Apollodorus', and I have chosen Statius' *Achilleid* over the summaries of the lost Epic Cycle poems. In other words, this anthology is conceived as a reader of ancient mythological *literature* and is not simply a myth sourcebook. It is for this reason that nonliterary inscriptions and other sources such as the bureaucratic Linear B tablets have been avoided. Egypt presents a special case in that, despite its vast corpus of texts written in a variety of ways (on papyri, walls of pyramids and other buildings, inside the panels of coffins, etc.), mythical narratives are usually not directly represented, especially in the earlier periods. To quote Ian Shaw (2004: 116), "Egyptian texts have a tendency to allude to various divine myths through references to rituals and the use of various epithets, but their literature is notoriously lacking in straightforward narrative-style myths. Reconstructing Egyptian mythology from ancient texts can be rather like piecing together the biblical account of the birth of Jesus from a series of Christmas cards and carols."

Regarding the translations themselves, a substantial contribution of this volume is that it offers new translations of important Egyptian, Hittite, and Ugaritic mythological texts that are generally not accessible to the public. Experts in these fields, such as Sam Meier (North-West Semitic) and Andrés de Diego (Egypt), have contributed new translations that reflect the latest advances in their fields. In the case of the Hittite texts, Mary Bachvarova has even offered a critical edition in which she produces new readings and proposes new reconstructions and arrangements of the fragments. For the translation of another fragmentary text, the Derveni Papyrus, two leading experts in that field, Alberto Bernabé and Miguel Herrero, have also contributed the latest readings of the damaged text. Other Greek texts have also been translated afresh by myself (Hesiod and the Homeric Hymns being my area of expertise in archaic literature), while new rhythmic translations of one book of Homer's *Iliad* and two of the *Odyssey* have been generously provided by Barry B. Powell, whose complete translations of the two works will appear soon with this press. Mark Anderson, a specialist in Greek philosophy, has translated Plato's myths. The translations of Pindar and Lucretius are also fresh contributions by Hanne Eissenfeld, who is currently working on Pindar. As for the general introductions to the thematic sections, those of Parts One to Six have been written by myself, while the shorter (section) introductions have been provided by the individual translators (but I introduce the Homeric passages) and by myself (all other texts).

Some translations for other texts have been taken from the Oxford's World Classics series, for instance, the Mesopotamian texts by Stephanie Dalley, Virgil's *Aeneid* (set in rhythmic verse by Frederick Ahl), and Apuleius' *Golden Ass* (by P. G. Walsh). I am also indebted to their notes, which I condensed and adapted. Minor editorial changes to these translations include regularization of the spelling and punctuation to conform to standard American practice. (See also the Note on Text Arrangement, Transliterations, and Chronology on page xxiii.)

Finally, in order to keep the cost of the anthology within limits, translations have been reused and adapted from the older volumes of the Loeb series and other out-of-copyright editions, usually for Latin texts, for instance, Ovid's *Metamorphoses* by F. J. Miller and Apollodoros' *Library* by J. Frazer, which are not inferior to more recent versions. In any event, the language has been updated to remove any archaisms. I also have annotated all of these texts, generally by using select notes from the existing edition, sometimes shortening them or adding my own clarifications.

ACKNOWLEDGMENTS

✦

THIS VOLUME would not have been realized without the vision, guidance, and contagious enthusiasm of executive editor Charles Cavaliere. I also thank other staff of Oxford University Press for their hard work at different stages of the edition and production, especially assistant editor Lauren Aylward, editorial assistant Karen Omer, production editor Shelby Peak, and photo researcher Francelle Carapetyan. In its early stages, this project greatly benefitted from comments and suggestions provided by several readers. I thank:

Eve A. Browning
   (University of Minnesota, Duluth)
Cristina Calhoon
   (University of Oregon)
Kevin Crotty
   (Washington and Lee University)
Fritz Graf
   (The Ohio State University)

Deborah Lyons
   (Miami University, Ohio)
Robin Mitchell-Boyask
   (Temple University)
Carl Ruck
   (Boston University)
Jackie Murray
   (Skidmore College)

I also thank those readers who wished to remain anonymous.

I cannot express enough gratitude to the wonderful and disciplined team of translators who contributed to this volume: Mark Anderson, Mary Bachvarova, Alberto Bernabé, Andrés Diego Espinel, Hanne Eisenfeld, Miguel Herrero de Jáuregui, Sam Meier, and Barry Powell. Other colleagues have given me invaluable advice on various matters connected with their areas of expertise (the more or less virtuous use of which is, of course, my own responsibility). My sincere gratitude goes to Simeon Chavel, Richard Fletcher, William Hansen, Tom Hawkins, Bruce Heiden, Robert Ritner, Andrea Seri, and Christopher Woods. I also thank Hanne Eisenfeld for her help with some editing and Justin Hanson for his help with the index. Ben Acosta-Hughes, Chair of OSU's Classics Department, has my deep gratitude for his support, especially during the last months of editing work, as do our assistants Erica Kallis and Wayne Lovely. Finally, as steady and patient as ever, Anthony Kaldellis has helped me make this project better in innumerable ways, especially with his careful reading of all my introductions. In case I forget to tell you every day, *gracias*.

I dedicate this volume to my children, Alfonso and Sarah, because stories, including these ones, entertained children for millennia and shaped the world they inherited, but also because in the last two years they had to share their mother's attention with these ancient authors. Thank *you*.

CAROLINA LÓPEZ-RUIZ
Columbus, Ohio
April 2013

NOTE ON TEXT ARRANGEMENT, TRANSLITERATIONS, AND CHRONOLOGY

✦

CUNEIFORM texts were written on clay tablets and arranged by columns. In Mesopotamian literary texts, the lines of those columns usually corresponded with verses. These verses, as in all Semitic languages (e.g., Ugaritic and Hebrew), do not constitute metrical units (like Greek verses), in terms of either syllable count or length (short-long syllable-alternation), nor are they marked by rhyme patterns. Instead, poetic language is marked by alliteration, the repetition of words or variations on the same idea (parallelism), metaphors, comparisons, and wordplay. Groups of lines are often united by sense and stylistic features, forming stanzas, which editors represent in clusters of lines or paragraphs, if space permits. In our case, these line (verse) divisions in the tablets have been sacrificed in favor of a more economical, run-in format. Ugaritic texts are less consistent than Mesopotamian in their verse/line arrangements, and the editors have had to choose how to group the lines. The translations for Ugaritic are in continuous lines as well. But precisely because of its nonmetric nature, most of the poetic language of these texts can be appreciated regardless of the line divisions. Even in the case of Greek poetry, which is metrical, a continuous (prose-like) translation has been chosen for Hesiod, the *Homeric Hymns*, and sections of tragedies, for only a poetic translation in English would really reflect the verse structure. Line divisions are, therefore, retained here only in those translations written in English verse (e.g., B. B. Powell's Homeric passages and F. Ahl's *Aeneid's* passages). Verse numbers in translations are often approximate and do not necessarily coincide exactly with the Greek divisions, as translators might break the lines differently for the sake of syntactical clarity.

Square brackets [. . .] indicate *lacunae* (gaps) in the text, whether these are a damaged word or a number of missing words, regardless of the length of the gap. When more than one line is missing, it is indicated by the translator or the editor. Other clarifications about the text or summaries of omitted sections are also inserted in parentheses and italics outside the translation. A parenthetical clarification is occasionally inserted in the translation by the translator or myself, for example, "the god (Apollo) said . . . " That means the clarification is not in the text but supplied when the reference is not clear.

✦

For the sake of simplicity, Near Eastern names and untranslatable words have been transliterated without using special diacritical signs, which are used by experts to represent particular characters and sounds with no equivalent in English. Since nonspecialists would not know what to make of these marks, I have decided to omit them.

Recent trends increasingly favor avoiding the Latinization of Greek names. I have rendered Greek names as close to their original forms as possible (Tartaros, Kottos, Boiotia, and not the Latinized Tartarus, Cottus, Boeotia), allowing for occasional exceptions in the case of very well-known Latinized names (Cyprus not Kypros, Achilles not Achilleus). I have standardized this spelling across all Greek translations, maintaining the Latin renderings of Greek names (Aeneas, Olympus) only when they appear in the works of Latin authors.

✦

Despite appearances, the chronology and even labeling of historical periods in the ancient world is not a settled matter. There are often alternative chronologies, higher or lower, for different periods and cultures. Israel's Iron Age, Greece's "Dark Ages" and archaic period, and Egyptian chronology are perhaps the most notable areas of debate. For the sake of simplicity, I have followed "standard" chronologies as represented in the main reference books, avoiding the extreme positions and the debates around them. Dates for Egypt, for instance, follow the chronology in Shaw (2000: 479–483), Mesopotamian dates usually conform to the Middle Chronology, and for the dating of the books of the Hebrew Bible I have followed the introductions by experts in the *Oxford Annotated Bible* (2007, 4th ed.). For Greek texts, such as those composed by Homer and Hesiod for which there is chronological controversy, I have followed fairly well-accepted positions and indicated the main issues under debate.

Finally, I use the chronological indicators BCE (Before Common Era) and CE (Common Era) instead of BC (Before Christ) and AD (Anno Domini). BCE/CE is more often adopted by Near Eastern scholarship and seemed appropriate in a volume that bridges the fields of Classical and Near Eastern studies. Recent surveys of Greek history have also adopted BCE/CE, such as *The Cambridge Companion to Archaic Greece* (ed. A. Shapiro, 2007) and Blackwell's *History of the Archaic Greek World: ca. 1200–479 BCE* (J. M Hall, 2007).

ABOUT THE EDITOR

✦

CAROLINA LÓPEZ-RUIZ is Associate Professor of Classics at The Ohio State University in Columbus, Ohio. She studied at the Universidad Autónoma of Madrid, Spain (Classics), the Hebrew University of Jerusalem and the University of Chicago (Ph.D. 2005, Committee on the Ancient Mediterranean World). López-Ruiz has published articles on Greek and Near Eastern literatures and mythology and the Phoenician presence in the Iberian Peninsula. She is the co-editor of *Colonial Encounters in Ancient Iberia: Phoenician, Greek, and Indigenous Relations* (University of Chicago Press, 2009, with M. Dietler) and the author of *When the Gods Were Born: Greek Cosmogonies and the Near East* (Harvard University Press, 2010). She is currently preparing a monograph on the pre-Roman culture of Tartessos in the Iberian Peninsula with co-author S. Celestino (Oxford University Press) and is working on a book project on cultural contact across the "orientalizing" Mediterranean during the eighth–seventh centuries BCE.

CONTRIBUTORS

✦

MARK ANDERSON is Associate Professor of Philosophy and Director of Classics at Belmont University in Nashville, Tennessee. He has published articles on Socrates, Plato, and Nietzsche and is author of the book *Pure: Modernity, Philosophy, and the One* (Sophia Perennis, 2009).

MARY R. BACHVAROVA is Associate Professor in the Department of Classical Studies at Willamette University in Salem, Oregon. She has published articles on Hittite and Greek literature (especially poetry) and linguistics and co-edited the volume *Anatolian Interfaces: Hittites, Greeks and Their Neighbors* (with eds. B. J. Collins and M. Woodbridge, Oxbow Press, 2008). Her monograph *From Hittite to Homer: The Anatolian Background of Greek Epic* is forthcoming from Cambridge University Press.

ALBERTO BERNABÉ is Professor in the Department of Greek Philology and Indo-European Linguistics at the Universidad Complutense in Madrid, Spain. He is an expert in Greek religion and mythology as well as Indo-European and Hittite linguistics, on all of which he has published extensively. Among his works are *Hieros logos: poesía órfica sobre los dioses, el alma y el más allá* (Akal, 2003) and the latest edition of the Orphic fragments, *Poetae Epici Graeci Testimonia et Fragmenta* Pars II: Fasc. 1. *Orphicorum et Orphicis similium testimonia* (Bibliotheca Teubneriana, 2004).

ANDRÉS DIEGO ESPINEL is a tenured researcher at the Spanish National Research Council (CSIC) in Madrid, Spain. His work focuses on Egyptian activities outside the Nile Valley during the Old and Middle Kingdoms, on which he has published articles and the books *Etnicidad y territorio en el Egipto del Reino Antiguo* (Universitat Autònoma de Barcelona, 2006) and *Abriendo los caminos de Punt: Contactos entre Egipto y el ámbito afroárabe durante la Edad del Bronce (ca. 3000 a.C.-1065 a.C.)* (Editorial Bellaterra, 2011). He works as epigraphist for the Spanish–Egyptian mission at Dra Abu el-Naga, Luxor.

HANNE EISENFELD is a Ph.D. candidate in the Department of Classics at The Ohio State University in Columbus, Ohio, with an interdisciplinary specialization in Religions of the Ancient Mediterranean. In her dissertation, "Only Mostly Dead: Immortality and Related States in Pindar's Victory Odes," she seeks to contextualize Pindar's mythological narratives within the Greek religious landscape.

MIGUEL HERRERO DE JÁUREGUI is Assistant Professor in the Department of Greek Philology and Indo-European Linguistics at the Universidad Complutense in Madrid, Spain. He has written articles on Greek epic and religion and is the author of *Orphism and Christianity in Late Antiquity* (De Gruyter, 2010) as well as a co-editor of *Tracing Orpheus: Studies of Orphic Fragments* (De Gruyter, 2011).

SAM MEIER is a Professor of Near Eastern Languages and Cultures at The Ohio State University in Columbus, Ohio. He is the author of articles on Ugaritic and Hebrew languages and literatures and broader Near Eastern topics as well as the monographs *The Messenger in the Ancient Semitic World* (Society of Biblical Literature, 1988), *Speaking of Speaking: Marking Direct Discourse in Biblical Hebrew* (Brill, 1992), and *Themes and Transformations in Old Testament Prophecy* (InterVarsity, 2009).

BARRY B. POWELL is the Halls-Bascom Professor of Classics Emeritus at the University of Wisconsin-Madison. He is a specialist in Homer and in the history of writing, as well as Greek mythology and Egyptian language and culture. He has published a number of widely used textbooks and handbooks on Classical myth and Greek civilization and is the author of *Homer and the Origin of the Greek Alphabet* (Cambridge, 1991) and *Writing: Theory and History of the Technology of Civilization* (Wiley-Blackwell, 2009). His annotated translations of Homer's *Iliad* and *Odyssey* are forthcoming from Oxford University Press.

TIMELINE

All dates are BCE unless noted. Dates, especially in the second and early first millennia BCE, are approximate. (Written sources and artistic developments are indicated in italics; r. before dates stands for "ruled.")

✦

Period	Mesopotamia	Egypt
Early Bronze Age 3300–2000	*3300–3100 Earliest forms of writing develop* *Sumerian culture* Dynasty of Akkad conquers Sumerian states (Sargon of Akkad, r. 2334–2279) 2300–2000 (Neo)-Sumerian Third Dynasty of Ur	*3300–3100* *Earliest forms of writing develop* 3000–2686 Early Dynastic Period: political unification 2686–2181 Old Kingdom 2181–2055 First Intermediate Period
Middle Bronze Age 2000–1550	Amorite Kingdoms 1800 Rise of Assyrian Empire in northern Mesopotamia (19th–18th centuries) Old Babylonian Empire, southern Mesopotamia (Hammurabi of Babylon, r. 1792–1750) Babylon sacked by Hittites (uncertain date)	2055–1650 Middle Kingdom 1650–1550 Second Intermediate Period (Hyksos Period)
Late Bronze Age 1550–1200	1365–1076 Assyrian Empire 1595–1155 Kassite Period in Babylon *Early versions of the* Epic of Gilgamesh, Enuma Elish, *and other Mesopotamian literature in circulation during the second millennium*	1550–1069 New Kingdom Amarna Period (Akhenaten, 1352–1336) Clashes with Hittites (Battle of Kadesh, 1274; Ramses XII: r. 1279–1213)

Anatolia, Canaan, Phoenicia, Israel	Greece	Italy
Hattians and other (pre-Indo-European and Indo-European) cultures in Anatolia Syria-Palestine under Egyptian sphere of influence; city-states flourish	3000–1900 Early Minoan (Protopalatial) Period in Crete and Early Cycladic in Cycladic islands	
1750 Rise of Hittite Empire *18th-century Proto-Sinaitic script: a "proto-alphabetic" script used to write a Canaanite language*	1900–1600 Middle Helladic Period in mainland; Middle Cycladic in Cycladic islands 1600? Eruption of volcano on Thera (Santorini) 1900–1700 First Palatial period of Minoan civilization in Crete 1700–1450 Second Palatial Period *Linear A script*	
Hittite Empire and Egypt compete for control of the Levant *Hittite texts* *Luwian culture attested in cuneiform and Luwian hieroglyphic inscriptions down to the Iron Age* 14th–12th centuries Canaanite state of Ugarit flourishes *Ugaritic texts* ca. 1200 Destruction of Hattusa, Ugarit, and other Near Eastern city states Troy/Ilion destroyed *(Homer's Trojan War?)* *Exodus narrative situated roughly at this time*	Mycenaean Civilization (Late Helladic Period) 1450 Mycenaean destruction of Minoan palaces *Linear B used in Crete and Mainland Greece to write Greek* 1200–1100 destruction and abandonment of Mycenaean centers	

TIMELINE *(cont.)*

Period	Mesopotamia	Egypt
	Assyrian expansion begins (Tiglath-pileser I: r. 1114–1076)	Invasion by Sea Peoples (Ramses III: r. 1184–1153), including Philistines
	10th–7th centuries Neo–Assyrian Empire	Egypt is conquered by Assyrians (671)
		664–332 Late Period
	Standard versions of the Epic of Gilgamesh, Enuma Elish, *and* Atrahasis	Saite Dynasty, 664–525
	745–722 Assyrian expansion in the Levant	
	Rise of Babylonia: captures of Assyrian capital Niniveh (612)	
	586–539 Neo-Babylonian Empire	
Iron Age *1200 –* *(Divided into various historical periods)*		

Anatolia, Canaan, Phoenicia, Israel	Greece	Italy
11th–7th centuries "Neo–Hittite" states in southeast Anatolia and Syria	1100–700 Geometric Period or "Dark Age"	1100–700 Villanovan culture in central–northern Italy
Israelites and Philistines settle in Canaan	*No written documents; Geometric style in art*	7th century Expansion of Etruscan culture
United monarchy of Israel (Saul, David, Solomon: late 11th–10th centuries) *David and Goliath episode set in this time*	1100 traditional date for "Dorian invasion"	
	1050 Greeks settle in coast of Asia Minor	700 *Etruscan alphabet (predecessor of Latin alphabet) is adopted from the Greeks*
	776 First Olympic Games	
Part of the Hebrew Bible may date from around this time; Early Hebrew inscriptions attested	750 Emergence of the *polis* (city-state) throughout Greece	753 Foundation of Rome (Romulus and Remus)
Phoenician, Aramean, Moabite and other states flourish in the region *Phoenician, Luwian, Aramaic inscriptions*	750 *Adoption of the Phoenician alphabet* 750–600 *Flourishing of the arts, orientalizing phenomenon*	753–509 Roman monarchic Period
925 Shishak I invades Palestine	750 – Greek colonization begins in Southern Italy and Sicily	
Phoenician colonial expansion in the West begins		
	750–700 works by Homer and Hesiod	
814 Foundation of Carthage		
Phrygian empire in central Anatolia (high point 8th century)	700–479 Archaic Period *Early 6th-century Lyric poets Sappho, Alcaeus; beginnings of Presocratic philosophy/natural philosophy and science*	
701 Assyrian capture of Judah		
586 Babylonian capture of Jerusalem	594 Solon's reforms in Athens	

TIMELINE *(cont.)*

Period	Mesopotamia	Egypt
	Persian Empire established by (Cyrus II "The Great": ca. 559–530)	525–404 First Persian Period
		403–344 Short phase of Egyptian rule
	539 Cyrus captures Babylon	343–332 Second Persian Period

Persian Period (539–333) in the EAST

Archaic to Classical Period in GREECE

Etruscan culture and Roman Republic in ITALY

Anatolia, Canaan, Phoenicia, Israel	Greece	Italy
Lydian empire (Croesus) falls to Cyrus in 545	546–510 Peisistratid tyranny in Athens	Etruscans dominate central Italy (until sack of Veii by Rome in 396)
538 Israelite exiles return from Babylon	508 Democratic reforms in Athens by Kleisthenes	509 Roman Republic begins
520–515 Second temple built ("Second Temple Period" begins)	499–494 Ionian revolt against Persians	509 First treaty between Rome and Carthage
(Part of the Hebrew Bible may have been redacted around this time)	490 First Persian invasion (Darius); battle of Marathon	496 Rome fights against the Latin League, continues expansion throughout Italy during 5th–4th centuries
	480–79 Second Persian invasion (Xerxes): battles of Thermopylae, Salamis, Plataia	
	479–323 Classical Period	390 Sack of Rome by Celts
	Athenian tragedians active: Aeschylus (484 on), Sophocles (460s on), Euripides (455 on)	
	Herodotos' Histories: Mid-5th century	
	Pindar's Odes: Early 5th century	
	478 Rise of Athenian Empire	
	462 Perikles' democratic reforms in Athens	
	448 Parthenon's construction starts	
	431–404 Peloponnesian War between Athens and Sparta and their allies (Athens defeated)	
	Thucydides writes his History of the Peloponnesian Wars	
	420s to 380s Aristophanes' comedies	
	399 Trial and execution of Socrates; *385 Plato starts teaching in Athens*	
	359 Rise of Macedonian Empire (Phillip II): controls Greece by 338	

TIMELINE *(cont.)*

Period	Mesopotamia	Egypt
	331 Alexander the Great captures Babylon	Conquered by Alexander the Great (campaigns 336–323)
	323 Alexander dies in Babylon	Ptolemaic kingdom
	Seleucid kingdom	*Alexandria becomes a center for the arts and literature; Library founded in the early 3rd century*
		Apollonios Rhodios, poet and librarian, writes the Argonautika
Hellenistic Period		

Anatolia, Canaan, Phoenicia, Israel	Greece	Italy
Various Hellenistic kingdoms divide Asia Minor, Syria and Palestine (Ptolemaic, Seleucid, Pergamon, Pontus, etc.)	336: Phillip II assassinated, Alexander becomes king and starts conquest of Persian Empire	264–241 First Punic War 237 Rome annexes Sardinia and Corsica
3rd century Gauls settle in Galatia, central Asia Minor	323 Alexander's death	
Revolt of the Maccabees in Israel (167–164)	Hellenistic Period Greece divided between kingdoms, cities, and leagues (e.g., Macedonia, Athens, Sparta, Achean and Aetolian Leagues)	218–201 Second Punic War; Hannibal invades southern Italy; defeated at Zama (201) by Scipio Africanus; Rome annexes Sicily, parts of Iberia
Hashmonean rule of Judah (165–137)		
150–146 Siege and Destruction of Carthage	214–167 series of Macedonian Wars with Rome	
Pompey conquers the Levant (66–62)	146 "Achaean War" with Rome; sack of Corinth: Rome gains control over Greece	146 Rome gains control over Greece
		150–146 Siege and destruction of Carthage (Scipio Aemilianus)
		Civil Wars between Marius and Sulla (80s) and Caesar and Pompey (40s)

TIMELINE *(cont.)*

Period	Mesopotamia	Egypt
	Parthia gradually assumes control	31 BCE–311 CE Roman Period
		31 Octavian (Augustus) conquers Egypt (defeats Marc Anthony and Cleopatra VII at Actium)
Roman Empire		

Anatolia, Canaan, Phoenicia, Israel	Greece	Italy
Herod the Great (r. 37 BCE–4 CE), rebuilds "Second Temple"	Greece is a Roman province	49 Julius Caesar named dictator; assassinated in 44
29 Augustus (re)founds Carthage as a Roman colony	*(Greek continues as the official and spoken language in Greece and all eastern Roman provinces)*	Roman Empire begins with Octavian (now called Augustus; r. 27 BCE–14 CE)
Year 1 CE Conventional date for the birth of Jesus	*Plutarch of Chaeronea, 46 –126 CE*	
First Jewish Revolt against Rome in Judah (66–73 CE), Second Temple destroyed by Titus (70 CE)		*Livy 59 BCE–17 CE Virgil 70 BCE–19 CE Ovid 43 BCE– 17 CE*
1st–2nd centuries CE: Philon of Byblos' Phoenician History*; Flavius Josephus' works on Jewish history*		*Apuleius from Madaura, 125 CE–, writes* The Golden Ass
		Hadrian, r. 117–138 CE, builds temple of Venus in Rome

MAPS

✦

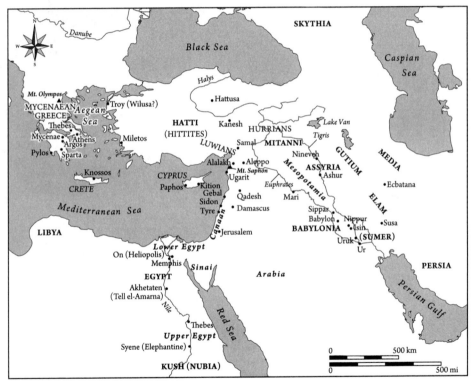

MAP 1 ✦ The Near East and the Aegean in the Late Bronze Age

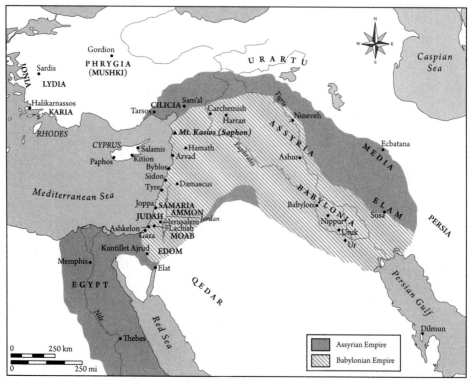

MAP 2 ✦ The Near East during the Assyrian and Babylonian Empires, eighth–sixth
centuries BCE

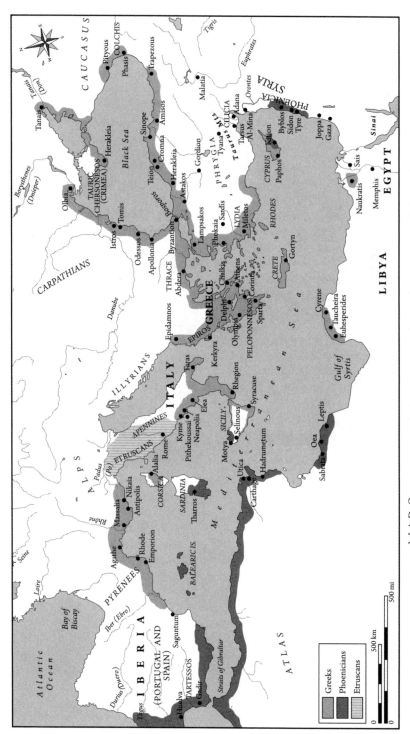

MAP 3 ✦ Greeks and Phoenicians in the Mediterranean, eighth–sixth centuries BCE

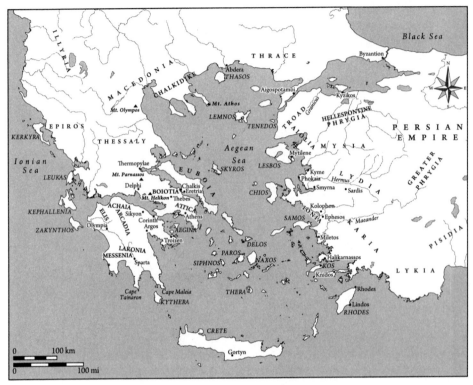

MAP 4 ✦ Greece and the Aegean in Archaic-Classical Times

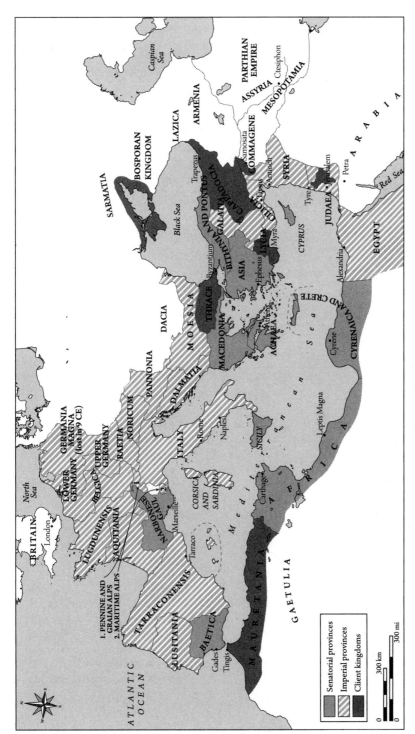

MAP 5 ✦ The Roman Empire at the Death of Augustus (14 CE)

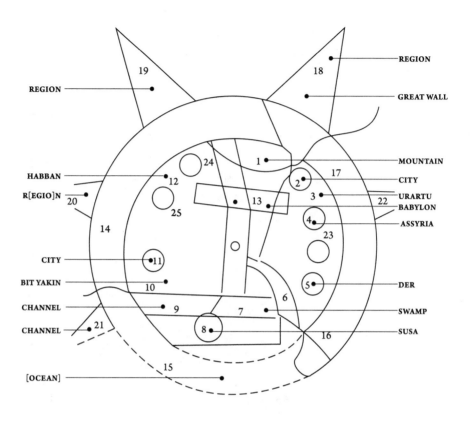

1. *ša-du-[ú]*	Mountain	18. BÀD.GU.LA	Great Wall
2. uru	city	⌈6⌉ *bēru*	6 leagues
3. *ú-ra-áš-tu[m]*	Urartu	*ina bi-rit*	in between
4. ᵏᵘʳaš+šurᵏⁱ	Assyria	*a-šar* ᵈ*šamaš*	where the Sun
5. dér(BAD.AN)ᵏⁱ	Der	*la innammaru*	is not seen
6. x-ra-[...		(nu.igi.lá)	
7. *ap-pa-r[u[*	swamp	19. *na-gu**-*ú**	Region
8. ⌈*š*⌉*uša[n]*(⌈M⌉ÚŠ.⌈EREN⌉ᵏ⌈ⁱ?⌉)	Susa	6 *bēru*	6 leagues
9. bit-qu	channel	*ina bi-rit*	in between
10. *bit-ia-ʾ-ki-nu*	Bit Yakin	20. *[na-gu]-ú*	[Regio]n
11. uru	city	[(...)]	[(...)]
12. *ha-ab-ban*	Habban	21. *[na]-gu-ú*	[Re]gion
13. TIN.TIRᵏⁱ	Babylon	[(...)]	[(...)]
14. ⁱᵈ*mar-ra-tum*	ocean	22. *na-gu-ú*	Region
15. [(ⁱᵈ)*mar-ra-tum*]	[ocean]	⌈8⌉ *bēru*	8 leagues
16. [(ⁱᵈ)m]*ar-ra-tum*	[o]cean	*ina bi-rit*	in between
17. *mar-r[a-tum]*	oce[an]	23-25. No inscription	
		*Signs visible on early photographs	

ANCIENT MAPS

MAP 6 ✦ The earliest surviving world maps are from Babylon. World maps, such as the famous example now in the British Museum, served as inspiration for the Greek ones. This is a schematic rendering of the map. It represents the known world from the perspective of Babylon, with labels written in Akkadian. As in Hecateus' map, the Ocean, in the shape of a cosmic river, surrounds the Earth, with regions or islands falling outside the map perhaps representing mythological regions (perhaps of the Netherworld?). This map was found in Sippar (southern Iraq) and dates to the late fifth century BCE.

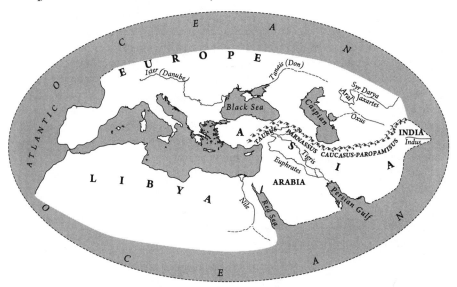

MAP 7 ✦ Map of the ancient world based on the one designed by Hecataeus of Miletos (Gr. Hekataios, b. 550 BCE). Hecataeus was among the first geographers-ethnographers, and his work *Travels around the Earth* was illustrated by cartography. According to Herodotos of Halikarnassos, such a map was engraved in bronze and carried off from Miletos to Sparta during the Ionian revolt against Persia. The map shows the widespread belief that the world was surrounded by the River Ocean (Okeanos). The idea of the world encircled by water shaped eschatological narratives throughout antiquity.

PART 1

AND SO IT BEGAN:

COSMOGONIES AND THEOGONIES

MOST CULTURES HAVE stories about creation or about beginnings; in fact, each culture usually has many such stories, which are not always compatible with each other. The texts presented in this part were selected because, despite their many differences, they are genealogically related to each other. They represent different branches and offshoots of a vast family tree of ancient creation literature whose origins lay in Mesopotamia and that flourished in the literary cultures of Greece and Rome. These texts were written by Babylonians, Egyptians, Hittites, Canaanites, Israelites, Greeks, and Romans. Across the huge chronological and cultural distances that separated them, authors reworked traditional themes, always enriching them with new elements and adapting them to contemporary concerns. All together they share many common motifs, which reveal the kinship, intense contact, and mutual influence among the peoples of the ancient Mediterranean.

Cosmogonies are stories about the birth of the cosmos. Most of them place the beginning of the world in natural elements or abstract states, such as Earth, Sky, the primordial waters, Chaos, or the Void. Sometimes these entities are presented as divine, but generally they lack the individual, **anthropomorphic** personalities that mythologized gods normally exhibit. Cosmogony is followed by **theogony**, which explains the birth and family relations of the gods, including their struggles for power. This stage sometimes leads to an account of the origin of mankind, or **anthropogony**, which, in turn, can lead to human **genealogies**, from the heroes to the founders of cities and kings of historical societies. For any culture, then, these myths and legends, taken together, can provide a "brief history of time," the backbone of which is genealogical succession and which can potentially stretch from the poet's age back to the origin of all things. The transition from cosmic and natural entities to anthropomorphic gods and then to human beings is paralleled by a perception that the universe has moved from simplicity toward complexity, from a less differentiated and defined state of being to a more orderly cosmos governed by a group of gods and heroes entangled in complex relationships.

All these creation myths, after all, are the products of **polytheist** societies, that is, societies that worshipped many gods at the same time. This pantheon normally formed one divine family (such as the gods of Olympos), sometimes with exiled ancestors and relatives, but in other traditions the gods are more like a group of political adversaries (such as in the *Baal Cycle*, Part 3, document 5.a). Even in the case of the Hebrew Bible, the canonical text of one of the earliest monotheist religions, most scholars agree that its account replaced a previous polytheist schema similar to that of other Near Eastern cultures of its time, traces of which still survive, for instance, in the book of Genesis and in some Psalms (e.g., Part 2, documents 3 and 4, and Part 3, document 6).

In these theogonies, at any time, one god rules over the cosmos, imposing his order on it; in other words, heaven is a monarchy. This most powerful god is represented as a king whose position must be accepted by his fellow gods (as when Zeus is acclaimed king in the *Theogony*, document 1.5) but whose power is often threatened and contested, sometimes by his son (Kronos by Zeus in the *Theogony*), by a more distant relation (Tiamat by Marduk in the *Enuma Elish*), by his cupbearer (Anu by Kumarbi in the *Kumarbi Cycle*, Part 3, document 4.b), or by a rival divine lord (Baal by Mot in the *Baal Cycle*). These contests are always ultimately resolved by the accession of a new king in heaven and the emergence of a new order. This divine hierarchy, of course, mirrored the predominant monarchic regimes of the societies that produced these creation myths. In fact, the chain of kings in heaven had a parallel in the Near Eastern and Greek king lists, only the former were much shorter, corresponding usually to the history of a single dynasty. (Some later Greek thinkers, labeled Euhemerists, would in fact argue that the gods were originally kings and their sons were later worshipped by their followers.)

The governing god is often in constant fear of losing control, and the struggles with his rivals are a persistent feature of these myths. This motif is sometimes called by scholars "Succession Myth" and is best exemplified in the Hittite "Song of Birth" that opens the Hurro-Hittite *Kumarbi Cycle* and Hesiod's *Theogony*. Rival gods are not the only threat that the king in heaven faces. He often has to fight off monsters created by rival gods, such as the giant rock Ullikummi and serpent Hedammu in the *Kumarbi Cycle* and the serpent monster Typhon/Typhoeus in the *Theogony*. Even clashes with other gods are not always fought in a warrior-like way, but sometimes include savage and unnatural acts, such as castrating the king (as Kronos does to Ouranos in the *Theogony*) and then even swallowing his genitals (as Kumarbi does with Anu), swallowing your own children (Kronos), or gobbling up a wife pregnant with a potential successor (as

Zeus does to Metis). These strange acts of violence in turn give place to unnatural births from male deities (Athena from Zeus' head and Teshub from Kumarbi). Such acts represent the rival's attempt to interrupt the natural continuity of his predecessor's rule, to take control over the female capacity of procreation, and to prevent the succession from passing from an older to a younger god in ways that can be emulated by others. The Hurro-Hittite story, however, has been included with the rest of the *Kumarbi Cycle* in Part 3 (document 4.b) in order to keep that group of texts together and because it does not deal with the creation of the world but only with the struggle between the gods.

The cosmogonic texts that actually survive from antiquity are a fraction of those that were produced, and even the written versions of these myths captured only a small part of a broader background of oral performance and religious knowledge. What authority did the written versions enjoy? The Book of Genesis (document 1.4), we all know, eventually became part of a people's scripture and for many people today remains the definitive account of the origin of the world. The *Enuma Elish* (document 1.1) was recited as a hymn in honor of Marduk at the New Year's Akitu festival in Babylon. But the religious authority or the canonical status of the other texts is difficult to establish. There were no mechanisms in Greece, for instance, to establish any kind of religious uniformity or to treat any one text as authoritative. This brings us to the question of authorship and the poet's engagement with tradition. You will notice, in this and later sections, that we do not always know who composed these texts. This is especially the case with the Near Eastern texts. We cannot always treat these works as the products of an individual's creative genius as we are habituated to do because of our relationship with modern literature. Many of these texts are literary versions of older, also anonymous, oral traditions. It is difficult to assess the degree to which the person who wrote them departed from the oral tradition, or how his version compared with other existing versions of the same story, because usually they have been lost. All we know is that one or more professional scribes, possibly commissioned by religious authorities, consolidated what they considered a "standard" version of a given myth at a given time in a process that could be repeated subsequently as views and needs changed. Sometimes, as with the *Baal Cycle* (Part 3, document 5.a) and the "standard" version of *Gilgamesh* (e.g., Part 3, document 1), we have the names of the scribes (Ilimilku and Sin-liqe-unninni, respectively), but it is not easy to evaluate their role as "authors." Yet given the quality and uniform style of the texts written by each, and based on a comparison with older versions in the case of *Gilgamesh*, some scholars believe that these scribes had an independent poetic voice.

Beginning with the Greek poets Homer and Hesiod, and continuing with the later Greek and Roman authors such as Apollonios, Virgil, and Ovid, literary works become more strongly identified with their individual authors. These poets definitely shaped their creations with the knowledge of existing myths and old traditions constantly in view, but they certainly adapted, adjusted, and innovated as they saw fit. It is not clear that the works of Hesiod represent what other Greeks were thinking about the gods at that time, as we have no Greek cosmogonies preserved prior to his, but their literary success quickly made them canonical. Subsequent Greek and Roman authors then found cosmogony to be a fascinating type of literature, which they incorporated, always with new twists, into their epic poetry, comedy, and philosophy.

The production of cosmogonies declined in later antiquity, though older texts were still preserved. In part this was because of a shift in religious thought. **Neoplatonism** promoted the belief in an eternal world, and, while it postulated a metaphysical hierarchy that stretched from the material world up to impersonal divine principles, the relationship among those elements was considered to be permanent. This system of thought was not compatible with cosmogony. At the same time, the rise of Christianity imposed a theological model according to which there was only one God who does not change and who does not face any (serious) rivals. "In the beginning was the Word, and the Word was with God, and the Word was God" (John 1.1). After the fourth century CE, the Father and the Son were declared to be one and the same deity, so the possibility of conflict within a divine family along Near Eastern and ancient Greek lines was forestalled. However, elaborations on God's creation of the world and on the role of Adam and Eve still occupied a central place in Jewish and Christian texts that fall outside the canonical books of the Hebrew Bible and the New Testament (Gnostic texts, Christian apocryphal texts, Jewish pseudepigrapha, Kabbalah, the Dead Sea Scrolls), which are still proliferating due to discoveries of new texts (mostly papyri) from the ancient world. ✦

1.1. BABYLONIAN EPIC OF CREATION: *ENUMA ELISH*

This narrative poem is called *Enuma Elish* after the first two words, "when above," "when on high" (as the book of Genesis in the Hebrew Bible was known as *Bereshit* "when first . . . "). The text, written in seven tablets in fairly complete condition, was discovered in 1849 in the ruins of the Neo-Assyrian palace of King Ashurbanipal at Nineveh (in today's Mosul, Iraq). It dates to the seventh century BCE. This was only one of several copies that were subsequently discovered at Assyrian and Babylonian sites, and there is little variation among the different copies. Although all existing copies date to the early first millennium BCE, the poem must have been composed in the late second millennium BCE (Late Bronze Age), since it is written in the Old Babylonian form of the Akkadian language. The *Enuma Elish*, like other Near Eastern poetic texts, did not use verses in the formal sense of the word (e.g., constrained by the number of syllables or specific metric patterns, like in Greek and Latin poetry). The poetic tone is instead marked by the distinctive language and figures of speech, such as alliteration (repeating the same sound), repetitions, parallelism (repeating the same idea with different words), word play or puns, metaphors, etc.

The *Enuma Elish* was one of many creation stories in circulation in ancient Mesopotamia. This particular cosmogony was connected with the city of Babylon and recited at the New Year festival at that city in the month of April. The poem narrates the succession and struggles of the first gods and the rise of Marduk (Ashur in the Assyrian version) as the champion who defeated the primeval goddess Tiamat and her allies, who represented the forces of chaos. Marduk is exalted as the new king of the gods and creator of the world as we know it, to whom all owe absolute obedience. The poem ends with the recitation of Marduk's fifty names. In the recitation at the New Year festival, the poem invoked the renewal of order in the universe and of the king's sovereignty, which mirrored the absolute power of Marduk over his allies.

SOURCE: S. Dalley, *Myths from Mesopotamia: Creation, The Flood, Gilgamesh, and Others* (Oxford World's Classics, Oxford and New York, 1989, rev. ed. 2000), with minor modifications.

TABLET I

When skies above were not yet named, nor earth below pronounced by name, Apsu, the first one, their begetter and maker Tiamat, who bore them all, had mixed their waters together, but had not formed pastures, nor discovered reed-beds; when yet no gods were manifest, nor names pronounced, nor destinies decreed, then gods were born within them. Lahmu (and) Lahamu emerged, their names pronounced.[1]

As soon as they matured, were fully formed, Anshar (and) Kishar were born, surpassing them. They passed the days at length, they added to the years. Anu their first-born son rivalled his forefathers: Anshar made his son Anu like

---

[1] Ea and Damkina in the Assyrian version.

himself,[2] and Anu begot Nudimmud (Ea) in his likeness. He, Nudimmud, was superior to his forefathers: Profound of understanding, he was wise, was very strong at arms.

Mightier by far than Anshar his father's begetter, he had no rival among the gods his peers. The gods of that generation would meet together and disturb Tiamat, and their clamour reverberated. They stirred up Tiamat's belly, they were annoying her by playing inside Anduruna. Apsu could not quell their noise and Tiamat became mute before them; however grievous their behaviour to her; however bad their ways, she would indulge them. Finally Apsu, begetter of the great gods, called out and addressed his vizier Mummu, "O Mummu, vizier who pleases me! Come, let us go to Tiamat!"

They went and sat in front of Tiamat, and discussed affairs concerning the gods their sons. Apsu made his voice heard and spoke to Tiamat in a loud voice: "Their ways have become very grievous to me, by day I cannot rest, by night I cannot sleep. I shall abolish their ways and disperse them! Let peace prevail, so that we can sleep."

When Tiamat heard this, she was furious and shouted at her lover; she shouted dreadfully and was beside herself with rage, but then suppressed the evil in her belly: "How could we allow what we ourselves created to perish? Even though their ways are so grievous, we should bear it patiently."

(Vizier) Mummu replied and counseled Apsu; the vizier did not agree with the counsel of his earth mother: "O father, put an end to (their) troublesome ways, so that she may be allowed to rest by day and sleep at night."

Apsu was pleased with him, his face lit up at the evil he was planning for the gods his sons. (Vizier) Mummu hugged him, sat on his lap and kissed him rapturously. But everything they plotted between them was relayed to the gods their sons. The gods listened and wandered about restlessly; they fell silent, they sat mute. Superior in understanding, wise and capable, Ea who knows everything found out their plot, made for himself a design of everything, and laid it out correctly, made it cleverly, his pure spell was superb. He recited it and it stilled the waters. He poured sleep upon him so that he was sleeping soundly, put Apsu to sleep, drenched with sleep. Vizier Mummu the counselor (was in) a sleepless daze. He (Ea) unfastened his belt, took off his crown, took away his mantle of radiance and put it on himself. He held Apsu down and slew him; tied up Mummu and laid him across him. He set up his dwelling on top of Apsu, and grasped Mummu, held him by a nose-rope.

When he had overcome and slain his enemies, Ea set up his triumphal cry over his foes. Then he rested very quietly inside his private quarters and named them Apsu and assigned chapels, founded his own residence there, and Ea and Damkina his lover dwelt in splendour. In the chamber of destinies, the hall of designs, Bel, cleverest of the clever, sage of the gods, was begotten. And inside Apsu, Marduk was created; inside pure Apsu, Marduk was born. Ea his father created him, Damkina his mother bore him.

---

[2] Assur (head of the Assyrian pantheon) was assimilated with Anshar from the eighth century onwards.

He suckled the teats of goddesses; the nurse who reared him filled him with awesomeness. Proud was his form, piercing his stare, mature his emergence, he was powerful from the start. Anu his father's begetter beheld him, and rejoiced, beamed; his heart was filled with joy. He made him so perfect that his godhead was doubled. Elevated far above them, he was superior in every way. His limbs were ingeniously made beyond comprehension, impossible to understand, too difficult to perceive. Four were his eyes, four were his ears; when his lips moved, fire blazed forth. The four ears were enormous and likewise the eyes; they perceived everything. Highest among the gods, his form was outstanding. His limbs were very long, his height (?) outstanding.

(Anu cried out) "Mariutu, Mariutu, son, majesty, majesty of the gods!"

Clothed in the radiant mantle of ten gods, worn high above his head five fearsome rays were clustered above him. Anu created the four winds and gave them birth, put them in his (Marduk's) hand: "My son, let them play!"

He fashioned dust and made the whirlwind carry it; he made the flood-wave and stirred up Tiamat. Tiamat was stirred up, and heaved restlessly day and night. The gods, unable to rest, had to suffer. . . . They plotted evil in their hearts, and they addressed Tiamat their mother, saying: "Because they slew Apsu your lover and you did not go to his side but sat mute, he has created the four, fearful winds to stir up your belly on purpose, and we simply cannot sleep! Was your lover Apsu not in your heart? And (vizier) Mummu who was captured? No wonder you sit alone! Are you not a mother? You heave restlessly but what about us, who cannot rest? Don't you love us? Our grip(?) [is slack], (and) our eyes are sunken. Remove the yoke of us restless ones, and let us sleep! Set up a [battle cry] and avenge them! Con[quer the enemy] and reduce them to nought!"

Tiamat listened, and the speech pleased her: "Let us act now, (?) as you were advising! The gods inside him (Apsu) will be disturbed, because they adopted evil for the gods who begot them."

They crowded round and rallied beside Tiamat. They were fierce, scheming restlessly night and day. They were working up to war, growling and raging. They convened a council and created conflict. Mother Hubur, who fashions all things, contributed an unfaceable weapon: she bore giant snakes, sharp of tooth and unsparing of fang (?). She filled their bodies with venom instead of blood. She cloaked ferocious dragons with fearsome rays and made them bear mantles of radiance, made them godlike,

(chanting this imprecation) "Whoever looks upon them shall collapse in utter terror! Their bodies shall rear up continually and never turn away!"

She stationed a horned serpent, a *mushhushu*-dragon, and a *lahmu*-hero, an *ugallu*-demon, a rabid dog, and a scorpion-man, aggressive *umu*-demons, a fish-man, and a bull-man bearing merciless weapons, fearless in battle. Her orders were so powerful, they could not be disobeyed. In addition she created eleven more likewise. Over the gods her offspring who had convened a council for her she promoted Qingu and made him greatest among them, conferred upon him leadership of the army, command of the assembly, raising the weapon to signal engagement, mustering combat-troops, overall command of the whole battle force. And she set him upon a throne:

"I have cast the spell for you and made you greatest in the gods' assembly! I have put into your power rule over all the gods! You shall be the greatest, for you are my only lover! Your commands shall always prevail over all the Anukki!"

Then she gave him the Tablet of Destinies and made him clasp it to his breast: "Your utterance shall never be altered! Your word shall be law!"

When Qingu was promoted and had received the Anu-power and had decreed destinies for the gods his sons, (he said): "What issues forth from your mouths shall quench Fire! Your accumulated venom (?) shall paralyse the powerful!"

(*Catchline*) Tiamat assembled his (*sic*) creatures

(*Colophon*) First tablet, "When skies above." [Written] like [its] original [and inspected].

Tablet of Nabu-balatsu-iqbi son of Na'id-Marduk.

Hand of Nabu-balatsu-iqbi son of Na'id-Marduk [. . .].

TABLET II

Tiamat assembled his (*sic*) creatures and collected battle-units against the gods his (*sic*) offspring. Tiamat did even more evil for posterity than Apsu. It was reported (?) to Ea that she had prepared for war. Ea listened to that report, and was dumbfounded and sat in silence. When he had pondered and his fury subsided, he made his way to Anshar his father; came before Anshar, the father who begot him and began to repeat to him everything that Tiamat had planned:

"Father, Tiamat who bore us is rejecting us! She has convened an assembly and is raging out of control. The gods have turned to her, all of them, even those whom you begot have gone over to her side, have crowded round and rallied beside Tiamat. Fierce, scheming restlessly night and day, working up to war, growling and raging, they have convened a council and created conflict. Mother Hubur, who fashions all things, contributed an unfaceable weapon: she bore giant snakes, sharp of tooth and unsparing of fang (?). She filled their bodies with venom instead of blood. She cloaked ferocious dragons with fearsome rays, and made them bear mantles of radiance, made them godlike,

(*chanting this imprecation*) " 'Whoever looks upon them shall collapse in utter terror! Their bodies shall rear up continually and never turn away!'

"She stationed a horned serpent, a *mushhushshu*-dragon, and a *lahmu*-hero, an *ugallu*-demon, a rabid dog, and a scorpion-man, aggressive *umu*-demons, a fish-man, and a bull-man bearing merciless weapons, fearless in battle. Her orders were so powerful, they could not be disobeyed. In addition she created eleven more likewise. Over the gods her offspring who had convened a council for her she promoted Qingu, made him greatest among them, conferred upon him leadership of the army, command of the assembly, raising the weapon to signal engagement, to rise up for combat, overall command of the whole battle force. And she set her (*sic*) upon a throne:

" 'I have cast the spell for you and made you greatest in the gods' assembly! I have put into your power rule over all the gods! You shall be the greatest, for you are my only lover! Your commands shall always prevail over all the Anukki!'

"She gave him the Tablet of Destinies and made him clasp it to his breast: 'Your utterance shall never be altered! Your word shall be law!'

"When Qingu was promoted and had received the Anu-power and had decreed destinies for the gods her sons, (he said): 'What issues forth from your mouths shall quench Fire! Your accumulated venom (?) shall paralyze the powerful!'"

Anshar listened, and the report was very disturbing. "Woe!" he cried, he bit his lip, his liver was inflamed, his belly would not rest. His roar to Ea his son was quite weak.

"My son, you who started the fight, you remain responsible for what you have done. You went and slew Apsu, and Tiamat, whom you enraged—where else is an opponent for her?"

Despairing of advice, the prince of good sense, creator of divine wisdom, Nudimmud, with soothing speech, words of appeasement, he answered Anshar his father nicely:

"Father, you are the unfathomable fixer of fates! The power to create and to destroy is yours! O Anshar, you are the unfathomable fixer of fates! The power to create and destroy is yours! For the moment stay quiet at the words I shall tell you. Bear in mind what a good thing I did. Before I slew Apsu, who else could he look to? Now (there are) these (monsters), before I can rush up and extinguish him (Qingu) he will surely have destroyed me! Then what?"

Anshar listened, and the speech pleased him. His heart prompted him to speak to Ea: "My son, your deeds were highly commendable, you can make a strike fierce, unbeatable. Ea, your deeds were highly commendable, you can make a strike fierce, unbeatable. But go towards Tiamat, sooth her uprising, may her fury abate at your spell."

He listened to the words of his father Anshar. He took the road, went straight on his way. Ea went, he searched for Tiamat's strategy, but then stayed silent and turned back. He entered into the presence of the ruler Anshar, in supplication he addressed him:

"My father, Tiamat's actions were too much for me. I searched for her course, but my spell was not equal to her. Her strength is mighty, she is completely terrifying. Her crowd is too powerful, nobody could defy her. Her noise never lessens, it was too loud for me. I feared her shout, and I turned back. But father, you must not relax, you must send someone else to her. However strong woman's strength, it is not equal to a man's. You must disband her regiments, confuse her advice, before she can impose her power on us."

Anshar shouted furiously, he addressed Anu his son: "Steadfast son, heroic *kashushu*-weapon, whose strength is mighty, whose attack is unfaceable, go against Tiamat and stand your ground! Let her anger abate, let her fury be quelled. If she will not listen to your word, speak words of supplication to her, that she may be calmed."

He listened to the words of his father Anshar. He took the road, went straight on his way. He went, he searched for Tiamat's strategy, but then stayed silent and turned back. He entered into the presence of the ruler Anshar, in supplication he addressed him:

"My father, Tiamat's actions were too much for me. I searched for her course, but my spell was not equal to her. Her strength is mighty, she is completely terrifying. Her crowd is too powerful, nobody could defy her. Her noise never lessens, it was too loud for me. I feared her shout, and I turned back. But father, you must not relax, you must send someone else to her. However strong a woman's strength, it is not equal to a man's. You must disband her regiments, confuse her advice, before she can impose her power over us."

Anshar was speechless, and stared at the ground; He gnashed his teeth (?) and shook his head (in despair) at Ea. Now, the Igigi assembled, all the Anukki.[3] They sat silently (for a while), tight-lipped.

(Finally they spoke) "Will no (other) god come forward? Is [fate] fixed? Will no one go out to face Tiamat with [. . .]?"

Then Ea from his secret dwelling called [the perfect] one (?) of Anshar, father of the great gods, whose heart is perfect like a fellow-citizen or countryman (?), the mighty heir who was to be his father's champion, who rushes (fearlessly) into battle: Marduk the Hero! He told him his innermost design, saying: "O Marduk, take my advice, listen to your father! You are the son who sets his heart at rest! Approach Anshar, drawing near to him, and make your voice heard, stand your ground: he will be calmed by the sight of you."

The Lord rejoiced at the word of his father, and he approached and stood before Anshar. Anshar looked at him, and his heart was filled with joy. He kissed him on the lips, put away his trepidation.

(Then Marduk addressed him, saying) "Father, don't stay so silent, open your lips, let me go, and let me fulfill your heart's desire. Anshar, don't stay so silent, open your lips, let me go, and let me fulfill your heart's desire."

(Anshar replied) "What kind of man has ordered you out (to) his war? My son, (don't you realize that) it is Tiamat, of womankind, who will advance against you with arms?"

(Marduk answered) "Father, my creator, rejoice and be glad! You shall soon set your foot upon the neck of Tiamat! Anshar, my creator, rejoice and be glad, you shall soon set your foot upon the neck of Tiamat."

(Anshar replied) "Then go, son, knowing all wisdom! Quell Tiamat with your pure spell! Set forth immediately (in) the storm chariot; let its [. . .] be not driven out, but turn (them?) back!"

The Lord rejoiced at the word of his father; his heart was glad and he addressed his father: "Lord of the gods, fate of the great gods, if indeed I am to be your champion, if I am to defeat Tiamat and save your lives, convene the council, name a special fate, sit joyfully together in Ubshu-ukkinakku: My own utterance shall fix fate instead of you! Whatever I create shall never be altered! The decree of my lip shall never be revoked, never changed!"

(Catchline)
Anshar made his voice heard
(Colophon)
Second tablet, 'When skies above'. [Written] according to [. . .]
[. . .] a copy from Assur.
(Last line damaged)

---

[3] The Anukki (also called Anunnaki, Anunna, and Enunaki) are Sumerian old chthonic deities of fertility and the Underworld, associated with Anu (Sky God). They became judges of the Underworld. They are often paired with the Igigi, a Sumerian group of younger Sky Gods, headed by Enlil.

TABLET III

Anshar made his voice heard and addressed his speech to Kakka his vizier:

"O Kakka, vizier who pleases me! I shall send you to Lahmu and Lahamu. You know how to probe, you are skilled in speaking. Have the gods my fathers brought before me; let all the gods be brought to me. Let there be conversation, let them sit at a banquet, let them eat grain, let them drink choice wine, (and then) let them decree a destiny for Marduk their champion. Set off, Kakka, go and stand before them, and everything that I am about to tell you, repeat to them:

'Anshar your son has sent me, he has told me to report his heart's message, to say: Tiamat who bore us is rejecting us! She has convened a council, and is raging out of control. The gods have turned to her, all of them, even those whom you begot have gone over to her side, have crowded round and rallied beside Tiamat. They are fierce, scheming restlessly night and day. They are working up to war, growling and raging. They convened a council and created conflict. Mother Hubur, who fashions all things, contributed an unfaceable weapon: she bore giant snakes, sharp of tooth and unsparing of fang (?). She filled their bodies with venom instead of blood. She cloaked ferocious dragons with fearsome rays, and made them bear mantles of radiance, made them godlike:

(chanting this imprecation) " 'Whoever looks upon them shall collapse in utter terror! Their bodies shall rear up continually, and never turn away!'

"She stationed a horned serpent, a *mushhushu*-dragon, and a *lahmu*-hero, an *ugallu*-demon, a rabid dog, and a scorpion-man, aggressive *umu*-demons, a fish-man, and a bull-man bearing merciless weapons, fearless in battle. Her orders were so powerful, they could not be disobeyed. In addition she created eleven more likewise. Over the gods her offspring who had convened a council for her she promoted Qingu, made him greatest among them, conferred upon him leadership of the army, command of the assembly, raising the weapon to signal engagement, to rise up for combat, overall command of the whole battle force. And she set him upon a throne:

" 'I have cast the spell for you and made you greatest in the gods' assembly! I have put into your power rule over all the gods! You shall be the greatest, for you are my only lover! Your commands shall always prevail over all the Anunnaki.'

"She gave him the Tablet of Destinies, and made him clasp it to his breast. 'Your utterance shall never be altered! His (! Your) word shall be law!'

"When Qingu was promoted and had received the Anu-power and had decreed destinies for the gods her sons (he said): 'What issues forth from your mouths shall quench Fire! Your accumulated venom (?) shall paralyze the powerful.'

"I sent Anu, but he was unable to face her. Nudimmud[4] panicked and turned back. Then Marduk, sage of the gods, your son, came forward. He wanted of his own free will to confront Tiamat. He addressed his words to me,

" 'If indeed I am to be your champion, to defeat Tiamat and save your lives, convene the council, name a special fate, sit joyfully together in Ubshu-ukkinakku: and let me, my own utterance, fix fate instead of you. Whatever I create shall never be altered! Let a decree from my lips never be revoked, never changed!'

---

[4] Sumerian name of Ea.

"Hurry and decree your destiny for him quickly, so that he may go and face your formidable enemy!' "

Kakka set off and went on his way, and before Lahmu and Lahamu the gods his fathers prostrated himself and kissed the earth in front of them, then straightened up and stood and spoke to them: "Anshar your son has sent me. He has told me to report his personal message, to say: 'Tiamat who bore us is rejecting us! . . . *(the same message given by Anshar to Kakka above, repeated verbatim, is skipped here).*' Hurry and decree your destinies for him quickly, so that he may go and face your formidable enemy."

Lahmu and Lahamu listened and cried out aloud. All the Igigi then groaned dreadfully: "How terrible! Until he (Anshar) decided to report to us, we did not even know what Tiamat was doing."

They milled around and then came, all the great gods who fix the fates, entered into Anshar's presence and were filled with joy. Each kissed the other: in the assembly [. . .] there was conversation, they sat at the banquet, ate grain, drank choice wine, let sweet beer trickle through their drinking straws. Their bodies swelled as they drank the liquor; they became very carefree, they were merry, and they decreed destiny for Marduk their champion.

(Catchline)
They founded a princely shrine for him

TABLET IV

They founded a princely shrine for him, and he took up residence as ruler before his fathers *(who proclaimed)*:

"You are honoured among the great gods. Your destiny is unequalled, your word (has the power of) Anu! O Marduk, you are honoured among the great gods. Your destiny is unequalled, your word (has the power of) Anu! From this day onwards your command shall not be altered. Yours is the power to exalt and abase. May your utterance be law, your word never be falsified. None of the gods shall transgress your limits. May endowment, required for the gods' shrines wherever they have temples, be established for your place.

"O Marduk, you are our champion! We hereby give you sovereignty over all of the whole universe. Sit in the assembly and your word shall be pre-eminent! May your weapons never miss (the mark), may they smash your enemies! O lord,[5] spare the life of him who trusts in you, but drain the life of the god who has espoused evil!"

They set up in their midst one constellation,[6] and then they addressed Marduk their son: "May your decree, O lord, impress the gods' command to destroy and to recreate, and let it be so! Speak and let the constellation vanish! Speak to it again and let the constellation reappear."

He spoke, and at his word the constellation vanished. He spoke to it again and the constellation was recreated. When the gods his fathers saw how effective his

[5] Bel (cf. Hebrew Baal). "Lord" was one of Marduk's titles.

[6] In other interpretations "one garment."

utterance was, they rejoiced, they proclaimed: "Marduk is King!" They invested him with scepter, throne, and staff-of-office. They gave him an unfaceable weapon to crush the foe: "Go, and cut off the life of Tiamat! Let the winds bear her blood to us as good news!"

The gods his fathers thus decreed the destiny of the lord and set him on the path of peace and obedience. He fashioned a bow, designated it as his weapon, feathered the arrow, set it in the string. He lifted up a mace and carried it in his right hand, slung the bow and quiver at his side, put lightning in front of him, his body was filled with an ever-blazing flame. He made a net to encircle Tiamat within it, marshalled the four winds so that no part of her could escape: South Wind, North Wind, East Wind, West Wind, the gift of his father Anu, he kept them close to the net at his side. He created the *imhullu*-wind (evil wind), the tempest, the whirlwind, the Four Winds, the Seven Winds, the tornado, the unfaceable facing wind. He released the winds, which he had created, seven of them. They advanced behind him to make turmoil inside Tiamat.

The lord raised the flood-weapon, his great weapon, and mounted the frightful, unfaceable storm-chariot. He had yoked to it a team of four and had harnessed to its side "Slayer," "Pitiless," "Racer," and "Flyer;" their lips were drawn back, their teeth carried poison. They know not exhaustion, they can only devastate. He stationed on his right Fiercesome Fight and Conflict, on the left Battle to knock down every contender (?). Clothed in a cloak of awesome armor, his head was crowned with a terrible radiance.

The Lord set out and took the road, and set his face towards Tiamat who raged out of control. In his lips he gripped a spell, in his hand he grasped an herb to counter poison. Then they thronged about him, the gods thronged about him; the gods his fathers thronged about him, the gods thronged about him. The Lord drew near and looked into the middle of Tiamat: he was trying to find out the strategy of Qingu her lover. As he looked, his mind became confused, his will crumbled and his actions were muddled. As for the gods his helpers, who march(ed) at his side,[7] when they saw the warrior, the leader, their looks were strained. Tiamat cast her spell. She did not even turn her neck. In her lips she was holding falsehood, lies, (wheedling):

"[How powerful is] your attacking force, O lord of the gods! The whole assembly of them has gathered to your place!"

(*But he ignored her blandishments*) The Lord lifted up the flood-weapon, his great weapon and sent a message to Tiamat who feigned goodwill, saying:

"Why are you so friendly on the surface when your depths conspire to muster a battle force? Just because the sons were noisy (and) disrespectful to their fathers, should you, who gave them birth, reject compassion? You named Qingu as your lover, you appointed him to rites of Anu-power, wrongfully his. You sought out evil for Anshar, king of the gods, so you have compounded your wickedness against the gods my fathers! Let your host prepare! Let them gird themselves with your weapons! Stand forth, and you and I shall do single combat."

---

[7] The scene of the chief god entering battle (in the Assyrian version Assur) accompanied by the gods was depicted on the doors of Senacherib's New Year Temple, which are described in an inscription.

When Tiamat heard this, she went wild, she lost her temper. Tiamat screamed aloud in a passion, her lower parts shook together from the depths. She recited the incantation and kept casting her spell. Meanwhile the gods of battle were sharpening their weapons.

Face to face they came, Tiamat and Marduk, sage of the gods. They engaged in combat, they closed for battle. The Lord spread his net and made it encircle her, to her face he dispatched the *imhullu*-wind, which had been behind: Tiamat opened her mouth to swallow it, and he forced in the *imhullu*-wind so that she could not close her lips. Fierce winds distended her belly; her insides were constipated and she stretched her mouth wide. He shot an arrow, which pierced her belly, split her down the middle and slit her heart, vanquished her and extinguished her life. He threw down her corpse and stood on top of her.

When he had slain Tiamat, the leader, he broke up her regiments; her assembly was scattered. Then the gods her helpers, who had marched at her side, began to tremble, panicked, and turned tail. Although he allowed them to come out and spared their lives, they were surrounded, they could not flee. Then he tied them up and smashed their weapons. They were thrown into the net and sat there ensnared. They cowered back, filled with woe. They had to bear his punishment, confined to prison. And as for the dozens of creatures, covered in fearsome rays, the gang of demons who all marched on her right, he fixed them with nose-ropes and tied their arms. He trampled their battle-filth (?) beneath him. As for Qingu, who had once been the greatest among them, he defeated him and counted him among the dead gods,[8] wrested from him the Tablet of Destinies, wrongfully his, sealed it with (his own) seal and pressed it to his breast.

When he had defeated and killed his enemies and had proclaimed the submissive (?) foe his slave, and had set up the triumphal cry of Anshar over all the enemy, and had achieved the desire of Nudimmud, Marduk the warrior strengthened his hold over the captive gods, and to Tiamat, whom he had ensnared, he turned back. The Lord trampled the lower part of Tiamat, with his unsparing mace smashed her skull, severed the arteries of her blood, and made the North Wind carry it off as good news.[9] His fathers saw it and were jubilant: they rejoiced, arranged to greet him with presents, greetings gifts.

The Lord rested, and inspected her corpse. He divided the monstrous shape and created marvels (from it). He sliced her in half like a fish for drying: half of her he put up to roof the sky, drew a bolt across and made a guard hold it. Her waters he arranged so that they could not escape. He crossed the heavens and sought out a shrine; he leveled Apsu, dwelling of Nudimmud.

The Lord measured the dimensions of Apsu and the large temple (Eshgalla), which he built in its image, was Esharra: in the great shrine Esharra, which he had created as the sky, he founded cult centers for Anu, Ellil, and Ea.

(Catchline)
He fashioned stands for the great gods
(Colophon)

---

[8] The precise implication of "dead gods" is not clear.

[9] In ancient Mesopotamia and Egypt the north wind was considered the most favorable wind.

146 lines. Fourth tablet 'When skies above.' Not complete. Written according to a tablet whose lines were cancelled.

Nabu-belshu (son of) Na'id-Marduk, son of a smith, wrote it for the life of himself and the life of his house, and deposited (it) in Ezida.

TABLET V

He fashioned stands for the great gods. As for the stars, he set up constellations corresponding to them. He designated the year and marked out its divisions, apportioned three stars each to the twelve months. When he had made plans of the days of the year, he founded the stand of Neberu to mark out their courses, so that none of them could go wrong or stray.

He fixed the stand of Ellil and Ea together with it, opened up gates in both ribs, made strong bolts to left and right. With her liver he located the heights; he made the crescent moon appear, entrusted night (to it) and designated it the jewel of night to mark out the days:

"Go forth every month without fail in a corona, at the beginning of the month, to glow over the land. You shine with horns to mark out six days; on the seventh day the crown is half. The fifteenth day shall always be the mid-point, the half of each month. When Shamash looks at you from the horizon, gradually shed your visibility and begin to wane. Always bring the day of disappearance close to the path of Shamash,[10] and on the thirtieth day, the [year] is always equalized, for Shamash is (responsible for) the year. A sign [shall appear (?)]: sweep along its path. Then always approach the [. . .] and judge the case. [. . .] the Bowstar to kill and rob.

(15 lines broken) At the New Year's Festival (. . . *fragmentary passage skipped).*

Marduk [. . .] He put into groups and made clouds scud. Raising winds, making rain, making fog billow, by collecting her poison, he assigned for himself and let his own hand control it. He placed her head, heaped up [. . .]. Opened up springs: water gushed out. He opened the Euphrates and the Tigris from her eyes,[11] closed her nostrils, [. . .]. He piled up clear-cut mountains from her udder, bored waterholes to drain off the catch water. He laid her tail across, tied it fast as the cosmic bond, and [. . .] the Apsu beneath his feet. He set her thigh to make fast the sky, with half of her he made a roof; he fixed the earth. He [. . .] the work, made the insides of Tiamat surge, spread his net, made it extend completely. He [. . .] heaven and earth [. . .] their knots, to coil [. . .]

When he had designed its cult, created its rites, he threw down the reins (and) made Ea take (them). The Tablet of Destinies, which Qingu had appropriated, he fetched and took it and presented it for a first reading (?) to Anu.[12] [The gods (?) of] battle whom he had ensnared were disentangled (?); he led (them) as captives into the presence of his fathers. And as for the eleven creatures that Tiamat had created, he [. . .], smashed their weapons, tied them at his feet, made images of them and had them set up at the door of Apsu: "Let this be a sign that will never in future be forgotten!"

[10] Alluding to the moon's disappearance on the eastern horizon (sunrise).

[11] The word for "eyes" also means "springs."

[12] Anu or Ea (reading is ambiguous).

The gods looked, and their hearts were full of joy at him. Lahmu and Lahamu and all his fathers embraced him, and Anshar the king proclaimed that there should be a reception for him. Anu, Enlil and Ea each presented him with gifts.

[. . .] Damkina his mother exclaimed with joy at him; she made him beam [inside (?)] his fine (?) house. He (Marduk) appointed Usmu, who had brought his greetings present as good news, to be vizier of the Apsu, to take care of shrines. The Igigi assembled, and all of them did obeisance to him. The Anunnaki, each and every one, kissed his feet. The whole assembly collected together to prostrate themselves.

[. . .] they stood, they bowed, "Yes, King indeed!" [. . .] his fathers took their fill of his manliness, [they took off his clothes] which were enveloped in the dust of combat. [. . .] the gods were attentive to him. With cypress [. . .] they sprinkled (?) his body. He put on a princely garment, a royal aura, a splendid crown. He took up a mace and grasped it in his right hand. [. . .] his left hand. [. . .] He set a [*mushhushu-dragon* (?)] at his feet, placed upon [. . .] slung the staff of peace and obedience at his side.

When the mantle of radiance [. . .] and his net was holding (?) fearful Apsu, a bull. [. . .] In the inner chamber of his throne. [. . .] In his cellar. [. . .] The gods, all that existed, [. . .] Lahmu and Lahamu [. . .] made their voices heard and spoke to the Igigi: "Previously Marduk was (just) our beloved son but now he is your king. Take heed of his command."

Next they spoke and proclaimed in unison: "LUGA-DIMMER-ANKIA is his name.[13] Trust in him! When they gave kingship to Marduk, they spoke an oration for him, for blessing and obedience. Henceforth you shall be the provider of shrines for us. Whatever you command, we shall perform ourselves."

Marduk made his voice heard and spoke, addressed his words to the gods his fathers: "Over the Apsu, the sea-green dwelling, in front of (?) Esharra, which I created for you, (where) I strengthened the ground beneath it for a shrine, I shall make a house to be a luxurious dwelling for myself and shall found his cult centre within it, and I shall establish my private quarters, and confirm my kingship. Whenever you come up from the Apsu for an assembly, your night's resting place shall be in it, receiving you all. Whenever you come down from the sky for an assembly, your night's resting place shall be in it, receiving you all. I hereby name it Babylon, home of the great gods. We shall make it the centre of religion."

The gods his fathers listened to this command of his,

(a very fragmented passage follows, in which the gods rejoice at Marduk's foundation of Babylon and once more acclaim him as king; skipped here)

(Catchline)

When Marduk heard the speech of the gods

(Colophon)

Fifth tablet, 'When skies above'

Palace of Assurbanipal, king of the world, king of Assyria.

---

[13] Sumerian for "King of the gods of heaven and earth."

TABLET VI

When Marduk heard the speech of the gods, he made up his mind to perform miracles. He spoke his utterance to Ea, and communicated to him the plan that he was considering: "Let me put blood together, and make bones too. Let me set up primeval man: Man shall be his name. Let me create a primeval man. The work of the gods shall be imposed (on him), and so they shall be at leisure. Let me change the ways of the gods miraculously, so they are gathered as one yet divided in two."

Ea answered him and spoke a word to him, told him his plan for the leisure of the gods: "Let one who is hostile to them be surrendered (up), let him be destroyed, and let people be created (from him). Let the great gods assemble, let the culprit be given up, and let them convict him."

Marduk assembled the great gods, gave (them) instructions pleasantly, gave orders. The gods paid attention to what he said. The king addressed his words to the Anunnaki: "Your election of me shall be firm and foremost. I shall declare the laws, the edicts within my power. Whosoever started the war, and incited Tiamat, and gathered an army, let the one who started the war be given up to me, and he shall bear the penalty for his crime, that you may dwell in peace."

The Igigi, the great gods, answered him, their lord Lugal-dimmer-ankia, counselor of gods: "It was Qingu who started the war, he who incited Tiamat and gathered an army!"

They bound him and held him in front of Ea, imposed the penalty on him and cut off his blood. He created mankind from his blood,[14] imposed the toil of the gods (on man) and released the gods from it.

When Ea the wise had created mankind, had imposed the toil of the gods on them—that deed is impossible to describe, for Nudimmud performed it with the miracles of Marduk—then Marduk the king divided the gods, the Anunnaki, all of them, above and below. He assigned his decrees to Anu to guard, established three hundred as a guard in the sky; did the same again when he designed the conventions of earth, and made the six hundred dwell in both heaven and earth.

When he had directed all the decrees, had divided lots for the Anunnaki, of heaven and of earth,[15] the Anunnaki made their voices heard and addressed Marduk their lord: "Now, O Lord, that you have set us free, what are our favors from you? We would like to make a shrine with its own name. We would like our night's resting place to be in your private quarters, and to rest there. Let us found a shrine, a sanctuary there. Whenever we arrive, let us rest within it."

When Marduk heard this, his face lit up greatly, like daylight: "Create Babylon, whose construction you requested! Let its mud bricks be moulded, and build high the shrine!" The Anunnaki began shoveling. For a whole year they made bricks for it. When the second year arrived, they had raised the top of Esagila in front of (?) the Apsu; they had built a high ziggurat for the Apsu. They founded a dwelling for Anu, Ellil, and Ea likewise.

---

[14] It is unclear whether the subject is Marduk or Ea.

[15] Inheritances and land were divided by lot (see also in *Atrahasis*, Part 2, document 1.a).

In ascendancy he settled himself in front of them, and his 'horns' look down at the base of Esharra.[16] When they had done the work on Esagila, (and) the Anunnaki, all of them, had fashioned their individual shrines, the three hundred Igigi of heaven and the Anunnaki of the Apsu all assembled. The Lord invited the gods his fathers to attend a banquet. In the great sanctuary which he had created as his dwelling: "Indeed, Bab-ili (is) your home too! Sing for joy there, dwell in happiness!"

The great gods sat down there, and set out the beer mugs; they attended the banquet. When they had made merry within, they themselves made a *taqribtu*-offering in splendid Esagila. All the decrees (and) designs were fixed. All the gods divided the stations of heaven and earth. The fifty great gods were present, and the gods fixed the seven destinies for the cult. The Lord received the bow, and set his weapon down in front of them. The gods his fathers looked at the net which he had made, looked at the bow, how miraculous her construction, and his fathers praised the deeds that he had done. Anu raised (the bow) and spoke in the assembly of gods, he kissed the bow. "May she go far!" He gave to the bow her names, saying: "May Long and Far be the first, and Victorious the second; her third name shall be Bowstar, for she shall shine in the sky."

He fixed her position among the gods her companions. When Anu had decreed the destiny of the bow, he set down her royal throne. "You are highest of the gods!" And Anu made her sit in the assembly of gods. The great gods assembled and made Marduk's destiny highest; they themselves did obeisance.

They swore an oath for themselves, and swore on water and oil, touched their throats.[17] Thus they granted that he should exercise the kingship of the gods and confirmed for him mastery of the gods of heaven and earth.

Anshar gave him another name: ASARLUHI: "At the mention of his name we shall bow down! The gods are to pay heed to what he says: his command is to have priority above and below. The son who avenged us shall be the highest! His rule shall have priority; let him have no rival!

"Let him act as shepherd over the black-headed people,[18] his creation. Let his way be proclaimed in future days, never forgotten. He shall establish great *nindabu*-offerings for his fathers. He shall take care of them, he shall look after their shrines. He shall let them smell the *qutrinnu*-offering, and make their chant joyful.

"Let him breathe on earth as freely as he always does in heaven. Let him designate the black-headed people to revere him, that mankind may be mindful of him, and name him as their god. Let their (interceding) goddess pay attention when he opens his mouth.

"Let *nindabu*-offerings be brought [to] their god (and) their goddess. Let them never be forgotten! Let them cleave to their god. Let them keep their country pre-

---

[16] Either the construction's pinnacles or an allusion to crowns with bull horns worn by the gods.

[17] A gesture that accompanied treaty oaths, as attested in the Old Babylonian Period.

[18] That is, dark-haired, which was a way of referring to human beings in general, though a deliberate contrast with fair-haired people predominating in other regions is possible.

eminent, and always build shrines. Though the black-headed people share out the gods.

"As for us, no matter by which name we call him, he shall be our god. Come, let us call him by his fifty names! His ways shall be proclaimed, and his deeds likewise!

"MARDUK

"Whose father Anu designated him at the moment of his birth, to be in charge of pasturage and watering places, to enrich their stalls, who overwhelmed the riotous ones with his flood-weapon and saved the gods his fathers from hardship.

"Let THE SON, MAJESTY OF THE GODS be his name! In his bright light may they walk forever more: The people whom he created, the form of life that breathes. He imposed the work of the gods (on them) so that they might rest. Creation and abolition, forgiveness and punishment—Such are at his disposal, so let them look to him.

"MARUKKA—he is the god who created them. He pleases the Anunnaki and gives rest to the Igigi.

"MARUTUKKU—he is the help of country, city, and his people. Him shall the people revere forever.

"MERSHAKUSHU—fierce yet considerate, furious yet merciful. Generous is his heart, controlled are his emotions.

"LUGAL-DIMMER-ANKIA—his name which we gave him in our assembly. We made his command higher than the gods his fathers.

"He is indeed BEL of the gods of heaven and earth, all of them, the king at whose instruction the gods are awed above and below.

"NARI-LUGAL-DIMMER-ANKIA is a name that we have given him as director of all the gods, who founded our dwellings in heaven and earth out of difficulties, and who shared out the stations for the Igigi and Anunnaki. At his names may the gods tremble and quake in (their) dwellings.

"ASARLUHI (first) is his name, which his father Anu gave him, he shall be the light of the gods, strong leader, who like his name is the protecting spirit of god and country. He spared our dwellings in the great battle despite difficulties.

"Second, they called him Asarluhi as NAMTILA, the god who gives life, who restored all the damaged gods as if they were his own creation. Bel, who revives dead gods with his pure incantation, who destroys those who oppose him but [. . .]s the enemy.

"Asarluhi third as NAMRU, whose name was given (thus), the pure god who purifies our path."

Anshar, Lahmu, and Lahamu called his three names; they pronounced them to the gods their sons:

"We have given him each of these three names. Now you, pronounce his names as we did!"

The gods rejoiced, and obeyed their command. In Ubshu-ukkinakku they deliberated their counsel:

"Let us elevate the name of the son, the warrior, our champion who looks after us!"

They sat in their assembly and began to call out the destinies, pronounced his name in all their rites.

(Catchline)

Asare, bestower of plough land, who fixes (its) boundaries

TABLET VII

(This tablet continues the recitation of the fifty names of Marduk. The names are difficult to interpret, belonging mostly to Sumerian gods into whom Marduk was assimilated, with the exception of Addu, the West Semitic Storm God also known as Haddad or Adad. Only the closing lines of the tablet are reproduced here.)

With fifty epithets the great gods called his fifty names, making his way supreme. May they always be cherished, and may the older explain (to the younger). Let the wise and learned consult together, let the father repeat them and teach them to the son. Let the ear of shepherd and herdsman be open, let him not be negligent to Man-Iuk, the Ellil of the gods. May his country be made fertile, and himself be safe and sound.

His word is firm, his command cannot alter; no god can change his utterance. When he is angry, he does not turn his neck (aside); in his rage and fury no god dare confront him. His thoughts are deep, his emotions profound; criminals and wrong-doers pass before him.

He (the scribe?) wrote down the secret instruction which older men had recited in his presence, and set it down for future men to read.

May the [people?]s of Marduk whom the Igigi gods created weave the [tale?] and call upon his name in remembrance (?) of the song of Marduk who defeated Tiamat and took the kingship.

1.2. MESOPOTAMIA: *THEOGONY OF DUNNU*

This story survives in a single copy found in the city of Sippar in the nineteenth century. Although the text itself is Late Babylonian (ca. 1000–750 BCE), it contains an older theogony from the city of Dunnu, a small city in Babylonia, prominent in the early second millennium BCE. This theogony shows how cosmogonic stories from different places and traditions within Mesopotamia could vary dramatically. In contrast with the Babylonian epic of creation *Enuma Elish* (document 1.1), this theogony presents earthly entities as the primordial creators, followed by a chain of sons who all kill their fathers and marry their mothers or sisters in a violent model of succession of kingship only broken at the New Year, when for the first time a son does not kill his father in order to succeed him. The story fits within the general pattern of the "Succession Myth" (e.g., Hesiod's *Theogony* in document 1.5 and the Hittite *Song of Birth* in Part 3, document 4.b). The *Theogony of Dunnu*, however, contains the longest and most homicidal chain of succession of all the comparable stories. The shift in *modus operandi* introduced by Hayyashum with the New Year (he imprisons his father), in turn, is comparable with Zeus' behavior toward his father Kronos in Hesiod's *Theogony* (document 1.5).

SOURCE: Stephanie Dalley, *Myths from Mesopotamia: Creation, The Flood, Gilgamesh, and Others* (Oxford World's Classics, Oxford and New York, 1989, rev. ed. 2000), with minor modifications.

At the very beginning (?) [Plough[19] married Earth] and they [decided to establish (?)] a family (?) and dominion. "We shall break up the virgin soil of the land into clods." In the clods of their virgin soil (?), they created Sea.

The furrows, of their own accord, begot the Cattle God. Together they built Dunnu forever (?) as his refuge (?).

Plough made unrestricted dominion for himself in Dunnu. Then Earth raised her face to the Cattle God his son and said to him, "Come and let me love you!" The Cattle God married Earth his mother, and killed Plough his father, and laid him to rest in Dunnu, which he loved. Then the Cattle God took over his father's dominion. He married Sea, his older sister.

The Flocks God, son of the Cattle God, came and killed the Cattle God, and in Dunnu laid him to rest in the tomb of his father. He married Sea his mother. Then Sea slew Earth her mother. On the sixteenth day of Kislimu, he took over dominion and rule.[20]

[The Flocks God][21] the son of the Flocks God married River, his own sister, and killed (his) father the Flocks God and Sea his mother, and laid them to rest in the tomb undisturbed (?). On the first day of Tebet, he seized dominion and rule for himself.

The Herdsman God son of the Flocks God married his sister Pasture-and-Poplar, and made Earth's verdure abundant, supported sheepfold and pen to feed (?) creatures of field and fen, and [. . .] for the gods' requirements. He killed [. . .] and River his mother and made them dwell in the tomb. On the [. . .] day of Shabat, he took over dominion and rule for himself.

Haharnum son of the Herdsman God married his sister Belet-seri and killed the Herdsman God and Pasture-and-Poplar his mother, and made them dwell in the tomb. On the sixteenth day of Addar, he took over rule (and) dominion.

[Then Hayyashum] son of Haharnum married [. . .] his own sister. At the New Year he took over his father's dominion, but did not kill him, and seized him alive. He ordered his city to imprison his father [. . .] and [. . .]

(about 38 lines missing, then 20 fragmentary lines which mention Nusku, Ninurta, and Ellil)

1.3. EGYPTIAN COSMOGONIES

The sources for Egyptian creation myths are too scattered and varied to give even a representative sample in the space afforded by this volume. Even though some creation myths (such as the Heliopolitan cosmogony) became widely known throughout the country, there was no unifying mythology. Each major city had its own unique pantheon and mythology. Allusions to creation

---

[19] *Harab,* "plough" in Akkadian, is related to North-West Semitic *hrb,* "sword" (e.g., in Hebrew), and Greek *harpe,* sickle, the instrument with which the castration of the Sky was performed in Hesiod's *Theogony.*

[20] The sequence of months corresponds to December–January–February–March, the last four months of their year, which began in April.

[21] Author's restoration: If the sequence follows a consistent pattern, there would have been two "Flocks" gods, as suggested by Lambert (see Dalley's note).

are ubiquitous in Egyptian funerary texts, ranging from the third-millennium BCE Pyramid Texts (Old Kingdom) and the later Coffin Texts (Middle Kingdom, first half of the second millennium BCE), to countless papyri with individualized selections of religious texts (e.g., from the so-called *Book of the Dead*). Before those texts could be read (after the different Egyptian scripts were deciphered in the early nineteenth century), all we knew about Egyptian religion was mediated by classical tradition, that is, through elaborations of Egyptian mythology by Greek and Roman authors (such as Plutarch's *On Isis and Osiris*, on which see Part 6, document 5).

1.3.a. The Memphite Theology: Ending of the Shabako Stone

The so-called Shabako stone is a breccia[22] slab from Wadi Hammamat (eastern Egyptian desert) carved with an inscription that, as stated in its heading, was discovered by the Twenty-fifth Dynasty king Shabako (ca. 716–702 BCE): "as their forefathers made (it), eaten by worms, it was not known/understood from the beginning to the end." According to the same text, Shabako ordered that it be reproduced "anew so that it became better than it had been before," on a slab which was placed in the temple of Ptah at Memphis. The date of the original document is unknown. Initially, it was unanimously dated to the Old Kingdom (ca. 2686–2125 BCE), but more recent studies place it later, probably in the Ramesside Period (ca. 1295–1069 BCE) or even in the Twenty-fifth Dynasty (ca. 747–656 BCE) itself. Re-used as a millstone, the slab has lost a great part of its carved surface. However, its legible parts, located at the edges of the stone, record the Memphite rendition of some important themes in Egyptian myths and religion. The first part, arranged as a dramatic text, refers to an episode of the myth of Osiris: the dispute between Horus and Seth over Egypt's government. The second part, translated here, describes Memphis' main deity, Ptah, as supreme divinity and creator (hence the name of this source: *Memphite Theology*), and underlines the political and religious role of the city as the religious and political center of Egypt.

On a lacunose (i.e., fragmentary) introductory column to the second part, Ptah is called "Ptah the great, who is the heart and tongue of the En[nead] [. . .]." This epithet anticipates the contents of the last section of the Shabako stone. It emphasizes the value given by the Egyptians to speech as a performative tool of creation and connects the text to similar narrations in *Enuma Elish* and Genesis 1 (see documents 1.1 and 1.4).

SOURCE: Shabako Stone (London, BM 498, cols. 53–64), translated and annotated by A. Diego Espinel.

(. . .) The one who came into being as the heart, and the one who came into being as the tongue, being like the image of Atum: it is Ptah, the great and powerful, who caused [all the gods] and their *kas* to [live] through this heart and this tongue.

---

[22] A type of rock composed by broken fragments of minerals or stones (gravel) cemented together naturally.

Horus came into being as Ptah through him, and Thot came into being as Ptah through him. It so happens that heart and tongue command over the li[mbs] [. . .], that he is the foremost of all the bodies and the foremost of all the mouths of all the gods, all the human beings, all the cat[tle], and all the reptiles that live, conceiving and ordering every matter he wishes. His Ennead of gods is in front of him as the teeth and lips. They are the semen and hands of Atum.[23] Atum's [En]nead[24] came int[o being] through his semen and fingers, since the gods are lips and teeth in this mouth that pronounced the name of everything. Shu and Tefnut originated from it, and it gave birth to the Ennead of gods.

The eyes are watching, the ears are listening, the nose is receiving the air, and they inform the heart. It is it what permits every kind of knowledge to originate. It is the tongue that repeats what the heart conceived. Thus all the gods were born and his Ennead of gods was completed, for every divine word has come into being as a conception of the heart and a command of the tongue. Thus the *kas* have been made and the *hemsuts* have been fixed,[25] (the ones) which create every provision and every offering by means of this word, (the ones) which make what is lovable and hateful. Thus, life has been given to the possessor of peace, and death has been given to the possessor of crimes. Thus every task and craft have been created: the action of the arms, the gait of the legs, and the motion of all the limbs (exist) according to what he has commanded, and to the word of conception of the heart which has been originated in his tongue and facilitates every thing.

It became so, that Ptah is called "the one who creates the totality and caused the gods to come into being." He is Ta-Tjenen,[26] the creator of the gods. Every thing has been originated from him as offerings and provisions, as offerings to the gods, and as every good thing. Thus it is found and known that his strength is more powerful than the gods. Thus Ptah was satisfied after his creation of every thing and every divine word. He has given birth to the gods, he has created the cities, he has founded the provinces, he has placed the gods in their temple(s), he has made prosperous their offerings, he has founded their sanctuaries, he has fashioned their bodies according to what rests in their hearts. Thus the gods have entered in their bodies, (made) of every kind of wood, every kind of precious stone, every kind of clay and all things that grow over him (i.e., Ptah), in which they have come into being. Thus all the gods and their *kas* were assembled for him, (and they are) satisfied and united with the lord of the Two Lands.

---

[23] According to some texts, divinities were created by Atum through masturbation. Other texts, for example document 1.3.b, mention Atum's saliva as a means of divine creation.

[24] Enneads of gods are frequently mentioned in Egyptian texts. Since the number three was employed by Egyptians as the plurality, nine (3 × 3) was considered the plural of plurals. Here the Ennead of gods refers to the Great Ennead of Heliopolis, which consisted of Atum himself, Shu, Tefnut, Geb, Nut, Osiris, Isis, Seth, and Nephthys.

[25] The *ka* is a complex concept of a nonphysical aspect of the gods and human beings. It was connected to the reproductive action, being also a link of his possessor with his forefathers. In the beyond, the *ka* was also tightly related to the sustenance of the deceased, since it was the recipient and consumer of the mortuary offerings. The *hemsut* is a more obscure term, which seems to be a female counterpart of the *ka*.

[26] A Memphite god, usually associated with Ptah, who symbolizes the emerging primeval mound.

(It is) the granary of the god Ta-Tjenen, the great throne that delights the heart of the gods, who are in the Domain of Ptah, the domain (lit. "the lady") of every life who has created the Life/Knot-of-the-Two-Lands (i.e., Memphis) in it, because of Osiris, who was drowned in its waters, and whom Isis and Nephthys spotted.[27] They beheld him and they looked after him. Horus ordered Isis and Nephthys to take Osiris and to put an end to his drowning. They turned their head in time, and they brought him to land. He entered the secret entrance of the lords of the eternity, according to the steps of the one who appears in the horizon, over the paths of Re in his great throne. He [entered] the palace, and he joined the gods, Ta-Tjenen, Ptah, lord of years. Thus Osiris came into being in the land of the Domain of the Sovereign, to the north of this land where he had come. His son Horus appears as king-*niswt*, and appears as king-*bity* in the arm of his father Osiris, with the gods who have preceded him and who will succeed him.

1.3.b. "A Hymn to Life": *Coffin Texts* Spell 80

The Egyptian *Coffin Texts* are a large and heterogeneous group of religious texts—hymns, litanies, and magical and ritual **spells**—which were mainly written on the walls of private coffins (but also on tomb walls, **stelai**, and papyri). They comprise more than a thousand different spells. The first secure examples date to the very end of the First Intermediate Period or Early Middle Kingdom (ca. 2125–2055 BCE), even though there are some possibly earlier examples. The texts have been found all across Egypt, but they disappear by the beginning of the Second Intermediate Period (ca. 1650 BCE). *Coffin Texts* **formulae** are also attested in previous *Pyramid Texts* and chapters of the later *Book of the Dead*. In all of these contexts, *Coffin Texts* spells had mostly a mortuary function. They combine ritual and magical practices with mythical and theological references. In this regard, the spells do not provide a balanced example of either aspect. While mythical references are well expressed, their ritual intentions and contexts are not explicitly mentioned (even though some possible connections with binding and fumigation of the deceased can be deduced). Concerning its mythological aspects, Spell 80 is a speech by Shu as "life," stating his pre-eminence over the *heh*-geniuses who hold Nut. This idea is described in detail in *The Book of the Heavenly Cow* (though in a section not included in the excerpt in Part 2, document 2.b). Shu is the air, which separates earth (Geb) from sky (Nut) and provides life. In his discourse he offers many references to Egyptian myths and religious ideas, such as some mythical aspects of the Heliopolitan theology (i.e., the Osirian myth or the fight of Re against the serpent Apep; see Part 6, document 4). However, the most relevant motif is that of Life as a creative power, which strengthens and revitalizes divine power and provides sustenance to every living being.

SOURCE: *Coffin Texts* Spell 80 (CT II 27–43), translated and annotated by A. Diego Espinel.

---

[27] Notice that this part of the Osirian myth, describing the death of Osiris, is not narrated in the "Great Hymn to Osiris," translated in Part 6, document 3.

"O, these eight *heh*-geniuses of millions of millions, who embrace the sky with their arms, who reunite the sky and horizon of Geb. Shu has begotten you from the *heh*-flood, from the primeval waters, from the darkness, from the gloom. He allots you to Geb and Nut, being Shu the eternity and Nut the infinity.[28]

"I am the soul of Shu, preeminent of the great cows, who ascends to the sky according to his desire, who descends to the earth when his heart wishes. Come in joy for greeting the god who is in me! As I am Shu, who is begotten of Atum, my dress is the breath of life which comes out of my environment, from Atum's mouth, and opens the winds which are over my paths.

"I am the one who made the sky light after the darkness; my skin is the pressure of the winds which come out behind me, from the mouth of Atum. My efflux is the storm cloud of the sky, and my smell is the rage of the dusk. The length of this sky is for my strides, and the breadth of this earth is for my foundations.

"I am the one whom Atum created, I will be a place of infinity, because I am the eternity who has begotten millions of millions![29] I am the one who repeats the ejection of Atum, who came out from his mouth when he used his hand, who has prevented his saliva from falling down to the earth."

Then Atum said: "Tefnut is my daughter who lives, and she will exist with her brother Shu. Life is his name and Maat is her name.[30] I live with my two children, and I will live with my two fledgelings, with me in their midst. One in my back, another in my belly. Life will rest with my daughter Maat, one in my interior, another around me. I will stand over them, and their arms will be around me. It is Geb, my son, who lives as I begot (him) from my name. He has known how to make the one who was inside the egg live in the corresponding belly, as the human beings who came out from my eye, which I sent because I was alone with the primeval waters in inactivity. I did not find a place where I could stay and I did not find a place where I could seat before Heliopolis had been created there yet; before the papyrus had been pulled together yet to sit over it; before Nut had been created to be over my head and had married Geb; before the first body was born; before the Ennead of primeval gods had come into being and they had began to stay with me."

Then Atum said to Nut: "I am floating, completely tired, and the *pat*-people is inert. It is my son, Life, who raises my heart, who will make my chest live when he has reunited these tired limbs of mine."

Nut said to Atum: "Kiss your daughter Maat and put her in your nose, so your heart will live. They are not far from you. They are your daughter Maat and your son Shu, whose name is Life. May you live on your daughter Maat. It is your son Shu who raises you."

"I indeed am Life, the son of Atum. He has begotten me from his nose, and I have come out from his nostrils. I will place myself in his neck in order that he can kiss me along with my sister Maat. He appears every day when he comes out from

[28] The spell starts with an invocation to the *heh*-geniuses by the god Shu.

[29] Some authors consider this point as a division between two different but closely connected spells (80A and 80B).

[30] Maat, Re's daughter, was the goddess who symbolized universal order and justice. In this spell Maat is Atum's daughter, since this primeval god was frequently identified with Re.

his egg and begets the god in the coming out (of the sun). Praises are said to him by the ones whom he created in the horizon. I have caused my father to live because the unwearying stars are the crew of his ship, the life of the living limbs.

"I am Life, who joins the heads, who reestablishes the necks, who causes the throats to live. I join Atum and I reestablish the head of Isis over her neck after I have joined the spine of Khepri for him, because I am the light of the ever-widening movements, who brings the sky to Atum, to the nostrils of Re, every day. I go and come, I open the path of Re when he sails to the western horizon. I am his nose, and my arms save him from Apep when he travels to the western horizon.[31] With my air-blow I make prosperous the neck of the one who is in the night boat and who is in the day boat, who came out today from the west and east of the body of Nut. The one who creates me every day, who places me in his nose, my father Atum. I joined his head, and I reestablished his neck. I reestablished the head of Isis over her neck, I joined the body of Osiris, and I reunited his bones. I strengthened his muscles, and I made his limbs healthy. I gave offerings to him, and I reestablished him, the bull of the west.

"I am Life, the possessor of years, the life of eternity and the possessor of infinity, whom Atum has made the elder among his souls, when he begot Shu and Tefnut in Heliopolis, when he was alone, and came into being as three, when he separated Geb from Nut, before the first body was born; before the Ennead of primeval gods came into being and they began to stay with me in my nose.

"He conceived me in his nose. I came out from his nostrils. He placed me in his neck and he did not permit me to be far from him. Life is my name, the son of the primeval god. I live in/as the *besnu*-material (?) of Atum. I am Life in his neck, the one who makes the throat flourish, whom Atum has made as Nepri,[32] when he makes me descend to this earth, to the island of fire, when my name came into being as Osiris, the son of Geb. I am Life, for whom the length of the sky and the width of Geb are made. The guidance of the offerings to the god came into being from me.

"My father Atum kisses me when he comes out from the eastern horizon, and his heart is pleased when he watches me while he is travelling in peace to the western horizon. When he finds me in his path, I join his head. I cause his *uraeus* to live.[33] I reestablish the head of Isis over her neck. I reunite the bones of Osiris and I make his limbs strong every day. I cause his limbs to flourish every day: Falcons live by means of birds, jackals by means of marauding, boars by means of the desert, hippopotami by means of the cultivated lands, human beings by means of the god Nepri, crocodiles by means of fish, fish by means of water, which is in the inundation, as Atum ordered.

"I will guide them, and I will make them live by means of my mouth, which is the life that is in their nostrils. I will guide my air-blow to their throats. I will reunite

---

[31] On this mythological motif, see Chapter 108 of the *Book of the Dead* (Part 6, document 4).

[32] Nepri is a grain and harvesting deity.

[33] The *uraeus* is a protective serpent placed on the forehead of the kings and gods. It is a mark of power and authority and a symbol of the Lower Egypt goddess Wadjet.

their heads by means of Hu,[34] who is in my mouth, whom Atum, who has come up from the eastern horizon, has given me. I will make the fish and the reptiles live on the back of Geb, as I indeed am Life, who is under Nut."

1.3.c. Excerpts from *The Teachings for Merikare*

The excerpts included below mention the role of god as creator and provider of life. They come from the longer work called *The Teachings for Merikare*. Although the origins of these narratives can be traced to the Heracleopolitan Period (Ninth/Tenth Dynasty, ca. 2160–2025 BCE), their literary composition probably dates to the Twelfth Dynasty (Middle Kingdom, ca. 1985–1773 BCE). In turn they are preserved only in New Kingdom papyri and **ostraca**. *The Teachings for Merikare* are a series of recommendations made by an unidentified king (probably called Khety) to his successor Merikare (possibly the last king of his dynasty). The realistic tone of the discourse highlights the king's mistakes and his political weakness. This description of royalty as a vulnerable and pragmatic institution contrasts with the respect for the divine realm, which is never questioned, as the following excerpts show. They depict a generic image of Egyptian gods (described here with the generic term "god") as powerful beings who have to be respected and worshipped because of their power and knowledge but also because they are the creators of the world and the foundation upon which royal authority rests.

Small caps correspond to parts of the original hieratic text written in red instead of black ink. In Egyptian literary texts, rubrics were usually employed for signaling the first verse of a stanza (as also, for instance, in the *Tale of the Shipwrecked Sailor* in Part 3, document 3).

SOURCE: *The Teachings for Merikare* (Pap. St-Petersburg 1116A), translated and annotated by A. Diego Espinel.

Pap. St-Petersburg 1116A, 123–127

(. . .) A generation follows another generation among human beings, while god, who knows (their) character, is hidden. No one can oppose the lord of the hand. He can attack whatever the eyes can see.

THE GOD ON HIS PATH SHOULD BE RESPECTED, made of precious stones, fashion[ed of cop]per; as water which is replaced by water, (thus) there is no channel which allows itself to be silted up, but instead it ruins the dyke in which it was hidden. (. . .)

Pap. St-Petersburg 1116A, 129–138

(. . .) Act for god, and he will act for you accordingly, with offerings that make the inscribed offering tables of stone flourish. It is the guidance of your name. God knows who is acting for him. Human beings are (well) provided, they are the cattle

---

[34] Hu is the divine authoritative and creative utterance. It is usually related to Sia, a concept that includes the ideas of knowledge, reason, and wisdom.

of god. He has made the sky and the earth for their hearts. He has driven off the crocodile from the waters. He has made the wind of the heart for their noses to live. They are his images, what originates from his limbs. He appears in the sky because of their hearts. He has created for them vegetables and cattle, fowl and fish to feed them. He killed his foes and [destr]oyed his children when they were conspiring to make a [rebe]llion.[35] He has made the day light for their hearts, and he sails in order to [se]e them. He has built his shrine around them, so when they weep, he is listening. He has made for them the governance from the egg, a leader to hold up the back of the weak. He has made for them magic words as weapons to repelling the effect of eventualities, vigilant about them night and day. He has killed the discontented among them, like a man who hits his son for the sake of his brother. God knows every name (. . .).

1.4. GOD'S CREATION, FROM THE BOOK OF GENESIS 1

The first book of the Hebrew Bible opens with a well-known creation story, one that has been revered as authoritative by the three monotheistic religions: Judaism, Christianity, and Islam. The Book of Genesis was called *Bereshit* after the first words of the Hebrew text ("when at first" or "in the beginning") and later called Genesis by Christian exegists. As is true for a great part of the Hebrew Bible and other ancient Near Eastern texts, there was no authorship originally attached to Genesis. Only in Hellenistic times was it attributed to Moses, as was the rest of the Pentateuch or Torah. Neither do we know the date of its composition. Like most of the Pentateuch and the Bible in general, Genesis was composed during a long period of time, stretching over the centuries from the time of David and Solomon (eleventh to tenth centuries BCE) to the exile in Babylon (sixth century BCE) and after. Detailed study of the biblical texts shows that the Pentateuch was redacted through the selection of older (now lost) texts and edited, synthesized, and expanded as needed. This was done by several editors or redactors (or groups of them), who are in turn divided by scholars into four different groups: the Jahwistic (J), Priestly (P), Elohistic (E), and Deuteronomistic (D) redactors, which differ in specific vocabulary (e.g., calling the Israelite god Yahweh or Elohim), literary style, and emphasis on different theological views.

The passages in Genesis 1–3 are the result of two layers of composition, with a creation narrative focused on cosmic order (Gen. 1–2.3), reproduced here, and a narrative focused on the creation of mankind and its relationship with God (Gen. 2.4–3.24), reproduced in Part 2, document 3. The first, seven-day, creation narrative (below) was probably redacted later than the second one (Gen. 2.4–3.24, the Adam and Eve story). It is attributed to the P (Priestly) source, which calls the Israelite god Elohim (translated as "God") and has him act in a distant, benevolent, and rational manner. The second (Adam and Eve) account (see Part 2, document 3) is probably older and written by the J

---

[35] A probable reference to the destruction of humankind narrated in the *Book of the Heavenly Cow* (for which see Part 2, document 2.b).

(Jahwistic) source and depicts a more anthropomorphic, harsh, and interventionist divinity. In that narrative the name *Yahweh* is used.

The creation stories of Genesis are not the only ones the Israelites told. Even though the Genesis version was deliberately placed at the beginning of the Torah and given canonical status, allusions to other creation stories show that there existed a wealth of oral and written traditions of which only a few made it into the preserved written corpus. For instance, in Job 38, the conflict between God and the sea is the first act of creation, evoking both the primordial waters of the *Enuma Elish* (document 1.1) and cosmic fights between Baal (Storm God) and Yamm (the Sea) in the Ugaritic texts (Part 3, document 5.a); likewise, order is established in the cosmos as Yahweh defeats the dragon-like Leviathan in Psalm 74 (see Psalm 29 in Part 3, document 6); in Proverbs 8 Wisdom (*hokhmah*) features as the force that was with God "from the beginning, from the origin of the earth" when "there was still no deep," etc.

SOURCE: The Hebrew Bible, New Revised Standard Version (NRSV), with minor modifications.

Genesis 1. (1) When at first God created the heavens and the earth,[36] (2) the earth was a formless void and darkness covered the face of the deep, while a wind from God swept over the face of the waters. (3) Then God said, "Let there be light"; and there was light. (4) And God saw that the light was good; and God separated the light from the darkness. (5) God called the light Day, and the darkness he called Night. And there was evening and there was morning, the first day.

(6) And God said, "Let there be a dome in the midst of the waters, and let it separate the waters from the waters." (7) So God made the dome and separated the waters that were under the dome from the waters that were above the dome. And it was so. (8) God called the dome Sky. And there was evening and there was morning, the second day.

(9) And God said, "Let the waters under the sky be gathered together into one place, and let the dry land appear." And it was so. (10) God called the dry land Earth, and the waters that were gathered together he called Seas. And God saw that it was good. (11) Then God said, "Let the earth put forth vegetation: plants yielding seed, and fruit trees of every kind on earth that bear fruit with the seed in it." And it was so. (12) The earth brought forth vegetation: plants yielding seed of every kind, and trees of every kind bearing fruit with the seed in it. And God saw that it was good. (13) And there was evening and there was morning, the third day.

(14) And God said, "Let there be lights in the dome of the sky to separate the day from the night; and let them be for signs and for seasons and for days and years, (15) and let them be lights in the dome of the sky to give light upon the earth." And it was so. (16) God made the two great lights—the greater light to rule the day and

[36] This opening clause can be interpreted as an independent sentence, "In the beginning God created . . . " or as a temporal sentence introducing the following one, "When in the beginning God created . . . " (even "When God started creating . . . "), which makes clearer that God's creation was not *ex nihilo* (out of nothing), but out of the chaotic primeval waters (*tohu-wa-bohu*). I slightly modify the NRSV translation, which chooses a middle solution: "In the beginning when God created . . . ."

the lesser light to rule the night—and the stars. (17) God set them in the dome of the sky to give light upon the earth, (18) to rule over the day and over the night, and to separate the light from the darkness. And God saw that it was good. (19) And there was evening and there was morning, the fourth day.

(20) And God said, "Let the waters bring forth swarms of living creatures, and let birds fly above the earth across the dome of the sky." (21) So God created the great sea monsters and every living creature that moves, of every kind, with which the waters swarm, and every winged bird of every kind. And God saw that it was good. (22) God blessed them, saying, "Be fruitful and multiply and fill the waters in the seas, and let birds multiply on the earth." (23) And there was evening and there was morning, the fifth day.

(24) And God said, "Let the earth bring forth living creatures of every kind: cattle and creeping things and wild animals of the earth of every kind." And it was so. (25) God made the wild animals of the earth of every kind, and the cattle of every kind, and everything that creeps upon the ground of every kind. And God saw that it was good.

(26) Then God said, "Let us make humankind in our image, according to our likeness; and let them have dominion over the fish of the sea, and over the birds of the air, and over the cattle, and over all the wild animals of the earth, and over every creeping thing that creeps upon the earth." (27) So God created humankind in his image, in the image of God he created them; male and female he created them. (28) God blessed them, and God said to them, "Be fruitful and multiply, and fill the earth and subdue it; and have dominion over the fish of the sea and over the birds of the air and over every living thing that moves upon the earth." (29) God said, "See, I have given you every plant yielding seed that is upon the face of all the earth, and every tree with seed in its fruit; you shall have them for food. (30) And to every beast of the earth, and to every bird of the air, and to everything that creeps on the earth, everything that has the breath of life, I have given every green plant for food." And it was so.

(31) God saw everything that he had made, and indeed, it was very good. And there was evening and there was morning, the sixth day.

Genesis 2. (1) Thus the heavens and the earth were finished, and all their multitude. (2) And on the seventh day God finished the work that he had done, and he rested on the seventh day from all the work that he had done. (3) So God blessed the seventh day and hallowed it, because on it God rested from all the work that he had done in creation. (4) These are the generations of the heavens and the earth when they were created.

(See continuation in Part 2, document 3.)

1.5. HESIOD'S *THEOGONY*

Hesiod's *Theogony* (or "birth of the gods") was probably composed at the end of the eighth or the beginning of the seventh century BCE. Together with Homer, Hesiod is the first Greek author whose works have survived. We know very little about the author himself, besides the (probably) autobiographical details he offers in his other poem, *Works and Days*, according to which he lived in Boiotia (west of Attica), where his father settled after coming from Kyme in Asia Minor. Like the *Iliad* and *Odyssey*, the *Theogony* is composed in **dactylic hexameters**, the standard verse for orally transmitted epic poetry. All of these epics invoke the Muses, daughters of Memory, illustrating the reliance of the singer of tales on his memory, crucial in a pre-literate world. Furthermore, the poems by Homer and Hesiod established a written tradition of hexametric poetry. Their style, including **formulae** and **epithets** for gods and heroes, became a model for future mythical narratives. The "Homeric" vocabulary and meter were later also used for magical spells, funerary epigraphs, and other expressions that echoed the authority of these ancestral mythical and heroic narratives.

The *Theogony* narrates both the origins of the universe and the gods and the struggle among the gods to hold power. Thus it starts off as a cosmogony, relying heavily on genealogies and in some aspects echoing the contemporaneous birth of natural philosophy, which sought to understand the origins and organizational principles of the physical world. Hesiod then moves on to a mythical story proper, revolving around the succession of fathers and sons: Ouranos (Sky), Kronos, and Zeus. In a sense, the poem could be considered a "Hymn to Zeus," since it climaxes with the figure of the Sky God as the young victorious figure who overthrows the old gods and establishes a new order in the world. In contrast, humankind appears only marginally, in the story about Prometheus, although arguably in a pivotal part of the epic.

In his poem, Hesiod collects and structures information that had previously circulated through oral tradition in songs and stories, and so the *Theogony* functions as a catalogue of supernatural beings (e.g., gods, nymphs, monsters) and their genealogies. Given the loss of those previous (nonwritten) stories, it is difficult to ascertain the degree of innovation by Hesiod in respect to his sources. Like Homer, he must have creatively re-worked, re-organized, and possibly completely altered existing traditions to his liking or that of his audience. The epic poems of Hesiod and Homer, like Greek poetry generally afterwards, were meant to be recited or sung with the accompaniment of music on social occasions such as banquets, funerals, artistic contests, games, and other festivities.

SOURCE: Hesiod, *Theogony*, translated and annotated by C. López-Ruiz.

(Invocation to the Muses)

Let us begin to sing of the Helikonian Muses, who hold high and sacred Helikon; around a dark-violet spring, with tender feet, they dance, and around the altar of the very powerful son of Kronos; after washing their delicate skin in the spring of Parmessos or of the Horse or of sacred Olmeios, at the highest point of Helikon they performed choral dances, beautiful, lovely ones, and they rolled down with their feet. Starting to move from there, covered in much mist, (10) they moved at night uttering a very beautiful voice, celebrating Zeus, aegis-bearing, and Lady Hera of Argos, who wears golden sandals, and the daughter of aegis-bearing Zeus, bright-eyed Athena, and Phoibos Apollo and Artemis, fond of arrows, and Poseidon, who holds the earth, the earth-shaker, and revered Themis and Aphrodite of vivid glance, and golden-crowned Hebe and fine Dione, and Leto and Iapetos, and crooked-minded Kronos and Dawn (Eos), and great Sun (Helios) and shining

Moon (Selene), (20) and Earth (Gaia) and great Ocean (Okeanos) and black Night (Nyx) and the holy family of the other ever-existing immortals.

(How the Muses gave Hesiod his song)

They are the ones who once taught Hesiod beautiful song as he was tending his sheep at the foot of sacred Helikon. This speech the goddesses addressed to me first, the Olympian Muses, daughters of aegis-bearing Zeus: "Rustic shepherds, base dishonor, mere stomachs! We know how to tell many false things that are like truths, and we know, whenever we want, how to sing out truths."

So they said, the articulate daughters of mighty Zeus, (30) and they gave me a branch of flourishing laurel for a scepter after plucking it, a remarkable one; then they inspired in me divine voice, so that I could celebrate the things to come and those past, and they ordered me to sing hymns of the family of the happy ever-existing ones, but to sing to *them* always first and last.

(Second invocation to the Muses; how the Muses are the poets of Olympos)

(Addressing himself) But what do I care about these things of tree or stone?[37] Hey, you! Let us begin with the Muses, who, singing hymns to father Zeus, cheer up his great heart inside Olympos, recounting the present, the things to come, and those past, coming together with their sound, as their tireless voice flows pleasant from their mouths; (40) the halls of their father, loud-sounding Zeus, rejoices at the flowery voice of the goddesses as it spreads out, and the peak of snowy Olympos resounds, the house of the immortals.

Sending forth their immortal voice, first they praise in their song the venerable race of the gods from the beginning, whom Earth and broad Sky (Ouranos) begat, and those who were born from them, gods, providers of goods. Then, secondly, they celebrate Zeus, father of gods and men, as they, the goddesses, start and end their song, how he excels among the gods and is the greatest in power. (50) And then, singing of the race of human beings and mighty Giants, they please the mind of Zeus inside Olympos, the Olympian Muses, daughters of Zeus who bears the aegis.

(The Muses' birth, place in Olympos, and names)

Mnemosyne (Memory) bore them in Pieria, sleeping with the father, the son of Kronos—she, the guardian of the hills of Eleuther—as a forgetfulness of evils and relief from troubles. For nine nights wise Zeus slept with her, climbing up into the sacred bed, away from mortals. But when a year had passed and the seasons turned around as the months wasted away, and many days were completed, (60) she bore nine girls, all of the same mind, with a spirit free of sorrow, in whose heart the song dwells, – at a small distance from the highest peak of snowy Olympos. There they have their radiant choruses and beautiful mansions, and by them the Graces and Desire have their houses in the midst of feasts; and they sing emitting from their mouths a lovely voice, and they celebrate the allotments and noble customs of all immortals, emitting their very lovely voice.

They then went to Olympos, rejoicing in their beautiful voice, with a divine song; and around them the black earth resounded as they sang, (70) and a lovely

---

[37] It is unknown what this allusion to "tree and stone" means. Hesiod is probably referring to a proverb that somehow encapsulates his previous digression.

sound rose from under their feet as they returned to their father. He is king in the sky; he himself holds the thunder and kindled lightning, after defeating by force his father Kronos. Fairly in each detail, he distributed to the immortals their portions and declared their privileges. These things, then, the Muses sang, they who hold Olympian mansions, the nine daughters begotten by great Zeus: Klio, Euterpe, Thalia, Melpomene, Terpsichore, Erato, Polymnia, Ourania, and Kalliope[38] – she is the principal among them all, (80) for she accompanies revered kings as well.

(The Muses give kings the gift of soothing and persuasive speech)

Whomever they honor, the daughters of great Zeus, and behold at the moment he is born among the Zeus-bred kings, they pour a sweet dew upon his tongue, and gentle words flow from his mouth; and from that moment all the people look up to him as he resolves disputes with right judgment; and, speaking confidently, he quickly puts an end even to a great quarrel. For this is why sensible men are kings,[39] because, when people are being wronged in the assembly, they manage to restitute things easily, (90) exhorting with smooth words. And as he goes up to the gathering, they appease him as a god, with gentle reverence, and he stands out among the gathered ones. Such is the sacred gift of the Muses to men.

(The Muses inspire poets, who soothe the afflictions of men)

For it is surely from the Muses and far-shooting Apollo that men who sing and play the lyre are at ease upon the earth, but kings owe it to Zeus; and fortunate is *that* man, whomever the Muses love; the voice flows sweet from his mouth. For if someone, even with sorrow in his recently-battered spirit, is drying up with affliction in his heart, yet when a poet, (100) a servant of the Muses, sings of the famous deeds of men of old and of the blessed gods who hold Olympos, right away he forgets his troubles and does not remember his sorrows at all; for the gifts of the goddesses quickly turned them away.

(Third invocation to the Muses)

Rejoice, daughters of Zeus, and give me a lovely song; celebrate the holy family of the ever-existing immortals, who were born of Earth and starry Sky, and of dark Night, those whom salty Sea (Pontos) nourished. Tell how at first the gods and the earth came into being, and the rivers and infinite sea, raging with waves, (110) and the shining stars and wide sky up there, and those who were generated from them, the gods who provide, and how they divided their resources and how they distributed their honors, and also how in the beginning they got hold of very rugged Olympos. Tell me these things, Muses who have Olympian dwellings, from the beginning, and say what came first of these things.

---

[38] Their names mean: "she who glorifies" (Klio), "she who delights well" (Euterpe), "the blooming one" (Thalia), "she who sings" (Melpomene), "she who delights in dance" (Terpsichore), "the lovely one" (Erato), "she of many hymns" (Polymnia), "the heavenly one" (Ourania), and "she of the noble voice" (Kalliope).

[39] The phrase is ambiguous and could be understood also as "this is why kings are sensible (wise, reasonable) men" or "this is why there are sensible kings."

(First elements and first gods)

Surely first of all Chaos[40] came into being, and then Earth (Gaia) of wide bosom, the always-safe sitting place of all the immortals who hold the peak of snowy Olympos, and steamy Underworld (Tartaros), at the bottom of the wide-pathed earth and Love (Eros), (120) who is the fairest among the immortal gods, the limb-looser, and among all the gods and men he dominates the mind and the thoughtful counsel in their breasts.

From Chaos Darkness (Erebos) and black Night were generated, and from Night in turn Aither and Day came forth, whom she bore becoming pregnant from her intimate union with Darkness. Earth engendered first starry Sky, equal to herself, to cover her from all sides, so as to be the ever immovable seat of the blessed gods, and she bore the high mountains, graceful shelters of the goddesses, (130) the Nymphs, who live on top of mountains of many glens. And she, without desirable love-making, also bore Pontos, the barren sea, raging with swell.

(Birth of the Titans, Cyclopes, and hundred-handed Giants)

But after that, lying in bed with Sky she bore Ocean of deep whirls and Koios and Kreios and Hyperion and Iapetos and Theia and Rhea and Themis and Mnemosyne and Phoebe of the golden wreath and lovely Tethys. And after these crooked-minded Kronos was born, the youngest, most terrible of the children, and he hated his vigorous begetter. And then she bore the Cyclopes, who have violent hearts, (140) Thunder and Lightning and tough-hearted Brightness, who gave Zeus thunder and contrived the thunderbolt. These were really similar to the gods in every other respect but a single eye was set in the middle of their forehead; "Cyclopes" was their assigned name, because one circled-shaped eye was set in their foreheads; strength and violence and contrivances accompanied their actions.

Earth and Sky engendered yet another three sons, great and mighty, not to be named: Kottos and Briareos and Gyges, arrogant children. (150) One hundred arms sprang from their shoulders, indescribable, and fifty heads for each one grew from their shoulders upon their sturdy limbs; and the mighty strength in their great form was unfathomable.

(Kronos castrates Ouranos, i.e., Sky)

And so, these were all those born from Earth and Sky, most frightful of children, and they were hated by their begetter from the start; and as soon as one of them was born, he would keep secluding them in Earth's hiding place, and would not let them come up, and Sky took pleasure in this evil deed; but she kept groaning inside, the tremendous Earth, (160) feeling bloated, and so she thought of a deceitful, evil trick.

At once fabricating a type of grey adamant she fashioned a sickle and showed it to her dear children. And she said, giving them courage, afflicted though she was in her own heart: "Children of mine and of a reckless father, if you would be willing to obey me, we would avenge your father's evil outrage; for he was the first to conceive unseemly actions."

---

[40] What Hesiod meant by *chaos* is uncertain, since this is its first appearance in Greek and later uses probably derive from Hesiod's. It is usually understood as "chasm, void."

So she said, and, as it turned out, fear got hold of them all, and not one of them made a sound. But great crooked-minded Kronos, taking courage, addressed his noble mother with answering words: (170) "Mother, I might be able to accomplish this task, if I undertake it, since I do not care for our abominable father; for he was the first to conceive unseemly actions."

So he said, and tremendous Earth rejoiced in her great chest. She made him sit and hid him in an ambush, and placed in his hands the sharp-toothed sickle, and she explained the whole trick to him. And great Sky came, bringing night along, and extended himself up against and around Earth, with desire for love-making, and stretched out in every direction; but his son reached out with his left hand, while he grasped in his right one the tremendous sickle, (180) long and sharp-toothed, and with vehemence he reaped the genitals away from his own father, and threw them back to be dispersed behind him.

(Creatures born from Sky's severed genitals, including Aphrodite)

And these (the genitals) did not escape his hand in vain: For as many drops of blood as shot forth from them, Earth received them all; and as the years sailed around she bore the mighty Erinyes and the great Giants, dazzling in their armor, holding long spears in their hands, and the Nymphs which they call Melian[41] upon the infinite earth.

As for the genitals, as soon as he had cut them off with the adamant and had thrown them down to the agitated sea, far from dry land, (190) the waters carried them for a long time, and around them a white foam rose up from the immortal flesh; and inside this grew a girl. First she approached divine Kythera, and from there she arrived later to Cyprus, surrounded by currents. And out came the beautiful revered goddess, and all around grass grew from under her delicate feet. Gods and men call her Aphrodite, the "foam-born"[42] goddess, and well-garlanded Kythereia (Aphrodite, because she grew in the foam; and then Kythereia, because she reached Kythera), and Cyprogeneia, because she was born in very wavy Cyprus, (200) and also "congenial," because she appeared from genitalia.[43] Eros (Love) accompanied her, and beautiful Desire, from the moment she was born and went into the tribe of the gods; and so from the start she had honor and received as her lot a fate among human beings and immortal gods: virginal secrets, smiles and deceits, sweet pleasure, love-making, and kindness.

And their father, great Sky, started calling his sons "Titans" as a nickname, thus reproaching them, whom he had begotten; for he said that they had "attempted"[44] to perform a great deed (210) with recklessness, and that there would be a punishment for it later on.

[41] These seem to be the Ash-Tree Nymphs, from whom humankind was born according to some traditions (see also *Theogony* 563, *Works and Days* 145).

[42] The name was thought to derive from the Greek word for foam, *aphros*.

[43] A pun is made between *philommeidea*, literally "lover of smiles," and *medea*, "genitals." We follow G. Most (Loeb edition, 2006), who renders her epithet as "genial" (my "congenial") to reflect a similar pun.

[44] The poet plays with *Titenas* (Titans) and *titainontas* "attempting" (from *teino*, "stretch by force; aim at"), resonating even with *tisin*, "punishment," in line 210.

(Night and her offspring)

Night bore frightful Doom and black Fate and Death, and bore Sleep, and brought forth the tribe of Dreams. Second, she bore Blame and painful Lament, – gloomy Night, without sleeping with any of the gods; and the Hesperides, who, beyond the glorious Ocean, take care of the beautiful golden apples and the trees that bear this fruit. And the Moirai (Destinies) and the ruthlessly avenging Fates: (the Moirai) Klotho, Lachesis, and Atropo, who give mortals good and evil to have, just as they are born, (220) and (the Fates) who follow closely the transgressions of men and gods, and the goddesses do not cease from their terrible anger until they exact a harsh punishment on whoever acts wrongly.

Deadly Night also gave birth to Nemesis (Retribution), a pain for mortal men; and afterwards she bore Deceit and Intimacy and wretched Old Age, and she bore stubborn-hearted Strife. And then abominable Strife bore painful Toil and Forget-fulness and Famine and tearful Sorrows, and Fights and Battles and Murders and Manslaughters and Quarrels and Lies and Stories and Polemics, (230) and Lawless-ness and Ruin, similar to one another, and Oath, who surely troubles earthly men the most, when someone deliberately swears a false oath.

(233–269 skipped: Account of the offspring of Sea (Pontos): Nereus, Thaumas, Phorkys, and Keto. Nereus, also called the "Old Man," is the father, with Doris, of the fifty sea nymphs called Nereids, whose names are given here; account of the offspring of Thaumas.)

(Offspring of Phorkys and Keto)

(270) To Phorkys Keto bore old women of beautiful cheeks, gray-haired from their birth, the ones whom immortal gods and men who walk on earth call Graias, and Pemphredo of the noble robe and Enyo with the saffron robe, and the Gorgons, who live beyond famous Ocean at the limit, towards the night, where the Hesperides of acute voice are: Sthenno and Euryale and Medusa, who suffered sorrows. She was mortal, while the other two are immortal and ageless; but only by her side the dark-haired one (Poseidon) lay down in the midst of a soft meadow and spring flowers.

(280) When Perseus cut her head off from her neck, great Chrysaor and the horse Pegasos sprang forth from it. The one had this given name because he was born besides the springs (*pegai*) of Ocean, and the other one for holding a golden sword (*chryseon aor*) in his hands. And the one (Pegasos) flew away, leaving behind the earth, mother of flocks, and reached the immortals; and he dwells in Zeus' house, bringing thunder and lightning to wise Zeus.

And Chysaor bore three-headed Geryon, mingling in love with Kallirhoe, the daughter of famous Ocean. This one, in turn, was slain by the force of Herakles (290) by his rolling-footed cattle in Erytheia, surrounded by currents, on that very day, when he drove the cattle of broad foreheads to sacred Tiryns, after crossing the strait of Ocean and killing Orthos and the cowherd Eurytion in the steamy stable beyond the famous Ocean.

And she[45] gave birth to another indescribable monster, in no way similar to mor-tal men or immortal gods, inside a hallow cave: Echidna, divine and strong-hearted,

---

[45] Unclear who is the subject, probably Keto or Medusa.

half a nymph of vivacious eyes and beautiful cheeks, but half a monstrous serpent, terrible, huge, (300) specked, bloodthirsty, under the hidden places of the blessed earth. Down there she has a cave, under a hollow rock, far from the immortal gods and from mortal men, for that is where the gods assigned her famous mansions to live in. And she keeps watch amidst the Arimoi, under the ground, baneful Echidna, undying nymph and unaging for all her days.

And they say that Typhon mingled in love with her, he who is terrible, arrogant, and lawless, with the maiden of vivacious eyes; and once impregnated she bore children of strong hearts: First she engendered the dog Orthos to serve Geryon, (310) and yet second she bore something indescribable, not to be mentioned, blood-thirsty Cerberus, the bronze-sounding dog of Hades, with fifty heads, shameless and powerful; and still third she engendered the Hydra of Lerna, of perverse mind, whom Hera, the goddess of white arms, raised, immensely irritated at Herakles' strength. Even this one the son of Zeus, scion of Amphytrion, wiped out with pitiless bronze, together with bellicose Iolaos; Herakles did, by the counsel of Athena, leader of hosts.

But she had also given birth to Chimaera, who breathes invincible fire, (320) terrible and huge, swift-footed and powerful. Three were her heads: one of a lion of flashing eyes, another of a she-goat, and another of a snake, a mighty dragon. [A lion in front, a dragon behind, and a she-goat in the middle, snorting a terrible force of burning fire.][46] Pegasos and excellent Bellerophon took the life of this one.

But, overpowered by Orthos, she (Echidna) in turn had given birth to the lethal Sphinx, ruin for the Kadmeians,[47] and to the lion of Nemea, whom Hera then raised, the illustrious spouse of Zeus, settling it in the hills of Nemea, a pain for human beings. (330) While living there it went about snaring the tribes of men, and ruled over Tretos of Nemea and over Apesas; but the vigor of the Heraklean force overpowered him. And lastly Keto, mingling in love with Phorkys, bore a terrible serpent, which guards the all-golden apples at the great limits in the caverns of the dark earth. This is the offspring of Ketos and Phorkys.

(Descendants of the Titans)

(Lines 337–382 skipped: Children of Ocean: Catalogue of rivers and spring nymphs, known as Oceanids, who protect youths; only a small portion of the thousands of rivers and Oceanids are provided, for "the name of all of them is difficult for a mortal man to say, but each of those who live around one of them knows them." Children of Theia with Hyperion: Helios [Sun], Selene [Moon], and Eos [Dawn]; children of Eurybe and Kreios; children of Eos [Dawn] and Astraios: the winds [Zephyros, Boreas, and Notos] and the stars.)

(Styx and her offspring, her connection with Zeus)

And Styx, daughter of Ocean, mingling with Pallas, gave birth in her mansions to Rivalry (Zelos) and Victory (Nike) of beautiful ankles, and she engendered also Power (Kratos) and Force (Bia), remarkable children. Their house is not apart from

---

[46] These lines probably did not belong in the original text but were added (interpolated) later and are identical with those in *Iliad* 6.181–182.

[47] The descendants of Kadmos, founder of Thebes, whom the Sphinx besieged until it was defeated by Oedipus.

Zeus, and there is neither residence nor path but that through which Zeus leads them, but they always sit by Zeus, the loud-thunderer. For this is how Styx planned it, the eternal daughter of Ocean, (390) on that day, when the Olympian lightener (Zeus) summoned the immortal gods to high Olympos, and said that, whoever of the gods would fight with him against the Titans, he would not deprive him of his privileges, but each one would keep what he had before among the immortal gods. And he added this, that whoever had been without honor and privilege under Kronos, would have honor as well as privilege, as it is right. So eternal Styx came first to Olympos with her children, by the counsel of her dear father; and Zeus honored her and gave her abundant gifts. (400) For he established her as the great oath of the gods, and for her children to live with him for all days. And so he fulfilled from start to end for everyone, just as he had promised; for he is greatly powerful and rules.

(Offspring of Phoebe and Koios)
And Phoebe in turn went to the very desirable bed of Koios; and thereafter, a goddess pregnant from the love of a god, gave birth to Leto of the dark robe, always soothing, kind to both human beings and immortal gods, soothing from the beginning, the nicest inside Olympos. And she gave birth to renowned Asteria, (410) whom Perse once led to his great house to be called his dear wife.

(Hakate and her powers)
And she (Asteria) became pregnant and bore Hakate, whom Zeus, son of Kronos, honored above all; for he procured for her magnificent gifts: to hold a share of the earth and of the barren sea. And she also received her share in honor from the starry sky, and she is most honored among the immortal gods. For even now, whenever one of the terrestrial men propitiates her performing good sacrifices according to tradition, he invokes Hakate; and great honor follows easily that man, whose prayers the goddess accepts with benevolence, (420) and she also bestows on him fortune, since she surely has this power. For as many as were born from Earth and Sky and obtained an honor, among them all she has a part, and not even the son of Kronos violated or took away all that she obtained among the Titans, the former gods, but she holds it, just as the partition was first made at the beginning. Neither did she, on account of being a single child, partake less in honor and privileges in the earth and the sky and the sea, but rather even more, since Zeus honors her.

By whomever she wishes, she stands grandly and helps him. (430) In the assembly, whoever she wishes excels among the people, and when men march armed into man-killing war, there the goddess is present, and to those she wishes she grants victory, in her benevolence, and offers glory. In a trial she sits next to revered kings. She is good, besides, when men compete in an athletic match; there the goddess also stands by their side and helps them; and the one winning by force and strength easily carries a handsome price and rejoices, and gives his parents glory.

And she is good at assisting horsemen, whomever she wishes. (440) And to those who work the gray turbulent sea and who pray to Hakate and the loud Earth-Shaker (Poseidon), she would easily grant abundant fish, the glorious goddess, but she easily would take it away just as it appeared, if so she fancied. And she is good at augmenting the livestock in the stables, together with Hermes. The herds of cattle and the broad flocks of goats, and the herds of wooly sheep, if she so wishes in her heart, from few she multiplies them, and from many she makes them fewer.

So is she honored, despite being the only child of her mother, with prerogatives among all the immortals. (450) And the son of Kronos established her as nurse of children, of all those who after her saw with their eyes the light of Dawn of many gleams. So was she a nurse of children from the start, and these were her prerogatives.

(Children of Rhea and Kronos [Olympian gods]; Kronos is deposed by Zeus)

Rhea, conquered by Kronos, bore illustrious children: Hestia, Demeter, and Hera of the golden sandals, and powerful Hades, who inhabits his residence under the earth and has a ruthless heart, and the resounding Earth-Shaker (Poseidon), and wise Zeus, father of both gods and men, due to whose thunder the wide earth trembles. But great Kronos started gulping them down, (460) as each of them reached their mother's knees coming out of her holy womb, with the following reasoning, that no other of the brilliant descendants of Sky might hold the royal honor among the immortals. For he had learned from Earth and starry Sky that he was bound to be overpowered by his own child, through the plans of great Zeus, no matter how mighty he was. And at least about this he was not neglectful, but keeping a close watch he kept swallowing his children; and Rhea felt horrible sorrow.

But when she was about to give birth to Zeus, father of both gods and men, at that moment she begged her own dear parents, (470) Earth and starry Sky, to think of a plan, so that she could go unnoticed as she gave birth to her dear son, and also avenge the vengeful spirits of her father and her children, whom great crooked-minded Kronos had gulped down. And they paid much heed to their dear daughter and obeyed her, and they both related to her everything that was bound to happen with king Kronos and his strong-hearted son. And they sent her to Lyktos, to the rich land of Crete, Just as she was about to give birth to the youngest of her children, great Zeus. Tremendous Earth received him in broad Crete, (480) to raise him and take care of him.

Carrying him through the swift black night, she arrived there, first to Lyktos; taking him in her arms she hid him in a deep cave, under the deep hiding places of divine earth in the Aigaian mountain, dense in woods. And, wrapping a great stone in swaddling-clothes, she delivered it to him, to the great lord son of Sky, king of the early gods; which then he took with his hands and put down into his belly, the wretch, without even suspecting that behind him, in place of the stone, undefeated and untroubled, his own son remained, (490) who soon was going to take away his privilege, conquering him with force and his hands, and then rule among the immortals.

And quickly thereafter the strength and splendid limbs of the lord grew; and, after a year had passed, fooled by the loquacious suggestions of Earth, great crooked-minded Kronos brought up again his offspring, defeated by his son's tricks and force. But first he vomited the stone, which he had swallowed last; this Zeus fixed on the earth of wide paths in sacred Pytho, in the valleys under mount Parnassos, (500) to be a memorial in the future, a wonder for mortal human beings. And he freed his fathers' brothers[48] from their horrible bonds, the sons of Sky, whom his father had bound foolishly. And they repaid him in gratitude for his kind deeds,

[48] Referring to the Cyclopes.

and gave him thunder and smoky thunderbolt and lightning, which huge Earth had concealed before. Relying upon these he rules over mortals and immortals.

(Children of Iapetos)

Iapetos married Klymene, beautiful-ankled daughter of Ocean, and climbed up into the same bed with her. And she bore him Atlas, a child of strong spirit, (510) and gave birth to the very famous Menoitios and to Prometheus ("Forethought"), versatile, of sharp mind, and to clumsy Epimetheus ("Afterthought"), who became a disgrace from the beginning for men who survive on bread. For he was the first to accept a woman designed by Zeus, a maiden. Far-sounding Zeus threw arrogant Menoitios down into the dark, smiting him with burning thunderbolt on account of his recklessness and his excessive prowess. Atlas, in turn, holds the broad sky by hard obligation, at the limits of the earth in front of the Hesperides of acute voice, making it stand with his head and his tireless arms. (520) For this is the portion that wise Zeus gave him. And he bound Prometheus with painful fetters, the resourceful plotter, with hard bonds which he dragged through the middle of a pillar. And he set on him a long-winged eagle: she would eat his immortal liver, but it would grow the same all through the night, as much as the long-winged bird had eaten the whole day. This one Herakles killed, the mighty son of Alkmene of beautiful ankles, who defended the son of Iapetos from the evil plague and liberated him from his afflictions; not without the consent of Olympian Zeus, who rules on high, (530) so that the fame of Theban-born Herakles would be even greater than before on the fertile earth. So in respect for this, he honored his celebrated son. Angry though he was, he ceased the rage he used to have before, as Prometheus would challenge the counsels of the powerful son of Kronos.

(Prometheus' tricks)

For when the gods and mortal men were sorting things out at Mekone,[49] he (Prometheus) presented a great ox, after dividing it with great anticipation, trying to trick Zeus' mind.

For first he set down for him the meat and the entrails, rich in fat, placed inside skin, hiding them in the ox's stomach. (540) And then, in turn, he set down for him the white bones of the ox, in a deceitful trick, well arranged, hiding them in gleaming fat. And surely then the father of men and gods addressed him: "Son of Iapetos, eminent among all lords, O friend, how unfairly have you divided up the portions." So he said teasing him, Zeus who knows eternal plans, to which in turn responded crooked-minded Prometheus, with a half smile, for he had not forgotten the deceitful trick: "Zeus, most glorious, greatest among the eternal-born gods, among these choose whichever your heart inside your chest bids you."

(550) So he said as he plotted deception; but Zeus, who knows eternal plans, realized it and did not fail to recognize the deceit. And he was contemplating in his spirit evils for mortal men, ones that he surely was going to accomplish. And finally with both hands he lifted the white fat, and became furious in his chest, and rage

---

[49] The precise meaning of these words is unclear, as *ekrinonto* (a plural middle voice form from *krino*, "split, divide, choose") can also mean "were separating," and we do not know what the object of the verb is. It could be gods and human beings themselves or something else, like adjudicating the sacrificial offerings to each group, as the story seems to indicate.

reached his spirit, when he saw the white bones of the ox, part of the deceitful trick. And since this moment the tribes of men upon the earth burn white bones for the immortals on top of smoky altars. And cloud-gatherer Zeus addressed him, greatly enraged: "Son of Iapetos, who knows counsels better than anyone, (560) O friend, it seems you did not forget your deceitful tricks yet."

So said in anger Zeus, who knows eternal plans. And from then onwards, always mindful of his rage, he did not give the Meliai[50] the force of relentless fire for mortal men who dwell upon the earth. But the noble son of Iapetos fooled him completely by hiding the far-seen flame of relentless fire in a hollow cane; this in turn bit deeply the spirit of high-thundering Zeus, and he was furious in his heart, when he saw among men the far-seen flame of fire.

(Creation of the first woman)

(570) But at once he prepared an evil for humanity, in exchange for the fire; for the very renowned Lame one (Hephaistos) fashioned from earth the likeness of a maiden, by the plans of the son of Kronos; and the goddess of bright eyes, Athena, girded her and adorned her, with a silvery dress; and with her own hands she hung down from her head an embroidered veil, a marvel to see. And around her temples Pallas Athena placed lovely flourishing garlands, flowers from the meadow. And around her head she placed a golden headband, one that the very renowned Lame one had made with his own hands, to please the father Zeus. (580) In it he had fashioned many designs, a marvel to see, all the terrible beasts that the main-land and the sea nourish; many of these he put in it, and beauty breathed upon them all, marvelous, looking like living creatures with voice.

But once he made a beautiful evil thing to pay for the good one,[51] he took her where the other gods and human beings were, embellished with the adornment of the bright-eyed one, fathered by a mighty one;[52] and wonder possessed both immortal gods and mortal men, when they saw the thorny deception, irresistible for men. (590) For the race of female women springs from this one, [for from her is the destructive race and tribe of women,][53] a great pain for mortals, dwelling together with men, no companions in destructive poverty but only in wealth. Just as when the bees inside vaulted beehives maintain the drones, who only partake in base deeds, and while the ones strive all day until the sun goes down, every day, and set up the white honey-combs, the others, remaining inside, sheltered by the hives, reap the labor of others into their own stomachs; (600) just in such way high-thundering Zeus set up women as an evil for mortal men, partakers in troublesome actions.

But another disgrace he provided in exchange for the good: whoever does not want to marry, escaping marriage and the mischievous works of women, arrives at deadly old age without an attendant; and he who did not lack sustenance while he was alive, now that he is dead his relatives share out his livelihood. But the one in whose destiny is marriage, and who acquires a decent wife, suited with intelligence, for this one, with the passing of time, the evil is balanced out with the good (610) in

---

[50] This refers to the Ash-Tree Nymphs (see note 41 on page 36).

[51] That is, to pay for the stolen fire.

[52] Athena.

[53] This (or the previous) line probably does not belong in the text.

a steadfast manner; and yet he who obtains shameless progeny lives with constant anguish in his mind, in his spirit, and in his heart, also an evil that has no relief.

Thus it is not possible to cheat or elude the mind of Zeus. For not even the son of Iapetos, Prometheus, the savior, escaped his heavy anger, but by necessity, astute though he was, a great chain held him down.

(Zeus' war with the Titans or Titanomachy)

When their father (Sky) first became irritated with Obriareos,[54] and with Kottos and Gyges,[55] he bound them with strong bonds, envious of their excessive prowess and also of their appearance and their size; (620) he made them dwell under the broad-pathed earth. There they were, withstanding pain, dwelling under the earth at the edge, at the limits of great earth, suffering much and for long, holding great grief in their heart. But the son of Kronos, together with the other immortal gods whom beautiful-haired Rhea bore in love with Kronos, brought them up to the light again, following the advice of Earth.

For she had explained to them everything in detail, that it was with these that they would attain victory and splendid boast. For they had long been fighting, enduring distressful pain, (630) the Titan gods and all those who were born from Kronos, confronting one another in mighty clashes; some, the illustrious Titans, from high Othrys, and the others from Olympos, the gods who give boons, whom beautiful-haired Rhea bore sleeping with Kronos.

By then, they had been fighting for ten full years, constantly enduring distressful battle against each other. Neither was there a solution for their difficult strife nor an end for either side, but the outcome of the war had been stretched even. However, when he offered them[56] supplies, (640) nectar and ambrosia, which the gods themselves eat, and the vigorous spirit had been restored in the chests of them all, [as they received the nectar and desirable ambrosia] then the father of men and gods addressed them:

"Listen to me, splendid sons of Earth and Sky, so I can say what my spirit in my chest tells me to. For a very long time already we have been fighting against each other, over victory and power, every day, the Titan gods and all of us descended from Kronos. But now show me your great strength and your invincible arms (650) in deadly combat against the Titans, remembering our kind friendship, and how you reached again the light after suffering so many things under an insufferable bond, thanks to our counsel, from under a murky fog."

So he said, and in turn blameless Kottos responded to him at once: "Sir, it is not an unknown thing that you are talking about, but we also know that you excel in thoughts and excel in intelligence, and that you emerged as the defender of the immortals against cold ruin. And through your careful plans we were released back again from under a murky fog, from under unpleasant bonds, (660) O son of the lord Kronos, after suffering hopeless pains. So also now, with determined mind and well-disposed spirit we will defend your power in dreadful battle, storming the Titans in mighty clashes."

---

[54] That is, Briareos, in a variant form of the same name.

[55] These are the Hundred-Handers, mentioned in *Th.* 147 ff.

[56] Zeus to Briareos, Kottos, and Gyges.

So he said; and the gods, givers of boons, approved after hearing his speech; for their spirit was craving war even more than before; and they provoked undesirable war, all of them, female and male alike, on that very day, the Titan gods and all those descendant from Kronos, and those whom Zeus brought to the light from the darkness under the earth, (670) terrible and powerful, who possessed a superb strength.

One hundred arms sprang from their shoulders, equal for all of them, and fifty heads for each one grew from their shoulders upon their sturdy limbs. Then they took position against the Titans in miserable combat, holding enormous rocks in their sturdy hands. And the Titans reinforced their ranks with determination; and both sides showed the work of their arms and their force, and the boundless sea resounded terribly, and the earth roared greatly, and the broad sky moaned as it trembled, (680) and high Olympos shook from the ground under the rush of the immortals, and the deep quake reached from their feet to steamy Tartaros, and the loud sound of the unspeakable clashes and of the powerful blows.

In such way they shot resounding missiles at each other. And the voice of both sides reached the starry sky as they called on each other; for they clashed in a loud war-cry. But Zeus could not contain his strength anymore; instead, his heart filled with strength at once and showed his full force; and he advanced at the same time from the sky and from Olympos (690) continuously shooting lightning, and the thunderbolts flew packed together out of his sturdy hand, with thunder and lightning, whirling about a sacred and intense flame. And all around the life-giving earth roared as it burned, and all around the immense woods crackled loudly. The whole earth boiled, and the streams of Ocean and the barren sea; and a hot breath surrounded the earthly Titans, and an unspeakable flame reached the divine aether, and the luminescent shine of the thunderbolt and lightning blinded their eyes, powerful though they were, (700) and an astonishing heat invaded the chasm, and to look directly at it with your eyes and to hear its sound with your ears seemed just like when earth and broad sky from above approached[57]; for this kind of great roar would arise from below as she was crushed down and he rushed down from above.

Such noise the gods produced as they merged in strife. At the same time, the winds spread the commotion and the dust and the thunder and the lightning and the lazing thunderbolt, the shafts of great Zeus, and brought the cry and the screaming to the middle of both sides. An unspeakable din of deadly strife (710) rose, and it became clear where the dominating action was. The battle tilted to one side; for before, charging against each other they had fought incessantly in mighty combats. But then Kottos, Briareos, and Gyges, insatiable of war, were among the first ones to provoke a violent battle; then they threw three hundred stones from their sturdy arms, one after the other, and they covered the Titans with their darts. Indeed, they sent them under the earth of wide paths and they bound them with hard bonds, after defeating them with their hands, high-spirited though they were, (720) so far below the earth as the sky is from the earth.

---

[57] Probably referring to when they mated in primordial times.

(Description of the Underworld and Styx)

For such is the distance to the steamy Underworld (Tartaros) from the earth: for a bronze anvil, falling from the sky for nine nights and days, would reach the earth on the tenth; [so in turn is the distance from the earth to the steamy underworld;] so in turn a bronze anvil, falling from the earth for nine nights and days, would reach the underworld on the tenth. Around it a bronze fence stretches out, and on both sides of it a three-layered night wraps it around its neck; what is more, above it grow the roots of the earth and the barren sea. There is where the Titans are hidden, under a dark fog, (730) by the designs of Zeus the cloud-gatherer, in a dank region, at the limits of the tremendous earth. And they have no way out, for Poseidon installed bronze gates, and a wall extends from both sides.

(Skipped 734–745: probably interpolated lines, which add no significant information)

In front of these (gates) the son of Iapetos[58] holds the wide sky, making it stand on his head and his tireless arms, immovable, just where Night and Day passing very close exchange greetings as they pass through the great bronze threshold; (750) the one is going to step inside, and the other is going out the doors, and never does the house hold them both inside, but always one of them, going out of the house, turns over the earth, while the other, going inside the house, awaits the time of her trip, until it arrives; the one holds for those on earth much-seeing light, while the other holds Sleep (Hypnos) in her arms, brother of Death (Thanatos), lethal Night, totally covered in murky fog. And inside the children of Night have their homes, Sleep and Death, terrible gods. (760) Never does the bright Sun look upon them with his rays when he goes up to the sky or down from the sky. While one of them goes around gently over the earth and the broad back of the sea, and is soothing for men, the other has an iron core, a bronze heart in his ruthless chest: he keeps whomever among mortals he gets hold of, and he is hateful even for the immortal gods.

There stand, in front, the resounding houses of the earthly god, [powerful Hades and awesome Persephone,] and a fearful dog guards them in the front, (770) ruthless, and he has an evil trick: upon those going in, he fawns in the same way with his tail and with both ears, but he does not let them go out again; instead he is vigilant and bites whomever he catches going outside the gates [of Powerful Hades and awesome Persephone].

There dwells a goddess hateful to the immortals, terrible Styx,[59] the oldest daughter of Ocean, of circular flow. Far from the gods, she dwells in a famous mansion vaulted with tall rocks; and from all sides around it leans on silver columns, approaching the sky. (780) And rarely swift-footed Iris, the daughter of Wonder (Thaumas), travels there with a message over the broad back of the sea. Whenever strife and quarrel arise among the immortals and then one of those who have Olympian mansions lies, Zeus would send Iris to bring a great oath from afar, the renowned water in a golden receptacle, cold, which flows from the high steep rock; and under the broad-pathed earth it flows abundant from the sacred river through

---

[58] Atlas.

[59] Hesiod makes a pun between the name Styx and the adjective *stygeros,* "hateful, abominable" (as if we had used "stigmatized," for instance).

the dark night. A branch of Ocean, a tenth part, she had been apportioned. (790) Nine times around the earth and the broad back of the sea, spinning in silver whirls he falls into the sea, and she, as one of them, flows forth from the rock, a great pain for the gods: Whoever among the immortals who hold the summit of snowy Olympos swears a false oath as he pours it, lies without breath for the duration of a full year, and he cannot go near the nourishment of ambrosia and nectar, but lies down without air and without voice in a covered bed, and an evil deep sleep covers him. And yet, when he has completed this malady at the end of the year, (800) a new trial replaces the other, a more difficult one: for nine years he stays apart from the gods, who live forever, and he never partakes in their council or in their banquets, for all of nine years; but on the tenth he participates again in the assemblies of the gods, who hold Olympian mansions. As such an oath the gods established the imperishable water of Styx, the one of old, which flows forth through a coarse region.

That is where the sources and the ends of the dark earth and the steamy underworld and the barren sea and the starry sky all lie in succession, (810) disturbing, dank, which even the gods hate. And that is where the marble gates and the bronze threshold are, unshakable, well fitted with unending roots, self-generated; and beyond, apart from all the gods, live the Titans, at the other side of the gloomy chasm. But the famous helpers of loud-crashing Zeus inhabit houses in the foundations of the Ocean, Kottos and Gyges; as for Briareos, since he was noble, the deep-sounding Earth-shaker made him his son-in-law, and he gave him to marry Wave-Walker (Kymopoleia), his daughter.

(War with Typhoeus or Typhonomachia)

(820) Yet after Zeus had driven the Titans away from the sky tremendous Earth bore her youngest child, Typhoeus,[60] in love with Tartaros, thanks to golden Aphrodite. His hands are of the kind that attain deeds by strength,[61] and his feet are tireless, those of this powerful god; and off his shoulders he has one hundred heads of a snake, a terrible serpent, licking with dark tongues; and on these awful heads two eyes glittered under his eyebrows like fire; and from each of his heads fire burned as he stared; (830) and the voices in all of the terrible heads uttered an indescribable sound of different kinds: for sometimes they would make a sound as if for the gods to understand,[62] but other times the sound of a proud, loud-bellowing bull, wild in his strength, and yet other times that of a lion who has pitiless spirit, and another in turn one similar to cubs, a marvel to hear, and another in turn he whistled, and the high mountains echoed from below.

And an incredible deed would have been accomplished on that day, and he would have ruled over mortals and immortals, if at that point the father of men and gods had not acutely realized it. He thundered hardly and loudly, (840) and all around the earth resounded in a terrifying way, and also the wide sky above and the sea and the streams of Ocean, and the underworld of the earth. And Olympos shook greatly

---

[60] Presumably the same creature as the one mentioned as Typhon in *Th.* 306.

[61] The Greek text of this line is corrupt and the meaning is not clear, so any translation is a mere guess.

[62] That is, like human speech.

under his immortal feet as the lord launched himself forward, and the earth groaned in response. And a fire took hold of the dark-blue sea under both the thunder and lightning and the fire from such a monstrosity of hurricanes and winds and flaming thunderbolt. The whole earth boiled, and also the sky and the sea; and then tall waves swelled on both sides of the coast, around and about, under the impetus of the gods, and a ceaseless commotion arose. (850) Hades trembled, he who rules over the deceased under the earth, and so did the underworld Titans, who live around Kronos, because of the ceaseless din and the terrifying fight.

But when Zeus indeed gathered his strength and took his weapons, thunder, lightning and flaming thunderbolt, he struck him jumping from Olympos; and so he wrapped in flames all the awful heads of the terrible monster. And when he had overpowered him, slashing him with blows, he collapsed with lame limbs, and tremendous earth groaned. A flame then emerged from the thundering lord (860) in the creeks of the rugged dark mountain, as it was hit, and the tremendous earth was much burned by the awful smoke, and it melted like tin heated with skill by vigorous men in well-perforated melting pots, or like iron, which, even being the hardest, overpowered by scolding fire in mountainous creeks, melts down on the divine earth by the works of Hephaistos. So now melted the earth with the spark of flaming fire. Then, aggravated in his spirit, Zeus hurled him into the broad underworld.

It is from Typhoeus that the humid force of blowing winds comes, (870) except that of Notos and Boreas and clearing Zephyros; for these are from the gods by lineage, a great benefit for mortals. But the other breezes blow randomly over the sea; these are the ones that, falling onto the murky sea, as a great sorrow for mortals, rush in a dangerous hurricane; and they all blow from here and there, scatter ships and destroy sailors; and there is no escape from the disaster for men who stumble upon them in the sea. And these, in turn, also upon the boundless, flower-bearing earth destroy the cherished works of dirt-born men, (880) filling them with dust and troubling confusion.

(Zeus secures his power)

Next, after the blessed gods had completed their toil and by force had assigned the prerogatives for the Titans, then surely they encouraged Zeus, the far-sounding Olympian, by the advice of Earth, to be king and rule over the gods; and he made a fair distribution of prerogatives for them.

(Zeus marries Metis and gives birth to Athena)

Then Zeus, as king of the gods, took Metis[63] as his first wife, who knows the most among both gods and mortal men. But just when she was about to give birth to the bright-eyed goddess Athena, he completely tricked her mind with deceit (890) and with wily words, and then he gulped her down into his belly, by the advice of Earth and starry Sky: for they had so advised him, lest another of the eternal-born gods hold the royal honor instead of Zeus. For it was decreed that children of superior mind would be born from her: first the bright-eyed girl, Tritogeneia,[64] possessing

---

[63] Metis, which means "Wisdom," "Skill," was born from Tethys and Okeanos, who were among the Titans (while Zeus and the Olympian gods descend from younger Titan Kronos) (*Th.* 133–137).

[64] Athena.

strength equal to her father and intelligent counsel, but after she was going to give birth to a son, a king of gods and men, who would have an arrogant heart. But before that Zeus gulped her down into his belly, (900) and so the goddess would advise him on both good and evil.

(Lines 901–924 are a list of the wives that Zeus takes after Metis and the children they bore to Zeus. These wives are Themis, Eurynome, Demeter, Mnemosyne, Leto, and Hera.)

But he himself, from his head, gave birth to bright-eyed Athena, (925) the terrible mistress, bellicose, army-leader, invincible, for whom din and wars and battles are pleasing. But Hera was both furious and aggravated with her husband, and without mingling in love, gave birth to famous Hephaistos, who excels among all in Olympos with his skills.

(Lines 930–962 continue the list of goddesses who bore children to Zeus; then follows a catalogue of goddesses or women descended from gods who bedded with mortal men and the god-like offspring they bore; the last lines, 1019–1022, are themselves the beginning of a separate poem that continues this genealogical theme, only partially preserved, called the Catalogue of Women.*)*

1.6. ORPHIC COSMOGONY: THE DERVENI PAPYRUS

In ancient Greece there existed an entire literary tradition that ascribed works to the mythical poet Orpheus. Orpheus was deemed to be the first poet and musician, whose music enchanted beasts and even stirred emotions in trees and rocks. He is famous for his nearly successful attempt to bring his wife Eurydice back from Hades (see his story in Part 6, document 12). Many of the texts called **"Orphic"** were concerned with the origins of the cosmos (cosmogonies) and the birth and genealogies of gods (theogonies). The existence of such traditions shows that the literary **genre** of cosmogonies went beyond Hesiod's *Theogony* and that many stories of this type were in circulation. The Orphic texts vary widely, but some common features stand out in several, such as the position of Night at the beginning of the cosmos, the appearance of a Time deity in the early stages of creation, the prominence of a cosmic egg from which a creator called Phanes or Protogonos was born, and a final succession of Heaven and Earth, Kronos, and Zeus, culminating in the god Dionysos, who is a central figure in Orphic theology. In some of the Orphic cosmic speculation we can see the effect of **Presocratic philosophy** (or "natural philosophy," seventh to sixth centuries BCE), as well as motifs that point to Near Eastern models, particularly Phoenician (where a Time deity and an egg appear; see documents 1.7.a and 1.7.b). Orphic cosmogonies were connected with intellectual and religious initiation groups (Orphic, Eleusinian, and Bacchic). They were well known by the fifth century BCE, when Plato talks about them, but their texts manifest a much older tradition comparable to that of Hesiod. The main problem for scholars is that the sources are for the most part very fragmentary and reconstructed from quotations by later authors (e.g., Damaskios, a Neoplatonist philosopher of the fifth to sixth centuries CE).

The Derveni Papyrus contains a unique, directly preserved, Orphic text. Discovered in an archaeological dig, this papyrus is the oldest preserved manuscript from Europe. Sometime around the middle of the fourth century BCE, it had rolled off the funerary pyre of a Greek nobleman in Derveni (northern Greece). The fire burned only part of the papyrus, carbonizing the rest, thus guaranteeing its preservation. The document, of unknown authorship, contains a philosophical commentary on an Orphic cosmogony, which is quoted and commented on and can be tentatively reconstructed. It should be noted, however, that scholars have proposed different arrangements and reconstructions of the damaged fragments, and also that the original cosmogony might not have been quoted in full or in even in the original order by the Derveni commentator. In any case, the whole document is a copy of an older text (given some scribal mistakes), and it follows that the cosmogony quoted in it, in turn, must be even older than the commentary, from at least around 500 BCE.

The brief theogonic text is written in hexameters and condenses mythological motifs known from other texts (e.g., the castration motif), sometimes alluding to them very briefly and assuming the reader knows more elaborated versions. The poem quoted by the Derveni author focuses on Zeus' glorious ascension to power in Olympos and his re-creation of the universe. The poem, therefore, seems to be a hymn or, more likely, a "sacred discourse" (*hieros logos*) of the type associated with Orphic initiation rituals, which are alluded to in the commentary. The preserved lines of the Orphic cosmogony are reproduced here.

SOURCE: The Derveni Papyrus, from the Greek text edited in A. Bernabé, *Poetae Epici Graeci Testimonia et Fragmenta* Pars II: Fasc. 1. *Orphicorum et Orphicis similium testimonia* (Bibliotheca scriptorum Graecorum et Romanorum Teubneriana, Munich and Leipzig, 2004), fragments 3–18, translated by Alberto Bernabé and Miguel Herrero.

(3) I will speak to the lawful, shut your doors, profane!

(4) those who were born from Zeus the almighty king [. . .]

(5) Zeus, when he took the prophesized power of his father
   in his hands, and the strength and the illustrious deity

(6) Zeus [. . . came to the cave where]
   Night was seated, who knew all oracles, immortal nurse of
   the gods [. . .] give oracles from the hidden place,
   she prophesized all which was lawful to accomplish
   how he would take the fine throne of snowy Olympos.

(7) Zeus, once he had heard the oracles of his father [. . .]

(8) [. . .] swallowed the phallus [of Ouranos/Sky]
   [of the first-born king,] which had first thrown out the aither [. . .]

(9–10) And from Earth was born Kronos, who did a terrible thing.
   [. . .] took away the kingship [. . .]
   Ouranos, son of Night, he was the first to reign;
   from him Kronos in his turn, and then prudent Zeus,

(11) getting intelligence and the royal honor among the blessed
[. . .] all the sinews

(12) [Zeus . . . swallowed the power]
of the phallus of the first-born king. And in him all
immortal blessed gods and goddesses were joined
and rivers and lovely springs and everything else
which had come to be; and he became the only one.

(13) Now he is king of all and will be everafter

(14) Zeus became the first, Zeus last, god of the shining bolt.
Zeus head, Zeus middle, Zeus is formed from all things,
Zeus breath of all, Zeus is destiny of all,
Zeus king, Zeus lord of all, god of the shining bolt.

(15) Zeus engendered through ejaculation
Persuasion and Harmony and heavenly Aphrodite,
and he contrived Earth and broad Heaven above,

(16) and he contrived the great might of broad-flowing Ocean
and he placed therein the sinews of silver-eddying Achelous,
from whom all seas [. . .]

(17) in the middle the (moon) of equal measure everywhere,
which is manifested to many mortals over the immense earth.

(18) But when the mind of Zeus had conceived all the works,
he wanted to unite in love with his own mother.

1.7. PHOENICIAN COSMOGONIES

The Phoenicians were a Semitic people of Canaanite origin from the area that roughly approximates the modern countries of Lebanon and northern Israel. Although they had a long and deeply influential presence in the Mediterranean, with colonies throughout northern Africa, Sicily, Sardinia, Spain, and Portugal (the most famous being Gadir and Carthage), we have very few Phoenician literary sources. They played a crucial role in transmitting to Greek culture both technologies (e.g., the alphabet) and mythological themes from the broader Near Eastern milieu. In contrast to the increasing archaeological information we have about them, their own literature has completely disappeared except for traces glimpsed through the lens of classical authors. Their history is also reconstructed from classical, Near Eastern, and biblical allusions, while the abundant Phoenician **epigraphical** evidence offers little historical and mythological information.

1.7.a. Philon of Byblos: Excerpts from the *Phoenician History*

Document 1.7.a contains a fragment of one of the few works by a Phoenician to have come down to us. Philon of Byblos was a scholar and antiquarian who lived during the early Roman Empire (64–141 CE). He wrote in Greek, as was usual in the eastern part of the Roman Empire. However, he claimed to be transmitting a Phoenician theogony originally written by one Sanchounia-thon over a thousand years before his time. His approach was to transform these myths into a historical account in which the gods were but ancient kings and inventors who were later divinized. This is called a **Euhemeristic** approach (after Euhemeros, a scholar active at the Macedonian court at the late fourth to early third centuries BCE, that is, the early Hellenistic period). Unfortunately, of his many works, the only substantial excerpts to survive are quotations from the beginning of his *Phoenician History*, quoted by the Christian bishop Eusebios of Caesarea (ca. 300 CE) in his *Praeparatio Evangelica*. He, in turn, was quoting the third-century CE Neoplatonic scholar Porphyry of Tyre, who dealt with Philon's writings in his works about philosophy and the history of religions.

The narrative of Philon was for long considered a mere reelaboration on Greek motifs with little genuine claims of antiquity or Phoenician authenticity. However, thanks to the discovery of Ugaritic texts from Late Bronze Age Syria, scholars now believe that Philon is basing at least part of his information on Phoenician archives and possibly earlier Canaanite traditions preserved in his own time. Names such as Sanchouniathon, Dagon, Demarous, Adodos, Baitylos, and many others are of Semitic origin. For instance, some appear in the Ugaritic epics, such as Demarous (Ugaritic Dimaranu or the like); Kronos, equated with Elos by Philon, is clearly the heir of the Canaanite god El (or Ilu in Ugaritic), head of the Canaanite pantheon; and the role of Pontos (the Sea) as cosmic enemy in the narrative is parallel with that of Yamm (Sea) in the Ugaritic *Baal Cycle*. Finally, the arrangement of the pantheon at the end of the cited passage implies that despite the cosmic fights, Elos/Kronos maintains his place as patriarchal leader of the gods, much as El/Ilu does in the Ugaritic epics (see *Baal Cycle* and *Aqhat Epic* in Part 3, documents 5.a and 5.b).

Yet with the castration of Ouranos (Sky) by Kronos and other allusions, Philon aligns his mythology with the Hesiodic tradition (which he sees as dependant on the Canaanite and not the reverse). Conscious of his "bicultural" stand, he draws constant equivalences (we call this ***interpretatio***) between Greek and Semitic gods. In turn, other aspects of his narrative reveal influences from Presocratic natural philosophy and later schools of thought, intertwined in a crowded account that combines elements assimilated over the centuries in the Eastern Mediterranean "melting pot." The motif of the "first inventors" (*protoi heuretai*) also occupies a good part of his account.

Finally, Phoenician cosmogonies seem to have shared basic concepts with Orphic ones, most remarkably the idea of a cosmic egg (see also Aristophanes in document 1.8) but also the mention of Time (here as Aion, "eternal time") and Protogonos, "First Born." The latter was the name some Orphic cosmogonies gave to Phanes ("The Shining One"), a divinity said to be born from the cosmic egg, which in turn was made by Time (Chronos—not to be confused with Kronos).

SOURCE: A. Kaldellis and C. López-Ruiz, *BNJ-FGrH* 790, *P. E.* 1.10.1–31 modified.

(Cosmogonic section)

(1) He (Philon) posits as the source of all things a dark and windy air or a gust of dark air and a foul and nether chaos.[65] These things were limitless and, for a long eon, had no boundary. He says, "But when the wind conceived an erotic desire for its own sources and a mixing together took place, that intertwining was called Desire (Pothos). And this was the source for the creation of all things. It itself was not aware of its own creation. And from his entwining with the wind Mot came into being. (2) Some say that this is mud, others the putrefaction of the liquid mixture. And from this mixture came all the sowing of creation and the birth of all things. There were animals with no sensation, from which came animals with intelligence. And they were called Zophasemin, which means "observers of the heavens." And they had the shape of an egg.[66] And Mot shone forth and the sun and the moon and the stars and the luminous bodies and the great stars." (3) Such was their cosmogony, outright introducing atheism.

Let us read what follows, what he says about the creation of animals. He says, (4) "And when the air was filled with light through the heating of both the sea and the earth, there came about winds and clouds and the greatest downpourings of the heavenly waters and floods. And then they parted and were removed from their proper place by the burning heat of the sun, and when all of them had mingled again in the air and collided there was thunder and lightning. And the crash of thunder awoke the intelligent animals that were mentioned before, and they were alarmed because of the noise and so then the male and the female began to move across the land and in the sea. (5) Such was their account of the generation of animals." To this the same author [i.e., Philon] adds that "these were found written in the cosmogony of Taautos[67] and his commentaries, which were based on conjectures and evidence, which his intellect perceived and illuminated for us."

(History of culture—first inventors)

(6) After this he states the names of the winds, the South wind, the North, and the rest, and adds: "But they were the first to dedicate what sprouted from the earth, and regarded them as gods, and worshipped them, things from which both they and their descendants and all their ancestors were sustained. And they made libations and offered incense. [They believed that pity and compassion and lamentation were appropriate for vegetation that separated itself from the earth and for the first generation of animals from the earth as well as their birth from each other, and their death, when they departed from life.]" (7) And he adds: "Such, then, were

---

[65] The "dark and windy air or gust" reminds of the biblical *tohu-wa-bohu*, "formless void and darkness," while chaos is found first in Hesiod's *Theogony*. Air and aether also appear in Orphic cosmogonies and in Phoenician ones (see document 1.7.b).

[66] Scholars see here a reference to the "world egg" or cosmic egg of Orphic cosmogonies (an egg also appears in the Egyptian cosmogony of Hermopolis). Zophasemim is West Smitic *zophei-shamaim*, "observers of heaven."

[67] Or Egyptian Thoth (*Tahawte* or *Djhwty*), associated with the art of writing and identified with Hermes in the Greek world (see note 70).

their notions regarding worship, corresponding to their weakness and the lack of spiritual daring of that time."

And then he says that from the Kolpias wind and his wife Baau (which he interprets as being the night) were born Aion and Protogonos (First-Born), who were mortal men called by these names. Aion discovered the food that grows on trees. Those born to these two he calls Genos and Generation, and they settled Phoenicia. But when there were droughts, they stretched their arms toward the heaven, to the sun. "For the latter," he says, "they held to be the only god, the lord of heaven, calling him Beelsamen, which in Phoenician means lord of heaven, or Zeus among the Greeks." (8) After these things he accuses the Greeks of error, saying, "It is not in vain that we have expounded on these things in different ways, because they relate to the later reception of the names that occur in these matters, which the Greeks, in their ignorance, have taken in a different way, misled by the ambiguity of translation." (9) Next he says that "from Genos, the offspring of Aion and First-Born, mortal children were born in turn, whose names are Light, Fire, and Flame. They," he says, "discovered fire by rubbing sticks together and taught its use to others. They gave birth to sons who were great in size and stature, whose names were given to the mountains over which they ruled; thus were named Mts. Kassios, Libanos, the Anti-Libanos, and Brathy. From them," he says, "were born Samemroumos, who is also called High-in-Heaven, [and Ousoos]. But," he says, "they called themselves after their mothers, given that women at that time coupled freely with whomever they chanced upon." (10) Then he says that "High-in-Heaven occupied Tyre, inventing huts from reeds, rushes, and papyrus. He rebelled against his brother Ousoos, who was the first to think of clothing his body using leather from animals that he managed to capture. When there was a downpour of rain and gusts of wind, the trees in Tyre rubbed against each other and caught fire, and their wood burned. Ousoos took a tree, trimmed it, and was the first to dare to sail on the sea. He dedicated two stelai to Fire and Wind, and worshipped them and made libations of blood to them from beasts he hunted. (11) And when these two died," he says, "their descendants dedicated staves to them, and worshipped these staves, and held annual festivals in their honor."

"But many years later there were born to the family of High-in-Heaven Hunter and Fisherman, the inventors of fishing and hunting, after whom hunters and fishermen are named. From them were born two brothers, the discoverers of iron and its working. One of them, Chousor, devised formulae and spells and prophesies. This was Hephaistos, who also invented the hook, bait, line and raft, and was the first of men to set sail. Hence they honored him even as a god after his death. (12) He was also called Zeus Meilichios. Some say that his brothers invented walls made of bricks. After these things, two young men were born to this family, of whom one was called Craftsman, the other Earthly Native. They invented the method of mixing staw and clay to make bricks, and hardening them in the sun. But they also invented roofs. From them sprung others, of whom one was called Field, the other Field Hero or just Hunter, of whom there is in Phoenicia an arcane and highly revered statue as well as a temple drawn by a pair of oxen. Among the Byblians he is named the greatest of the gods. (13) These two conceived the notion of adding courtyards to houses as well as enclosures and dens. From them came hunters and those who hunt with dogs. They are also called Drifters and Titans. From them were born Amynos and Magos, who introduced villages and flocks. From them were born Misor and Sydyk, namely Supple and Just. They discovered the use of salt. (14) From Misor was born Taautos, who invented the first script for writing, whom the Egyptians call Thoyth, the Alexandrians Thoth, and the Greeks Hermes. From Sydyk were born the Dioskouroi, who are also the Kabeiroi, Korybantes, and Samothracians. They," he says, "were the first to invent a boat. From them others were born, who discovered herbs and how to heal dangerous bites and spells."

(History of Kronos)

"Around this time there lived a certain Elioun, also called Most High,[68] and a woman named Berouth, who settled in the area of Byblos. (15) From them was born Terrestrial Native, whom they later called Ouranos (Sky) and after him, on account of his surpassing beauty, the element up above us was named 'heaven.' A sister was born to him from the parents mentioned above, who was named Ge (Earth). And on account of her beauty," he says, "the earth, which has the same name, was named after her. Their father, Most High, died in an encounter with wild beasts and was deified; his children offered libations and sacrifices to him. (16) Ouranos succeeded to his father's rule and married his sister Earth, and begat from her four children: Elos, who is also Kronos, Baitylos, Dagon, who is also Grain,[69] and Atlas. And with other wives Ouranos produced numerous offspring. Hence Earth (Ge) was grieved and rebuked Ouranos in jealousy. As a result, they separated from each other. But even after Ouranos had left her he would violently approach and rape her at will, and then leave her again. He also tried to destroy his children by her, but Earth defended herself many times, making an alliance for her protection. And when Kronos became a man, he relied on Hermes Trismegistos[70] as a councilor and aid—for he was his secretary—and punished his father Ouranos in defense of his mother."

(18) "The children of Kronos were Persephone and Athena.[71] The first died as a virgin. As for Athena, with her advice and that of Hermes Kronos made a sickle and a spear. Then Hermes used words of magic on Kronos' allies and instilled in them the desire to fight against Ouranos on behalf of Earth. And so Kronos waged war against Ouranos and drove him from power, succeeding him in the kingship. Ouranos' lovely concubine, who was pregnant,[72] was captured in the battle, and Kronos gave her to be the wife of Dagon. (19) While with him she bore the child that Ouranos had sown and called him Demarous."

"After these events, Kronos surrounded his own dwelling with a wall and founded the first city, Byblos in Phoenicia. (20) After these things, Kronos suspected his own brother Atlas, and on the advice of Hermes buried him deep in the

---

[68] Compare with Phoenician and Hebrew *Elyon*, "Most High" (e.g., Gen. 14.18). The Greek *hypsistos* was used as a cultic divine title in the Hellenistic period.

[69] The identification of El and Kronos appears in many ancient sources; Baitylos here is a god, not the sacred stone or baetyl, mentioned below; Dagon is a Semitic god of fertility and grain (cf. Hebrew *dagan*, "grain").

[70] Hermes Trismegistos ("Three-times-greatest") became the authority for the later Hermetic esoteric movement. Here Hermes is again identified with Taautos (Thoth).

[71] The goddesses, especially Athena, reflect the attributes of Ugaritic Anat (see Part 3, document 5.b).

[72] Seemingly Earth (Ge), the wife mentioned above.

earth. At this time the descendants of the Dioskouroi built rafts and ships and sailed away. They were cast ashore near Mt. Kassios, where they consecrated a temple. Now, the allies of Elos, that is of Kronos, were called Eloeim, just as those who were called after Kronos were the Kronians. (21) Kronos has a son, Sadidos, whom he killed with his own steel, as he regarded him with suspicion. He deprived him of life, becoming the killer of his own son. Likewise he decapitated his own daughter, so that all the gods were shocked by Kronos' state of mind. (22) Time had passed when Ouranos, who was in exile, sent his maiden daughter Astarte along with two sisters of hers, Rhea and Dione, to kill Kronos through trickery. But Kronos captured them and made them, who were sisters, his lawful wives. (23) When Ouranos learned this he marshaled Fate and Season along with other allies against Kronos. But Kronos apporpiated them too and kept them by his side. Moreover," he says, "the god Ouranos invented baetyls, devising stones imbued with soul. Kronos had seven daughters with Astarte, the Titanids or Artemids. (24) And again to him with Rhea he had seven children, the youngest of whom was worshipped as soon as he was born. And with Dione he had . . . daughters, and with Astarte again he had two sons, Desire and Eros. (25) But Dagon discovered grain and plough, and was called Zeus Ploughman. One of the Titanids coupled with Sydyk the so-called Just and gave birth to Asklepios. (26) In addition, three sons were born to Kronos in Peraia: Kronos, who had the same name as his father, Zeus Belos, and Apollo. In that time there also lived Pontos (Sea), Typhon,[73] and Nereus, the father of Pontos and son of Belos. (27) To Pontos was born Sidon, who was the first to discover how to sing a hymn on account of the surpassing beauty of her voice, and Poseidon. To Demarous was born Melkathros, who is also Herakles."[74]

(28) "And then Ouranos again wages war against Pontos and, withdrawing, allies with Demarous.[75] Demarous attacks Pontos, but Pontos routs him. Demarous vowed to offer a sacrifice for his escape.[76] (29) In the thirty-second year of his dominion and reign, Elos, that is Kronos, trapped his father Ouranos in an inland location and, having him in his power, castrated him in the vicinity of some springs and rivers. This is where Ouranos was deified and his spirit was finished. The blood of his genitals dripped into the springs and the waters of the rivers. And the place is shown to this day. (31) Greatest Astarte and Zeus, Demarous and Adodos[77] the king of the gods, were ruling the land with the consent of Kronos." (. . .)

[73] See the role of Typhon/Typhoeus in Hesiod's *Theogony* (document 1.5) and the *Hymn to Apollo* (Part 3, document 9); here the role of the monstrous divine enemy is taken by Pontos (see below).

[74] The identification of Herakles with the Phoenician god Melqart (whose name means "City-king") is well attested in Greek and Greco-Phoenician sources.

[75] Presumably in the war agaist Kronos.

[76] See the theme of the sacrifice to Zeus Soter ("Savior") by Molorchos so that Herakles would return safely from his fight with the Nemean lion (Part 3, document 11.b).

[77] These seem to be epithets or alternative names for Zeus, which appear in North-West Semitic sources as variations (hyposthases) of the Storm God: *Dmrn* appears in Ugaritic texts in parallel with Baal Haddad, and Philo's Adodos is Semitic Haddad or Adad, the Storm God in the Levant.

(The text of Philon continues through Eusebius' P.E. 1.10.53, containing the account of rulers after Kronos, as well as a segment about child sacrifice, allegedly practiced by the Phoenician rulers in times of crisis, and a section on the wondrous nature of snakes.)

1.7.b. Phoenician Cosmogonies Mentioned by Damaskios

This document provides the only textual source for Phoenician cosmogonies outside Philon. These accounts were circulating in Greek in late antiquity (presumably translated from the original Phoenician). Our source this time is Damaskios, the late fifth- to early sixth-century CE Neoplatonic philosopher, who, in turn, paraphrases or quotes previous authors as sources for Phoenician mythology: he refers to Eudemos of Rhodes, the fourth-century BCE writer and pupil of Aristotle, and to Mochos, a legendary Phoenician wise figure of uncertain date. In this brief text, we can see again some of the Semitic names that appeared in Philon (Chousoron, Oulomos) and elements that surface in Orphic cosmogony, such as the cosmic egg. Desire (Pothos) also seems to have had a special place in Phoenician cosmogonies, judging by these two sources, which is comparable with the prominent place of Eros in Hesiod's *Theogony*, standing among the four primordial elements.

SOURCE: Carolina López-Ruiz, *BNJ-FGrH* 784 F4, Damaskios, *De principiis* 125c.

The Sidonians, according to the same writer (i.e., Eudemos) set before everything Time, Desire, and Mist, and they say that from the union of Desire and Mist, as dual principles, emerged Air and Breeze, implying that Air is the unmixed part of the intelligible, whereas Breeze, moving out of it (i.e., of Air), is the vital pattern (prototype) of the intelligible. And they say that, in turn, from these two an egg was born, corresponding, I think, to the intelligible intellect.

Outside of Eudemos, I found the mythology of the Phoenicians, according to Mochos, to be as such: at the beginning there was Aither and Air, two principles themselves, from whom Oulomos was born, the intelligible god, himself, I think, the peak of the intelligible. From him, they say, mating with himself, was born first Chousoron, the opener, then an egg; the latter, I think, they call the intelligible intellect, and the opener Chousoron they call the intelligible force, as it was the first to differentiate undifferentiated nature. Unless after these two principles the highest is the one Wind, while the middle are the two winds Lips and Notos—for they make even these somehow precede Oulomos. As for Oulomos, he would be the intelligible intellect himself, and the opener Chousoros would be the first order after the intelligible, and the egg would be the sky; for they say that Ouranos (Sky) and Ge (Earth) were born from the egg as it broke in two, each one from one of the two halves.

1.8. COSMOGONY IN ARISTOPHANES' *BIRDS*

Aristophanes (446–386 BCE) was a comic playwright in classical Athens, the only surviving representative of the genre known as Old Comedy. In many of his comedies he parodies contemporary characters such as politicians and philosophers (e.g., Socrates), as well as popular trends in politics (speaking against ongoing wars), thought (sophistry, natural philosophy), and religion (the role of the gods, the mysteries), always questioning the conventional and ridiculing the new fashions. In his comedy *Birds* (414 BCE), these animals claim their rightful place among the gods, on the grounds that they have come into being before all other gods. In this passage, the chorus of birds sings a cosmogony (for ignorant men to hear), which places them directly in relation with the primordial entities of the universe. This cosmogony parodies those that circulated in Aristophanes' time. The primordial place of Night and Darkness resonates as Orphic, as does the cosmic egg, a feature salient in Phoenician cosmogonies, while the place of Tartaros and Eros (Love) as primordial entities harkens back to Hesiod, but also to Phoenician cosmogonies.

SOURCE: Aristophanes, *Birds*, 688–702, translated by Carolina López-Ruiz.

(. . .) turn your mind to us, always-existing immortals,

to us the ethereal, the un-aging, the ones of eternal thoughts,

(690) so that you hear from us correctly everything about the celestial things. Once you know correctly the nature of the birds, the origin of the gods and the rivers, and of Chaos and Darkness (Erebos), tell Prodikos[78] on my behalf to cry till the end. At the beginning there was Chaos, Night, black Darkness, and broad Tartaros; Earth, Air and Heaven were not yet; but from Darkness, black-winged

(695) Night, in its limitless bosom, bore first of all an egg full of air (empty), out of which, as the seasons were completed, grew desired Eros (Love), his back refulgent with his two golden wings, like a swift whirlwind. And this one, mingling with winged gloomy Chaos in broad Tartaros, hatched our race, and it was the first one he brought to light.

(700) For earlier there was no race of immortals, before Eros brought everything together; and as they were mixing, the ones with the others, the sky was born and the ocean, and the earth, and the whole imperishable race of the blessed gods.

1.9. SHORT COSMOGONY IN APOLLONIOS OF RHODES' *ARGONAUTIKA*

Apollonios was a poet and librarian in Alexandria (Egypt) in the third century BCE (known as Rhodios, "of Rhodes," because he spent part of his life on that island). His poem the *Argonautika* is the only epic poem preserved from Hellenistic times. The poem relates the story of Jason and the Argonauts, focusing on their quest for the Golden Fleece and the love story between Jason and Medea. In book one, Orpheus (the legendary poet and enchanter, who accompanied the Argonauts) sings the following cosmogony. His singing is intended to calm down his comrades who were engaged in a heated argument. After Orpheus sings, they are pacified and spellbound, and they turn to offering proper

[78] Prodikos of Kos was a famous sophist who had interests in natural philosophy.

libations to Zeus and go to sleep peacefully. The dramatic context sheds light on the soothing qualities imparted by the recitation or singing of epic poetry, and especially the enchanting effect of cosmogonies, which turns the mind to dwell on mysterious events at the beginning of time. The cosmogony itself is rather eclectic and seems to combine elements akin to Hesiodic, Empedoclean, Orphic, and Egyptian traditions.

SOURCE: Apollonios of Rhodes' *Argonautika*, 1.493–515, translated by Carolina López-Ruiz.

> (. . .) And it would have turned into a quarrel,
>> had their comrades, and the son of Aison himself (Jason), not restrained them
> (495) by calling on the contenders, and had Orpheus, holding the lyre in his left hand, not begun singing. He sang how the earth, the sky, and the sea,
>> at first joined together in one body, were separated
>> from each other as the result of a terrible quarrel;
>> and how in heaven the stars have a fixed course forever,
> (500) as do the moon and the paths of the sun;
>> and how the mountains sprang up, and how the resounding rivers
>> with their nymphs and all creeping creatures came into being.
>> And he sang how at first Ophion and Ocean's daughter
>> Eurynome held the power over snowy Olympos,
> (505) and how, through strength of arms, the one yielded his prerogative to Kronos,
>> and the other to Rhea, and then they both sank under the Ocean's waves;
>> and these two in the meantime ruled over the blessed Titan gods,
>> while Zeus, still a lad, still with childish thoughts in his mind,
>> dwelled under the Diktean cave; and the earthborn
> (510) Cyclopes had not yet strengthened him with the thunderbolt,
>> with thunder and lightning, for these bring glory to Zeus.
>> So he said, and he stopped his lyre together with his immortal voice;
>> but they, even though he had ceased, still eagerly bent their heads
>> forward, all at once with upright ears, keeping quiet
> (515) under a spell; such an enchantment of a song he had left them.

1.10. CREATION MYTH IN OVID'S *METAMORPHOSES*, BOOK 1

Ovid is one of the greatest poets of the Augustan era (on par with Virgil and Horace). He was born in 43 BCE and died in 17 CE after nine years in exile in the Black Sea region. Ovid's most acclaimed work is the *Metamorphoses* ("Transformations"), but his production was vast and included, among other extant and lost works, the *Heroides* (letters of heroines), the *Ars Amatoria* ("Art of Love"), the *Fasti* ("Calendar," about Roman festivals and rituals), and the *Tristia* ("Sorrows," written from exile).

In the fifteen books of poems called *Metamorphoses*, Ovid narrates the transformations suffered by mythological characters. Written in dactylic hexameters, in the traditional epic style of Homer and Hesiod, Ovid's main model for this type of poetic collection of stories lies in Hesiod's *Theogony* and *Catalogue of Women*. However, the poem is considered to some degree a mock-epic, in which Love overpowers and often ridicules even the great Olympian gods. Ovid displays his vast knowledge of Greek and Roman literature and mythology in his unique poetic re-elaborations of traditional stories, with a poetic voice whose wit and versatility have rarely been matched.

Book 1 opens with a short invocation to the gods, a convention of cosmogonic and epic singing (see the beginning of Hesiod's *Theogony*, document 1.5), followed by a rather eclectic cosmogony, which echoes a long and varied tradition, ranging from Hesiod (Chaos at the beginning) to the **Epicurean** philosophical poetry of Lucretius (see *De rerum natura* 5.416 ff.; on this work see Part 5, document 7).

SOURCE: Ovid, *Metamorphoses*, Book 1.1–88. F. J. Miller, *Ovid, Metamorphoses* (Loeb Classical Library, Cambridge, MA; London, 1921, 2nd ed.), with minor modifications.

My mind is bent to tell of bodies changed into new forms. You gods, for you yourselves have wrought the changes, breathe on these my undertakings, and bring down my song in unbroken strains from the world's very beginning even unto the present time.

Before the sea was, and the lands, and the sky that hangs over all, the face of Nature showed alike in her whole round, which state have men called chaos: a rough, unordered mass of things, nothing at all save lifeless bulk and warring seeds of ill-matched elements heaped in one. No sun as yet shone forth upon the world, nor did the waxing moon renew her slender horns; not yet did the earth hang poised by her own weight in the circumambient air, nor had the ocean stretched her arms along the far reaches of the lands. And, though there was both land and sea and air, no one could tread that land, or swim that sea; and the air was dark. No form of things remained the same; all objects were at odds, for within one body cold things strove with hot, and moist with dry, soft things with hard, things having weight with weightless things. God—or kindlier Nature—composed this strife; for he rent asunder land from sky, and sea from land and separated the ethereal heavens from the dense atmosphere. When thus he had released these elements and freed them from the blind heap of things, he set them each in its own place and bound them fast in harmony. The fiery weightless element that forms heaven's vault leaped up and made place for itself upon the topmost height. Next came the air in lightness and in place. The earth was heavier than these, and, drawing with it the grosser elements, sank to the bottom by its own weight. The streaming water took the last place of all, and held the solid land confined in its embrace.

When he, whoever of the gods it was, had thus arranged in order and resolved that chaotic mass, and reduced it, thus resolved, to cosmic parts, he first molded the earth into the form of a mighty ball so that it might be of like form on every side. Then he bade the waters to spread abroad, to rise in waves beneath the rushing winds, and fling themselves around the shores of the encircled earth. Springs, too, and huge, stagnant pools and lakes he made, and hemmed down-flowing rivers within their shelving banks, whose waters, each far remote from each, are partly swallowed by the earth itself, and partly flow down to the sea; and being thus received into the expanse of a freer flood, beat now on shores instead of banks. Then he bid plains to stretch out, valleys to sink down, woods to be clothed in foliage, and the rock-ribbed mountains to arise. And as the celestial vault is cut by two zones on the right and two on the left, and there is a fifth zone between, hotter than these, so did the providence of God mark off the enclosed mass with the same number of zones, and the same tracts were stamped upon the earth. The central zone of these may not be dwelt in by reason of the heat; deep snow covers two, two he placed between and gave them temperate climate, mingling heat with cold.

The air hung over all, which is as much heavier than fire as the weight of water is lighter than the weight of earth. There did the creator bid the mists and clouds to take their place, and thunder, that should shake the hearts of men, and winds which with the thunderbolts make chilling cold. To these also the world's creator did not allot the air, that they might hold it everywhere. Even as it is, they can scarcely be prevented, though they control their blasts, each in his separate tract, from tearing the world to pieces. So fiercely do these brothers strive together. But Eurus[79] drew off to the land of the dawn and the realms of Arabia, and where the Persian hills flush beneath the morning light. The western shores, which glow with the setting sun are the place of Zephyrus; while bristling Boreas betook himself to Scythia and the farthest north. The land far opposite is wet with constant fog and rain, the home of Auster, the South-wind. Above these all he placed the liquid, weightless ether, which has naught of earthy waste.

Scarce had he thus parted off all things within their determined bounds, when the stars, which had long been lying hidden crushed down beneath the darkness, began to gleam throughout the sky. And, that no region might be without its own forms of animate life, the stars and divine forms occupied the floor of heaven, the sea fell to the shining fishes for their home, earth received the beasts, and the mobile air the birds. A living creature of finer stuff than these, more capable of lofty thought, one who could have dominion over all the rest, was lacking yet. Then man was born: whether the god who made all else, designing a more perfect world, made man of his own divine substance, or whether the new earth, but lately drawn away from heavenly ether, retained still some elements of its kindred sky—that earth which the son of Iapetus mixed with fresh, running water, and molded into the form of the all-controlling gods. And, though all other animals are prone, and fix their gaze upon the earth, he gave to man an uplifted face and bade him stand erect and turn his eyes

---

[79] Eurus is the east wind, Zephyrus the west wind, Boreas the north wind, and Auster the south wind (Notus/Notos in Greek tradition).

to heaven. So, then, the earth, which had but lately been a rough and formless thing, was changed and clothed itself with forms of men before unknown.

1.11. TWO SHORT COSMOGONIES, FROM VIRGIL'S *AENEID* AND *ECLOGUES*

Roman poet Virgil (Publius Vergilius Maro, 70–19 BCE), born in a village near Mantua in northern Italy, is perhaps best known for his epic poem the *Aeneid*. In the *Aeneid*, Virgil narrates the adventures of the Trojan hero Aeneas, who escapes from burning Troy with his father, Anchises, and son, Ascanius, and a group of companions. Aeneas ultimately reaches Italy, where he defeats the Latins in war. He becomes the progenitor of the Roman people and of the Julio-Claudian dynasty through his son Ascanius/Iulus (Julius Caesar, Augustus, Tiberius, Caligula, Claudius, and Nero are all members of this family). Written in dactylic hexameters and organized into twelve books, the *Aeneid* is a Roman adaptation of Homeric motifs, especially the "Returns" (*Nostoi*) of heroes after the Trojan War, the theme also followed by Homer in the *Odyssey*. While the survival and future destiny of Aeneas was part of the epic cycle, Virgil's elaboration integrates the mythical story with explicit and implicit allusions to Roman history and recent events leading to (and legitimizing) Augustus' imperial position. Homeric in inspiration, Virgil produces a very different type of epic, strongly historicizing and concerned with the fate of existing nations (not of heroes alone). It is imbued with philosophical reflection and self-conscious literary perfectionism, even though, according to tradition, the work was not in its final form when it reached Augustus' hands after Virgil's death.

His other two main works, also preserved in full, are the *Eclogues* and the *Georgics*. They are collections of poems of pastoral and agricultural inspiration, respectively, in which the poet infuses older Greek traditions with Italian elements, in a century when Roman poetry found its own voice and reached unsurpassed levels, most notably in the writings of Catullus, Horace, Ovid, and Virgil.

1.11.a. A "Tyrian" Cosmogony, from *Aeneid*, Book 1

In the following passage, Aeneas and his men are at Queen Dido's court at Carthage, partaking of a banquet. After an invocation and libation to Jupiter and other gods, Dido asks for the Carthaginians (here called Tyrians, as Carthage was founded by Phoenicians from Tyre) and Trojans to be bound in friendship (for more on Aeneas and Dido, see Part 5, document 8). As they all join in drinking, a Tyrian bard starts singing, and his song is a cosmogony. Both Tyrians and Trojans rejoice at the song, and the banquet continues until late at night while Dido entices the Trojans to tell her about the Trojan War and its famous heroes and battles. With some emphasis on celestial phenomena, the imagined "Phoenician" cosmogony here resembles Apollonios' cosmogony in the *Argonautika* (see document 1.9), with Virgil substituting a Tyrian poet for Orpheus, and a mythologized Atlas (a mountain range in western North Africa) for the inspirational Greek Muses who dwell in the Helikon or Olympos mountains.

SOURCE: Virgil, *Aeneid*, Book 1.740–747. F. Ahl, *Virgil, Aeneid* (Oxford World Series, Oxford and New York, 2007), with minor modifications.

> While other lords follow suit, a student of Atlas, the maestro,
>
> Livens the air with his gilded harp. For the long-haired Iopas
>
> Sings of the unpredictable moon, of the sun and its labors,
>
> Origins human and animal, causes of fire and of moisture,
>
> Stars (Lesser, Greater Bear, rainy Hyades, also Arcturus),
>
> Why in the winter the sun so hurries to dive in the Ocean,
>
> What slows winter's lingering nights, what blocks and delays them.
>
> Tyrians encore, applaud. Thus cued, Troy's men show approval.

1.11.b. Cosmic Song of Silenus, from *Eclogues* 6

The *Eclogues* (also called the *Bucolics*) are one of the major works by the Roman poet Virgil (70–19 BCE), inspired by the bucolic (i.e., "pastoral") Greek literary genre represented by Theocritus (third century BCE). Virgil's ten *Eclogues* are charged with political and erotic discourse and feature herdsman-poets (sometimes incarnated as mythological and historical characters) engaging in monologues and dialogues in the form of poetic competitions and set in a rural idealized setting. In this excerpt from *Eclogue* 6, the drinking satyr-god Silenus is playfully held hostage by nymphs and satyrs, who demand that he sing. He begins with a cosmogony and continues by telling of other famous myths until night falls before he has finished singing.

SOURCE: Virgil, *Eclogues* 6.31. H. R. Fairclough, *Virgil. Eclogues, Georgics, Aeneid 1–6* (Loeb Classical Library, Cambridge, MA and London, 1916), with minor modifications.

For he sang how, through the vast void, the seeds of earth, and air, and sea, and liquid fire were gathered together; how from these elements nascent things, yes all, and even the young globe of the world grew together; how the earth began to harden, to shut off the Sea God in the deep, and little by little to assume the shape of things; how next the lands are astounded at the new sun shining and how rains fall as the clouds are lifted higher, when first woods begin to arise and here and there living creatures move over mountains that know them not.

PART 2

MANKIND CREATED, MANKIND DESTROYED

STORIES ABOUT THE creation of humanity, also called anthropogonies, appear in many cosmogonies and theogonies (in a progression from the cosmos to the genealogies of gods to the creation of humankind). For instance, the creation of man and woman is showcased prominently as part of both creation narratives in Genesis 1.1–2.3 and 2.4–3.24 (Part 1, document 4, and document 2.3 below). The place of human beings in relation to the rest of the creation, however, and of man in relation to woman varies greatly in both stories. The Babylonian creation epic *Enuma Elish* (Part 1, document 1) also includes the creation of people by Marduk out of the remains of his cosmic enemies Tiamat and her consort Qingu. However, in *Atrahasis* (below) men are created from mud as laborers for the gods by the Womb Goddess—as if they were bricks, with the blood and flesh of a lesser god thrown into the mix.

In the ancient Mediterranean, the disparity of traditions about the origin of humankind was even greater than between traditions about the origins of the world. There were multiple variations within each culture. This might be due in part to the fact that the origins of mankind are often linked to the origin of particular groups of people, that is, to genealogical traditions from a given city or region. The multiplicity of local traditions may have made it difficult or irrelevant in some cases to accept universal ideas about the origins of humankind.

A remarkable case of silence regarding the origin of mankind can be found in Hesiod's *Theogony*, which, though it does not include an anthropogony per se, does mention the creation of women by Hephaistos (with the help of other gods). This story, repeated in a slightly different variant in the *Works and Days* (document 2.5), implies that men and women descend from Pandora and Epimetheus, the brother of Prometheus and son of the titan Iapetos. The problem this poses is that men had appeared earlier in the narrative (*Theogony* 535), and so it is not clear who created those men. But logic and consistency are not the priorities of the poem (or of creation stories in general). In turn, in Apollodorus' *Bibliotheke* ("Library"), a compendium of Greek myths written in prose some time in the first to second centuries CE, Prometheus is said to have created human beings out of clay, which constitutes a variant of the Hesiodic version (see *Library* 1.7.1). The motif of a demiurge or artisan-like creator is also adopted by philosophers such as Plato (see the *Timaeus* in Part 7, document 1).

The "Five Races of Men" in Hesiod's *Works and Days*, like the *Theogony*, does not focus on the moment or mode of creation of humanity. This is a folk motif that pairs the degradation of the human race with the degradation of metals, from gold to silver and then bronze and iron, with the race of heroes breaking the sequence between bronze and iron. This passage, however, shares with the story of Eden in Genesis the idea that human beings were once closer to the gods and that their purity and divine element disappeared at some point, creating an environment in which the distance between the divine and human realms is insuperable. The idea of different human ages finds parallels in the Indo-Iranian world, which may be explained by the Greeks' Indo-European heritage or, more likely, by historical contact with Persian beliefs and traditions. Thus, in Iranian tradition, Ahura Mazda explains to Zoroaster his vision of a tree with branches of gold, silver, steel, and iron as representing the ages of the world (*Bahman Yasht* 1.2–5, 2.14–22). A similar idea appears in the biblical story about the vision of Babylonian king Nebuchadnezzar II (reigned ca. 605–562 BCE), who dreamed of a statue made of metals, progressively deteriorating from the gold head to the clay feet. The image is used in the story by the prophet Daniel to explain the steady decline of the kingdoms that will succeed his own (Dan. 2.31–45) (this work was redacted in the second century BCE and was almost certainly influenced by Hesiod). In India a more distantly related motif (the ages or *yugas*, symbolized by colors) also presents the world's ages as decreasing in longevity and righteousness.

Some common motifs in many of these anthropogonies are the use of mud or dirt as the material for creation (in Genesis, *Atrahasis*, Hesiod and Apollodorus) and the descent of people from lesser gods (in Hesiod, the Orphic anthropogony, the *Enuma Elish* and *Atrahasis*). In the Eden story in Genesis 2–3 (document 2.3) and in Hesiod's Pandora story (document 2.5.), woman is portrayed negatively. She is the cause of eternal grief for man. In the case of the Flood story at least, it is fairly clear that the versions we have in Israel, Greece, and Rome, all stem from the Mesopotamian tradition (via Greece in the case of Rome). Interestingly, the human survivor in each case (Atrahasis, Noah, Deukalion) is aided by a god who is favorable to human beings (Enki/Ea in the *Atrahasis* and Gilgamesh versions, Prometheus in Apollodorus), while in the monotheistic elaboration of the Flood, for obvious reasons, the god who saves Noah is the one who condemned the human race in the first place. The Flood (or several of them) was regarded by Greeks as a historical fact that, moreover, connected them with other cultures: Plato mentions it in the story of Atlantis, when the wise man Solon is told about it by Egyptian priests (see Part 7, document 3); the Hellenistic Egyptian priest and antiquarian Manetho posited the Greek flood as one of the common points (or synchronisms) between Greek tradition and Egyptian history; the historian Diodorus Siculus (active ca. 60–30 BCE) also mentions the deluge and the creatures that emerged from the soil afterward in his account of Egypt; and in the second century CE, Lucian (a satirist from Syria) starts his treatise *De Dea Syria* with a curious retelling of the *Atrahasis* flood story. The Mesopotamian story of Adapa presents yet another narrative about early men and their place in relation to the gods. Adapa is a wise man, the first of the antediluvian "seven sages" (a tradition echoed later in the Greek world), who is sent by the god Ea to the city of Eridu in order to introduce religious rites to humankind. He is close to receiving immortality from the gods but fails to do so in the end.

Cosmogony and anthropogony also occupied a central place in Jewish and Christian texts outside the canonical books of the Hebrew Bible and the New Testament. Gnostic texts, Christian apocryphal texts, Jewish pseudepigrapha, the Kabbalah, and the Dead Sea Scrolls elaborate in varied ways on the creation and the place of Adam and Eve in the divine plan. In the Greek world especially, where there were no canonical religious texts to limit the direction of creation stories, the possibilities were endless. Human beings emerged from the stones thrown by Deukalion and Pyrrha over their shoulders after the Flood (see document 2.6); the people of Thebes grew from the teeth of a dragon sowed in the ground by Kadmos (see Part 4, document 10); and the Athenians claimed as their founder and first king the half-snake, earth-born figure Kekrops. In the legends of Argos, on the other hand, the first man, called Phoroneus, was said to have been born from the local river Inachos.

These myths, in which human beings underscored their ties to the land, were quite popular in Greece. Through them, entire populations claimed to be **autochthonous,** that is, indigenous to the land they inhabited. An opposite, astral, elaboration was put by Plato in the mouth of the comedian Aristophanes in the *Symposium* (see Part 7, document 4), according to which the original three (not two) genders of human beings were descended from the sun (males), the earth (females), and the moon (androgynous gender). Still another anthropogony seems to have circulated in Orphic texts, which tied the origin of human beings to the Titans and Dionysos (document 2.7). Meanwhile, natural philosophers tried to explain things without the intervention of the gods. A rather evolutionary version of the origins of human beings was attributed to the Presocratic philosopher Anaximander, whereby people emerged from fishy creatures. According to the testimonies, he postulated " . . . that there arose from heated water and earth either fish or animals very like fish. In these human beings grew and were kept inside as embryos up to puberty. Then finally they burst and men and women came forth already able to nourish themselves."[1]

Such a huge variety of views and traditions cannot begin to be represented in the present volume. Only a sample of the Mesopotamian, biblical, and Greco-Roman traditions is offered here. The reader can explore other texts through the Bibliography at the end of the book. ✦

---

[1] Censorius, *On the Day of Birth* 4.7 (= DK 12A30). Translation by R. D. McKirahan, *Philosophy before Socrates* (Indianapolis, IN, 1994).

2.1. MESOPOTAMIAN FLOOD STORIES

The following texts contain the earliest known stories about a great Flood and the destruction of mankind. The first document, *Atrahasis*, is embedded in a longer narration of the creation of the human race as a solution to alleviate the labor of the lesser gods, who worked as servants for the superior gods, and the series of plagues sent by the gods to diminish humankind's numbers, culminating in the Flood. The main character, Atrahasis ("Super-wise"), saves himself and his family with the aid of the clever god Enki. The gods then decide to control the life span, birth rate, and infant mortality of humankind so as to avoid the overpopulation problem that had led to the decision to annihilate them in the first place.

This story of Atrahasis is preserved in Akkadian in its Old Babylonian Version (OBV), dated to around 1700 BCE. Later fragments come from the Standard Babylonian Version (SBV), written in the early first millennium BCE. These follow the older version closely and are used here to fill some gaps. They were found at the library of the Assyrian king Ashurbanipal at Nineveh (seventh century BCE). Another, more complete, version of the same story was incorporated in the standard version of the *Epic of Gilgamesh* (Tablet XI) (excerpted in document 2.1.b). This version is narrated by the survivor of the Flood, Ut-napishtim, to Gilgamesh in their Underworld encounter (for which see Part 6, document 1). He is the only immortal human, exceptionally granted this favor by Enlil himself (Ellil here) after the Flood. This version in *Gilgamesh* offers the closest parallels with the Genesis Flood story (document 2.4). The text was in fact the first fragment of the *Epic of Gilgamesh* to be discovered among the cuneiform tablets unearthed at the Library at Nineveh by explorer Austen H. Layard in the mid-nineteenth century. Announced in 1872 as "The Chaldean Account of the Deluge," it brought to scholarly attention the existence of a pre-biblical Flood tradition, establishing the study of the Ancient Near East as an essential foundation for understanding the world of the Hebrew Bible and resulting in the development of Assyriology as an independent field of study.

The author named in the final **colophon** (a sort of rubric) of *Atrahasis*, Ipiq-Aya, probably wrote the text in the city of Sippar. He was surely reworking older traditional materials, not composing it as an original author in the modern sense. The main character, Atrahasis, is most likely an elaboration on a historical figure (as in the case of Gilgamesh). The Sumerian king lists feature his father or grandfather (Ubara-Tutu) and Atrahasis himself (called Ziusudra in Sumerian) as kings of Shuruppak (in central-southern Mesopotamia) before a great flood took place. The disaster is recorded in the lists as a historical event (though not a universal one necessarily), and traces of one or several floods have been found by archaeologists in layers of soil from different sites dating to the early third millennium. The legendary figure and his savior role in the Flood became so famous that the character appears in different versions of the story and with different names: he is the Ut-napishtim and Uta-na'ishtim (meaning "he who found life") of the *Epic of Gilgamesh* (document 2.1.b); the same character forms the basis of the later Xisuthros (from an account of Babylonian history written in Greek in Hellenistic times by an author called Berossos); and it possibly also forms the basis for the biblical Noah and Prometheus, whose name, meaning "fore-thinking," is perhaps a Greek version of Atrahasis.

The OBV is used for *Atrahasis*, with some insertions from the SBV. *Atrahasis* is written on three tablets, divided into eight columns each (four in obverse and four in reverse, numbered i, ii, etc.). The excerpt from the *Epic of Gilgamesh* comes from Tablet XI (divided in columns too). (For the versions of the *Epic of Gilgamesh*, see the headnote to Part 3, document 1.)

SOURCE: S. Dalley, *Myths from Mesopotamia: Creation, The Flood, Gilgamesh, and Others* (Oxford World's Classics, Oxford and New York, 1989, rev. ed. 2000), with minor modifications.

2.1.a. *Atrahasis*

TABLET I

(OBV) (i) When the gods instead of man[2] did the work, bore the loads, the gods' load was too great, the work too hard, the trouble too much, the great Anunnaki made the Igigi carry the workload sevenfold.[3]

Anu their father was king, their counselor warrior Ellil, their chamberlain was Ninurta, their canal-controller Ennugi. They took the box (of lots) [. . .], cast the lots; the gods made the division.[4] Anu went up to the sky, [and Ellil (?)] took the earth for his people (?). The bolt which bars the sea was assigned to far-sighted Enki.

When Anu had gone up to the sky, [and the gods of] the Apsu had gone below, the Anunnaki of the sky made the Igigi bear the workload. The gods had to dig out canals, had to clear channels, the lifelines of the land, the Igigi had to dig out canals, had to clear channels, the lifelines of the land.

The gods dug out the Tigris river (bed) and then dug out the Euphrates.[. . .] in the deep [. . .] they set up [. . .] the Apsu [. . .] of the land [. . .] inside it [. . .] raised its top [. . .] of all the mountains they were counting the years of loads; [. . .] the great marsh, they were counting the years of loads. For 3,600 years they bore the excess, hard work, night and day. They groaned and blamed each other, grumbled over the masses of excavated soil:

"Let us confront our [. . .] the chamberlain, and get him to relieve us of our hard work! Come, let us carry [the Lord (?)], the counselor of gods, the warrior, from his dwelling. Come, let us carry [Ellil], the counselor of gods, the warrior, from his dwelling."

Then Alla made his voice heard and spoke to the gods his brothers,

[2] The openings of the *Enuma Elish* and the *Theogony of Dunnu* are very similar (see Part 1, documents 1 and 2).

[3] The Anunnaki (also called Anunna, Anukki, and Enunaki) are Sumerian chthonic deities of fertility and the Underworld. See also note 3 on page 11.

[4] Inherited land was apportioned by casting lots in ancient Mesopotamia (cf. Homer's *Iliad* 15.187–193, where Poseidon claims that the world had been divided by lot between himself, Zeus, and Hades).

(gap of about 8 lines)

(ii) "Come! Let us carry the counselor of gods, the warrior, from his dwelling. Come! Let *us* carry Ellil, the counselor of gods, the warrior, from his dwelling. Now, cry battle! Let us mix fight with battle!"

The gods listened to his speech, set fire to their tools, put aside their spades for fire, their loads for the fire-god, they flared up. When they reached the gate of warrior Ellil's dwelling, it was night, the middle watch, the house was surrounded, the god had not realized. It was night, the middle watch, Ekur was surrounded, Ellil had not realized.

Yet Kalkal was attentive, and had it closed, he held the lock and watched [the gate]. Kalkal roused [Nusku]. They listened to the noise of [the Igigi]. Then Nusku roused his master, made him get out of bed: "My lord, your house is surrounded, a rabble is running around your door! Ellil, your house is surrounded, a rabble is running around your door!"

Ellil had weapons brought to his dwelling. Ellil made his voice heard and spoke to the vizier Nusku: "Nusku, bar your door, take up your weapons and stand in front of me."

Nusku barred his door, took up his weapons and stood in front of Ellil. Nusku made his voice heard and spoke to the warrior Ellil: "O my lord, your face is (sallow as) tamarisk! Why do you fear your own sons? O Ellil, your face is (sallow as) tamarisk! Why do you fear your own sons? Send for Anu to be brought down to you, have Enki fetched into your presence."

He sent for Anu to be brought down to him, Enki was fetched into his presence, Anu king of the sky was present, Enki king of the Apsu attended. The great Anunnaki were present. Ellil got up and the case was put. Ellil made his voice heard and spoke to the great gods: "Is it against me that they have risen? Shall I do battle [. . .] ? What did I see with my own eyes? a rabble was running around my door!"

Anu made his voice heard and spoke to the warrior Ellil:

(iii) "Let Nusku go out and [find out] word of the Igigi who have surrounded your door. A command [. . .] to [. . .]"

Ellil made his voice heard and spoke to the vizier Nusku: "Nusku, open your door, take up your weapons [and stand before me!] In the assembly of all the gods, bow, then stand [and tell them]: 'Your father Anu, your counselor warrior Ellil, your chamberlain Ninurta and your canal-controller Ennugi have sent me to say: Who is in charge of the rabble? Who is in charge of the fighting? Who declared war? Who ran to the door of Ellil?'"

[Nusku opened] his door, [took up his weapons,] went [before (?)] Ellil. In the assembly of all the gods [he bowed], then stood and told the message: "Your father Anu, your counsellor warrior Ellil, your chamberlain Ninurta and your canal-controller Ennugi have sent me to say: 'Who is in charge of the rabble? Who is in charge of the fighting? Who declared war? Who ran to the door of Ellil?'" *(one line missing)* Ellil *(rest of line missing)*

"Every single one of us gods declared war! we have put [a stop] to the digging. The load is excessive, it is killing us! Our work is too hard, the trouble too much! So every single one of us gods has agreed to complain to Ellil."

Nusku took his weapons, went [and returned to Ellil]: "My lord, you sent me to [. . .]. I went [. . .] I explained [. . .] saying: 'Every single one of us gods declared war. We have put [a stop] to the digging. The load is excessive, it is killing us, our work is too hard, the trouble too much, so every single one of us gods has agreed to complain to Ellil!'"

Ellil listened to that speech. His tears flowed. Ellil spoke guardedly (?), addressed the warrior Anu: "Noble one, take a decree (iv) with you to the sky, show your strength—while the Anunnaki are sitting before you call up one god and let them cast him for destruction!"

Anu made his voice heard and spoke to the gods his brothers: "What are we complaining of? Their work was indeed too hard, their trouble was too much. Every day the earth (?) [resounded (?)]. The warning signal was loud enough, we kept hearing the noise. [. . .] do [. . .] tasks (?)"

(gap partly filled, partly overlapped by the following two SBV [5] *fragments)*

(SBV) "(While) the Anunnaki are sitting before you, and (while) Belet-ili the womb-goddess is present, call up one and cast him for destruction!"

Anu made his voice heard and spoke to [Nusku]: "Nusku, open your door, take up your weapons, bow in the assembly of the great gods, [then stand] and tell them [. . .]: 'Your father Anu, your counsellor warrior Ellil, your chamberlain Ninurta and your canal-controller Ennugi have sent me to say: Who is in charge of the rabble? Who will be in charge of battle? Which god started the war? A rabble was running around my door!'"

When Nusku heard this, he took up his weapons, bowed in the assembly of the great gods, [then stood] and told them [. . .]: "Your father Anu, your counselor warrior Ellil, your chamberlain Ninurta and your canal-controller Ennugi have sent me to say: 'Who is in charge of the rabble? Who is in charge of the fighting? Which god started the war? A rabble was running around Ellil's door.'"

(gap of uncertain length)

(SBV) Ea made his voice heard and spoke to the gods his brothers: "Why are we blaming them? Their work was too hard, their trouble was too much. Every day the earth (?) [resounded (?)]. The warning signal was loud enough, [we kept hearing the noise.] There is [. . .] Belet-ili the womb-goddess is present—Let her create primeval man so that he may bear the yoke [. . .], so that he may bear the yoke, [the work of Ellil], let man bear the load of the gods!"

(gap)

(OBV) "Belet-ili the womb-goddess is present, let the womb-goddess create offspring, and let man bear the load of the gods!"

They called up the goddess, asked the midwife of the gods, wise Mami: "You are the womb-goddess (to be the) creator of mankind! Create primeval man, that he may bear the yoke! Let him bear the yoke, the work of Ellil, let man bear the load of the gods!"

---

[5] The Standard Babylonian Version is used here, that is, the standardized version circulating in Assyria and Babylonia during the fist half of the first millennium BCE.

Nintu made her voice heard and spoke to the great gods: "It is not proper for me to make him. The work is Enki's; he makes everything pure! If he gives me clay, then I will do it."

Enki made his voice heard and spoke to the great gods: "On the first, seventh, and fifteenth of the month I shall make a purification by washing. Then one god should be slaughtered. And the gods can be purified by immersion. Nintu shall mix clay with his flesh and his blood. Then a god and a man will be mixed together in clay. Let us hear the drumbeat forever after,[6] let a ghost come into existence from the god's flesh, let her proclaim it as his living sign, and let the ghost exist so as not to forget (the slain god)."

They answered "Yes!" in the assembly, the great Anunnaki who assign the fates. On the first, seventh, and fifteenth of the month, he made a purification by washing. Ilawela who had intelligence, they slaughtered in their assembly. Nintu mixed clay with his flesh and blood. They heard the drumbeat forever after. A ghost came into existence from the god's flesh, and she (Nintu) proclaimed it as his living sign.

(v) The ghost existed so as not to forget (the slain god). After she had mixed that clay, she called up the Anunnaki, the great gods. The Igigi, the great gods, spat spittle upon the clay. Mami made her voice heard and spoke to the great gods: "I have carried out perfectly the work that you ordered of me. You have slaughtered a god together with his intelligence. I have relieved you of your hard work, I have imposed your load on man. You have bestowed noise on mankind. I have undone the fetter and granted freedom."

They listened to this speech of hers, and were freed (from anxiety), and kissed her feet: "We used to call you Mami but now your name shall be Mistress of All Gods."

Far-sighted Enki and wise Mami went into the room of fate. The womb-goddesses were assembled. He trod the clay in her presence.[7]

(SBV) She kept reciting an incantation, for Enki, staying in her presence, made her recite it. When she had finished her incantation, she pinched off fourteen pieces (of clay), (and set) seven pieces on the right, seven on the left. Between them she put down a mud brick. She made use of (?) a reed, opened it (?) to cut the umbilical cord, called up the wise and knowledgeable womb-goddesses, seven and seven. Seven created males, seven created females, for the womb-goddess (is) creator of fate. He [. . .]-ed (crowned/veiled?) them two by two, [. . .]-ed them two by two in her presence. Mami made (these) rules for people:

"In the house of a woman who is giving birth the mud brick shall be put down for seven days. Belet-ili, wise Mami shall be honored. The midwife shall rejoice in the house of the woman who gives birth and when the woman gives birth to the baby, the mother of the baby shall sever herself.

"A man to a girl [. . .]

(OBV) "[. . .] her bosom [. . .]

---

[6] Perhaps meaning the "heartbeat," "pulse."

[7] This alludes to the procedure of brick-making. According to an incantation, the brick god, Kulla, was created by Enki by pinching off clay. Clay bricks were the main building material in Mesopotamia.

"A beard can be seen (?) on a young man's cheek. In gardens and waysides a wife and her husband choose each other."

The womb-goddesses were assembled and Nintu was present. They counted the months, called up the tenth month as the term of fates.

(vi) When the tenth month came, she slipped in (?) a staff and opened the womb.[8] Her face was glad and joyful. She covered her head, performed the midwifery, put on her belt, said a blessing. She made a drawing in flour and put down a mud brick:

"I myself created (it), my hands made (it). The midwife shall rejoice in the house of the *qadishtu-priestess*. Wherever a woman gives birth and the baby's mother severs herself, the mud brick shall be put down for nine days. Nintu the womb-goddess shall be honored. She shall call their [. . .] 'Mami.' She shall [. . .] the womb-goddess, lay down the linen cloth (?). When the bed is laid out in their house, a wife and her husband shall choose each other. Ishtar shall rejoice in the wife-husband relationship in the father-in-law's house. Celebration shall last for nine days, and they shall call Ishtar 'Ishhara.' [On the fifteenth day (?)], the fixed time of fate she shall call [. . .]."

(gap of about 23 lines)

A man [. . .] Clean the home [. . .] The son to his father [. . .] They sat and [. . .] He was carrying [. . .]

(vii) He saw [. . .] Ellil [. . .] They took hold of [. . .], made new picks and spades, made big canals to feed people and sustain the gods.

(gap of about 13 lines)

600 years, less than 600, passed,[9] and the country became too wide, the people too numerous. The country was as noisy as a bellowing bull. The God grew restless at their racket, Ellil had to listen to their noise. He addressed the great gods: "The noise of mankind has become too much, I am losing sleep over their racket. Give the order that *shuruppu-disease* shall break out . . . "

(gap of about 3 lines)

Now there was one Atrahasis whose ear was open (to) his god Enki. He would speak with his god and his god would speak with him. Atrahasis made his voice heard and spoke to his lord: "How long (?) [will the gods make us suffer]? Will they make us suffer illness forever?"

Enki made his voice heard and spoke to his servant: "Call the elders, the senior men! Start [an uprising] in your own house, let heralds proclaim [. . .] let them make a loud noise in the land: Do not revere your gods, do not pray to your goddesses, but search out the door of Namtara. Bring a baked loaf into his presence. May the flour offering reach him, may he be shamed by the presents and wipe away his 'hand.'"[10]

---

[8] The word used for "staff" also means a "term" or recurrent period of time.

[9] The round number 600 fits with the sexagesimal system used by the ancient Mesopotamians. This tradition is reflected in the Genesis Flood story (Genesis 6–8; see document 2.4), where Noah is said to be 600 years old when the Flood happened. Notice that repetition of numbers is also a literary device (e.g., in the *Epic of Gilgamesh*).

[10] "Hand" (of a god) is in Akkadian an expression for disease.

Atrahasis took the order, gathered the elders to his door. Atrahasis made his voice heard and spoke to the elders: "I have called the elders, the senior men! (viii) Start [an uprising] in your own house; let heralds proclaim [. . .] let them make a loud noise in the land: Do not revere your gods! Do not pray to your goddesses! Search out the door of Namtara. Bring a baked loaf into his presence. May the flour offering reach him; may he be shamed by the presents and wipe away his 'hand.'"

The elders listened to his speech; they built a temple for Namtara in the city. Heralds proclaimed. [. . .] They made a loud noise in the land. They did not revere their god, did not pray to their goddess, but searched out the door of Namtara, brought a baked loaf into his presence. The flour offering reached him. And he was shamed by the presents. And wiped away his "hand."

The *shuruppu-disease* left them, [the gods] went back to their [(regular) offerings]
(2 lines missing to end of column)
(Catchline)
600 years, less than 600 passed

TABLET II

(OBV) (i) 600 years, less than 600, passed, and the country became too wide, the people too numerous. The country was as noisy as a bellowing bull. The God grew restless at their clamor, Ellil had to listen to their noise. He addressed the great gods:

"The noise of mankind has become too much. I am losing sleep over their racket. Cut off food supplies to the people! Let the vegetation be too scant for their hunger![11] Let Adad wipe away his rain. Below (?) let no flood-water flow from the springs. Let wind go, let it strip the ground bare, let clouds gather (but) not drop rain, let the field yield a diminished harvest, let Nissaba stop up her bosom. No happiness shall come to them. Let their [. . .] be dejected."
(gap of about 34 lines to end of column)
(ii) (gap of about 12 lines at beginning of column)
"Call the [elders, the senior men], start an uprising in your house, let heralds proclaim [. . .] Let them make a loud noise in the land: Do not revere your god(s)! Do not pray to your goddess! Search out the door of Adad, bring a baked loaf into his presence. May the flour offering reach him, may he be shamed by the presents and wipe away his 'hand.' (Then) he will make a mist form in the morning and in the night he will steal out and make dew drop, deliver (?) the field (of its produce) nine-fold,[12] like a thief."

They built a temple for Adad in the city, ordered heralds to proclaim and make a loud noise in the land. They did not revere their god(s), did not pray to their goddess, but searched out the door of Adad, brought a baked (loaf) into his presence. The flour offering reached him; he was shamed by the presents and wiped away his

---

[11] These lines were used separately in an incantation against drought, according to later sources.

[12] Notice the repeated use of nine, as in the nine months of the pregnancy and the nine days in which the brick was put down.

"hand." He made mist form in the morning and in the night he stole out and made dew drop, delivered (?) the field (of its produce) nine-fold, like a thief.

[The drought] left them, [the gods] went back [to their (regular) offerings].

(SBV) (iii) Not three epochs had passed. The country became too wide, the people too numerous. The country was as noisy as a bellowing bull. The gods grew restless at their noise. Enlil organized his assembly again, addressed the gods his sons: "The noise of mankind has become too much, sleep cannot overtake me because of their racket. Command that Anu and Adad keep the (air) above (earth) locked, Sin and Nergal keep the middle earth locked. As for the bolt that bars the sea, Ea with his *lahmu*-creatures shall keep it locked."

He ordered, and Anu and Adad kept the (air) above (earth) locked, Sin and Nergal kept the middle earth locked. As for the bolt that bars the sea, Ea with his *lahmu*-creatures kept it locked.

Then the very wise man Atrahasis wept daily. He would carry a *mshakku*-offering along the riverside pasture, although the irrigation-water was silent. Halfway through the night he offered a sacrifice. As sleep began to overtake him (?) he addressed the irrigation-water: "May the irrigation-water take it, may the river carry it, may the gift be placed in front of Ea my lord. May Ea see it and think of me! So may I see a dream in the night."

When he had sent the message by water, he sat facing the river, he wept (?), the man wept (?) facing the river as his plea went down to the Apsu. Then Ea heard his voice. [He summoned his *lahmu*-creatures] and addressed them: "This man whose [prayers reach me (?)] – Do go quickly and bring me news of him, and ask him to give me a report about his country."

They crossed the wide seas [until they arrived] at the harbor of Apsu. They repeated Ea's message to Atrahasis: "Are you the man who is weeping? Is it your plea that went down to the Apsu? Ea has heard your voice and he has sent us to you."

"If Ea has really heard me, what [has reached him]?"

They answered straight away, they addressed Atrahasis: "As sleep began to overtake (you) the irrigation-water took (the offering), the river carried (it), the gift was placed in front of Ea your lord. Ea saw it and thought of you, and so he sent us to you."

The *lahmu*-creatures [returned] into the seas. Ea made his voice heard and spoke, he addressed Usmu his vizier: "Go out to Atrahasis and tell him my order, saying: 'The state of the country is according to the behavior of its people.'"

Usmu, Ea's vizier, addressed Atrahasis saying: "The state of the country is according to the behavior of its people. If water has left it, if grain has left [the fields (?), it is because [. . .] to me, [. . .] they have left them. The country is like a young man who falls flat on his face, he has fallen down [and is not nourished] from the teats [of the sky]. The land has been shaken off like a dried fig onto [the ground]. Above, the teats of the sky are sealed, and below, the water from the depths is bolted, it does not flow. (That is why) the dark ploughland has whitened, (that is why) in the pastureland grass does not sprout."

(OBV) (iv) Above, [rain did not fill the canals (?)], below, flood-water did not flow from the springs. Earth's womb did not give birth, no vegetation sprouted [. . .] People did not look [. . .], the dark pastureland was bleached, the broad countryside filled up with alkali.[13] In the first year they ate old grain, in the second year they depleted the storehouse. When the third year came, their looks were changed by starvation, their faces covered with scabs (?) like malt.

They stayed alive by [. . .] life. Their faces looked sallow. They went out in public hunched, their well-set shoulders slouched, their upstanding bearing bowed. They took a message [from Atrahasis to the gods].

In front of [the assembly of the great gods], they stood [and . . .]. The orders [of Atrahasis they repeated] in front of [. . .]

(gap of about 32 lines to end of column)

(SBV) (iv) [600 years, less than 600 years, passed. The country became too wide, the people too numerous.] He grew restless at their noise. Sleep could not overtake him because of their racket. Ellil organized his assembly, addressed the gods his sons:

"The noise of mankind has become too much. I have become restless at their noise. Sleep cannot overtake me because of their racket. Give the order that *shuruppu-disease* shall break out, let Namtar put an end to their noise straight away! Let sickness: headache, *shuruppu, ashakku,* blow in to them like a storm."

They gave the order, and *shuruppu-disease* did break out. Namtar put an end to their noise straight away. Sickness: headache, *shuruppu, ashakku,* blew into them like a storm. The thoughtful man, Atrahasis kept his ear open to his master Ea; he would speak with his god, [and his god (?)] Ea would speak with him. Atrahasis made his voice heard and spoke, said to Ea his master:

"Oh Lord, people are grumbling! Your [sickness] is consuming the country! Oh Lord Ea, people are grumbling! [Sickness] from the gods is consuming the country! Since you created us [you ought to] cut off sickness: headache, *shuruppu* and *ashakku.*"

Ea made his voice heard and spoke, said to Atrahasis: "Order the heralds to proclaim, to make a loud noise in the land: Do not revere your gods, do not pray to your goddesses![. . .] withhold his rites! [. . .] the flour as an offering [. . .] to her presence [. . .] say a prayer [. . .] the presents [. . .] his 'hand.'"

Ellil organized his assembly, addressed the gods his sons:

"You are not to inflict disease on them again, (even though) the people have not diminished—they are more than before! I have become restless at their noise, sleep cannot overtake me because of their racket! Cut off food from the people, let vegetation be too scant for their stomachs! Let Adad on high make his rain scarce, let him block below, and not raise flood-water from the springs! Let the field decrease its yield, let Nissaba turn away her breast, let the dark fields become white, let the broad countryside breed alkali, let earth clamp down her womb so that no vegetation sprouts, no grain grows. Let *ashakku* be inflicted on the people, let the womb be too tight to let a baby out!"

They cut off food for the people, vegetation [. . .] became too scant for their stomachs. Adad on high made his rain scarce, blocked below, and did not raise flood-

---

[13] Referring to salination, that is, the crystallization of salts on the topsoil when drainage of irrigation water is inadequate.

water from the springs. The field decreased its yield, Nissaba turned away her breast, the dark fields became white, the broad countryside bred alkali. Earth clamped down her womb: No vegetation sprouted, no grain grew. *Ashakku* was inflicted on the people. The womb was too tight to let a baby out.

(v) Ea kept guard over the bolt that bars the sea, together with his *lahmu*-heroes. Above, Adad made his rain scarce, blocked below, and did not raise flood-water from the springs. The field decreased its yield, Nissaba turned away her breast, the dark fields became white, the broad countryside bred alkali. Earth clamped down her womb: No vegetation sprouted, no grain grew. *Ashakku* was inflicted on the people. The womb was too tight to let a baby out.

(gap of 2 lines)

When the second year arrived they had depleted the storehouse. When the third year arrived [the people's looks] were changed [by starvation]. When the fourth year arrived their upstanding bearing bowed, their well-set shoulders slouched, people went out in public hunched over.

When the fifth year arrived, a daughter would eye her mother coming in; a mother would not even open her door to her daughter. A daughter would watch the scales (at the sale of her) mother, a mother would watch the scales (at the sale of her) daughter. When the sixth year arrived, they served up a daughter for a meal, served up a son for food. [. . .]

Only one or two households were left. Their faces were covered with scabs (?) like malt. People stayed alive by [. . .] life. The thoughtful man Atrahasis kept his ear open to his master Ea. He would speak with his god, and his god Ea would speak with him. He left the door of his god, put his bed right beside the river, (for even) the canals were quite silent.

(gap of about 25 lines)

(vi) When the second year arrived, they had depleted the storehouse. When the third year arrived, the people's looks were changed by starvation. When the fourth year arrived, their upstanding bearing bowed, their well-set shoulders slouched, people went out in public hunched over.

When the fifth year arrived, a daughter would eye her mother coming in; a mother would not even open her door to her daughter. A daughter would watch the scales (at the sale) of her mother, a mother would watch the scales (at the sale) of her daughter. When the sixth year arrived, they served up a daughter for a meal, served up a son for food. [. . .]

Only one or two households were left. Their faces were covered with scabs (?) like malt, the people stayed alive by [. . .] life. They took a message [. . .] entered and [. . .] the order of Atrahasis [. . .] saying: "How long [. . .]"

(gap of about 36 lines to end of tablet)

(OBV) (v) He (Ellil) was furious [with the Igigi]: "We, the great Anunna, all of us, agreed together on [a plan]. Anu and [Adad] were to guard [above], I was to guard the earth [below]. Where Enki [went], he was to undo the [chain and set (us) free], he was to release [produce for the people]. He was to exercise [control (?) by holding the balance (?)]."

Ellil made his voice heard and [spoke] to the vizier Nusku: "Have the fifty (?) *lahmu*-heroes (?) [. . .] fetched for me! Have them brought in to my presence!"

The fifty (?) *lahmu*-heroes (?) were fetched for him. The warrior [Ellil] addressed them: "We, the great Anunna, [all of us], agreed together on a plan. Anu and Adad were to guard above, I was to guard the earth below. Where you [went, you were to undo the chain and set (us) free, you were to release produce for the people, you were to exercise control (?) by holding the balance (?)]."

[. . .]. The warrior Ellil [. . .].

(gap of about 34 lines)

(vi) "Adad made his rain pour down,[. . .] filled the pasture land and clouds (?) veiled [. . .] do not feed his people, and do not give Nissaba's corn, luxury for people, to eat."

Then [the god (?)] grew anxious as he sat, in the gods' assembly worry gnawed at him. [Enki (?)] grew anxious as he sat, in the gods' assembly worry gnawed at him.

(3 lines fragmentary)

[They were furious with each other], Enki and Ellil. "We, the great Anunna, all of us, agreed together on a plan. Anu and Adad were to guard above, I was to guard the earth below. Where you went, you were to undo the chain and set (us) free! You were to release produce for the people! [You were to exercise control (?)] by holding the balance (?)."

[. . .]. The warrior Ellil [. . .].

(gap of 30 lines)

(vii) "[You] imposed your loads on man, you bestowed noise on mankind, you slaughtered a god together with his intelligence, you must . . . and [create flood]. It is indeed your power that that shall be used against [your people!]. You agreed to [the wrong (?)] plan! Have it reversed! (?) Let us make far-sighted Enki swear . . . an oath."

Enki made his voice heard and spoke to his brother gods: "Why should you make me swear an oath? Why should I use my power against my people? The flood that you mention to me— What is it? I don't even know! Could I give birth to a flood? That is Ellil's kind of work! Let him choose [. . .] Let Shullat and [Hanish] march [ahead] [Let Erakal pull out] the mooring poles, let [Ninurta] march, let him make [the weirs] overflow . . . " *(gap of 2 or 3 lines to end of column)*

(viii) *(gap of 31 lines beginning next column)*

" . . . The assembly [. . .] Do not listen to [. . .] The gods gave an explicit command. Ellil performed a bad deed to the people."

(Catchline)

Atrahasis made his voice heard and spoke to his master

TABLET III

(OBV) (i) *(gap of about 10 lines)*

Atrahasis made his voice heard and spoke to his master: "Indicate to me the meaning of the dream, [. . .] let me find out its portent (?)"

Enki made his voice heard and spoke to his servant: "You say: 'I should find out in bed (?).' Make sure you attend to the message I shall tell you! Wall, listen constantly to me! Reed hut, make sure you attend to all my words! Dismantle the house, build a boat, reject possessions, and save living things. The boat that you build [. . .] *(2 lines fragmentary)* Roof it like the Apsu so that the Sun cannot see inside it! Make upper decks and lower decks. The tackle must be very strong, the bitumen strong, to give strength. I shall make rain fall on you here, a wealth of birds, a hamper (?) of fish."

He opened the sand clock and filled it, he told him the sand (needed) for the Flood was seven nights' worth. Atrahasis received the message. He gathered the elders at his door. Atrahasis made his voice heard and spoke to the elders:

"My god is out of favor with your god. Enki and [Ellil (?)] have become angry with each other. They have driven me out of [my house]. Since I always stand in awe of Enki, he told (me) of this matter. I can no longer stay in [. . .], I cannot set my foot on Ellil's territory (again). [I must go down to the Apsu and stay] with (my) god (?). This is what he told me."

(gap of 4 or 5 lines to end of column)

(ii) *(gap of about 9 lines beginning next column)*

The elders [. . .]. The carpenter [brought his axe,] the reed worker [brought his stone, a child brought] bitumen. The poor [fetched what was needed.]

(9 lines very damaged)

Everything there was [. . .] everything there was [. . .] Pure ones [. . .] fat ones [. . .] he selected [and put on board. The birds] that fly in the sky, cattle [of Shak] kan, wild animals (?) [. . .] of open country, [. . . he] put on board [. . .] He invited his people [. . .] to a feast. [. . .] he put his family on board.

They were eating, they were drinking. But he (Atrahasis) went in and out, could not stay still or rest on his haunches, his heart was breaking and he was vomiting bile. The face of the weather changed. Adad bellowed from the clouds.

When (?) he (Atrahasis) heard his noise, bitumen was brought and he sealed his door. While he was closing up his door Adad kept bellowing from the clouds. The winds were raging even as he went up (and) cut through the rope, he released the boat.

(iii) *(6 lines missing at beginning of column)*

Anzu was tearing at the sky with his talons, [. . .] the land, he broke [. . .] the Flood [came out (?)].

The *kashushu*-weapon went against the people like an army. No one could see anyone else, they could not be recognized in the catastrophe. The Flood roared like a bull, like a wild ass screaming the winds [howled]. The darkness was total, there was no sun.

[. . .] like white sheep. [. . .] of the Flood.

(2 lines fragmentary)

[. . .] the noise of the Flood. [. . .]

[Anu (?)] went berserk, [the gods (?)] [. . .] his sons [. . .] before him. As for Nintu the Great Mistress, her lips became encrusted with rime. The great gods, the Anunna, stayed parched and famished. The goddess watched and wept, midwife of the gods, wise Mami:

"Let daylight (?) [. . .] Let it return and [. . .]! However, could I, in the assembly of gods, have ordered such destruction with them? Ellil was strong enough (?) to give a wicked order. Like Tiruru he ought to have cancelled that wicked order! I heard their cry leveled at me, against myself, against my person. Beyond my control (?) my offspring have become like white sheep."

"As for me, how am I to live (?) in a house of bereavement? My noise has turned to silence. Could I go away, up to the sky and live as in a cloister (?)? What was Anu's intention as decision-maker? It was his command that the gods his sons obeyed, he who did not deliberate, but sent the Flood, he who gathered the people to catastrophe [. . .]"

(iv) *(3 lines missing at beginning of column)*

Nintu was wailing [. . .]: "Would a true father (?) have given birth to the [rolling (?)] sea (so that) they could clog the river like dragonflies?[14] They are washed up (?) like a raft overturned, they are washed up like a raft overturned in open country! I have seen, and wept over them! Shall I (ever) finish weeping for them?"

She wept, she gave vent to her feelings, Nintu wept and fuelled her passions. The gods wept with her for the country. She was sated with grief, she longed for beer (in vain). Where she sat weeping, (there the great gods) sat too, but, like sheep, could only fill their windpipes (with bleating). Thirsty as they were, their lips discharged only the rime of famine.

For seven days and seven nights the torrent, storm, and flood came on.

(gap of about 58 lines)

(v) He put down [. . .], provided food [. . .]

The gods smelt the fragrance, gathered like flies over the offering. When they had eaten the offering, Nintu got up and blamed them all: "Whatever came over Anu who makes the decisions? Did Ellil (dare to) come for the smoke offering? (Those two) who did not deliberate, but sent the Flood, gathered the people to catastrophe—You agreed the destruction. (Now) their bright faces are dark (forever)."

Then she went up to the big flies[15] which Anu had made, and (declared) before the gods: "His grief is mine! My destiny goes with his! He must deliver me from evil, and appease me! Let me go out in the morning (?) [. . .]

(vi) "Let these flies be the lapis lazuli of my necklace, by which I may remember it (?) daily (?) [forever (?)]."

The warrior Ellil spotted the boat and was furious with the Igigi: "We, the great Anunna, all of us, agreed together on an oath! No form of life should have escaped! How did any man survive the catastrophe?"

Anu made his voice heard and spoke to the warrior Ellil: "Who but Enki would do this? He made sure that the [reed hut] disclosed the order."

Enki made his voice heard and spoke to the great gods: "I did it, in defiance of you! I made sure life was preserved [. . .]

(5 lines missing)

"Exact your punishment from the sinner. And whoever contradicts your order

(12 lines missing)

"I have given vent to my feelings!"

Ellil made his voice heard and spoke to far-sighted Enki: "Come, summon Nintu the womb-goddess! Confer with each other in the assembly."

---

[14] The drowning of dragonflies is also mentioned by Ut-napishtim in *Gilgamesh*, Tablet X.vi (Part 6, document 1).

[15] This allusion is not understood. It may refer to the gods abandoning humankind.

Enki made his voice heard and spoke to the womb-goddess Nintu: "You are the womb-goddess who decrees destinies.[16] [. . .] to the people. [Let one-third of them be . . .] [Let another third of them be . . .].

(vii) In addition let there be one-third of the people, among the people the woman who gives birth yet does not give birth (successfully); let there be the *pashittu*-demon among the people, to snatch the baby from its mother's lap. Establish *ugbabtu, entu, egisitu*-women:[17] They shall be taboo, and thus control childbirth."

(26 lines missing to end of column)

(viii) *(8 lines missing at beginning of column)*

" . . . How we sent the Flood. But a man survived the catastrophe. You are the counselor of the gods; on your orders I created conflict. Let the Igigi listen to this song in order to praise you, and let them record (?) your greatness. I shall sing of the Flood to all people: Listen!"

(Colophon)[18]

The End.

Third tablet, "When the gods instead of man;" 390 lines; total 1,245 for the three tablets. Hand of Ipiq-Aya, junior scribe. Month Ayyar [x day], year Ammi-saduqa was king. A statue of himself [. . .]

2.1.b. Flood Story from the *Epic of Gilgamesh*, Tablet XI

(i) (. . .) "Let me reveal to you a closely guarded matter, Gilgamesh, and let me tell you the secret of the gods. Shuruppak is a city that you yourself know, situated [on the bank of] the Euphrates. That city was already old when the gods within it decided that the great gods should make a flood. There was Anu their father, warrior Ellil their counselor, Ninurta was their chamberlain, Ennugi[19] their canal-controller.

"Far-sighted Ea swore the oath (of secrecy) with them, so he repeated their speech to a reed hut: 'Reed hut, reed hut, brick wall, brick wall, listen, reed hut, and pay attention, brick wall (this is the message): Man of Shuruppak, son of Ubara-Tutu, dismantle your house, build a boat. Leave possessions, search out living things. Reject chattels and save lives! Put aboard the seed of all living things, into the boat. The boat that you are to build shall have her dimensions in proportion, her width and length shall be in harmony, roof her like the Apsu.'

"I realized and spoke to my master Ea: 'I have paid attention to the words that you spoke in this way, my master, and I shall act upon them. But how can I explain myself to the city, the men and the elders?'

"Ea made his voice heard and spoke, he said to me, his servant: 'You shall speak to them thus: "I think that Ellil has rejected me, and so I cannot stay in your city,

---

[16] From this point on men will have a limited life span, whereas before they were primeval men (*lullu*) who could live for centuries (as did Atrahasis himself).

[17] These were females devoted to temples, usually not allowed to have children. Such priestesses were famous, for instance, at the temple of Shamash (Sun God) at Sippar, where this text probably originated.

[18] Brief colophons existed for other tablets of *Atrahasis*, but only this one is translated here.

[19] Sumerian deity and throne-bearer of Enlil.

and I cannot set foot on Ellil's land again. I must go down to the Apsu[20] and stay with my master Ea. Then he will shower abundance upon you, a wealth of fowl, a treasure of fish. [. . .] prosperity, a harvest, in the morning cakes/darkness, in the evening a rain of wheat/heaviness he will shower upon you." [21]

"When the first light of dawn appeared, the country gathered about me. The carpenter brought his axe, the reed-worker brought his stone, the young men [. . .] oakum (?), children carried the bitumen, the poor fetched what was needed [. . .].

(ii) "On the fifth day I laid down her form.[22] One acre was her circumference, ten poles each the height of her walls, her top edge was likewise ten poles all round. I laid down her structure, drew it out, gave her six decks, divided her into seven. Her middle I divided into nine, drove the water pegs into her middle. I saw to the paddles and put down what was needed: Three *sar* of bitumen I poured into the kiln,[23] three *sar* of pitch I poured into the inside. Three *sar* of oil they fetched, the workmen who carried the baskets.

"Not counting the *sar* of oil which the dust (?) soaked up, the boatman stowed away two more *sar* of oil. At the [. . .] I slaughtered oxen. I sacrificed sheep every day. I gave the workmen ale and beer to drink, oil and wine as if they were river water. They made a feast, like the New Year's Day festival. When the sun [rose (?)] I provided hand oil.

"[When] the sun went down, the boat was complete. [The launching was (?)] very difficult; launching rollers had to be fetched (from) above (to) below. Two-thirds of it [stood clear of the water line (?)]. I loaded her with everything there was, loaded her with all the silver, loaded her with all the gold, loaded her with all the seed of living things, all of them. I put on board the boat all my kith and kin. Put on board cattle from open country, wild beasts from open country, all kinds of craftsmen.

"Shamash had fixed the hour: 'In the morning cakes/darkness, in the evening a rain of wheat/heaviness (I) shall shower down: Enter into the boat and shut your door!' That hour arrived; in the morning cakes/darkness, in the evening a rain of wheat/heaviness showered down. I saw the shape of the storm; the storm was terrifying to see. I went aboard the boat and closed the door. To seal the boat I handed over the (floating) palace with her cargo to Puzur-Amurru the boatman.[24]

"When the first light of dawn appeared, a black cloud came up from the base of the sky. Adad kept rumbling inside it. Shullat and Hanish were marching ahead, marched as chamberlains (over) (?) mountain and country. Erakal pulled

---

[20] The fresh primordial waters, originally paired with Tiamat (see *Enuma Elish* in Part 1, document 1), and the realm of Ea and the Seven Sages.

[21] Puns are made between the very similar sounding words for a kind of cake and "darkness," and for "wheat" and "heaviness."

[22] An enormous version of the reed rafts and boats that the Mesopotamians built for river floatation (as opposed to timber ships).

[23] Three *sar* is about 24,000 gallons.

[24] No boatman is mentioned in *Atrahasis*, but he might have played a more important role in other versions.

out the mooring (?) poles, Ninurta marched on and made the weir(s) overflow. The Anunnaki had to carry torches, they lit up the land with their brightness.[25] The calm before the Storm-god came over the sky, everything light turned to darkness. [. . .]

(iii) "On the first day the tempest [rose up], blew swiftly and [brought (?) the flood-weapon], like a battle force [the destructive *kashusu*-weapon] passed over [the people]. No man could see his fellow, nor could people be distinguished from the sky. Even the gods were afraid of the flood-weapon. They withdrew; they went up to the heaven of Anu.[26] The gods cowered, like dogs crouched by an outside wall. Ishtar screamed like a woman giving birth; the Mistress of the Gods,[27] sweet of voice, was wailing: 'Has that time really returned to clay, because I spoke evil in the gods' assembly? How could I have spoken such evil in the gods' assembly? I should have (?) ordered a battle to destroy my people[28]; I myself gave birth (to them), they are my own people, yet they fill the sea like fish spawn!' The gods of the Anunnaki were weeping with her. The gods, humbled, sat there weeping. Their lips were closed and covered with scab.

"For six days and [seven (?)] nights the wind blew, flood and tempest overwhelmed the land; when the seventh day arrived, the tempest, flood and onslaught, which had struggled like a woman in labor, blew themselves out (?). The sea became calm, the *imhullu*-wind grew quiet, the flood held back. I looked at the weather; silence reigned, for all mankind had returned to clay. The flood-plain was flat as a roof. I opened a porthole and light fell on my cheeks. I bent down, then sat. I wept. My tears ran down my cheeks. I looked for banks, for limits to the sea. Areas of land were emerging everywhere (?).

"The boat had come to rest on Mount Nimush.[29] The mountain Nimush held the boat fast and did not let it budge. The first and second day the mountain Nimush held the boat fast and did not let it budge. The third and fourth day the mountain Nimush held the boat fast and did not let it budge. The fifth and sixth day the mountain Nimush held the boat fast and did not let it budge.

"When the seventh day arrived, I put out and released a dove. The dove went; it came back, for no perching place was visible to it, and it turned round. I put out and released a swallow. The swallow went; it came back, for no perching place was visible to it, and it turned round. I put out and released a raven. The raven went, and saw the waters receding. And it ate, preened (?), lifted its tail and did not turn round.

---

[25] Adad was the Weather God (Haddad and Adad in West Semitic cultures; in Ugaritic sources Haddad is a title of Baal). Shullat and Hanish are paired minor deities, servants of the sun god and the Weather God, respectively. Erakal (also known as Nergal) was the chief god of the Underworld. Ninurta was the Sumerian warrior god, also god of shepherds, and son of Enlil/Ellil. He was the leader of the Anunnaki, who in turn are old Underworld deities.

[26] In ancient Mesopotamia there were upper, middle, and lower heavens, the upper being the domain of Anu.

[27] Belet-ili ("mistress of the gods") is the great Mother Goddess, also called Nin-hursag ("mountain lady"), Ninmah ("supreme lady"), Nintu ("birth lady"), and Mammi ("mummy"), among other names (see her role in *Atrahasis* in document 2.1.a).

[28] Or "did I order a catastrophe to destroy my people?"

[29] Probably Pir Omar Gadrun, north of Suleimaniyah, northeast of Kirkuk (in modern Iraq).

"Then I put (everything ?) out to the four winds, and I made a sacrifice, set out a *surqinnu*-offering upon the mountain peak, arranged the jars seven and seven; into the bottom of them I poured (essences of ?) reeds, pine, and myrtle.[30] The gods smelt the fragrance, the gods smelt the pleasant fragrance, the gods like flies gathered over the sacrifice. As soon as the Mistress of the Gods arrived, (iv) she raised the great flies, which Anu had made to please her: 'Behold, O gods, I shall never forget (the significance of) my lapis lazuli necklace, I shall remember these times, and I shall never forget. Let other gods come to the *surqinnu*-offering but let Ellil not come to the *surqinnu*-offering, because he did not consult before imposing the flood, and consigned my people to destruction!'

"As soon as Ellil arrived[31] he saw the boat. Ellil was furious, filled with anger at the Igigi gods[32]: 'What sort of life survived? No man should have lived through the destruction!'

"Ninurta made his voice heard and spoke, he said to the warrior Ellil: 'Who other than Ea would have done such a thing? For Ea can do everything!'

"Ea made his voice heard and spoke, he said to the warrior Ellil: 'You are the sage of the gods, warrior, so how, O how, could you fail to consult, and impose the flood? Punish the sinner for his sin, punish the criminal for his crime, but ease off, let work not cease; be patient, let not [. . .]. Instead of your imposing a flood, let a lion come up and diminish the people. Instead of your imposing a flood, let a wolf come up and diminish the people. Instead of your imposing a flood, let famine be imposed and [lessen] the land. Instead of your imposing a flood, let Erra[33] rise up and savage the people. I did not disclose the secret of the great gods, I just showed Atrahasis a dream, and thus he heard the secret of the gods.'

"Now the advice (that prevailed) was his advice. Ellil came up into the boat, and seized my hand and led me up. He led up my woman and made her kneel down at my side. He touched our foreheads, stood between us, blessed us: 'Until now Utnapishtim was mortal, but henceforth Ut-napishtim and his woman shall be as we gods are. Ut-napishtim shall dwell far off at the mouth of the rivers.'"

2.2. EGYPTIAN TEXTS ON THE CREATION AND DESTRUCTION OF MANKIND

2.2.a. Excerpts from the *Coffin Texts*

The following passages are excerpts from several larger *Coffin Texts* spells. They record different mythical notions about the origins of mankind. The most common one is the creation of humanity from the tears of Re, the sun god, following an **etiology** based on the similarity between the word for "humankind" (*rmt*), and the word for "tears" (*rmyt*). Spell 714 does not mention this fact

---

[30] There is evidence that libations were made *into* jars.

[31] In the Hittite version of Gilgamesh, Kumarbi takes the place of Ellil here.

[32] The Igigi gods are a group of Sumerian "younger" sky-gods headed by Ellil; they are often paired with the Anunnaki. See note 3 on page 11.

[33] God of war, hunting, and plague.

explicitly, but it is clear because of a paratactic connection (i.e., juxtaposition) between both terms. The same can be said of Spell 80 (Part 1, document 3.b), where human beings are said to come out of Atum's eye. On the other hand, the reference in Spell 1130 is self-evident. Nonetheless, the creation of humanity by the gods in a moment of extreme grief does not seem to have affected Egyptian concepts about Life, which were mainly positive.

Despite its fragmentary condition, the excerpt from Spell 996 mentions another mythical explanation for the creation of humanity through the action of the god Khnum. These texts and later references point out that this god was not considered the creator of humanity in general terms, but as the fashioner (literally, "the potter") of every human being in the womb, a concept that resembles the creation acts of the Greek **demiurge** (Part 7, documents 1 and 2) and of the Hebrew God in the second Genesis 2–3 account (document 2.3).

SOURCE: Excerpts from the *Coffin Texts*, translated and annotated by A. Diego Espinel.

Excerpt from *Coffin Texts* Spell 714 (CT VI 344f–g)

(Human beings come from Re's tears)

(. . .) "I (Re) caused my coming into being by myself, by means of my powers. I am the one who made myself and who built myself according to the desire of my heart. What has been originated from me is under my supervision. As for the tears, they have been made out of anger against me; human beings, who belong to the blindness which is behind me, are [my] cat[tle] (?)" (. . .)

Excerpt from *Coffin Texts* Spell 1130 (CT VII 462d–465a)

(Human beings come from Re's tears)

(. . .) "I (the demiurge god) have done four good deeds inside the portal of the horizon:

"I have created the four winds so that every human being can breathe in his environment. This was one of my deeds.

"I have created a great flood so that the poor as well as the great may be powerful. This was one of my deeds.

"I have created every human being equal to his brother and I have ordered them not to do evil, although their hearts disobey what I said. This was one of my deeds.

"I have created (them) in such a way that their hearts do not forget the west (i.e., the Afterlife), and that they make divine offerings to the gods of the provinces. This was one of my deeds.

"I caused the gods to come into being from my sweat, and human beings from the tears coming out of my eye." (. . .)

Excerpt from *Coffin Texts* Spell 996 (CT VII 212e–g)

(The god Khnum as a potter creator of mankind)

(. . .) The *qerhet*-jar is in the kiln, and Khnum is in his entrance. He has modelled m[e] [. . .] he forms me during a year. (. . .)

2.2.b. Excerpt from the *Book of the Heavenly Cow*

The so-called "Story of the Destruction of Mankind" is included in the ritual text known as *Book of the Heavenly Cow*. This is a religious composition found in different New Kingdom royal tombs (Tutankhamun, Sety I, Ramesses II, Ramesses III, and Ramesses VI) (ca. 1336–1136 BCE) and in two papyri from Deir el-Medina dated to Ramesside times, currently kept in Turin. It constitutes one of the few coherent narrative examples of Egyptian religious texts. The date of its original composition is unknown. The myth is already mentioned in the Middle Kingdom (see the *Teachings for Merikare* in Part 1, document 3.c), and its actual composition has been dated either to the Middle Kingdom itself (ca. 2055–1650 BCE) or later, to the Eighteenth Dynasty (ca. 1550–1295 BCE). The text is divided into two different sections. The first part, translated here in full, describes the rebellion of human beings against Re, the consequent dispatch by the sun god of his eye against the rioters, and the decision of the god to save humanity from his eye (personified by a goddess), by causing her to become drunk. The second part, not translated in this volume, refers to the reordering of the world by Re after leaving the earth and settling in the sky on the heavenly cow. This cow is Nut, the Sky Goddess, who is supported by the god Shu and eight *heh*-gods (see *Coffin Text* spell 80 in Part 1, document 3.b).

SOURCE: *Book of the Heavenly Cow* (excerpt), translated and annotated by A. Diego Espinel.

It so happens that Re, who came into being by himself, appeared after he became the king of human beings and gods mixed together. Then mankind conspired words against Re when his majesty, life! integrity! health! (hereafter l.i.h.),[34] was old, and his bones (were) of silver, his limbs of gold, and his hair of real lapis lazuli. When his majesty, l.i.h., learned about the words of conspiracy by the human beings, he said to the ones who were in his retinue: "Summon to me my eye, Shu, Tefnut, Geb, and Nut, along with the fathers and mothers who existed with me in the primeval waters, and with the god Nun. Let him bring his entourage with him, and let you bring them secretly, lest human beings discover (it) and their hearts become discouraged. Come with them to the great domain, thus they will say their decisive advice. Let me return to the primeval waters, to the place where I came into being."

Then these gods were brought [. . .] and these gods [were placed] on both sides of him, touching the earth with their forehead, in front of his majesty so he could say his speech in front of the father of the senior gods (i.e., Nun), the maker of human beings, the king of plebeians. Then they said to his majesty: "Speak to us so we can hear you about it."

Then Re said to Nun: "O, senior god who created me, and ancestral gods! Look, human beings, who came into being from my eye,[35] have conspired words against

---

[34] The l.i.h. desiderative formula (i.e., for "desiring" or "wishing" something) was frequently employed following generic mentions of kings, their palaces, and their personal names.

[35] This sentence could be a reference to the creation of humankind from the tears of Re mentioned in several *Coffin Texts* spells, as in document 2.a.

me. Tell me what you would do against it. Look, I am searching for (a plan). I will not have them killed until I have heard what you can say about it."

Then the majesty of Nun said: "My son, a god more powerful than the one who made him, elder than the one who created him, sit on your throne, as the terror you inspire is great. Your eye will act against the ones who conspire against you."

Then the majesty of Re said: "Look, they have fled to the desert lands and their hearts are terrified for what I said to them."

Then [they] said to his majesty: "Let your eye go, may she[36] smite them for you, those who conspired badly. There is no eye more prominent than it to smite them for you. It will descend as Hathor."

Then this goddess went to him after she had killed humankind in the desert, and the majesty of this god said: "Come, come in peace, Hathor, who has carried out this task! May I come to her!"

Then this goddess said: "As you live for me,[37] I have defeated humanity. It was a pleasure for my heart."

Then the majesty of Re said: "I will govern (*sekhem*) them as king by diminishing them." *And so, Sekhmet, the breadpaste of night, came into being in order to wade across their blood from Herakleopolis.*[38]

Then Re said to the summoned ones: "Look! Messengers! Runners! Couriers! May they flee as the shadow of the body!" Then these messengers were brought immediately and the majesty of this god said: "Run to Elephantine and bring to me *didi*-ochre in great quantity."

This *didi*-ochre was brought to him and the majesty of this great god ordered to the "Locked One" who is in Heliopolis to mill this *didi*-ochre, while maidservants grind barley for the beer. Then this *didi*-ochre was put in this beverage, and it became as human blood. Then seven thousand *hebenet*-jars of beer were made (in this way).

Then the majesty of the Dual King, Re, came with these gods in order to see these jars of beer. It was the dawn of the destruction of mankind by the goddess, in their (*sic*) days of travelling southward. Then the majesty of Re said: "How good it is! I will protect humankind from her."

Then Re said: "Transport them to the place where she said she was going to kill humankind."

Then the majesty of the Dual King, Re, woke up early in the deepest of night in order to pour this sleep-inducing beverage, and the fields were three palms (in depth) filled with the liquid by means of the power of this god. Then, the goddess came at dawn and she found this inundation, and her face became happy. She drank the liquid, and it was a pleasure for her heart. Then she became so drunk that she couldn't recognize the human beings, and the majesty of Re said to this goddess:

---

[36] "Eye" in Egyptian is a feminine noun. It can be also read as "action"; therefore, the Eye of Re is the means of acting of the sun god.

[37] A common Egyptian oath formula.

[38] Italics signal the religious and mythical etiologies in the narrative. Since they are usually based on wordplays, transliterations of the relevant words have been included in parentheses. In this paragraph Re changes his mind and wants only to diminish humankind. From this point on, the story mentions how Re tries to appease his eye.

"Come, come in peace, the charming one (*iamet*)!" *And so the beautiful women/goddesses from Iamu[39] came into being.*

Then the majesty of Re told to this goddess: "Sleep-inducing beverages will be made for her in the seasonal year festival and maidservants will be in charge of it." *And so, the making of sleep-inducing beverages came into being and maidservants will be in charge in the festival of Hathor, (made) by every human from the first day.*

Then the majesty of Re told to this goddess: "Is the pain of fire (fever?) the cause of the illness?" *And so, respect came into existence because of the pain.*

Then the majesty of Re said: "As I live for myself, my heart is very tired to stay with them, so I could kill them with no exception. The embrace of my arm won't be slender."[40]

This is what the gods who were in his entourage said: "Don't flee in your disappointment, as you will have power over whatever you want."

Then this god said to the majesty of Nun: "My limbs are weak for the first time. I won't come until another reaches me."

Then the majesty of Nun said: "My son Shu, [your] eye for [your] father is your protection. My daughter Nut put him [. . .]"

Then Nut said: "How, my father Nun?"

And Nut said: "Do not [. . .]" *And so Nut came into being as [a cow].*

Then the majesty of Re [placed himself] on her back. These human beings [came back] [. . .] and they saw him on the back of th[is] cow. Then these human beings said to him: "[. . .] [Come] to us and we will defeat your woes that conspired words against the one who made them."

His majesty proceeded to the palace [. . .] of this cow. He [did not] come with them. Then the land fell in darkness. When the land got light, these human beings went up with bows and weapons [. . .] and they [. . .] for shooting to the enemies. Then the majesty of this god said: "your despicable act is on you, oh killers, may the terror be far [. . .] be the terror over the human beings."

Then this god said to Nut: "I have placed myself in [your] back in order to be raised up." "How is this? (*petwi*)" asked Nut. *And so [she] came into being as the double sky (peti).*

The majesty of this god [said]: "Get away (*heri*) from them! Raise me up! Watch me!" *And so she came into being as the firmament (herit).*

Then the majesty of this god watched her interior and she said: "If you could satisfy me with many human beings!" *[And so the] [. . .] came into being. (. . .)*[41]

2.3. ADAM AND EVE, FROM GENESIS 2–3

The creation of humankind by Yahweh is narrated in Genesis 1–3 in two different ways. In the opening creation story (Gen. 1–2.3, for which see Part 1, document 4), the Hebrew God creates the world in an act of speech and in an orderly and symmetrical manner, with man and woman created

---

[39] Current Kom el-Hisn, in the Western Delta.

[40] Re decides to leave the earth. In order to settle in the sky, Nut, the Sky Goddess, is fashioned as a heavenly cow. Abandoned by the gods, human beings fall into strife.

[41] Subsequently, the text refers to the creation of three different spheres in the cosmos by Re: the sky, governed by himself and Thoth; the earth, led by the king and Shu; and the netherworld, under the command of Geb and Osiris.

equal (1.27) after the other creatures. That narrative by the so-called Priestly redactors is placed before the probably older narrative by the Jahwistic redactors, the Adam and Eve story reproduced here (Gen. 2.4–3.24), in which Yahweh's interaction with man is emphasized and man's position in the creation is superior to that of the other creatures and of woman (see Figure 20). The Hebrew God is here always called "Yahweh Elohim," conventionally translated "the Lord God" because the *tatragrammaton* (four letters YHWH) is often read as Adonai, "Lord" to avoid pronouncing his name. The conventional translation is maintained here, however, to avoid the awkward rendering "Yahweh God."

SOURCE: The Hebrew Bible, Genesis 2.4–3.24, New Revised Standard Version, with minor modifications.

Genesis 2. (4) In the day that the Lord God made the earth and the heavens, (5) when no plant of the field was yet in the earth and no herb of the field had yet sprung up—for the Lord God had not caused it to rain upon the earth, and there was no one to till the ground; (6) but a stream would rise from the earth, and water the whole face of the ground—(7) then the Lord God formed man from the dust of the ground,[42] and breathed into his nostrils the breath of life; and the man became a living being. (8) And the Lord God planted a garden in Eden, in the east; and there he put the man whom he had formed. (9) Out of the ground the Lord God made to grow every tree that is pleasant to the sight and good for food, the tree of life also in the midst of the garden, and the tree of the knowledge of good and evil.

(10) A river flows out of Eden to water the garden, and from there it divides and becomes four branches. (11) The name of the first is Pishon; it is the one that flows around the whole land of Havilah, where there is gold; (12) and the gold of that land is good; bdellium and onyx stone are there. (13) The name of the second river is Gihon; it is the one that flows around the whole land of Cush. (14) The name of the third river is Tigris, which flows east of Assyria. And the fourth river is the Euphrates.

(15) The Lord God took the man and put him in the garden of Eden to till it and keep it. (16) And the Lord God commanded the man, "You may freely eat of every tree of the garden; (17) but of the tree of the knowledge of good and evil you shall not eat, for in the day that you eat of it you shall die."

(18) Then the Lord God said, "It is not good that the man should be alone; I will make him a helper as his partner." (19) So out of the ground the Lord God formed every animal of the field and every bird of the air, and brought them to the man to see what he would call them; and whatever the man called every living creature, that was its name. (20) The man gave names to all cattle, and to the birds of the air, and to every animal of the field; but for the man there happened to be no helper as his partner.[43] (21) So the Lord God caused a deep sleep to fall upon the

---

[42] Note the etymological play between Hebrew *'adam*, "man," and *'adamah*, "dirt, ground" (see pun on the name of "woman" below).

[43] NRSV "there was not found a helper . . . . "

man, and he slept; then he took one of his ribs and closed up its place with flesh. (22) And the rib that the Lord God had taken from the man he made into a woman and brought her to the man.[44] (23) Then the man said, "This at last is bone of my bones and flesh of my flesh; this one shall be called Woman, for out of Man this one was taken."

(24) Therefore a man leaves his father and his mother and clings to his wife, and they become one flesh. (25) And the man and his wife were both naked, and were not ashamed.

Genesis 3. (1) Now the serpent was more crafty than any other wild animal that the Lord God had made. He said to the woman, "Did God say, 'You shall not eat from any tree in the garden'?" (2) The woman said to the serpent, "We may eat of the fruit of the trees in the garden; (3) but God said, 'You shall not eat of the fruit of the tree that is in the middle of the garden, nor shall you touch it, or you shall die.'" (4) But the serpent said to the woman, "You will not die; (5) for God knows that when you eat of it your eyes will be opened, and you will be like God, knowing good and evil." (6) So when the woman saw that the tree was good for food, and that it was a delight to the eyes, and that the tree was to be desired to make one wise, she took of its fruit and ate; and she also gave some to her husband, who was with her, and he ate. (7) Then the eyes of both were opened, and they knew that they were naked; and they sewed fig leaves together and made loincloths for themselves.

(8) They heard the sound of the Lord God walking in the garden at the time of the evening breeze, and the man and his wife hid themselves from the presence of the Lord God among the trees of the garden. (9) But the Lord God called to the man, and said to him, "Where are you?" (10) He said, "I heard the sound of you in the garden, and I was afraid, because I was naked; and I hid myself." (11) He said, "Who told you that you were naked? Have you eaten from the tree of which I commanded you not to eat?" (12) The man said, "The woman whom you gave to be with me, she gave me fruit from the tree, and I ate." (13) Then the Lord God said to the woman, "What is this that you have done?" The woman said, "The serpent tricked me, and I ate."

(14) The Lord God said to the serpent, "Because you have done this, cursed are you among all animals and among all wild creatures; upon your belly you shall go, and dust you shall eat all the days of your life. (15) I will put enmity between you and the woman, and between your offspring and hers; he will strike your head, and you will strike his heel." (16) To the woman he said, "I will greatly increase your pangs in childbearing; in pain you shall bring forth children, yet your desire shall be for your husband, and he shall rule over you." (17) And to the man he said, "Because you have listened to the voice of your wife, and have eaten of the tree about which I commanded you, 'You shall not eat of it,' cursed is the ground because of you; in toil you shall eat of it all the days of your life; (18) thorns and thistles it shall bring forth for you; and you shall eat the plants of the field. (19) By the sweat of your face you shall eat bread until you return to the ground, for out of it you were taken; you

---

[44] The name of "woman" in Hebrew, *'ishah*, is here connected with the similar sounding word for "man," *'ish*.

are dust, and to dust you shall return." (20) The man named his wife Eve, because she was the mother of all living.[45] (21) And the Lord God made garments of skins for the man and for his wife, and clothed them.

(22) Then the Lord God said, "See, the man has become like one of us, knowing good and evil; and now, he might reach out his hand and take also from the tree of life, and eat, and live forever"—(23) therefore the Lord God sent him forth from the garden of Eden, to till the ground from which he was taken. (24) He drove out the man; and at the east of the garden of Eden he placed the cherubim,[46] and a sword flaming and turning to guard the way to the tree of life.

2.4. THE STORY OF NOAH, FROM GENESIS 6–9

After a number of generations of extremely long-lived descendants of Adam and Eve, Yahweh sends the great flood to annihilate the human race. The story revolves around the extraordinary survival of Noah and his family in a floating ark, thanks to Yahweh's mercy and detailed instructions. Thus, a second chance for humankind begins when Yahweh blesses Noah and his sons and tells them to "Be fruitful and multiply, and fill the earth, etc." (Gen. 9.1 ff.) after which "the whole earth was peopled" from Noah's three sons, Shem, Ham, and Japheth (9.18–19).

The similarity between the Genesis and the Mesopotamian flood stories was noticed as soon as the tablets of the latter were first deciphered. One major difference between the two accounts is that in the monotheistic account a single god (Yahweh) decrees the destruction of humanity, sends the flood, and mediates to save the chosen virtuous human, while in the Mesopotamian account these functions were fulfilled by the gods Enlil/Ellil and Ea/Enki, respectively. The Genesis account also introduces the factors of corruption and violence as causes for the annihilation. The narration in Genesis 6–8 interweaves parallel accounts belonging to the Jahwistic and the Priestly traditions. Instead of placing one version after the other, as in Genesis 1–3 with the creation stories, here the redactor has integrated them so as to avoid narrating two consecutive floods. This results in some inconsistencies, such as the specific inclusion of extra pairs of clean (unpolluted) animals beside the unclean (polluted) animals in the ark, to provide for the final sacrifice (8.20), alongside a version (Priestly) where no such distinction is made (6.19–20; 7.14–15) and in which only one pair of each is included (7.9), so logically Yahweh's covenant includes no animal sacrifice (see 9.1–17). Notice also that the entrance of Noah, his family, and the animals in the ark is narrated twice (7.7–9 and 7.13–16). The Hebrew God is here called some times Yahweh but more often Elohim, that is "God."

SOURCE: The Hebrew Bible, Genesis 6–9.1, New Revised Standard Version, with minor modifications.

---

[45] The name of Eve in Hebrew (*Hawwah*) can also mean "living thing," from the verb "to live" (*hayah*). Here she is the mother of "all living things" (*kol-hay*).

[46] The *cherubim* were composite winged creatures (with a combination of human and other animal features), like those said to have guarded the entrance to Solomon's temple in Jerusalem, described in Ezekiel 10.

Genesis 6. (1) When man began to multiply on the face of the ground,[47] and daughters were born to them, (2) the sons of God(s)[48] saw that they were fair; and they took wives for themselves of all that they chose. (3) Then Yahweh said, "My spirit shall not abide in mortals for ever, for they are flesh; their days shall be one hundred and twenty years." (4) The Nephilim[49] were on the earth in those days— and also afterwards—when the sons of God(s) went in to the daughters of human beings, who bore children to them. These were the heroes that were of old, warriors of renown.

(5) Yahweh saw that the wickedness of humankind was great in the earth, and that every inclination of the thoughts of their hearts was only evil continually. (6) And Yahweh was sorry that he had made humankind on the earth, and it grieved him in his heart. (7) So Yahweh said, "I will blot out from the earth the human beings I have created—people together with animals and creeping things and birds of the air, for I am sorry that I have made them." (8) But Noah found favor in the sight of Yahweh.

(9) These are the descendants of Noah. Noah was a righteous man, blameless in his generation; Noah walked with God. (10) And Noah had three sons, Shem, Ham, and Japheth. (11) Now the earth was corrupt in God's sight, and the earth was filled with violence. (12) And God saw that the earth was corrupt; for all flesh had corrupted its ways upon the earth.

(13) And God said to Noah, "I have determined to make an end of all flesh, for the earth is filled with violence because of them; now I am going to destroy them along with the earth. (14) Make yourself an ark of cypress wood; make rooms in the ark, and cover it inside and out with pitch. (15) This is how you are to make it: the length of the ark three hundred cubits, its width fifty cubits, and its height thirty cubits. (16) Make a roof for the ark, and finish it to a cubit above; and put the door of the ark in its side; make it with lower, second, and third decks. (17) For my part, I am going to bring a flood of waters on the earth, to destroy from under heaven all flesh in which is the breath of life; everything that is on the earth shall die. (18) But I will establish my covenant with you; and you shall come into the ark, you, your sons, your wife, and your sons' wives with you. (19) And of every living thing, of all flesh, you shall bring two of every kind into the ark, to keep them alive with you; they shall be male and female. (20) Of the birds according to their kinds, and of the animals according to their kinds, of every creeping thing of the ground according to its kind, two of every kind shall come in to you, to keep them alive. (21) Also take with you

---

[47] Separate words "ground" and "earth" are used in the translation to distinguish between two Hebrew terms, 'adamah ("ground, dirt") and 'erez ("earth, land"). The name of "man," 'adam, comes from the first term, here standing close to it to emphasize the association.

[48] *Elohim* is a plural word originally meaning "gods" but used in the Hebrew Bible as a singular noun for "God." However, this and a handful of other passages reveal the polytheistic background of inherited traditions (see Yahweh's use of the expression "one of us" in Gen. 3.22 and 11.7).

[49] The Nephilim are one of the several races of giants mentioned in the Bible (see Num. 13.33; Deut. 2.10–11). The idea of a primeval race of semi-divine human beings later extinguished by a god or by their own violence is akin to Greek ideas about a heroic race of demigods existing before the present race of men (see the "Five Races of Men" in Hesiod's *Works and Days*, document 2.5).

every kind of food that is eaten, and store it up; and it shall serve as food for you and for them." (22) Noah did this; he did all that God commanded him.

Genesis 7. (1) Then Yahweh said to Noah, "Go into the ark, you and all your household, for I have seen that you alone are righteous before me in this generation. (2) Take with you seven pairs of all clean animals, the male and its mate; and a pair of the animals that are not clean, the male and its mate; (3) and seven pairs of the birds of the air also, male and female, to keep their kind alive on the face of all the earth. (4) For in seven days I will send rain on the earth for forty days and forty nights; and every living thing that I have made I will blot out from the face of the ground." (5) And Noah did all that Yahweh had commanded him.

(6) Noah was six hundred years old when the flood of waters came on the earth. (7) And Noah with his sons and his wife and his sons' wives went into the ark to escape the waters of the flood. (8) Of clean animals, and of animals that are not clean, and of birds, and of everything that creeps on the ground, (9) two and two, male and female, went into the ark with Noah, as God had commanded Noah. (10) And after seven days the waters of the flood came on the earth.

(11) In the six-hundredth year of Noah's life, in the second month, on the seventeenth day of the month, on that day all the fountains of the great deep burst forth, and the windows of the heavens were opened. (12) The rain fell on the earth for forty days and forty nights. (13) On the very same day Noah with his sons, Shem and Ham and Japheth, and Noah's wife and the three wives of his sons, entered the ark, (14) they and every wild animal of every kind, and all domestic animals of every kind, and every creeping thing that creeps on the earth, and every bird of every kind—every bird, every winged creature. (15) They went into the ark with Noah, two and two of all flesh in which there was the breath of life. (16) And those that entered, male and female of all flesh, went in as God had commanded him; and Yahweh shut him in.

(17) The flood continued for forty days on the earth; and the waters increased, and bore up the ark, and it rose high above the earth. (18) The waters swelled and increased greatly on the earth; and the ark floated on the face of the waters. (19) The waters swelled so mightily on the earth that all the high mountains under the whole heaven were covered; (20) the waters swelled above the mountains, covering them fifteen cubits deep. (21) And all flesh died that moved on the earth, birds, domestic animals, wild animals, all swarming creatures that swarm on the earth, and all human beings; (22) everything on dry land in whose nostrils was the breath of life died. (23) He blotted out every living thing that was on the face of the ground, human beings and animals and creeping things and birds of the air; they were blotted out from the earth. Only Noah was left, and those that were with him in the ark. (24) And the waters swelled on the earth for one hundred and fifty days.

Genesis 8. (1) But God remembered Noah and all the wild animals and all the domestic animals that were with him in the ark. And God made a wind blow over the earth, and the waters subsided; (2) the fountains of the deep and the windows of the heavens were closed, the rain from the heavens was restrained, (3) and the waters gradually receded from the earth. At the end of one hundred and fifty days the waters had abated; (4) and in the seventh month, on the seventeenth day of the month, the ark came to rest on the mountains of Ararat. (5) The waters continued to abate until the tenth month; in the tenth month, on the first day of the month, the tops of the mountains appeared.

(6) At the end of forty days Noah opened the window of the ark that he had made (7) and sent out the raven; and it went to and fro until the waters were dried up from the earth. (8) Then he sent out the dove from him, to see if the waters had subsided from the face of the ground; (9) but the dove found no place to set its foot, and it returned to him to the ark, for the waters were still on the face of the whole earth. So he put out his hand and took it and brought it into the ark with him. (10) He waited another seven days, and again he sent out the dove from the ark; (11) and the dove came back to him in the evening, and there in its beak was a freshly plucked olive leaf; so Noah knew that the waters had subsided from the earth. (12) Then he waited another seven days, and sent out the dove; and it did not return to him any more.

(13) In the six hundred and first year, in the first month, on the first day of the month, the waters were dried up from the earth; and Noah removed the covering of the ark, and looked, and saw that the face of the ground was drying. (14) In the second month, on the twenty-seventh day of the month, the earth was dry. (15) Then God said to Noah, (16) "Go out of the ark, you and your wife, and your sons and your sons' wives with you. (17) Bring out with you every living thing that is with you of all flesh—birds and animals and every creeping thing that creeps on the earth—so that they may abound on the earth, and be fruitful and multiply on the earth." (18) So Noah went out with his sons and his wife and his sons' wives. (19) And every animal, every creeping thing, and every bird, everything that moves on the earth, went out of the ark by families.

(20) Then Noah built an altar to Yahweh, and took of every clean animal and of every clean bird, and offered burnt-offerings on the altar. And when Yahweh smelled the pleasing odor, Yahweh said in his heart, "I will never again curse the ground because of humankind, for the inclination of the human heart is evil from youth; nor will I ever again destroy every living creature as I have done. As long as the earth endures, seedtime and harvest, cold and heat, summer and winter, day and night, shall not cease."

Genesis 9. (1) God blessed Noah and his sons, and said to them, "Be fruitful and multiply, and fill the earth . . . . "

2.5. HESIOD'S PROMETHEUS, PANDORA, AND FIVE RACES OF MANKIND, FROM *WORKS AND DAYS*

In his poem *Works and Days*, the Greek poet Hesiod (probably active in the late eighth to the early seventh centuries BCE) aligns himself with a different literary tradition from his *Theogony* (see Part 1, document 5), though their styles are similar and they are both set in hexameters. This is the genre of so-called "wisdom literature," or didactic literature, attested in many ancient cultures. The closest parallels to Hesiod appear in the ancient Near East, in texts such as the Sumerian *Father and His Misguided Son*, the Egyptian *Instructions of Ankh-sheshonq*, the books of Job, Proverbs, and Ecclesiastes in the Hebrew Bible, and the story of *Ahiqar*. As a "wisdom poem," *Works and Days* focuses on the ethical behavior of human beings toward each other and their place in the real world, rather than on stories about gods or heroes (as in the *Theogony* or Homer's works, though ethical issues are of course present in those compositions as well, especially in Homer). In the wake of these literary traditions, Hesiod frames his poem as a series of pieces of advice he gives to his mischievous brother Perses, whom he accuses of having taken more than his allotted share of their family inheritance, and to the kings he has allegedly bribed. After the moral exhortations in the first third of the poem (including the passages below), *Works and Days* offers practical instructions on how to work the land, navigation, and the propitious and unpropitious days of the month, all accompanied by mythological folk material.

These passages immediately follow Hesiod's harangue to his brother, jumping from the specific situation between the brothers to the broader topic of the state of the human race and the troublesome presence of women in it. The story of Prometheus and Pandora also appears in Hesiod's *Theogony* 535–616 (see Part 1, document 5) (see Figures 17 and 23). There, Prometheus' conflict with Zeus starts with the deceit about a sacrificial offering, not mentioned in the *Works and Days*. Woman's creation in the *Theogony* is similar but narrated in less detail, and she is not given a name. The motif of the jar full of evils appears only in the *Works and Days* (although it is mentioned as if it were a known theme), and particular attention is paid to the puzzling presence of Hope in the jar. The *Theogony*'s passage, on the other hand, elaborates on the ambivalent gift of women and the snares of marriage. Both accounts end with similar sentences about the impossibility of evading the will of Zeus. The story of the Five Races (also called "Five Ages") insists on the idea that gods and men had "a common origin" and that human beings grew distant from the divine realm (compare with stories of the Flood and of Adam and Eve above). This condition did not increase with every generation but was temporarily reversed by the race of heroes. It was mainly through **hybris** and unjust behavior that humankind fell into its present disgraceful state, in which the poet and his brother lived.

SOURCE: Hesiod, *Works and Days* 42–201, translated and annotated by C. López-Ruiz.

(Prometheus and Pandora)

In fact, the gods hold back people's livelihood, hiding it from them; for you would otherwise easily work even in one day enough to have for one year, even without working; soon you would place your steering-oar[50] on top of the fireplace and the work of the oxen would die out, as that of the hard-working mules. But Zeus hid it, when he became angry in his heart that crooked-minded Prometheus (Forethought) had deceived him.

---

[50] A part of the plowing device.

It was for this reason that he devised sorrowful miseries for human beings. (50) So he hid fire; this in turn the benevolent son of Iapetos[51] stole for mankind from Zeus the counselor in a hollow cane, unnoticed by Zeus who enjoys the thunderbolt.

But the cloud-gatherer, Zeus, spoke to him in anger: "Son of Iapetos, who has more ideas than anyone, you rejoice that you have stolen fire and cheated my mind: a great sorrow (this will be) for yourself and for men to come! To them I will give an evil to pay for the fire, in which all of them will take pleasure in their hearts, while embracing their own suffering."

So he said, and he burst out laughing, the father of men and gods. (60) Then he told renowned Hephaistos to quickly moisten earth with water, and to put in it the voice and strength of a human, and to make its face like those of the immortal goddesses: the beautiful, desirable form of a maiden. And he told Athena to teach her skills, to weave a very intricate cloth; and Aphrodite to pour grace around her head, and painful desire and paralyzing cares; and he urged Hermes, the envoy, slayer of Argos, to put in it a bitchy mind and a cunning character.

So he spoke, and they obeyed him, Zeus, the lord, son of Kronos. (70) And at once, out of dirt, the famous Lame One[52] modeled the likeness of a modest maiden, according to the plans of Kronos' son. The bright-eyed goddess, Athena, girdled her and adorned her. All around the divine Graces and Lady Persuasion placed on her skin golden necklaces, and all around the beautiful-haired Seasons crowned her with Spring flowers; and Pallas Athena arranged all the adornment on her body. And then into her breast the envoy, slayer of Argos, placed lies and flattering words and a cunning character, according to the plans of loud-thundering Zeus. And so a voice (80) he put into her, the herald of the gods, and this woman he named Pandora (All-Gift), since all who have mansions in Olympos gave her gifts,[53] a sorrow for bread-eating men.

After he had completed the utter, impossible deception, the father sent the famous slayer of Argos (i.e., Hermes) to Epimetheus (Afterthought), carrying the gift, like the swift messenger of the gods that he is; and Epimetheus did not consider that Prometheus had told him not ever to accept a gift from Olympian Zeus, but to send it back, lest somehow some evil befalls mortals. Only after he had received it, when he had the evil, he understood.

(90) For before this the tribes of men used to live far apart from evils and apart from harsh pains and from distressful diseases, which now give death to men. [For in anguish mortals quickly turn old.][54] But the woman scattered them, after she lifted the great lid of the jar with her hands. And so she conceived miserable sorrows for humankind.

Only Hope[55] remained there, in its indestructible home, under the rim of the jar, and it did not fly away; for, before it could, Pandora put the lid back on the jar by

---

[51] Prometheus.

[52] Hephaistos.

[53] Hesiod thus makes clear the etymology of her name from *doron*, "gift."

[54] Probably not an authentic line (= *Odyssey* 19.360).

[55] Greek *elpis* can also be translated as "expectation." It is not clear how this "hope" should be interpreted and what it was doing among the evils that Pandora spilled, nor why it stays in the jar by Zeus' will.

the plans of the aegis-bearer, the cloud-gatherer Zeus. (100) But another thousand miseries roam about among human beings; for the earth is full of evils, and full is the sea; and sicknesses for human beings spontaneously come and go, some by day, some by night, bringing evils to mortal men in silence, since the counselor Zeus took away their voice.

In such a way it is not at all possible to evade the mind of Zeus.

(Five Races of Mankind)

And if you want, I will top it off with yet another story, one I know well too—and try to keep it at heart: how gods and mortal men have one common origin.

Golden was, at first, the race of mortal people, (110) which the immortals, who hold Olympian mansions, made. They lived in the time of Kronos, when he used to be king in heaven. Just like gods they used to live, with their spirits free of sorrows, far apart from effort and pain; nor did wretched old age befall them, but, since their legs and arms were always the same, they enjoyed themselves in parties, free from all afflictions; and they died as if overcome by sleep. Everything was good for these ones; the fertile land produced its fruit all by herself, abundant and rich; while they, voluntarily peaceful, shared out their tasks together with their many goods, (120)—wealthy in sheep, dear to the blessed gods.

But ever since the earth covered up this race, they act as spirits by the will of great Zeus; favorable guardians of mortal people on earth, who watch out for punishments and base deeds, covered in mist, walking around everywhere upon the earth, as granters of wealth, for they also kept this kingly honor.

Then came a much worse race, a silver one, which those who hold Olympian mansions made afterwards, not like the golden one in either body or mind. (130) On the contrary, for a hundred years a child would be raised by his caring mother, pampered, a big baby in his own house. But as soon as he would grow up and reach the point of youth, he would live for a tiny little time, and so they endured the sorrows of their foolishness. For they were not capable of keeping their reckless arrogance from each other, nor did they want to attend to the immortals or sacrifice on the altars of the blessed ones, which is a divine law for people throughout their dwellings.

Later, Zeus the son of Kronos concealed these ones, enraged because they did not honor the blessed gods who hold Olympos. (140) So after the earth had also covered up this race, they are the second ones called subterranean blessed mortals, though all the same honor accompanies them too.

Father Zeus made another, third, race of mortal people, a bronze one, not like the silver one at all, from the ash-trees,[56] terrible and powerful, who cared for the wailing works of Ares and for outrages; they did not even eat bread, but had a strong-hearted spirit of adamant; monstrous they were; and great strength and unreachable arms grew from their shoulders on their sturdy bodies. (150) Of bronze was their armor, and of bronze their houses, and they worked with bronze; for there used to be no black iron.

---

[56] Or ash-tree Nymphs; see Hesiod's *Theogony* 187 and note on page 36.

And yet, overpowered by their own hands they went to the dank house of cold Hades, nameless; for black death seized them, impressive though they were, and they left the light of the bright sun.

So after the earth had also covered up this race, Zeus, the son of Kronos, made yet again another, a fourth one, on the much-nourishing earth, more just and superior, a divine race of hero-men, who are called (160) half-gods, the race preceding (ours) upon the infinite earth. Evil war and terrible combat also destroyed these ones, some under seven-gated Thebes, in the land of Kadmos, fighting for the sake of Oedipus's flocks, and others when war carried them in ships, over the deep abyss of the sea, for the sake of Helen of the beautiful hair.

There certainly the end of death covered some of them completely, but on others Zeus, the son of Kronos, bestowed a life and dwellings far from people, and he, the father, settled them at the limits of the earth; (170) and so they live there with a care-free heart, in the Isles of the Blessed, beyond the Ocean of deep-currents; happy heroes, for whom the grain-giving field bears honey-like fruit that flourished three times per year.

[Far from the immortals; and Kronos is king over them; for the father of men and gods freed him; and now he is always honored among them, as is fitting. And in turn Zeus placed another race of mortal men, all who now have come into being upon the much-nourishing earth.][57]

After this, I wish I did not have to be among the fifth group of men, but that I had died before or been born after. For now indeed the race is of iron; and never during the day do they rest from toil and hardship, nor by night, when they are worn out, as the gods will give them troublesome worries. Though, all the same, these will also have good things mixed with the bad ones.

(180) But Zeus will destroy this race of mortal people too, at the time when those who are born come out with gray temples. And the father will not be akin to his children, nor the children at all (to him), nor the guest to his host and the companion to his companion, nor will the brother be a friend, just as he was before.

And they will dishonor their parents as soon as they grow old; and then they will insult them addressing harsh words to them, - cruel people, who do not know fear of the gods; they would not even repay their aging parents for their rearing. With justice in their own hands, they will plunder each other's city; (190) nor will there be any favor for he who keeps his oath, nor for the just man or the noble one, but rather the wrong-doer and the man who transgresses they will honor; justice will be in their hands and there will be no shame; a base person will harm the better one by speaking with crooked arguments, and on top of them he will swear an oath.

And Envy will accompany all miserable people, badmouthing envy, who delights in disgraces, the one of hateful gaze. And then they will surely go to Olympos from the wide-pathed earth, the two of them covering their fair skin with white mantles to join the tribe of immortals, leaving human beings behind: (200) Shame and

---

[57] These five lines are probably a later addition (the first one is in the manuscript tradition, while the following four come from two papyri); numbered 169 a–e, they fit better after 173.

Indignation,[58] while sorrowful pains will be left behind for mortal people, and there will be no defense against evil.

2.6. OVID'S AGES OF MANKIND AND THE FLOOD, FROM *METAMORPHOSES*, BOOK 1

The Roman poet Ovid (first century BCE to first century CE, on whom see Part 1, document 10) elaborates here a new (Latin) version of the story of the Five Races (or Ages) of Mankind, which Hesiod made famous (see document 2.5), followed by his version of the Greek story of the Flood and its survivors, Deukalion and Pyrrha (attested in Greek sources but not in a poetic elaboration such as Ovid's). This section follows the account of the creation of the world at the beginning of the *Metamorphoses* (see Part 1, document 10). The Flood narrative traveled and served as poetic inspiration from second millennium BCE Mesopotamia to Israel, Greece, and finally Rome. In contrast with Ovid's verses on the creation of life, which is brief and directed by divine will, his portrayal of the evolution of the earth after the Flood reveals the influence of natural philosophy (heat and moisture as sources of life, etc.), especially of the type articulated by the **Epicurean** Roman philosopher Lucretius in his poem *De rerum natura* (on which see headnote to Part 5, document 7). The insertion of the story of Lycaon (the first human story in the *Metamorphoses*) in the context of the Flood introduces humanity's depravity as a justification of the divine punishment.

SOURCE: Ovid, *Metamorphoses*, Book 1.89–451. F. J. Miller, *Ovid, Metamorphoses* (Loeb Classical Library, Cambridge, MA and London, 1921, 2nd ed.), with minor modifications.

(The Ages of Mankind)

Golden was that first age, which, with no one to compel, without a law, of its own will, kept faith and did the right. There was no fear of punishment, no threatening words were to be read on brazen tablets; no suppliant throng gazed fearfully upon its judge's face; but without judges lived secure. Not yet had the pine-tree, felled on its native mountains, descended thence into the watery plain to visit other lands; men knew no shores except their own. Not yet were cities girded with steep moats; there were no trumpets of straight, no horns of curving brass, no swords or helmets. There was no need at all of armed men, for nations, secure from war's alarms, passed the years in gentle ease.

The earth herself, without compulsion, untouched by hoe or plowshare, of herself gave all things needful. And men, content with food which came with no one's seeking, gathered the arbute fruit, strawberries from the mountain-sides, cornel-cherries, berries hanging thick upon the prickly bramble, and acorns fallen from the spreading tree of Jove.[59] Then spring was everlasting, and gentle zephyrs with warm breath played with the flowers that sprang unplanted. Soon the earth, untilled,

---

[58] *Aidos* can mean "shame, respect, reverence" and *Nemesis* "divine punishment, indignation."

[59] The oak is associated with Zeus (equated with Roman Jove), especially at the oracle at Dodona.

brought forth her stores of grain, and the fields, though unfallowed, grew white with the heavy, bearded wheat. Streams of milk and streams of sweet nectar flowed, and yellow honey was distilled from the verdant oak.

After Saturn[60] had been banished to the dark land of death, and the world was under the sway of Jove, the silver race came in, lower in the scale than gold, but of greater worth than yellow brass. Jove now shortened the bounds of the old-time spring, and through winter, summer, variable autumn, and brief spring completed the year in four seasons. Then first the parched air glared white with burning heat, and icicles hung down congealed by freezing winds. In that age men first sought the shelter of houses. Their homes had heretofore been caves, dense thickets, and branches bound together with bark. Then first the seeds of grain were planted in long furrows, and bullocks groaned beneath the heavy yoke.

Next after this and third in order came the brazen race, of sterner disposition, and more ready to fly to arms savage, but not yet impious. The age of hard iron came last. Straightway all evil burst forth into this age of baser vein: modesty and truth and faith fled the earth, and in their place came tricks and plots and snares, violence and cursed love of gain. Men now spread sails to the winds, though the sailor as yet scarcely knew them; and keels of pine which long had stood upon high mountain-sides, now leaped insolently over unknown waves. And the ground, which had hitherto been a common possession like the sunlight and the air, the careful surveyor now marked out with long-drawn boundary-line. Not only did men demand of the bounteous fields the crops and sustenance they owed, but they delved as well into the very bowels of the earth; and the wealth which the creator had hidden away and buried deep amidst the very Stygian shades was brought to light, wealth that pricks men on to crime. And now baneful iron had come, and gold more baneful than iron; war came, which fights with both, and brandished in its bloody hands the clashing arms. Men lived on plunder. Guest was not safe from host, nor father-in-law from son-in-law; even among brothers it was rare to find affection. The husband longed for the death of his wife, she of her husband; murderous stepmothers brewed deadly poisons, and sons inquired into their fathers' years before time. Piety lay vanquished, and the maiden Astraea,[61] last of the immortals, abandoned the blood-soaked earth.

And, that high heaven might be no safer than the earth, they say that the Giants essayed the very throne of heaven, piling huge mountains, one on another, clear up to the stars. Then the Almighty Father hurled his thunderbolts, shattered Olympus, and dashed Pelion down from underlying Ossa. When those dread bodies lay overwhelmed by their own bulk, they say that Mother Earth, drenched with their streaming blood, informed that warm gore anew with life, and, that some trace of her former offspring might remain, she gave it human form. But this new stock, too, proved contemptuous of the gods, very greedy for slaughter, and passionate. You might know that they were sons of blood.

---

[60] Equivalent to Greek Kronos and occupying here the same position as Kronos in the *Theogony* (banished by Zeus) and in Hesiod's "Five Races."

[61] Goddess of Justice.

When Saturn's son from his high throne saw this he groaned, and, recalling the infamous revels of Lycaon's table—a story still unknown because the deed was new—he conceived a mighty wrath worthy of the soul of Jove, and summoned a council of the gods. Nothing delayed their answer to the summons. – There is a high way, easily seen when the sky is clear. It is called the Milky Way, famed for its shining whiteness. By this way the gods fare to the halls and royal dwelling of the mighty Thunderer. On either side the palaces of the gods of higher rank are thronged with guests through folding-doors flung wide. The lesser gods dwell apart from these. Fronting on this way, the illustrious and strong heavenly gods have placed their homes. This is the place, which, if I may make bold to say it, I would not fear to call the Palatines[62] of high heaven.

So, when the gods had taken their seats within the marble council chamber, the king himself, seated high above the rest and leaning on his ivory scepter, shook thrice and again his awful locks, wherewith he moved the land and sea and sky. Then he opened his indignant lips, and thus he spoke:

> I was not more troubled than now for the sovereignty of the world when each one of the serpent-footed giants was in laying his hundred hands upon the captive sky. For, although that was a savage enemy, their whole attack sprung from one body and one source. But now, wherever old Ocean roars around the earth, I must destroy the race of men. By the infernal streams that glide beneath the earth through Stygian groves, I swear that I have already tried all other means. But that which is incurable must be cut away with the knife, lest the untainted part also draw infection. I have demigods, rustic divinities, nymphs, fauns and satyrs, and sylvan deities upon the mountain-slopes. Since we do not yet esteem them worthy the honor of a place in heaven, let us at least allow them to dwell in safety in the lands allotted them. Or do you think that they will be safe, when against me, who wield the thunderbolt, who have and rule you as my subjects, Lycaon, well known for savagery, has laid his snares?

All trembled, and with eager zeal demanded him who had been guilty of such bold infamy. So, when an impious band was mad to blot out the name of Rome with Caesar's blood,[63] the human race was dazed with a mighty fear of sudden ruin, and the whole world shuddered in horror. Nor is the loyalty of thy subjects, Augustus, less pleasing to you than that was to Jove. After he, by word and gesture, had checked their outcry, all held their peace. When now the clamor had subsided, checked by his royal authority, Jove once more broke the silence with these words:

---

[62] The Palatine (Lat. *Palatium*, here in plural *Palatia*) was the hill in Rome where Augustus and the emperors who followed him established their residences, from where we formed our word "palace."

[63] A reference to Julius Caesar's murder in 44 BCE, although it could also refer to a failed attempt against Augustus.

He (Lycaon) has indeed been punished; have no care for that. But what he did and what his punishment I will relate. An infamous report of the age had reached my ears. Eager to prove this false, I descended from high Olympus, and as a god disguised in human form travelled up and down the land. It would take too long to recount how great impiety was found on every hand. The infamous report was far less than the truth. I had crossed Maenala, bristling with the lairs of beasts, Cyllene, and the pine-groves of chill Lycaeus. Thence I approached the seat and inhospitable abode of the Arcadian king, just as the late evening shades were ushering in the night. I gave a sign that a god had come, and the common folk began to worship me. Lycaon at first mocked at their pious prayers; and then he said: "I will soon find out, and that by a plain test, whether this fellow be god or mortal. Nor shall the truth be at all in doubt."

He planned that night while I was heavy with sleep to kill me by an unexpected murderous attack. Such was the experiment he adopted to test the truth. And not content with that, he took a hostage who had been sent by the Molossian race, cut his throat, and some parts of him, still warm with life, he boiled, and others he roasted over the fire. But no sooner had he placed these before me on the table than I, with my avenging bolt, overthrew the house upon its master and on his guilty household. The king himself flies in terror and, gaining the silent fields, howls aloud, attempting in vain to speak. His mouth of itself gathers foam, and with his accustomed greed for blood he turns against the sheep, delighting still in slaughter. His garments change to shaggy hair, his arms to legs. He turns into a wolf, and yet retains some traces of his former shape. There is the same grey hair, the same fierce face, the same gleaming eyes, the same picture of beastly savagery.

One house has fallen; but not one house alone has deserved to perish. Wherever the plains of earth extend, wild fury reigns supreme. You would deem it a conspiracy of crime. Let them all pay, and quickly too, the penalties which they have deserved. So stands my purpose.

When he had done, some proclaimed their approval of his words, and added fuel to his wrath, while others played their parts by giving silent consent. And yet they all grieved over the threatened loss of the human race, and asked what would be the state of the world bereft of mortals. Who would bring incense to their altars? Was he planning to give over the world to the wild beasts to despoil? As they thus questioned, their king bade them be of good cheer (for the rest should be his care), for he would give them another race of wondrous origin far different from the first.

(The Flood)

And now he was on the point of hurling his thunderbolts against the whole world; but he stayed his hand in fear lest perchance the sacred heavens should take fire from so huge a conflagration, and burn from pole to pole. He remembered also that it was in the fates that a time would come when sea and land, the unkindled palace of the sky and the beleaguered structure of the universe should be destroyed by fire. And so he laid aside the bolts, which Cyclopean hands had forged. He preferred a different punishment, to destroy the human race beneath the waves and to send down rain from every quarter of the sky.

Straightway he shuts the North-wind up in the cave of Aeolus and all blasts that put the clouds to flight; but he lets the South-wind loose. Forth flies the South-wind with dripping wings, his awful face shrouded in pitchy darkness. His beard is heavy with rain; water flows in streams down his hoary locks; dark clouds rest upon his brow; while his wings and garments drip with dew. And, when he presses the low-hanging clouds with his broad hands, a crashing sound goes forth; and next the dense clouds pour forth their rain. Iris, the messenger of Juno, clad in robes of many hues, draws up water and feeds it to the clouds. The standing grain is overthrown; the crops which have been the object of the farmers' prayers lie ruined; and the hard labor of the tedious year has come to naught.

The wrath of Jove is not content with the waters from his own sky; his sea-god brother aids him with auxiliary waves. He summons his rivers to council. When these have assembled at the palace of their king, he says:

> Now is no time to employ a long harangue. Put forth all your strength,
> for there is need. Open wide your doors, away with all restraining dykes,
> and give full rein to all your river steeds.

So he commands, and the rivers return, uncurb their fountains' mouths, and in unbridled course go racing to the sea.

Neptune himself smites the earth with his trident. She trembles, and at the stroke flings open wide a way for the waters. The rivers overleap all bounds and flood the open plains. And not alone orchards, crops and herds, men and dwellings, but shrines as well and their sacred contents do they sweep away. If any house has stood firm, and has been able to resist that huge misfortune undestroyed, still do the over-topping waves cover its roof, and its towers lie hid beneath the flood. And now the sea and land have no distinction. All is sea, but a sea without a shore.

Here one man seeks a hill-top in his flight; another sits in his curved skiff, plying the oars where lately he has plowed; one sails over his fields of terrain or the roof of his buried farmhouse, and one takes fish caught in the elm-tree's top. And sometimes it chanced that an anchor was embedded in a grassy meadow, or the curving keels brushed over the vineyard tops. And where recently the slender goats had browsed, the ugly seals rested their bulk. The Nereids are amazed to see beneath the waters groves and cities and the haunts of men. The dolphins invade the woods, brushing against the high branches, and shake the oak-trees as they knock against them in their course. The wolf swims among the sheep, while tawny lions and tigers are borne along by the weaves. Neither does the power of his lightning stroke avail the boar, nor his swift limbs the stag, since both are alike swept away by the flood; and the wandering bird, after long searching for a place to alight, falls with weary wings into the sea.

The sea in unchecked liberty has now buried all the hills, and strange waves now beat upon the mountain peaks. Most living things are drowned outright. Those who have escaped the water slow starvation at last overcomes through lack of food.

(Deucalion and Pyrrha)

The land of Phocis separates the Boeotian from the Oetean fields, a fertile land, while still it was a land. But at that time it was but a part of the sea, a broad expanse of sudden waters. There Mount Parnasus lifts its two peaks skyward, high and steep, piercing the clouds. When here Deucalion and his wife, borne in a little skiff, had come to land—for the sea had covered all things else—they first worshipped the Corycian nymphs and the mountain deities, and the goddess, fate-revealing Themis, who in those days kept the oracles. There was no better man than he, none more scrupulous of right, nor than she was any woman more reverent of the gods.

When now Jove saw that the world was all one stagnant pool, and that only one man was left from those who were recently so many thousands, and that but one woman too was left, both innocent and both worshippers of God, he rent the clouds asunder, and when these had been swept away by the North-wind he showed the land once more to the sky, and the heavens to the land. Then too the anger of the sea subsides, when the sea's great ruler lays down his three-pronged spear and calms the waves; and, calling sea-hued Triton, showing forth above the deep, his shoulders thick overgrown with shell-fish, he bids him blow into his loud-resounding conch, and by that signal to recall the floods and streams. He lifts his hollow, twisted shell, which grows from the least and lowest to a broad-swelling whorl—the shell which, when in mid-sea it has received the Triton's breath, fills with its notes the shores that lie beneath the rising and the setting sun. So then, when it had touched the sea-god's lips wet with his dripping beard, and sounded forth the retreat which had been ordered, it was heard by all the waters both of land and sea; and all the waters by which it was heard it held in check. Now the sea has shores, the rivers, bank full, keep within their channels; the floods subside, and hill-tops spring into view; land rises up, the ground increasing as the waves decrease; and now at length, after long burial, the trees show their uncovered tops, whose leaves still hold the slime which the flood has left.

The world was indeed restored. But when Deucalion saw that it was an empty world, and that deep silence filled the desolated lands, he burst into tears and thus addressed his wife:

> O sister, O my wife, O only woman left on earth, you whom the ties of common race and family,[64] whom the marriage couch has joined to me, and whom now our very perils join: of all the lands which the rising and the setting sun behold, we two are the throng. The sea holds all the rest. And even this hold, which we have upon our life is not as yet sufficiently secure. Even yet the clouds strike terror to my heart. What would be your feelings, now, poor soul, if the fates had willed that you be rescued all alone? How would you bear your fear, alone? Who would console your grief? For be assured that if the sea held you, I would follow you, my wife, and the sea should hold me also.

[64] Deucalion and Pyrrha were cousins, which is sometimes expressed as "sister" when referring to a female cousin.

O, would that by my father's arts[65] I might restore the nations, and breathe, as did he, the breath of life into the molded clay. But as it is, on us two only depends the human race. Such is the will of Heaven: and we remain sole samples of mankind.

He spoke; and when they had wept awhile they resolved to appeal to the heavenly power and seek his aid through sacred oracles. Without delay side by side they went to the waters of Cephisus' stream, which, while not yet clear, still flowed within their familiar banks. From this they took some drops and sprinkled them on head and clothing. So having done, they bent their steps to the goddess's sacred shrine, whose gables were still discolored with foul moss, and upon whose altars the fires were dead. When they had reached the temple steps, they both fell prone upon the ground, and with trembling lips kissed the chill stone and said:

If deities are appeased by the prayers of the righteous, if the wrath of the gods is thus turned aside, O Themis, tell us by what means our race may be restored, and bring aid, O most merciful, to a world overwhelmed.

The goddess was moved and gave this oracle:

Depart hence, and with veiled heads and loosened robes throw behind you as you go the bones of your great mother.

Long they stand in dumb amazement; and first Pyrrha breaks the silence and refuses to obey the bidding of the goddess. With trembling lips she prays for pardon, but dares not outrage her mother's ghost by treating her bones as she is bid. Meanwhile they go over again the words of the oracle, which had been given so full of dark perplexities, and turn them over and over in their minds. At last Prometheus' son comforts the daughter of Epimetheus with reassuring words:

Either my wit is at fault, or else (oracles are holy and never counsel guilt!) our great mother is the earth, and I think that the bones which the goddess speaks of are the stones in the earth's body. It is these that we are bidden to throw behind us.

Although Pyrrha is moved by her husband's surmise, yet hope still wavers; so distrustful are they both as to the heavenly command. But what harm will it do to try? They go down, veil their heads, ungird their robes, and throw stones behind them just as the goddess had bidden. And the stones—who would believe it unless ancient tradition vouched for it?—began at once to lose their hardness and stiffness, to grow soft slowly, and softened to take on form. Then, when they had grown in size and become milder in their nature, a certain likeness to the human form, indeed, could be seen, still not very clear, but such as statues just begun out of marble have, not sharply defined, and very like roughly blocked-out images. That part of them, however, which was earthy and damp with slight moisture, was changed to flesh; but what was solid and

---

[65] Prometheus, who was said to have created the first human beings out of clay.

incapable of bending became bone; that which was just now veins remained under the same name. And in a short time, through the operation of the divine will, the stones thrown by the man's hand took on the form of men, and women were made from the stones the woman threw. Hence come the hardness of our race and our endurance of toil; and we give proof from what origin we are sprung.

As to the other forms of animal life, the earth spontaneously produced these of diverse kinds; after that old moisture remaining from the flood had grown warm from the rays of the sun, the slime of the wet marshes swelled with heat, and the fertile seeds of life, nourished in that life-giving soil, as in a mother's womb, grew and in time took on some special form. So when the seven-mouthed Nile has receded from the drenched fields and has returned again to its former bed, and the fresh slime has been heated by the sun's rays, farmers as they turn over the lumps of earth find many animate things; and among these some, but now begun, are upon the very verge of life, some are unfinished and lacking in their proper parts, and ofttimes in the same body one part is alive and the other still nothing but raw earth. For when moisture and heat unite, life is conceived, and from these two sources all living things spring. And, though fire and water are naturally at enmity, still heat and moisture produce all things, and this inharmonious harmony is fitted to the growth of life. When, therefore, the earth, covered with mud from the recent flood, became heated up by the hot and genial rays of the sun, she brought forth innumerable forms of life; in part she restored the ancient shapes, and in part she created creatures new and strange.

She, indeed, would have wished not so to do, but you also she then bore, you huge Python, you snake unknown before, who were a terror to new-created men; so huge a space of mountain-side did you fill. This monster the god of the glittering bow[66] destroyed with arms never before used except against does and wild she-goats, crushing him with countless darts, well-nigh emptying his quiver, till the creature's poisonous blood flowed from the black wounds. And, that the fame of his deed might not perish through lapse of time, he instituted sacred games whose contests throngs beheld, called Pythian from the name of the serpent he had overthrown. At these games, youth who had been victorious in boxing, running, or the chariot race received the honor of an oaken garland. For as yet the laurel-tree[67] did not exist, and Phoebus was wont to wreathe his temples, comely with flowing locks, with a garland from any tree.

2.7. AN ORPHIC ANTHROPOGONY

A peculiar anthropogony seems to have circulated in Orphic texts, although it is only attested in a very late source and reconstructed (with some uncertainty) from possible allusions to it in earlier texts as early as Pindar (ca. 522–443 BCE) and Plato (424–348 BCE). Orphic texts provided theological elaborations

---

[66] Apollo, who established his most important sanctuary, oracle, and pan-Hellenic games (called Pythian Games) at Delphi. Pythia was also the name of the priestess who delivered the oracles at Delphi. See *Hymn to Apollo* in Part 3, document 9.

[67] The laurel, *daphne* in Greek, provides the link with the next story told, that of Daphne and Apollo.

connected with the mysteries (secret, initiatory, cults dedicated to Persephone and Dionysos) and were in circulation and proliferating in late antiquity, co-existing with the spread of Christianity. According to this text (and possibly to earlier Orphic ideas), human beings were made of the remains of the Titans, who had devoured the baby Dionysos (also called Zagreus). This is understood by many as a key reason for the mention in earlier sources of the "ancient grief" of Persephone (Dionysos' mother in this story—he is the son of Semele in other stories), which the initiates need to appease (see Dionysos in the Underworld in Figure 11). The difficulty in reconstructing the story is precisely due to its connection with secret rites, which are exclusive and secretive by definition. Whatever its reach in antiquity, this anthropogony is a variant of the more generally accepted ideas that 1) Dionysos was born twice (in the Semele version she is killed while pregnant and he is sewn into Zeus' thigh from where he is born), and 2) humankind descends from or was made by the Titans, as in the stories of Prometheus and Epimetheus (e.g., document 2.5). The material composition of human beings from the Titan's dead matter has a precedent in the Mesopotamian tradition, where people are made out of the bodies of lesser gods, while the insistence on the link between humanity and an original crime that needs to be redeemed, along with the death of Dionysos and his rebirth in different variants, brings Orphism close to Christian theology, a resemblance that has been much studied.

Olympiodoros, a Neoplatonic scholar who wrote in sixth-century CE Alexandria, included this story in his commentary on Plato's *Phaedo*, more specifically in the section in which Socrates says that suicide is wrong and alludes to a myth that "cannot be told," which our author believes to be the following Orphic myth.

SOURCE: Olympiodoros, *Commentary on Plato's Phaedo* 1.3; 41 (Westerink = *OF* 304 I, 318 III, 320 I, commenting on *Phaedo* 62b), translated and annotated by C. López-Ruiz.

(. . .) There is also such a mythological argument: Four kingdoms are transmitted by Orpheus. The first one was the one of Ouranos, which Kronos received after cutting off the genitals of his father; after Kronos Zeus was king, having thrown his father into Tartaros. Then Zeus was succeeded by Dionysos, whom they say that, by the plotting of Hera, the Titans who were around him[68] tore into pieces and ate. And Zeus, outraged at them, struck them with his thunderbolts, and (they say that) human beings were born from the soot of the smoke that arose from them, as a matter formed (from it). Therefore, we should not commit suicide, not because (as the sentence [by Socrates] seems to say) we are in a prison in our body (for this is evident, and he [Socrates] would not call this "secret"), but (it says) that we should not commit suicide on account of our bodies being Dionysiac. For we are part of him (Dionysos), to the degree that we are composed from the soot of the Titans after they had eaten his flesh.

---

[68] The text is ambiguous as to "around whom" the Titans were, whether Zeus or Dionysos, their victim.

PART 3 ✦ EPIC STRUGGLES: GODS, HEROES, AND MONSTERS

THIS SECTION INCLUDES stories about gods, heroes, and monsters. In each story, the main character strives against opposing forces to overcome numerous obstacles, thus gaining legitimacy and power. These extraordinary adventures are the most popular and can be found in myths from all around the world; it should not be surprising, therefore, that this part is the longest in the volume. Part Three, for the most part, brings together narratives centered on epic fights, which are not only "epic" in a general sense, but usually partake in the **epic** genre of poetry in the stricter sense, consisting of long narrative poems about deeds of gods and heroes. Other texts included here narrate divine or heroic struggles that cannot be labeled as "epic" but nonetheless represent important stories about gods' rivalries and about the position of human and divine "heroes" in the world.

In some of these stories, therefore, the gods confront obstacles set by other gods or by monsters, such as in the fight between Horus and Seth in the Egyptian texts, Baal against Mot and Yamm in the Ugaritic epics, and the various feats of Kumarbi and the Storm God in the Hittite epics. The figure of Yahweh in Psalm 29 fits into this type as well. A subtype within these divine feats is the god's fight with a snake-like monster (anticipating the popular dragon-slaying motif in later traditions). Some examples, included here, are the fights of Zeus with Typhon in the *Theogony* (Part 1, document 5), of Apollo with Python in the *Hymn to Apollo* (document 3.9), that of Marduk with Tiamat in the *Enuma Elish* (Part 1, document 1), and of the Hittite gods against various serpentine monsters (Illuyanka and Hedammu, documents 3.4.a and 3.4.b). In turn, other clashes are part of a story of the "succession myth" type, that is, fights between the different generations of gods in order to establish a new order. The *Kumarbi Cycle* starts with one such story (the *Song of Birth*, document 3.4.b), and the *Baal Cycle* (document 3.5.a) follows the pattern to some degree as well, but others are included in Part 1 given their importance as creation stories, such as the Babylonian *Enuma Elish* and Hesiod's *Theogony* (Part 1, documents 1 and 5). The rivalry between Horus and Seth (document 3.2) as well as the murder of Osiris at the hands of Seth (in Part 6, document 5) also share in this theme. Yet another group of texts present narratives wherein the gods seek to establish their position not among gods but among humans, such as in the *Homeric Hymn to Apollo* (document 3.9) and the two texts about Dionysos (documents 3.10.a and 3.10.b). This reminds us of the interdependency of gods and humans, since mortals need their gods' favor but gods crave human worship and even need it for survival (as seen in the *Hymn to Demeter*, in Part 6, document 8).

Other texts presented here deal with human heroes, whose stories take so many different turns that they cannot be easily categorized. To outline some general patterns only, while most heroes represented here are warriors, broader themes surface in each epic story, some of them shared, such as the journey through dangerous and sometimes fantastic lands (the Shipwrecked Sailor, Gilgamesh, Odysseus, Herakles, etc.), the direct or indirect confrontation with gods who attack or try to doom the hero (Aqhat, Diomedes, Herakles), and the difficult acceptance of the hero's mortal condition (Gilgamesh), a dilemma that even affects the gods, who strive to protect their human children or protégées (as in the *Iliad*).

Many of these stories would fall into what folklorists and narratologists have called the "hero pattern," which takes specific forms, but basically entails the well-known trajectory of alienation, overcoming of obstacles, and victorious return that makes for a good adventure. Often this adventure takes the form of a journey, as in the *Homeric Hymns*, the *Odyssey*, *Gilgamesh*, and other stories (Theseus, Herakles, Perseus, even Dionysos in the *Bacchae*). In what sometimes is called the "journey for power," the central character becomes a better king, or a king at all, or an honored god, or, exceptionally, an immortal, such as Herakles. In turn, there is a deep gap between these exceptional humans, who in fact interact with the gods, and regular humans, who are limited to a mediated interaction with the divine through ritual actions (sacrifices, divination, prayer) and dreams. The *Homeric Hymns* are good examples of the exceptional trespassing of these boundaries by the gods, who manifest themselves to humans directly in epiphanies of different sorts (often beginning with a first contact in disguise). In the regular mortal's imagination, these heroes, often sons of gods, are almost but not quite like gods, the difference being the mortality with which the heroes themselves have a hard time coming to terms. We do not know what the Greek word for hero (*heros*) meant exactly, or its etymology, but we know that in Greece these heroes were perceived not only as characters worthy of an epic (Homer calls all the Achaeans "heroes") but as worthy of special honors, as supported by the archaeological and literary evidence. The "hero cult" category is often discussed and surely comprised very different types of local practices, from the offerings left at Mycenaean tombs (reinterpreted in the Iron Age as belonging to Homeric heroes) to a centralized polis cult to Theseus. In other cultures, most notably in Egypt, kings enjoyed divine status as well, and ancestor cults are well attested in the Canaanite world, while in Rome ancestors were firmly integrated into aristocratic family rituals and state religion.

For reasons of space, important heroic sagas have been left out of this Part: the *Iliad*, *Odyssey*, and *Aeneid* are only partly represented here and should be read in their entirety; they are required reading in many high schools and colleges. After the Trojan War cycle, the other main Greek epic saga concerned the city of Thebes. An archaic epic poem called *Thebaid* has been lost to us, but many great works and narratives engage with this cluster of stories (e.g., Aeschylus' *Seven against Thebes*, Sophocles' *Oedipus King* and *Antigone*, Statius' *Thebaid*, etc.). These can be independently read in abundant available translations. The importance of this city in the mythical landscape emerges in our texts in the story of Kadmos and the associations of Dionysos and Herakles with Thebes. The great saga of the Argonauts, most completely elaborated in Apollonios of Rhodes' *Argonautika*, is not included here except in allusions to it by the characters Medea and Jason in the *Medea* (Part 5, document 6) and the brief cosmogony from the *Argonautika* (Part 1, document 9). The story of Romulus and Remus, whose heroic pattern fits this part, is instead included in Part 4 (documents 13.a and 13.b) in connection with the foundation of Rome. While other Roman texts would have been appropriate additions to this part (e.g., Ovid's treatment of Theseus, Jason, Herakles, and others in the *Metamorphoses*), Roman epic heroes are generally elaborations on the Greek ones, even if sometimes integrated into Italic traditions (e.g., Aeneas and Herakles), while the intrinsically Roman heroic characters are mostly historical figures, who inhabited an altogether different world from that of the fantastic demi-gods of older Mediterranean myths. ✦

3.1. THE *EPIC OF GILGAMESH* (SELECTIONS)

The *Epic of Gilgamesh* is the greatest literary work from ancient Mesopotamia. Its roots extend back to the earliest literary traditions at the end of the third millennium BCE (writing in cuneiform itself is attested since around 3000 BCE). Gilgamesh was in fact the name of one of the early kings of Sumerian Uruk, attested in king lists. As often happens with mythical traditions, a semi-legendary king becomes a hero around whom fantastic stories grow, including stories imbued with epic motifs: the transformation of the hero into a noble king, battles with monstrous creatures, the value of friendship held up and extolled, the harsh consequences of divine punishment, and the inevitability of death.

The stories about Gilgamesh became enormously popular throughout the entire ancient Near East and some of its motifs even reached the Greek world. The textual history of what we call the *Epic of Gilgamesh*, therefore, is complex, as copies and translations of it circulated throughout the Near East. The texts we have do not form a single version but come from different times and places, often representing fragmentary texts. The oldest fragments are written in Sumerian and probably go back to traditions from the Ur III period (Third Dynasty of Ur) at the very end of the third millennium BCE (2094–2047 BCE). These were independent shorter stories about Gilgamesh (called Bilgamesh in Sumerian) and were preserved mostly by later Babylonian writers in the eighteenth century BCE whose language was Akkadian but who preserved Sumerian texts because of their prestige and cultural importance for the Babylonians. New versions in Akkadian, in turn, were created during the second millennium BCE, including the one known as "Surpassing all other kings." It was during the Late Bronze Age (ca. 1550–1200 BCE) that the epic was most broadly copied, even for use in school and sometimes for ritual use. Fragments in Akkadian and in some cases translations in other languages have been found in the Levant and Anatolia: at Ugarit, Emar, Meggido, and Hattusa.

Finally, an even newer version, creatively expanding on the previous ones, circulated in the royal libraries of Assyria and Babylonia in the early to mid-first millennium BCE. The British explorer and diplomat Austen H. Layard found the first tablets containing this version in 1849 in the ruins of the palace of Ashurbanipal (685–627 BCE) at Nineveh. Also written in Akkadian, the text is fairly standardized throughout and thus is known as the "Standard Babylonian Version" (SBV), though in ancient times it was known as "He who saw the Deep," after its opening line. This version forms the basis for most modern translations, with some of its gaps filled by other extant versions. Although the copies we have date to the first millennium BCE, the originals are probably older, likely dating to some time between the thirteenth and eleventh centuries BCE, and are attributed in some documents to a scribe called Sin-liqe-unninni. Although not an "author" in the modern sense, as Mesopotamian literary texts were largely anonymous, the scribes that wrote all the versions must have had a degree of creative leeway in modifying, expanding, and editing the existing texts.

The influence of the *Epic of Gilgamesh* on Near Eastern and Greek literatures and myths cannot be overstated. Besides the ubiquitous artistic representations of scenes of Gilgamesh and his friend Enkidu (e.g., fighting Humbaba or the Bull of Heaven), found most frequently on reliefs and cylinder seals (see Figures 3, 4, and 7), many of the narrative tropes of the Gilgamesh story were adapted by Canaanites and Hittites in the Late Bronze Age and most probably also by their Iron Age heirs (Phoenicians, Aramaeans, Luwians, etc.), whose literature is largely lost. The Greeks, too, adapted elements from the Gilgamesh story: Achilles and his lament over his soulmate Patroklos, Odysseus' many adventures and his visit to the Underworld, Herakles and Perseus as monster-slayers (see Figure 8), and Diomedes and Hippolytus, who harm or offend the Love Goddess Aphrodite, are just a few examples. In fact, the *Epic of Gilgamesh* and the Mesopotamian writing tradition more generally may have inspired the Greeks (perhaps Homer himself) to undertake the writing of the long Homeric epics, originally based in oral tradition.

The SBV is used here unless otherwise noted. The text was written in eleven tablets, each divided into six columns (numbered i, ii, etc.). Our selection includes tablets I, II, V, VII, and VIII. Tablet VI (Gilgamesh and Ishtar) is included in Part 5, document 1, with other Love stories; tablets X–XI (Gilgamesh's journey to the Netherworld) appear in Part 6, document 1, with the travels to the Underworld; and the excerpt that narrates the Flood is included in Part 2, document 1.b, with the other flood stories.

SOURCE: S. Dalley, *Myths from Mesopotamia: Creation, The Flood, Gilgamesh, and Others* (Oxford World's Classics, Oxford, 1989, rev. ed. 2000), with minor editorial modifications. Notes are largely based on Dalley's, which should be consulted for further details.

TABLET I

(SBV) (i) He who saw the Deep, the country's foundation, [who] knew [. . .], was wise in all matters! [Gilgamesh, who] saw the Deep, the country's foundation, [who] knew [. . .], was wise in all matters![1]

He searched (?) lands (?) everywhere. He who experienced the whole gained complete wisdom. He found out what was secret and uncovered what was hidden. He brought back a tale of times before the Flood.[2] He had journeyed far and wide, weary and at last resigned. He engraved all toils on a memorial monument of stone. He had the wall of Uruk built, the sheepfold of holiest Eanna, the pure treasury.

See its wall, which is like a copper band, survey its battlements, which nobody else can match. Take the threshold, which is from time immemorial. Approach Eanna, the home of Ishtar, which no future king, nor any man, will ever match! Go up on to the wall of Uruk and walk around! Inspect the foundation platform and

---

[1] These first lines are quoted from the translation by George (1999, rev. 2003), since they reflect what is now known to be the title of the Standard Version of Gilgamesh, "He who saw the Deep." Dalley has: "[Of him who] found out all things, I [shall te]ll the land, [Of him who] experienced everything, [I shall tea]ch the whole."

[2] See episode with Ut-napishtim the flood survivor in Tablet XI (Part 2, document 1.b).

scrutinize the brickwork![3] Testify that its bricks are baked bricks, and that the Seven Counsellors[4] must have laid its foundations! One square mile is city, one square mile is orchards, one square mile is claypits, as well as the open ground of Ishtar's temple. Three square miles and the open ground comprise Uruk.

Look for the copper tablet-box, undo its bronze lock, open the door to its secret, lift out the lapis lazuli tablet and read it: the story of that man, Gilgamesh, who went through all kinds of sufferings. He was superior to other kings, a warrior lord of great stature; a hero born of Uruk, a goring wild bull. He marches at the front as leader; he goes behind, the support of his brothers; a strong net, the protection of his men; the raging flood-wave, which can destroy even a stone wall.

Son of Lugalbanda, Gilgamesh, perfect in strength. Son of the lofty cow, the wild cow Ninsun. He is Gilgamesh, perfect in splendor,[5] who opened up passes in the mountains, who could dig pits even in the mountainside; who crossed the ocean, the broad seas, as far as the sunrise; who inspected the edges of the world, kept searching for eternal life; who reached Ut-napishtim the far-distant, by force; who restored to their rightful place cult centers (?) which the Flood had ruined.

There is nobody among the kings of teeming humanity who can compare with him, who can say "I am king" beside Gilgamesh. Gilgamesh (was) named from birth for fame.

(ii) Two-thirds of him was divine, and one-third mortal. Belet-ili[6] designed the shape of his body, made his form perfect, [. . .] was proud [. . .]

(2 lines missing)

In Uruk the Sheepfold he would walk about, show himself superior, his head held high like a wild bull. He had no rival, and at his *pukku*[7] his weapons would rise up, his comrades have to rise up. The young men of Uruk became dejected in their private [quarters (?)]. Gilgamesh would not leave any son alone for his father. Day and night his [behavior (?)] was overbearing. He was the shepherd (?) [. . .] He was their shepherd (?) yet [. . .] Powerful, superb, [knowledgeable and expert], Gilgamesh would not leave [young girls alone], the daughters of warriors, the brides of young men.

The gods often heard their complaints. The gods of heaven [. . .] the lord of Uruk: "Did [Aruru[8] (?)] create such a rampant wild bull? Is there no rival? At the *pukku* his weapons rise up, his comrades have to rise up. Gilgamesh will not leave any son alone for his father. Day and night his [behavior (?)] is overbearing. He is the shepherd of Uruk the Sheepfold, he is their shepherd, yet [. . .] Powerful, superb, knowledgeable [and expert], Gilgamesh will not leave young

---

[3] Mesopotamians used baked mud bricks only for high-quality construction.

[4] Probably the Seven Sages, who taught humankind craftsmanship.

[5] In the Hittite version of Gilgamesh he is attributed divine qualities and is described as a giant.

[6] Belet-ili, "mistress of the gods," was the great Mother Goddess (cf. her role in *Atrahasis*).

[7] If the reading is correct (another possible reading is *puqqu*, "when he was alerted"), this refers to the *pukku* and *mekku* game played with sticks at weddings. The game was associated with Isthar and fertility, but the clash of the objects employed (the *pukku* and *mekku*) is used here and elsewhere as a metaphor for the clash of battle.

[8] Another name for the Mother Goddess.

girls [alone], the daughters of warriors, the brides of young men. Anu often hears their complaints."

They called upon great Aruru: "You, Aruru, you created [mankind (?)]! Now create someone for him, to match (?) the ardor (?) of his energies! Let them be regular rivals, and let Uruk be allowed peace!"

When Aruru heard this, she created inside herself the word (?) of Anu. Aruru washed her hands, pinched off a piece of clay, cast it out into open country. She created a [primitive man], Enkidu the warrior: offspring of silence (?), sky-bolt of Ninurta.[9]

His whole body was shaggy with hair, he was furnished with tresses like a woman. His locks of hair grew luxuriant like grain. He knew neither people nor country; he was dressed as cattle are. With gazelles he eats vegetation; with cattle he quenches his thirst at the watering place. With wild beasts he presses forward for water.

A hunter, a brigand, came face to face with him beside the watering place. He saw him on three successive days beside the watering place. The hunter looked at him, and was dumbstruck to see him. In perplexity (?) he went back into his house and was afraid, stayed mute, was silent, and was ill at ease, his face worried. [. . .] the grief in his innermost being. His face was like that of a long-distance traveller.

(iii) The hunter made his voice heard and spoke, he said to his father: "Father, there was a young man who came [from the mountain (?)]. [On the land] he was strong, he was powerful. His strength was very hard, like a sky-bolt of Anu. He walks about on the mountain all the time; all the time he eats vegetation with cattle; all the time he puts his feet in (the water) at the watering place. I am too frightened to approach him. He kept filling in the pits that I dug [. . .]; he kept pulling out the traps that I laid. He kept helping cattle, wild beasts of open country, to escape my grasp. He will not allow me to work [in open country]."

His father spoke to him, to the hunter: "[. . .] Uruk, Gilgamesh. [. . .] his open country. [His strength is very hard, like a sky-bolt of Anu.][Go, set] your face [towards Uruk]. [. . .] the strength of a man, [. . .] lead (her) forth, and [. . .] the strong man. When he approaches the cattle at the watering place, she must take off her clothes and reveal her attractions. He will see her and go close to her. Then his cattle, who have grown up in open country with him, will become alien to him."

[He listened] to the advice of his father [. . .]. The hunter went off [to see Gilgamesh (?)]. He took the road, set [his face] towards Uruk; entered the presence (?) of Gilgamesh [. . .]:

"There was a young man who [came from the mountain (?)]. On the land he was strong, he was powerful. His strength is very hard, like a sky-bolt of Anu. He walks about on the mountain all the time; all the time he eats vegetation with cattle; all the time he puts his feet in (the water) at the watering place. I am too frightened to approach him. He kept filling in the pits that I dug; he kept pulling out the traps that I laid. He kept helping cattle, wild beasts of open country, to escape my grasp. He did not allow me to work in the open country."

---

[9] These are epithets alluding to Enkidu, which might be connected with cultic vocabulary.

Gilgamesh spoke to him, to the hunter: "Go, hunter, lead forth the harlot Shamhat,[10] and when he approaches the cattle at the watering place, she must take off her clothes and reveal her attractions. He will see her and go close to her. Then his cattle, who have grown up in open country with him, will become alien to him."

The hunter went; he led forth the harlot Shamhat with him, and they took the road, they made the journey. In three days they reached the appointed place. Hunter and harlot sat down in their hiding place (?). For one day, then a second, they sat at the watering place. Then cattle arrived at the watering place; they drank.

(iv) Then wild beasts arrived at the water; they satisfied their need. And he, Enkidu, whose origin is the mountain, (who) eats vegetation with gazelles, drinks (at) the watering place with cattle, satisfied his need for water with wild beasts.

Shamhat looked at the primitive man, the murderous youth from the depths of open country: "Here he is, Shamhat, bare your bosom, open your legs and let him take in your attractions! Do not pull away, take wind of him! He will see you and come close to you. Spread open your garments, and let him lie upon you; do for him, the primitive man, as women do. Then his cattle, who have grown up in open country with him, will become alien to him. His love-making he will lavish upon you!"

Shamhat loosened her undergarments, opened her legs and he took in her attractions. She did not pull away. She took wind of him, spread open her garments, and he lay upon her. She did for him, the primitive man, as women do. His love-making he lavished upon her. For six days and seven nights Enkidu was aroused and poured himself into Shamhat.

When he was sated with her charms, he set his face towards the open country of his cattle. The gazelles saw Enkidu and scattered; the cattle of open country kept away from his body. For Enkidu had stripped (?); his body was too clean. His legs, which used to keep pace with (?) his cattle, were at a standstill. Enkidu had been diminished, he could not run as before. Yet he had acquired judgement (?), had become wiser.

He turned back (?), he sat at the harlot's feet. The harlot was looking at his expression, and he listened attentively to what the harlot said. The harlot spoke to him, to Enkidu: "You have become [profound] Enkidu, you have become like a god. Why should you roam open country with wild beasts? Come, let me take you into Uruk the Sheepfold; to the pure house, the dwelling of Anu and Ishtar, where Gilgamesh is perfect in strength, and is like a wild bull, more powerful than (any of) the people."

She spoke to him, and her speech was acceptable. Knowing his own mind (now), he would seek for a friend. Enkidu spoke to her, to the harlot: "Come, Shamhat; invite me to the pure house, the holy dwelling of Anu and Ishtar, where Gilgamesh is perfect in strength, and is like a wild bull, more powerful than (any of) the people. Let me challenge him, and [...]"

---

[10] Shamhat (used as a personal name here) means "voluptuous woman, prostitute." In Mesopotamia, prostitutes were devotees of Ishtar and part of her temple personnel, where "sacred prostitution" was practiced.

(v) *(Enkidu still speaking)* "(By saying:) 'In Uruk I shall be the strongest! I shall go in and alter destiny: One who was born in open country has [superior(?)] strength!'"

Shamhat answered: "Come on, let us go forth, and let me please you! [. . .] there are, I know. Go, Enkidu, into Uruk the Sheepfold, where young men are girded with sashes and every day is a feast day; where the drums are beaten and girls (?) [show off] (their) figures, adorned with joy and full of happiness. In bed at night great men [. . .] O Enkidu! You who [know nothing (?)] of life! Let me show you Gilgamesh, a man of joy and woe! Look at him, observe his face; he is beautiful in manhood, dignified, his whole body is charged with seductive charm. He is more powerful in strength of arms than you! He does not sleep by day or night. O Enkidu, change your plan for punishing him! Shamash loves Gilgamesh, and Anu, Ellil, and Ea made him wise!

"Before you came from the mountains, Gilgamesh was dreaming about you in Uruk. Gilgamesh arose and described a dream, he told it to his mother: 'Mother, I saw a dream in the night. There were stars in the sky for me. And (something) like a sky-bolt of Anu kept falling upon me! I tried to lift it up, but it was too heavy for me. I tried to turn it over, but I couldn't budge it. The country(men) of Uruk were standing over [it]. [The countrymen had gathered (?)] over it; the men crowded over it; the young men massed over it; they kissed its feet like very young children. I loved it as a wife, doted on it, [I carried it], laid it at your feet; you treated it as equal to me.'

"[The wise mother of Gilgamesh], all-knowing, understood. She spoke to her lord. [The wise wild cow Ninsun] all-knowing, understood. She spoke to Gilgamesh: '[When there were] stars in the sky for you, and something like a sky-bolt of Anu kept falling upon you, you tried to lift it up, but it was too heavy for you; you tried to turn it over, but you couldn't budge it. [You carried it], laid it at my feet; I treated it as equal to you, and you loved it as a wife, and doted on it.'

(vi) *(Ninsun continues)* '(It means) a strong partner shall come to you, one who can save the life of a friend; he will be the most powerful in strength of arms in the land. His strength will be as great as that of a sky-bolt of Anu. You will love him as a wife, you will dote upon him. [And he will always] keep you safe (?). [That is the meaning] of your dream.'[11]

"Gilgamesh spoke to her, to his mother: 'Mother, I have had a second dream. An axe was thrown down in the street (?) of Uruk the Sheepfold and they gathered over it; the country(men) of Uruk stood over it. The land gathered together over it; the men massed over it. [I carried it], laid it at your feet. I loved it as a wife, doted upon it. And you treated it as equal to me.'

"The wise mother of Gilgamesh, all-knowing, understood; she spoke to her son. The wise wild cow Ninsun, all-knowing, understood; she spoke to Gilgamesh: 'The copper axe which you saw is a man. You will love it as a wife, you will dote upon it, and I shall treat it as equal to you. A strong partner will come to you, one who can save the life of a comrade. He will be the most powerful in strength of arms in the land. His strength will be as great as that of a sky-bolt of Anu.'

---

[11] Or "your dream [was favorable and very significant]."

"Gilgamesh spoke to his mother: 'Let it fall, then, according to the word of Ellil the great counselor. I shall gain a friend to advise me.' Ninsun retold his dreams."

Thus Shamhat heard the dreams of Gilgamesh and told them to Enkidu. "[The dreams mean that you will lo]ve one another."

TABLET II

(Tablet II.i not extant; gap of about 45 lines)

(ii) Enkidu was seated before her in Tirannu [. . .] tears [. . .] trusted Mulliltu

(gap of a few lines, and next 8 lines very fragmentary)

She (i.e., Shamhat) held him (by the hand (?)) and like gods [. . .] To the shepherds' hut [. . .] The shepherds were gathered around him of their own accord, and by themselves— "The young man-how like Gilgamesh in build, mature in build, as sturdy (?) as battlements. Why was he born in the mountains? He is just as powerful in strength of arms as a sky-bolt of Anu!"

They put food in front of him; [. . .] They put drink in front of him; [. . .] Enkidu would not eat the food; he narrowed his eyes and stared.

(A passage follows with several gaps and very fragmentary lines)

[He stood] in the street of Uruk [the Sheepfold][. . .] the strong [. . .] He barred the way [of Gilgamesh]. The country of Uruk was standing around him; the country gathered together over him; the men massed (?) over him; the young men crowded over him, kissed his feet like very young children.

When the young man [. . .] The bed was laid at night for Ishhara and for godlike Gilgamesh an equal match was found. Enkidu blocked his access at the door of the father-in-law's house. He would not allow Gilgamesh to enter. They grappled at the door of the father-in-law's house, wrestled in the street, in the public square. Doorframes shook, walls quaked.

(iii) *(about 37 lines missing)*

"He was the most powerful in strength of arms in the land. His strength was as great as that of a sky-bolt of Anu; a build as sturdy as battlements [. . .]."

The [wise] mother of Gilgamesh, [all-knowing (?)]. Spoke [to her son]. The wild cow Ninsun [spoke to Gilgamesh]: "My son, [. . .] Bitterly [. . .]

(iv) [. . .] Seized [. . .]. He brought up to his door [. . .] Bitterly he was weeping [. . .]; "Enkidu had no [. . .] His hair is allowed to hang loose [. . .] He was born in open country, and who can prevail over him?"

Enkidu stood, listened to him speaking, pondered, and then sat down, began to cry. His eyes grew dim with tears. His arms slackened, his strength [. . .]. (Then) they grasped one another, and embraced and held (?) hands. [Gilgamesh made his voice heard and spoke], he said [to] Enkidu: "[Why are your eyes] filled [with tears]?"

(about 29 lines missing)

(v) "Ellil has destined him to keep the Pine Forest[12] safe, to be the terror of people. Humbaba, whose shout is the flood-weapon, whose utterance is Fire, and

---

[12] More usually translated as "cedar." S. Dalley defends the rendering "pine" on the grounds that pines were more frequently used in construction and were abundant in the Amanus and Zagros mountains (while cedars are more confined to Lebanon).

whose breath is Death, can hear for a distance of sixty leagues[13] through (?) the . . . of the forest, so who can penetrate his forest? Ellil has destined him to keep the Pine Forest safe, to be the terror of people: Debility would seize anyone who penetrated his forest."

Gilgamesh spoke to him, to Enkidu: "Are you saying that [. . .]?"

(gap of about 34 lines)

(vi)[. . .] Gilgamesh [made his] voice heard [and spoke to Enkidu]: "My friend, are there not [. . .] Are there no children (?) [. . .]?"

Enkidu made his voice heard and [spoke to Gilgamesh]: "My friend, were we to go to him, [. . .] Humbaba [. . .]"

Gilgamesh made his voice heard [and spoke to Enkidu]: "My friend, we really should [. . .]"

(gap of a few lines)

They sat and pondered on [. . .] "We made a hassinnu-axe [. . .] A *pashu-axe* with a whole talent of [bronze for each half (?)] Their swords weighed a whole talent each; [. . .] Their belts weighed a whole talent each; their belts [. . .] *(new break)* . . . *(new break)* . . . [. . .][14]

"Listen to me, young men; young men of Uruk who know [. . .] I am adamant: I shall take the road [to Humbaba]. I shall face unknown opposition, [I shall ride along an unknown] road. Give me your blessing, since I [have decided (?)] on the course, that I may enter the city-gate of Uruk [again in future (?)] and [celebrate] the New Year Festival once again in [future] years (?),[15] and take part in the New Year Festival in years [to come] (?). Let the New Year Festival be performed, let joy [resound, . . .] Let *illuru-cries*[16] ring out in [. . .]."

Enkidu gave advice to the ciders, the young men of Uruk ["Tell him not to go to the [Pine] Forest, that journey is not to be undertaken! A man [. . .] The guardian of the Pine [Forest . . .]

(gap of a few lines)

The great counselors of Uruk rose up and gave an opinion to [Gilgamesh]: "You are [still young (?), Gilgamesh, you are impetuous to [. . .], but you do not know what you will find [. . .]. Humbaba, whose shout is the flood-weapon, whose utterance is Fire and whose breath is Death, can hear for up to sixty leagues the sounds of his forest. Whoever goes down to his forest [. . .] or two. Who, even among the Igigi,[17] can face him? Ellil destined him to keep the Pine Forest

---

[13] Literally "hours," as the Mesopotamians divided the day into 12 hours (1 hour =2 of our hours) and measured distance by the time it would take to cover it.

[14] "New break" is a comment introduced by the scribe, copying from a damaged tablet.

[15] The Akitu festival just meant "festival" at first, but by the time the tablets were written in Nineveh it referred to the New Year festival. During this festival, the king's officials swore an oath of allegiance for the coming year, and the king, identified with the god (Marduk in Babylonia, Assur/Ashur in Nineveh), probably participated in a sacred marriage ritual with a priestess of Ishtar. The *Enuma Elish* (epic of creation; see Part 1, document 1) was recited at this occasion.

[16] An exclamation of the "Halleluyah" type.

[17] On the Igigi gods, see footnote 3 in Part 1, document 1.

safe, to be the terror of people." Gilgamesh listened to the speech of the great counselors.

(gap of a few lines)

(Tablets III and IV skipped here: in Tablet III the elders of the city offer advice to Gilgamesh and entrust Enkidu with his safety. Tablet IV narrates the friends' journey toward the forest where Humbaba lives; during the trip, Gilgamesh has three dreams, which Enkidu interprets; the first two are favorable but the third one is upsetting.)

TABLET V

(SBV) (i) They stood at the edge of the forest, gazed and gazed at the height of the pines; gazed and gazed at the entrance to the pines, where Humbaba made tracks as he went to and fro.

The paths were well trodden and the road was excellent. They beheld the Pine Mountain, dwelling-place of gods, shrine of Irnini.[18] The pines held up their luxuriance even on the face of the mountain. Their shade was good, filling one with happiness. Undergrowth burgeoned, entangling the forest.

(8 fragmentary lines, then gap; when the text resumes, they have entered the forest and found Humbaba—for Humbaba's face, see Figure 4)

(LV)[19] Humbaba made his voice heard and spoke; he said to Gilgamesh: "The fool Gilgamesh (and (?)) the brutish man ought to ask themselves, why have you come to see me? Your [friend] Enkidu is small fry who does not know his own father! You are so very small that I regard you as I do a turtle or a tortoise which does not suck its mother's milk, so I do not approach you.

"[Even if I] were to kill (?) you, would I satisfy my stomach? [Why, . . .], Gilgamesh, have you let (him) reach me, [. . .] so I shall bite [through your/his] windpipe and neck, Gilgamesh, and leave [your/his body] for birds of the forest, roaring (lions), birds of prey and scavengers."

Gilgamesh made his voice heard and spoke; he said to Enkidu: "My friend, Humbaba has changed his mood and [. . .] has come upon him [. . .] and my heart [trembles lest he . . .]suddenly!"

Enkidu made his voice heard and spoke; he said to Gilgamesh: "My friend, why do you talk like a coward? And your speech was feeble (?), and you tried to hide (?). Now, my friend, he has drawn you out (?) with the (blow)pipe of the coppersmith for heating (?) to count back each league swollen (?) with the heat (?), each league of cold, to dispatch the flood-weapon, to lash with the whip! Don't retrace your footsteps! Don't turn back! [. . .] Make your blows harder!"

(gap of a few lines?)

---

[18] A goddess of war, assimilated to Ishtar.

[19] LV = Late Version, i.e., texts from Babylonia, dating between 612 BCE and the Seleucid era (Hellenistic times). The sections drawn from the LV are hardly preserved in the SBV. The Hittite version at this point shows that Humbaba has been alerted of the heroes' presence by the sound of crushing trees.

(SBV) His (Gilgamesh's) tears flowed before Shamash [( )]: "Remember what you said in Uruk! Stand there (?) and listen to me! (?)"

[Shamash] heard the words of Gilgamesh, scion of Uruk, [and said]: "As soon as a loud voice from the sky calls down to him, rush, stand up to him, let him not [enter the forest (?)], let him not go down to the wood, nor [. . .]. [Humbaba] will [not] be clothed in seven cloaks, he will be wearing [only one]; six are taken off (?). Like a charging wild bull which pierces [. . .] he shouts only once, but fills one with terror. The guardian of the forests will shout [. . .] *(one line missing)* Humbaba like [. . .] will shout."

(gap of uncertain length)

(ii) As soon as the swords [. . .] from the sheaths [. . .] streaked with verdigris (?) [. . .] dagger, sword [. . .] one [. . .] they wore [. . .] Humbaba [made his voice heard and spoke (?)]: "He will not go (?) [. . .] He will not go (?) [. . .]

(7 lines illegible)

"May Ellil [. . .]."

Enkidu [made] his voice heard [and spoke], [he addressed his speech (?)] to Humbaba: "One alone (?) [cannot . . .] They are strangers (?) [. . .] It is a slippery path, and [one] does not [. . . but two . . .] two [. . .] A three-stranded cord [is hardest to break (?)] A strong lion [cannot prevail over (?)] two of its own cubs."

(3 broken lines, then gap of uncertain length, then 2 broken lines)

(LV) He struck (?) (his) head (?), and matched him [. . .] They stirred up the ground with the heels of their feet; Sirara and Lebanon[20] were split apart at their gyrations; white clouds grew black, death dropped down over them like a fog.

Shamash summoned up great tempests against Humbaba: South Wind, North Wind, East Wind, West Wind, Moaning Wind, Gale, *shaparziqqu*-Wind, *imhullu*-Wind, . . . –Wind, Asakku, Wintry Wind, Tempest, Whirlwind, thirteen winds rose up at him and Humbaba's face grew dark.

He could not charge forwards, he could not run backwards. Thus the weapons of Gilgamesh succeeded against Humbaba. Humbaba gasped for breath, he addressed Gilgamesh: "You are young, Gilgamesh; your mother gave birth to you, and you are the offspring of [. . .]. You rose (?) at the command of Shamash, Lord of the Mountain and you are the scion of Uruk, king Gilgamesh. [. . .] Gilgamesh [. . .] Gilgamesh [. . .]. I shall make (them) grow luxuriantly for you in [. . .]. As many trees as you [. . .]. I shall keep for you myrtle wood, [. . .], timbers to be the pride [of your palace (?)]."

Enkidu made his voice heard and spoke; he said to Gilgamesh: "[My friend], don't listen to [the words] of Humbaba."

(3 broken lines, gap of about 15 lines; when it resumes Humbaba is speaking to Enkidu)

(iii) "You have found out the nature of my forest, the nature [of my dwelling] and (now) you know all their . . . -s. I should have taken you (and) slain you at the entrance to my forest's growth; I should have given your flesh to be eaten by the

---

[20] Names of mountains, both in the Lebanon area. A pun is made between Sirara/Saria (Mt. Hermon, also known to Mesopotamians as "Pine Mountain") and the verb *saru*, "to dance, to gyrate."

birds of the forest, roaring (lions), birds of prey, and scavengers. But now, Enkidu, it is in your power (?) to . . . , so tell Gilgamesh to spare my life (?)!"

Enkidu made his voice heard and spoke; he said to Gilgamesh: "My friend, finish him off, slay him, grind him up, that [I may survive] Humbaba the guardian of the [Pine] Forest! Finish him off, slay him, grind him up that [I may survive] Humbaba, the guardian of the forest. (Do it) before the leader Ellil hears, [(. . .)] [Lest (?)] the gods (?) be filled with fury at us [(. . .)]. Ellil in Nippur, Shamash in [Sippar]. Set up an eternal [memorial] to [tell] how Gilgamesh [slew] Humbaba!"

Humbaba listened, and [. . .]

(gap of about 20 lines)

(iv) *(gap of about 24 lines; again Humbaba speaks to Enkidu)*

"You sit like a shepherd [. . .] and just like [. . .]. Now, Enkidu, thus settle (?) your own release (?) and tell Gilgamesh that he may save his life."

Enkidu made his voice heard and spoke; he said [to Gilgamesh]: "My friend, [finish off] Humbaba, the guardian of the Pine Forest, [finish him off], slay him [and grind him up, that I may survive]. (Do it) before the leader Ellil hears, [. . .] lest (?) the gods (?) be filled with fury at us [. . .]. Ellil in Nippur, Shamash in Sippar. [Set up an eternal memorial] to tell how Gilgamesh [slew (?)] Humbaba."

Humbaba listened and [. . .]

(v) *(gap of about 13 lines; when they resume Humbaba is cursing the two friends)*

"Neither one of them shall outlive his friend! Gilgamesh and Enkidu shall never become (?) old men (?)."

Enkidu made his voice heard and spoke; he said to Gilgamesh: "My friend, I talk to you but you don't listen to me!"

(2 broken lines)

[. . .] of his friend. [. . .] at his side. [. . .] until he pulled out the entrails. [. . .] he/it springs away. [. . .] sharpens (?) teeth [. . .] abundance (?) fell on to the mountain. [. . .] abundance (?) fell on to the mountain.

(8 lines missing to end of column)

(vi) *(gap of about 22 lines)*

[. . .] their dark patch (?) of verdigris. Gilgamesh was cutting down the trees; Enkidu kept tugging at the stumps. Enkidu made his voice heard and spoke; he said to Gilgamesh: "My friend, I have had a fully mature pine cut down, the crown of which butted against the sky. I made a door six poles high and two poles wide; its doorpost is a cubit . . . , its lower and upper hinges are (made) from a single [. . .]. Let the Euphrates carry [it] to Nippur; Nippur [. . .]."

They tied together a raft, they put down [. . .]. Enkidu embarked [. . .] and Gilgamesh [. . .] the head of Humbaba.

(Catchline)

He washed [his filthy] hair, [he cleaned his gear]

(Colophon)

Fifth tablet, series [of Gilgamesh].

(Tablet VI is reproduced in Part 5 with the Love stories; it narrates how the goddess Ishtar tries to seduce Gilgamesh, followed by the fight with the Bull of Heaven. After Gilgamesh and

Enkidu kill the bull, they lie down and Enkidu has a dream, about which he talks to Gilgamesh at the beginning of Tablet VII.)

TABLET VII

"My friend, why are the great gods consulting together?"

(gap of about 20 lines, which may partly be filled in essence from a Hittite version, which is given here)

Then daylight came. [And] Enkidu said to Gilgamesh: "O my brother, what a dream [I saw] last night! Anu, Ellil, Ea, and heavenly Shamash [were in the assembly]. And Anu said to Ellil: 'As they have slain the Bull of Heaven, so too they have slain Huwawa,[21] who [guarded] the mountains pla[nted] with pines.' And Anu said: 'One of them [must die].' Ellil replied: 'Let Enkidu die, but let Gilgamesh not die.'

"Then heavenly Shamash said to valiant Ellil: 'Was it not according to your word that they slew the Bull of Heaven and Huwawa? Should now innocent Enkidu die?' But Ellil turned in anger to heavenly Shamash, saying: '(The fact is), you accompanied them daily, like one of their comrades.'"

Enkidu lay down before Gilgamesh, his tears flowing like streams. "O my brother, my brother is so dear to me. But they are taking me from my brother." And: "I shall sit among the dead, I shall [. . .] the threshold of the dead; never again [shall I see] my dear brother with my own eyes."

(End of Hittite insertion)

Enkidu made his [voice heard and spoke], He said to [his friend Gilgamesh]: "Come, [. . .] In [. . .] The door [. . .] Because [. . .]"

(3 broken lines)

(ii?) Enkidu lifted up [. . .]. He discussed [. . .] with the door: "Door, don't [you] remember the words? Are not. . . . . . . [. . .]? I selected the timber for you over twenty leagues, until I had found a fully mature pine. There is no other wood like yours! Your height is six poles, your width two poles.[22] Your doorpost, your lower and upper hinge (?) are made [from a single tree]. I made you, I carried you to Nippur [. . .]. Be aware, door, that this was a favor to you, and this was a good deed done for you [. . .]. I myself raised the axe, I cut you down, loaded you myself on to the raft, [. . .] I myself [. . .] temple of Shamash [. . .] I myself set (you) up in his gate [. . .] I myself [. . .] And in Uruk [. . .]"

(2 broken lines)

"Now, door, it was I who made you, I who carried you to Nippur. But the king who shall arise after me shall go through you; Gilgamesh shall [go through] your portals and change (?) my name, and put on his own name!"

He tore out (?) [the door (?) and] hurled(?) [. . .]. He kept listening to his words, [. . .] straight away Gilgamesh kept listening to the words of his friend Enkidu, and his tears flowed. Gilgamesh made his voice heard and spoke; he said to Enkidu [. . .]:

"You, who used to be reasonable, [now speak] otherwise! Why, my friend, did your heart speak otherwise (?). The dream was very precious, and the warning awful;

---

[21] Name of Humbaba in the Hittite version.

[22] Either 36 meters or 54 meters depending on the measurement applied.

your lips buzzed like flies (?)! The warning was awful, the dream was precious. They have left a legacy of grieving for next year. The dream has left a legacy of grief for next year. [I shall go] and offer prayers to the great gods; I shall search out [your goddess (?)], look for your god, [. . .] the father of the gods; to Ellil the counsellor, father of the gods [. . .]. I shall make a statue of you with countless gold [. . .]."

[The words] he spoke were not like [. . .]; [what] he said did not go back, did not [alter (?) the . . .] that he cast (?) did not go back, he did not erase. [. . .] to the people [. . .].

At the first light of morning Enkidu [raised] his head, wept before Shamash, his tears flowed before the rays of the Sun: "I hereby beseech you, Shamash, because my fate is different (?), [because] the hunter, the brigand, did not let me attain as much as my friend,

(iii) "Let the hunter never attain as much as his friend! Make his advantage vanish, make his strength less! [. . .] his share from your presence, let [. . .] not enter, let it go out through the window!"

When he had cursed the hunter as much as he wanted, he decided to curse the harlot too: "Come, Shamhat, I shall fix a fate for you! [Curses (?)] shall not cease for ever and ever. I shall curse you with a great curse! Straight away my curses shall rise up against you! You shall never make your house voluptuous again; you shall not release [. . .] of your young bulls; you shall not let them into the girls' rooms. Filth shall impregnate your lovely lap (?); the drunkard shall soak your party dress with vomit, [. . .] fingers (?); [your cosmetic paint (?) shall be] the potter's lump of clay (?); you shall never obtain the best cosmetic [oil (?);] bright silver, people's affluence, shall not accumulate in your house.

"The [. . .] of your [. . .] shall be your porch; the crossroads (?) shall be your only sitting place; waste ground your only lying place, the shade of a city wall your only sitting place. Thorns and spikes shall skin your feet; the drunkard and the thirsty shall slap your cheek;[23] [. . .] shall shout out against you. The builder shall never plaster the [walls (?) of your house;] owls will nest [in your roof beams (?);] feasting shall never take place in your house . . .

(about 4 broken lines)

"Because you defiled me when I was pure; because you seduced me in the open country when I was pure."

Shamash heard the utterance of his mouth. Immediately a loud voice called down to him from the sky: "Enkidu, why are you cursing my harlot Shamhat, who fed you on food fit for gods, gave you ale to drink, fit for kings, clothed you with a great robe, then provided you with Gilgamesh for a fine partner? And now Gilgamesh, the friend who is a brother to you will lay you to rest on a great bed and lay you to rest on a bed of loving care, and let you stay in a restful dwelling, the dwelling on the left.[24]

"Princes of the earth will kiss your feet. He will make the people of Uruk weep for you, mourn for you; will fill the proud people with woe, and he himself will

---

[23] Notice identical curses issued in the *Ishtar's Descent* (Part 6, document 2).

[24] See the similar idea of different paths in the Underworld in the Gold Tablets, the *Aeneid*, and the Myth of Er (Part 6, documents 9 and 13, and Part 7, document 5).

neglect his appearance after you(r death). Clothed only in a lionskin, he will roam the open country."

Enkidu listened to the speech of Shamash the warrior. [His anger abated (?)]; his heart became quiet.

(about 2 lines missing)

(iv) "Come, Shamhat, I shall change your fate! My utterance, which cursed you, shall bless you instead. Governors and princes shall love you; the single-league man shall smite his thigh (for you); the double-league man shall shake out his locks (for you). The herdsman shall not hold back for you, he shall undo his belt for you. He shall give you ivory, lapis lazuli, and gold, rings (and) brooches (?) shall be presents for you. Rain shall pour down for him (?), his storage jars shall be heaped full. The diviner shall lead you into the palace (?) of the gods. Because of you, the mother of seven, the honored wife, shall be deserted."

Then Enkidu [wept (?)], for he was sick at heart. [. . .] he lay down alone. He spoke what was in his mind to his friend: "Listen again, my friend! I had a dream in the night. The sky called out, the earth replied, I was standing in between them. There was a young man, whose face was obscured. His face was like that of an Anzu-bird. He had the paws of a lion, he had the claws of an eagle. He seized me by my locks, using great force against me. I hit him, and he jumped like a *keppu*-toy, he hit me and forced me down like an [onager (?)], like a wild bull he trampled on me, he squeezed my whole body. (I cried out:) 'Save me, my friend, don't desert me!' But you were afraid, and did not [help me (?)], you [. . .]

(3 broken lines)

"[He hit me and] turned me into a dove. [. . .] my arms, like a bird. He seized me, drove me down to the dark house, dwelling of Erkalla's god, to the house which those who enter cannot leave, on the road where travelling is one way only, to the house where those who stay are deprived of light, where dust is their food, and clay their bread. They are clothed, like birds, with feathers, and they see no light, and they dwell in darkness. "Over the door [and the bolt, dust has settled.] I looked at the house that I had entered, and crowns were heaped up. I [. . .] those with crowns who had ruled the land from time immemorial; [priests (?) of] Anu and Ellil regularly set out cooked meats, set out baked (bread), set out cold water from waterskins. In the house of dust that I had entered Dwelt the *enu* and *lagaru*-priests, dwelt the *isippu* and *lumahhu*-priests, dwelt the *gudapsu*-priests of the great gods, dwelt Etana, dwelt Shakkan, dwelt Ereshkigal, the Queen of Earth.[25] Belet-seri, the scribe of Earth, was kneeling before her. She was holding [a tablet] and kept reading aloud to her. She raised her head and looked at me: '[Who (?)] brought this man?'

(gap of about 50 lines for column v)

(vi) *(gap of about 2 lines)*

(Enkidu) "[. . .] experienced all kinds of troubles, remember me, my friend, and do not forget what I went through."

---

[25] Etana was a king of Kish and Shakkan a cattle-god (no myths are known about their presence in the Underworld). Ereshkigal is the wife of Nergal, the god of the Underworld (which was called "the Earth" among other names); Nergal was also called "Lord of Erkalla" (or "Great City," mentioned a few lines earlier).

(Gilgamesh) "My friend saw an in[describable] dream."

From the day he saw the dream, his [strength] was finished. Enkidu lay there the first day, then [a second day. The illness] of Enkidu, as he lay in bed, [grew worse, his flesh weaker.] A third day and a fourth day, the [illness] of [Enkidu grew worse, his flesh weaker (?),] a fifth, sixth and seventh day, eighth, ninth [and tenth.] The illness of Enkidu [grew worse, his flesh weaker (?)]. An eleventh and twelfth day [his illness grew worse, his flesh weaker.] Enkidu, as he lay in bed, [. . .] Gilgamesh cried out and [. . .]: "My friend is cursing me, [. . .] Because in the midst of [. . .] I was afraid of the fight [. . .] My friend, who [was so strong (?)] in the fight, [cursed me (?)] I, in [. . .]"[26]

(gap of up to 30 lines)

TABLET VIII

(i) When the first light of dawn appeared,[27] Gilgamesh said to his friend: "Enkidu, my friend, your mother a gazelle, and your father a wild donkey sired you, their milk was from onagers; they reared (?) you, and cattle made you familiar with all the pastures. Enkidu's paths [led to] the Pine Forest.

"They shall weep for you night and day, never fall silent, weep for you, the elders of the broad city, of Uruk the Sheepfold. The summit will bless (us) after our death, They shall weep for you, the [. . .]s of the mountains, they shall mourn [. . .] [The open country as if it were your father], the field as if it were your mother. They shall weep for you, [myrtle (?)], cypress, and pine, in the midst of which we armed ourselves (?) in our fury.

"They shall weep for you, the bear, hyena, leopard, tiger, stag, cheetah, lion, wild bulls, deer, mountain goat, cattle, and other wild beasts of open country. It shall weep for you, the holy river Ulaya, along whose bank we used to walk so proudly. It shall weep for you, the pure Euphrates, with whose water in waterskins we used to refresh ourselves.

"They shall weep for you, the young men of the broad city, of Uruk the Sheepfold, who watched the fighting when we struck down the Bull of Heaven. He shall weep for you, the ploughman at [his plough (?)] who extols your name with sweet Alala. He shall weep for you, [. . .] of the broad city, of Uruk the Sheepfold, who will extol your name in the first . . .

"He shall weep for you, the shepherd, the herdsman (?), who used to make (?) the beer mixture (?) for your mouth. She shall weep for you, [the wet-nurse (?)] who used to put butter on your lower parts. He (?) shall weep for you, the elder (?) who used to put ale to your mouth. She shall weep for you, the harlot [. . .] by whom you were anointed with perfumed oil. They shall weep for you, [parents]-in-law

---

[26] Gilgamesh implies here and again in Tablet IX.i that his cowardice caused Enkidu's illness, alluding to an episode that is not preserved (possibly the heroes were attacked by lions in their way to Humbaba's forest or in some later episode).

[27] Much of Tablet VIII is preserved in school tablets containing student errors. The stock opening phrase is reminiscent of the Homeric formula "as soon as rosy-finger dawn appeared" (e.g., *Od.* 9.149 in document 3.8.b, translated as "When early-born dawn appeared, who has fingers like roses").

who [comfort (?)] the wife . . . of your loins (?). They shall weep for you, the young men, [like brothers (?)] they shall weep for you and tear out (?) their hair over you. For you, Enkidu, I, (like?) your mother, your father, will weep on your (lit. his) plains [. . .]

(ii) "Listen to me, young men, listen to me! Listen to me, elders of Uruk, listen to me! I myself must weep for Enkidu my friend, mourn bitterly, like a wailing woman. As for the axe at my side, spur to my arm, the sword in my belt, the shield for my front, my festival clothes, my manly sash: Evil [Fate (?)] rose up and robbed me of them. My friend was the hunted mule, wild ass of the mountains, leopard of open country. Enkidu the strong man was the hunted wild ass of [the mountains, leopard of open country].

"We who met, and scaled the mountain, seized the Bull of Heaven and slew it, demolished Humbaba the mighty one of the Pine Forest, now, what is the sleep that has taken hold of you? Turn to me, you! You aren't listening to me! But he cannot lift his head. I touch his heart, but it does not beat at all."[28]

He covered his friend's face like a daughter-in-law. He circled over him like an eagle, like a lioness whose cubs are [trapped] in a pit, he paced back and forth. He (?) tore out and spoilt (?) well-curled hair, he stripped off and threw away finery as if it were taboo.[29]

When the first light of dawn appeared, Gilgamesh sent out a shout through the land. The smith, the [. . .], the coppersmith, the silversmith, the jeweler (were summoned). He made [a likeness (?)] of his friend, he fashioned a statue of his friend. The four limbs of the friend were [made of . . .], his chest was of lapis lazuli, his (?) skin was of gold [. . .]

(gap of about 12 lines)

(iii) "[I will lay you to rest] on a bed [of loving care] and will let you stay [in a restful dwelling, a dwelling of the left]. Princes of the earth [will kiss your feet]. I will make the people [of Uruk] weep for you, [mourn for you]. [I will fill] the proud people with sorrow for you. And I myself will neglect my appearance after you(r death); clad only in a lionskin, I will roam the open country."

When the first light of dawn appeared, Gilgamesh arose and [went to his treasury], he undid its fastenings and looked at the treasure. He brought out carnelian, flint, alabaster,

[. . .] kept making (?) [. . .] for his friend [. . .]

(Seventeen lines are very fragmentary and list/describe the materials for Enkidu's splendidly rich statue. The last columns of the tablet are very damaged, and only a few lines of column v are preserved, in which Gilgamesh is making an offering to Shamash. A new fragment of about 73 lines, perhaps belonging somewhere in column iv, lists burial goods, animal sacrifices, and items offered to individual deities after being displayed for Shamash. Each deity is asked to welcome Enkidu and walk by his side in the Underworld, so that he will not be sick at heart.)

---

[28] This line has been compared to *Iliad* 18.317, when Achilles puts his hands on the breast of his dead friend Patroklos. The mourning of Achilles for Patroklos and that of Gilgamesh bear many other resemblances (neither wants to bury his friend, they are both compared with anxious lions deprived of their cubs, and they both wail like women).

[29] According to other variants, this sentence seems to be corrupt.

(In Tablet IX Gilgamesh mourns Enkidu and is in anguish at the thought of his own mortality; he decides to travel to the Underworld in search of the only immortal man, the survivor of the flood, for which see Part 6, document 1.)

3.2. THE DISPUTES BETWEEN HORUS AND SETH (FROM THE *PYRAMID TEXTS* AND PAPYRI)

The following excerpts come from different kinds of texts and periods, but all of them refer to the homosexual episode between Horus (Osiris' son) and Seth, which was omitted in Plutarch's version of the Osiris myth (for which see Part 6, document 5). These sexually charged episodes could have been included in Part Five of this volume (about love and sexuality), but in turn they represent a famous episode in the struggle for power between the two Egyptian gods who competed for the dominion of the universe after Osiris's death. The first text is a spell from the *Pyramid Texts*, a corpus of religious texts originally inscribed on the walls of the pyramids of the last kings of the Old Kingdom and some of their wives. This brief formula is only attested in the pyramid of king Pepy I (ca. 2321–2287 BCE), where it is a mythical motif embedded in a longer protective spell against snakes. It briefly alludes to the episode as a consensual action between the two gods. The second text, a papyrus, is the only surviving fragment of a longer literary piece, dating to the Twelfth Dynasty (Middle Kingdom, ca. 1985–1773 BCE). It is one of the earliest and rarest known examples of a narrative account of an Egyptian myth. The third text is an excerpt from the *Contendings of Horus and Seth*, a Ramesside story preserved on the *Papyrus Chester Beatty* I, and dated to the end of the Nineteenth Dynasty of the New Kingdom (ca. 1200 BCE). It includes this episode as part of a much longer account of the long-running dispute between Seth and Horus, who both want to succeed Osiris as king of the gods, resulting in the final victory of Osiris' son (see also allusion to Horus' victory in Part 6, document 3). These three texts on the same divine anecdote show how the treatment of the motif evolved over the centuries: from a ritual funerary spell in the first text to a mythical narrative in the second, and finally to a more elaborated—but folk-oriented—narrative in the last of the three sources.

SOURCES: *Pyramid Texts* Spell 1036, *Pap. London UCL* 32158, and *Papyrus Chester Beatty* I, translated and annotated by A. Diego Espinel.

Pyramid Texts Spell 1036 from the pyramid of Pepy I (P/A/E 30)

Words to be said: Horus complains because of the eye in his body, when he had eaten [. . .] the gods. Seth sobs because of his testicles. Horus has introduced his penis into Seth's anus, and Seth has introduced his penis into Horus' anus (. . .)

Pap. London UCL 32158 (1, x+8–2, 9)

(. . .) [. . .] Then the majesty of Seth said to the majesty of Horus: "How beautiful are your buttocks. Broad are your legs [. . .]"

Then the majesty of Horus said: "Take care, I will say [. . .] to their palace."

Then the majesty of Horus said to his mother I[sis]: "[. . .] Seth wants to have sex with me!"

Then she said to him: "Watch out! Do not let him enter. After he says it to you again, you will say to him: 'It is entirely painful to me because you are heavier than me. My strength cannot equal your strength.' So you will say to him. After he has given to you (his) strength, you will shove your fingers up your butt. Look, placing [. . .] to him as [. . .] [. . .] Look, it will be sweet to his heart, more than the height (?) [. . .] [. . .] [the sem]en which has came out from his phallus without letting Re see it [. . .]" [. . .]

Pap. Chester Beatty I (Dublin, Chester Beatty Library) 11, 1–13, 5

(. . .) Then Seth said to Horus: "Come! Let's make a pleasant day at my home!"
Then Horus said to him: "Let's do it. Certainly, let's do it, let's do it!"

Now, when the time of dusk had passed, a mat was set down for them and both men lay down. During the night Seth made his phallus erectile, and he put it in between the thighs of Horus.

Then Horus put his two hands in between his thighs and he took the semen of Seth, and Horus went to tell his mother Isis: "Come, Isis, my mother! Come and see what Seth has done against me!" He opened his two hands and let her see the semen of Horus. She shouted out loud and she took her knife and cut his hand.[30] She threw it to the water and provided him with another similar hand.

Then she brought some sweet ointment and put it on the phallus of Horus, and[31] she caused him an erection; then she put his phallus into a jar and he let his semen pour into it. Then in the morning, Isis went with the semen of Horus to the garden of Seth and she said to the gardener of Seth: "What plants does Seth eat here with you?" Then the gardener said to her: "He does not eat any plant here with me, apart from the lettuces."[32]

Isis poured the semen of Horus on them. Then Seth came according to his daily routine, and ate the lettuces he used to eat, and he became pregnant because of the semen of Horus.

Then Seth went to say to Horus: "Come! Let's go that I may contest in Court!"
Then Horus said to him: "Let's do it. Certainly, let's do it, let's do it!"

Then they went to Court, both men, and they stood in the presence of the Great Ennead of gods. They were told: "Speak!"

Then Seth said: "Let the office of ruler, l.i.h.!, be given to me; as for Horus, present here, I have done a male's action against him."

Then the Great Ennead of gods shouted aloud, and they spat at the face of Horus, (but) then Horus laughed at them, and Horus swore an oath by the god saying: "Everything Seth has said is false! May the semen of Horus be summoned and let's see from where it answers. Let's summon mine and let's see from where it answers."

---

[30] The wording here and in the following sentence could refer to one or both hands.

[31] Literally "then." I have translated it occasionally as "and" in order to avoid excessive reiterations.

[32] Lettuce sap is milky and looks like semen.

THEN Thot, the lord of the divine words (i.e. writings), the scribe of truth of the Ennead of gods, put his hand on the shoulder of Horus and said: "Come out, semen of Seth!" And it answered from the water, from the interior of the cucumbers field (?).

THEN Thot put his hand over the shoulder of Seth and said: "Come out, semen of Horus!" AND it said to him: "Where will I come out from?"

THEN Thot said to it: "Come out from his ear," AND it said to him: "Will I come out from his ear, I who am a divine liquid?"

THEN Thot said to it: "Come out from the top of his head!" AND it came out as a sun disk of gold over the head of Seth.

THEN Seth became extremely angry and extended his hand trying to seize the sun-disk of gold, AND Thot took it, and he put it as a crown over his head.

THEN the Ennead of gods said: "Horus is right, Seth is wrong."

THEN Seth became extremely angry and he shouted aloud to the god(s) when they said: "Horus is right, Seth is wrong."

THEN Seth swore a great oath by the god saying: "The office won't be given to him until he has been dismissed outside with me, and after we have built ships of stone and raced each other, both men. The one who overcomes his rival, *he* will be given the office of ruler, l.i.h.!" (. . .)

3.3. EGYPT: *TALE OF THE SHIPWRECKED SAILOR*

This story is known only through the *Papyrus St-Petersburg* 1115, dated to the late Twelfth Dynasty (ca. 1985–1773 BCE). It is one of the most important and puzzling compositions of Middle Kingdom literature. Extensive scholarly efforts have been made to study and interpret it due to its original theme and composition, its complex chronological structure, the absence of names for its few characters, and its sudden and pessimistic ending. The story is formed, like a set of Russian *matrioshka* dolls, by three different stories inserted into one another. The framing story starts *in medias res*, very much like the *Odyssey* (see document 3.8.b), as a dialogue between a junior officer (the main character) and his superior officer or commander (called "prince"). They have just arrived in Egypt (possibly at Elephantine at the First Cataract of the Nile) after an apparently unsuccessful expedition to Nubia, south of Egypt. In order to encourage the commander, who is worried about facing the king at his return, the junior officer (or "able follower" in the opening line) tells him an experience of his, which constitutes the central story. He mentions how he became shipwrecked during an expedition to Sinai. As the sole survivor, he arrived at an island where a divine snake lived. During his encounter, the giant snake related to the sailor a third story describing his own misadventure on the island. Finally, an Egyptian ship arrives at the island and the sailor returns to Egypt loaded with many precious products. At his return he is promoted as "follower" of the king. At that point we return to the framing story, which ends abruptly when the commander, despite the shipwrecked sailor's account, expresses his fatalistic feelings regarding the immediate future.

With its unusually pessimistic ending, *The Shipwrecked Sailor* contains numerous esoteric references and motifs, which scholars have linked to aspects of Egyptian religion and culture as well as to Near Eastern and African traditions. The original intention and meaning of the text, however, remain a mystery, as well as its sources of inspiration and its influence on other Egyptian literary texts. This story is indeed difficult to place within any of the thematic units of this volume, but perhaps it fits best in this section. Although the shipwrecked sailor is not a conventional "hero," his strange experience brings to mind Odysseus' encounters with supernatural beings in fantastic geographical settings. The lesson given by the serpent and the sailor himself is akin to the *carpe diem* message already present in the *Epic of Gilgamesh* (see quotation in Part 6, page 430). Moreover, this sailor is one of the few human literary characters in Middle Egyptian literature who experience direct contact with the supra-human sphere, since the talking serpent is a divine being possibly connected with the Sun God. Hence, this text is a rare representative of mythological narrative from ancient Egypt.

SOURCE: *The Shipwrecked Sailor* (*Pap. St-Petersburg* 1115, 1–189), translated and annotated by A. Diego Espinel.

THEN THE ABLE follower SAID: "Be heartened, my prince! Look, we have reached the residence. The mallet has been taken, the mooring-post has been staked, and the prow-rope has been placed on the ground. Thanks have been given and god has been praised. Every man embraces his companion. Our crew has returned safely, with no losses among the members of our expedition. We have reached Wawat,[33] and we have passed Biga.[34] Look at us now, we have come successfully! It is our land that we have reached!

"LISTEN NOW TO ME, my prince. I am not exaggerating. Wash yourself and put water on your fingers! So you can answer when you are asked, and you can speak to the king with self-command, and answer without stammering. The mouth of a man can save him, and his words can cause compassion (lit. "can cover his face"). But you act as you wish, it is useless to speak to you.

"Now I WILL RELATE to you something similar that happened to myself. I went to the Mining Region[35] of the sovereign and I descended the Great Green[36] on a ship a hundred and twenty cubits long and forty cubits broad.[37] There was on board a crew of a hundred and twenty men, among the best of Egypt. They looked at the sky and they looked at the land, and their hearts were braver than lions. THEY COULD FORETELL a gale before it happened, a storm before it brewed, but a gale came up while we were in the Great Green, before we could reach land. The wind

---

[33] Lower Nubia—the region between the First and Second Cataracts of the Nile.

[34] A Nile island in the southern part of the First Cataract, near Aswan.

[35] Lit. "Bia," usually referring to the mining region of Sinai.

[36] In Egyptian texts, "Great Green" usually refers to a beneficent aspect of the Nile inundation. However, it can be translated as "sea" in some cases, such as here.

[37] Approximately 60 meters × 20 meters.

raised and it made a continued howling. A wave of eight cubits was in it.[38] As for the mast, I reached for it. Then the ship wrecked, and no one of those who were inside (survived). Then I was placed on an island by a wave of the Great Green. I spent three days alone, with my heart as my sole companion. I passed the night inside a tent of wood, and I embraced the shade. Then I stretched my legs in order to find out what I could put in my mouth. I FOUND figs and grapes there, and every good vegetable: common sycamore figs there, and notched sycamore figs; cucumbers (?) as if they were cultivated, fish there and fowl. There was nothing that was not in it. Then I ate until I was satisfied and I had to set (some of the food) on the ground because it was too much for my arms. I took a fire drill and lit a fire, and I made a holocaust to the gods.

"THEN I HEARD a noise of thunder. I thought it was a wave of the Great Green; the trees were splintering, and the ground was trembling. I uncovered my face and I discovered that a serpent was approaching. He was thirty cubits (long) and his beard was longer than two cubits.[39] His body was overlaid with gold, and his eyebrows were of real lapis lazuli. He was bent up in front (of me).

"HE OPENED his mouth toward me, while I was prostrated on my belly in front of him. He told me: 'Who brought you? Who brought you, commoner? Who brought you? If you delay in telling me who brought you to this island, I will make you know yourself as ashes, turned into one who cannot be seen!' <I said:> 'You (lit. "He") speak to me, but I cannot hear you. I am in front of you, but I do not recognize myself!'[40] Then he put me in his mouth and took me to his place of rest. He set me down without touching me. I was intact, with no (parts) taken away from me.

"HE OPENED his mouth toward me, while I was prostrated on my belly in front of him. Then he told me: 'Who brought you? Who brought you, commoner? Who brought you to this island of the Great Green whose two sides are in the water?' Then I answered to him this, with my arms bent before him. I told him: 'I was descending to the Mining Region on a mission of the sovereign on a ship a hundred and twenty cubits long and forty cubits broad. There was in it a crew of a hundred and twenty men, among the best of Egypt. They looked at the sky and they looked at the land, and their hearts were braver than lions. THEY COULD FORETELL a gale before it happened, a storm before it brewed. Every one had a more courageous heart and a braver arm than his companion's. There was no fool among them. But a gale came up while we were in the Great Green, before we could reach land. The wind raised and it made a continued howling. A wave of eight cubits came with it. As for the mast, I reached for it. Then the ship wrecked, and no one of those who were inside (survived) but me, and look, I am beside you. THEN I was brought to this island by a wave of the Great Green.'

"Then he said to me: 'Do not be afraid! Do not be afraid, commoner! Do not cover your face, as you have reached me. Look, it is god who has allowed you to

---

[38] Approximately 4 meters.

[39] The snake would be approximately 15 meters long, and its beard would be approximately 1 meter tall.

[40] The sailor is totally astounded and frightened as he is in the presence of a divine being.

live.[41] He has brought you to this island of the *ka*. There is nothing that is not in it. It is plentiful in every good thing. Look, you will spend month upon month until you have completed four months on this island. (Then) a boat will come from the Residence (i.e., Pharaoh's palace) with sailors aboard whom you know; you will go with them to the Residence, and you will die in your city.

(The snake continues) 'How FORTUNATE is he who can relate what he has experienced when misfortunes have (already) passed! Now I will relate to you something similar that happened in this island.[42] I was in it with my companions and children, in the midst of them: We were seventy-five serpents in total, with my children and my brothers, without mentioning to you a little daughter whom I fetched wisely.[43]

'THEN A STAR fell down and they went up in a flame coming from it. It happened when I was not with <them>, and they burnt when I was not among them. Then I fell away (lit. 'I died') because of them, when I found them as a single pile of corpses. If you are courageous and your heart is firm, you will embrace your children, kiss your wife, and see your house. That is better than anything. You will reach the Residence and you will be in the midst of your companions. May you experience this.' "I (i.e., the sailor) stretched out my body, and I touched the ground in front of him.

(The sailor continues) "THEN I TOLD TO YOU (*sic*):[44] 'I will report your power to the sovereign, and I will let him know your power. I will send you *ibi*-oil, *hekenu*-oil, *iudeneb*-resin, *khesayt*-resin, and resin of terebinth of the temples with which every god is appeased. I will tell what has happened to me, what I have seen of his (*sic*) powers. I will praise god for you in the city before the council of the entire land. I WILL SLAUGHTER bulls for you as a holocaust, and I will strangle fowls for you. I will bring to you a fleet laden with every noble thing of Egypt, as is done to a god who loves human beings in a distant land which people do not know.'

"THEN HE LAUGHED AT ME FOR WHAT I HAD SAID as it was foolishness to him. He said to me: 'You are not rich in *antyu*-resin and in every existing kind of terebinth resin. I am the ruler of Punt![45] *Antyu*-resin is mine, that *hekenu*-oil you said you were going to bring is the greatness of this island. Moreover, it will so happen that when you move away from here, you will never see this place, which will be transformed into water.'

"THEN THAT BOAT came as he had foretold previously, and I went and climbed a tall tree, and I recognized those who were aboard. Then I went to report it <to him>, but I found he knew it (already), and he said to me: 'Fare well! Fare well com-

---

[41] It is difficult to ascertain if "god" is a reference to a precise divinity here. As in many other texts, the word "god" seems to be a generic term (see *The Teachings for Merikare* in Part 1, document 3.c).

[42] The serpent is still talking, and he starts to tell the shipwrecked sailor his story.

[43] A later royal composition, the *Litany of Re*, enumerates the seventy-five names of the Sun God Re, which coincides with the number of serpents in the island. The odd reference to the serpent's daughter could be an allusion to Maat, Re's daughter and personification of universal order (see *Coffin Text* spell 80 and note 30 there (Part 1, document 3.b).

[44] In other words, "Then I (the sailor) said to him (the serpent)," or perhaps "Then I tell you."

[45] Punt was a region from which Egypt imported exotic products, mainly aromatic resins. It was possibly located on the eastern Sudanese coast or on the western coast of the Arabian peninsula, but the name was used generically (such as the *Indias* later on) for areas around the Red Sea, which produced the coveted resins.

moner to your house, and see your children! Make me a good name in your city. Look, this is my request to you.'

"THEN I POSTRATED MYSELF on my belly, with my arms bent before him, and he gave me a load of *antyu*-resin, *hekenu*-oil, *iudeneb*-resin, *khesayt*-resin, *ti-shepses*-wood, *shaasekh*-product (?), *kohol*, tails of giraffes, great lumps of resin of terebinth, tusks of ivory, hounds, monkeys, apes, and every noble product.

"THEN I LOADED IT aboard this ship, and I prostrated on my belly to praise god for him. Then he said to me: 'Look, you will reach the Residence in two months. You will embrace your children, will grow young in the Residence, and will be buried.' Then I went down to the shore, near the ship, and I called out to the members of the expedition who were aboard. On the shore I said fairwell to the lord of this island, and those who were aboard did the same.

"WE SAILED northwards, to the Residence of the sovereign. We reached the Residence in two months, according to every thing he had said. Then I went in to the sovereign, and brought him these products that I had brought from this island, and he praised god for me before the council of the entire land. Then I was appointed a (king's) follower, and his personnel was assigned to me. Look at me after what I have experienced! Listen to my [speech], for it is good to listen to people!"

Then he (the commander) said to me[46]: "Do not act cleverly, my mate! Who would give water to a bird at dawn, when its slaughter will be in the morning?"

(Colophon) It CAME from its start to its end, just as it was found written, [as] a writing of the scribe of skilful fingers, Ameny's son, Amenaa, l.i.h.

3.4. HITTITE MYTHS

Hittite is an Indo-European language from Anatolia, for which we have evidence dating to the second millennium BCE, making it the earliest attested Indo-European language. Archaeological exploration of the Hittite capital, Hattusa, located about 150 kilometers east of Anakara (the capital of Turkey), began at the end of the nineteenth century, and in 1906 clay tablets broken into some 2,500 fragments were unearthed, leading to the discovery of a major Bronze Age empire that, at its peak, around 1200 BCE, extended from northwest Anatolia to Syria. The Hittite language was deciphered in 1915, but work continues on the other eight languages inscribed on clay tablets and stone monuments found at Hattusa. The Hittite empire was a multicultural and multilingual entity, and the Hittite court took great interest in Mesopotamian learning in Akkadian and Sumerian, and in archaic and local Anatolian traditions, collecting texts in Hattic, Luwian, and Palaic. The selection of mythological texts in this anthology, in fact, represents both native Anatolian magical and religious traditions and Hurro-Hittite literature. The Hurrians, in turn, were the primary rivals of the Hittites as the latter attempted to expand east and south at the beginning of the sixteenth century. The Hurrian empire was eventually subordinated to the Hittite empire in Cilicia in the fifteenth

---

[46] We return to the framing story, so the commander makes this remark to the sailor, who has told this whole story.

century, and it proved to be a key conduit of Syro-Mesopotamian traditions to the Hittite court.

Note about text arrangement and numbering: Texts are extant in multiple copies or versions, mostly fragmentary. Because the texts presented here are composites of the different sources, scholars use a rather complicated system of labeling the fragments. Hence, the "best" source (the most complete) is labeled "A," while other exemplars are designated by other letters. Paragraph numbering (§1, etc.) is the key method to keep track of where we are in the tablet, but if a tablet is broken at the top or bottom, the paragraph number cannot represent the original paragraph. Thus, a tablet for which the opening of column i is missing begins its paragraph and line numbering at, for example §1', i 1'–3'. If in addition there is another gap, the paragraph number adds a second apostrophe, for example §6'', while two gaps in a single column causes the line number to gain another apostrophe, for example i 4''–7''. Since line numbering is not consistent between the different copies or versions, line numbers are given for all exemplars used.

SOURCE: Translated and annotated by M. Bachvarova. Unless otherwise noted, all translations of Hittite texts are based on the edition of CTH 348 by E. Rieken et al. at the online database Konkordanz der hethitischen Texten (http://www.hethport.uni-wuerzburg.de/hetkonk/), with some new joins. The numbering of the fragments is Bachvarova's. Some unplaced fragments and unintelligible paragraphs are omitted.

3.4.a. Anatolian (Hattic) Myth of *Illuyanka*

The term *illuyanka*, of Indo-European origin, means "eel-snake." Two variants of the Hittite story about the water snake are recorded on a single tablet, extant in at least eight copies. Each tells how the Storm God (Hurrian Teshub, Hittite Tarhun(na), Luwian Tarhunt) was at first defeated at the hands of the water snake and then eventually prevailed. In both cases the Storm God receives aid from a mortal who suffers from his connection to the gods. In one story, he is helped by the goddess of the wilderness, Inara, who is helped in turn by a man named Hupasiya. In the other, the Storm God creates a son with the daughter of a poor man, then marries him into the snake's family. While the stories have obvious parallels with other Indo-European traditions, their roots in the pre-Hittite, Hattic layer of Anatolian culture in north-central Anatolia are shown by the geographic and divine names mentioned. The first version was used as the **etiology** (or ***aition***) for the Hattic-derived springtime *purulli* festival (cf. Hatt. *pur* "land"), and the second one may have actually been acted out by cult performers, as "the daughter of a poor man" is mentioned in a list of cult disbursements. As with the Telipinu *mugawar* (in Part 6, document 6), this story is imbedded in a frame referring to real-life cultic activities.

The stories are variants of the mythical battles between light and dark, order and chaos, fertility and natural disaster, in which a heroic male battles a snake or dragon. Many are extant in Indo-European and Near Eastern languages, including the Hurro-Hittite *Song of Hedammu*, translated in the next document. Greek parallels include the battle between Zeus and Typhon (Hesiod's *Theogony* in Part 2, document 5), between Apollo and Python (document 3.9), and between Bellerophon ("snake killer") and the Chimaera. The fight of Baal with Yamm (document 3.5.a) and of Yahweh with the sea (document 3.6) also conform to the same motif. The role of Inara has parallels with that of Anzili in the *Kumarbi Cycle*, and the theme of humans used as pawns by the gods is also found in the *Song of Release* (in Part 4, document 2) as well as broadly in Greek and other Near Eastern mythologies.

(§1, A i 1–8, F i 1–5) [T]hus Kell[a, the anointed priest[47] o]f the Storm God of Nerik,[48] the story of *purulli*, [. . . o]f Ta[rhun] of Heaven: When they speak as follows: "Let the land thrive (and) prosper. Let the land be protected." So that it thrive and prospers, they celebrate the *purulli* festival.

(Tarhun, fighting the snake alone, is at first defeated by him, and the gods refuse to help the Storm God. Inara, however, comes up with a plot to trick the snake and destroy him along with his children, but she needs the help of a human, who is willing to help her only if she sleeps with him.)

(§2, A i 9–11, F i 6–7, E i 1'-2') When Tarhun and the snake fell into conflict with each other in Kiskilussa, the snake overcame Tarhun.

(§3, A i 12–14, E i 3'-4') But, Tarhun invoked al[l] the gods, "Come on, take my side!" So, Inara made a feast.

(§4, A i 15–18, E i 6', D i 1'-3') She prepared a lot of everything, vessels of wine, vessels of *marnuwan*, vessels of [*wa*]*lhi*,[49] and [she] m[ade] an abundance i[n] the vessels.

(§5, A i 19–20, D i 4'-5') Inara went to [Z]iggaratta, and she found Hupasiya, a human.

(§6, A i 21–23, D i 6'-8') Thus Inara: "Hupasiya, I am about to do such and such a matter, you also join with me!"

(§7, A i 24–26, D i 9'-10', B i 1'-2') Thus Hupasiya to Inara: "If I slee[p] with you, I will go and do (that) of your heart." So, h[e] slept with her.

(§8, B i 3'-8', A i 27–29, C i 1'-3') Inara led Hupas[iya a]way, and she hid him. Meanwhile, Inara adorned herself, and she called up the snak[e] from his hole, "I am making a feast here now, so come to eat (and) drink."

(§9, B i 9'-12', C i 4'-7') The snake with [his children] came up, and they ate (and) dran[k] their fill. [They] dran[k] of all the vessels, and they were intoxicated.

(§10, B i 13'-18', C i 1'-13', H 1'-5', G 1'-2') They did not want[50] to go down in the hole again. And, Hupasiya came, and he bound the snake with a rope. Tarhun came, and he killed the sna[k]e, and the gods were with him.

(§11, B i 19'-25', C i 14'-22', G 3'-9', H 6'-9') Inara built at house for herself on top of a rock, in the land of Tarukka, and she settled Hupasiya inside the house, and Inara repeatedly orders him, "When I go to the steppe, you for your part do not

---

[47] The "anointed priest" ([LÚ]GUDU₁₂ or *kumra*) officiated in rites from the Hattic cultural layer.

[48] This local Storm God from the Hattic town of Nerik was named Nerak or Nerikkil, but it is unclear what he is called in the story, since his name is hidden behind the Sumerian sign for "Storm God."

[49] *Marnuwan* and *walhi* are two beer-like beverages typical of Hattic culture.

[50] Or "were unable."

look out from the window. But, if you look out, you wi[ll] see your wife (and) your children.

(§12, C i 23–24, A ii 5') When the twentieth day went by, that one for his part peeked out [from] the wind[ow], and [he saw] his wife (and) his children.

(§13, C i 25'-27', A ii 6'-8') [W]hen Inara on the one hand came back from the steppe, that one on the other hand began to weep, "Release me [b]ack to my house."

(§14, A ii 9'-14') [Th]us Ina[ra to Hupasiya, " . . .] away [. . . w]ith the offense [. . .] the m[ead]ow of Tarhun [. . .] that one (subj.). Him/her [. . .]

(The following paragraph makes the transition from the story to its ritual frame. The house on the cliff that Inara builds may have been a cult place located close to a spring representing the primordial waters over which the snake had control. The water necessary for crops, and therefore the prosperity of the kingdom, was ensured by the king's close relationship with the goddess, maintained by cult offerings. Mountains, as weather-makers, were included in the worship of the Storm God and received offerings of their own.)

(§15, A ii 15'-20') Inara [went] to Kiskil[ussa]. As she se[t] her house [and] the [course] of the flood [in] the hand of the king, therefore we enact the f[i]rst *purull[i]*, and the hand [of the king does X to the house] of Inara and the course of the flood.

(§16, A ii 21'-24') Mount Zaliyanu is fore[most] of all. When the rain pours in Nerik, the [M]an of the Staff[51] sends thick bread from Nerik.

(§17, A ii 25'-30') He requested rain from Mount Za[liyan]u, and he brings it, [thick] bread, to him. He sets it [. . .], and he does [X . . .] to it. He [do]es [X . . .]

(Column ii of exemplar A breaks off before paragraph end, and there is a gap of approximately 40 lines before the story is picked up in D, which unfortunately prevents us from understanding how Kella viewed the relationship between the two stories.)

(§18', D iii 1') *(One sign visible.)*

(§19', D iii 2'-5, A iii 1'-3') [And] what [. . . Kella] said: The s[nake] defeated [Tarhun, and] he took [his heart and eyes], and Tarhun [also X-ed] him.

(§20', A iii 4'-8', D iii 6'-8') He took for himself as wife the daughter of a poor man, and she gave birth to a son, and when he grew up, he took for himself in marriage a daughter of the snake.

(§21', A iii 9'-12', D iii 9'-10') Tarhun orders his son repeatedly, "When you go in the house of your wife, request from them the heart and eyes."

(§22', A iii 13'-19') So, when he went, he requested from them the heart, and they gave it to him. Afterwards, he also requested the eyes from them, and they gave them also to him. He brought them back to Tarhun, his father, and Tarhun took back for himself the heart and his eyes.

(§23', A iii 20'-28') When he was rendered healthy in his body as formerly, he went to the sea[52] finally in ba[t]tle. When he gave battle to him, he had finally defeated him, the snak[e], and the son of Tarhun was with the snake, and he called up to heaven, to his father.

---

[51] The Staff could be the ritual implement that we know symbolized Zaliyanu.

[52] The Black Sea.

(§24', A iii 29'-33') "Include me too! Don't have mercy on me!" So, Tarhun killed the snake and his son,[53] and here now, that one, Tarhun [. . .]

(We return to the story frame again.)

(§25', A iii 34'-35') Thus Kell[a, the anointed priest of the Storm God of Nerik]: "When the gods [. . .]

(Column iii of exemplar A breaks off before paragraph end and a gap follows. Kella now explains why the town of Tanipiya receives cult disbursements and about the cult place for Mount Zaliyanu at a particular spring. Anatolian cult places often combined worship for a male mountain divinity and a female spring divinity, who may be the goddess Tazzuwasi mentioned here.)

(§26", D iv 1'-4') They made the [forem]ost god[s the hi]ndmost [ ], and the [hi]ndmost they made the foremost gods.

(§27", D iv 5'-7', A iv 1'-3') The provisions of Zaliyanu are a lot and his wife, (that) of Zaliyanu, Zashapuna, is greater than the Storm God of Nerik.

(§28", D iv 8'-10', C iv 1–4, A iv 4'-7') Thus the gods to the anointed priest Tahpurili: "When we go to the Storm God of Nerik, where shall we sit down?"

(§29", D iv 11'-16', C iv 5–10, A 8'-13') Thus the anointed priest Tahpurili: "When you sit down on the basalt throne, and when the anointed priests draw the lot, which anointed priest holds Mount Zaliyanu—the basalt throne lies above the spring—`and he will sit down there."

(§30" A iv 14'-17', D iv 17'-19', C 11'-14') All the gods will arrive there, and they will draw the lot. Of all the gods of Kastama, Zashapuna is greatest.

(§31", A iv 18'-21', D iv 20'-25', C iv 15'-17') Also, because she is his wife, (that) of Zaliyanu, (and) Tazzuwasi is his concubine, these three men[54] remain in Tanipiya, and a field is returned by the king.

(§32", A iv 24'-28', C iv 20–23) A field (the size of) six *kapanu*s, a gar[den] (the size of) one *kapanu*, a house and a threshing floor, three houses (for) the slave[s]. But, it is [on] a tablet. I also have reverence for the w[ord]s, and I said these.

(Colophon)

(§33", A iv 29'-32') First tablet, finis[hed], of the word of Kella, the anointed priest. Pihaziti, [scribe,] before Walwaziti, overseer of the scr[ibe]s, wrot[e] (it).

3.4.b. Hurro-Hittite Narrative Song: *Kumarbi Cycle*

The narrative tradition to which the *Kumarbi Cycle* belongs was brought by the Hurrians to Anatolia and then adopted by the Hittite court, where scribes wrote down both Hurrian and Hittite versions. The *Song of Release* (Part 4, document 2) also belongs to this group. These texts represent an oral-derived tradition that could be performed in either Hurrian or Hittite, which amalgamated Mesopotamian, Syrian, and Hurrian beliefs and motifs. When it was adapted to Hittite interests, some of its main characters were replaced by Anatolian equivalents, such as "Ishtar" (Hurrian Shawushka), who was replaced by Anzili, and the

---

[53] The referent of "his" is ambiguous: has the man become the son of the snake, now that he has entered his household?

[54] In other words, the priests of the three gods.

Hurrian Storm God Teshub (*Teshshub*), who was replaced by Hittite and Luwian Tarhun(t) (see his smiting image in Figure 6).

This set of texts has at least four parts, three of which are extant, telling of the Storm God's rise to power and subsequent battles to retain kingship in heaven. The first member, the *Song of Birth* (previously labeled as the "Song of Kingship in Heaven" or the "Song of Kumarbi" by scholars, before we learned its original title), describes the conception and birth of the Storm God and other members of his generation. We are missing the second part, the *Song of the Sea*, describing the Storm God's battle with the Sea, although we know its plot from a summary in another text. The Sea remains a key ally of Kumarbi, the Storm God's "mother," as he strives to remove the Storm God from power by creating new sons in the *Song of Hedammu* and the *Song of Ullikummi*. The cycle has parallels with Mesopotamian creation stories (e.g., *Enuma Elish*, Part 1, document 1), with the Ugaritic *Baal Cycle* (document 3.5.a), with Hesiod's *Theogony* (Part 1, document 5), and also with Caucasian folk tales. Its connections with the Anatolian *Illuyanka* myth are also discussed in the introduction to that story (document 3.4.a).

The Song of Birth

This narrative sets the stage for the Storm God's subsequent battles with the **chthonic** god Kumarbi, telling of his bizarre conception, when Kumarbi bites off the genitals of Anu ("Heaven"), and his birth from Kumarbi's "good place." Several other divine beings are also born from Anu's sperm, including the river Tigris (Aranzah) and the Storm God's brother and vizier Tashmishu, also known as Suwaliyatt, who come out of the mountain on which Kumarbi spits out the sperm. The birth of Shawushka (Anzili), the Storm God's sister, is also mentioned, if we take "the Powerful One" in §13' as an epithet applying to her. (Indeed, the name Shawushka means "powerful one" in Hurrian.) Only the first tablet of the multi-tablet work was preserved, and the text is very fragmentary towards its end, but we can see that the birth of two other beings is described, coming from Earth, who possibly was impregnated by the Storm God's Wagon, the constellation Ursa Major, which is drawn by the bulls Sherish and Tilla.

(The song opens by addressing the Former Gods, who have been deposed and sent underground by the Storm God. The poet lists them by name and calls upon them to listen to his story of how the Storm God was born.)

(§1, A i 1–4) [I sing of Kumarbi, father of the gods.] Let them who are the [F]o[r]mer Gods, [. . .], the powerful [Form]er Gods listen. Let Na[ra, Napshara, Mink]i, Ammunki listen, let Amme[z]zadu, [Alulu,] father (and) mother of [X],[55] listen.

(§2, A i 5–11) Let [Enlil (and) Abad]u, father (and) mother of Ish[h]ara, listen. Let Enlil [(and) Ninli]l, who are powerful (and) ete[r]nal gods [below] and [ab]ove, [. . .] and [the S]hining One listen. Long ago, i[n f]ormer years, Alalu was king in

---

[55] I use X to indicate a single missing noun or verb, when it can be assumed.

heaven. Alalu was on the throne, and Powerful Anu, their foremost, (that) of the gods, stood before hi[m], and he kept bow[i]ng down at his feet, and he kept putting drinking cups in his hand.

(§3, A i 12–17) As just nine years were counted off, Alalu was king in heaven, and in the ninth year Anu [w]ent in batt[le] against Alalu. He defeated him, Alalu, and he ran away before him, and he went down into the dark earth. He went down into the dark earth, while Anu seated himself on the throne. Anu was sitting on the throne, and powerful Kumarbi kept giving him to drink. He kept bowing down at his feet and putting drinking cups in his hand.

(§4, A i 18–24) As just nine years were counted off Anu was king in heaven, and in the ninth year Anu went in battle against Kumarbi.[56] Kumarbi, the seed of Alalu, went in battle against Anu, and Anu was no longer able to withstand the eyes of Kumarbi. He broke away from Kumarbi and from his hands. He ran, Anu, and he set off for heaven. Kumarbi assaulted him from behind, and he grabbed Anu (by) the feet, and he dragged him down from heaven.

(§5, A i 25–29) He bit his butt-cheeks and his manliness fused with Kumarbi's heart like bronze.[57] When Kumarbi swallowed down the manliness of Anu, he rejoiced, and he laughed. Anu turned back to him and began to say <to> Kumarbi, "Did you rejoice before [yo]ur heart because you swallowed my manliness?

(§6, A i 30–36) "Don't rejoice before your heart. I have put a burden inside your heart. First, I have impregnated you with Tarhun, the august one. Secondly, I have also impregnated you with the River Aran[z]ah, not to be resisted. Thirdly, I have also impregnated you with august Tashmishu. I have also placed three terrifying gods as burdens inside your heart. You will go and finish (the pregnancy?) by smashing the cliffs of Mt. Tassa with your head."

(§7, A i 37–41) When Anu finished speaking, he we[nt] up to heaven and he concealed himself. [K]um[arbi], the wise king, spat forth from his mouth, he spat forth from his mouth s[pit and manliness] mixed together. What Kumarbi s[pat] forth, [M]t. Kanzura acce[pted] as a fearsome god.

(§8, A i 42–46) [Kuma]rbi, upset (?), [went to] Nipp[ur . . . he] went, and on the lordly . . . him [. . .] sat down, Kumarbi . . . not [. . .] [c]ounts off. The seventh month arriv[ed . . .] in his heart [. . .].

(Gap of about 45 lines. Now the birth of the Storm God is described. Inside Kumarbi, he debates what his outlet will be.)

(§9', A ii 1–3) "[. . .] Kumarbi, and from his vigorous [. . .] come [f]orth, or come [f]orth from his 'swelling', or come forth from his 'good place'!"

(§10', A ii 4–15) A.GILIM[58] [began] to speak words before Kumarbi, in his heart, "May you be living, l[or]d of wisdom (and) the headwaters! When [. . .] to come out, Kumarbi, you bit below. Which ones [. . .]. Earth will give me her power. Heaven will g[ive] me [hi]s h[er]oism, and Anu will give me his manliness, and Kumarbi will

---

[56] Has the scribe slipped here, switching the two gods?

[57] Anu's white sperm and Kumarbi's red heart (equivalent to the ancient idea of the female's contribution to the fetus, menstrual blood) are equated with white tin and red copper, the components of bronze.

[58] An epithet of Tarhun.

give me his wisdom. Nara will give me his powerfulness, and Napshara will give me [his X]. En[li]l will give me his power, [his . . .], his fearsomeness, and his wisdom. [. . .] of all the heart, [and X will give me his/her X] and mind [. . .].

(§11', A ii 16–22) [. . .] they do [X] to the bull Sherish [. . .] Mount [. . .] one time [. . .] wagon [. . .] august . . . (will) give [(plural obj.)].[59] (")Let them stand [. . .] me. Suwaliya[t . . .]. When s/he gave me [. . .], s/he . . . me [. . .]."

(§12', A ii 23–28) A[nu] began to speak, "[. . .], come! I feared you [. . .], frowning (thing). You (will) do [X]. Which ones [. . .] I gave everything. [. . .] come, heaven[. . .]. They (will) do [X . . .] to him like a woman (obj.). Come forth with [. . .], likewise come, Tarhun, the city [. . .], come! [. . .] Come forth with thunder. [. . .] every[. . .] come! If it is good, [com]e from the 'good place'."

(§13', A ii 29–38) He began to speak to Kumarbi in his heart, "[. . .] they stand . . . the place. If I [come f]orth [from X,] he will break [the X thing]s like a reed. I[f] I come [f]orth [from] the 'good place' I will defile myself by that way also. In heaven, on earth [. . .]. I will defile myself inside by means of the ear. But, if I come forth from the 'good place' [. . .] l[ike] a woman (subj) [. . .] he will cry out (with birth pangs) for my sake. When I/me, Tarhun of Heaven, withi[n . . .] he decreed it/them within. S/he broke him, Kumarbi, [li]ke a stone, (at) his skull, and s/he came up from him by means of his skull, Powerful One, the heroic king."[60]

(Kumarbi is extremely upset at the birth of a rival and demands the child from the wise god Ea, a member of the earlier generation of the gods, so he can destroy Tarhun. Kumarbi attempts to swallow a basalt rock, perhaps given to him as a substitute for his son, but the hard rock injures his teeth and he is reduced to tears. Ea creates a cult for the rock, probably represented by a baetyl stone.)

(§14', A ii 39–54) When he went, he stood before Ea. Kumar[bi b]owed, and he fell down, Kumarbi. Because [of anger his X] was [a]ltered. [Kumarb]i so[ught] out the god Abundance. Before Ea [he began to] speak, "Give me the [ch]ild. I will eat [hi]m up. Which woman to me [doe]s [X]. And which ones to me, Tarhun (obj.) [. . .] I will eat [u]p. Like [a brittle re]ed I will crus[h him]. You [did X . . .] I will wound (on the head) in front [. . . he d]ecreed [. . .] he fin[is]hed, Ea [. . .], ask! With his mind did he gather him up? [. . .] Kumarbi (obj.) [. . .], Ea (subj.)." [He began] to l[ook] at him. Kumarbi began to eat [. . .], but the [basal]t [broke off/damaged] Kumarbi's teeth in his mouth. [W]hen his teeth in his mouth were [broken/injured . . .], he began to weep.

(§15', A ii 55–70) [. . . Kum]arbi (subj.). [He began to] spea[k] words, "I was afraid of [X . . .] I will do [X . . .]." Like old age Kumarbi (subj.) to/for [. . .]. To Kumarbi he began to speak, "Let them call [it X]. Let it lie in [X place]." And he threw the basalt in [. . . a hol]e. "Let [wea]lthy [men], heroes, (and) lords [sac]rifice cattle [(and) sheep] to you, and let poor men make offerings with [meal] to you. Is/are it/they not like [. . .]-ness? What [. . .] Kumarbi (obj.)

---

[59] Direct object. I indicate if the word is subject (subj.) or object (obj.) when relevant.

[60] The Powerful One may be the bi-gendered Shawushka (Anzili). Since the event is narrated in the past tense, the speaker does not seem to be discussing the future birth of the Storm God. I suggest that Shawushka has already been born out of Kumarbi's head, and that the Storm God should come from the same place. Other scholars assume that Tarhun is being referred to here.

from his mouth, no one afterwards [. . .] Kumarbi said, "[. . .] it happened in your body. They do [X . . .] to the lands up and down."

(§16', A ii 71–75) [The rich men] began to sacrifice with cattle (and) sheep, [while the poor men] began to make an offering [. . .] with [m]eal. They began to [. . .]. His skull like a garment [they closed up]. They closed up Kumarbi, his skull. From [the "good] place" heroic Tarhun came forth.

(§17', A ii 76–87) [. . . Fa]te-[Goddess]es. His "good place" like a garment [they closed up], his [pl]ace (obj.) like [. . .], the second place [. . .] and for the Aranzah River afterwards [. . .] it (the river?) went forth. [The Fate Goddesses] birthed it (the river) [. . . Kumarbi did X] like a woman of the [(child-)be]d. When [they did X] to Kumarbi, [a]nd for Mount Kanzura [. . . , the Fate Goddesses birthed] it, Mount Kanzura, [and Suwaliyat]t, the hero, came (out) [. . .] from the "good place" also he ca[me] forth, [. . .], and he [rejoic]ed, Anu [] he looks at [. . . begins] to [. . .].

(Column ii breaks off before paragraph end, fairly close to the bottom edge of the obverse side of the tablet. When the story continues, the Storm God is grown up and engaged in subduing the other gods. The Tutelary Deity of the Steppe, a god of wild spaces, conveys Tarhun's arrogant words to Ea, who is offended.)

(§19" A iii 2'-21') [. . . " . . .] we will [destr]oy. Anu (subj.) [. . .], and w[e will] destroy [. . .], and him, among you (pl.) [. . .]. The god Abundance [we will] destroy like [. . .] When [. . .] which [wor]ds he/you spoke [. . .] you will destroy Kumarbi [. . .] on my throne [. . .] Kumarbi (obj.). Who to us [. . .] Tarhun (obj.). But, when he grows up [. . .] someone [el]se they will make [. . .] leaves alone [. . . . A]bandon him [. . .] the lord (subj.) of wisdom (and) the headwaters [. . .] make [X] king! [. . .] of the word [. . .] on a shoe-sole[61] [. . .]." When Tarhun [heard the words . . .], he felt bad in his heart. [. . .] he said to the [bu]ll Sherish.

(§20", A iii 22'-29', B r. col. 1'-5') [. . .] they will come in battle against [. . .] he will [co]nquer, Kumarbi (subj.) also [. . . he] will rise [u]p, Ea (subj.) also, [. . .] the child and the Sun God (subj.) [. . .] in the time [. . .] I chased. Him [. . .] I [co]nquered, Zababa[62] (obj.) also [. . .]. When I [b]rought him to the city, now who (pl.) [. . .] will do battle again [agains]t me?"

(§21", A iii 30'-39', B r. col. 6'-16') The bull Sherish [spoke] in [turn] to Tarhun, "[. . .] my lord, why do [you] curse them? [. . .], the gods (subj.)? My lord, why [do you curse] them? [. . .], why do yo[u] curse Ea also? [. . .] he heard, Ea (subj.) [. . .] with . . . likewise not [. . . an]ything . . . (his) great mental [force] is as large as the land. For you forceful [. . .] will come. [. . .] you will go and not be a[ble] to lift your neck[63] [. . .] he will say [. . .] I [will do X]. He is wise [. . .] Ea (subj.) [. . .]

(Break of approximately 20 lines. The creation of a divine statue is apparently demanded, probably by Tarhun, which is offensive to Ea.)

(§23"', A iii 62"-63") [. . . fi]ghting [. . . E]a (subj.) [. . .] within [. . .]

(§24"', A iii 64"-66") "[X]-bird of [. . .] let him release inside (of it), and eyebrows [. . .] let him ma[k]e [X] out of gold."

---

[61] Perhaps we have here a reference to an act expressing humble obedience; cf. *Song of Ullikummi* 3, §11"'.

[62] A war-god.

[63] To "lift one's neck" means to be strong and proud.

(§25''', A iii 67''-72'') When Ea h[eard] the word[s], in his heart he felt bad. Ea began to speak in turn to the Tutelary Deity of the Steppe, "Don't you say curses repeatedly to me! He who cursed me, [. . .] curses me. You who [(verb) (object)] to me in turn, you curse me. Underneath a pot of beer [(subject?) (verb)], that pot boils over."

(Column iii ends. There is a large gap before the text picks up again in the second half of column iv. Another set of births is described, with the reward given to the messenger who brings the news to Ea. How this relates to the activities or Tarhun is unclear.)

(§26'''', A iv 1'-5') [. . .] he d[oes X . . . W]agon [. . . wit]h the Wagon [. . .]

(§27''', A iv 6'-16') [When] the sixth [mon]th came, the Wagon [. . .] the manli[ness] of the Wagon [. . .] the Wagon [went?] back to the city A[bzu . . .]. He took [wis]dom to his mind [. . .] Ea, lord of wis[dom . . .] did [X]. But Earth set [off] to Abzu [. . . kn]ows. And Ea, [lord of] wisdom, [c]ounts [the months]. The first month, the [second month, the third month went]. The fourth [mo]nth, the fifth month, the sixth month went. [The seventh month], the eighth [m]onth, the ninth month went. The tent[h] month [arrived]. In the tenth month Earth [began to] cry out.

(§28''', A iv 17'-27') When Earth cried out [. . . s]he gave birth to [two] children. A messenger went. [. . .] he approved on [h]is throne, E[a . . .] he brough[t] the fine word: "[. . .] Earth h[as] borne two children [. . .]." Ea [he]ard the words. To him [. . .] by [mo]uth the mess[enger . . .] who went, [. . .] the king ga[v]e gifts. To him a garment [for his] b[ody . . .]. To him a pull-over garment for his chest [. . .], and an *ipantu*-garment of silver fo[r the mes]senger. Around h[is] middle he wind[s X garment].

(Colophon)

(§29'''', A iv 28'-35') First tablet of the Song of Birth, not finished. Hand of Ashapala, son of Tarhuntassa, grandson of Kuruntapiya, and great-grandson of War-siya, student of Ziti. This tablet (from which I copied) was damaged. I, Ashapa<l>a, wrote it in the presence of Ziti.

Song of Hedammu

This story must have been popular among Hittite scribes, since there are many copies and/or versions extant. Although there are only fairly small, discontinuous fragments, the basic outline of large parts of the plot can be made out: Kumarbi decides to create a rival to Tarhun and arranges a marriage between himself and the daughter of the Sea God, Shertapshuruhi, the product of which is the ravenous sea snake Hedammu. Kumarbi attempts to conceal his son from Anzili and Tarhun and arranges for a nursemaid, provided by the Sea, but somehow Anzili spies the monster and reports the existence of a rival to her brother Tarhun. Anzili is called on to seduce the monster and goes to the seaside to show him her beautiful naked body and administer some type of potion to him. What we do not know is how the story ends, although we assume that the sister–brother team were successful in vanquishing Hedammu.

Nor do we know how the story begins. One tablet, Fragment 2, shows that, in this version, at least an entire tablet's worth of action occurs before the betrothal of Shertapshuruhi to Kumarbi. This tablet starts *in medias res* with the marriage discussion between the Sea and Kumarbi. It may be that in this version the entire plot of the conflict between the Sea and Tarhun was told as a preliminary to the story of Hedammu's creation.

If the assignments of the fragments to various tablets provided in the electronic concordance of Hittite texts (Konkordanz der hethitischen Texten) are correct, two of the tablets tell versions of the story about Hedammu that are quite different from each other. In one, "Version X," almost an entire tablet was devoted to the seduction scene(s) involving Hedammu and Anzili. In the other tablet, "Version Y," the seduction scene was considerably more brief, leaving room for a discussion involving Ea, who serves as the elder among the gods, trying to impress upon Kumarbi and Tarhun the harmful consequences of their conflict on humans and therefore the gods (who depend upon their offerings); it would also include a meeting between Kumarbi and the Sea.

Since research establishing the relationship of the various fragments and copies or versions to each other is ongoing, the various fragments have not been interwoven here into a single coherent narrative. First a scene is presented that could precede the betrothal scene, referring to a (verbal) conflict between Kumarbi, Tarhun, and Ea. (In fact, this scene could belong to a later stage, in which Hedammu is already alive, as Version Y, §§6²–7² shows.) The betrothal scene, which appears at the beginning of the tablet, is presented next, along with the close of its tablet. Then, scenes that seem to occur directly after Hedammu's birth, but before Anzili administers the potion to Hedammu, are presented. After these fragments, those belonging to the tablet with "Version Y" follow, then those from the tablet presenting "Version X."

Fragment 1[64]

(This scene provides the motivation for Kumarbi to create Hedammu. He ruminates on how he is being insulted among the gods, and possibly among humans, and thinks that if he could create a rival to Tarhun, he would be able to preserve his prestige.)

(1, §1' A 1'-2') [. . .] when/if [. . .]

(1, §2' A 3'-9') Kumarbi [began to speak] words be[fore his mind], "Me, Kumarbi . . . would [. . .], if in the place of assembly [. . .] heatedly, if he perhaps struck me, Ea [. . .] king of wisdom would [. . .]. If humankind perhaps [. . .] Ea also foremost [. . .]."

(1, §3' A 10'-19') Kumarbi [began to] sp[eak] to before his mind, "Me, Kumarbi, son of A[lalu . . .], but to me Ammezzadu (wife of Alalu) [. . . ."] And, among the gods Kumarb[i . . . I]f for Tarhun a riva[l . . .] for Tarhun, heroic (subj.) [. . .] would [. . .] he eats/will eat [. . .]

(The fragment breaks off before the paragraph ends.)

Fragment 2[65]

(Exemplar A consists only of the beginning of column i and the end of iv. It opens with the scene in which the betrothal of Kumarbi to Shertapshuruhi is discussed. The close of the tablet suggests a scene of violence. Does it describe the depredations of Hedammu? His birth and early upbringing would have been described in the lost intervening sections.)

[64] 1.A = KUB 33.110 1'-2'.

[65] 2.A = KBo 26.70 + KUB 33.109 + KUB 33.94; B = KUB 43.65.

(2, §1' B 1'-5') [. . .] awa[y . . .]. "They ate him/it. [. . .] d[id] not fall on the ground [. . .], but they ate him/it up. [. . .] s/he wen[t] under the [ear]th."

(2, §2' A i 1–15, B 6'-9') [The Sea] heard. [His mind rejoi]ced [inside]. [He pu]t his foot [. . .] on a s[tool]. They put a rhyton in his hand for the Sea. The grea[t Sea began to] spe[ak] words in turn to Kumarbi, "[To u]s the matter is good, Kumarbi, [fathe]r [of] the gods. Come to me on the seventh day, to my house, [. . .] my daughter [She]rtapshuruhi (obj.), and [she is . . .] in length and in [wi]dth she is one DANNA.[66] Her, [Sh]ert[ap]shuruhi, [you will drink] like sweet milk." When Kumarbi heard, [his mind] rejoiced [in]side, and when night time arrived [. . . . They] led [fo]rth the great Sea from Ku[ma]rbi's house with [. . .], *arkammi*-drums, and bronze g[*algaltur*]*i*-cymbals, and with (toasts from) bronze rhyta. They led him away [t]o his house. I[n his hous]e he sat on a beautiful chair. The Sea looked forward to Kumarbi('s visit) on the seventh day.

(2, §3' A i 16–18) Kumarbi beg[an] to speak [words] to his vizier, "Mukishan[u, my vizier, which wor]ds [I speak] to y[ou, hold your ear cocked to my words . . .]

(Column i breaks off before paragraph end.)

(2, §4' (A iv 1'-8') [. . .]s [. . .] Sea [. . .] strike[. . .] drag[. . . with]in [. . .], but [. . .]

(Colophon)

2, §5''' (A iv 9''-10'') [. . . Song of He]da[mmu . . .] First tablet, no[t finished.]

(The tablet number in the colophon must be a mistake; the tablet starts in the middle of a scene.)

Fragment 3[67]

(This fragment belongs before the scene in which Kumarbi decides to consult with the Sea over the choice of a nurse for his child, following the order of events of Song of Ullikummi *[1, §§8''-9''], in which, as soon as Ullikummi is born, he is dandled on his father's knee, then the question of a nurse for him is pondered. It appears that Hedammu was born in the house of his grandfather [which makes sense for a sea monster who must remain immersed in his natural element], for Kumarbi goes down to the Sea to meet him, after rewarding the messenger who reports the event to him [cf.* Song of Birth *§28'''].)*

(3, §1' A 1'-5', B 1'-5') [. . .] s/he wen[t . . .] t[o] Kumarbi [. . .] from the pillar [. . .]. S/he to Kumarbi [. . .]. The words of the [S]ea [. . .] likewise [r]emem11ber[. . .]

(3, §2' A 6'-10', B 6'-9') [W]hen Kumarbi heard [the wor]ds [of] the S[ea . . .] the messenger (obj.) seven ti[mes . . .] for him a wreath [. . .] gold [. . .] Kumarbi (subj.) the mes[senger . . .] downwards secretl[y . . .]

(3, §3' A 11'-16', B 10'-12') [Kumar]bi came dow[n] to the Sea. [They] ga[ve] him to eat (and) to drink [. . .] s/he lifted the boy. [On] the k[nees] of Kumarbi [. . .] him. [Kumarbi] for himself the boy (obj.) [. . .]

(Fragment breaks off before paragraph end.)

---

[66] One DANNA = 1,500 meters.

[67] 3.A = KBo 26.80; B = KBo 57.230 + FHL 25.

Fragment 4[68]

(In this scene, Kumarbi hopes to set up a location in Nippur where he can discuss the raising of his child with the Sea without being overheard by Anzili in Nineveh or Tarhun in Kummi.)

(4.1, §1', A ii 1'-6') [. . . s/he] come[s . . .] would [. . .] snake [. . .] s/he did [X . . .] s/he did [Y].

(4.1, §2', A ii 7'-14') [. . .] The Sea for himself [. . .], and for him/her [. . .], and . . . forth [. . . (pl. obj.) . . .] s/he [m]oved [. . . heave]n a[nd] earth [. . .]

(4.1, §3', A ii 15'-16') [. . .] s/he [sear]ches [. . .] s/he went.

(Column ii breaks off before paragraph end.)

(4.1 §4", A iii 1'-2') [. . .] s/he went [i]n the temple.

(4.1, §5", A iii 3'-12') [Kumarbi] began to speak [words to] his [vizi]er, ["Muk-ishanu, my vizier,] go in the [t]emple [of Nippur . . . drive away snakes], and drive (them) away from [. . .], from the walls. [. . .] drive (them) away from the pegs (and) from the walls [t]o [release the walls], drive (them) away from [X . . .], but [which windows are facing] Kummi, let them be closed, [and which doors] are fac-ing [Nineveh, let them be shut off] with a cloth of Byblos, let Anzili of Nineveh not he[a]r [this matter, and inside of the house] prepare [a l]ot [to eat (and) to drink. Call] the great S[ea]. I will give [the boy into the care] of a nurse."

(4.1, §6", A iii 13'-16') [Mukishanu hear]d [the words]. He promptly [stood] u[p . . .] the nether go[ds . . . . He entered the temple of Ni]ppur [. . .] bronze knife [. . .]

(4.2, §1', A 1'-15') [. . .] he did [X. . . . snak]es from the foundations [. . .] from the [wa]lls t[o] release [. . .] h[e dr]ov[e away], and from [X], from the peg(s), fr[om] the ceiling [he d]rove away [. . .], and from the foremost [X] they did [X, a]nd . . . fort[h . . .] the *azupanku*s with wo[oden . . .], a[nd whic]h windows we[re] fac-ing [Kum]mi, [they] were closed up, and which [doors] and [window]s were facing Nineveh, they shut [off with a cloth] of Byb[los], and inside of the house he [prepa]red [a lot] to eat (and) [to] drink, and [he] fill[ed] vessels with wine-beer, and t[hey] pil[ed] with bread the laid [tab]les. [Muk]ishanu car[ried] out the words of Kumarbi, [and] h[e] brought [ba]ck word to Kumarbi.

(4.2, §2', A 16'-19') [Mukish]anu [began to] spe[ak] words to Kumarbi, "Where you [sent] me, [I have] carr[ied out] everything [in that very spot], also [inside] of the house [I have prepared (things)] to eat (and) drink, [as] the will [of] my lord [had] commanded."

(4.2, §3', A 20'-23') [Kum]arbi [began to speak] words to Muki[shanu, " . . . do]es [X . . .] one time [. . .] festival [. . .]

(Fragment breaks off before paragraph end.)

Fragment 5[69]

(This fragment has been associated with the following one because of the mention of Duddula, a town in northern Mesopotamia. It appears to describe the establishment of a festival in the town, perhaps where Hedammu is raised; just as in the Song of Birth *the birth of Tarhun is followed by the establishment of a sacrifice [§§15'-16'].)*

---

[68] 4.1 A = KBo 26.94; 4.2 A = KBo 26.83.

[69] 5.A = KBo 26.82.

(5, §1 A, 1–13) [Kumarbi] be[g]an to [speak] words to [Mukishanu, his vizier], "Mukish[anu, my vizier], which [wor]ds I say to you, to my wo[rds hold your ear cocked. . . .] with *ussandur* [. . .], and [s]ixty young men from Duddula [. . .], and for the sixty young men weapons . . . with a snake [. . .], and [s]ixty young women from Duddula [. . .], and give them [j]ars of wine, of lapis lazuli. On the[ir] lip (i.e., the jars') [. . .] l[let the]m be [X]-ed, an[d] let the sixty young women [. . .] with [X] be seized. [. . .] to the great Sea [let them] b[ring them.]

(Fragment breaks off before paragraph end.)

Fragment 6[70]

(This scene describes the upbringing of Hedammu, who proves to have a monstrous appetite.)

(6, §1', A 1'-23') [. . . to Kuma]rbi . . . s/he did obeisance. [. . . ba]ck to Kummi, the cit[y . . .] and to Duddulla, the cit[y . . .] s/he did [X], but [in front] of [. . .] they raise Hedammu. They place [. . .] in oil [. . .]. They place him in water. [. . .]. Like an apple tree [they protect] him from the cold. They [gi]ve him to eat two thousand cows [and horses], and which goats and sheep [. . . the]y [give] him, there is no counting at all. He eat[s cows] and horses by the thousand. [He eats horr]ible lizards (and) frogs [. . .] forth like a spear, he does [X . . .]. In water he does [X . . .], and an IKU's worth[71] of fish, the "dog of the river" [. . .], and by the [thous]and he eats [. . .] like [hon]ey [he] swallow[s them] down, [li]ke [. . .] he laps [. . . he] finish[es] eating. [H]e does [X . . .]. He do[es Y . . .]

(Fragment ends at paragraph end.)

Fragment 7[72]

(Before this scene, Anzili seems to have learned of the existence of Hedammu. She arrives at a god's house, presumably her brother Tarhun's, too agitated to eat or drink, and warns him that a rival has been created. His destructive activities are mentioned. The god weeps at the news.)

(7, §1', C iii 1'-5') [. . .] ri[ver . . .] in fr[ont of . . .] gods [. . .] t[o] Tarhun [. . .]

(7, §2', C iii 6'-7') [. . .] god [. . .]

(Column iii of C breaks off.)

(7, §3", A 1'-15', C iv 1'-8', B 1'-6') [. . .] does [X . . .], Anzili (subj.), [queen of] N[ineveh . . . "Let them place a throne for her to sit], and let them [l]ay a table for her, to [e]at." And, [whi]le [they were speaking in this way, An]zili arrived at their side, but she [did] n[ot speak] to Tarhun. They placed a throne [for h]er [to sit]. She did not sit [. . . , and] they laid [a table for her, to eat], but [she did n]ot reach forth. They [offere]d [her a cup], but she d[id] not set her lip (to it), [the queen of] Ni[neveh . . . X] began to [spe]ak, "Why do [you] not ea[t . . . , why] do you not drink?" "My lord, [. . .] eating, and what drinking . . . not [. . .] the Sea (obj.) again[st] the gods . . . they did [X . . .]. He in heaven [(and) in] eart[h . . .]. In the sea, what riv[al (obj.) . . .] by [what s]ign will I speak of [him]?" She described Hedam[mu . . .], and Anzili recounted [. . .] (about) him.

---

[70] 6.A = KUB 8.67.

[71] One IKU = 15 meters, but its value as a measurement of area is unknown.

[72] 7.A = KBo 19.112; B = KBo 19.112A + KBo 60.323; C = KBo 26.142.

(End of column iv for C.)

(7, §4", A 16'-19') [. . .] he heard Anzili. [. . . " . . . he (i.e., Hedammu)] ravages completely. [. . . " . . . And, hi]s [tears flowed] forth [like] canals. [. . .]

(Fragment breaks off before paragraph end.)

Fragment 8[73]

(Here Tarhun seems to have heard that an enemy has come into being and is oppressing the land because of his great appetite. The Storm God meets with Kumarbi in a hospitable setting to ask about him. Kumarbi apparently is just returning from a visit to the Sea, where he has refused to address a matter put before him.)

(8, §1', A 1'-14', B 1'-8') [. . .] awa[y . . .]. Him the lor[d . . . w]ord hear[. . . , p]ower [. . .] they sent down in the Dark Earth [. . .] Kumarbi (subj.) did [X] with regard to the matter of the watch [. . .]. He was simply silent. [Be]fore hi[m . . .] he did not speak. Kumarb[i] went [u]p from the Sea. Kumarbi placed his feet up [. . .]. Tarhun, heroic king [of Kummi], went before him. [. . .] began to speak to Kumarbi, "[. . . father of the god]s, where were you [. . . wh]o is he, the enemy?"

(8, §2', A 15'-17') [K]umarbi [beg]an [to speak] words in re[ponse] to Tarhun, "From Mt. Hurshana [. . . a s]nake (obj.) [. . .]

(The fragment breaks off before paragraph end. A small [?] gap follows.)

(8, §1', A 18"-20") [. . .] like a mill[st]one [. . .] i[n] the lands [. . .] Hedammu (obj.) [. . .]

(8, §2', A 21"-29") [. . . began to speak words] in tur[n] to the Sea, [" . . .] to him because of hunger [. . .] s/he arrives. To hi[m . . . a]sk! But, if to hi[m . . .]. But you . . . it . . . m[e . . .] he eats a cow [. . .] he eats [. . .]s [by the] thous[and . . .]

(Fragment breaks off before paragraph end.)

"Version Y"[74]

(This set of five passages consists of a piece of columns i and ii from the obverse and a larger piece of iv from the reverse from one tablet, which are filled out by eight other fragments containing parallel passages. The narrative represents a fairly succinct version of the story. First there is a hospitality scene, in which the guest is so upset by the news that he or she refuses to enjoy the food and drink served. Then, Anzili apparently spots Hedammu for the first time and is afraid. In the next passage Ea scolds Tarhun and Kumarbi for the damage they do to mankind. As in Atrahasis (Part 2, document 1.a), humans are envisioned as necessary to the gods. Then, Kumarbi arranges a secret meeting with the Sea. The next passage humorously presents the complaints of humans buffeted by the meteorological manifestations of the conflict among the gods. The final scene is Anzili's seduction of Hedammu, who is so aroused at the sight of her nakedness that he ejaculates copiously, and his sperm [which may be imagined as frog eggs] appears to blanket the land.)

---

[73] 8.A = KUB 8.64 (+) KBo 26.79; B = KBo 26.109.

[74] A = KBo 19.109 + KBo 109a (+) KBo 26.72 + Bo 6404 + KUB 33.84; B = KBo 56.6 + KUB 8.65; C = KUB KUB 33.100 + KUB 36.16; D = KUB 33.103; E = KUB 33.116; F = KUB 33.122; G = KUB 26.71 + KUB 12.65; H = KBo 26.73; I = KBo 19.111. For "Version Y" and "Version X" I use superscript numbers instead of the convention of a raised stroke or strokes after the paragraph number to indicate a break in the numbering.

(Y, §1¹, A i 1'-6') [. . .] 3 DANNAs [. . .] tooth [. . .] everything [. . .]

(Y, §2¹, A i 7'-14', B i 1'-8') [. . .] in front of the [X]-s [. . .] and [. . .], but [. . . doe]s [X . . . hea]ven and earth [. . . eve]rything [. . .], but s/he stepped [. . .] under the Black Earth [. . .]. When s/he arrived under the dark earth [. . . s/he did not eat yet], nor did s/he drink anyth[ing . . .]. The wind e[a]ts it, the peg.

(Y, §3¹, B i 9'-14', A i 15'-18') [. . .] up to Enli[l . . .] s/he does [not] eat [ye]t, [nor] doe[s] s/he eat [anything . . .] no one (subj.). [. . . tong]ues . . . h[uma]nkind [. . .] under the sea [. . .] to Hedammu [. . .] he devours.

(Y, §4¹, B i 15'-27', A i 19'-20') [. . .] Anzili [of Nineveh . . .] goes [a]way . . . the go[d . . .] did [X]. The sea [. . .] does [X . . . ,] he eats. When the god [. . .], s/he [began] to speak before his/her mind, [" . . . . W]hich god from under the sea [. . .]. The empty cities [. . .]. While Hedammu [. . .]. But, Anzili [went] f[orth] to the sea [. . . Hedammu] saw Anzili. [Hedammu . . .]. Heaven upwards [. . .] "I fear them, the s[nakes . . .]."

(Exemplars A and B break off before paragraph end. A gap follows before passages from other fragments pick up the narrative.)

(Y, §5², C iii 1'-7') [. . .] b[asalt-]stone [. . .] off[ering . . .] mountains [. . . so] meone some[thing . . . s/he look[s a]t [. . . spins] like the wheel [of a pot]ter.

(Y, §6², D ii 1–8, C iii 8'-16', E ii 1'-8') [Ea], king of wisdom, spoke among the gods. [Ea] began to [spe]ak, "Why do y[ou (pl.)] destroy it, [mankind?] They will not give offerings to the gods, and they will not burn cedar incense for us. [A]nd, [if] you destroy mankind, they will no long[er worship] the gods. Also, no one will offer [thick-brea]d (and) libation to us. And, Tarhun, heroic king of Kummi, will go and grasp the plow [himse]lf. And, Anzili and Hebat will go and grind the [grind]stone themselves."

(Y, §7², D ii 9–16, C iii 17'-26') [E]a, king of wisdom, began to speak to Kumarbi, "What is the reason why [y]ou, Kumarbi, purs[ue] mankind for evil? Doesn't mankind make pile(s) of grain, and don't [the]y pr[om]ptly off[er] (it) to you, Kumarbi? Also, inside the temple, in joy, to you alone, Kumarbi, father of the gods, they promptly made offerings. Don't they make offerings to Tarhun, the canal inspector of ma[nk]ind? And, don't they mention me, Ea the king, by name? [. . .] you put the wisdom of all after [. . .] the blood (and) tears of mankind [. . . K]umarb[i . . .]

(Both exemplars break off before paragraph end. A gap follows.)

(Y, §8³, F ii 1'-5', E iii 1'-3', G iii 1') *(Kumarbi tells Mukishanu to convey the following message to the Sea:)* [. . . " . . . make your way away] under [river] (and) earth. [Let Kusuh[75]], Istanu,[76] [and the gods] of the earth [not see you]. Go up to Kum[arbi] under [river (and) eart]h."

(Y, §9³, F ii 6'-9', G iii 2'-4', E iii 4"-8") [Mukishanu] heard [the wor]ds. He p[romptly stood] up. [He] made his way away under river and earth. Kusuh, Istanu, and the gods of the earth did [not s]ee him. [He] went down to the Sea.

(Y, §10³, G iii 5'- 16', F iii 1–8, E iii 10"'-14", A ii 1'-2') Mukishanu began to speak in turn the words of Kumarbi to the Sea, "Come, the father of the gods, Kumarbi, calls you, and for which matter he calls you, it is an urgent matter. Come

---

[75] The Moon God.

[76] The Sun God.

promptly. Come away under river and earth. Let not Kusuh, Istanu, and the gods of the earth see you." When the great Sea heard the words, he stood up promptly, and he w[ent] away down by the path of earth and of river. He completed it at one go. He came up to Kumarbi from below, from the pillar(?), from the earth, to [his] throne. They set a throne for the Sea, for him to sit. The grea[t Sea] sat on his throne. He [s]ets a laid table for him, t[o] eat. And the cup-bearer give[s] him sweet wine to drink. Kumarbi, the father of the gods, and the great Sea [s]i[t]. They eat (and) drink their fill.

(Y, §11³, G iii 17'-22', H 1'-5', A ii 3'-7') Kumarbi began to [s]peak words to his vizier, "Mukishanu, my vizier, which words I speak to y[ou], hold your ear cocked to my words. Draw shut the doorbo[lt . . .], and thro[w to] the (door)-bars [. . .] in the palace [. . .] like a [s]cent le[t] him/her/it [not] do [X]. Word[s . . .] like a *puspusi* (obj.) [. . .] poor men [. . .]"]

(Y, §12³, H 6'-8', G iii 23'-24', A ii 8'-10') Mukish[a]nu [heard] the word[s]. He prompt[ly stood . . .] he began to [X]. The doo[rb]olt (subj.), the p[eg . . . b]ronze withi[n . . .]

(All passages break off before paragraph end. A gap follows before column iv of exemplar A picks up the narrative.)

(Y, §13⁴, D iii 1'-7') [. . . " . . .] strikin[g . . . . B]ut, the lightni[ng] and [th]under of Tarhun and Anzili, with the water, is not going away from us yet, s[o . . .] we are not able to go yet. Our knees keep [s]haking, and our heads spin like the [whe]el of a potter, and our cocks are limp!"

(Bottom of column iii reached in D.)

(Y, §17⁷, A iv 3'-10', I iv 1–8) [. . .] in [heave]n the clouds [. . .] from the [powe]rful waters [. . .] s/he did. Whe[n Anzil]i, the queen of Nineveh thought it good, she sprinkled love, *sahi*, and [*parnull*]*i*[77] in the powerful waters, and the love, *s[ahi]*, (and) *parnulli* dissolved in the waters. When Hedammu tasted the sc[e]nt, the beer, [a sweet] dream seized victorious Hedammu, h[is] mental powers. He was dreaming like an ox or an ass. [. . .] he recognized [no]thing, and he was eating his fill of frogs and lizards.

(Y, §18⁷, A iv 11'-19', I iv 9–10) [Anzil]i began to speak to Hedammu, "C[ome] up again, fr[om] the powerful [water]s [. . .] come straight up, and cutting through the middle." 90,000 [. . .] pulls . . . the place from the earth, and Anzili holds forth [before Hedammu her naked limb]s. Hedammu (subj.) [. . .] his manliness springs forth. His manline[ss]. He impregnates repeatedly [(pl. obj.) . . .] 130 towns [. . . he] did [X]. And, with his belly/embryo(s) . . . 70 towns [. . .] in . . . he finished off [(pl. obj.) . . .] heaps of heads he [h]eap[ed] up.

(Y, §19⁷, A iv 20'-25') [. . .] on the pedestal s/he was struck. Anzili, queen of Nineveh . . . in two [. . .] approached at the feet [of Hedam]mu [. . .], she was going in front of him, [Anzili, queen of Nineveh . . .] she [ap]proached, Anzili, while Hedammu behind her [. . .] when/like [. . .] he keeps pouring out with te[rrifying . . .]. Them on the ground, terrifying floods, [. . .] they do [X]. From the throne, down from the sea he went, Hedammu, victorious one [. . .] away [. . .] he went.

---

[77] *Sahi* and *parnulli* are two fragrant plant-based substances.

(Y, §20[7], A iv 26'-30') [Hedamm]u [bega]n [to speak] to Anzili, "Young woman, if to you lov[e . . .] lov[e . . .] give. Come in the strong [waters . . . . Anzili] began to speak in turn [to Heda]mmu. [. . . (pl. obj.)] like [. . .]

(Column iv breaks off before paragraph end.)

"Version X"[78]

(Most extant fragments of this tablet, preserved in six pieces that are extended by two fragments from other tablets with parallel passages, discuss activities involving Anzili and Hedammu. One passage mentions Hedammu and his mother, and the first fragments of another passage refer to songs being sung and obeisance being done, seemingly to Hedammu, since the intention is to soothe him. This scene may not involve Anzili, although it is consistent with how her activities are described elsewhere.)

(X, §1[1], B rev.[?] 1'-6', A i 1'-4') [..] s/he did [X]. S/he [. . .] w[e] (will) step [. . .] I (will) do [X . . .]. I (will) do [Y . . .] to Hedammu. If H[edamm]u (obj.) [. . .], but if Heda[mmu . . . m]y si[n].

(X, §2[1], B rev.[?] 7'-11', A i 5'-10') [When . . .] finished [speaki]ng, s/he [went] away [. . .], while [Anzil]i wen[t] into the bath-house. [. . .] she went in to bathe. She bathed herself [. . .] she did [X . . .], while with sweet fine oil she anointed herself. She [ador]ned [herself], and love was running after her as puppies do.

(X, §3[1], B rev.[?] 12'-16', A i 11'-16') [Anzili] began to speak [to Ninatta (and) K]ulitta, [" . . .] take the [*galgaltu*]*ri*-cymbals. [On] the shore of the sea with the *arkammi*-drum strike [on the right side], and on the [le]ft strik[e] the *galgalturi*-cymbals [. . .] fo[r] kingship [. . .]. [I]f perhaps [he] hear[s] our message [. . .] we will see him, when [. . .].

(X, §4[1], B rev.[?] 17'-18') [. . . Nina]tta [(and)] Kulitta [. . .]

(The fragment breaks off before paragraph end. In the following passage Hedammu may be discussing Anzili with his mother.)

(X, §5[2], A i 17"-19") [. . .] Hedammu . . . the Se[a . . .] Shertapsh[uruhi . . .]

(X, §6[2], A i 20"-26") [. . .] Hedammu [. . .] began to [. . . the h]eroic god (obj.) [. . .] fills [. . .] s/he did [X]. "My mother [. . .], but [y]ou [. . .]

(The fragment breaks off before paragraph end. The story continues with songs and attention paid to Hedammu and a seductive baring of breasts.)

(X, §8[4], C ii 1–8) [. . .] they keep singing [. . .] songs. [. . .] of [h]eaven (and) earth [. . .]s [. . . a]ll of them [keep] bowing. [Dow]n for him [. . .] they [strew p]ebbles (and *patturi*s [. . .] (her) breast(s) [. . .] does [X . . .] waters [. . .]

(X, §9[4], C ii 9, 10'-16') [. . .] s/he [. . .] did [X]. W[e] (will) go [. . .]s, a[nd] together [. . .]. S/he the mountains [. . .] we (will) sleep [. . .], and the [X (obj.)] soothe[. . .], and the fig (subj.) . . . him/her (obj.) [. . .]

(Column ii of C breaks off here, only two paragraphs into column ii, and there is a large gap before C picks up again as Anzili lures Hedammu with her naked body.)

(X, §10[5], C ii 1'-5') [. . .] trembl[e . . .]. Down for him [. . .]. Anzili [. . .]. Heda[mmu . . .] in the deep waters [. . .]

---

[78] A = KBo 26.74 (+) KBo 19.110 (+) IBoT 2.135 + KUB 36.57 (+) KBo 22.51 (+) KUB 8.66 + KUB 33.86 (+) KUB 33.85 + KBo 26.75; B = KUB 33.88; C = KUB 36.95.

(X, §11[5], A ii 6'-10', C iii 1'-6') When Hedammu does [X . . .]. Hedammu [. . . raised] his head from the wave. He saw Anzili. Anzili hel[d] up her naked limbs before [Hed]ammu.

(X, §12[5], A ii 11'-16', C iii 7'-18') Hedammu [began to] spea[k] to Anzili in turn, "Which god are you also? Are you no[t] afraid [. . .]?" In the sea [. . .]. For himself/ herself strik[e . . .]. For him lik[e] for an ox. [. . .] and not [. . .] we do [X . . .] spear . . . his penis within [. . .] the scent soothed [. . .] in the future a dream will not release [. . .] limbs away . . . spear [. . .] s/he does [X].

(C reaches the bottom of the column. The seduction scene appears to be turning violent in the following passage.)

(X, §13[6], A ii 17"-28") [. . .] everlast[ing . . .]. But, black/night [. . .] they (will) [d]ie. [. . . s/he] is/will be [a]ngry [. . .] You will die, you will perish [. . .] s/he goes/will go [. . .] they do not/will not do . . . [insid]e of the house. [. . .] The Fate Goddesses, the Great Goddesses [. . .] likewise did not d[o].

(X, §14[6], A ii 29"-43") Hedammu began to speak to [Anz]ili, "You, woman, go [. . .] far away, I will eat you up! [. . .] angry. It/them to me [. . .]

(Bottom edge of ii is reached.)

(X, §15[6], A iii 2'-14') [. . .] in the place [. . .] Nineveh (obj.) [. . .] people [. . .] I (will) brin[g]. [. . .] dried [. . .] Hedammu (subj.) [. . .]

(The fragment breaks off before paragraph end.)

(X, §17[7], A iii 16"'-22"') [H]edammu [began to] spea[k] words to Anzili, "What woman are you?" Anzili began to speak [in turn] to Hed[ammu], "I am an an[gry] young woman. For me foliag[e does X to] the mountains like *sharauwar*." She says it. Anzili [does] obeisance [. . .] to Hedammu. Him with the speech [. . .] she intoxicates.

(X, §18[7], A iii 23"'-30"') Hedammu [began to] spe[ak] to Anzili, "What woman are you? [Tell me] your name. I [. . .] say[. . .] t[hey] say [. . . " . . .] s/he [sa]id [. . .] "Up [. . .] run[. . .] above [. . .] Anzili [. . .]

(Column iii breaks off before paragraph end.)

(X, §20[8], A iv 1'-6') [. . .] we (will) [c]all as witness [. . . *parnul*]*li* (obj.) fro[m] the powerful [waters . . .] Hedamm[u . . .]

(The fragment breaks off before paragraph end.)

(X, §22[10], A iv 12"'-15"') [. . .] For us the head [. . .] within, the fig [. . . X] ten thousands s/he does/will not release [. . . s/he/it] spring[s].

(X, §23[10], A iv 16"'-19"') Hedammu (subj.) [. . .]. Of the [w]atch [. . .]

(Column iv breaks off before paragraph end.)

Song of Ullikummi

Once again Kumarbi creates another son to oppose the Storm God, this time from a rock. The new stone-like monster, Ullikummi (Hurrian for "destroy Kummi!"), will be immune to the tricks of Anzili. It appears that at first Ulli-kummi is successful against the Storm God and his allies, repelling a large force of gods, but the Storm God has recourse to the knowledge of Ea, gaining access to the primordial copper cutting tool, with which heaven and earth were sepa-rated, in order to cut the stone monster apart from the earth. The copper implement is analogous to the sickle used by Kronos to castrate Ouranus (Hesiod's *Theogony*, Part 1, document 5).

SOURCE: Translation is based on the transliteration by Rieken et al. (2009) of CTH 345 on the electronic Konkordanz der hethitischen Texten. Some unplaced fragments are omitted.

TABLET I

(1, §1, B i 1–8, A i 1–8) [I shall] s[ing of X, in whose [mi]nd [is X], and he takes wisdom in his mind, the head (and) father of all the gods, Kumarbi. Kumarbi takes wisdom with his mind, he who raises up an evil day. He takes evil for himself against Tarhun, and he raises a rival against Tarhun.

(1, §2, B i 9–20, A i 9–19) Kumarbi [takes] wisdom with his mind, and he lines it up like jewel bead(s). When Kumarbi took wisdom before his mind, he promptly rose up from his throne. He took his staff with his hand, [and] he put o[n his feet] the swift wind[s] as shoes. He set off from Urkesh, the city, and he arrived at the Cool Lake,[79] and when Kumarb[i . . . . I]n the Cool La[ke] a great cliff [l]ies. In length it is three DANNAs, [and] in width [it is . . . DANNAs] and half a DANNA. What it holds below, his desire sprang forth [to sleep with it]. He slept with the r[ock]. To it [. . .] his manliness withi[n]. He took it five times, [again] he took it ten times.

(1, §3, B i 21–22) [. . .] he [too]k that staff [. . .]

(Column i breaks off before paragraph end, with approximately 30–35 lines missing, before the beginning of column ii. At this point Kumarbi's child appears to be gestating, and Kumarbi's old ally, the Sea, is involved, along with the Sea's vizier Impaluri, although at the beginning of this section the Sea appears to have upset Kumarbi in some way and must placate him. It could be that the sea is again the place in which the fetus gestates.)

(1, §4′, A ii 1–8) [. . . Kumarbi], father of the gods, sits. [. . .] he saw Kumarbi. [. . .] he set off to the Sea.

(1, §5′, C ii 1–21, B ii 1–17, A ii 9–30) Impaluri began [to] speak [words] in turn to the [S]ea, "Kumarbi sits on his [th]rone, father of the gods." The Sea began to speak in turn to Im[pal]uri, "Impaluri, listen to these words from me. Go, emphasize them in front of Kumarbi. Go, say to Kumarbi, 'Why did you come against the house, angry? Trembling seized the house, and fear seized the slave women. Awaiting you, the cedar-incense is already broken, and awaiting you the stews are already cooked, and, awaiting you, [da]y and night the singers are holding [u]pright their lyres. Stand up! Come away to my house.'" Kumarbi stood up. Impaluri goes in front of him, and Kumarbi goes from his house. He set off, Kumarbi, and he went into the house of the Sea.

(1, §6′, C ii 22–37, B ii 18–30) The Sea spoke, "Let them place a stool for Kumarbi to sit, and let them place a table in front of him. Let them bring to h[im] to eat (and) to [d]rink, and let them bring beer for him to drink." The cooks brought stews, while the cupbearers brought sweet wine for him to drink. They drank once, they drank twice, they drank three times, they drank four times, they drank five times, they drank six times, they drank seven times. Kumarbi b[egan] to speak to Mukishanu, his vizier, "M[ukishanu], my [vizi]er, which matter I speak to you, hold

---

[79] Identified with Lake Van in far eastern Turkey.

[forth] your ea[r] to me. Take your staff with your hand, and put your shoes [on your feet]. G[o . . .]. In the waters [. . .]. Speak [these wo]rds in fro[nt of] the waters [. . . Ku]marbi[. . .]

(The column breaks off before paragraph end. When the story is continued in column iii, the time of childbirth has arrived. The Fate Goddesses, who were also called the Irsirra Goddesses, again serve as midwives. The child is given to the goddesses to be nurtured and placed upon the shoulder of Ubelluri, an Atlas-like figure, to grow up. His rapid growth, as a volcanic rock outcropping in the sea, is noticed by the gods.)

(1, §7", A iii 1'-9') [. . . w]hen/[i]f the nigh[t . . . the (time of the) wa]tch a[rrived . . . ar]rived [. . .] rock (subj.?) . . . the rock (obj.) [. . .] birt[h] him. [. . .] the rock (subj.) away [. . .] the child . . . Kumarbi . . . lig[ht . . .]

(1, §8", A iii 10'-25', E 1'-7') The [mid]wives birthed him. The Fate Goddesses, the G[reat] Goddess[es, lifted the child]. They bounce[d him] on [K]um[arbi's k]nees. [Kumar]bi beg[an] to amuse thi[s s]on. [He] be[gan] to sit him upright. He began to [g]ive [the child] a fine name. Kumarbi began to [sp]eak before [his] mi[nd], "What name [shall I give] him? Which child the Fate Goddesses, the Great Goddesses, gave to me, [he] sprang from my body like a spear. Com[e], let his name be Ullikummi. Let him go up to [kingsh]ip in heaven, let him crush flat Kummi, [the beau]tiful city, and let him strike Tarhun. Let him grind [him (i.e., Tarhun)] up like [c]haff, and let him pulverize him with his foot [like] an ant, and let him shred apart Tashmishu like a britt[le re]ed, and let him scatter all the gods down from [heaven] like birds, let him sha[t]ter them [like] empty vessels."

(1, §9", A iii 26'-36') When Kumarbi fi[nish]ed spe[akin]g words, he [began] to speak before his mind, "To [who]m shall I give him, this child? Who [will take] him for themselves, will treat [hi]m as a gift, [will do X], will [take] him into the [dark] earth? L[et] Istanu of [Heaven and Kus]uh [n]ot s[e]e him, and le[t] Tarhun, the [h]eroic king [of] Kumm[i], not [see him]. Let him not kill him. Let Anzili, queen of Nineveh, woman of inc[ant]ations, no[t] see him. Let her not shred him apart l[i]ke a brittle reed.

(1, §10", A iii 37'-45') Kumarbi began to speak to Impal[ur]i, "Impaluri, which word[s] I speak [to you], hold your ear c[o]cked to my words. Take your staff with your hand and pu[t] the swift winds o[n yo]ur [feet] as shoes. Go down to the Irsirra Goddesses and say in front of the Irsirra Goddesses these weight[y] words, 'Come, Kumarbi, father of the gods, cal[l]s you to the house of the gods. For which ma[tt]er he calls you, [you don't know it]. Come promptly!'

(1, §11", A iii 46'-48', C iii 1'-8') "[The Irsirra Goddess]es will take [him], the child. Those ones [will take] him [down into the dark] earth, and the Irsirra Goddesses [. . .] the heroes (obj.), eyes [. . .], and not the great ones [. . .]." [When] Impaluri [hear]d [the words, he took] his staff with his hand, he put [his shoe]s [on his feet. He wen]t [forth], Impaluri. [He] arrived at [the Irsirr]a [Goddesses.]

(1, §12", C iii 9'-19', B iii 2'-9') [Impaluri] began to [speak the wor]ds [in turn] to the Irsirra Goddesses, "Come, Kumar<b>i, father of the gods, [calls yo]u, and for which matter [he calls] you, you do not [know] it. Hurry! Come!" When [the Irs]irra Goddesses heard the words, [they hurried,] they [h]astened. They [rose up] from their thrones, and they completed it at one go, and they arrived [at] the side of Kumarbi. Kumarbi began to speak to the [I]rsirra Goddesses.

(1, §13", B iii 10'-19', C iii 20'-28', A iv 1'-5') "[T]ake this [child] and trea[t] him as a gift. Tak[e] him to the dark earth. Hurry, hasten. Place him as a spear on Ubelluri's right shoulder. In one day [l]et him grow a cubit, and in one month [le]t him grow an IKU, and whatever rock strikes his head, let his eyes be covered (against it)."

(1, §14", A iv 6'-12') When the Irsirr[a] Goddesses heard the [wo]rds, they took [the child] from Kumarb[i's k]nees, and the Irsir[ra] Goddesses lifted the child. They pressed [him] in [their] bosom like a garment. They lifted him [lik]e the wind[s]. They bounced him on Enlil's knees. [En]lil raised his eyes and see[s] the child. He was standing in f[ro]nt of the divinity, and his body was made of stone, of b[a]salt.

(1, §15", A iv 13'-18', D iii 1'-5') Enlil began to speak before [h]is [mi]nd, "Who is this child? Wh[om] have the Fate Goddesses, the Great Goddesses, raised again? Who will look [again] on the weighty battle[s] of the great gods? Of no one else, of Kumarbi alone is i[t], an [evi]l thing. As Kumarbi raised Tarhun, now against [him] this basalt rival [he has] rai[sed]."

(1, §16", A iv 20'-21', D iii 6'-7') When Enlil [finished spea]king the word[s, they placed] the child as a s[pear] on Ubelluri's right shoulder.

(1, §17", A iv 22'-26', D iii 8'-11') And, the basalt grows up. The powerful waters make him grow, and in one day he grows a cubit taller, and in one month he [g]rows an IKU taller, and whatever rock strikes his head, his eyes [ar]e [c]overed (against it).

(1, §18", A iv 27'-32', D iii 12'-17') When it go[t] to the fifteenth day, the stone was grown tall. He [sto]od l[ike] a spear in the sea up to his knees. He stuck out of the water, the stone. He is in height like [. . .]. The sea wraps around his waist like a garment. He s[h]oots up like a mushroom (?), the stone. In heaven above he reaches the temples and the *ku*[*n*]*tarra*-building.

(1, §19", A iv 33'-36', D iii 18'-22') Istanu [l]ooks [down] fr[om] heaven. He sees Ullikummi, [and] Ullik[ummi s]ees Istanu of [H]eaven. Istanu [began] t[o] speak [before] his [mind], "What god [. . .], rapidly (growing), [stands] in the sea? His limbs do not resemble [the X] of [g]ods."

(1, §20", A iv 37'-40', D iii 23'-26') Istanu of Heaven turned his ray[s]. He went forth to the sea. Whe[n] Istanu arrived at the sea, Istanu held his hand in front of his brow. [He saw U]ll[iku]mmi i[n the sea . . .], and because of anger his [X] was a[l]tere[d].

(1, §21", A iv 41'-50', C iv 1'-12', D iii 27'-38') [Whe]n Istanu [of] Heaven saw the god in [the se]a, Istanu for a second time [tur]ned bac[k] his rays. He set f[or]th [. . .]. He set out, down to Tarhun, [Istanu. When] he saw Istanu coming towards him, Tashmishu began [to] spea[k to] Tarhu[n], "Why is he coming, Istanu of Heaven, [king of] the land[s], and for what matter is he coming? It is an [important] matte[r]. It is [n]ot one to be cast aside. The struggle is weighty, [and] the battle is weighty. And, it is a ferment of heaven, and it is famine of the land and death." Tashmishu began to speak to Tarhun, "Let them place a throne for him to sit, and l[et the]m lay a table for him, for eating."

(1, §22", A iv 51'-54', D iii 39'-41') [W]hile they were speaking in this way, Istanu arrived [i]n [the house] to them. They placed a throne for him to sit, but he did not [sit, a]nd they laid a table for him, to eat, but he did not re[ac]h forth. They gave him a cup, but he di[d] not set his lip (to it).

(1, §23", A iv 55'-58') Tarhun began to speak in turn to Istanu, "Is the chamberlai[n b]ad, [wh]o placed [the throne], so that you didn't sit? Is the tab[le]-man bad, [who p]laced [the table], so that you didn't eat? Is the cupbearer ba[d], who gave [the cup], so that y[ou] didn't drink?"

(Colophon)

(1, §24", A left edge 1–2, C iv 13') First tablet, Song (of) Ullikumm[i, not finished . . .]

TABLET II

(The same hospitality scene involving Tarhun and the Sun God Istanu continues when the story is picked up in the second tablet.)

(2, §1', B i 1') [. . .] s/he/it is [. . .]

(2, §2', B i 2'-8') Tarhun in turn to [. . . said . . .] yo[u did] not eat. [. . .] f]in[e . . . in] turn [he] spok[e . . . awa]y [. . .]

(Exemplar B breaks off before the end of the paragraph.)

(2, §3", A i 1') [. . .] for [wh]ich matter [. . .]

(2, §4", A i 2'-13') [. . .] Tarhun heard. [Because of] ange[r . . .] his [X was alt] ered. Tarhun began to speak [in tur]n [to Istanu of Heaven, "]Let [the bread on the table] be [f]ine! Eat up! Let [the sweet wine] in [the cup] be fine! [. . . E]at up! And drink, so you are slaked! [. . .] G[o] up to heaven!" [. . . he] heard, Istanu of Heaven [. . .] rejoiced within. [The bread on the tab]le was fine, so he ate [his fill, and the swe]et [wine in the cup] was fine, so he d[ran]k. [Istanu] stood [u]p, and he went up to hea[ve]n.

(2, §5", A i 14'-28', C iv 1'-23') [Istanu] of Heaven [. . . aft]erwards. Tarhun t[ook wis]dom before his mind. Tarhun a[nd] Tashmishu took each other [b]y the h[and]. [Fro]m the *kuntarra*, from the temple they went forth [. . .], while Anzili cam[e] away from heaven with heroicness. [An]zili spoke in turn to her mind, "Inside wher[e] are they running, the two brothers?" She sw[ift]ly (?) stood, Anzili. Before her two [brothers] she rose up. They to[o]k each other by the hand. They went up Mount Hazzi,[80] and the king of Kummi kept setting his eyes, he kept setting his eyes on the dreadful basalt. He saw the dreadful basalt, and because of anger his [X] was altered [. . .]

(2, §6", A i 29'-42') Tarhun sat on the ground, and his tears were flowing [for]th like canals, and Tarhun, [w]eeping, speaks a word, "Who will see [aga]in the strife caused by this one? Who will [do b]attle again? Who will see again the fearsome qualities of [thi]s one?" Anzili speaks [in tu]rn to Tarhun, "My brother, he does not [kn]ow even a little mental force, although heroism[81] has been given to him tenfold. [. . .] which child they are birthing [. . .] you do not know his mental force. [. . .] we were in the house of Ea [. . . If] I were a man, [I] would [do X] to you [. . .]. I will go [. . .].

(After about 26 unintelligible lines, we pick up the narrative in column ii of version A, as Anzili attempts to seduce the rock monster.)

---

[80] Mt. Casius or Jebel Aqraa in northern Syria, near Ugarit. This mountain plays an important role in the *Baal Cycle*, where it is called Mt. Zapan or Saphon (see document 3.5.a below).

[81] "Heroism:" UR.SAG-*tar* = *hastaliyatar*, lit. "bone-hardness."

(2, §7''', A ii 1'-4') [. . .] mus[hroom (?) . . .] which one[s] (subj.) like/when [. . .] let them be [. . .]

(2, §8''', A ii 5'-12') She got dressed. [She] a[dorned herself . . .]. She [went away] from Nineveh. [She took] her lyre (and) *galgalturi*-cymbals [with her] ha[nd.] Anz[ili] set out [to the sea]. She burne<d> cedar as incense, and she struck her [ly]re (and) *galgal[turi]*-cymbals. She made her gold (ornaments) f[lu]tter. She took up a [s]ong, so that heave[n] and [e]arth [we]re singing in response to her.

(2, §9''', A ii 13'-25') Anzili sings, and she puts on a stone of the sea and a pebble. There is a great wav[e] from the sea. The great wave says to Anzili, "Before whom are you singing, and before whom are you filling your mouth with wi[nd]? The man is deaf, so he doe[s not] hear. He is blind in his [ey]es, so he does not see. He h[as] no graciousness. Go away, Anzili, and [r]each your brother, while he is not yet bone-hard, while the skull of his head has not yet become terrifying."

(2, §10''', A ii 26'-30') When Anzili heard this much, she extinguished the c[edar], and she threw away her lyre (and) [*ga*]*lgalt[uri]*-cymbals, and [she did X to] her gold (ornament)s. Wailing, [. . .] she set out [. . .].

(Column ii breaks off before the end of the paragraph, with 2–3 lines lost. Column iii starts about 8 lines down from the top edge as Tarhun prepares his wagon for battle, which is envisioned as a terrible thunderstorm.)

(2, §11'''', A iii 1'-14') [. . . Tarhun spoke a word to Tashmishu, . . .] "Let them mix the fodder. [Let t]hem [bring] the swe[et] oil. Le[t] them anoint the horns of the bull Sherish, and let them plate the tail of the bull Tella with gold, and let them set the axle turning. Let them move the powerful things within, and let them release the powerful stones on the *harshandanahit*[82] outside, and let them summon forth the thunder. Let them call the rains (and) the winds, which break up rocks in an area of 90 IKUs and cover 800, and the [l]ightning, which flashes terribly, let them bring it forth from the bedchamber. Let them set forth the wagon, and then prepare it (and) set it up. Bring back word to me."

(2, §12'''', A iii 15'-25') When Tashmishu heard the words, he hurried, he [ha]stened, and [he drove] the bull Sherish from the pasture, and [he drove the bull T]ella from Mount Imgarra. [. . .] in the outer gatehouse [. . .] he brought sweet oil, and [he anointed the horns] of the bull Sherish, and he [plat]ed the tail [of] the bull Tella [with gold], and he [X]-ed the axle, [and he] relea[sed the strong st]ones [on the *harshandanahit*] outside [. . . whic]h [break up rocks] in [an area of 90 IKUs . . .]

(Column iii breaks off before paragraph end.)

(2, §13'''', A iv 1'-14') [. . .] eight [. . .] 1,000 *gipes[sars*[83] . . .] he [pl]aced [. . .] to fight. Furthermore, he gathered [u]p the tools of w[ar], and he gathered up the parts of the wagon. [He] brough[t] the clouds out from [hea]ven. Tarhun set his [eye]s on the [basalt] st[one. He] sa[w] it. It in height [. . . X]-ed, and furthermore [. . .] its . . . in height three times [. . .] he [t]urned.

(2, §14''''', A iv 15'-22') Tarhun [b]egan to [spea]k to T[ashmishu . . .] wagon [. . .] wind [. . .] let them [g]o. [. . .] call[. . .]. He went [. . . wor]d[s . . .]

---

[82] A piece of chariot apparatus.

[83] A *gipessar* is approximately 50 centimeters.

(Column iv breaks off before paragraph end. Approximately 20 lines are missing.)
(Colophon)
(2, §15""", A left edge) Second tablet, not finished, of the S[ong (of) Ullikummi.]

TABLET III

(Approximately 30 lines are missing from the top of column i. When the story continues the gods' unsuccessful battle against Ullikummi is being described. Ullikummi grows so large he is able to threaten the Syrian goddess Hebat, the divine consort of the Storm God.)

(3, §1', A i 1') [. . . " . . .] I (will) do [X . . .] heave[n . . .]"

(3, §2', A i 2'-24') When the gods h[eard] the matter, they put together the parts of the wagon. [. . .] they handed (it) over [to Ashtabi . . .]. Ashtabi[84] sprang up [like a whorl on a spindle shaft]. He [. . .] the wago[n . . . he] set the shaft whirling. [. . .] He thunders, Asht[abi . . .]. Thundering, A[shtabi . . .] he released [. . .] downward to the sea. [. . .] they bailed [. . .]. Ashtabi (subj.) [. . .] seventy gods seized [. . .]. He stil[l . . .] did not succeed [in doing X]. A[shtabi . . .], and the seventy gods [fell] do[wn] in the sea. [. . .] the basalt . . . h[is] limbs [. . .] does [X . . .]. He mad[e] heaven tremble. He [tu]rned [heaven]. He [. . .] tore [a]part heaven [l]ik[e] an [e]mpty garment. The basal[t] gre[w] taller. Before, his height was 1,000 and 900 DANN[A]s, [but afterwards his height is X DA]NNAs. [. . .] he stands on the dark earth below. The basalt shoo[t]s up like a mu[s]hroo[m]. He reaches the *kuntarra* and the houses of the gods. His height is 9,000 DANNAs. The basalt . . . , and his width is 9,000 DANNAs. He stood in [f]ront of the city gates at Kummi like a spear. The basalt approached Hebat in her temple, so Hebat could no longer hear the message of the gods, and she could not see Tarhun and Suwaliya[t] with her own eyes.

(3, §3', A i 25'-29') Hebat bega[n] to speak wo[rds] to Takiti,[85] "[I] cannot he[ar] the [w]ord of Tarhun, the important matter, and I cannot [hea]r the message of Suw[aliya]t and of all the gods. This one, whom [they] speak of as Ullikummi the basalt, has he perhaps de[f]eated my husband, the august [Tarhun]?"

(3, §4', A i 30'-33') Hebat began to [s]peak [in turn] to Takit[i], "[Li]sten to m[y] words. [Ta]ke your sta[ff] with your hand, and p[ut o]n your feet the sw[i]ft [w]inds as shoes. [. . .] go! Has the [b]asa[lt] perh[aps ki]lled [my husband, Tarhun the augu]st king? [Bring back] w[ord] to me."

(3, §5', A i 34'-37') [And when Takiti hear]d [the words], she hurried, [she] has[tened . . .] draw[. . .] forth [. . .] she [g]oes. There is no path at all [. . .] she did [X]. [She went back] to Hebat.

(3, §6', A i 38'-40') [Takiti b]egan [to speak in turn to Hebat], "My lady, to m[e . . .]

(Column i breaks off before paragraph end, with approximately 20 lines lost, which appear to have related more details of Tarhun's defeat at the hands of Ullikummi. Next, Hebat's concern for her husband is vividly portrayed. Then, Tarhun appears to discuss with his vizier on what mountain they might sit to discuss their plans without being overheard. Alternatively, they may be

---

[84] Ashtabi is a north Syrian god, equated on the one hand with the male instantiation of Ishtar and on the other with Ninurta, the martial Sumerian god of thunderstorms.

[85] Takiti is a member of Hebat's entourage, here a sort of feminine equivalent to a "vizier" for a male god.

discussing where they can take up residence, having been forced out of heaven, since the Storm God was envisioned as living on top of a mountain. They decide to visit the wise Ea in Abzu.)

(3, §7", A ii 1–26, E 1'-13') [Whe]n [Tash]mishu h[eard] the words of Tarhun, he promptly rose up. [He took] his staff with his hand, and he put [o]n his feet the swif[t winds] as shoes. He wen[t] up to the tall watch tower, and he took [his place] in front of Hebat, "[Tarhun orders] me t[o] go to the narrow confines (of the grave), until he completes the years which are decreed for him." When Hebat saw Tashmishu, Hebat nearly fell down from the roof. [I]f she had taken a step, she would have fallen down from the roof, but her maids seized her and did not release her. When Tashmishu finished speaking the words, he set off down from the watch tower, and he went down to Tarhun. Tashmishu began to speak in turn to Tarhun, "[W]here shall we sit down on top of Mount Kandurna? [If] we sit down on top of Mount Kandurna, will [anot]her sit on top of Mount Lalapaduwa? [W]here specifically shall we move [X]? Will there be no king above in heaven? [. . . " . . .] sits down. [Tashmish]u began to speak in turn to Tarhun, "Tarhun, my lord, [listen] to my words. Which [w]ords I speak to you, hold [your ear coc]ked to my words. Come on, let's go to the city Abzu, in the presence of Ea. Then, we will ask [Ea] about the tablets of ancient words. [When] we arrive in front of the gate of the house of Ea. . . . Ea's door [. . .], we will bow five times to the inner doors of Ea. We will arrive inside to Ea, and we will bow fifteen times to Ea. Perhaps we will be pleasing to Ea. Perhaps Ea [will listen], and he will be merciful to [u]s, and he will hand over to us the ancient [tablet.]"

(3, §8", A ii 27–32) [When Tarhun] heard the words [of Tashmish]u, he hurried, [he hastened.] He promptly rose up from his [th]rone. [Tarhun] and [Tashmishu] took each other by the hand. [They] comple[ted] it at one go. They [arrived] at Abzu. [Tarhun] went [to] the house of Ea. He [bowed five times at] the fron[t doors], and he bowed five times at the [inne]r doors, [and when] they reached the presence of Ea, [he] bo[wed before Ea fif]teen times.

(3, §9", A ii 33–45') [. . .] st[ood u]p [. . . he] bega[n] t[o speak . . .] Ea (subj.) [. . .] no[t . . .] not [. . .]

(3, §10", A ii 46'-49') [. . . began] to speak [. . .], "For me the matter [. . . he s] ets. For me, you, Tarhun [. . .] let him arise in front. The matt[er . . .]

(3, §11"', A ii 50'-55') When Tashmishu [heard] the word[s of Ea . . . he] ran forth. [He kissed] his knees three ti[mes], and he kissed the soles of his feet four times. [. . . he] embraced [X]. For him [. . .]. For him while within [. . .] for the basalt death on his right [shoulder . . .]

(3, §12"', A ii 56'-62') Ea [began to] sp[eak] in turn to Tashmishu, "On [top of] Mount Kandur[na . . .] on t[op of] Mount Lalapaduwa [. . .] on the dark earth [. . .] the fatherly, the grandfatherl[y storehouse. Let them take] for[th] the saw [. . .] the [m]en . . . down away [. . .]"

(3, §13"', A ii 63'-67') [Whe]n Ea [finished speaking] the word[s . . . Tarhun] a[nd Tashmish]u [sat] on [top of] Mou[nt Kandurna . . . on top of Mo]unt Lalapaduw[a . . . b]efore his mind [. . .]

(The column breaks off before paragraph end, but the scene with Ea is also described in another fragment. This may present another version of the scene or refer to a second meeting between Ea and Tarhun.)

(3, §14"", F i 1'-8') [. . . ma]tter [in] mind n[ot . . .]. Ea [took] wisdom [before] his [mind]. He stood up. [He] went [forth . . .] in the courtyard, Ea. [. . .]. All the gods s[t]ood up [in front of] him, and Tarhun, heroi[c] king [of Kummi stood up] in front [of him.]

(3, §15"", F i 9'-11') Ea saw Tarhun, [and his X] alte[red] because of [anger]. The god [. . .]

(The fragment breaks off, and we return to exemplar A in column iii. Ea speaks to Enlil, who belongs to the eldest generation of the gods. Ea then goes to visit Ubelluri to see Ullikummi for himself.)

(3, §16"", A iii 1'-10') The god [Ea . . .] the[n . . .]. They [took each other] by the hand. [. . .]. While/Until [. . .]. He ca[me] away from the assembly. [. . .]. He b[egan] to wail. [. . .] "Be living, Ea! [. . .] who com[es] back in front [. . .], and to the gods the scent [. . .]. Why di[d you/he] cross it? [. . .]"

(3, §17"", A iii 11'-18', D 1'-4') Ea [began] to [s]peak to Enl[il, "Do y]ou [not know, Enlil? Has no one brought] the matter to you? [Do you not know], w[hich] riv[a]l [Kum]arbi [has] cr[eated] against Tarhun, [which basal]t has matured [in the water]? He is [9,000 DANNAs in] heig[ht, and he] shoots up like [a mushroom (?), and . . .]. Again[st] you [. . . f]orm[er . . . who is he, this rap]idly (growing) [god]?"

(3, §18"", A iii 19') [Ea and E]nlil (subj.) [. . .]

(3, §19"", A iii 20'-22') [. . .] Ea [said to X, "What] shall I [say to you]? Who [. . . ? . . .] the pure tem[ples . . . "]

(3, §20"", A iii 23'-29') When Ea [finished speaking] the wo[rds, he went] to the side of Ubelluri [. . .]. Ubelluri [lifted] his eyes, [he saw Ea]. Ubelluri [began to speak words] to E[a], "Be living, Ea!" [And, he stood] u[p. Ea bega]n [to greet] Ubelluri [in turn, "Be] li[ving, Ubelluri, on the dark ear[th, . . .] upon whom [the ear]th is built."

(3, §21"", A iii 30'-39') Ea began to [spea]k [in turn] to Ubelluri, "Do you not know, Ubelluri, and has no one brought the matter to you? Do you not know, which rapidly (growing) god Kumarbi has created against the gods? Because Kumarbi . . . seeks death against Tarhun, he is creating a rival against him. The one who has matured as basalt in the water, do you not know him? He shoots up like a mushroom (?). He has blocked off heaven, the pure temples, and Hebat. Because you, Ubelluri, are distant from the dark earth, do you not know this ra[p]idly (growing) god?"

(3, §22"", A iii 40'-44') Ubelluri began to speak in turn t[o E]a, "When they built heaven and earth on top of me, I didn't notice anything, and when they went and cut apart heaven and eart[h] with the copper *kuruzza*-tool, there too I [did]n't notice (anything), but [n]ow something hurts me on my shoulder, and [I] don't know who he is, this god."

(3, §23"", A iii 45'-47') [W]hen Ea heard the words, he bent Ubelluri's [righ]t shoulder over, and the basalt stood on Ubelluri['s righ]t shoulder like a spear.

(3, §24"", A iii 48'-55a', B 1'-8') Ea began to speak in turn to the Former Gods, "[L]isten to my words, Former Gods, the ancient words which you [k] now: Open it up, the ancient, fatherly, grandfatherly storehouse. Let them bring the seal of the ancestors, [and] let them unseal [i]t. Let them take [for]th the ancient copper saw, with which they cut apart heaven and earth. [We will] cut off Ullikummi, the basalt, at his feet, at the bottom, whom [K]umarbi rai[sed] as a r[i]v[a]l against the gods. [When the Former Gods heard] the [words of] E[a, the For]mer [Gods . . .]

(Column iii breaks off before paragraph end, followed by a gap of approximately 23 lines. Here the events of the second battle between Ullikummi and the other gods, apparently sufficiently cataclysmic to crack open the earth and reveal the dead, would have been described. Ea appears to have played a decisive role in it.)

(3, §25"""", A iv 1'-3') [] Ea [. . .]

(3, §26"""", A iv 4'-8') But, Tashmishu [. . .] did [o]beisance [. . .] bega[n] to [s]peak [. . .], "In his [b]ody [X] is chan[g]ed wi[thin, and] on [his] head his hair has c[han]ged [. . .].

(3, §27"""", A iv 9'-12') Ea began to speak in turn to Tashmishu, "Go forth, my son, don't stand [in] front of m[e]. Inside me my mind [is] sickened, because I have seen with my own eyes the dead on the dark earth. They stand like dust and ashes(?)."

(3, §28"""", A iv 13'-20') Ea began to speak in turn to Tashmishu, "I repelled him once [. . .], Ullikummi, the basalt. You (pl.) go, do battle with him again! Let him not stand as a spear any longer at the gates of [X]." Tashmishu [he]ard, and he began to rejoice. He shouted aloud three times, and the gods above in [heav]en heard. They shouted aloud twice, and Tarhun, heroic king of Kummi, heard. They went into the place of assembly, and all the gods began to bellow like oxen at Ullikummi, the basalt.

(3, §29"""", A iv 21'-22', C 1'-4') Tarhun sprang up like a whorl on a spindle shaft. Thundering, he moved down towards the sea, and Tarhun does battle with him, the basalt.

(3, §30"""", A iv 23'-24', C 5') The basalt began to speak in turn to Tarhun, "What shall I say to you, Tarhun? Strike and carry out (that) of your desire! Ea, king of wisdom, stands with you.

(3, §31"""", A iv 25'-28'; 3.2. §4", A iii 6'-13') "What shall I say to you, Tarhun? My desire likewise I have held as follows; before my mind I lined up wisdom like jewel bead(s): 'I will go up to heaven to kingship. I will take for myself Kummi and the pure temples of heaven and the [*k*]*untarra*, while I will scatte[r] the gods down from heaven like meal.'"

(The final section of the story is not fully intelligible, but it appears that Ullikummi renders a prophecy about what will happen to the parts of his body once he is killed. Perhaps he establishes a baetyl cult. There are similarities with of the Song of Birth, §15.)

(3, §32"""", A iv 29'-36') Ullikummi bega[n] to speak in [t]urn t[o Tarhun], "[Stri]ke over and over a[gai]n like a man, and carry out [(that) of your desire!] Ea, king [of] wisdom, stan[ds] with you. [. . .] tak[es] away!" They . . . on [a]ll the mounta[in]s [. . .]. Let [them] go and [c]all in the land, abov[e] (and) [be]low, the her[o . . .]. But, my liver (and) lu[ngs . . . whi]ch upwards [. . .]. Let them go and [ca]ll in the land [X. But, m]ly [X body part a]nd my kidne[ys (?)], which upwards [X]-ed. Let them go and call [in the] l[and X].

(3, §33"""", A iv 37'-45') The basalt began to [spea]k in turn to Tarhun, "Because you have already destroyed me [. . . he] will take [som]ething. What name I give him, let them go and call the basa[l]t [. . . . Let them go and c]all [. . .]. In [. . .]. Because the hero [. . .]. You (obj.) [. . .] to them [. . .]

(Colophon)

(3, §34'''''', A iv 46') [Third tablet of the Song of Ullikummi, finished . . .]

3.5. UGARITIC EPIC POEMS

During the Late Bronze Age (1550–1200 BCE) Ugarit was a cosmopolitan port city on the northeast Mediterranean coast (in modern Syria, 37 kilometers south of the Turkish border). Ugarit lay at the intersection of multiple cultures, with strong ties with the Aegean to the west, the Hittites to the north, Egypt and Canaan to the south, and Mesopotamia to the east. Texts discovered at the site were written in half a dozen languages, including the North-West Semitic language (Ugaritic) spoken by the inhabitants of the city, a language that was inscribed with a stylus on clay tablets in cuneiform (wedge-shaped) signs which, unlike the Mesopotamian script, represented an early alphabet (a system spread by the Phoenicians later on). These Ugaritic texts provide the single most extensive primary documentation for the literary and religious heritage of the North-West Semitic world in the second millennium BCE. The language, lexicon, poetry, religion, and concepts found in these texts overlap in thousands of ways with those in the Hebrew Bible, revolutionizing biblical studies that focus on an area only 400 kilometers to the south.

Because Ugarit was never again inhabited after its destruction in the early twelfth century BCE, the remains of the city are accessible not too far beneath the present ground level. Indeed, the discovery of the site in 1928 resulted from a farmer's plow striking 3,000-year-old remains. French excavations began the following year at the site (modern Ras Shamra) and continued with periodic interruptions throughout the twentieth century. The first tablets written in Ugaritic were discovered in 1929. Their script and language were deciphered in 1930 primarily under the leadership of Hans Bauer, who utilized his extensive knowledge of foreign languages in conjunction with skills he developed in cryptanalysis for German intelligence in World War I. Since then, some 1,400 tablets have been uncovered and read, containing not only long narrative poems (i.e., epic poems) such as the *Baal Cycle* and the *Aqhat* and *Kirta/Keret* poems (the latter not included here) but also a multitude of ritual, economic, and legal texts as well as letters and other shorter literary pieces.

All of the material translated here is poetry, one of whose distinguishing features, "parallelism," is the repetition of a given line with sometimes different or slightly modified words. The scribes did not always format the tablet to reflect the poetic structure, and consequently this translation will follow suit in aiming for a more readable rendering, aiming for accuracy while smoothing out some of the tedious repetition. The numbers that appear in the text identify the tablet and column (e.g., 4.III signifies the fourth tablet, third column). Brackets [. . .] indicate a portion of the text that is missing (weather shorter or longer); any translation found within brackets results from the restoration based on parallel passages that are better preserved.

SOURCE: Ugaritic *Baal Cycle* (*CAT* 1.1–1.6) and *Aqhat Epic* (*CAT* 1.17–1.19), translated and annotated by S. Meier. This is not a critical edition of the texts; for further details consult more comprehensive studies of these texts (see the Bibliography at the end of this volume).

3.5.a. The *Baal Cycle*

The longest preserved epic poem from Ugarit, the *Baal Cycle* is written in a series of tablets (only one copy or version of each is extant), signed by the scribe Ilimilk, who also wrote down the other two long poems preserved (*Aqhat* and *Kirta*). This poetic myth narrates the rise of Baal to the throne of the Ugaritic pantheon, under the surveillance of the "older" god, El (whose name means "god" and can also be read as Ilu). The struggle between Baal and first Sea (Yamm) and then Death (Mot) are similar to the cosmic battles between other Storm/Weather Gods (Zeus, Marduk, Teshub), while Baal's death (causing a great drought) and return place him among the ubiquitous "dying and rising gods" of ancient mythologies (see *Hymn to Demeter*, Isis and Osiris myth, *Ishtar's Descent*, etc., all in Part 6).

The nature of the Ugaritic pantheon is similar to that of the Olympian Greek gods, with El as the head of a family clan with complicated familial and political tensions: they hold assemblies, send messages to one another, and compete for power. The figure of El is weaker than that of the enthroned Zeus, however, which can be seen in this story about the rise of Baal as the champion of the gods. The pantheon is also governed by kingship, and therefore competition for power fits into the "Kingship in Heaven" pattern or "Succession Myth" seen in this volume in Hesiod's *Theogony* (Part 1, document 5) and the Hittite *Kumarbi Cycle* (document 3.4.b). Even with Baal's success, El remains the patriarch of the gods, bearing the epithet "bull" (the most powerful of animals). Athirat is El's consort. Her legacy as divine matriarch seems to have survived in first-millennium-BCE Canaanite religion in the figure of Asherah, even permeating in Israelite religion, where she might have been associated with Yahweh (see Figure 9). Her two assistants are Qudsh ("holy") and Amrar ("most blessed"), often identified together as Qudsh-wa-Amrar. Sun (Ugaritic "Shapsh") is a goddess, while Baal (meaning "lord" or "master"), also known as Haddu (in other Semitic sources called Haddad and Adad), is a storm deity who brings the rain that makes life possible. His two servants are "Vine" (*Gapn*) and "Field" (*Ugar*). His epithet, "cloud-rider," recalls that of Zeus as "cloud-gatherer," and this characterization appears later in the figure of Yahweh, as in Psalm 29 in document 3.6. (See also Figure 5.)

In contrast, the Sea (Ugaritic "Yamm") is a powerful manifestation of death: one cannot survive by drinking sea water, its depths are dark and mysterious, those who stay there too long drown, and its waves are uncontrollable in a storm and crash destructively on the shore. Since rivers flow into the sea, the deity Sea by extension is frequently identified by the designation River (Ugaritic "Nahar"). Another hostile deity is Death (Ugaritic "Mot"), who succeeds in subduing Baal, if only temporarily. Dagan (meaning "grain") is a grain god. Anat is a goddess of sex and violence, features that she shares with another goddess, Athtart (corresponding to Akkadian Ishtar, Phoenician Ashtart). Kothar-wa-Hasis ("skill-and-insight," also appearing as Hayin-wa-Hasis) is the god of metallurgy, sometimes identified simply as Kothar and sometimes simply as Hasis. Other goddesses mentioned in the texts translated here include Pidray, daughter of Light, Tallay, signifying "belonging to the dew," and Arsay, "earthy." Athtar (not the same as Athtart) is a male god associated with the planet Venus and rules the underworld.

(2.I) *(The beginning of the myth is not preserved, and the first tablet that is often associated with it is too fragmentary for a coherent translation here. There are very good reasons to doubt that the second tablet is actually an integral part of the literary unity found in tablets four, five, and six, but it is presented here since there are many thematic correspondences between the texts. The first 10 lines of the first column are too fragmentary for a coherent translation.)*

Sea sent messengers, judge River dispatched an embassy that rejoiced greatly [. . .]. "Leave without delay, lads. Set out for the council assembled in the midst of Mount Lalu. Neither bow at El's feet nor do homage to the assembled council, but remaining erect, say what you have to say and repeat your instructions. Repeat what I say to bull El, my father, and the assembled council: 'This is the message of Sea, even judge River, your lord and master. Hand over the one you obey, you multitude of gods. Hand over Baal, Dagan's son, so that I may humiliate him and become heir to his gold.'"

The lads left without delay. They set out for the midst of Mount Lalu, to the assembled council.

The holy gods, in the meantime, had sat down to feast and dine, while Baal stood by El. What a sight! The gods saw Sea's messengers, even judge River's embassy. The gods lowered their heads to their knees, even to their royal thrones.

Baal rebuked them: "Gods, why are you lowering your heads to your knees, even down to your royal thrones? The gods can respond as one to the tablet that Sea's messengers bring, even judge River's embassy. Gods, lift up your heads from your knees and royal thrones! I at least will be one who will respond to Sea's messengers, even judge River's embassy."

The gods lifted their heads from their knees and royal thrones.

Then Sea's messengers arrived, judge River's embassy. They neither bowed at El's feet nor did homage to the assembled council, but remaining erect, they said what they had to say and repeated their instructions. In appearance they seemed to be a fire, two fires, their tongues sharpened swords. They gave the message to bull El, his father: "This is the message of Sea, even judge River, your lord and master. Hand over the one you obey, you multitude of gods. Hand over Baal, Dagan's son, so that I may humiliate him and become heir to his gold."

Bull El, his father, answered: "Oh, Sea! Oh, River! Baal is your servant, Dagan's son is your captive! It is he who will bring the tribute owed to you, he will bring the gifts and offerings owed to you like the holy gods."

At this, Baal became angry and grabbed a butcher's knife with his hand, a bludgeon in his right hand. He attacked the lads, but Anat grabbed his right hand and his left: "Why are you striking Sea's messengers?"

(The 8 lines remaining in the column are too fragmentary for a coherent translation, and little remains from the next two columns, 2.II and 2.III, that can be clearly connected with the plot.)

(2.IV) *(The first 4 lines are either damaged or insufficiently lucid for confident translation; the unidentifiable speaker is discussing conflict with Sea and closes with the following words.)*

[. . .] "My strength will fall to the earth, even my power to the dust."

The words of this speech had not passed his/her lips or left his/her mouth when she spoke: "May he sink under prince Sea's throne."

Kothar-wa-Hasis said: "Prince Baal, I have something to say to you. Cloud-rider, let me repeat it. Baal, now you can strike your enemy, now you can destroy your adversary. You can take your eternal kingship, your dominion that will endure forever."

Kothar fashioned two maces and uttered their names: "As for you, your name is 'Expeller' (Yagarrish). Expeller, expel Sea from his throne, expel River from the seat of his dominion! You will swoop from Baal's hands and fingers like a vulture. Strike prince Sea's shoulders between judge River's arms."

The mace swooped from Baal's hands and fingers like a vulture. It struck prince Sea's shoulders between judge River's arms. But Sea was strong. He did not slump, his joints did not tremble, his frame did not collapse.

Kothar had fashioned two maces and uttered their names: "As for you, your name is 'All-banisher' (Ayyamur). All-banisher, banish Sea from his throne, banish River from the seat of his dominion! You will swoop from Baal's hands and fingers like a vulture. Strike prince Sea's head between judge River's eyes, so that Sea crumples and falls to the ground."

The mace swooped from Baal's hands and fingers like a vulture. It struck prince Sea's head between judge River's eyes. Sea crumpled and fell to the ground. His joints trembled, his frame collapsed. Baal gave the coup-de-grâce and dismembered Sea, annihilating judge River.

Athtart rebuked him by name: "Scatter him, Baal, mighty one, cloud-rider! Prince Sea, even judge River, is indeed our captive!"

Mighty Baal went out and scattered him. [. . .] "Sea is dead! Baal will rule as king [. . .].

(The final 10 lines of the column are too fragmentary for coherent translation, and the subject of the opening verbs that follow is unclear.)

(3.I) He served the mighty one, Baal, and took care of the prince and lord of the earth. When he stood up, he took some portions and gave him food to eat, while with a sharp knife he carved a breast and a slice of the fattened calf in his presence. He arose, arranged the feast, supplied him with drinks: he put a cup in his hand, goblets in both his hands, a stunningly large vessel, a rhyton for mighty men, a sacred cup that is neither for women to view nor for Athirat to look upon. He drew a thousand pitchers of wine and mixed ten thousand in his mead-bowl. When he stood up, he selected a tune and sang to cymbals in a musician's hands. The hero sang with melodious voice of Baal on Zapan's peaks.

Baal turned an eye to his daughters, gazing first at Pidray, daughter of light, then at Tallay, daughter of rain [. . .].

(Some 45 intervening lines are missing or too fragmentary for translation.)

(3.II) [. . .] Anat closed the gates of the house and met the youths at the foot of the mountain. What a scene! Anat engaged in battle in the valley and fought between the two cities, striking the people of the west and decimating the men of the east: severed heads under her like balls, severed hands above her like locusts, warrior hands like mounds of grasshoppers. Attaching the heads to her back and fastening the hands to her belt, she mopped up in warrior blood to the knees, even up to the neck in the soldier's gore. With a mace and her bowstring, she drove off the captives and defeated foes.

Another sight to behold: when Anat reached her house and the goddess returned to her palace, she was not satisfied with her battle in the valley and her fighting between the two cities. So she arranged chairs for warriors, and arranged tables for soldiers and footstools for heroes. Again she engaged in violent combat and fought, and then she looked about victoriously and made a conqueror's survey. Anat's liver swelled with her laughter at the victory, her heart filled with joy. She mopped up in warrior blood to the knees, even up to the neck in the soldier's gore, until she was satisfied with the battle in her house and the fighting between the tables.

The warrior-blood was wiped from the house, and the oil of peace was poured from a bowl. Virgin Anat, kin to the peoples, washed the warrior-blood and the soldier's gore from her hands and fingers, then arranged chairs with chairs, tables with tables, and footstools with footstools. When she had drawn water, she washed with heaven's dew, earth's oil, rain of the cloud-rider (i.e., Baal); upon her the heavens poured dew and the stars poured rain.

(3.III) She enhanced her beauty with the murex's purple dye, a product from a thousand acres of the sea.

(Some 20 lines are missing; Baal begins to instruct his messengers what to tell Anat.)

"[. . .] the love of the mighty one, Baal; the desire of Pidray, daughter of Light; the affection of Tallay (Dewy), daughter of Rain; the love of Arsay (Earthy), daughter of Wide-world. As is appropriate for youths, then, enter, bow, and fall down at Anat's feet. You will prostrate yourselves, honoring her, and repeat what I say to virgin Anat, kin to the peoples: 'This is the message of the mighty one, Baal, supreme among warriors:

"'Remove war from the earth and plant love in the dust, pour out peace in the midst of the earth and harmony in the steppes. Be quick, hurry, and make all speed! Let your feet and legs run speedily to me, for I have a message to tell you and a matter to relate: message of tree and whisper of stone, the sighing of heaven with earth, and the ocean depths with the stars. I understand the lightning, something the heavens do not know, a message which humans and earth's masses neither know nor understand. So come! I will explain it in the sacred place within the beautiful mountain of my inheritance and my victory, Divine Zapan.'"[86]

---

[86] Zapan (or Saphon) is Jebel Aqraa, a mountain north of Ras Shamra-Ugarit. It also features in Hurro-Hittite myths as Mt. Hazzi and later in classical sources as Mt. Kasios (Lat. Casius).

(The scribe incised 2 lines here, perhaps to indicate a formulaic element to be filled in, specifically the account of the gods traveling to Anat.)

As soon as Anat saw the gods, her feet slipped out from under her, sinews snapped about her, her face ran with perspiration above her, her sinew links trembled, her back muscles went limp. She raised her voice and exclaimed: "How is it that Gapn and Ugar have come here? What enemy or foes rise up against Baal, the cloud-rider? I destroyed El's beloved, Sea, didn't I? I annihilated River, the great god, didn't I?

"I muzzled the Dragon and harnessed him, didn't I? I destroyed Serpent, the twisting one, the tyrant with seven heads! I destroyed El's beloved, Desire; I terminated El's calf, Rebel; I destroyed El's bitch, Fire; I annihilated El's daughter, Flame. I engaged in battle for silver, I acquired gold!

"Has someone, putting Baal (3.IV) to flight like a bird, expelled him from his domain, Zapan's heights, driven him from his regal throne, his place of rest, his seat of dominion? Who is the enemy or foe who has risen against Baal, the cloud-rider?"

The youths responded and said: "No enemy or foe has risen against Baal, the cloud-rider. This is the message of the mighty one, Baal, supreme among warriors:

"'Remove war from the earth and plant love in the dust, pour out peace in the midst of the earth and harmony in the steppes. Be quick, hurry, and make all speed! Let your feet and legs run speedily to me, for I have a message to tell you and a matter to relate: message of tree and whisper of stone, a message which humans and earth's masses neither know nor understand, the sighing of heaven with earth, and the ocean depths with the stars. I understand the lightning, something the heavens do not know. So come! I will explain it in the sacred place within the mountain of my inheritance, Divine Zapan.'"

Virgin Anat, kin to the peoples, replied: "I, for my part, will remove war from the earth, will plant love in the dust, and will pour out peace in the midst of the earth and harmony in the steppes. Let Baal the cloud-rider put his [. . .] let him set fire to [. . .]. I, for my part, will remove war from the earth, will plant love in the dust, and will pour out peace in the midst of the earth and harmony in the steppes. Although there is another matter that I will address, go quickly, divine attendants - you are slow, and I am off! Ugar and Inbab (i.e., Anat's location) are quite a journey, you gods: two measures under earth's springs, three distances of caves."

At that point, she set out for Baal on Zapan's heights. At a distance of a thousand acres, even ten thousand hectares, Baal discerned the approach of his sister, his father's daughter. He dismissed the women from his presence, then set an ox and a fatted calf before her.

When she had drawn water, she washed with heaven's dew and earth's oil; upon her the heavens poured dew and the stars poured rain. She enhanced her beauty with the murex's purple dye, a product from a thousand acres of the sea.

(Some 15 lines are missing.)

Yet he (i.e., Baal) cries out, groaning, to his father, bull El, the king who established his legitimacy, and to the goddess Athirat along with her children and kin: "Baal has neither house nor court like the gods and Athirat's children, El's residence

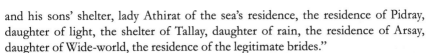

and his sons' shelter, lady Athirat of the sea's residence, the residence of Pidray, daughter of light, the shelter of Tallay, daughter of rain, the residence of Arsay, daughter of Wide-world, the residence of the legitimate brides."

Virgin Anat answered: "The bull El, my father, will answer me or (3.V) I will wrestle him to the ground like a lamb. I will make his gray hair and beard run with blood and gore, unless he gives to Baal a house and court like those that belong to the gods and Athirat's children."

When she stamped her feet, the earth shook. She then set out for El amid the sources of the rivers and the channels of the abysses. Upon her arrival at El's abode, she entered the pavilion of the Father of Years with an angry shout, repeating the cry to the lord of the gods. Her father, bull El, heard her voice and responded from the seven chambers and the eight portals of the enclosures: "[. . .] at the feet of the lads [. . .] Sun, the light of the gods, burns hot while the skies succumb in the hands of Death, El's son."

Virgin Anat replied: "El, don't be too happy with your fine house and your palace's great height. With my long, strong right hand I will seize it. I will smash your head and make your grey hair and beard run with blood and gore."

From the seven chambers El answered, from the eight portals of the enclosures: "I know you, daughter, that you act all too human, for your volatile nature is otherwise not to be found among goddesses. What do you wish, virgin Anat?"

Virgin Anat replied: "El, your decree is wise, your wisdom is enduring, and a life of good fortune is yours to decree. The mighty one, Baal, is our king and judge, with no one above him: it is all of us who bring his chalice and bear his cup. Yet he cries out, groaning, to his father, bull El, the king who established his legitimacy, and to the goddess Athirat along with her children and kin: Baal has neither house nor court like the gods and Athirat's children, El's residence and his sons' shelter, lady Athirat of the sea's residence, the residence of Pidray, daughter of light, the shelter of Tallay, daughter of rain, the residence of Arsay, daughter of Wide-world, the residence of the legitimate brides."

(At least 20 lines are missing from the end of the column, so that El's response is unknown: Did he respond favorably or otherwise to Anat's request? Although most of the next column (3.VI) is also missing, enough is preserved to show that Athirat's messengers, Qudsh-wa-Amrar, are sent to the god of metallurgy, Kothar-wa-Hasis, to enlist his assistance.)

(4.I) *(The first 3 lines are missing, but the messengers convey their request to the god of metallurgy, concluding about Baal that)* "he cries out, groaning, to his father, bull El, the king who established his legitimacy, and to the goddess Athirat along with her children and kin: Baal has neither house nor court like the gods and Athirat's children, El's residence and his sons' shelter, lady Athirat of the sea's residence, the residence of the legitimate brides, the residence of Pidray, daughter of light, the shelter of Tallay, daughter of rain, the residence of Arsay, daughter of Wide-world."

"There is yet a second matter about which I should speak with you: Provide gifts and presents for the great lady, Athirat of the sea, for her who created the gods."

With tongs in his hands, Hayin-wa-Hasis went up to the bellows where he cast silver and poured gold by the thousands, even ten-thousands, of shekels. He cast a canopy and a bed, a divine dais weighing twenty-thousand shekels that was covered with silver and coated with red gold, a divine throne of glistening gold, a divine footstool laminated with electrum, an exquisite divine portable couch where even the carrying poles were of gold, a divine table filled with creatures who were denizens of the deepest earth, and a divine bowl finely wrought as in Amurru and fashioned as in the land of Yam'an with decorations of myriads of wild oxen.

———————————————

(The scribe here incised 2 lines at the bottom of the column, perhaps to indicate a formulaic element to be filled in.)

(4.II) *(Some 20 lines are missing from the top of this column before Athirat's activities become apparent as she does something with her garments and her distaff.)*

She (i.e., Athirat) put a pot on the fire, a cooking pot on top of the coals. She enticed bull El, the compassionate, and prepared to petition the one who created all creatures. When she lifted her eyes and looked, Athirat saw the approach of Baal and Anat, kin to the peoples. Her feet slipped out from under her, sinews snapped about her, her face ran with perspiration above her, her sinew links trembled, her back muscles went limp.

She raised her voice and exclaimed: "How is it that the mighty one, Baal, and virgin Anat have come here? Are those who would strike me the ones who have already struck my children, the ones who destroy my kin?"

When Athirat, however, saw the gleam of silver and the glimmer of gold, lady Athirat of the sea was delighted and called aloud to her servant: "O fisherman of lady Athirat of the sea, look at the craftsmanship from the channels of the abysses. Take a large net with your hands, and into the Sea, El's beloved [. . .]

(Some 30 lines are missing, or are too fragmentary to make sense, at the end of column two and the top of column three. After the break, Anat seems to be speaking to Baal as they journey to Athirat.)

(4.III) [. . .] god who is king."

The mighty one, Baal, the cloud-rider, replied: "He stood up and insulted me by spitting on me in the assembly of the gods. At my table I drank humiliation from my cup. Now, cloud-rider Baal hates two kinds of feasts—no, three: a feast where shame is present, a feast where dissension is present, and a feast where the serving girls whisper. Truly, there shame was seen, along with the whispering of the servant girls."

At this point, the mighty one, Baal, and virgin Anat arrived and offered presents and gifts to Lady Athirat of the sea, the one who created the gods.

Lady Athirat of the sea replied: "How is it that you offer presents and gifts to Lady Athirat of the sea, the one who created the gods? Have you offered presents and gifts to bull El, the compassionate, the one who created all creatures?"

Virgin Anat responded: "Lady Athirat of the sea who created the gods, to you we offer presents and gifts, [. . .] to him we offer presents."

[. . .] The mighty one, Baal [. . .] lady Athirat of the sea [. . .] virgin Anat [. . .] the gods ate and drank, a suckling was served, with a sharp knife a slice of the fattened calf. They drank wine, the blood of vines, from goblets and golden cups.

(Some 30 lines are missing from the bottom of this column and the top of the next column.)

(4.IV) [. . .] Lady Athirat of the sea replied: "Listen, Qudsh-wa-Amrar, you fisherman of lady Athirat of the sea, saddle a donkey, harness an ass, put on the silver ropes and the golden bindings, and make ready my jenny's ropes."

Qudsh-wa-Amrar heard her, and saddled a donkey, harnessed an ass, put on the silver ropes and the golden bindings, and made ready her jenny's ropes. Having taken Athirat in his arms and set her on the donkey's beautifully prepared back, Qudsh-wa-Amrar then took the lead, burning bright as star, with virgin Anat coming behind. As for Baal, he departed for Zapan's heights.

Thus Athirat set out for El amid the sources of the rivers and the channels of the abysses. Upon her arrival at El's abode, she entered the pavilion of the Father of Years. She bowed and fell down at El's feet, prostrating herself and honoring him.

What a sight unfolded! As soon as El saw her, he unfurrowed his brow and laughed. He put his feet on the footstool and wiggled his toes, raising his voice and exclaiming: "How is it that lady Athirat of the sea has come here? How does it happen that the one who created the gods has made this trip? Perhaps you are famished after your travels, or really thirsty from your journey? Eat or drink: there is food for you to eat on the tables and wine, the blood of the vine, in the golden goblets to drink. On the other hand, perhaps King El's passion stirs you and love for the bull arouses you?"

Lady Athirat of the sea replied: "El, your decree is wise, you are eternally wise, and a life of good fortune is yours to decree. The mighty one, Baal, is our king and judge, with no one above him: it is all of us who bring his chalice and bear his cup. Yet he cries out, groaning, to his father, bull El, the king who established his legitimacy, and to the goddess Athirat along with her children and kin: Baal has neither house nor court like the gods and Athirat's children, El's residence and his sons' shelter, lady Athirat of the sea's residence, the residence of the legitimate brides, the residence of Pidray, daughter of light, the shelter of Tallay, daughter of rain, the residence of Arsay, daughter of Wide-world."

The beneficent one, El the compassionate, answered: "So, I'm a servant, am I? Am I Athirat's assistant, a servant who works with tools? Or is it that Athirat is a servant girl who makes bricks? Let a house and court be built for Baal (4.V) like the gods' and Athirat's children."

Lady Athirat of the sea responded: "El, you are both great and wise, and your grey hair, on beard and chest, instructs you well. As a result, Baal will abundantly provide his rain and showers in downpours, and he will make his voice (i.e., thunder) heard in the clouds as he hurls lightning bolts to earth. If it is a house of cedars, let him finish it; if a house of bricks, let him lay its courses. Let them tell the mighty one, Baal: 'Summon a caravan with its wares to your palatial house so that the mountains and hills may bring to you abundant silver and the finest gold, so that they may bring to you precious stones—and then build the house with the silver, the gold, and the purest lapis lazuli!'"

Virgin Anat was happy. When she stamped her feet, the earth shook, and thus she set out for Baal on Zapan's heights, over a distance of a thousand acres, even ten thousand hectares. Virgin Anat laughed, raising her voice and exclaiming: "Baal, good news for you! I bring you good news! A house and court have been granted to you like your brothers' and kin! Summon a caravan with its wares to your palatial house so that the mountains and hills may bring to you abundant silver and the finest gold—and then build the house with the silver, the gold, and the purest lapis lazuli!"

The mighty one, Baal, was delighted! When he summoned a caravan with its wares to his palatial house, the mountains and hills brought to him abundant silver, the finest gold, and precious stones. He sent a message to Kothar-wa-Hasis.

And then return to the account "When the lads were sent"[87]

At this point, Kothar-wa-Hasis arrived. Baal placed an ox and a fatted calf before him. When a throne was prepared, he was seated to the right of the mighty one, Baal, while the gods ate and drank.

The mighty one, Baal, the cloud-rider, said: "Kothar, quickly build and erect the palatial house! In the midst of Zapan's peaks, quickly, you must build and erect the palatial house! Let the palatial house encompass a thousand acres, even ten thousand hectares!"

Kothar-wa-Hasis responded: "Oh, mighty one, Baal who rides the clouds, listen and understand: shall I not put a window or a clerestory in the palatial house?"

The mighty one, Baal, answered: "Do not put a window or a clerestory in the palatial house [...]."

(4.VI) Kothar-wa-Hasis responded: "You will come around to my advice."

Kothar-wa-Hasis repeated his question: "Oh, mighty one, Baal who rides the clouds, please listen: shall I not put a window or a clerestory in the palatial house?"

The mighty one, Baal, answered: "Do not put a window or a clerestory in the palatial house lest Pidray, daughter of light, and Tallay, daughter of rain [...] Sea, El's beloved [...] he scorned me and spat [...]."

Kothar-wa-Hasis responded: "You will come around to my advice."

His palatial house was quickly built and erected. He went to Lebanon and Siryan for their choicest trees and cedars. A flame, indeed, a fire was set in the palatial house. For one day and then two, the flame and fire consumed the palatial house. On the third and fourth day, the flame and fire consumed the palatial house. On the fifth and sixth day, the flame and fire consumed the palatial house. Finally, on the seventh day, the flame and fire were extinguished in the palatial house: the silver had turned into tiles and the gold had become bricks.

The mighty one, Baal, was ecstatic: "I have built my palatial house of silver and gold!"

---

[87] The scribe incised two horizontal lines on the tablet at this point before inserting instructions to the reader to return to a formulaic scene (not preserved here) describing the sending of messengers and the delivery of their message, a verbatim account that the scribe did not wish to repeat. He followed this note with another single line to separate his comment from the narrative that then resumed.

Baal-Haddu completed the preparations of his palatial house: he slaughtered large and small cattle, he felled bulls and fatling rams, yearling calves, skipping lambs and kids. He invited his brothers and kin to his palatial house, the seventy sons of Athirat. He provided the gods and goddesses with rams, ewes, bulls, cows, thrones, chairs, jars of wine, and pitchers. While the gods ate and drank, sucklings were served with a sharp knife, slices of the fattened calf. They drank wine, the blood of vines, from goblets and golden cups. [. . .]

(The next dozen lines or so are either fragmentary or lacking entirely.)

(4.VII) [. . .] Baal passed from city to city and returned from town to town: sixty-six, seventy-seven, eighty, ninety cities and towns he captured, then returned to the palace.

The mighty one, Baal, said: "Kothar, son of the sea and son of the mingled waters, I have something to install: let a clerestory window be opened in the palatial house, let a rift open in the clouds in accord with Kothar-wa-Hasis' word."

Kothar-wa-Hasis laughed, raised his voice, and exclaimed: "I warned you, O mighty one, Baal: 'You will come around to my advice.'"

Baal opened a clerestory window in the palatial house, a rift in the clouds. Baal made his holy voice (i.e., thunder) heard, then he repeated his utterance, which covered the earth, causing the mountains to tremble and the high places of the earth to shake. Those who hate Baal-Haddu, his enemies, took to the forests and the mountainsides.

The mighty one, Baal, said: "Why do you tremble, you enemies of Haddu who wield weapons against Dimaranu?" Baal gazes straight ahead as his right hand brandishes the cedar-weapon. In this way Baal was enthroned in his palace.

"Will a king or usurper establish dominion on the earth? I will send a messenger to El's beloved son, the champion Death, so that he (El) may call out to beloved Death of the cavernous throat that I am the only one who rules over the gods, who fattens gods and humans, and who satisfies the earth's throngs." Baal cried aloud to his lads: "Observe, Gapn and Ugar, sons of [. . .]

(The next dozen lines are either unintelligible or missing as Baal gives instructions to Gapn and Ugar.)

(4.VIII) "[. . .] Set out for Mount Targuzizi and Mount Tharrummagi, two mounds at the edge of the earth. With the palms of your hands, lift the forested mountain so that you may descend to earth's quarantine, where you will be numbered among those who descend to the underworld. At that point, set out for the interior of his city Swamp, to Sinkhole his enthronement seat, and to Slime, the land of his ancestral heritage. But be vigilant, divine assistants: do not come too close to El's son Death, lest he pop you in his mouth like a lamb and you be devoured in his crushing throat like a kid. Sun, the light of the gods, burns hot while the skies succumb in the hands of Death, El's beloved. From a distance of a thousand acres, even ten thousand hectares, bow and fall down at Death's feet. You will prostrate yourselves and honor him, and repeat what I say to El's beloved, the champion Death:

'This is the message of the mighty one, Baal, supreme among warriors: "I have built my palatial house of silver and gold!"'

(Some 30 lines are illegible or missing, with Death's message to Baal appearing when the narrative resumes.)

["I will pierce you . . .] (5.I) as you struck and overpowered Lotan,[88] the fleeing and twisting serpent, the one who wields power with seven heads. Let the heavens wither and languish, for I am the one who will crush you in pieces and consume you from head to toe. You will certainly descend into the watery depths of the throat of El's beloved son, the champion Death."

The gods left without delay. They set out for Baal on Zapan's heights where Gapn and Ugar said: "This is the message of El's beloved son, the champion Death: 'My throat is the throat of a lion in a desolate land! If it is the craving of the dolphin in the sea, or bulls approaching a pool and deer coming to a spring, if my appetite truly consumes a heap, then I truly will eat with both my hands, whether seven bowls are my portion or my cup is mixed with a river! So give a summons, Baal, and invite me with my brothers and kin: dine and drink wine with my brothers and kin. Thus let us drink, Baal. I will pierce you [. . .] as you struck and overpowered Lotan, the fleeing and twisting serpent, the one who wields power with seven heads. Let the heavens wither and languish, for I am the one who will crush you in pieces and consume you from head to toe. You will certainly descend into the watery depths of the throat of El's beloved son, the champion Death.'"

(Some 40 lines are missing before the text resumes with messengers reporting to Baal the decree that he must submit to Death.)

(5.II) "[. . .] One lip to earth, one lip to heaven, [. . .] tongue to the stars. Baal will go inside him, descending into his mouth like a dried olive, something the earth produces and trees bear as fruit."

The mighty one, Baal, the cloud-rider was terrified: "Depart, repeat what I say to El's beloved son, the champion Death: 'This is the message of the mighty one, Baal, supreme among warriors: "Greetings, Death, son of El. I am your servant forever."'"

The gods left without delay. They set out for Death, son of El, to the interior of his city Swamp, to Sinkhole his enthronement seat, and to Slime, the land of his ancestral heritage. They raised their voices and exclaimed: "This is the message of the mighty one, Baal, supreme among warriors: 'Greetings, Death, son of El. I am your servant forever.'"

Death, son of El, was delighted. He raised his voice and exclaimed: "How is it that Baal gives me a summons and invites me with my brothers and kin [. . .].

(Some 175 lines are illegible, missing, or only partially preserved in the remainder of 5.II, all of 5.III and 5.IV, and the top of 5.V. Enough is preserved in column four to indicate that festive dining took place, and when a coherent text resumes, the speaker is addressing Baal in anticipation of Baal's death.)

(5.V) [. . .] "I will put him[89] in a hole of the gods in the earth, but you take your clouds, wind, bolts, rains, and with you your seven lads and eight adjutants, along with Pidray, daughter of light, and Tallay, daughter of rain. Then set out

---

[88] Lotan or Litan is a serpentine sea monster and cosmic enemy of the Storm God, which appears in the Hebrew Bible as Leviathan, whom the God of Israel defeats (Isa. 27.1). The fight of a god with this type of monster is seen also in Hesiod's *Theogony* (Part 1, document 5), the *Hymn to Apollo* (document 3.9), and several of the Hittite texts (*Iluyanka, Song of Hedammu;* see documents 3.4.a and 3.4.b).

[89] We do not know to whom this "him" refers.

for Mount Knkny, and with the palms of your hands, lift the forested mountain so that you may descend to earth's quarantine, where you will be numbered among those who descend to the underworld. The gods will know that you have died."

The mighty one, Baal, heard. He made love with a heifer in the steppe, the field bordering Death's domain, lying with the cow seventy-seven times. She aroused him eighty-eighty times and conceived, giving birth to Mathu. The mighty one, Baal, clothed him [. . .]

(Some 50 lines are missing. The text resumes with messengers reporting Baal's demise to El.)

(5.VI) "[. . .] We came upon the earth's most pleasant region, the steppe, the most beautiful field bordering Death's domain. We came upon Baal fallen to the earth. The mighty one, Baal, is dead. The prince, the lord of the earth has perished."

Then the beneficent one, El the compassionate, came down from his throne and sat on the footstool, then from the footstool he sat on the earth. He poured dirt and dust on his head, appropriate for sorrowful mourning, covered his loins with a mourning garb, scratched incisions in his skin with a stone razor, gashed his cheeks and chin, gouged his upper arms, plowed his chest like a garden, and gouged his back like a valley. He raised his voice and exclaimed: "Baal, Dagan's son, is dead! What does this mean for the multitudes of people? I must go down to the underworld."

At that time, Anat was roaming as she hunted over every hill and mountain to the core of earth and field. She came upon the earth's most pleasant region, the steppe, the most beautiful field bordering Death's domain. She came upon Baal fallen to the earth. She covered her loins with a mourning garb, (6.I) scratched incisions in her skin with a stone razor, gashed her cheeks and chin, gouged her upper arms, plowed her chest like a garden, and gouged her back like a valley: "Baal, Dagan's son, is dead! What does this mean for the multitudes of people? We must go down to the underworld."

Sun, the light of the gods, went down to her. When she had sobbed to surfeit, drinking her tears like wine, she called aloud to Sun, the light of the gods: "Burden me with the mighty one, Baal!"

Sun, the light of the gods, heard and lifted the mighty one, Baal, placing him on Anat's shoulder. Weeping over him, she carried him up to Zapan's peaks and buried him, placing him in a hole of the gods in the earth. She slaughtered seventy wild bulls, seventy oxen, seventy sheep, seventy deer, seventy gazelles, and seventy asses as a ritual offering of the mighty one, Baal. [. . .] She then set out for El amid the sources of the rivers and the channels of the abysses. Upon her arrival at El's abode, she entered the pavilion of the Father of Years. She bowed and fell down at El's feet, prostrating herself and honoring him. She raised her voice, and exclaimed: "Now let the goddess Athirat rejoice along with her children and kin, for the mighty one, Baal, is dead. The prince, the lord of the earth has perished."

El calls out to lady Athirat of the sea: "Listen, lady Athirat of the sea, give one of your sons that I might install him as king."

Lady Athirat of the sea responded: "Shall we not install Yadi-yalhan as king?"

The beneficent one, El the compassionate, replied: "He is too weak to run or wield a spear in comparison with Baal, Dagan's son."

Lady Athirat of the sea responded: "Shall we not install Athtar the terrifying as king? Athtar the terrifying shall be king!" At that point, Athtar the terrifying ascended the peaks of Zapan and sat on the throne of the mighty one, Baal. His feet did not reach the footstool, nor did his head reach its top.

Athtar the terrifying said: "I cannot be king on the peaks of Zapan." Athtar the terrifying descended from the throne of the mighty one, Baal, but he became king of the underworld, god of it all.

(Six lines are unintelligible.)

(6.II) [. . .] One day passed, then two, and the maid, Anat, looked diligently for him. As a cow's heart for her calf, and a ewe's for her lamb, so was Anat's heart longing after Baal. She seized the fringe of Death's garment, grabbing the edge of his robe, and raised her voice and exclaimed: "You! Death! Give me my brother!"

Death, El's son, replied: "Virgin Anat, what is it you want? I was roaming as I hunted over every hill and mountain to the core of earth and field. My appetite was deprived of humans, the earth's multitudes. I came upon the earth's most pleasant region, the steppe, the most beautiful field bordering Death's domain. I was the one who drew near to the mighty one, Baal. I was the one who popped him in my mouth like a lamb, devoured in my crushing throat like a kid."

Sun, the light of the gods, burned hot while the skies succumbed in the hands of Death, El's son. One day passed, then two, then days became months. The maid, Anat, had looked diligently for him. As a cow's heart for her calf, and a ewe's for her lamb, so was Anat's heart longing after Baal.

She seized Death, El's son, and split him with a sword. She winnowed him with a sieve, she burned him in the fire, she ground him down with a millstone, and sowed him in the field. Birds ate what remained of him, fowl devoured his parts, the remnants called out to the remnants.

(The scribe incised here 2 lines at the bottom of the column; the top of the next column lacks some 40 lines, which conclude with a presentation of two possible dreams that El might see indicating Baal's status.)

(6.III) "[. . .] Then I will know that the mighty one, Baal, the prince and lord of the earth has perished and that he is dead.

"But if the mighty one, Baal, the prince and lord of the earth is alive and well, let the heavens rain oil and the wadis flow with honey in El's dream, the vision of the beneficent one, the compassionate one who created all creatures. Then I will know that the mighty one, Baal, the prince and lord of the earth is alive and well."

The heavens rained oil and the wadis flowed with honey in El's dream, the vision of the beneficent one, the compassionate one who created all creatures. Beneficent El, the compassionate one, was delighted. He put his feet on the footstool, unfurrowed his brow and laughed. He raised his voice and exclaimed: "I can sit down and relax and my inner turmoil can subside, for the mighty one, Baal, the prince and lord of the earth is alive and well."

El called out to virgin Anat: "Listen, virgin Anat, give this message to Sun, the light of the gods: (6.IV) 'Sun, the furrows in El's fields remain dry. Baal neglects the furrows of the plowed land. Where is the mighty one, Baal? Where is the prince and lord of the earth?'"

Virgin Anat left and set out for Sun, the light of the gods. She raised her voice and exclaimed: "This is the message of bull El, your father, the beneficent one who fathered you: 'Sun, the furrows in El's fields remain dry. Baal neglects the furrows of the plowed land. Where is the mighty one, Baal? Where is the prince and lord of the earth?'"

Sun, the light of the gods, replied: "Pour pleasing wine in goblets, let your kin bring garlands: I will search for the mighty one, Baal."

Virgin Anat replied: "Wherever you go, Sun, wherever you go, El will protect you!"

(Nearly 40 lines are either fragmentary or entirely missing in the remainder of the column that recounted Baal's reappearance.)

(6.V) Baal seized Athirat's children. He struck the great ones with a scimitar, he struck Sea's militia with a mace, he struck Sea's small ones to the earth.

At last Baal returned to his royal throne, his resting place, the seat of his dominion.

Days became months, months became years. Then in the seventh year, Death, El's son, approached the mighty one, Baal. He raised his voice and exclaimed: "Because of you I endured shame. Because of you I endured winnowing with a sieve. Because of you I endured splitting with a sword. Because of you I endured burning in the fire. Because of you I endured grinding with a millstone. [. . .] Because of you I endured scattering in the field. Because of you I endured sowing in the sea. Give me one of your brothers so that I may feed, so that my furious anger may turn aside. If you do not give me one of your brothers, then I will consume multitudes [. . .]."

(Nearly 40 lines are either fragmentary or entirely missing in the remainder of the column and the top of the final column. When a coherent passage resumes, Death seems to be talking about how Baal tricked him.)

(6.VI) [. . .] Death, El's son. "Look! Baal gave me own brothers as my food! It was my mother's sons that he gave me to consume!"

He returned to Baal on Zapan's peaks. He raised his voice and exclaimed: "Baal, you gave me own brothers as my food! It was my mother's sons that you gave me to consume!"

They eyed each other like seasoned warriors; Death was strong, Baal was strong.

They collided like wild bulls; Death was strong, Baal was strong.

They bit like serpents; Death was strong, Baal was strong.

They grappled like swift competitors; Death fell, Baal fell.

Up above, Sun called out to Death: "Listen well, Death, son of El! How can you engage in battle with the mighty one, Baal? How will your father, bull El, not hear you? He will certainly remove the supports for your enthronement, overturn your royal throne, and smash your scepter of judgment."

El's beloved son, the champion Death, began to fear and became terrified. At the sound of her voice, Death rose, raised his voice and cried out: "Let Baal be enthroned on his royal throne, his resting place, the seat of his dominion." [. . .]

(A half-dozen lines are too fragmentary for translation, after which a hymn of praise to Sun closes the narrative, followed by a colophon identifying the scribe and the king of Ugarit.)

> [. . .] You will also eat the food that is offered,
> You will drink the wine that is presented.
> Sun, you exercise authority over the deceased,
> Sun, you exercise authority over the gods.
> Deities are in your company,
> The dead are in your company.
> Kothar is your companion,
> Hasis is your close friend.
> In the sea are Desire and the Dragon[90]
> Where Kothar-wa-Hasis cast them,
> Where Kothar-wa-Hasis cut them off.

(Colophon)

The scribe: Ilimilk from Shubban, student of Attan, the diviner, chief of the priests, chief of the herdsmen, an official of Niqmaddu, king of Ugarit, master of YRGB, lord of THRMN.

3.5.b. The *Aqhat Epic*

The *Aqhat* (or *Aqhatu*) epic is preserved in a series of tablets signed by the scribe Ilimilk, like the other two preserved epic poems from Ugarit (the *Baal Cycle* and the *Keret* epic). Unlike for the *Baal Cycle*, we do not have the final tablets of this epic. In contrast to the mythic dimensions of the *Baal Cycle* with its nearly exclusive focus on the gods, this narrative revolves around a family of humans on earth and the crises that jeopardize their lives over many years, in all of which the gods are intimately involved. In this sense, the poem reflects a heroic world akin to that of the later Homeric epics.

The patriarch of this story, Dan'il (or Danilu), is introduced as pious but with no male heir. The meaning and significance of the repeated epithets for Dan'il as the "man of Rapa' . . . man of the Harnamite" remain unclear to us. Aqhat is the son whom El, head of the pantheon, graciously gives to Dan'il at the instigation of Baal, the Storm God associated with fertility. The Kotharat ("skillful ones") are goddesses associated with birth who make the divinely supervised birth of Aqhat possible. Dan'il also receives from the gods a special bow with arrows, manufactured by the gods of metallurgy and crafts (Kothar, Hasis, and Hayin), a gift that Dan'il passes on to his son, Aqhat. The goddess of sex and violence, Anat, insists on possessing the bow for herself, but Aqhat insultingly refuses to surrender it, which causes the family's and the land's misfortune. Unfortunately, the final tablet of the text has not been found, so the story breaks

---

[90] Anat mentioned in 3.III that she had earlier subdued these two creatures.

off when Pughat (Aqhat's sister) is trying to exact vengeance on her brother's murderers.

(17.I) *(Some 10 lines are missing from the beginning of the story.)*
Then Dan'il, the man of Rapa', the champion, the man of the Harnamite, in proper attire provided food and drink for the gods, the holy ones. He cast aside his garment, went up to his bed and lay down. He cast aside his clothing and slept through the night.

Not just once! One day and then two days, Dan'il in proper attire provided food and drink for the gods, the holy ones. Three days and then four, Dan'il in proper attire provided food and drink for the gods, the holy ones. Five days and then six, Dan'il in proper attire provided food and drink for the gods, the holy ones. Dan'il cast aside his garment, went up to his bed and lay down. He cast aside his clothing and slept through the night.

A new development on the seventh day! Baal approached El with his petition: "Oh, the anguish of Dan'il the man of Rapa'! Oh, the groaning of the champion, the man of the Harnamite! For he has no son as do his brothers, nor offspring as do his kin. In proper attire he provided food and drink for the gods, the holy ones. O, bull El, my father, bless him! You who created all creatures, strengthen him so that there can be a son and offspring in his palatial house who will raise a stele in the sanctuary for his divine ancestor, even a votive memorial for his clan, one who will bring his spirit out of the underworld and protect his steps from the dust, who will shut the jaws of any who malign him and who will expel any who wrong him, who will grasp his hand when he is drunk and support him when he has had too much wine, who will partake of his meal-offering in Baal's temple and his portion in El's temple, who will plaster his roof when it becomes muddy and wash his gear when it becomes dirty."

El grasped a cup in his hand, a goblet in his right hand, and generously blessed his servant. He blessed Dan'il the man of Rapa' and strengthened the champion, the man of the Harnamite: "May Dan'il live, the man of Rapa', the champion, the man of the Harnamite! [. . .] Let him go up to his bed and lie down: while kissing his wife, let her become pregnant, and while embracing her, let her conceive. Let there be a son and offspring in his palatial house who will raise a stele in the sanctuary for his divine ancestor, even a votive memorial for his clan, one who will bring his spirit out of the underworld and protect his steps from the dust, who will shut the jaws of any who malign him and who will expel any who wrong him, who will grasp his hand when he is drunk and support him when he has had too much wine, who will partake of his meal-offering in Baal's temple and his portion in El's temple, who will plaster his roof when it becomes muddy and wash his gear when it becomes dirty."

(Some 15 missing lines cannot be reconstructed at the end of this column and the beginning of the next column, although the words first spoken by Baal and then repeated by El as a blessing upon Dan'il are repeated a third time to Dan'il, who responds as follows.)

(17.II) Dan'il's face expressed joy, as above his countenance glowed. He unfurrowed his brow and laughed. He put his feet on the footstool, raising his voice and exclaiming: "Even I can now sit and rest at ease, and my soul can rest at ease within me. For a son will be born to me just like my brothers, offspring just like my kin, one who will raise a stele in the sanctuary for my divine ancestor, even a votive memorial for my clan, one who will bring my spirit out of the underworld and protect my steps from the dust, who will shut the jaws of any who malign me and who will expel any who wrong me, who will grasp my hand when I am drunk and support me when I have had too much wine, who will partake of my meal-offering in Baal's temple and my portion in El's temple, who will plaster my roof when it becomes muddy and wash my gear when it becomes dirty."

Dan'il reached his house and came into his palace. The Kotharat entered his house, the dazzling daughters of the crescent moon. At that point, Dan'il the man of Rapa', the champion, the man of the Harnamite, slaughtered an ox for the Kotharat. He provided food and drink for the Kotharat, dazzling daughters of the crescent moon.

Not just once! One day and then two days, he provided food and drink for the Kotharat, dazzling daughters of the crescent moon. Three days and then four, he provided food and drink for the Kotharat, dazzling daughters of the crescent moon. Five days and then six, he provided food and drink for the Kotharat, dazzling daughters of the crescent moon.

A new development on the seventh day! The Kotharat, dazzling daughters of the crescent moon, left his house [. . .] the pleasures of the bed [. . .] the delights of the bed of childbirth. Dan'il sat down and counted her months: one month and a second, a third month and a fourth, the months arrived [. . .].

(Some 10 lines are missing from the end of this column. The next two columns, 17.III–IV, are missing entirely and must have contained material that included information about Aqhat's birth to Dan'il and his growth to maturity, as well as introducing the significance of a very special bow.)

(17.V) *(After a dozen lines or so missing from the top of the column, Kothar-wa-Hasis is finishing a speech.)*

"[. . .] I will take the bow there, I will quadruple the arrows."

At that point, when the seventh day came, Dan'il the man of Rapa', the champion, the man of the Harnamite, raised himself up and sat among the nobles in the entrance to the city gate where he judged the widow's case and enacted justice for the orphan. When he raised his eyes and looked over a distance of a thousand acres, even ten thousand hectares, he perceived Kothar's coming, the stride of Hasis.

A sight to behold! He was bringing the bow, and he had quadrupled the arrows! Then Dan'il the man of Rapa', the champion, the man of the Harnamite, raised his voice and called out to his wife: "Listen, Lady Danatay, prepare a lamb from the flock for Kothar-wa-Hasis' appetite, for the desire of Hayin, the one skillful with his hand. Provide food and drink for the gods. Honor and take care of them, lords of Memphis, gods of it all."

Lady Danatay heard and prepared a lamb from the flock for Kothar-wa-Hasis' appetite, for the desire of Hayin, the one skillful with his hands.

At this point, Kothar-wa-Hasis arrived. He placed the bow in Dan'il's hands and put the arrows on his knees. Then Lady Danatay provided food and drink for the gods. She honored and took care of them, lords of Memphis, gods of it all. Kothar departed for his own tent, Hayin departed for his own residence.

Then Dan'il the man of Rapa', the champion, the man of the Harnamite [. . .] the bow [. . .] upon Aqhat [. . .] the best of your hunt, son [. . .] the best of your game [. . .] the game in his palace [. . .].

(Some 35 lines are either missing or are too fragmentary for sustained translation in the remainder of this column and the beginning of the next column, 17.VI, but enough is clear to indicate that in the midst of a banquet in progress, Anat sees the bow that is in Aqhat's possession.)

She emptied her cup on the ground, raised her voice, and called out: "Listen carefully, champion Aqhat. Ask for silver and I will give it to you, or gold and I will grant it to you, but give your bow to Anat. Let the kin to the peoples take your arrows."

Aqhat the champion responded: "I will donate ash-trees from Lebanon, tendons from wild oxen, horns from mountain goats, sinews from a bull's heels, and reeds from a great swamp. Give these to Kothar-wa-Hasis so that he can fashion a bow and arrows for Anat, kin to the peoples."

Virgin Anat replied: "Ask for life, champion Aqhat! Ask for life and I will give it to you, even immortality and I will grant it to you. I can make it possible for you to count the years with Baal. You will be able to count the months with El's sons. Like Baal, the one who lives will live indeed: they will make a feast and provide him with drink, a minstrel will chant and sing over him." She answered him: "I am the one who will give life to Aqhat the champion."

Aqhat the champion replied: "Do not lie to me, virgin, for to this champion your lies are worth spit. What can a man take at the end? At the close, what can a man take? Glaze will be poured on my head, lime on the top of my skull,[91] and I will die the death that comes to all. I am one who will surely die. Nevertheless, I have something further to say: bows are for warriors! What? Will women hunt?"

Anat laughed out loud, but in her heart she fashioned a plot: "Think again, champion Aqhat, think again and go with care. Should I ever find you acting the rebel or behaving proudly, I will be the one to make you fall beneath my feet, you handsome boy, strongest of men."

When she stamped her feet, the earth shook. She then set out for El amid the sources of the rivers and the channels of the abysses. Upon her arrival at El's abode, she entered the pavilion of the Father of Years. She bowed and fell down at El's feet, prostrating herself and honoring him. Virgin Anat slandered Aqhat the champion, the child of Dan'il man of Rapa', as she spoke, raising her voice and calling out: "Aqhat [. . .]."

(Some 20 lines are missing from the remainder of the column, although the final letters of a scribe's colophon identifying himself are preserved on the edge of the tablet: "Scribe: Ilimilk of Shubban, student of Attan the diviner.")

(18.I) *(The initial five lines are largely missing.)*

Virgin Anat replied: "El, don't be too happy with your fine house and your palace's great height. With my long, strong right hand I will seize it. I will smash your head and make your gray hair and beard run with blood and gore. Call upon Aqhat, son of Dan'il, so that he deliver you or protect you from virgin Anat's hand!"

---

[91] This description does not correspond to known burial practices in the second millennium BCE and may be a metaphor for the white hair of old age.

The beneficent one, El the compassionate, answered: "I know you, daughter, that you act all too human, and your volatile nature is otherwise not to be found among goddesses. Be gone, impious daughter! You will seize whatever you wish and attain whatever you desire. Anyone who stands in your way will be utterly annihilated."

So virgin Anat departed. At that point, she set out for Aqhat the champion over a distance of a thousand acres, even ten thousand hectares. Virgin Anat laughed as she raised her voice and called out: "Listen, champion Aqhat, you are my brother and I [am your sister . . .] your seven kin [. . .] my father I fled [. . .] you will hunt [. . .] I will instruct you [. . .] the city Abilum, the city of Prince Moon where a tower [. . .]."

(Some 20 lines are missing from the end of this column, as well as all the lines in the next two columns, 18.II–III.)

(18.IV) *(The first 4 lines of this column are fragmentary.)* Virgin Anat departed, heading for Yatpan, the Sutu warrior.[92] She raised her voice and called out: "May Yatpan return [. . .] the city Abilum, the city of Prince Moon. How will Moon not be renewed? [. . .] in right horn [. . .] his head."

Yatpan, the Sutu warrior, replied: "Listen, virgin Anat, it is you who will strike him for his bow and deprive him of life for his arrows. The admirable champion has prepared a meal [. . .] he remained alone in a tent [. . .]."

Virgin Anat answered: "Return, Yatpan [. . .], I will put you like a vulture on my belt, like a bird of prey in my scabbard. As for Aqhat, son of Dan'il, when he sits down to eat the meal, vultures will circle over him and a flock of carrion birds will fix their eyes. Among the vultures I, too, will be circling. I will maneuver you over Aqhat. Strike him twice on the skull, three times above the ear. Like an executioner, spill his blood even to his knees, like a butcher, so that his life goes out from his nose like the wind, his soul like vapor and smoke. I will not let him live."

She took Yatpan, the Sutu warrior. She put him like a vulture on her belt, like a bird of prey in her scabbard. As Aqhat, Dan'il's son, sat down to eat the meal, vultures circled over him and a flock of carrion birds fixed their eyes. Anat was circling among the vultures, and she maneuvered Yatpan over Aqhat. Yatpan struck him twice on the skull, three times above the ear. Like an executioner, he spilled his blood even to his knees, like a butcher. His life went out from his nose like the wind, his soul like vapor and smoke.

[. . .] Aqhat. She wept [. . .] "I struck you for your bow, I did not let you live on account of your arrows."

(The last 2 lines of the column are fragmentary, along with the first 7 lines of the next tablet [19.I], followed by a further 6 lines whose meaning is not clear.)

[. . .] into the water it fell [. . .] the bow was broken [. . .] virgin Anat returned [. . .] her hand like [. . .], her fingers like a singer a lyre [. . .].

[. . .]. "I struck him for his staff, I struck him for his bow, I did not let him live on account of his arrows. Yet his bow was not given to me, and in death [. . .] the first fruits of summer [. . .] an ear of grain in its husk."

---

[92] Yatpan is apparently a mercenary from the nomadic Sutu people.

At that point, Dan'il, the man of Rapa', the man of the Harnamite, raised himself up and sat among the nobles in the entrance to the city gate where he judged the widow's case and enacted justice for the orphan.

(Four lines are missing.)

Pughat[93] raised her eyes and saw the harvest withered on the threshing floor, drooping and dried up. Over her father's house vultures circled and a flock of carrion birds fixed their eyes. Pughat wept in her heart, crying within. She tore Dan'il's garment, the man of Rapa', even the clothes of the champion, the man of the Harnamite.

It was then that Dan'il, the man of Rapa', prayed for clouds in the heat of the season, that the clouds might provide the early rain and that the dew might moisten the grapes in summer. For seven years, even eight, Baal the cloud-rider had failed: no dew, no showers, no surging of ground water, no welcome sound of Baal's voice (i.e., thunder).

She indeed tore Dan'il's garment, the man of Rapa', even the clothes of the champion, the man of the Harnamite. Dan'il cried aloud to his daughter: (19.II) "Listen, Pughat, water-bearer, gatherer of dew for barley, discerner of the stars' transit.[94] Saddle a donkey, harness an ass, put on the silver ropes and my golden bindings."

Pughat heard, she the water-bearer, gatherer of dew for barley, with insight into the stars' transit. As she profusely wept, she saddled a donkey and harnessed an ass. Weeping, she lifted her father and set him on the back of the donkey, on the ass's splendid back.

As Dan'il went around his parched land, he spotted a ripening stalk in the parched and desiccated land. He embraced the ripening stalk and kissed it: "Would that the ripening stalk and plant might flourish in the parched and desiccated land, that Aqhat the champion's hand would harvest you and put you in the granary!"

As Dan'il went around his devastated land, he spotted an ear of grain in the devastated dry land. He embraced the ear of grain and kissed it: "Would that the ear of grain and plant might flourish in the devastated and dry land, that Aqhat the champion's hand would harvest you and put you in the granary!"

The words of this speech had not passed his lips or left his mouth when Pughat raised her eyes and saw two lads coming.

(The next 10 lines are poorly preserved with only bits of narrative and dialogue clear.)

"He struck twice on the skull, three times above the ear." [. . .]

Tears flowed like quarter-shekels. [. . .]

"I bring you news, Dan'il. [. . .]. She caused his life to go out from his nose like the wind, his soul like vapor and smoke."

They arrived, raised their voices and called out: "Listen, Dan'il man of Rapa', Aqhat the champion is dead. Virgin Anat caused his life to go out like the wind, his soul like vapor."

---

[93] Pughat is Aqhat's sister.

[94] The connection between dew and stars is not random, for dew (like rain) was perceived as coming from the sky (Deut. 33.28; Prov. 3.20; Hag. 1.10; Zech. 8.12) so that one speaks of "the dew of heaven" (Gen. 27.28, 39; Dan. 4.15, 23, 25, 33 [Heb. 4.12, 20, 30]; 5.21; see Deut. 32.2; 33.13).

His feet slipped out from under him, his face ran with perspiration above him, his sinews snapped about him, his sinew links trembled, his back muscles went limp. He raised his voice and called out: "Smitten [. . .]."

(Six lines are missing.)

As he lifted his eyes, he looked and spied vultures in the clouds. (19.III) He raised his voice and called out: "May Baal break the vultures' wings and pinions so that they fall beneath my feet. I will split their bellies and inspect them carefully. If there is fat or bone, I will weep and bury him and place him in a hole of the gods in the earth."

The words of this speech had not passed his lips or left his mouth when Baal broke the vultures' wings and pinions so that they fell beneath his feet. He split their bellies and inspected them carefully. There was neither fat nor bone.

He raised his voice and called out: "May Baal reconstruct the vultures' wings and pinions. Vultures, take wing and fly!"

As he lifted his eyes, he looked and spied Hargab, father of vultures. He raised his voice and called out: "May Baal break Hargab's wings and pinions so that he falls beneath my feet. I will split his belly and inspect it carefully. If there is fat or bone, I will weep and bury him and place him in a hole of the gods in the earth."

The words of this speech had not passed his lips or left his mouth when Baal broke Hargab's wings and pinions so that he fell beneath his feet. He split his belly and inspected it carefully. There was neither fat nor bone.

He raised his voice and called out: "May Baal reconstruct Hargab's wings and pinions. Hargab, take wing and fly!"

As he lifted his eyes, he looked and spied Samal, mother of vultures. He raised his voice and called out: "May Baal break Samal's wings and pinions so that she falls beneath my feet. I will split her belly and inspect it carefully. If there is fat or bone, I will weep and bury him and place him in a hole of the gods in the earth."

The words of this speech had not passed his lips or left his mouth when Baal broke Samal's wings and pinions so that she fell beneath his feet. He split her belly and inspected it carefully. There was fat! There was bone! He removed Aqhat from them [. . .] He wept and prepared a grave, burying him [. . .]. He raised his voice and called out: "May Baal break the vultures' wings and pinions if they fly over my son's grave and disturb him in his sleep."

The king cursed Qor-Maym[95]: "Woe to you, Qor-Maym, who share responsibility for the assault on Aqhat the champion! Perpetually look for asylum in El's temple! Be a fugitive now and forever, now and for all generations!" Finally, he gestured with the staff in his hand.

He arrived at Mrrt-tgll-bnr. He raised his voice and called out: "Woe to you, Mrrt-tgll-bnr, who share responsibility for the assault on Aqhat the champion! May your root not sprout from the ground, may your head droop under the hand of any who plucks you! Be a fugitive now and forever, now and for all generations!" Finally, he gestured with the staff in his hand.

---

[95] Dan'il curses three cities in the vicinity of the discovery of his son's remains, their mere proximity indicating their need to exonerate themselves from the crime (see Deut. 21.1–9).

(19.IV) He arrived at the city Abilum, the city of Prince Moon. He raised his voice and called out: "Woe to you, city Abilum, who share responsibility for the assault on Aqhat the champion! May Baal strike you with blindness from this moment and forever, now and for all generations!" Finally, he gestured with the staff in his hand.

Dan'il arrived at his house and came into his palace. Women who weep and mourn entered his palatial house, as into his court did men who lacerate their skin. They wept for Aqhat the champion, shedding tears for the child of Dan'il man of Rapa'. Days turned into months, months became years. As many as seven years they wept for Aqhat the champion, shedding tears for the child of Dan'il man of Rapa'.

Then, in the seventh year, Dan'il the man of Rapa' spoke! The champion, the man of the Harnamite, responded, raising his voice and calling out: "Be gone from my palatial house, you women who weep and mourn, from my court you men who lacerate your skin!"

He offered a sacrifice to the gods and made incense ascend to heaven; the man of the Harnamite's incense ascended even to the stars.

(Three lines are damaged.)

Pughat the water-bearer replied: "My father offered a sacrifice to the gods and made incense ascend to heaven; the man of the Harnamite's incense ascended even to the stars. Bless me so that I may go blessed, empower me so that I may go empowered: I will strike the one who struck my brother and annihilate the one who annihilated my mother's child."

Dan'il the man of Rapa' replied: "May Pughat live, water-bearer, gatherer of dew for barley, discerner of the stars' transit [. . .], may she strike the one who struck her brother and annihilate the one who annihilated her mother's child. [. . .]"

She washed and rouged herself with shellfish, a product from a thousand acres of the sea. She took a champion's gear for clothes, inserted a dagger in its sheath, put a sword in its scabbard, and over them she put on a woman's garment.

Pughat reached the steppe-dwellers as the Sun darkened. As the light of the gods set, Pughat arrived at the tents.

Word was brought to Yatpan: "The woman who hired us has come to your pavilion and has come among the tents."[96]

Yatpan, the Sutu warrior, responded: "Escort her in so that she can give me wine to drink. Take the cup from my hand, the goblet from my right hand."

Pughat was escorted in and gave him to drink. She took the cup from his hand, the goblet from his right hand.

Yatpan, the Sutu warrior, responded: "The god who created encampments will place in the wine [. . .]. The hand that struck Aqhat the champion will strike the enemy by the thousands."

[. . .]. She gave him mixed wine to drink a second time.

(The narrative continued on another tablet that has not been found.)

---

[96] There is considerable ambiguity in the remaining lines that are preserved, a function of not having the entire narrative at our disposal. One possible interpretation is that Pughat disguised herself as the warrior goddess, Anat, but this is by no means certain.

3.6. YAHWEH AS A STORM GOD: PSALM 29

The Book of Psalms opens the third part of the Hebrew Bible's canon. These pieces of varying length and type (mainly hymns, petitions, and thanksgivings) were composed at various times and places during the first half of the first millennium BCE. Many of them are attributed to King David and other authors, but we do not know who composed them or who put together the anthology in which they have come down to us. "Psalms" is their Greek name (*Psalmoi*), meaning "songs played on a stringed instrument," which emphasizes their musicality. In Hebrew they are called *Tehillim*, "praises," given their religious character, but the language of singing and music is central in them as well. The hymn here, for instance, is entitled *mizmor le-David*, "a melody for/of David," even if it is conventionally translated as "psalm."

This psalm illustrates the tradition in which Yahweh is celebrated as a Storm God, much like Ugaritic Baal, Greek Zeus, Hittite Teshub, and Babylonian Marduk. The "heavenly beings" (or "sons of gods") praise the Lord as he brings rain and fertility through, acknowledging him as he returns to the assembly of divine beings (cf. Ps. 82.1, 89.5–7). Scholars have seen this hymn as a direct heir of Canaanite poetry, adapted by the early Israelites to their Yahwistic creed (for Canaanite features, see also Figure 9). The storm is represented as an event of cosmic proportions, which shakes nature (see representation of Baal in Figure 5). Yahweh is here a cloud-rider (see Zeus the "cloud-gatherer" and Baal the "cloud-rider") and his voice, like that of the other Storm Gods, is thunder itself (cf. Zeus "loud-sounding" and "broad-seeing/sounding"). His dominion over the sea ("over the flood" in verse 10) also reminds one of the cosmic fight between Baal and Yam in the *Baal Cycle* (document 5.a above) and the older Mesopotamian traditions in which the primordial waters were subdued. Similar Canaanite features can be traced in other parts of the Hebrew Bible, especially in Psalms 104 and 74, Job 41.1–34, and Isaiah 27.1. This poem is also a very good example of the poetic device of parallelism, typical of North-West Semitic as well as Mesopotamian literatures. This means repetitions and variations on those repetitions were irregularly used for poetic effect.

SOURCE: The Hebrew Bible, New Revised Standard Version, with minor modifications.

A Psalm of David

> (1) Ascribe to Yahweh,[97] O heavenly beings,[98]
>   ascribe to Yahweh glory and strength.
> (2) Ascribe to Yahweh the glory of his name;
>   worship Yahweh in holy splendor.

---

[97] The name of Yahweh has been maintained here (editor's modification), instead of the traditional rendering "the Lord."

[98] Literally, the Hebrew reads "sons of god(s)" (*bnei 'elim*).

(3) The voice of Yahweh is over the waters;
   the God of glory thunders,
   Yahweh, over mighty waters.

(4) The voice of Yahweh is powerful;
   the voice of Yahweh is full of majesty.

(5) The voice of Yahweh breaks the cedars;
   Yahweh breaks the cedars of Lebanon.

(6) He makes Lebanon skip like a calf,
   and Sirion[99] like a young wild ox.

(7) The voice of Yahweh flashes forth flames of fire.

(8) The voice of Yahweh shakes the wilderness;
   Yahweh shakes the wilderness of Kadesh.[100]

(9) The voice of Yahweh causes the oaks to whirl,[101]
   and strips the forest bare;
   and in his temple all say, 'Glory!'

(10) Yahweh sits enthroned over the flood;
   Yahweh sits enthroned as king for ever.

(11) May Yahweh give strength to his people!
   May Yahweh bless his people with peace!

3.7. DAVID AND GOLIATH: 1 SAMUEL 17

The two books of Samuel are part of the so-called Deuteronomistic History, that is, the compilation and edition of previous traditions into a single running narrative covering the history of Israel from the conquest of the land to the end of the kingdoms of Israel and Judah (including the books of Deuteronomy, Joshua, Judges, 1 and 2 Samuel, 1 and 2 Kings). The prevailing theory is that this book, like the others of this group, was written by a number of (now anonymous) authors, probably after the Babylonian exile (587–538 BCE), although others argue for a more complex chronology with earlier stages of composition. The stories about the rise of David, such as the episode included here, present him as an innocent and unambitious though extremely successful young hero who owes his prowess to his God's favor. The Lord anoints him and is always

---

[99] Mount Hermon, in southern Lebanon.

[100] This is the desert east of Kadesh (or Qadesh) in central-west Syria. The city was destroyed at the end of the Bronze Age, so the reference here also points to the antiquity of the tradition to which this poem belongs.

[101] Or "causes the deer to calve," in a different interpretation.

with him (perhaps as a retrospective apologetic view for his later expansionistic tendencies). Even though David had already been in King Saul's court as his lyre player and armor bearer, and though Saul "loved him greatly" (1 Sam. 16.14–23), the narrative about Goliath here seems to introduce David anew, and Saul does not seem to know the lad, which means that the source is a once-independent story in which the two had not yet met. Here David is presented as an unarmed shepherd, which contrasts with the previous episode in which he is an arm-bearer of the king and hence a soldier.

The combat between David and Goliath presents several elements that make it one of the more "Hellenic" sounding stories of the entire Hebrew Bible. The enemy, Goliath, is a Philistine. The Philistines' origins, about which much has been written, lie in the Aegean, or perhaps Cyprus (see Amos 9.7), as corroborated by archaeological and epigraphical evidence (for example, by their early Mycenaean-style pottery and different diet and possible Greek divine names). The name Goliath appears only here and is itself a non-Semitic name. It is probably Indo-European, and it has been compared with the name of Lydian King Alyattes. Two names (*alwt* and *wlt*), inscribed in potsherds from ancient Gath (modern site of Tell es-Safi), seem to confirm the historicity of this type of name in the area of Philistine settlement. Besides being portrayed by the Israelites as alien to their religion and customs, the whole scene of the single combat between the giant and David is reminiscent of the Homeric epics (see the story of young Nestor defeating the giant Ereuthalion, *Il.* 7.132–160). Moreover, the bronze and unusual armor, described in detail in 17.5–7, is seen as reflecting some kind of Greek panoply as well, whether Late Bronze Age (Mycenaean) or Iron Age; as with Homer's heroes, the extant traditions are hard to pin down chronologically as they both contain historical information but are re-elaborated through the centuries, presenting a rather composite picture. It is possible that this heroic motif reached Israel with the spread of the Homeric epics in the eastern Mediterranean, coloring whatever earlier traditions about the Philistines might have informed the Deuteronomistic writers.

SOURCE: The Hebrew Bible, New Revised Standard Version.

Now the Philistines gathered their armies for battle; they were gathered at Socoh, which belongs to Judah, and encamped between Socoh and Azekah, in Ephes-dammim. (2) Saul and the Israelites gathered and encamped in the valley of Elah, and formed ranks against the Philistines. (3) The Philistines stood on the mountain on one side, and Israel stood on the mountain on the other side, with a valley between them. (4) And there came out from the camp of the Philistines a champion named Goliath, of Gath, whose height was six cubits and a span.[102] (5) He had a helmet of bronze on his head, and he was armored with a coat of mail; the weight of the coat was five thousand shekels of bronze. (6) He had greaves of bronze on his legs and a javelin of bronze slung between his shoulders. (7) The shaft of his spear was like a weaver's beam, and his spear's head weighed six hundred shekels of iron; and

---

[102] That would make him 9.5 feet (3 meters) tall. The Greek version (*Septuagint*) has four cubits, more realistically.

his shield-bearer went before him. (8) He stood and shouted to the ranks of Israel, "Why have you come out to draw up for battle? Am I not a Philistine, and are you not servants of Saul? Choose a man for yourselves, and let him come down to me. (9) If he is able to fight with me and kill me, then we will be your servants; but if I prevail against him and kill him, then you shall be our servants and serve us." (10) And the Philistine said, "Today I defy the ranks of Israel! Give me a man, that we may fight together." (11) When Saul and all Israel heard these words of the Philistine, they were dismayed and greatly afraid.

(12) Now David was the son of an Ephrathite of Bethlehem in Judah, named Jesse, who had eight sons. In the days of Saul the man was already old and advanced in years. (13) The three eldest sons of Jesse had followed Saul to the battle; the names of his three sons who went to the battle were Eliab the firstborn, and next to him Abinadab, and the third Shammah. (14) David was the youngest; the three eldest followed Saul, (15) but David went back and forth from Saul to feed his father's sheep at Bethlehem. (16) For forty days the Philistine came forward and took his stand, morning and evening.

(17) Jesse said to his son David, "Take for your brothers an ephah[103] of this parched grain and these ten loaves, and carry them quickly to the camp to your brothers; (18) also take these ten cheeses to the commander of their thousand. See how your brothers fare, and bring some token from them."

(19) Now Saul, and they, and all the men of Israel, were in the valley of Elah, fighting with the Philistines. (20) David rose early in the morning, left someone in charge of the sheep, took the provisions, and went as Jesse had commanded him. He came to the encampment as the army was going forth to the battle line, shouting the war cry. (21) Israel and the Philistines drew up for battle, army against army. (22) David left the things in charge of the keeper of the baggage, ran to the ranks, and went and greeted his brothers. (23) As he talked with them, the champion, the Philistine of Gath, Goliath by name, came up out of the ranks of the Philistines, and spoke the same words as before. And David heard him.

(24) All the Israelites, when they saw the man, fled from him and were very much afraid. (25) The Israelites said, "Have you seen this man who has come up? Surely he has come up to defy Israel. The king will greatly enrich the man who kills him, and will give him his daughter and make his family free in Israel." (26) David said to the men who stood by him, "What shall be done for the man who kills this Philistine, and takes away the reproach from Israel? For who is this uncircumcised Philistine that he should defy the armies of the living God?" (27) The people answered him in the same way, "So shall it be done for the man who kills him."

(28) His eldest brother Eliab heard him talking to the men; and Eliab's anger was kindled against David. He said, "Why have you come down? With whom have you left those few sheep in the wilderness? I know your presumption and the evil of your heart; for you have come down just to see the battle." (29) David said, "What have I done now? It was only a question." (30) He turned away from him towards another and spoke in the same way; and the people answered him again as before.

---

[103] Ancient Hebrew dray measure, equivalent to approximately 23 liters.

(31) When the words that David spoke were heard, they repeated them before Saul; and he sent for him. (32) David said to Saul, "Let no one's heart fail because of him; your servant will go and fight with this Philistine." (33) Saul said to David, "You are not able to go against this Philistine to fight with him; for you are just a boy, and he has been a warrior from his youth." (34) But David said to Saul, "Your servant used to keep sheep for his father; and whenever a lion or a bear came, and took a lamb from the flock, (35) I went after it and struck it down, rescuing the lamb from its mouth; and if it turned against me, I would catch it by the jaw, strike it down, and kill it. (36) Your servant has killed both lions and bears; and this uncircumcised Philistine shall be like one of them, since he has defied the armies of the living God." (37) David said, "The Lord, who saved me from the paw of the lion and from the paw of the bear, will save me from the hand of this Philistine." So Saul said to David, "Go, and may the Lord be with you!"

(38) Saul clothed David with his armor; he put a bronze helmet on his head and clothed him with a coat of mail. (39) David strapped Saul's sword over the armor, and he tried in vain to walk, for he was not used to them. Then David said to Saul, "I cannot walk with these; for I am not used to them." So David removed them. (40) Then he took his staff in his hand, and chose five smooth stones from the wadi, and put them in his shepherd's bag, in the pouch; his sling was in his hand, and he drew near to the Philistine.

(41) The Philistine came on and drew near to David, with his shield-bearer in front of him. (42) When the Philistine looked and saw David, he disdained him, for he was only a youth, ruddy and handsome in appearance. (43) The Philistine said to David, "Am I a dog, that you come to me with sticks?" And the Philistine cursed David by his gods. (44) The Philistine said to David, "Come to me, and I will give your flesh to the birds of the air and to the wild animals of the field." (45) But David said to the Philistine, "You come to me with sword and spear and javelin; but I come to you in the name of the Lord of hosts, the God of the armies of Israel, whom you have defied. (46) This very day the Lord will deliver you into my hand, and I will strike you down and cut off your head; and I will give the dead bodies of the Philistine army this very day to the birds of the air and to the wild animals of the earth, so that all the earth may know that there is a God in Israel, (47) and that all this assembly may know that the Lord does not save by sword and spear; for the battle is the Lord's and he will give you into our hand."

(48) When the Philistine drew nearer to meet David, David ran quickly towards the battle line to meet the Philistine. (49) David put his hand in his bag, took out a stone, slung it, and struck the Philistine on his forehead; the stone sank into his forehead, and he fell face down on the ground. (50) So David prevailed over the Philistine with a sling and a stone, striking down the Philistine and killing him; there was no sword in David's hand. (51) Then David ran and stood over the Philistine; he grasped his sword, drew it out of its sheath, and killed him; then he cut off his head with it.

When the Philistines saw that their champion was dead, they fled. (52) The troops of Israel and Judah rose up with a shout and pursued the Philistines as far as Gath and the gates of Ekron, so that the wounded Philistines fell on the way from Shaaraim as far as Gath and Ekron. (53) The Israelites came back from chasing the

Philistines, and they plundered their camp. (54) David took the head of the Philistine and brought it to Jerusalem; but he put his armor in his tent.

(55) When Saul saw David go out against the Philistine, he said to Abner, the commander of the army, "Abner, whose son is this young man?" Abner said, "As your soul lives, O king, I do not know." (56) The king said, "Inquire whose son the stripling is." (57) On David's return from killing the Philistine, Abner took him and brought him before Saul, with the head of the Philistine in his hand. (58) Saul said to him, "Whose son are you, young man?" And David answered, "I am the son of your servant Jesse the Bethlehemite."

3.8. HOMER'S GODS AND HEROES

Homer is (with Hesiod) the earliest poet known in the history of Greek literature. From very early on, his influence was so great that many works were attributed to him, though only the *Iliad* and the *Odyssey* are now thought to be his (some scholars believe the *Odyssey* belongs to a different poet). We know nothing for sure about his life, origins, exact date, or manner of composition, and these problems (called "the Homeric question") have provoked endless scholarly debates throughout history. Archaeological discoveries have revolutionized our knowledge of the Bronze Age Aegean and opened up the possibility that some of the traditions in Homer might allude to the Mycenaean world and especially the turbulent wars before its collapse around 1200 BCE. For instance, rich citadels and palaces were discovered at Late Bronze Age sites that figure prominently in Homer, such as Mycenae, Pylos, and Troy itself, which suffered several destructions. Moreover, the decipherment of Linear B tablets from mainland Greece and Crete in the 1950s also proved that the rulers of those sites were Greek speakers. Our knowledge of the impoverished Iron Age, which followed (also called "Geometric" because of its pottery styles), at the end of which Homer was composing, has also increased. It is, therefore, safe to say that some Homeric motifs (the siege and destruction of Troy itself, many geographical and personal names, pieces of armor and other artifacts, etc.) go back to Mycenaean times, while many (or most) relate to Iron Age society and its fascination with a glorious past as it was then imagined. In a similar way, Homer's poems are composed in an artificial poetic language that contains archaisms dating to earlier stages of the Greek language as well as a combination of dialectal forms, with Ionic (from the central coast of Asia Minor) predominating and Aiolic (further north in Asia Minor) being the second most common—hence the idea that Homeric poetry was formed somewhere in the northeast Aegean.

Homer and Hesiod share the distinction of being the earliest Greek poets whose works survive. One difference between them, however, is that Homer's verses do not include any self-allusions or biographical details (whether real or fictional). They both composed soon after the alphabet was introduced in Greece in the mid-eighth century BCE, which makes the written version of their poems datable to some time in the second half of that century or around the turn of the seventh, according to most theories. Before that, all mythology and poetry was composed, recited, and passed down orally. Although there is a common idea that Homer preceded Hesiod, there is really no evidence to know for sure the exact date of either poet or who came first. Early Greek epic poetry exhibits features of oral tradition, especially the repetitive use of formulae and epithets. Formulae are sentences or phrases such as "When early-born dawn appeared, who has fingers like roses" or "and he stood before him and he spoke." Epithets are adjectives or short compounds attached to particular characters, such as "Zeus the son of Kronos," "Hektor, tamer of horses," and "swift-footed Achilles" (one Greek word is often translated using more than one word in English).

Both Homer and Hesiod, and other epic poets afterwards (e.g., in the *Homeric Hymns*), used the epic verse par excellence, the dactylic hexameter: each line consists of six units (called "feet"), each foot consisting of one long syllable and two short ones (or alternatively two long ones). The length of the syllables in Greek is determined by the length of the vowels (Greek vowels could be long or short) and their position in closed or open syllables (in relation to different clusters of consonants). Hence, formulae and epithets helped the poet (bard or singer) fill up whole verses or parts of a verse with ready-made phrases with predictable metrics. In the translations here, Barry B. Powell reproduces some of the rhythmic flow of the hexameters through a five-beat verse.

SOURCE: Homer, *Iliad*, Book 5 and *Odyssey*, Book 9.105–end, translated and annotated by B. B. Powell, with minor modifications. His full translations of the *Iliad* and *Odyssey* are forthcoming from Oxford University Press in Fall 2013.

3.8.a. The Aristeia of Diomedes: *Iliad*, Book 5

Homer's *Iliad* is an epic poem in twenty-four books, set during the ten-year-long siege of Troy (in the north-west coast of Asia Minor) by a contingent of Greek allies, a siege caused by the abduction of Helen (of Sparta) by the Trojan prince Alexander. The action of the *Iliad*, however, focuses on only a few days toward the end of the war (in the ninth year) and on the figure of Achilles. The poem revolves around the falling out between Achilles and Agamemnon (leader of the Greeks, brother of Menelaos, whose wife was Helen); Achilles' decision to withdraw from battle in order to punish the Greeks and restore his honor; and the dramatic death of Achilles' friend Patroklos, which causes the return of Achilles to battle and his awaited combat with Hektor, whom he kills.

In Book 5 the Greek warrior Diomedes features as "the best of the Acheans" in the place of Achilles (who is not fighting). This is one of several episodes that focus on the battle exploits (*aristeia*, from Greek *aristos*, "best") of particular heroes besides Achilles in the *Iliad*. Book 5 is included here as an example of the Homeric representation of heroes and gods because it is here where mortals and immortals are represented in closest proximity, with the heroes being capable of threatening and wounding the gods (literally speaking) and the gods displaying the anthropomorphic qualities that characterize them in Homer. As the reader will notice, the gods in the *Iliad* have taken sides for or against the Trojans and the Greeks (in general, Hera, Athena, and Poseidon help the Greeks, while Aphrodite, Ares, and Apollo help the Trojans) with Zeus remaining neutral or free to act in whichever way he sees fit in a case-by-case basis.

The Greeks in Homer are never called "Greeks" (Gr. *Hellenes*) and are represented as a mosaic of different peoples led by various kings or chiefs; the general names applied to the contingent are Argives, Achaeans, and Danaans. The Trojans are called Trojans or Dardanians, and Troy is also called Ilion (a Bronze Age name for the city perhaps attested in Hittite sources as *Wilusa*); hence, *Iliad* is "a poem about Ilion/Troy." Main heroes are often called by the name of their fathers (e.g., the son of Tydeus, i.e., Diomedes). In turn, many of the names that appear in the battle scenes are "stock" minor names that do not reappear. The more important ones are explained, while the more famous characters and the Olympian gods are not.

> Well then Pallas Athena gave to Diomedes,
> the son of Tydeus, strength and boldness, that he might
> stand out among all the Argives and that he might win
> high praise. She kindled from his helmet and his shield
> 5 an unwearying fire, like the harvest star that shines
> above all others when it has bathed in Ocean.[104] Just such
> a flame did she enkindle from his head and his shoulders,
> and she sent him into the thick of it where the most men
> were encamped.
>   There was among the Trojans a certain
> 10 Dares, rich and blameless, a priest of Hephaistos.
> He had two sons, Phegeus and Idaios, both of them
> experienced in every kind of battle. These two
> separated from the throng and went after Diomedes.
> The two men drove their car, but Diomedes went on foot
> 15 upon the ground. When they got near, advancing
> against each other, Phegeus threw his long-shadowed spear
> first. The point of the spear went over the left shoulder
> of the son of Tydeus and did not hit him. Then the son
> of Tydeus threw his bronze. Nor did the weapon fly
> 20 in vain from his hand, but struck Phegeus on the chest
> between the nipples. He dropped him from the car.
> Idaios sprang back and quit the very beautiful chariot.
> He did not dare to stand over his dead brother.
> Nor would he himself have escaped black fate,

---

[104] The harvest star is Sirius, also called "Orion's dog." Ocean is the river that surrounds the earth. When Sirius is not visible, it is said to bathe in Ocean.

25 except Hephaistos saved him. Hephaistos hid him
    in night so that their aged father might not be ruined
    by grief. But the son of magnificent Tydeus drove off the horses
    and gave them to his companions to take to the hollow ships.
            When the big-hearted Trojans saw that one of the sons of Dares
30 ran off and the other was dead beside the car,
    panic struck them. But blue-eyed Athena took mad Ares
    by the hand and spoke to him: "Ares, Ares—
    murderer of men, blood-stained stormer of walls,
    ought we not now to leave the Trojans and the Achaeans
35 to fight?[105] Zeus can give glory to whichever side
    he chooses. But let us withdraw and avoid the anger
    of Zeus." So speaking, she led mad Ares from the battle.
    She sat him down on the banks of the sandy Skamander.
            The Danaans turned the Trojans into flight. Each man
40 of the captains got his man. First the king of men,
    Agamemnon, knocked down the leader of the Halizones, the great
        Odios,
    who had turned to flee. The spear got him in the back
    between the shoulders, and the shaft drove through his chest.
    He fell with a thud and his armor clanged about him.
45 Idomeneus took down Phaistos, the son of Boros
    the Maionian, who had come from deep-soiled Tarne.[106] Idomeneus,
    famous for his spear, pierced him with the long shaft
    as Phaistos mounted his car. Idomeneus struck his
    right shoulder. He tumbled from the car. Hateful darkness
50 encompassed him. The followers of Idomeneus stripped the body.
            Then Menelaos, the son of Atreus, hit the son of Strophios,
    Skamandrios, cunning in the hunt, with his sharp spear.
    Artemis had taught Skamandrios how to strike down
    all the wild animals that the forest nurtures in the mountains.
55 But Artemis, who pours forth arrows, was not good to him
    then, nor the archery in which he had earlier excelled.
    But Menelaos, the son of Atreus, famous for his spear,
    stabbed him in the back with his spear as he ran away
    before him, right between the shoulders, and he drove it through

---

[105] In Book 4, Ares had roused the Trojans, and Athena the Achaeans. Now Athena wants Ares off the field so that Diomedes can show his brilliance, to which Ares complies.

[106] Idomeneus, from Knossos in Crete, kills Phaistos, who has the name of a rival Cretan town! The location of Tarne is unknown.

60 to the other side. Skamandrios fell on his face
and his armor clanged around him.
                                    Meriones killed Phereklos,
the son of Hermonides the carpenter. Phereklos knew how
to make all kinds of delicate things with his hands,
for Pallas Athena loved him above all men.
65 Phereklos had made the well-balanced ships for Alexander,
the beginning of harm, which became an evil for all the Trojans
and for himself.[107] For he did not know the oracles of the gods.
Meriones pursued Phereklos and when he came up
Meriones hit Phereklos in the right buttock. The spear
70 went through to the bladder beneath the bone. Phereklos groaned
and fell to his knees. Death concealed him. Meges
killed Pedaios, a son of Antenor. Although he was
a bastard, but the excellent Theano[108] raised him with care,
as if he were her own child, to please her husband.
75 Meges, famous for his spear, came up close and struck
Pedaios with his sharp spear on the back of his head.
Straight through the teeth the bronze cut off his tongue.
He fell in the dust. He seized the cold bronze with his teeth.
                    Eurypylos, the son of Euaimon, then killed the good
80 Hypsenor, son of the brave Dolopion, who was
made priest of Skamandros. He was honored like a god
by the people. Eurypylos, the brilliant son of Euaimon,
struck Hypsenor on the shoulder with his sword as he ran
before him, rushing on him. Eurypylos cut off the heavy arm.
85 Blooded, the arm fell to the ground. A purple
death came over his eyes and overpowering fate
seized him. And so it went as they labored in the relentless
battle.
                    As for the son of Tydeus, you could not say
which side he was on, whether he was the fellow of the Trojans
90 or the Achaeans. For he raged across the plain like a winter river
in flood, which in its swift flow wears away the embankments.
The embankments, though tightly packed, cannot withstand
the water's force, nor can the walls of the fruitful gardens
as it comes roaring, when the rain of Zeus drives it on.

[107] An allusion to the cause of the war (Paris' abduction of Helen from Sparta).
[108] A priestess of Athena, we learn in Book 6.

95 Many are the handsome works of men brought to ruin.
Even so were the thick ranks of the Trojans driven in rout
by the son of Tydeus. The Trojans did not await him,
even though they were many. But when Pandaros, the good son of
    Lykaon,
100 saw Diomedes raging across the plain and driving
the Trojan ranks before him, he stretched the curved bow
against the son of Tydeus. He hit him in the right shoulder
as he rushed onwards, on the plate of his bronze cuirass.
The bitter arrow flew through the plate, it went straight
105 on its way, and the bronze cuirass was drenched in blood.
Then the glorious son of Lykaon boasted over him:
        "Get up and go, you great-hearted Trojans, goaders
of horses! I have wounded the best of the Achaeans. I don't
think he can long endure the powerful shaft,
110 if truly the king, the son of Zeus, sent me forth when I came
from Lykia."[109] So he said in boast. But the sharp arrow
did not subdue Diomedes. Pulling back, he took
his stand beside his horses and his car. He spoke to Sthenelos,
the son of Kapaneus: "Come down, son of Kapaneus, from the car
115 and draw this arrow from my shoulder." So he spoke, and Sthenelos
jumped to the ground from the chariot. He stood beside him
and drew the sharp arrow all the way through the shoulder. The blood
spurted up through the supple shirt.
                    Then Diomedes, good
at the cry, prayed: "Hear me, unwearied one,
120 the daughter of Zeus who carries the goatskin-fetish[110]—
if ever with good thoughts you stood beside my dear father
in the fury of war, then now be kind to me,
Athena. Grant that I take my man, that he come
within the cast of my spear, whoever it was who hit
125 me on the sly and boasts of his blow. He doesn't
think I shall long behold the sunlight." So he spoke
in prayer, and Athena heard him. She made his limbs

---

[109] The "king" is Apollo, archer-god and sponsor of archers such as Pandaros. This "Lykia" is northeast of Troy, not in the far southeast where the important fighter Sarpedon comes from (as we will see).

[110] This is the translation of the *aegis* (so this epithet appears in translations as "aegis-bearing"), a puzzling protective cape or shield worn by Zeus and Athena, often represented in art as having the Gorgon's face on it and snake-tassels. See description in lines 742–747 below.

to be light, and his feet and hands too. Standing
near him she spoke words that went like arrows:
130   "Have the courage to go up against the Trojans now.
For in your breast I have placed the strength of your father,
who never turned aside, such as had the horseman
Tydeus, wielder of the shield. I have removed the mist
from your eyes which lay upon them, so you can recognize who
135 is a god and who a man. So if any god comes
here to make trial of you, don't attack the deathless god—
unless the daughter of Zeus, Aphrodite, should come into the war,
stab her with the sharp bronze!"

So speaking, blue-eyed
      Athena
went away. The son of Tydeus went back and tangled with
140 the foremost fighters. Although before he was eager to fight
the Trojans, now three times the rage came upon him, like a lion
that a shepherd guarding his wooly sheep in the field has wounded
as it leapt over the wall of the sheepfold, but he did not kill him.
He has roused its might and the shepherd gives up his defense
145 and lurks between the outbuildings, and the flock, having no
      protection,
tries to flee. But they are heaped in piles next
to each other while in his rage the lion leaps up
from the high-walled courtyard. Even with such fury did
the powerful Diomedes tangle with the Trojans.

To begin
150 he killed Astynoos and Hypeiron, shepherd of the people.
The first he hit above the nipple, striking with the brazen spear.
The second he struck with his great sword on the collar bone
beside the shoulder, and he cut away the shoulder from the neck
and from the back. He let them go and went after
155 Agas and Polyeidos, sons of Eurydamas, the old man
who prophesied from dreams. But he interpreted no dreams for
      their homecoming—
for the powerful Diomedes killed them. Then he went after
Xanthos and Thoon, both of them sons of Phainops,
born late in his life. Now he was worn down by grievous old age
160 and fathered no other son to make his heir.
Diomedes killed the sons, he took away their dear lives,
both of them, and he left to the father moaning

and pain, for he did not receive them alive returning
from the battle. The near of kin divided the inheritance.

165   Then he took two sons of Priam, the son of Dardanos,
in a single chariot, Echemmon and Chromios. Just as
a lion leaps among a herd of cattle and breaks
the neck of a calf as the herd grazes in a woodland
pasture, even so did Diomedes drive the two
170 of them helter-skelter from their car, quite unwilling.
Then he took their armor. He gave the horses to his companions
to drive to the ships.

               Aeneas saw him throwing into chaos
the ranks of men. He went through the battle and the tumult
of spears looking for godlike Pandaros, to see
175 if he could find him somewhere. At last he found him,
blameless and strong, and he stood before him and he spoke:

       "Pandaros, where is your bow and your winged arrows
and your fame? No man here dares compete with you
in this, nor does any one in Lykia boast that he
180 is better than you. But come now, lifting your hands
to Zeus, fire an arrow at this man, who is doing such
violence and ferocious harm to the Trojans. He has loosed
the knees of many noble young men. Maybe
it is a god angered with the Trojans because of some sacrifice.
185 The wrath of a god can be harsh."

                 The fine son of Lykaon
then answered him: "Aeneas, good counselor to the Trojans
who wear shirts of bronze, this man looks like the valiant son
of Tydeus to me. I can tell from his shield and his helmet
with its crest, and his horses. Of course I can't tell if it is
190 a god. If this is the man I think, the valiant
Diomedes, it is not without some god's help that he rages.
But some one of the deathless ones who live on high Olympos
must stand near him, shoulders hidden in a cloud.
This god turned aside the sharp shaft as it made
195 its way to the mark. For I have already fired a shot.
I hit him in the right shoulder, and the arrow went straight through
the plate of his bronze cuirass. I thought that I had cast
him down to the House of Hades, but I did not subdue him.
It must be some angry god! I have no horses

200 and no car that I could mount, though in Lykaon's halls
there are eleven brand-new chariots, just made. Cloths
cover them. Beside each stand a yoke of horses
munching on white barley and wheat. The old spearman Lykaon
ordered me again and again before I set off
205 to war from the well-built house—he commanded me to mount
horse and car and to lead the Trojans[111] through the bitter
conflicts. But I wouldn't listen. It would have been better
if I had! I spared the horses. I was afraid that they
would lack feed in the midst of so many men
210 when they are used to eating their fill. So I left
them and came to Troy on foot, trusting to my bow,
which was to do me no good at all. For already I have fired
at two captains, the son of Tydeus and the son
of Atreus. From both I drew real blood when I hit them,
215 but that only excited them the more. With bad luck I took
my curved bow from its peg on that day when I led
my Trojans to lovely Ilion, bearing pleasure to shining
Hector. If I return home and see with my own eyes
the land of my fathers and my wife and my high-roofed house,
220 may some utter stranger cut off my head
if I do not smash this bow with my hands and cast
it into the blazing fire. It is worthless to me,
like the wind!"

Aeneas, a Trojan captain, answered:
"Don't talk like that! Things will be no different until
225 we go up against this Diomedes with horse and car
and take him on in our armor. So come, get in my car,
that you might see what sort of horses are these
horses of Tros.[112] They know full well how to pursue
swiftly, and to retreat here and there over the plain.
230 They will carry us safely to the city, if Zeus again
grants glory to Diomedes, the son of Tydeus. But come,
take the whip and the shining reins. I will descend

---

[111] That is, his own people, the inhabitants from around Zeleia on the slopes of Mount Ida northeast of the city of Troy (Ilion) proper, who are called "Trojans."

[112] The divine breed of horses was begun by Aeneas' great-great-grandfather Tros, to whom Zeus gave horses in recompense for Zeus' snatching of Ganymede, a beautiful prince of the house of Troy (see lines 271–273).

from the car in order to fight him.[113] Or you can attack him,
and I will care for the horses."

The good son of Lykaon

235 then answered: "Aeneas, you hold onto the reins yourself
and keep control of your own horses. They will better pull
the car made of bent rods when they recognize who is holding
the reins, if we have to flee from the son of Tydeus.
I am afraid that they may panic and run wild

240 and be unwilling to bear us out of the war
because they miss your voice, and I fear that the son
of Tydeus might then waylay and kill us both
and drive off the single-hoofed horses.[114] So must you
drive your car and control your horses. I'll take

245 Diomedes on with my sharp spear as he comes at me."

So speaking they mounted into the ornate car.
Eagerly they turned the swift horses against the son
of Tydeus. Sthenelos, the fine son of Kapaneus, saw them,
and at once he spoke to the good Diomedes with words

250 that flew like arrows: "Diomedes, son of Tydeus,
dear to my heart, I see two powerful men
eager to fight you, men with boundless strength.
One is Pandaros, a straight shot with the bow. He boasts
of being the son of Lykaon. The other is Aeneas,

255 who boasts of being the son of blameless Anchises,
with Aphrodite for a mother. But come, let us withdraw in the car.
Don't rage in this way among the frontline troops or you may lose
your life."

Powerful Diomedes glowered beneath his brows

and said: "Don't speak of flight! I don't think you will

260 persuade me. It is not in my blood to fight by running
away, nor to squat cringing. My strength is still steadfast.
I am not going to mount a car, but I will go against them
just as I am. Pallas Athena will not let me be afraid.
As for these two, their swift horses will not carry them back

265 from us again, even if one or the other gets away.
I'll tell you something else—please pay attention to what I say.

---

[113] Chariots in Homer are mostly used as transportation to and from the battlefield and not as fighting machines. Chariots confer prestige and social power on their owners.

[114] Probably as opposed to the cloven hoofs of cattle, sheep, and goats.

If wise-counseling Athena gives me the glory of killing
both these men, then you hold back our swift horses
by wrapping their reins around the rail. And remember to rush
270 upon the horses of Aeneas and drive them from the Trojans to the
    Achaeans
with their fancy shinguards. For they are of the race that Zeus,
whose voice reaches far, gave to Tros as recompense for his son
Ganymede. They are the best horses beneath the dawn or sun.
The king of men Anchises[115] stole from this line
275 when unknown to Laomedon he had them cover some of his mares.
From these were born a stock of six in Anchises'
halls. Four of these he reared himself at the stall,
and he gave two to Aeneas, the deviser of rout.
If we can capture these horses, we will gain a handsome
280 reputation."

        So they spoke to one another. Just then they closed,
driving their swift horses. The good son of Lykaon[116]
spoke to Diomedes first: "Son of lordly Tydeus,
stalwart and wise, I guess my sharp arrow did not
finish you off, the bitter shaft! Now I will try to hit you
285 with my spear, to see if I can take you down." He spoke,
balanced the long-shadowed spear, and cast. He struck
the son of Tydeus on his shield. The bronze spear-point
went straight through and reached the bronze cuirass.
The good son of Lykaon shouted aloud over him:
290 "Got you, right through the belly! You won't last long!
You've given me great glory."

        Without fear powerful Diomedes
   answered:
"But you missed the mark! You did not hit me! I don't
think that you two will be done before one or the other
will glut Ares with his blood, the warrior-god who carries
295 the shield." So speaking, Diomedes cast. Athena
guided the missile onto Pandaros' nose next to the eye,
and it pierced his white teeth. The unyielding bronze cut the tongue

[115] Aeneas' father. He was also a descendant of Tros through his mother Themiste, daughter of
Ilos (son of Tros). The breed of horses was inherited by Laomedon (uncle of Anchises), who was
the son of Ilus and father of Priam, the king of Troy at the time of the Trojan War.
[116] Pandaros.

off at the root and the point came out beside the lower part
of the chin. Pandarus tumbled from the car. His armor
300   clanged about him—bright, flashing—and the swift-footed
horses turned aside. His breath-soul and his strength
were loosened. Aeneas jumped down with shield and long spear,
fearing that Achaeans would snatch the corpse from him.
He hovered over Pandarus like a lion trusting in its might.
305   He held his spear and shield before him, well-balanced
and round, impatient to kill whoever should come
against him. He screamed terribly.

>   The son of Tydeus
picked up a boulder in his hand, a mighty deed,
a stone that two men might carry such as mortals
310   are today. But he easily hefted it by himself.
With it he struck Aeneas on the hip where the thigh
bone rotates on the hip bone—they call it the 'cup.'
The stone smashed the cup, and it smashed the two tendons.
The jagged stone peeled away the skin. Then the warrior
315   fell on his knees, and he stayed there. He rested with his thick
hand on the earth. Black night enclosed his eyes.

>   And now Aeneas, the king of men, would have died
if the daughter of Zeus, Aphrodite, had not caught sight
of him. His mother, who bore him to Anchises when he was
320   herding cattle.[117] Around her beloved son
Aphrodite placed her pale forearms. She covered him with a fold
of her shining dress spread before him as a protection,
in case any Danaan with swift horses should throw the bronze
into his chest and take away his breath-soul.
325   She then carried her beloved son out of the war.

>   But the son of Kapaneus, Sthenelos, did not forget
the agreements he had made with Diomedes, good at the war cry.
He held back his own single-hoofed horses from the fray,
lashing their reins to the rail. He ran up to the horses
330   of Aeneas, with beautiful manes, and drove them out
from the Trojans to the Achaeans with fancy shinguards. He gave
them to Deipylos to drive to the hollow ships,

---

[117] For the romance between Aphrodite and Anchises, from which Aeneas was born, see the
Homeric Hymn to Aphrodite in Part 5, document 5.

his dear companion, whom he honored above all his age-mates
because they were likeminded. Then Sthenelos mounted

335 his own car and took the flashing reins. Swiftly
he drove the horses with strong hooves, eagerly seeking
the son of Tydeus. But Diomedes had gone in pursuit
of Cypris[118] with his pitiless bronze, recognizing that she
was a god without strength, not one of those who dominate in the war

340 of men—no Pallas Athena, nor city-sacking Enyo.[119]
When he came upon her, pursuing through the immense crowd,
he thrust with his sharp spear as he leapt upon her. The son
of great-souled Tydeus pierced the skin on her delicate
hand. Immediately the spear went into the flesh,

345 passing through the deathless clothes that the Graces
themselves had made, injuring the wrist above
the palm. Immortal blood flowed from the goddess,
ichor, which flows in the veins of the blessed gods.
For gods do not eat bread or drink the shining wine.

350 Thus they are without blood and are called deathless.

   With a loud cry Aphrodite let her son Aeneas
fall from her. Phoibos Apollo took Aeneas
in his arms from a dark cloud, so that no one of the Danaans
with their fast horses might throw the bronze into his chest

355 and kill him. Over her Diomedes, good at the war cry,
shouted aloud: "Get out of here, daughter of Zeus,
leave this battle and the war! Isn't it enough that you deceive
strengthless women? If you are going to enter into battle,
I think you will shudder soon even to hear the word,

360 even should you hear it at a distance!"

   So he spoke,
and she left, beside herself and much distressed.
Wind-footed Iris[120] took her and brought her out
of the throng, wracked with pain. Her beautiful skin
turned black. She found mad Ares on the left of the battle,

---

[118] Another name for Aphrodite because she was born on Cyprus (see Hesiod's *Theogony* 189–200 in Part 1, document 5, and *Hymn to Aphrodite* in Part 5, document 5). She is called "Cypris" five times in this book, and never again in the *Iliad*.

[119] A war-goddess, feminine counterpart of Ares, also called *Enyalios*.

[120] Goddess who stands for the rainbow and serves as messenger of the gods.

365 sitting down. He had leaned his spear against a cloud
and his swift horses were there. Falling on her knees, Aphrodite
fervently begged her dear brother for his horses with head-pieces[121]
of gold: "My beloved brother, save me! Give me your horses
to go to Olympos and the seat of the deathless ones. I am much
370 pained because of a wound that a mortal man has given me,
the son of Tydeus, who now would fight even with father Zeus."
      So she spoke, and Ares gave her the horses
with golden head-pieces. She got in the car, much distraught
at heart. Iris got in beside her and took the reins
375 in her hands. She lashed the horses to drive them on.
The two sped onward. Quickly they arrived at steep
Olympos, the seat of the gods. There wind-footed Iris
stayed the horses and set them free from the car
and cast before them immortal food. But divine
380 Aphrodite threw herself on the knees of her mother Dione,[122]
who held her daughter close and stroked her with her hand.
Then Dione said: "Dear child, who of the heavenly ones
has foolishly done this to you, as if you were doing something
evil in full view?" Laughter-loving Aphrodite answered her:
385 "The bold Diomedes, the son of Tydeus, has wounded me,
because I rescued my own beloved son from the war,
Aeneas, who of all people is by far the most dear to me.
The dread battle is no longer between Trojans and Achaeans,
but now the Danaans fight against the deathless ones!"
390   Then Dione, the great goddess, answered her: "Endure,
my child, and hold up for all your suffering. Many
of those who live on Olympos, in bringing dire pain
to one another, have suffered from men. Ares suffered
when mighty Otos and Ephialtes, the sons of Aloeus,
395 bound him in powerful bonds.[123] He lay tied up in a bronze
jar for thirteen months. And Ares, insatiate for war,

---

[121] A decoration that fell over the horse's brow.

[122] According to Hesiod (*Theogony* 188 ff.), Aphrodite was born from the foam around the severed genitals of Ouranos. Dione is the feminine form of Zeus ("Mrs. Zeus"). She, not Hera, was the consort of Zeus at the oracle of Dodona. The Mesopotamian Sky God Anu had Antu as consort, the feminine form of his name, and some have seen similarities between this passage and the one in the *Epic of Gilgamesh*, where Ishtar is offended by the hero and complains to Anu and Antu (see Part 5, document 1).

[123] Iphimedeia was married to Aloeus but bore Poseidon twin giant sons, who threatened to reach Olympos and attack the gods. Apollo killed them before they reached maturity.

would have died, if the twins' very beautiful step-mother
Eeriboia[124] had not told Hermes. He stole away Ares,
already much worn down, for the harsh bonds had overcome him.
400 Hera suffered when Herakles, the powerful son of Amphitryon,
wounded her in the right breast with a three-barbed arrow.
Incurable pain overcame her. Monstrous Hades
too suffered the sharp arrow when that same man,
Herakles, the son of Zeus, the cloud-gatherer, hit Hades
405 in Pylos among the dead and gave him over to pain.[125]
Hades went to the house of Zeus and to high Olympos,
lamenting in his heart and pierced with pains, for the arrow
had fixed in his strong shoulder and distressed his spirit.
Paieon[126] applied a pain-killing poultice and healed him—
410 for he was not made to die. Scoundrel, doer of violence!
He cares not if he does evil! With his arrows he caused pain
to the gods who possess Olympos. Now blue-eyed Athena
has set this man upon you—fool! Diomedes
knows not in his heart that he who goes up against
415 the gods does not last. His children do not call him
'papa' as they hover about his knees, when he returns
from the war and the dread battleground. For all that he
is mighty, let him take care that he not go up
against someone stronger than you, or for sure the wise
420 Aigialeia, daughter of Adrestus, will wake
from sleep. She will rouse with her wailing all those in her house,
crying for her wedded husband, the best of the Achaeans—
even she, the strong wife of Diomedes, tamer of horses."[127]
    She spoke and with both her hands she wiped away
425 the *ichor*. The arm was healed and the pains were lessened.
When Athena and Hera saw her, they thought to irritate
Zeus, the son of Kronos, with mocking words. The blue-eyed

---

[124] Eeriboia was the granddaughter of Hermes and second wife of Aloeus, hence stepmother of the monstrous Otos and Ephialtes.

[125] It is unknown why or when Herakles shot Hera in the breast. His wounding of Hades is also obscure, as well as the mention of Pylos.

[126] A healing god known from the Mycenaean Linear B tablets; he appears only in this book and in *Odyssey* 4. Paieon or Paian (see *Hymn to Apollo*, document 3.9) eventually became a title of Apollo as healer. A *paieon* (paean) is also a song to Apollo.

[127] In spite of Dione's warning, Diomedes comes to no harm through his attack on the gods. In fact nothing is known of the death of Diomedes.

goddess Athena began to speak among them:

    "Father Zeus, I wonder if what I will say will make you angry?

430 It seems to me that Cypris has been urging someone of the Achaean

women to follow after the Trojans,[128] whom she now loves so much . . .

and while stroking a certain one of the Achaean women,

who wear fine gowns, she has scratched her delicate hand

against a golden brooch."

          So she spoke. The father

435 of men and gods smiled. He called to golden

Aphrodite and said: "The works of war are not

for you, my child. Follow after the lovely works

of marriage. Let all these other things be the concern

of swift Ares and Athena." And so they conversed with one another.

440   Diomedes good at the war cry leapt on Aeneas,

realizing that Apollo himself held his two arms

over Aeneas. But Diomedes had no regard

for the great god. He was eager to kill Aeneas

and to strip off his famous armor. Three times he leapt

445 on him, desiring to kill him; three times Apollo

beat back his shining shield. But when for a fourth time

Diomedes rushed on him like a god, Apollo,

who works from a long way off, said, shouting

terribly: "Only think, son of Tydeus, and withdraw!

Don't wish to be like the gods. The races of immortal

450 gods and of men who walk the earth are not the same."

    So he spoke. The son of Tydeus withdrew a little backward,

avoiding the anger of Apollo, who strikes from afar.

Apollo set Aeneas apart from the crowd in sacred

Pergamos, where his temple was built. Leto and Artemis,

455 who showers arrows, healed him in the great sanctuary,

and they glorified him. But Apollo of the silver bow made an image

of him, just like Aeneas himself and wearing

the same armor. Around that image the Trojans

and the good Achaeans struck their shields made of bull's hide

460 that protected their breasts, both rounded shields and long ones

with feathers attached.[129]

---

[128] Alluding to Helen.

[129] The meaning of the Greek is not clear.

                Then Phoibos Apollo spoke to
mad Ares: "Ares, Ares, murderer of men,
blood-stained stormer of walls—will you not go into
the battle and withdraw this man, Tydeus' son,
465 who now would fight even with Father Zeus? First
in a close fight he wounded Cypris on the hand
at the wrist, and then he leapt on me as if he were a god!"
        So speaking he sat down at the top
of Pergamos while deadly Ares went among the ranks
470 of the Trojans and urged them on. He took on the likeness
of Akamas, the swift leader of the Thracians. He urged on
the sons of Priam:
                "O sons of Zeus-nurtured King Priam,
how long will you let your people be slaughtered by the
    Achaeans?
Are you waiting until the fight is at the foot of the finely crafted
    gates?
475 A man lies here whom we honor as we honor good Hector,
Aeneas, the son of generous-hearted Anchises. But come,
let us save our fine comrade from the fight." So speaking
he roused up the strength and spirit in each man.
                        Then Sarpedon[130]
sternly reproved good Hector: "Hector, where has
480 that strength gone that once you had? You said that
without armies and allies you would hold the city alone
with your brothers-in-law and your brothers. But of these I am
unable to see or note anyone. But they cower
like dogs around a lion. We do the fighting, who are but allies
485 among you. I myself come as an ally from very far off.
For Lykia is far, along the eddying Xanthos, where I left
my beloved wife and my infant son, and my many
possessions, which anyone covets who lacks. Still I urge
on the Lykians and I long myself to fight my man,
490 although there is nothing here of mine that the Achaeans
wish to drive off or take. Yet there you stand
and you do not urge your people to hold their ground
or defend their wives. Beware you do not become
a prey and a spoil to your enemies, as if caught in the meshes

---

[130] Sarpedon was a son of Zeus and Laodamia and king of Lykia in Asia Minor (not the Lykia where Pandaros came from, but the region in southern Anatolia).

495 of a net that ensnares all. They soon will sack your well-populated
city. These cares should weigh on you day and night.
You should beseech the captains of your far-famed allies to hold
their ground without flinching, and so put aside all strong
criticism of your command."

So spoke Sarpedon.

500 His word stung Hector in his heart. At once he leapt
from the chariot in full armor to the ground. Brandishing
his two
sharp spears, he went everywhere through the army, urging
the Trojans to fight. He roused the dread din of battle.
They rallied and took their stand opposite the Achaeans.

505 The Argives waited for them in gangs, they did
not flee. Even as the wind carries the sacred
chaff across threshing floor and men as they winnow,
which light-haired Demeter separates as the winds drive on,
the grain from the chaff, and the chaff grows white in piles—

510 even so were the Achaeans whitened in the upper part of their
bodies
with dust that the hooves of the horses kicked up between them
to the bronze-colored heaven as again they contended in war.

The charioteers wheeled around. The strength of
their hands
they bore straight forward. Mad Ares covered the battle

515 with the veil of night to help out the Trojans. He went
everywhere. Thus he accomplished the command of Phoibos
Apollo,
he of the golden sword,[131] who urged him to enliven
the spirit of the Trojans when he saw that Pallas Athena
had left the field of battle, for she had been helping the Danaans.

520   Apollo himself sent forth Aeneas from his very rich sanctuary,
and Apollo put courage in the breast of the shepherd of the people.
Aeneas took
his place among the companions. They rejoiced when they saw
him coming back alive and whole and with an abundant courage.
They asked no questions. Another sort of labor prevented them

---

[131] An odd epithet for a god whose typical weapon is the bow. It recurs only once in the *Iliad* (in Book 15), but it appears also in the *Hymn to Apollo* (document 3.9). This is also the name (*Chrysaor*) of the figure who springs from the severed head of Medusa, along with Pegasos.

525   that he of the silver bow roused up, and Ares
      the destroyer of men, and Eris[132] who rages without cease.
          On the other side, the two Ajaxes and Odysseus and Diome-
      des stirred
      the Danaans to the fight. They did not fear the ferocity
      of the Trojans, nor their pursuit, but thus they held their ground,
530   like clouds that the son of Kronos in quiet weather has placed
      motionless on the tops of mountains, at a time when North Wind
      is asleep and the other violent winds that blow and scatter
      the shadowy clouds with their shrill blasts—even so
      the Danaans held their ground and did not flee.
535   Agamemnon, the son of Atreus, went through the crowd
      giving
      many orders: "My friends, be men! Show a strong heart!
      Have shame before one another in the ferocious battle.
      Of men with shame more are saved than perish. Of those
      who flee there is no fame, no use." He spoke
540   and Agamemnon quickly hurled his spear. He hit
      a leading fighter, a companion of Aeneas, Deikoon,
      son of Pergasos, whom the Trojans honored like the sons
      of Priam, for he was eager to fight among the foremost.
      King Agamemnon struck him on the shield with his spear.
545   The shield did not stop the spear, but the bronze passed
      straight through. He drove it through the belt into
      the lower belly. Deikoon fell with a thud.
      His armor clanged around him.
                     Then Aeneas killed two
      of the best men of the Danaans, the sons of Diokles, Krethon
550   and Orsilochos, whose father dwelled in well-built Pheme,
      rich in substance. He came from the line of the river
      Alpheios, which passes through the land of Pylos, broad
      in its flow.[133] Alpheios bore Ortilochos as a king ruling many.
      Ortilochos bore Diokles, great of heart, and from Diokles

---

[132] Eris is "Strife." She was the one provoking the "judgment of Paris" at the wedding of Thetis and Peleus, when she (uninvited to the party) threw the "apple of discord" between the goddesses Hera, Aphrodite, and Athena.

[133] The Alpheios was the largest river in the Peloponnese, linking the regions of Arcadia and Elis in the western Peloponnese. It also appears in connection with Pylos in the *Hymn to Apollo* (document 3.9). Rivers are in Greek mythology often divinized and personified, like here (and like Skamandros, especially in *Iliad*, Book 21).

555 came the twin sons, Krethon and Orsilochos, experienced
in every kind of battle. When the two came of age,
they followed the Argives on the black ships to Ilion with its fine
horses,
to bring honor to Agamemnon and Menelaos, the sons of Atreus.
There the end of death concealed them. Like two lions
560 on the peak of a mountain who are raised by their mother in the
thickets
of a deep forest—they snatch cattle and fine sheep and make havoc
of the farms of men, until they are killed at the hands
of men wielding sharp bronze—even so did these two
men fall at the hands of Aeneas, like fir trees.

As they fell
565 Menelaos, beloved of Ares, took pity on them.
He stalked through the foremost fighters, decked out in splendid
bronze, shaking his spear. Ares roused up the bravado
of Menelaos, thinking he would fall to Aeneas. Antilochos,
the son of Nestor, saw Menelaos, and he stalked
570 through the forefighters. He feared greatly for Menelaos,
that something should happen to him and all their effort
be for nothing. Menelaos and Aeneas held out their hands
and their sharp spears against one another, eager
to do battle, when Antilochos stood close to the shepherd of the
people.
575 Aeneas backed off, though he was a fast warrior, when he saw
the two men holding their ground side by side.

Menelaos and Antilochos dragged the corpses to the
Achaean side.
They placed the luckless two men in the hands of their companions,
then themselves turned back to fight in the forefront. The two
580 of them killed Pylaimenes, the equal to Ares,
leader of the great-hearted Paphlagonian shield men.
Menelaos, Atreus' son, famous for his spear,
thrust at him as he stood, hitting him in the collarbone.

Antilochos hit Mydon, Aeneas' charioteer,
585 the noble son of Atymnios, as he was turning the single-hoofed
horses. He hit him with a stone smack on his elbow.
The reins, white with ivory, dropped from his hands
to the ground in the dust. Then Antilochos jumped on the car
and drove his sword into Mydon's temple. Gasping

590 for air, Mydon fell from the well-built car headlong
in the dust on his forehead and shoulders. He stood propped
there for a long time, for he had fallen into deep
sand. Finally the horses kicked him and he fell
to the ground in the dirt. Antilochos drove the horses
595 into the army of the Achaeans. Hector saw them
through the ranks. He rushed on them, screaming.
The strong battalions of the Trojans followed, Ares
in the lead and revered Enyo, who brought with her Kudoimos,[134]
shameless in carnage. Ares wielded in his hands
600 an enormous spear, going now before, now behind Hector.
Diomedes, good at the war cry, shivered when he saw him.

As when a man crossing a vast plain
stands helpless at the edge of a swift-flowing river,
flowing to the sea, and he sees it seethe with foam
605 and starts back, so did Diomedes draw back, and he spoke
to his people: "My friends, how we marveled at the good Hector
for being a spearman and a brave fighter! Ever by
his side is one of the gods, who wards off ruin.
And now Ares is at his side in the form of a mortal man.[135]
610 Let's back off, keeping our faces to the Trojans. Don't take
on the gods in your rage."

So he spoke. The Trojans came close.
Hector killed two men experienced in war
in a single car, Menesthes and Anchialos.
As they went down, the great Telamonian Aiax took pity
615 on them. He went up close and cast his shining
spear, and he struck Amphios the son of Selagos,
who lived in Paisos, rich in possessions, rich
in wheat land. But his fate led him to come to the aid
of Priam and his sons. Telamonian Aiax hit him
620 on the belt. The far-shadowed spear penetrated his lower
belly. He fell with a thump. The glorious Aiax
ran up to strip the armor. The Trojans poured
their spears upon Aiax, sharp, gleaming. Many
struck his shield. Aiax planted his heel on Amphios

---

[134] "Uproar," an allegorical figure.

[135] Athena gave Diomedes the power to tell the difference between men and gods earlier in this book.

625 and drew out the bronze spear, but he could not take
the handsome armor from the shoulders. Missiles oppressed him.
Aiax feared the powerful defense of the Trojans,
who opposed him in great numbers, standing nobly,
their spears aloft, driving Aiax back,
630 though he was tall and strong and brave. Aiax reeled
and retreated. And so they labored in the savage strife.

But a strong fate urged Tlepolemos,[136] the son of Herakles,
valiant and tall, against Sarpedon, like to a god.
When they came near to each other, the son and the grandson
635 of Zeus who gathers the clouds, Tlepolemos was first
to speak:

"Sarpedon, adviser to the Lykians,
why do you skulk around, being a man with little
experience of battle? They lie who say you are
a son of Zeus who carries the goatskin fetish,
640 for you are far inferior to those men who were begotten
of Zeus in the old days, among men of former times.
But they say that mighty Herakles was a different kind of man,
my father, who always held on, whose heart was like a lion.
Once he came here because of the horses of Laomedon
645 with only six ships and fewer men. He sacked
the city of Ilion, he emptied the street.[137] You have
the heart of a coward. Your people are dying. I don't think
your coming here from Lykia will prove a defense for the Trojans,
not even if you are very strong. But overcome
650 by my hand you shall pass the gates of Hades."

Sarpedon,

captain of the Lykians, answered him back: "Tlepolemos,
Herakles truly destroyed holy Ilion, through the folly
of the good Laomedon. He insulted one who had done
him a favor, and he did not relinquish the horses on account

---

[136] Tlepolemos, a son of Herakles, was a leader of the Rhodians. Herakles himself had attacked Troy before (see next note).

[137] Troy was threatened by a sea monster to whom Hesione, daughter of Laomedon, was offered as a sacrifice. Herakles killed the monster and freed the girl in exchange for the divine horses that Zeus had given to Tros, but Laomedon would not surrender the horses, so Herakles returned with an army and destroyed the city. He killed Laomedon and all his sons except Priam, who was "ransomed" by Hesione (Priam's name sounded like it meant "the ransomed one"). See the exploits of Herakles in document 3.11.b.

655 of which he had come from afar. As for you, I expect
that my hands will fashion death and black fate. Conquered
by my spear you will be a boast for me, and your breath-soul
will belong to Hades, famous for his steeds." So spoke
Sarpedon. Tlepolemos raised his spear made of ash.
660 The long missiles sped at the same time from their hands.
Sarpedon's hit Tlepolemos full on the neck. The terrible
point went through. Dark night fell over his eyes.

Tlepolemos had hit Sarpedon on the left thigh
with his long spear. The point eagerly went through
and grazed the bone, but his father Zeus warded
665 off death. The good companions carried out Sarpedon,
like a god, from the war. The long spear caused him much pain
as they dragged him along, for no one thought or noticed
in their haste to draw out the ashen spear from his thigh,
so he could walk. For they were having much difficulty
670 taking care of him. On the other side the Achaeans dragged
the dead Tlepolemos from the fighting.

Odysseus saw
what was happening, and, having an enduring spirit,
his heart raged within. He wondered in his breast
and in his spirit whether he should pursue Sarpedon,
675 the son of thunderous Zeus, or whether he should take
the lives of more Lykians. But it was not allotted to big-hearted
Odysseus to kill the burly son of Zeus
with his sharp bronze, and so Athena turned
his mind to the numerous Lykians. He killed Koiranos
680 and Alastor and Chromios and Alkandros and Halios and Noemon
and Prytanis.[138] And the good Odysseus would have killed more
of the Lykians, had not great Hector of the sparkling helmet
been quick to see what was happening. He stalked through the foremost
fighters, armed in shining bronze, bringing terror
685 to the Danaans.

Sarpedon, the son of Zeus, was cheered

---

[138] The name of Sarpedon may in fact be Lykian; the other names are Greek and many recur, later applied to other minor characters. They are mostly "speaking" names referring either to battle—Alastor, "eternal foe"; Chromios, "thunderer"; Alkandros, "strong man"— or to social ranking—Koiranos, "ruler"; Noemon, "adviser"; Prytanis, "leader." Halios is "the man of the sea."

when Hector came up, and he spoke a pathetic word:
"Son of Priam, don't let me lie here a prey
to the Danaans, but help me. May life leave me in your city,
because I may not return home to the dear land
690　of my fathers, to delight my own wife and my infant son."
So he spoke, but Hector of the sparkling helmet
did not answer him at all. He hastened past,
anxious as soon as possible to drive back the Argives,
to take the lives of many. His good companions
695　placed Sarpedon, like a god, beneath a most beautiful
oak of Zeus who carries the goatskin fetish.
Able Pelagon, a dear companion, forced
the ashen spear out of Sarpedon's thigh.
The breath-soul left his body. A mist poured
700　over his eyes. Then he revived, and the breath
of North Wind brought him back to life by blowing
on him who had painfully breathed forth his spirit.[139]
　　　　　　　　　　　　　　　　The Argives
before the attack of Ares and Hector armored in bronze
did not turn back to the black ships, nor did they
705　hold out in the fight, but always they edged backward
when they heard that Ares was with the Trojans. Well then,
who first and who last did Hector, the son of Priam,
and brazen Ares kill? Teuthras, who was like
a god, and then Orestes, driver of horses, and Trechos,
710　the Aetolian warrior, and Oinomaos and Helenos son
of Oinops, and Oresbios with the flashing belly-protector, who lived
in Hyle where he took good care of his great wealth
on the edge of the Kephisian lake.[140] Nearby lived
other Boiotians on a land that is exceedingly rich.
715　　　　　Now the goddess white-armed Hera saw what was happening,
how the Argives were being destroyed in the terrible combat.
Right away she spoke words to Athena that went like arrows:
"Alas, O daughter of Zeus who carries the goatskin fetish!
Unwearied one, I think that we spoke to no purpose when
　　we promised

---

[139] The next time around he will not be miraculously saved (despite Zeus' temptation to do so), when he is fatally wounded by Patroklos in *Iliad*, Book 16.

[140] The large Lake Kopais in northern Boiotia.

720 Menelaos that he would sail home after sacking Ilion,
    if we thus permit this ruinous Ares to rage.
    But come let us two think of savage valor!"
              So Hera spoke, and the blue-eyed Athena, divine,
    did not disobey her, but went back and forth harnessing
725 her horses with head-pieces of gold. Hebe[141]quickly
    fitted the curved wheels to either side of the car. The wheels
    were made of bronze with eight spokes, and the axle was made
    of iron. The rim was of imperishable gold, and on top
    of it were fitted tires of bronze, a marvel
730 to see. The hubs were made of silver, spinning
    around on either side. The body was woven
    of gold and silver strips. Two rails ran around it.
    The pole was made of silver, and from its tip
    she bound a beautiful golden yoke, and cast
735 on the yoke beautiful breast-collars. Beneath the yoke
    Hera led horses with lightning feet, eager
    for strife and the cry of war.
                        But Athena, the daughter
    of Zeus, let her soft embroidered gown fall
    to her father's floor. She herself had made it
740 with her own hands. She put on the shirt of Zeus
    who gathers the clouds. She armed herself for tearful war.
    Around her shoulders she cast the tasseled goatskin
    fetish, an object of terror, crowned by Rout,
    where inside is Eris, inside is Valor. Inside
745 is icy Attack, and inside is the head of the dreadful
    monster, the Gorgon, hideous and awful, a wonder
    of Zeus who carries the goatskin fetish. On her head
    Athena placed a helmet with ridges on either side and four
    golden plates, fitted with foot soldiers of a hundred cities.[142]
750 She stepped into the flaming chariot. She took up the spear—
    heavy, large, powerful—with which she overcomes
    the ranks of men, of warriors with whom she is angry,
    she of the mighty father. Swiftly Hera
    touched the horse with the lash. The gates of heaven

---

[141] "Youth," a child of Zeus and Hera and wife of Herakles after he was made a god.

[142] To indicate the large size of the helmet? (the Greek is obscure).

755 groaned open. The Horai[143] keep them, to whom
are entrusted the great heaven and Olympos, whether to throw
open the thick cloud or whether to shut it up.

There
through the gates they drove their horses, tolerant
of the goad. They found the son of Kronos sitting apart
760 from the other gods on the topmost peak of Olympos,
which has many ridges. Staying her horses,
the white-armed goddess Hera questioned the exalted
son of Kronos, Zeus: "Zeus, father,
don't you resent Ares for his violent acts?
765 He has destroyed so great and good an army of the Achaeans,
recklessly and not according to the right order of things,
to my sorrow. In the meanwhile, Cypris and Apollo of the silver bow,
free from care, take delight in having sent down this mad man
without respect for any law. Zeus, father,
770 will you be angry if I give Ares a good cuffing and chase him
out of the battle?" Zeus the cloud-gatherer answered:
"Well then, rouse up Athena, the gatherer of loot.
It's her habit most to bring Ares close to evil
pains."

So he spoke, and the white-armed goddess Hera
775 did not disobey. She applied the lash.
The two horses, not unwilling, flew between
the earth and starry heaven. As far as a man
can see into the misty distance, sitting on a place
of outlook and looking over the sea dark as wine,
780 just so far did the high-whinnying horses leap
in a single bound. But when they came to Troy
and the two flowing rivers, where the Simoeis and the Skamandros
join their streams, there white-armed Hera stayed
her horses, loosing them from her car, and she poured
785 about them a thick mist. Simoeis sent up
ambrosia[144] for them to graze on. The two goddesses
went like nervous pigeons in their walk,
anxious to help the Argive men. But when
they came to where the most and best men stood

---

[143] The "hours" or "seasons," a personification of time, here as the gatekeepers of heaven.

[144] The word means "immortal," the special food of the gods, or (like here) other divine beings, even horses.

790 crouched around powerful Diomedes, tamer of horses,
like lions who eat raw flesh, or wild boars,
hardly weaklings, there white-armed Hera
stood and shouted in the likeness of greathearted Stentor,[145]
whose voice was like bronze, so loud it was like fifty men
795 shouting: "Shame on you Argives, a bitter reproach,
good only to look at! So long as Achilles came into
the battle, the Trojans did not come forth before the Dardanian
Gate.
They feared his powerful spear. But now far from the city
they fight near the hollow ships." So speaking she excited
800 the strength and spirits of every man.
                                        The blue-eyed goddess
Athena leapt to the side of Tydeus' son.
She found Diomedes beside his horses and his car
cooling the wound he had received from the arrow of Pandaros.
For the sweat poured on beneath the strap of his round shield.
805 He was bothered by it and his arm grew tired. He raised up the strap
and wiped away the dark blood. The goddess lay hold
of the yoke of his horses and said: "Surely Tydeus
begot a son little like himself. Tydeus
was short in stature, but a fighter. Once I would
810 not let him fight or shine forth, when he went alone
as a messenger to Thebes among the many Kadmeians. I urged
him to dine, to be cheerful in the halls. But having his strong
spirit as of old, he challenged the youths of the Kadmeians,
and he easily defeated them. I was such a helper to him.
815 As for you, I stand at your side and protect you,
and I am glad to urge you to fight against the Trojans.
But either too many assaults have drenched your limbs in weariness
or a spiritless fear possesses you. You are no son of Tydeus,
the wise son of Oineus!"
                                        The mighty Diomedes
820 answered her in this way: "I know who you are,
goddess, daughter of Zeus who carries the goatskin fetish.
And so I will happily tell you my thought and I will not
conceal it. No spiritless fear possesses me,
nor any unwillingness to engage. But I am always mindful

---

[145] Although later proverbial (he spoke in a "stentorian voice"), this character only appears here.

825 of the instructions that you laid upon me. I am not to fight
face to face with the blessed gods, unless
the daughter of Zeus, Aphrodite, should come into the battle—
her I should wound with the sharp bronze. For this reason
I have withdrawn from the fighting and urged the other Argives to
     gather.
830 For I see that Ares is lording it over the battlefield."
        Then the blue-eyed goddess Athena answered him:
"My Diomedes, son of Tydeus, the darling of my heart,
don't be afraid of Ares nor any other of the deathless ones,
so powerful a helper to you am I going to be.
835 So come, turn your single-hoofed horses right away
against Ares. Fight him hand-to-hand.
Have no respect of great mad Ares—this raving one,
this evil made to order, this good for nothing. Just now
he was telling me and Hera that he was going to fight against
840 the Trojans and give aid to the Argives, but as it is
he's mingling with the Trojans. The others are forgotten."
So speaking, with her hand she drew back Sthenelos and shoved
him from his car to the ground. Speedily he jumped.
She got in the car next to good Diomedes,
845 a goddess anxious for battle. The great axle, made of oak,
groaned beneath the burden. For it carried a goddess and the best
of men. Pallas Athena took up the lash and the reins
and right away she headed the horses toward Ares.
He was just then stripping the armor from the huge Periphas,
850 by far the best of the Aetolians, the fine son of Ochesios.
Ares, dripping with blood, was stripping the corpse,
but Athena put on the cap of Hades so that powerful
Ares could not see her. When the murderous Ares saw
the good Diomedes, he let the huge Periphas lie
855 there where in killing him he had let loose his breath-soul.
        He headed straight for Diomedes, the tamer of horses.
When they came near, advancing against one another,
first Ares drove over the yoke and the reins of Diomedes'
horses, eager with his bronze spear to take away
860 the other's life. But the blue-eyed goddess Athena
took the spear in her hand and thrust it above the car,
to fly away in vain. Next, Diomedes, good at the war cry

thrust at Ares with his bronze spear. Pallas
Athena sent it into his lower belly near the buckle
865 of the belly-protector. There he wounded him, and he cut
the beautiful skin. Then Diomedes pulled out the spear.
  Brazen Ares bellowed as much as nine thousand
or ten thousand men yell in battle when they join
in the battles of Ares. A trembling got hold of the Achaeans
870 and Trojans. They were afraid, so loudly did Ares
roar, insatiate of war. Even as when
a black air appears from the clouds after a heat wave,
when a blustery wind arises—even so the brazen
Ares appeared to Diomedes, son of Tydeus,
875 as he went together with the clouds into the broad sky.
  Soon he arrived at the seat of the gods, steep Olympos,
and he sat down next to Zeus, the son of Kronos,
pained at heart. He showed him the immortal blood
running down out of the wound, and with a wailing
880 he spoke words that went like arrows: "Zeus, father,
doesn't it anger you to see these violent acts?
Always we gods suffer shivery things from the will
of one another, whenever we show favor to men.
We are all at war with you! You gave birth to that insane
885 and destructive daughter,[146] always concerned with evil acts.
All the gods who are in Olympos obey you
and are subject to you. But you pay no attention to her,
neither in word nor in deed, but you encourage her—
because you yourself begot this destroying child.
890 Now she has set Diomedes, high of heart,
the son of Tydeus, to rage against the deathless gods.
First he wounded Cypris in the close fight on the hand
near the wrist, but then, like a god, he raged against
me myself. Luckily I was able to run away.
895 Otherwise I would have suffered pains there for a long time
amidst the vile heaps of the dead, or I would
have been alive, but without strength from the blows of the bronze."
  Thus Zeus answered him, glowering beneath his brows:
"Ares, don't sit beside me and whine, you good for nothing.

---

[146] Athena.

900 You are most hated to me of the gods who inhabit
     Olympos! Always dear to you are strife
     and wars and battles. You have the mind of your mother
     Hera, intolerable, unyielding. I can scarcely control
     her with words. Therefore I think that you
905 are suffering these things because of her suggestions.
     Nonetheless I will not let you continue to endure
     these agonies. You are of my blood. Your mother bore
     you to me. If you were born of any other god,
     destructive as you are, then long before now you would be lower
910 than the Ouraniones!"[147]
                              Zeus spoke and he asked Paieon
     to heal Ares. Paieon spread a poultice over the wound
     and healed him, for surely Ares was not made to be mortal!
     Even as the juice of the wild fig quickly makes to grow
     thick the white milk that is liquid, but soon curdles as a man
915 stirs it, even so swiftly did he heal mad Ares.
     Hebe bathed him, and placed lovely clothes upon him.
     He sat beside Zeus, the son of Kronos, exulting
     in his glory.
                              Back to the house of great Zeus went Argive
     Hera and Alalkomenian[148] Athena, having put
920 an end to man-killing Ares' murderous rampage.

3.8.b.   Odysseus and the Cyclops: *Odyssey*, Book 9

Homer's *Odyssey* is an epic poem in twenty-four books that narrates the adventures of Odysseus and his companions after the sack of Troy as they try to return to their home, Ithaca, an island in western Greece. The encounter with the Cyclops is the third adventure of many that befall the travelers after they leave Troy. First Odysseus and his men (sailing on twelve ships, as we learn below) raid the land of the Kikones in Asia Minor; after that point, all the places Odysseus visits are fantastic and not attached to a real geographical referent, although scholars since antiquity have tried to identify them with specific areas of the Mediterranean. Finally, Odysseus is ferried by the Phaeacians, another fantastic people, and he arrives at Ithaca.

The structure and chronology of the *Odyssey* are not linear but complicated. Odysseus is narrating his adventures in first person to the Phaeacians. He

---

[147] The "heavenly gods," here not the Olympians but Kronos and the other Titans, the children of Ouranos whom Zeus imprisoned in underworld Tartaros, according to the story told in Hesiod's *Theogony* (for which see Part 1, document 5).

[148] A title meaning "protectress."

had reached them after his seven-year forced stay on the island of the goddess Kalypso, where he had arrived after losing all his companions in various
ordeals. In Books 9–12 Odysseus narrates his adventures to the friendly Phaeacians, before they convey him to Ithaca (in Book 13).

The name Cyclops (Cyclopes in plural) literally means "round-eye" or "round-
face." Though Homer never explicitly says that the Cyclops whom Odysseus
confronts has only one eye, the story of his blinding makes it obvious. It is not
clear whether Homer's Cyclopes are related to the Cyclopes in Hesiod's *Theogony*
(see Part 1, document 5), who were Titans and who helped Zeus by forging
the thunderbolt. The adventure excerpted below reflects central themes of the
Odyssey, especially the importance of complying with the rules of ritual **xenia**
(hospitality), and the triumph of the civilized intelligence and skill (technical
and linguistic) of Odysseus over the primitive and uncivilized Cyclops. The
hybris of Odysseus toward the end also brings about the wrath of Poseidon and
the disapproval of Zeus, which condemns the hero to many more years of wandering before he can reach his home.

*(In the opening lines, 1–105, Odysseus tells the Phaeacians how he and his men left Troy and
waged war with the Kikones.)*

(105)   "From there we sailed on, grieving in our hearts. We came
to the land of the arrogant and lawless Cyclopes. Trusting
in the deathless gods they neither plant with their hands nor do
    they plow,
but all these things spring up for them, unsown
and unplowed—wheat and barley and vines that bear grapes

(110)   for a fine wine and the rain of Zeus makes them grow.
They do not have assemblies where they discuss policy, nor do
they establish rules, but they live on the peaks of high mountains
in hollow caves, each man laying down the law to his own
children and wives, nor do they care about one another.

(115)   "There is a fertile island that stretches outside the harbor,
not close, not far from the land of the Cyclopes, wooded.
Countless goats live there, wild goats. The comings
and goings of men do not drive them away, nor do hunters
go there, men who suffer jeopardy in the woods as they tramp

(120)   upon the peaks of the mountains. The island is not occupied
by flocks, nor covered by plowland, but unsown and unplowed.
The island is every day empty of men, and it feeds
the bleating goats. For the Cyclopes have no red-cheeked
ships,[149] nor do builders of ships live among them who might build

---

[149] Because their sterns are painted red.

(125)   ships with fine benches to provide them everything
   they want, journeying to the cities of men, as men often
   cross the sea in ships to visit one another. Such men
   would have made of this island a pleasant place. It is by no means
   a poor place, but would bear every fruit in season. There are
    meadows
(130)   in it, watered and soft, beside the shores of the gray sea.
   Vines will never fail there. The land is level and suitable
   for plowing. One could harvest a bumper crop every season,
   for the soil is rich.

        "There is a secure harbor. There is
   no need of mooring ropes, nor need of throwing out
(135)   anchor stones, nor of making fast the sterns of ships.
   You need only draw the ships up on the shore, then wait
   for the time that your spirit urges you again to put to sea,
   when the winds blow fair. At the head of the harbor a spring
   of shining water flows from beneath a cave.
(140)   Poplars grow around it. There we sailed. Some god
   guided us through the dark night, for there was no light
   by which to see. A thick mist covered the island all around,
   and the cloud-hidden moon did not appear in the night sky.
   No one had seen the island, nor the long waves
(145)   rolling onto the dry land until we ran our ships
   with fine benches up onto the shore. When we had beached
   the ships, we took down the sails and ourselves went ashore
   on the edge of the sea. There we fell asleep and awaited
   the bright dawn.

        "When early-born dawn appeared,
(150)   who has fingers like roses, we wandered over the island,
   wondering at it. Nymphs, the daughters of Zeus who carries
   the goatskin fetish,[150] roused up the mountain goats so that my
    companions
   could have something to eat. Immediately we took out our bent
    bows
   and javelins with long sockets from the ships. We split up into three
(155)   groups and set to throwing our missiles. Soon
   the god had given us enough game to satisfy our hearts.

        Twelve ships followed me, and to each nine goats fell by lot.

---

[150] The Greek is *aegis*, on which see note on *Iliad*, Book 5, line 120.

For me alone they chose out ten. Then we spent
the whole day dining on endless flesh and sweet wine
(160) until the sun went down. The red wine from our ships
had not yet run out, some was still left. For we had taken
a lot of it in jars for each crew when we sacked the sacred
city of the Kikones.[151] We looked across to the land
of the Cyclopes, who lived nearby. We saw smoke and heard voices
(165) and the sound of sheep and goats. When the sun went down
and darkness came on, we lay down to rest on the edge
of the sea.

"When early-born dawn appeared, whose fingers
were like roses, I called an assembly and spoke thus
to all: 'The rest of you stay here, my trusty companions,
(170) while I take a ship and some companions and appraise these men,
to see who they are, whether they are violent and savage
and unjust, or whether they are friendly to strangers and have
minds that fear the gods.'

"So speaking I got
in my ship and commanded my companions to embark,
(175) to release the stern-cables. They quickly got in and sat down
on the benches. Sitting in order they struck the gray sea
with their oars. And when we had reached the place nearby,
there, at the edge of the land, we espied a cave
close to the sea, high up, overgrown by laurels.
(180) Many flocks were accustomed to sleep there. A high wall surrounded
the cave, made of stones set deep in the earth, and tall pines
grew there, and high-crowned oaks. A huge man
slept alone in that place, and herded his animals there,
all alone. He had no doings with others, but lived
(185) in solitude, without laws. For truly he was an
unearthly monster, not like a man who lives by bread,
more like a wooded peak of a high mountain range that stands
out alone above all others.

"I ordered the remainder
of my trusty companions to stay by the ship and to guard it
(190) while I went off, having selected twelve of my best men.
I had with me a goatskin of dark sweet wine which Maron

---

[151] People around the city of Ismaros, in Thrace just northwest of Troy, the first stop that Odysseus and his men make on their return journey.

had given me, the son of Euanthes, priest of Apollo,
who used to watch over Ismaros.[152] He gave it because
out of respect we protected him, along with his wife and child.

(195) He lived in a wood of Phoibos Apollo, and he gave me
splendid gifts. Of finely worked gold he gave me
seven talents,[153] and he gave me a silver wine-mixing
bowl, and beside these he filled twelve jars with wine,
a divine drink—sweet, unmixed. No one in his household

(200) knew about this wine, neither slave nor servant,
only his wife and the housekeeper. Whenever they drank
honeyed red wine, he would pour one cup of the wine
into twenty of water, and a wondrous odor would come up
from the mixing bowl.[154] Then one could hardly resist

(205) drinking it. With this wine I filled a large skin
and took it along, also provisions in a leather sack.
For my proud spirit imagined confronting a man
clothed in mighty strength, a savage, not subjecting himself
to laws or regulations.

                                   "We quickly arrived at the cave, but did not

(210) find him inside, for he was shepherding his fat flocks
in the fields. Coming into the cave we marveled at everything—
there were crates filled with cheeses, and pens groaned
with sheep and kids. Each kind were penned separately—
the older by themselves, the younger by themselves, the newborn

(215) by themselves as well. Vast jars were brimful in whey, and the milk pails
and bowls, finely made, into which he milked. Then my comrades
begged me to grab the cheeses and to leave that place—
to drive the kids and lambs quickly out of the pens
to our swift ship, and to sail away across the salt water.

(220) But I was not persuaded—it were better I had been!—
because I wanted to see him, in case he might give me gift-tokens.[155]
As it happened, his appearance was not to be a pleasing one
to my companions!

---

[152] City of the above-mentioned Kikones.

[153] "Talent" is from a Greek word meaning "scale, balance." It stood for a very large value.

[154] Ordinarily wine was mixed in proportion of two parts wine to three parts water.

[155] The aristocratic traveler could expect to be entertained and given a gift, often precious, that would ever thereafter bind the traveler and his descendants to the host. Such a relation was called *xenia*, "the rules of guest-friendship." The *Odyssey*, and the Cyclops episode, are much concerned with *xenia* and the violation of its rules.

"We made a fire and offered

sacrifice. We took some of the cheeses and ate them.

(225) We sat inside and waited until he should return

from herding his flocks. He finally arrived with a large load

of dried wood, useful at dinner time. He threw the wood inside

the cave with a crash. In terror we shrank back into a deep recess

of the cave. He drove his fat flock of sheep, all those

(230) he needed to milk, deep into the wide cavern, leaving

the males outside, the rams and the billys, in the deep

courtyard. Then he placed a huge boulder in the opening

of the cavern, lifting it on high, gigantic. Twenty-two

fine four-wheeled carts could not have dislodged it from

(235) the ground—such a towering mass of rock he placed

before the door. Then he sat down and milked his sheep

and the bleating goats, all in turn, and he placed

a suckling beneath each. And he smartly curdled half

the white milk,[156] gathered it and stored it in woven baskets,

(240) and the other half he put in vessels so that he could use it

for drink, so that it might serve him for dinner.

"When he had

finished

his tasks, he built a fire and, finally, he saw us—and he asked:

'Strangers, who are you? From where do you sail the watery

paths? Are you on some mission, or do you cross

(245) the sea at random, like pirates who wander around

endangering their lives while doing evil to men of other lands?'[157]

"So he spoke—and our hearts were frozen in fear of his rumbling

voice and his immense size. Nonetheless I answered

in this way: 'We are Achaeans returning from Troy.

(250) We have been buffeted by winds from every direction across

the great depth of the sea. Longing to go home, we have travelled

on a false course, by many stages. For so Zeus devised.

We are followers of Agamemnon, the son of Atreus,

whose fame is now the greatest under the heaven.

---

[156] Presumably by adding a fermenting agent, such as fig juice.

[157] Apollo uses the exact same words when he addresses the sailors in the *Hymn to Apollo*, 452–455 (document 3.9). Cyclops inverts all the rules of *xenia*. In polite society the host entertains and feeds the guest before asking the stranger's identity.

(255)   He has sacked a city of great size and destroyed
        its many people. We come to you on our knees,
        as suppliants, in the hope you might give us a gift-token or some other
        present, as is the custom among strangers. Respect the gods,
        O mighty man! We are your suppliants, and Zeus
(260)   is the avenger of suppliants and strangers—Zeus the god
        of strangers, who always stands by respectable voyagers.'
                "So I spoke, and he answered me immediately with a piti-
        less
        heart: 'You are a fool, stranger, or you must come from faraway,
        inviting me to fear or shun your gods. The Cyclopes
(265)   have no care for Zeus who carries the goatskin fetish,
        nor for any other of your gods, because we are more powerful
            than they!
        Not to avoid the hatred of Zeus would I spare you
        or your companions, if my spirit did not so urge me.
        But tell me, so that I may know—where did you anchor
(270)   your well-made ship, far away, or nearby?'
                "Thus he spoke, testing me, but he did not fool
        my great cunning. I answered him with crafty words:
        'Poseidon, the rocker of the earth, shattered my ship,
        throwing it against the cliffs at the edge of your land,
(275)   driving it onto a headland. For a wind arose
        from the sea, but I, along with my men, escaped
        dread destruction.'
                        "So I spoke. He did not answer
        from his pitiless heart, but leaping up he seized two of my companions,
        raised them high, then dashed them to the ground as if
(280)   they were puppies. Their brains ran out onto the ground,
        wetting the earth. Cutting them limb from limb, he readied
        his meal. He ate them like a lion raised in the mountains,
        not leaving anything—not the guts nor the flesh nor the bones
        rich with marrow.
                        "Wailing, we held up our hands
(285)   to Zeus, seeing this vile deed and helpless to do anything about it.
        But when Cyclops had filled his great belly by eating the flesh
        of two of our men, and then drinking pure milk, he lay stretched
        out among the sheep in the cave. I contemplated in my great
        heart going up close to him, drawing my sharp sword

(290)   from my thigh, and stabbing him in the chest where the belly
      shields the liver, feeling along with my hand to find
      the right place. But a second thought came to me—
      we would die then a grisly death! For our hands would be
      incapable of budging the heavy stone he had set in place
(295)   against those high doors. So, groaning miserably, we awaited
      the bright dawn.

               "When early-born dawn appeared
      and spread her fingers of rose, Cyclops stirred up
      the fire and milked his glorious herds, all in order,
      again setting the young to each dam. When he had
(300)   finished his tasks, he again seized two of my men
      for his meal. After he had made his meal, he drove out
      the fat herds, easily lifting away the huge stone.
      Then he put it back again, as if shutting the lid
      on a quiver. With a loud whistle Cyclops turned
(305)   his flocks toward the mountains.

                    "I was left there devising evil
      in the depths of my heart, wondering how I could take revenge,
      if Athena would grant me glory. Thinking on it,
      I devised the following plan: A great club of Cyclops lay
      beside a sheep pen, green, made of olive wood.
(310)   He had cut it to carry, once it dried out. Looking at it
      we considered it to be as big as a mast of a black
      ship with twenty oars—a big merchantman that crosses over
      the great gulf, so great it was in length
      and in breadth to look at. I went up to it and cut off
(315)   about six feet and gave the length to my companions.
      I told them to strip off the bark and make it smooth,
      while I stood by it and sharpened the point. Then I at once
      placed the stake in the blazing fire to harden it.
      Then I laid it away, hiding it beneath some dung
(320)   that was spread in big heaps all over the cave. I ordered
      the others to select by lot who would dare to assist me
      in hoisting the stake and grinding it into his eye
      when sweet sleep overcame him. They selected the very ones
      I myself would have chosen, four solid men,
(325)   and I the fifth among them.

                    "At dusk Cyclops returned

from the fields, leading his herds with beautiful fleece.
He drove the fat sheep into the broad cave, all of them
this time, leaving none of them outside in the deep court,
either because he had a foreboding, or some god urged him on.

(330) Then he lifted high the huge rock and set it back in place.
He sat down and milked his ewes and bleating goats,
all in order, again placing each young beneath the teat
of every mother. When he had finished his tasks, he snatched
two of my men and prepared his meal.

         "Then I spoke

(335) to Cyclops, standing near him, holding in my hands
a bowl of ivy wood filled with black wine: 'Cyclops,
take this wine, drink it after your meal of human flesh,
so that you might know what manner of drink our ship
contained. I was bringing it to you as a drink offering,

(340) in hopes you would take pity on me and send me homeward.
But as it is you are mad past bearing! Vile monster!
How then will anyone else from all the multitudes of men
ever come here again when you have behaved so badly?'

   "So I spoke. He took the wine and drank it.

(345) He was tremendously pleased quaffing the sweet drink,
and again he asked me: 'Give me some more, be a good fellow,
and tell me your name right away so that I may give you a gift-token
that will make you happy. Surely the rich plowland bears a fine grape
for the Cyclopes, and the rain of Zeus makes the grape grow, but this

(350) is equal to the food of the gods!' So he spoke, and again
I poured for him the flaming wine. Three times
I brought it and gave it to him, three times he drank
it in his mindless folly.

       "When the wine had gone
to his head, I spoke to him with honeyed words:

(355) 'Cyclops, you ask about my famous name,
so I will tell you and then you will give me a gift-token,
just as you promised. *Nbdy* is my name.
My mother and my father and everyone else calls me *Nbdy*.'

   "So I spoke, and he at once answered me from his pitiless heart:

(360) '*Nbdy*, I will eat you last among your comrades, the others first.
That will be your gift-token!'

       "He spoke and then, reeling over,

fell on his back. He lay there, bending his thick neck,
and sleep, who overcomes all, took hold of him. From his throat
dribbled wine and bits of human flesh. Drunk, he vomited.

(365) "I then pushed the stake I'd made into the hot ashes
until it glowed hot. I encouraged my companions, so that no man
would hold back from fear. Then, as soon as the stake was nearly
afire—although it was green, and glowed terribly—
then, I went up close and took it from the fire, my comrades

(370) attending me. A god breathed into us strong courage.

  "They took the stake of olive wood, sharp on its point,
and thrust it into his eye. I threw my weight
on it from above and spun it around, as when
a man drills a ship's timber with a drill, and those

(375) beneath keep the drill spinning with a thong, holding
the thong from either end, and the drill runs around
unceasingly—just so we took hold of that fiery stake
and spun it around in his eye, and his blood
streamed all around the heated thing. The flame

(380) singed his eyelid and eyebrow and the eyeball popped and its
  roots
crackled in the fire. As when a bronze-worker dips
a great ax or an adze in the cold water and the metal hisses
as he tempers it—from there comes the strength of iron[158]—so did
Cyclops' eye hiss around the olive stake.

(385) "He screamed horribly, and the rock echoed his cry.
In terror we drew back as he ripped out the stake from his eye,
mixed with a huge amount of blood. He wrenched
it from his eye and threw it away, throwing his hands about
wildly. Cyclops called aloud to the Cyclopes who lived

(390) nearby in caves in the windy heights. Hearing
his cry, they assembled from here and there, and standing
outside his cave they asked him what was the matter:

  'What is so bothering you, Polyphemos, that you cry out
through the immortal night and wake us all up?

---

[158] At the time that Homer was composing in the eighth century BCE, iron was replacing bronze, so the bronzesmith is said to quench an ax. In Homer weapons are always of bronze, but everyday implements could be made of iron. The word translated "tempers" really means "to treat with a drug," that is, with something dissolved in water. The effectiveness of tempering iron was thought to come from substances dissolved in water into which the hot metal was plunged, not from the sudden cooling of the metal.

(395)   Can it be that some man is driving off your flocks against
    your will? Or is someone killing you by trickery or by force?'
        "The powerful Polyphemos answered them from the
    cave:
    'My friends, *Nbdy* is killing me by trickery, not by force.'
        "And they answered with words that went like arrows: 'If
    nobody
(400)   is assaulting you in your loneliness—well, you cannot
    escape a sickness sent by great Zeus. Pray
    to our father Poseidon, the king.' So they spoke and went away.
        "My heart laughed, my made-up name and my cunning
    device had deceived him. Cyclops, groaning, in terrible pain,
(405)   fumbled around with his hands, then took away the stone
    blocking his door. He sat down in the doorway with arms
    outstretched, to catch anyone who might try to get out
    of the door along with the sheep—so much did he hope
    in his heart to find me a fool!
        "But I considered what would be
(410)   the best plan to devise a foolproof escape
    for my companions and for myself. I considered
    every kind of trick and device, as is usual in matters
    of life and death. A great evil was near! Now this
    seemed to me to be the best plan. Here are his well-fed
(415)   rams with thick wool, handsome and large, with fleece
    dark as violet. In silence I bound these together,
    taking up three at a time, with twisted stems
    on which the huge Cyclops, who knows no laws,
    used to sleep. The sheep in the middle would carry a man,
(420)   the two on the outside would go along, saving
    my comrades. Thus each three sheep bore a man.
        "As for me—there was a ram, by far the best of the flock,
    and I climbed up on his back and then squirreled around
    to his shaggy belly, where I lay, my hands clinging
(425)   constantly, with a steady heart, to the wonderful fleece.
        "Thus we waited, wailing, until the bright dawn.
    When early-born dawn appeared and stretched forth her fingers
    of rose, the rams hastened out to pasture.
    But the ewes, unmilked, bleated in the pens, for their udders
(430)   were full to bursting. Their master, worn down by savage pain,
    felt along the backs of all the sheep as they stood before him—

the fool! He did not realize that my men were bound
beneath the breasts of the wooly sheep. Last of all
the ram went out the door, burdened by the weight
(435) of its fleece and my own devious self. Feeling
along his back, the mighty Polyphemos said:
      'My dear ram, why do you go out of the cave
last of the entire flock? In the past you would never lag
behind the sheep, but you always went out the very first
(440) to graze on the tender bloom of the grass, taking
long strides. You always came first to the flowing rivers,
and you were always the most eager to return to the fold at evening.
But now you are the last of all. Perhaps you regret
the eye of your master that an evil man blinded,
(445) along with his miserable companions, overcoming my brain
with wine! *Nbdy*, who has not yet, I think,
escaped destruction! If you could think as I do,
and you had the power of speech to tell me where
that man flees from my wrath, then would his brains
(450) be smeared all over the ground of this cave
when I hit him, and my heart could take rest from the agony
that this good-for-nothing *Nbdy* has brought.'
                              "So saying
he sent the ram forth from the door. When we had gone a short
    distance
from the cave and the fold, I was first to loose myself
(455) from the ram, and then I cut free my companions. Quickly
we drove off the long-legged sheep, rich with fat,
turning constantly around, until we came to the ship.
Our friends were glad to see us, who had escaped death,
but they bewailed those who were lost. I would not let them weep,
(460) but I nodded at each, ordering them to load aboard the herds
with beautiful fleece so we might sail away over the salt sea.
They got back in and sat on their benches, and sitting
all in a row they struck the gray sea with their oars.
      "But when we were so far away you can barely hear a man
(465) when he shouts, then I called to Cyclops with these contemptuous
words: 'Cyclops, it turns out that you did not eat
the companions of a man without strength, in your hollow cave,
taking them by might and by violence! Surely your evil
deeds were bound to come back to you, wretch! You did not

(470) shrink from devouring strangers in your own house!
       For this Zeus, and the other gods, have punished you.'
                                      "So I spoke,
       and more anger boiled from his heart. He ripped off the peak
       of a high mountain, and he threw it. It landed just forward
       of our ship with its dark prow. The sea surged
(475) beneath the rock as it came down. The wave carried
       the boat back toward the shore, on that flood from the deep,
       driving it onto the dry land. But I seized a long pole
       in my hands and thrust the ship off land again.
       I nodded to my comrades, directing them to fall to their oars
(480) so that we might escape this evil. They set to their oars
       and rowed. When we were twice as far away,
       traveling over the sea, then I wanted to speak
       to Cyclops again, but my comrades, one after the other, tried
       to stop me with gentle words: 'Weirdo! Why
(485) do you want to stir up this savage man? Just now
       he has thrown a rock into the sea and brought our ship
       back to the dry land, and, truly, we thought
       we were done for. If he had heard even one of us uttering
       even one sound, he would have thrown a jagged rock
(490) and smashed our heads and all the timbers of our ship!
       He's a mighty thrower!'
                                      "So they cowered, but they did not
       persuade my great-hearted spirit. I shouted back
       at him with an angry heart: 'Cyclops, if any mortal man
       ever asks about the disgraceful blinding of your eye, you can say
(495) that Odysseus, sacker of cities, did it, the son of Laertes,
       whose home is in Ithaca.'
                                      "So I spoke,
       and groaning he gave me this answer: 'Yes, yes—!
       Now I remember an ancient prophecy. A prophet
       once came here, a good man, a tall man, Telemos, the son
(500) of Eurymos, who was better at prophecy than anyone. He grew old
       among the Cyclopes. He told me that all this would happen
       sometime in the future, that I would lose my sight at the hands
       of Odysseus. I always thought that some big man,
       and handsome, would come here, dressed in mighty power.
(505) As it is, a little man, a man of no consequence, a feeble little guy
       has blinded my eye after he got me drunk on wine!

But do return, O Odysseus, so that I can give you some guest-
    tokens . . .

And I can ask Poseidon, the famous shaker of the earth,

to give you a good trip home . . . For I am his son,

(510) you know, and he is my father. He himself will heal me,

if he wishes it—no other of the blessed gods, nor mortal human.'

      "So he spoke, and I said in reply: 'Would

that I might rob you of your breath-soul and your life

and send you to the house of Hades, as surely as the earth-shaker

(515) shall never heal your eye!'

            "So I spoke. He then raised

his hands into the starry heaven and prayed to Poseidon

the king: 'Hear me, Poseidon, holder of the earth,

you with the dark locks—if truly I am your son

and you are my father, grant that Odysseus, the son of Laertes,

(520) the sacker of cities, never reach his home, which he says

is in Ithaca. But if it is fated that he see his friends

again, and arrive to his well-built house, returning

to the land of his fathers—may he come after a long time,

and in big trouble, having lost all his companions, on someone else's

(525) boat, and may he find grief in his own house!'

      "So he spoke in prayer, and the dark-haired one

heard him. Right away Cyclops picked up a much bigger

stone, twirled it around, and put all his strength

into the throw. The rock this time fell behind the ship

(530) with its dark prows just a little bit, missing the blade

of the steering-oar. The sea surged as the stone submerged

and its wake drove the ship forward and onto dry land.

      "But when we came back to the island,[159] the other ships

with fine benches were waiting, grouped together, and around

(535) sat our comrades wailing, awaiting us constantly.

We dragged the ship up onto the sand. We ourselves

got out of the ship and onto the shore of the sea. Then

we took the sheep out of the hollow boat and divided

them up so that no man, as far as I was able, would go

(540) deprived of an equal share. My companions, who wear fancy

shinguards, gave the ram to me alone as a special gift

when the division took place. I sacrificed the ram

---

[159] The island opposite the Cyclops' cave, from where Odysseus set out.

on the shore to Zeus of the dark thundercloud, the son
of Kronos, who rules over all, and I burned the thigh pieces.

(545) He did not heed the offering but pondered how all
the ships with their fine benches might be destroyed,
along with my trusty companions.

        "So we spent the whole day
until the sunset, dining on endless flesh and sweet wine.

(550) When the sun went down and darkness came on, then we went
to bed on the shore of the sea. When early-born dawn
came and spread her fingers of rose, I roused up
my companions and ordered them to disembark, to loosen the stern-ropes.

Quickly they boarded the goats and sat down on the benches,

(555) and all in a row they struck the gray sea with their oars.

        "From there we sailed further, grieving at heart—glad to have
escaped death, but sorry for our dear companions who did not."

3.9. APOLLO'S JOURNEY: THE *HOMERIC HYMN TO APOLLO*

The so-called *Homeric Hymns* are anonymous poems of various length, dedicated to specific gods. Most of them were composed between the seventh and the fifth centuries BCE, with others as late as the Hellenistic period. They were traditionally attributed to Homer, and they indeed follow the Homeric epic style, in dactylic hexameters and using similar formulaic language in general (see headnote to document 3.8). However, internal evidence such as linguistic and stylistic differences, as well as independent ancient testimonies, show that they were composed by different poets who followed Homer, some soon after (the oldest being the hymns to Aphrodite, Apollo, and Demeter), and others much later. A few of them are long enough to constitute epic poems in themselves (Demeter, Apollo, Hermes, and Aphrodite) and contain longer mythical narratives, while the other extant hymns are much shorter (Dionysos, Pan, Athena, Artemis, Hera, Asklepios, and others) and probably served as opening invocations to the particular god, prefacing other longer pieces, perhaps at poetic (i.e., singing) competitions at festivals. Indeed, many of the hymns' endings directly allude to a next song, for example, "having started with you, I will now move on to another hymn" or "I will remember you and also another song." Furthermore, some of the hymns, especially the long ones, seem to be connected with particular sanctuaries and rituals (e.g., Eleusinian Mysteries of Demeter and Kore, sanctuaries of Apollo at Delphi and at Delos), although the exact relationship between poem and cult is a topic of unresolved scholarly debate.

The long *Homeric Hymn to Apollo* (*HH* 3) is one of the oldest hymns, probably dating to the very early seventh century BCE. This rough date is deduced from internal references and language, although some sources attribute it to one Kynthaios from Chios in the sixth century BCE. Already in Homer, Apollo is a central god, and the spread of his cult throughout Greece is well attested archaeologically by 700 BCE. Apollo was the son of Zeus and Leto and twin brother of Artemis. His figure was romanticized in modern culture as the "purest" image of a Greek god, with the sculptures of his naked young figure holding the lyre admired as visual representations of a classical ideal, often contrasted with the Dionysiac image of disorder and lust. However, Apollo is a more complex and ambivalent god. Bright as the sun with whom he is associated, he sponsors music (especially the lyre) and singing. But he is also responsible for plagues, which he shoots with his deadly arrows. This side of the god is represented at the opening of the hymn, when his sudden entrance into Olympos terrifies the gods, and at the beginning of the *Iliad*, when he marches down to the Greek camp, bow and arrows clashing on his shoulders, looking angry and dark "like the night" (*Il.* 1.43–49). His power as an oracular deity is also crucial and highlighted in the hymn. He is associated with healing and is the father of the healing god Aklepios. Paradoxically, unlike Dionysos, Apollo has not been identified so far in the Linear B tablets, and hence speculation as to where and when he arrived to Greece is still open. His figure combines features that make him similar to the Syrian and Hittite smiting and pestilence gods as well as to Egyptian solar deities, while he also seems to fit into Indo-European (especially Dorian?) religion. His standard epithet, Phoibos (Lat. Phoebus), means "bright, shinning." It sometimes stands for his name and points both to his association with the sun and his descent from Phoibe (mother of Leto).

The *Hymn to Apollo* has two distinct parts, which has led scholars to debate its original unity. The first part (down to line 178), which some think is the oldest, is dedicated to the birth of Apollo at Delos and his important cult on that Cycladic island, while the rest of the hymn narrates Apollo's search for a place to establish an oracle and how he takes possession of the sites of Krisa and Delphi and establishes his sanctuary and oracle there, after defeating the monster Python. Both parts contain detailed itineraries that mirror each other, first of Leto's search for a place to give birth, then of Apollo's search for his cultic place. A digression on Zeus' fight with the monster Typhaon (305–355) in the second part of the hymn has puzzled scholars. Whether it originated in a separate song or not, it is nicely integrated by the hymnist. The monster, after all, was raised by Python. Just as Zeus' defeat of Typhon introduced a new order of things (see Hesiod's *Theogony* in Part 1, document 5), Apollo's overcoming of Python leads to his establishment of a new sanctuary and oracle. The archaic poet worked with existing oral traditions and creatively combined them and modified them. As Susan Shelmerdine (1995:59) put it: "the extant hymn is an intentional blend of two separate traditions which has kept the language of each (Delian and Pythian) distinct in many places, yet consciously structured the narrative to connect the most important themes and events of the two."

The connection between the poem and the sanctuaries of Apollo at Delos and Delphi is obvious. The hymn celebrates the foundation of historical centers of Apollo's cult. These sanctuaries remained important throughout antiquity. In this sense, the hymn has relevance to the foundation stories explored in Part 4. Moreover, both sites, Delos and Delphi, are represented as underprivileged by nature (bare and barren) but privileged by the god's choice and destined to be sustained by the constant flow of worshippers ("out of a foreign hand," 59–60). As in the *Hymn to Demeter* (Part 6, document 8), *Aphrodite* (Part 5, document 5), and *Dionysos* (document 3.10.b), the story includes an **epiphany** of the deity to human beings, in different stages, as the gods appear first in human or animal disguise, only to reveal their real identity later on, followed by specific instructions to the people they appear to.

SOURCE: Homeric *Hymn to Apollo* (*HH* 3), translated and annotated by C. López-Ruiz.

(Delian section)

I will remember and not forget far-shooter Apollo, at whose entrance the gods tremble around the house of Zeus; and so they jump up from their seats, all of them, as he comes near, when he bends his splendid bow. Leto alone would stay by Zeus, who loves thunder, and she unstrung his bow and shut his quiver, and, taking the archery equipment from his mighty shoulders, she hung it on a column of his father, from a golden peg. And she led him and had him sit on a chair. (10) Then his father Zeus gave him nectar in a golden cup, acknowledging his son, and after that the other deities take their seats there. And so Lady Leto is joyful, because she was bringing to the world a bow-bearing and powerful son.[160]

Hail, blessed Leto, for you gave birth to glorious children, lord Apollo and arrow-pouring Artemis, her on Ortygia,[161] him on steep Delos, reclining against a high mountain and the Kynthian hill,[162] close to a palm tree by the streams of Inopos.

How should I, then, sing to you, who are celebrated with hymns in every possible way? (20) For in every direction, Phoibos, a field of song is laid out for you, be it throughout the calf-nourishing mainland or through the islands. All high viewpoints please you, the high headlands of lofty mountains and the rivers flowing down to the sea, as well as the peaks inclined toward the sea and the harbors of the ocean.

Perhaps I should sing, first of all, of how Leto bore you, a joy for mortal people, leaning against the Kynthos mountain, in a rocky island, sea-girt Delos? And from either side a dark wave came out to the dry-land with whistling winds; rushing on from there, you rule over all mortals[163]:

(30) As many people as Crete has in it and the province of the Athenians, as well as the island of Aigina and Euboia, famous for its ships; and Aigai, Eiresiai and coastal Peparethos; and Thracian Athos and the high peak of Pelion; and Samothrace and the shady mountains of Ida; and Skyros, Phokaia, and the steep mountain of Autokane; also well-built Imbros, barren Lemnos, and holy Lesbos, seat

---

[160] The alternation of present and past tenses (which I maintain) makes it unclear whether this refers to a recurrent reaction to Apollo's presence or to the first entrance of Apollo into Olympos.

[161] Probably the island of Rhenaia, meaning "Quail Island," near Delos.

[162] On which, according to tradition, she gave birth to both Apollo and Artemis.

[163] A catalogue of places mostly around the Aegean coast follows, many of them places where Apollo's cult was established, mirroring the "tour" of Apollo in the Pythian section later.

of Makar, son of Aiolos;[164] and Chios, which lies in the sea as the brightest of the islands; and rugged Mimas, and the high peak of Korykos; (40) dazzling Klaros and also the steep mountain of Aisagee; also refreshing Samos and the elevated heights of Mykale; Miletos and Kos, a city of Meropian people; also elevated Knidos and windy Karpathos, Naxos, Paros, and rocky Rhenaia; to so many places did Leto arrive while in labor with the far-shooter, in case one of these lands may set up a home for her son. But they were trembling and absolutely terrified, and none dared to receive Phoibos, even though they were more fertile, until Lady Leto happened to set foot on Delos, (50) and questioned her pronouncing winged words:

"Delos, if only you were willing to be the home for my son Phoibos Apollo, and establish inside you a rich temple. . . . For no one else will ever take you, as you will notice, nor will you be rich in cattle or sheep, I should think, nor will you bear corn, or grow abundant crops. But if you hold a temple of far-shooting Apollo, all people indeed will bring hecatombs, coming together here, and the indescribable scent of fat will constantly rise, and you will feed those who dwell in you out of a foreign hand, (60) since you are certainly not rich under your soil."[165]

So she said, and Delos rejoiced, and answered saying: "Leto, most honorable daughter of great Koios,[166] I for one would happily welcome the birth of the far-shooting lord, for I am terribly, truly badly-reputed by men, while in this way I might become highly honored. However, I do fear this rumor, Leto, and I won't hide from you: they say that this Apollo will be excessively reckless, and that he will very much hold sway over immortals and mortal men alike over the fertile land. (70) So I am terribly afraid in my heart and in my spirit, lest when he first sees the light of the sun, despising the island because I am indeed rocky, he might overturn me with his feet and toss me into the open sea. There a great wave will keep washing me away with its abundant force, while he will arrive at another land, whichever pleases him, to get for himself a temple and woody sacred groves; and octopuses will make their chambers in me, and black seals their homes, undisturbed in the absence of people.[167] But if you, goddess, dared to swear for me a great oath, (80) that he will build here first a truly beautiful temple to become an oracle for mankind,[168] then . . . (*lacuna*; let him establish temples and woody sacred groves?) among all people, since surely he will be widely renowned." So she (Delos) said; and Leto swore the great oath of the gods: "Let Earth know this now, and the wide Sky above, and the water of Styx,[169] flowing down, which is the greatest and most terrible oath among the

---

[164] A legendary king of Lesbos and, as son of Aiolos, forefather of the Aiolians (one of the main Greek linguistic and ethnic groups, along with the Dorians and the Ionians).

[165] Delos will live of the offerings of worshippers, in contrast to more fertile islands, which rejected Leto's request.

[166] Both parents of Leto, Koios and Phoibe, were among the Titans born from Gaia and Ouranos (Hesiod, *Th.* 133–137; see Part 1, document 5).

[167] Delos was believed to have been a wandering and untraceable island until it became fixed and visible after Apollo's birth (associating its name with Gr. *delos*, "clear, visible").

[168] Delos was not famous for an oracle, though one is attested epigraphically in Hellenistic times.

[169] A river in the Underworld. See Hesiod's *Theogony* 775–806.

blessed gods: it is in this place indeed that there will be forever a fragrant altar and a sacred precinct of Phoibos, and he will honor you above all the rest."

Then when she had sworn and completed the oath, (90) Delos rejoiced greatly at the birth of the far-shooting lord, while Leto for nine days and nine nights was pierced with hopeless labor cramps. And the goddesses were inside, all who were the best: Dione, Rhea, Themis Ichnaia, and much groaning Amphitrite, and other immortal goddesses, save white-armed Hera; for she had been sitting in the palace of cloud-gathering Zeus. But Eileithyia[170] alone had not heard, the goddess of labor-pains, for she was sitting in high Olympos under golden clouds by the designs of white-armed Hera, (100) who kept her back due to her jealousy that Leto, of the beautiful locks, was at that time going to give birth to a blameless and powerful son.

But the goddesses sent Iris[171] forth from the well-built island in order to bring Eileithyia, promising her a nine-cubit[172] long necklace strung with golden linen-threads. And they bid her to call her aside from white-armed Hera, lest she might make her turn around with her words as she is leaving. As soon as she heard this, swift Iris of wind-like feet set out to run and quickly covered the whole distance. When she thus arrived at the seat of the gods, steep Olympos, (110) at once calling her out from the palace to the doors, she told her everything with winged words, just as the goddesses who hold Olympian homes had instructed. And then and there she persuaded her heart in the dear chest, and off they went with timid feet, like pigeons in their steps. Then, when the goddess of labor-pains, Eileithyia, set foot on Delos, right then labor overtook Leto, and she was eager to give birth. She threw both her arms around a palm tree, propped her knees on the soft grass, and the earth below smiled; and out he rushed into the light, and all the goddesses cried out loud. (120) There the goddesses washed you, shooter Apollo, with good water, in a holy and pure way and they wrapped you in a white cloth, smooth and made for the occasion, and they threw a golden band around you. And his mother did not nurse Apollo of the golden sword,[173] but instead Themis[174] poured nectar and lovely ambrosia with her immortal hands; and so Leto is joyful, because she was bringing to the world a bow-bearing and powerful son.

Surely when you devoured the divine food, Phoibos, the golden bands would not retain you anymore as you struggled, not even chains would hold you back, but all bonds loosened up. (130) And right away Phoibos Apollo said to the goddesses: "May the lyre and the curved bow be mine, and I will prophesize to mankind the infallible will of Zeus." After thus speaking he started to stride from the wide-

---

[170] She was the daughter of Hera and Zeus (along with Hebe and Ares) and goddess of childbirth.

[171] See note 120 above.

[172] Fifteen feet approximately (a cubit was roughly the length of the forearm, 17–22 inches).

[173] It is not clear why this epithet (Greek *chrysaor*) is used for Apollo, whose weapon was the bow, not the sword. Chrysaor is also the person or creature who springs from the severed head of Medusa, along with Pegasos.

[174] Themis, a Titan and Zeus' second wife, is closely associated with Apollo and his oracle. She is the goddess of "right, customary law."

pathed earth, Phoibos of the long hair, who shoots from afar; and the goddesses were astonished, and in turn all of Delos blossomed with gold,[175] as when the top of a mountain does with forest flowers.

(140) And so you, lord of the silver bow, Apollo who shoots from afar, sometimes walk on rugged Kynthos, other times you go roaming about islands and men. Many are your temples and woody sacred groves, and dear to you are all high viewpoints and high headlands of lofty mountains and rivers flowing down to the sea; but in Delos you, Phoibos, delight the most in your heart, where Ionians of flowing robes come together with their own children and respectable wives.[176] They please you as they commemorate you with wrestling, dancing, and singing, (150) whenever they set up a contest. Someone would say that they were immortal and forever ageless, if he came upon them when the Ionians were gathered; for he would see the grace in all of them, and would be pleased in his spirit looking upon the men and beautifully-girded women and their swift ships and many possessions. And there is a great marvel besides this, which fame will never perish: the Delian girls, servants of the far-shooter; whenever they first sing of Apollo (and in turn of Leto and arrow-pouring Artemis), (160) singing of men and women of old too, they sing a hymn and they enchant the tribes of people. For they know how to emulate of all humans the voices and rattlings[177]; so each one would say that he himself is speaking! Such a beautiful song is composed by these.

But come, let Apollo, with Artemis, be gracious, and all of you maidens, farewell! And later remember me always, whenever one of the earthly human beings asks you, arriving here as a much-suffering visitor: "girls, who is the man that, for you the sweetest of bards, (170) comes here and pleases you the most?" Then you all surely answer about me: "a blind man, and he lives in rocky Chios,[178] and all his songs will be the best in posterity." And I (*lit.* we) will carry your fame for as long as on earth I keep visiting well-inhabited cities of people; and they will of course be persuaded, since this is even true. But I will not stop singing of far-shooting Apollo, the bow-bearer, whom beautiful-haired Leto bore.

(Pythian section)
O lord, you hold both Lykia and coveted Maionia and Miletos,[179] (180) pleasant city by the sea, while you yourself are in turn great lord of Delos, all around washed by the waves.

The son of glorious Leto marches towards stony Pytho,[180] playing with a hollow lyre, wearing divine garments, full of scent; and his lyre has a lovely tone at the touch of the golden plectrum. From there, he darts like a thought from earth to Olympos, to the house of Zeus to join the gathering of the others; and instantly the

---

[175] Three lines here are omitted, which are considered an expansion on line 139.

[176] The affluence of worshippers from the Ionian cities in Asia Minor is attested since the archaic period.

[177] Literally "rattling of castanets," the instruments or the rhythm of their speech.

[178] This precise line started the tradition that Homer was a blind man from the island of Chios.

[179] All in Asia Minor.

[180] Delphi. The origin of this name is explained in the story below.

immortals care for the lyre[181] and the song. The Muses,[182] all responding together with beautiful voice, (190) then and there start singing of divine gifts and sufferings of people, as many as they endure from the immortal gods as they live senseless and helpless, for they cannot find a cure for death and a defense for old age; then the well-mained Graces and cheerful Seasons,[183] and Harmonia, Hebe, and the daughter of Zeus, Aphrodite,[184] are dancing holding their arms around each other's wrists. In the midst of them is singing one neither ugly nor lesser, but rather impressive to look upon and admirable in her shape, arrow-pouring Artemis, reared with Apollo. (200) And among them Ares and sharp-eyed Argos-slayer (Hermes) are playing around; then Phoibos Apollo keeps playing the lyre, while taking graceful and high steps, and a radiance shines around him, sparklings coming from his feet and his well-spun robe. And golden-haired Leto[185] and wise Zeus take great pleasure in their hearts as they watch their dear son playing[186] with the immortal gods.

How should I, then, sing to you, who are celebrated with hymns in every possible way? Should I sing of you among wooers and in the realm of romance, how you went courting the daughter of Azan, (210) teaming up with the god-like son of Elatos, Ischys, of the good horses? Or with Phorbas born to Triops, or with Ereutheus? Or with Leukippos and Leukippos' wife, she on foot, but he on horses? - and indeed he did not fall short of Triops.[187]

Or (shall I sing) of how, looking for an oracle for humans, you first walked on the earth, far-shooting Apollo? First you came down to Pieria from Olympos; you passed by sandy Lektos and Ainianes and through the land of the Perrhaiboi; quickly you arrived at Iolkos, and stepped on Kenaios, of Euboia, famous for its ships; (220) and you stood on the Lelantian plain, which did not please your heart, at least not to set up a temple and wooded sacred groves. From there, crossing the Euripos, far-shooting Apollo, you walked on a holy green mountain; and soon you went down from it to Mykalessos and Teumessos, padded with grass. Then you arrived at the site of Thebes, covered in woods; for, as it happened, there were not yet trails or roads along the wheat-bearing plain of Thebes, but there was a forest instead.

---

[181] Two words alternate for Apollo's lyre: *phorminx* and *kytharis*.

[182] The nine Muses were daughters of Zeus and Mnemosyne. See the beginning of Hesiod's *Theogony* (Part 1, document 5) for their birth and function.

[183] Greek Charites (Graces) and Horai (Seasons).

[184] Harmonia was daughter of Ares and Aphrodite and wife of Kadmos (founder of Thebes). Hebe (Youth) became Herakles' wife on Olympos. Here Aphrodite is a daughter of Zeus, unlike in Hesiod's *Theogony* and the *Hymn to Aphrodite* (Part 5, document 5), where she is born from Ouranos' castrated genitals.

[185] Leto here assumes the role of the principal partner of Zeus, since placing Hera in the same scene would make the idyllic episode awkward.

[186] The verb here (*paizo*) can mean to play music, play a sport, or simply "play," as well as dance.

[187] We know little about these characters and their role in Apollo's romantic adventures.

From there you went forward, far-shooting Apollo, (230) to Onchestos,[188] the glorious grove of Poseidon. There, a newly-broken colt catches his breath, oppressed as he is as he carries a beautiful chariot, and his driver, skilled as he is, jumping to the ground from the car goes his way; and the horses for a while rattle the empty chariots, as they are free from dominance. If they drive the chariot into the forest of trees, they tend to the horses, but they prop up the vehicles and leave them there; for so was the ritual from the beginning; then they pray to the lord, and the car will then form part of the lot of the god.

But from there you went further, far-shooting Apollo; (240) for then you reached Kephissos of beautiful stream, which makes its sweet water flow down from Lilaia[189]; crossing it and very fortified Okalea, you, worker from afar, arrived from there to grassy Haliartos. Then you stepped on Telphousa[190]; the peaceful place there at least pleased you for setting up a temple and wooded sacred groves. You stood very close to her and addressed to her these words:

"Telphousa, I am surely thinking to set up here a remarkably beautiful temple, an oracle for mankind, who will always bring for me here perfect hecatombs, (250) all those who occupy the rich Peloponnesos[191] as well as all those throughout Europe[192] and the sea-girt islands, in order to receive an oracle. To them all I would prophesize infallible advice, issuing oracles in the rich temple."

After he said this, Phoibos Apollo laid out the foundations, broad and very long from end to end; and when she saw it, Telphousa was outraged in her heart and said this:

"Phoibos, Lord who works from afar, I will at least put a word in your mind, since you intend to set up here a remarkably beautiful temple to be an oracle for mankind, (260) who will always bring for you here perfect hecatombs; still I shall speak out, and you, keep it in your heart: the pounding of swift horses will always spoil it for you, and the mules, drinking from my sacred springs; there some people will prefer to admire the well-made chariots and the pounding of swift-footed horses than a large temple and all the possessions inside it. However, if I might in any way persuade you - for you are a more powerful and war-like lord than me, and your strength is the greatest – build it in Krisa,[193] under the fold of Parnassos. (270) There, neither beautiful chariots will rattle nor will there be pounding of swift-footed horses around the well-built altar. Instead, the famous tribes of people will

---

[188] Northwest of Thebes in Boiotia. The rite described here is otherwise unknown and has to do with Poseidon's domain over horses and charioteers. See, for instance, the story of Hippolytos, who is killed in a chariot accident due to Poseidon's designs (see Apollodorus E.1.19 in document 3.11.c).

[189] The river god Kephissos is born in Lilaia at the foot of Mount Parnassos.

[190] A spring at the foot of Mount Helikon in Boiotia.

[191] "The island of Pelops," which appears here for the first time as a single word.

[192] Here referring to "the continent," mainland Greece. In Hesiod, Europa is a nymph born from Tethys and Ocean (*Th.* 357), and in later tradition she is a Phoenician princess kidnapped by Zeus and brought westward. The name might be Semitic (from *'erev*, "evening, west").

[193] On the coast, in a fertile valley down from Mt. Parnassos. That place became the harbor of Delphi, which is up on the mountain.

surely bring you gifts as "Iepaieon,"[194] and you, with utterly delighted spirit, would receive the noble sacrifices from the people of the area."

Having said this, she persuaded the mind of the far-shooter, so that she would have fame in her land and not the far-shooter. So you went on from there, far-shooting Apollo, and arrived at the city of arrogant men of Phlegyes, who used to inhabit the land with no regard for Zeus, (280) in a fine glen close to the Kefisian lake. Quickly from there you advanced towards the mountain ridge, rushing, and reached Krisa under snowy Parnassos, a shoulder of it projecting westwards; a rock hangs over it, and a hallow, rugged gorge runs under it. There the lord Phoibos Apollo resolved to make for himself a desirable temple, and he said:

"It is here that I am considering building a remarkably beautiful temple to be an oracle for mankind, who will always bring me perfect hecatombs, (290) all those who occupy the rich Peloponnesos as well as all those throughout Europe and the sea-girt islands, in order to receive an oracle. To them all I would prophesize infallible advice, issuing oracles in the rich temple."

After he said this, Phoibos Apollo laid out the foundations, broad and very long from end to end; then Trophonios and Agamedes, sons of Erginos,[195] dear to the immortal gods, set a stone threshold on them; and countless tribes of people dwelled around the temple, to be forever sung for its stone construction. (300) Nearby there was a spring, where the lord, son of Zeus, killed a serpent with his mighty bow: a robust, huge, wild monster, who kept causing many calamities to the people in the land, many to the men themselves and many to their long-shanked sheep, for she was a murderous misery.[196]

(Digression about Typhaon)

Even one day she received and raised terrible and troublesome Typhaon[197] from Hera of the golden throne, a calamity for mortals, whom she (Hera) once bore when angry at father Zeus because the son of Kronos had in turn engendered famous Athena in his head. Lady Hera was immediately enraged (310) and even spoke so in the midst of the assembled immortals:

"Pay heed to me, all of you gods and all of you goddesses, how cloud-gathering Zeus starts to dishonor me first, after he made me his attentive wife: now without me he has even given birth to owl-eyed[198] Athena, who stands out among all the blessed immortals – while that one has grown weaker among all the gods, my child

---

[194] An unclear epithet, with the word *paieon* in it, on which see document 3.8.a, note 126 (on *Iliad* 5.409). The song *paian* or *paieon*, dedicated to the god, might lie under this epithet too (see lines 500 and 517).

[195] Famous architects to whom is attributed the construction of an archaic temple of Apollo (destroyed by fire in 548 BCE according to Pausanias) and of other temples.

[196] The word used (*drakaina*) means "she-dragon," referring to a serpent, not a four-legged dragon.

[197] He is called Typhoeus below and in Hesiod's *Theogony* (Part 1, document 5), where Gaia (Earth) bore him with Tartaros.

[198] Her epithet *glaukopis* derives from the little owl (*glaux*) and is often translated as "gray/blue-eyed" or "bright/gleaming-eyed."

Hephaistos,[199] shriveled of feet, whom I myself bore. Taking him in my hands, I tossed him and threw him into the wide ocean; but the daughter of Nereus, silver-footed Thetis,[200] (320) welcomed him and looked after him together with her sisters (if only she had pleased the blessed gods in another way . . .). O shameful crooked minded, what else will you devise now? How did you dare to beget owl-eyed Athena alone? Would I not have born her? – indeed I was called yours anyway, at any rate among the immortals, who hold the broad sky.[201] Be careful now, lest I conceive some mischief for you from now on. Now I will also devise how a child of mine might be begotten who may excel over the immortal gods, without shaming your sacred bed or my own, for I will not go to your bed, (330) but I will rather join the company of the immortal gods, keeping away from you."

After so saying, she went far away from the gods, mad as she was. Immediately afterwards she prayed, cow-eyed lady Hera, and with her hand turned down, she hit the ground and made an utterance: "Hear me now Earth and broad Sky above it, and Titan gods, who inhabit under the earth about great Tartaros, from whom men and gods are[202]; all of these, hear me now and give me a child without Zeus, in no way falling short of him in strength, but let him be superior (to him) as much as broad-sounding Zeus to Kronos." (340) After pronouncing these words, she struck the ground with her sturdy hand; and so the fertile Earth was moved, and Hera was pleased in her heart as she saw it, for she believed it would be fulfilled.

After this point, then, for one complete year she never went to the bed of wise Zeus, neither did she keep suggesting witty plans, never sitting by his decorated throne, as she used to; instead, staying in her temples, full of supplicants, she delighted in the offerings, the cow-eyed mistress Hera. But surely when the months and days were completed, (350) with a year finishing its cycle, and the season arrived, she bore terrible and frightening Typhaon, resembling neither gods nor mortals, a calamity for humans. Picking him up immediately, cow-eyed mistress Hera gave him away, adding an evil to an evil, and the serpent received him; and he went around doing much damage through the famous tribes of people.

(Back to the serpent Python)

As for he who would confront the serpent, his fated day would carry him, at least until the lord Apollo, who works from afar, cast an arrow at her – and a powerful one it was; and she, torn by harsh pain, lay down, panting heavily, twisting on the ground. (360) And a divine-sounding voice emerged, unspeakable, and she kept coiling here and there through the thick forest, and she was abandoning her bloody spirit, expiring, when he, Phoibos Apollo, boasted:

"Rot now in this place on men-sustaining earth, and you at least shall not be a mischievous bane for living mortals, who feed on the fruits of the very fertile earth

---

[199] It is unclear whether Zeus is here the father of Hephaistos (as in Homer) or Hera alone (as in Hesiod).

[200] A sea nymph and mother of Achilles.

[201] In an emended version of this line, "she (Athena) would have been called yours anyway . . . "

[202] Many of the gods and lesser divine beings generated from the Titans, and some traditions traced to them the origin of humans (see Orphic anthropogony in Part 2, document 7).

and will bring here perfect hecatombs, nor will Typhoeus or infamous Chimaera[203] defend you from a painful death, but black Earth and beaming Hyperion[204] will make you rot, it seems, here."

(370) So he said making a boast, and darkness covered her eyes. And so the sacred force of Helios rotted her completely on that spot, after which now it is called Pytho, and they call the lord by the eponym[205] "Pythian," because it was there that the force of piercing Helios rotted the monster.[206] And then of course he knew in his heart, Phoibos Apollo, why the nicely-flowing spring had deceived him; so he walked up to Telphousa in anger, and quickly reached her; and he stood very close to her and addressed her thus:

"Telphousa, you were not, as it turns out, going to deceive my mind (380), keeping a desirable place to pour your nicely-flowing water. Indeed my fame will also exist here, not only yours." He said, and the lord Apollo, who works from afar, pushed a protruding rock over her, with showering stones, and he covered up her stream, and he built an altar in the wooded sacred grove, very near the nicely-flowing spring. In that place they all make their prayers to the lord by the title "Telphousios," since he humiliated the sacred stream of Telphousa.

Surely at that time Phoibos Apollo was considering in his heart which people he might bring in as ministers, (390) who would serve him in rocky Pytho; so while mulling these things over he noticed a fast ship over the wine-dark sea; in it there were men, many and noble, Cretans from Minos' Knossos (who later are the ones who perform sacrifices for the lord and who announce the prophecies of Phoibos Apollo of the golden sword, whatever he might say as he issues oracles from the laurel[207] of the valleys under Parnassos).[208] They were sailing on their black ship in the direction of sandy Pylos and the Pylos-born people for business and goods; but then Phoibos Apollo joined them: (400) in the sea he leapt onto their swift ship, looking like a dolphin in his shape, and lay there as a great and frightful portent; and when any of them would have the intention to devise something in their heart,[209] he (the god/dolphin) would swing and shake the ship's timber in all directions. So they sat in the ship silently, scared, and they did neither release the gear along the concave black ship, nor released the sail of the dark-prowed ship; instead, just as they had set things up at the start, with ox-hides, so they kept sailing; but a hasty southern wind (Notos) pushed the swift ship from behind.

[203] See Hesiod's *Theogony* 319–324, where the Chimaera (Gr. *Chimaira*, lit. "she-goat") was the daughter of Typhoeus and Echidna.

[204] A Titan and father of Helios (Sun), both often used interchangeably for the Sun.

[205] A name given after someone else, such as "**eponymous** ancestor" (e.g., Doros for the Dorians).

[206] The etymology is drawn from the verb *pytho*, to rot.

[207] According to some sources, the laurel leaf was chewed by the Pythia. The absence of any mention of the Pythia in the hymn is puzzling. See footnote 25 on page 315.

[208] There was a cult of Apollo Delphinios ("Delphic") at Knossos in Crete. We do not know of any central role of Cretans in the cult at Delphi.

[209] The sense of this line is not clear. I am translating *noesai* as "devising" something (i.e., when one of them tried to throw the dolphin overboard or the like); others translate as "recognize" or "perceive" (the god?).

First they left on one side Cape Maleia,[210] (410) and near the Lakonian land they reached the sea-crowned citadel and territory of Helios, who delights humans, Tainaron, and where the deep-fleeced sheep of lord Helios are always grazing and have a desirable place. They naturally wanted to stop the ship there and, disembarking, ponder over the great marvel and see with their eyes if the prodigy stayed on the deck of the hallow ship or it would jump about towards the waves of the sea, full of fish; but the well-built ship did not obey the rudders,[211] and instead went her way, keeping the fertile Peloponnese on one side, (420) and so the lord Apollo, who works from afar, easily kept her straight with the breeze; and the boat, making its course, reached Arene and desirable Argiphea; also Thryon, ford of the Alpheios river, and well-constructed Aipy; and sandy Pylos and the Pylos-born people; and it went passed Krounoi and Chalkis, passed Dyme and passed radiant Elis where the Epeians rule. When it was heading towards Pherai, honored by Zeus' breeze, even under the clouds the steep peak of Ithaca, Doulichion, Same and woody Zakynthos became visible to them. (430) But surely when it passed the entire Peloponnese and, in the direction of Krisa, the boundless gulf[212] came into view, which closes off the rich Peloponnese all across, a great clear western wind (Zephyros) came by the will of Zeus, blowing impetuous from the upper air, so that the ship would quickly complete the journey as it rushed over the salty water of the sea. Indeed they begun to sail back in the direction of dawn and the sun,[213] and the lord, son of Zeus, Apollo, was guiding them.

So they arrived at wide-open Krisa, rich in vines, to its harbor, and the seafaring ship nearly touched the sand. (440) There, the lord Apollo, who works from afar, jumped off the boat, resembling a star in mid-day; for many sparks flew out from him, and his radiance reached the sky. He then entered all the way into his sacred chamber[214] amidst priceless tripods. There it so happened that he lit a flame, displaying its rays, and the brightness took hold of all of Krisa; and the wives and well-girded daughters of the Krisans raised a cry at the impetus of Apollo; for he inspired great fear in each of them.

From there, he leapt again to fly like a thought onto the ship, looking like a vigorous and powerful man, (450) early in his youth, his mane covering the broad shoulders. Even addressing them he pronounced winged words:

"Strangers, who are you? From where do you sail the watery ways? Are you on some mission, or do you cross the sea at random, like pirates who wander around endangering their lives while doing evil to people of other lands? Why on earth are you sitting in such sorrow, and you neither disembark on land nor stow the gear of

---

[210] The eastern-southernmost cape of the Peloponnese, which they reached coming from Crete. The next list of places follows the western coast of the Peloponnese, though not in exact sequence.

[211] Plural because boats used to have two of these steering pieces.

[212] The Gulf of Corinth. The area of Krisa and the sanctuary of Delphi are on its northern side.

[213] "Again" or "back" because Crete, where they sailed out from, is in the east.

[214] I use "sacred chamber" for the Greek word *adyton*, "(place) not to be entered," which was the innermost room of a sanctuary. The verb used for entering, *katadyo*, is also used for the setting sun, continuing with the description of the god as a "day-star," i.e., the sun.

your black ship? This is at least the norm among enterprising men, whenever they come to land from the sea in their black ship, (460) exhausted from their work, for immediately a desire for sweet bread takes over them around their core."

So he said, and he instilled courage in their chests. Indeed the leader of the Cretans answered him saying in turn:

"Stranger, since you are not at all like mortal beings, either in shape or stature, but like the immortal gods, health and great joy be with you, and may the gods grant you prosperity! Please tell me this truthfully, so that I may know for sure: What community is this? What land? What humans are born here? For it was with a different destination in mind that we were sailing the great deep sea, (470) to Pylos from Crete, where we can boast our race is from; but now we have arrived here with our ship, not at all by our will, as we yearn for our return through another path, another way; but one of the immortals led us here, even if we didn't wish it."

And in reply to them, Apollo, who works from afar, said: "Strangers, who used to live around the very wooded Knossos before, however now you will no longer return back to your beloved city, each to your noble homes, to your dear wives, but *here* you shall keep my rich temple, which is honored by many people. (480) I am the son of Zeus, Apollo I boast to be, and I brought you here over the great abyss of the sea, not at all with ill intention, but so that here you shall keep my rich temple, greatly honored by all humankind, and you shall know the decrees of the immortals, for whose sake you will always be honored, permanently, for all time. But come now, at once obey what I say: first, loosen the ox-hides and lower the sail, and then drag the swift ship onto the shore, take out your possessions and the gear of the balanced ship, (490) and build an altar on the sea shore, lighting a fire and making a burnt offering of white barley on it; then certainly pray standing around the altar. Since it was first on the misty sea that I sprang onto the swift ship in the shape of a dolphin, so pray to me as 'Delphinios'[215]; moreover the altar itself will always be 'delphinian' and conspicuous forever. Afterwards dine by the black ship and make libations to the blessed gods who hold Olympos. Then, when you have cast aside your desire for heart-pleasing food, (500) come with me and sing the 'Ie Paian'[216] until you reach the place where you will keep my temple."

So he said; and they naturally paid much heed to him and obeyed him: first they lowered the sails, then they loosened the ox-hides, and brought down the mast onto the mast-holder, pulling it with the forestays; next they themselves stepped down on the shore of the sea, and dragged the swift ship from the water and onto the dry land, high on the sand, they stretched the long stays next to it, and they built an altar on the shore of the sea; lighting a fire and making burnt offerings of white barley, (510) they started to pray as he ordered, standing around the altar. Next they took their meal by the fast, black ship, and they made a libation to the blessed gods who hold Olympos.

---

[215] Delphis means "dolphin" in Greek; hence, the connection is drawn between his apparition as a dolphin, the title of Apollo Delphinios, protector of sailors, and the name of Delphi, where the sanctuary is located (although it is never called by this name in the hymn).

[216] "Ie" is an exclamation of enthusiasm attached specifically to the cult to Apollo and his song the paian (as if "hail paian, hooray paian," or the like). See also note 194 above.

But when they had cast aside their desire for drink and food, they set out to go; and the lord Apollo, son of Zeus, started up among them, holding the lyre in his hands, playing it in a lovely way, stepping elegantly and high. And beating the ground[217] the Cretans kept following toward Pytho and singing the "Ie Paian," like the Cretan paian-singers and like those in whose heart the Muse has placed sweet-voiced song. (520) Tireless they treaded the ridge with their feet, and soon they reached Parnassos and the coveted place where he would dwell, honored by many people. And leading them he showed them his sacred chamber and rich temple. But their heart was agitated in their dear chest; in fact the leader of the Cretans talked to him asking:

"O lord, since indeed you have led us far away from our relatives and our father land – it was so that somehow your heart desired it – how do we even make a living now? Explain this, we beg you. This is not a desirable land at least in its wealth of crops or good pastures, (530) so as to live well and at the same time be of service to people!"

Smiling at them, the son of Zeus, Apollo, said: "Foolish human beings, poor penitents who want nothing but sufferings and sorrowful efforts and tensions in your spirit; I will simply say one thing to you, and you fix it in your hearts: everyone of you, holding a knife in your very right hand, slaughter sheep without stop; for they will all be plentiful, as many as the very famous tribes of people bring for me.[218] But guard my temple, and receive the tribes of people here gathering and most of all my guidance (. . . *lacuna?*)

(540) "If there shall be any purposeless word or any deed, and arrogance,[219] which is the norm among mortal people, other men will then be your masters, by whom you will be overpowered by necessity for all time. All has been said to you, and you guard it in your hearts."

So farewell to you too, son of Zeus and Leto; but I shall remember both you and another song.[220]

3.10. DIONYSOS IN DISGUISE

Dionysos is the Greek god of wine and the theater, as well as frenzied mad-ness, which he allegedly induced in his female worshippers, as famously dramatized in Euripides' *Bacchae*. The god is often represented as an exiled young god who returns to his birthplace after wandering through Asia. His exotic, foreign origins, postulated by ancient authors, were disproved when his name appeared among other Greek gods in the Mycenaean Linear B tablets. His semi-exotic and threatening presence, rather, is an intrinsic part of his iden-

---

[217] That is, dancing.

[218] Like Delos, Delphi is not fertile but will be rich in offerings from visitors, who had to purchase and offer a sacrificial animal and who deposited votive offerings and treasures throughout the shrine for the fame of individuals and cities.

[219] The word used is *hybris*. The warning by Apollo is in harmony with the "wisdom" of the maxims inscribed on the walls of his temple at Delphi: "know yourself" and "nothing in excess."

[220] Notice the formulaic ending, indicating with respect (the god will not be forgotten) the transition to another song, as in the *Hymn to Demeter* (Part 6, document 8).

tity as a god of "the other," one who transforms regular states of mind, both through the power of wine and through drama, where actors alter their identity on stage and provoke a change in their audience's emotions.

The most widely known story of Dionysos' birth from Zeus and Semele (daughter of Kadmos, the founder of Thebes; see Part 4, document 10) held that Semele, impregnated with Dionysos, asked Zeus to reveal himself to her in his true form, which caused her to die instantly before Zeus' blazing presence (see Figure 24). Zeus rescued the unborn baby and implanted ("sawed") him in his own thigh, whence Dionysos was born, hence his moniker "twice-born." His birth and return from exotic lands is vividly dramatized at the opening of Euripides' *Bacchae* (document 3.10.a). In an alternative tradition, reconstructed from scattered allusions in texts related to Orphism, Dionysos is the son of Persephone and Zeus. In this version, in which he is called Zagreus, he was killed as a baby by the jealous Titans (since he was the heir of Zeus) and brought back to life in various possible ways (see story in Part 2, document 7).

The importance of the Dionysos cult cannot be overstated. In Athens, drama was born under his auspices, and the famous classical tragedies and comedies we have were first performed in festivals dedicated to him (part of the City Dionysia and the Lenaia). Banqueting and wine, which were also his domain, were central to Greek society not merely for recreation but also as facilitators of social and political relations, what can be called "social lubricants." Initiation groups of Dionysos worshippers (or *bacchoi*) proliferated throughout the Greek and Roman world, though we do not know much about their rituals beyond the exaggerated depictions we find in Euripides' *Bacchae*. Through the connection with Persephone, perhaps, and his story of death and rebirth, Dionysos became a central figure in Orphic theology and eschatology (on which see Part 2, document 7 and Part 6, document 9).

Dionysos is typically portrayed in banqueting scenes, often depicted on cups, bowls, and vases. He usually appears with vine wreaths and cups, and sometimes with wild animal skins and holding a *thyrsus*, which was a long staff covered by ivy and other leaves, topped with a pine cone. It was a symbol of the god as well as related **Maenads** and **Satyrs**. In archaic representations, as well as in the *Hymn to Dionysos* (document 3.10.b), Dionysos is shown as a dark-haired young man or a bearded older man, more in tune with the Apollo of the *Hymn to Apollo* (document 3.9). This contrasts with the youthful, effeminate, and blond Dionysos that predominates in Classical and Hellenistic times, such as in his portrayal in Euripides' *Bacchae* here.

3.10.a. The Opening of Euripides' *Bacchae*

Euripides is the youngest of the three Athenian playwrights whose works have been preserved (the other two being Aeschylus and Sophocles). Born ca. 480 BCE (died in 407/06), he was only seventeen years younger than Sophocles (497/96–406/05), and much of their work overlapped in the second half of the fifth century. By the chance of textual transmission we have more plays by Euripides than by the other two playwrights, with nineteen plays preserved (out of the ninety or so he wrote). Euripides' style, like that of his predecessors, is highly distinctive. The least successful playwright of the three in his time (judging by his much fewer victories), he is the most "modern" in his interest in human psychology, especially female, and his realistic view of human existence as trapped in moral and emotional conflicts. Euripides was portrayed already in antiquity (in Aristophanes' *Frogs*) as a bookish intellectual who represented humans "as they are," in contrast to Sophocles, who represented them "as they ought to be" (according to Aristotle *Poet.* 1460^b33ff.).

In the opening scene of the *Bacchae*, the god is arriving at Thebes in order to avenge his mother Semele, which he will accomplish by driving the women of the town mad as Bacchants (followers of Bacchus, i.e., Dionysos) or Maenads ("raving women") and setting a trap for king Pentheus, who does not recognize the god's authority. This play was written in Euripides' final years in Macedonia, and it was represented after his death in the City Dionysia festival some time between 408 and 406 BCE, together with *Iphigeneia at Aulis* and *Alcmaeon in Corinth* (though not forming a thematic trilogy). These were his last plays. The *Bacchae* not only won first prize in the dramatic contest that year but is one of the most popular and controversial works of the author, especially in regard to his striking and unusually powerful representation of the divine (from an author who was otherwise rationalistic and not particularly pious like his predecessors). In a way, both texts here, the tragedy and the hymn, show the terrifying and demanding god in his interaction with humans.

SOURCE: Euripides, *Bacchae*: 1–63, translated and annotated by C. López-Ruiz.

(The scene is set before the palace of King Pentheus in Thebes. On stage, a monument to Semele can be seen, with a flame on top and remains of a burned building around it [for her death, see Figure 24]. Dionysos enters with a crown of ivy on his head and a thyrsus in his hand.)

DIONYSOS:
> Here I've come, the son of Zeus, to this Theban land;
> Dionysos! whom once bore the daughter of Kadmos,
> Semele, whose labor was induced by a lightning fire.
> Changing from a god into a mortal shape
> (5) I am at the spring of Dirke and the waters of Ismenos.
> I see my mother's tomb here near the palace,
> thunder-stricken as she was, and the ruins of her chambers,
> smoking with the flame of Zeus' fire, still living
> —as is the imperishable offense[221] of Hera against my mother.

---

[221] The word used is *hybris* (more frequently used for what mortals do against other mortals or against the gods).

(10) But I do praise Kadmos, who made this ground

sacred,[222] a precinct in honor of his daughter. And so I have covered it

all around with grape-bearing shoots.

After I left the gold-teeming fields of the Lydians

and the Phrygians,[223] and went across the sun-scorched plains of the
Persians,

(15) and the Bactrian walls, and the troublesome land

of the Medes, and happy[224] Arabia,

and the whole of Asia, which lies along the salty

sea-shore, with beautifully fortified cities

full of Greeks and barbarians mingling together,

(20) to this city of the Hellenes I have arrived first.

- I already danced and established my rites

in those places, so that I may be a popular divinity among mortals.

In all the Greek lands, I have raised my shout

first in Thebes, hanging a fawn skin upon my body

(25) and taking the *thyrsos* in my hand, a missile of ivy:

for my mother's own sisters (of all people!),

went around saying that Dionysos was not the child of Zeus,

that Semele, "wedded" by some mortal man,

attributed the mistake of her bedding to Zeus,

(30) —astute idea of Kadmos—for which Zeus killed her,

they kept boasting, since she had lied about her marriage!

Well then, these women I have goaded out of the house

in frenzy, and they occupy the hills, deranged in their minds.

I have ordered them to wear the attire of my mysteries,

(35) and all the Kadmeian female offspring,[225] as many women

as there were, I have driven mad from their houses;

and mingling with the daughters of Kadmos

they sit under green pine trees, on top of roof-less rocks.

For this city must fully realize, even if it doesn't want to,

---

[222] Lit. "not to be stepped in." The word used, *abaton*, was also used for the innermost (restricted)
area of a temple.

[223] Two regions of Asia Minor, particularly famous for their gold, as exemplified in the story
about King Midas, who turned whatever he touched into gold.

[224] The adjective *eudaimon* is difficult to translate (see note on its meaning in Plato in Part 7,
document 4). Here it means "happy" and "rich," "fortunate."

[225] All the women of Thebes, as Kadmos was not only the father of Semele and her sisters but
the founder of the city.

(40)   that it is *not* initiated into my Bacchic rites,

and that I vindicate my mother Semele,

by appearing to mortals as the god whom she bore to Zeus.

Kadmos, as it turns out, has given his prerogative

and his rule to Pentheus, the offspring of his daughter,[226]

(45)   who wages war against the gods regarding my rites, and drives me away

from his libations, and has no regard for me in his prayers.

Because of this, I will demonstrate to him and to all the Thebans

that I am god-born. Then I will move my feet

onto another land, having set things right here,

(50)   manifesting myself. But if the city of Thebes,

in its anger, seeks to drive the Bacchae down from the mountain

by force, I will join the Maenads as their commander in battle.

For this reason I have changed into a mortal appearance,

and transformed my shape into the figure of a man.

(55)   But come, O you who left Tmolos,[227] bulwark of Lydia,

my sacred band,[228] women whom I rescued from the barbarians

as companions of table and travels for me,

lift your drums, invention of mother Rhea and myself

and native to the country of the Phrygians,

(60)   and beat them as you walk around this palace

of Pentheus, so the city of Kadmos pays attention!

And so I will go to the gorges of Kythairon,

where the Bacchae are, and will dance with them.

3.10.b. The *Homeric Hymn to Dionysos*

(For the *Homeric Hymns* in general, see headnote to document 3.9.) This is one of several short *Homeric Hymns* dedicated to Dionysos (*Homeric Hymn* 7). It narrates an episode that is also transmitted in other literary sources with variations in the details (e.g., Euripides' *Cyclops*, Apollodorus' *Library*, and Ovid's *Metamorphoses*, Book 3). As with other *Homeric Hymns*, the story at least partly serves as an *aition* of a ritual, in this case one attested since the sixth century BCE, in which the god was carried or rolled on a boat wreathed with ivy, with his priest acting as helmsman. Whether the story explains the pre-existing ritual or the ritual

---

[226] Agave, one of Semele's sisters.

[227] A legendary king of Lydia and a mountain named after him.

[228] *Thiasos*, translated here as "sacred band," was a group that celebrated the rites of a divinity, a fraternity/sorority of sorts, including the appropriate banqueting, dancing, music, and processions.

enacts the popular story is impossible to know. We have no evidence to date the hymn accurately, and arguments can be made for dates ranging from the seventh to the fifth centuries BCE.

SOURCE: *Homeric Hymn to Dionysos* (*HH* 7), translated and annotated by C. López-Ruiz.

About Dionysos, the very famous son of Semele, I will remember how he appeared by the shore of the barren sea, on a projecting headland, looking like a lad in the bloom of his youth. His beautiful mane was floating about him; it was dark, and he was wearing a cloak on his sturdy shoulders, a red one. And soon from a well-decked ship some men were approaching quickly over the sea, Tyrsenian[229] pirates. A wretched fate was leading them. For as they saw him, they nodded at each other and rushed out quickly, and snatching him at once they threw him onto the ship, (10) rejoicing in their hearts. For it seemed to them that he was the son of Zeus-nurtured kings, so they intended to tie him with hard bonds. But the bonds did not hold him and fell far from his arms and legs, and he sat, smiling with his dark eyes, and so the helmsman, immediately— understanding—called out to his companions and shouted at them:

"Madmen, who is this powerful god you have kidnapped and tied up? Not even the well-crafted ship can carry him! For this one is either Zeus or Apollo of the silver bow or Poseidon, (20) since he is not like mortal human beings, but like the gods who hold Olympian homes. But come, let us immediately release him on the black dry land, and do not set your hands on him, lest he becomes at all angry and stirs up troublesome winds and a great hurricane."

So he said, but the captain rebuked him with severe words: "Fool, look at the fair wind! So go with it and hoist the sail of the ship after you pick up all the gear; and as for this one here, the men will worry about him. I am guessing he is going to Egypt or perhaps to Cyprus or to the Hyperboreans,[230] or further! (30) In the end, at some point, he will give away his friends and all his possessions and his siblings, since a deity has thrown him at us!"

Having said this, he had the mast and the sail of the ship hoisted. And so the wind started to blow into the center of the sail and they stretched the lines on both sides of it; but soon amazing things started appearing to them. First, throughout the fast black ship, wine was dripping, delicious and fragrant, and a divine scent started to arise; and astonishment took hold of all the sailors as they noticed it. Then at once a vine extended here and there at the top of the sail, and abundant clusters of grapes were hanging from it; (40) and a dark ivy plant started twining around the mast, blooming with flowers, its graceful fruit springing from it; even the oar-locks all had wreaths. And the sailors, as they saw it, already then started to beg the helmsman to take the ship to land; but it so happened that the god turned into a dreadful lion inside the ship, at the bow, and it was roaring loudly, and then,

---

[229] Probably Etruscans from Italy.

[230] A legendary people that the Greeks located in the far north (their name probably means "those beyond the Boreas wind," which was the north wind).

showing his signs,[231] he created a shaggy bear in their midst; and it stood up raging, while the lion was on the highest point of the deck, with a frightfully menacing stare. So they were put to flight towards the stern, and stood there, naturally shocked, around the helmsman, who had a sensible mind. (50) And he (the god/lion) suddenly leaping onto the captain seized him, and they, trying to escape an evil fate, all at once jumped out as soon as they saw it, to the shiny water, and they became dolphins. But having mercy on the helmsman, he held him back and made him all-fortunate, and told him:

"Courage! (noble Aktor?[232]), you who have gratified my heart: *Dionysos* is who I am! the loud-roaring one whom a Kadmeian mother bore, Semele, mingling in love with Zeus."

Farewell, child of fair-faced Semele; it is in no way possible for the one who forgets *you* to compose sweet song.

3.11. THE EXPLOITS OF PERSEUS, HERAKLES, AND THESEUS, FROM APOLLODORUS' *LIBRARY*

The *Library* (*Bibliotheke*) is the most important complete collection of Greek myths, written in three books and an added *Epitome* (or summary), which narrate Greek mythology from the creation to the Dorian invasion. The *Library* was attributed to one "Apollodorus the Grammarian" by the Byzantine scholar and patriarch Photius in the mid-ninth century CE. Photius thought this Apollodorus to be the famous Athenian grammarian (180–120 BCE) who had written a treatise *On the Gods*. However, for different reasons modern scholars are now sure that the author of the *Library* is not the Athenian Apollodorus of the second century BCE. For this reason he is often called "Pseudo-Apollodorus." In other words, we know nothing about the actual author or the date of this work, though a hypothetical date some time in the second century CE seems to be the current consensus.

The *Library* is written in an encyclopedic style. It is a straightforward account of what must have been standard versions of Greek myths circulating throughout the Mediterranean not only orally but also in previous texts. Oddly enough, no Roman stories are included in this collection. This sort of manual of Greek myths was not appreciated in its time as a literary work, but it would have been a useful companion to literary and artistic works. It was an educational tool that provided a handy reference for elites who needed to carry on learned conversations—a sort of "Mythology for Dummies" for the ancient world. The genre of ancient **mythography** has deep roots in epic poetry, as we see in Hesiod's *Theogony* and *Catalogue of Women*. The deliberate collection of myths in prose, however, flourished in the Classical period with the fifth- and fourth-century BCE genealogists (e.g., Hekataios, Pherekydes of Athens, Hellanikos) and the so-called Atthidographers (historiographers of Attika), who elaborated

---

[231] The word used here, *semata*, can mean "sign," "token," or "omen," here meaning the indexes by which the gods' identity could be identified (the wild animals, the ivy, and the vines).

[232] The text is corrupt here, perhaps originally containing the name of the helmsman.

compendia of chronologically organized data (with the aid of king and archon lists) integrated with mythical traditions. These sources were extensively used by later **mythographers**, who sometimes quoted them or mentioned their sources. The genre reached its apogee during the Hellenistic period and the Roman Empire, from which most of our texts come, such as Apollodorus' *Library*.

The preserved manuscripts include two types of mythographic works: some were written as aids or commentaries of important literary texts, such as those by Homer, Pindar, and Euripides, and are today preserved as *scholia* (notes in the margins) of the Byzantine manuscripts of those authors. The other type are self-standing compendia of myths, such as the *Library* and *Epitome* or, in Roman times, the superb poetic rendering of myths in Ovid's *Metamorphoses* and the mythologic handbook by Hyginus known as the *Fabulae*.

SOURCE: Apollodorus' *Library*, excerpts from Books 2, 3, and Epitome. Sir J. G. Frazer, *Apollodorus. The Library* (Loeb Classical Library, Cambridge, MA and London, 1921), with minor modifications.

3.11.a. Perseus

Apollodorus' *Library* is our most detailed source for the traditions concerning Perseus. The hero is connected particularly to the Argolid region as the founder or fortifier of Mycenae and as the king of Tiryns, two important Mycenaean strongholds. In historical times, Perseus was the subject of hero worship in the area, with a shrine and a spring dedicated to him, according to Pausanias. According to tradition, his adventures take place a couple of generations before Herakles. Both the human father (or stepfather) of Herakles, Amphitryon, and Eurystheus, the king of Tiryns who imposes the Twelve Labors on Herakles, were grandsons of Perseus. His exploits are set at the beginning of civilization, when the slaying of monsters (the Gorgon and the sea monster) accompanies the establishment of a new cosmic order under Zeus and the Olympian gods.

The origin of the name of Perseus is obscure, perhaps derived from non-Greek indigenous traditions in the Peloponnese, or perhaps it is pre-Greek— a Proto-Indo-European name preserved and brought by the Greeks. His association with the Persians is a later invention. The story of Perseus was a favorite subject for artistic representations since Archaic times, particularly the motif of Perseus beheading Medusa with the help of Athena. The myth of Perseus, including the killing of the Gorgon and the figures born from her, Pegasos and Chrysaor, displays a number of Near Eastern connections, from Andromeda's location in Joppe (Japho), the Gorgon's similarity to Mesopotamian monsters such as Lamashtu and Humbaba, and Pegasos' possible connection to the Luwian-Hittite Storm God Pihassassi (in Hesiod Pegasos carries Zeus' lightning). The *kibisis* (satchel, wallet) and the sickle (*harpē*) that Perseus uses may also be traced etymologically to Semitic roots. Most notably, the popular representation of Gilgamesh and Enkidu killing the monster Humbaba (on which see document 3.1) seems to have served as a model for archaic representations of Perseus slaying the Gorgon (see Figure 8).

(2.4.1) When Akrisios[233] inquired of the oracle (at Delphi) how he should get male children, the god said that his daughter would give birth to a son who would kill him. Fearing that, Akrisios built a brazen chamber under ground and there guarded Danae.[234] However, she was seduced, as some say, by Proetus, whence arose the quarrel between them (i.e., Akrisios and Proteus); but some say that Zeus had intercourse with her in the shape of a stream of gold which poured through the roof into Danae's lap. When Akrisios afterwards learned that she had got a child Perseus, he would not believe that she had been seduced by Zeus, and putting his daughter with the child in a chest, he cast it into the sea. The chest was washed ashore on Seriphos, and Diktys took up the boy and reared him.

(2.4.2) Polydektes, brother of Diktys, was then king of Seriphos and fell in love with Danae, but could not get access to her, because Perseus was grown to man's estate. So he called together his friends, including Perseus, under the pretext of collecting contributions towards a wedding gift for Hippodamia, daughter of Oinomaos. Now Perseus having declared that he would not stick even at the Gorgon's head, Polydektes required the others to furnish horses, and not getting horses from Perseus ordered him to bring the Gorgon's head. So under the guidance of Hermes and Athena he made his way to the daughters of Phorkys, namely, Enyo, Pephredo, and Deino; for Phorkys had them by Keto,[235] and they were sisters of the Gorgons, and old women from their birth. The three had but one eye and one tooth, and these they passed to each other in turn. Perseus got possession of the eye and the tooth, and when they asked them back, he said he would give them up if they would show him the way to the nymphs. Now these nymphs had winged sandals and the *kibisis*, which they say was a wallet. [But Pindar and Hesiod in *The Shield* say of Perseus: – "But all his back had on the head of a dread monster, <The Gorgon,> and round him ran the *kibisis*." The *kibisis* is so called because dress and food are deposited in it.][236] They had also the cap <of Hades>. When the Phorkydes had shown him the way, he gave them back the tooth and the eye, and coming to the nymphs got what he wanted. So he slung the wallet (kibisis) about him, fitted the sandals to his ankles, and put the cap on his head. Wearing it, he saw whom he pleased, but was not seen by others. And having received also from Hermes an adamantine sickle he flew to the ocean and caught the Gorgons asleep. They were Sthenno, Euryale, and Medusa. Now Medusa alone was mortal; for that reason Perseus was sent to fetch her head. But the Gorgons had heads twined about with the scales of dragons, and great tusks like swine's, and brazen hands, and golden wings, by which they flew; and they turned to stone such as beheld them. So Perseus stood over them as they slept, and while Athena guided

---

[233] King of Argos and father of Danae, the mother of Perseus. The story of Danae, mother of Perseus, was the theme of tragedies by Sophocles and Euripides, of which we have fragments only.

[234] Compare Soph. *Ant.* 944 ff. Horace represents Danae as shut up in a brazen tower (*Carm.* 3.16.1 ff.).

[235] See Hesiod's *Theogony* 270 ff. (Part 1, document 5) for the offspring of Phorkys and Keto.

[236] The word *kibisis* is derived by the writer from *keisthai* and *esthes* (though the word is probably Semitic; cf. Hebrew *qbẓ* "gather"). The gloss (in brackets) is probably an interpolation, and the reference is to Hesiod (*Shield* 223 ff.).

his hand and he looked with averted gaze on a brazen shield, in which he beheld the image of the Gorgon, he beheaded her. When her head was cut off, there sprang from the Gorgon the winged horse Pegasos and Chrysaor, the father of Geryon; these she had by Poseidon.[237]

(2.4.3) So Perseus put the head of Medusa in the wallet (*kibisis*) and went back again; but the Gorgons started up from their slumber and pursued Perseus: but they could not see him on account of the cap, for he was hidden by it.

Having come to Ethiopia, of which Kepheus was king, he found the king's daughter Andromeda set out to be the prey of a sea monster.[238] For Cassiopea, the wife of Kepheus, vied with the Nereids in beauty and boasted to be better than them all; hence the Nereids were angry, and Poseidon, sharing their wrath, sent a flood and a monster to invade the land. But Ammon having predicted deliverance from the calamity if Cassiopeia's daughter Andromeda were exposed as a prey to the monster, Kepheus was compelled by the Ethiopians to do it, and he bound his daughter to a rock. When Perseus beheld her, he loved her and promised Kepheus that he would kill the monster, if he would give him the rescued damsel to wife. These terms having been sworn to, Perseus withstood and slew the monster and released Andromeda. However, Phineus, who was a brother of Kepheus, and to whom Andromeda had been first betrothed, plotted against him; but Perseus discovered the plot, and by showing the Gorgon turned him and his fellow conspirators at once into stone. And having come to Seriphos he found that his mother and Diktys had taken refuge at the altars on account of the violence of Polydektes; so he entered the palace, where Polydektes had gathered his friends, and with averted face he showed the Gorgon's head; and all who beheld it were turned to stone, each in the attitude which he happened to have struck. Having appointed Diktys king of Seriphos, he gave back the sandals and the wallet (*kibisis*) and the cap to Hermes, but the Gorgon's head he gave to Athena. Hermes restored the aforesaid things to the nymphs and Athena inserted the Gorgon's head in the middle of her shield. But it is alleged by some that Medusa was beheaded for Athena's sake; and they say that the Gorgon was fain to match herself with the goddess even in beauty.

(2.4.4) Perseus hastened with Danae and Andromeda to Argos in order that he might behold Akrisios. But he, learning of this and dreading the oracle, forsook Argos and departed to the Pelasgian land. Now Teutamides, king of Larissa, was holding athletic games in honor of his dead father, and Perseus came to compete. He engaged in the pentathlon, but in throwing the quoit he struck Akrisios on the foot and killed him instantly. Perceiving that the oracle was fulfilled, he buried Akrisios outside the city, and being ashamed to return to Argos to claim the inheritance of him who had died by his hand, he went to Megapenthes, son of Proetus, at Tiryns and effected an exchange with him, surrendering Argos into his hands.

---

[237] See Hesiod's *Theogony* 280 ff. Note that Perseus does not originally fly on Pegasos (Bellerophon does), although he is associated with the winged horse early on and in medieval and later representations.

[238] Others set this episode in Joppe (Japho), modern Israel, where Andromeda's fetters were still exhibited in Roman times, according to Josephus (*Jewish War* 3.9.2).

So Megapenthes reigned over the Argives, and Perseus reigned over Tiryns, after fortifying also Midea and Mycenae.[239]

(2.4.5 skipped: catalogue of the children of Perseus and Andromeda, among them Alkaios, Sthenelos, and Elektryon, who are the fathers of Amphitrion, Eurystheus, and Alkmene, respectively, all characters connected with Herakles. After mentioning the birth of Eurystheus to Sthenelos, the author reports as follows:)

(End of 2.4.5) For when Herakles was about to be born, Zeus declared among the gods that the descendant of Perseus then about to be born would reign over Mycenae, and Hera out of jealousy persuaded the Eileithyias to retard Alkmene's delivery, and contrived that Eurystheus, son of Sthenelos, should be born a seven-month child.

(The narrative continues with the birth of Herakles, reproduced in the following document.)

3.11.b. Herakles

The *Homeric Hymn to Herakles the Lion-Hearted* provides a synthetic overview of the most popular hero in the entire Mediterranean world:

> I will sing of Herakles, son of Zeus, the best of earthly men by far, whom Alkmene bore in Thebes, a place of lovely dances, when she mingled with the dark-clouded son of Kronos. Wandering first through the ineffable land and sea at the orders of king Eurystheus, he performed many reckless actions himself, and many he suffered; but now he lives in the noble dwelling of snowy Olympos, enjoying himself, and has (for wife) Hebe of beautiful ankles. Greetings, lord, son of Zeus! Grant me excellence and fortune." (Translated by C. López-Ruiz)

Herakles was a demi-god that struggled with human and animal forces, was both brutish and resourceful, blessed and cursed by the gods, noble and insanely violent. He was not only a destroyer of cities, animals, and monsters, but he also represented the human ability to dominate nature and, in his exceptional case, even death. Scholars have placed him among mythical figures connected with the domestication of animals, cattle-raiding, and even **shamanism** (given his contact with the Beyond), arguably going back to the emergence of complex sedentary societies during the Neolithic Revolution.

According to the popular Greek interpretation of his name, "Herakles" means "Famous because of Hera," from "Hera" and *kleos*, "glory" (a common prefix or suffix in names; cf. Peri-*kles*, *Kleo*-patra, etc.). Given the goddess's hatred for the hero, it is possible that the real etymology of the name is different, even non-Greek. Some have suggested that Herakles is somehow connected with the chief Mesopotamian Underworld god Nergal, also called Erakal (or Lord of Erkalla, the "Great City"), who at some point was partly assimilated with Gilgamesh. Indeed, much of the imagery of Herakles' fights is found earlier in Near Eastern iconography: for example, a figure fighting a seven-headed snaky

---

[239] For the exchange of kingdoms and the fortification of Mycenae, see Pausanias 2.16.2–3.

monster strikingly similar to the Hydra appears in paintings from Mesopotamia and Ugarit; the above-mentioned god Nergal is often represented with a lion, bow, and club attires, just like Herakles; Marduk in *Enuma Elish* (Part 1, document 1) fights and kills twelve enemies (Tiamat and her eleven allies), the same number as Herakles' labors (though the number has other independent connotations, mainly astrological); and both he and Gilgamesh kill monsters and travel to the end of the world and the Underworld. Broader, Indo-European parallels are also evident: for instance, the Vedic myth of Indra or Trita, who fought a three-headed monster and carried away the cows hidden in a cave, offers a striking parallel for the story of Herakles and the cattle of the three-headed Geryon. In the end, we are dealing with a very old and ever-growing, shape-shifting, cluster of myths that pivot around a figure who trespasses our ideas of cultural boundaries.

Herakles is an extraordinarily versatile figure, whose myths traveled and multiplied easily, assimilating local myths from all over the Mediterranean (and beyond?). By placing Herakles' feats in their own landscapes, new peoples entered the circuit of Greek culture and acquired heroic prestige. His close association with colonization and the foundation of cities prompted the identification of Herakles with the Phoenician god Melqart, and the hero indeed was considered a civilizing force in the places he visited, which extended from Italy and Iberia to Asia Minor and Syro-Palestine. He became not only a pan-Hellenic hero but a pan-Mediterranean hero, and monumental temples bear witness to his cult across the Greek and Roman world from Agrigentum in Italy to Aman in Jordan. Dionysios of Halikarnassos (*Antiq. Rom.* i.40.6) wrote: "And in many other parts of Italy (besides Rome) precincts are consecrated to the god, and altars are set up both in cities and beside roads; and hardly will you find a place in Italy where the god is not honored." Not only Romans but also the Carthaginians (especially Hannibal) (cf. Figure 14) used the iconography of Herakles to represent their own colonizing and civilizing mission in the western Mediterranean. Moreover, the Phoenician god Melqart had long been identified with Herakles, with its most famous temple standing in the old Phoenician colony of Gadir, right outside the Pillars of Herakles, thus marking the limits of Herakles' wanderings and also of the known world and the extent of the Carthaginian area of influence. Carthaginians and Romans, including later emperors, often followed in the footsteps of Alexander the Great, who had already represented himself with the lion-head gear of Herakles as he marched on to spread Hellenic civilization across eastern lands (see also Alexander represented as the Egyptian god Amon in Figure 13).

The exploits of Herakles are mentioned and elaborated on by a host of classical authors, and cross-references to these have been reduced (in the notes) to a minimum, privileging those included in this volume. Some of the main literary works that could have been included here are Hesiod's *Shield of Herakles* and the tragedies *Herakles Insane* by Euripides and *Trachiniae* (or *Women of Trachis*) by Sophocles. The role of Herakles/Hercules in Virgil's *Aeneid* (Book 8, also in Livy I.7 ff.), as he defeats the violent giant Cacus, is a good example of how the Greek hero was embraced as a civilizing figure by non-Greek peoples as they adapted their own mythologies to fit Hellenic models.

Even if references to Herakles' feats are ubiquitous, Apollodorus' *Library* provides the most useful synthesis preserved. The narrative translated below continues with the account of the fate of the descendants of Herakles (*Library* 2.8.2–2.8.5). This is one of the sources for the theme of the "Return of the Heraclidae," also known as the "Dorian invasion," a story that was foundational for the Doric Greeks (the Spartans among them) and their claims of legitimate hegemony over a great part of the Peloponnese.

(Amphytrion, father of Herakles)

(2.4.6) When Elektryon reigned over Mycenae, the sons of Pterelaos came with some Taphians and claimed the kingdom of Mestor, their maternal grandfather, and as Elektryon paid no heed to the claim, they drove away his cattle; and when the sons of Elektryon stood on their defence, they challenged and slew each other. But of the sons of Elektryon there survived Likymnios, who was still young; and of the sons of Pterelaos there survived Eueres, who guarded the ships. Those of the Taphians who escaped sailed away, taking with them the cattle they had lifted, and entrusted them to Polyxenos, king of the Eleans[240]; but Amphitryon ransomed them from Polyxenos and brought them to Mycenae. Wishing to avenge his sons' death, Elektryon purposed to make war on the Teleboans, but first he committed the kingdom to Amphitryon along with his daughter Alkmene, binding him by oath to keep her a virgin until his return.[241] However, as he was receiving the cows back, one of them charged, and Amphitryon threw at her the club which he had in his hands. But the club rebounded from the cow's horns and striking Elektryon's head killed him.[242] Hence Sthenelos laid hold of this pretext to banish Amphitryon from the whole of Argos, while he himself seized the throne of Mycenae and Tiryns; and he entrusted Midea to Atreus[243] and Thyestes, the sons of Pelops, whom he had sent for.

Amphitryon went with Alkmene and Likymnios to Thebes and was purified by Kreon[244] and gave his sister Perimede to Likymnios. And as Alkmene said she would marry him when he had avenged her brothers' death, Amphitryon engaged to do so, and undertook an expedition against the Teleboans, and invited Kreon to assist him. Kreon said he would join in the expedition if Amphitryon would first rid the Kadmeia[245] of the vixen; for a brute of a vixen was ravaging the Kadmeia. But though Amphitryon undertook the task, it was fated that nobody should catch her.

---

[240] Elea (Gr. Eleia) or Elis is the area in the western Peloponnese, where Olympia is located (not to be confused with Elea in Italy).

[241] In Hesiod's *Shield*, 14 ff. Amphitryon should not go to his wife Alkmene until he had avenged the death of her brothers.

[242] According to other versions (e.g., Hesiod's *Shield*), the men quarreled over the cattle and Amphitryon killed Elektryon in rage.

[243] This Atreus is the father of Agamamnon and Menelaos, Greek leaders in the Trojan War.

[244] In other words, for the killing of Elektryon.

[245] Kadmeia stands for Thebes and its area, after Kadmos, its founder (on which see Part 4, document 10).

(2.4.7) As the country suffered thereby, the Thebans every month exposed a son of one of the citizens to the brute, which would have carried off many if that were not done. So Amphitryon betook him to Kephalos, son of Deioneus, at Athens, and persuaded him, in return for a share of the Teleboan spoils, to bring to the chase the dog which Prokris had brought from Crete as a gift from Minos; for that dog was destined to catch whatever it pursued. So then, when the vixen was chased by the dog, Zeus turned both of them into stone. Supported by his allies, namely, Kephalos from Thorikos in Attica, Panopeus from Phokis, Heleios, son of Perseus, from Helos in Argolis, and Kreon from Thebes, Amphitryon ravaged the islands of the Taphians. Now, so long as Pterelaos lived, he could not take Taphos; but when Comaitho, daughter of Pterelaos, falling in love with Amphitryon, pulled out the golden hair from her father's head, Pterelaos died, and Amphitryon subjugated all the islands. He slew Comaitho, and sailed with the booty to Thebes,[246] and gave the islands to Heleios and Kephalos; and they founded cities named after themselves and dwelt in them.

(Birth and upbringing of Herakles)

(2.4.8) But before Amphitryon reached Thebes, Zeus came by night and prolonging the one night threefold he assumed the likeness of Amphitryon and bedded with Alkmene[247] and related what had happened concerning the Teleboans. But when Amphitryon arrived and saw that he was not welcomed by his wife, he inquired the cause; and when she told him that he had come the night before and slept with her, he learned from Teiresias[248] how Zeus had enjoyed her. And Alkmene bore two sons, namely, Herakles, whom she had by Zeus and who was the elder by one night, and Iphikles, whom she had by Amphitryon. When the child was eight months old, Hera desired the destruction of the babe and sent two huge serpents to the bed. Alkmene called Amphitryon to her help, but Herakles arose and killed the serpents by strangling them with both his hands. However, Pherekydes says that it was Amphitryon who put the serpents in the bed, because he would know which of the two children was his, and that when Iphikles fled, and Herakles stood his ground, he knew that Iphikles was begotten of his body.

(2.4.9) Herakles was taught to drive a chariot by Amphitryon, to wrestle by Autolykos, to shoot with the bow by Eurytos, to fence by Kastor, and to play the lyre by Linos. This Linos was a brother of Orpheus; he came to Thebes and became a Theban, but was killed by Herakles with a blow of the lyre; for being struck by him, Herakles flew into a rage and slew him. When he was tried for murder, Herakles quoted a law of Rhadamanthys, who laid it down that whoever defends himself against a wrongful aggressor shall go free, and so he was acquitted. But fearing

---

[246] In the sanctuary of Ismenian Apollo at Thebes, Herodotos saw a tripod bearing an inscription in "Kadmeian letters" (i.e., archaic Greek letters, derived from the Phoenician "Kadmeian" alphabet), which said that the vessel had been dedicated by Amphitryon from the spoils of the Teleboans (Hdt. 5.59).

[247] This motif was the theme of Plautus' extant comedy *Amphitryio*.

[248] Teiresias is the famous blind seer from Thebes who features prominently in the stories of Oedipus (e.g., Sophocles' *Oedipus King*) and Dionysos (e.g., Euripides' *Bacchae*) among many others.

he might do the like again, Amphitryon sent him to the cattle farm; and there he was nurtured and outdid all in stature and strength. Even by the look of him it was plain that he was a son of Zeus; for his body measured four cubits, and he flashed a gleam of fire from his eyes; and he did not miss, neither with the bow nor with the javelin.

(First exploits as adult)

While he was with the herds and had reached his eighteenth year he slew the Kithaironeian lion, for that animal, sallying from Kithairon, harried the cattle of Amphitryon and of Thespios.

(2.4.10) Now this Thespios was king of Thespiai, and Herakles went to him when he wished to catch the lion. The king entertained him for fifty days, and each night, as Herakles went forth to the hunt, Thespios bedded one of his daughters with him (fifty daughters having been borne to him by Megamede, daughter of Arneos); for he was anxious that all of them should have children by Herakles. Thus Herakles, though he thought that his bed-fellow was always the same, had intercourse with them all. And having vanquished the lion, he dressed himself in the skin and wore the gaping mouth as a helmet.[249]

(2.4.11) As he was returning from the hunt, there met him heralds sent by Erginos to receive the tribute from the Thebans. Now the Thebans paid tribute to Erginos for the following reason. Klymenos, king of the Minyans, was wounded with a cast of a stone by a charioteer of Menoikeos, named Perieres, in a precinct of Poseidon at Onchestos; and being carried dying to Orchomenos, he with his last breath charged his son Erginos to avenge his death. So Erginos marched against Thebes, and after slaughtering not a few of the Thebans he concluded a treaty with them, confirmed by oaths, that they should send him tribute for twenty years, a hundred cattle every year. Falling in with the heralds on their way to Thebes to demand this tribute, Herakles outraged them; for he cut off their ears and noses and hands, and having fastened them by ropes from their necks, he told them to carry that tribute to Erginos and the Minyans. Indignant at this outrage, Erginos marched against Thebes. But Herakles, having received weapons from Athena and taken the command, killed Erginos, put the Minyans to flight, and compelled them to pay double the tribute to the Thebans. And it chanced that in the fight Amphitryon fell fighting bravely. And Herakles received from Kreon his eldest daughter Megara as a prize of valor, and by her he had three sons, Therimachos, Kreontiades, and Deikoon.[250] But Kreon gave his younger daughter to Iphikles, who already had a son Iolaos by Automedousa, daughter of Alkathos. And Rhadamanthys,[251] son of Zeus, married Alkmene after the death of Amphitryon, and dwelt as an exile at Okaleai in Boiotia.

---

[249] The lion-head headgear is the main way of recognizing Herakles in iconography (along with the club and sometimes other weapons).

[250] The number and names of his children by Megara vary by author. The Thebans celebrated an annual festival in their honor.

[251] A son of Zeus and Europa, brother of Minos, with whom he was a judge in the Underworld.

Having first learned from Eurytos the art of archery, Herakles received a sword from Hermes, a bow and arrows from Apollo, a golden breastplate from Hephaistos, and a robe from Athena; for he had himself cut a club at Nemea.

(Twelve labors)

(2.4.12) Now it came to pass that after the battle with the Minyans Herakles was driven mad through the jealousy of Hera and flung his own children, whom he had by Megara, and two children of Iphikles into the fire[252]; wherefore he condemned himself to exile, and was purified by Thespios, and repairing to Delphi he inquired of the god where he should dwell. The Pythian priestess then first called him Herakles, for hitherto he was called Alkeides.[253] And she told him to dwell in Tiryns, serving Eurystheus for twelve years and to perform the ten labors imposed on him, and so, she said, when the tasks were accomplished, he would be immortal.

(2.5.1) When Herakles heard that, he went to Tiryns and did as he was bid by Eurystheus. First, Eurystheus ordered him to bring the skin of the Nemean lion[254]; now that was an invulnerable beast begotten by Typhon. On his way to attack the lion he came to Kleonai and lodged at the house of a day-laborer, Molorchos; and when his host would have offered a victim in sacrifice, Herakles told him to wait for thirty days, and then, if he had returned safe from the hunt, to sacrifice to Saviour Zeus, but if he were dead, to offer it to him as to a hero.[255] And having come to Nemea and tracked the lion, he first shot an arrow at him, but when he perceived that the beast was invulnerable, he heaved up his club and made after him. And when the lion took refuge in a cave with two mouths, Herakles built up the one entrance and came in upon the beast through the other, and putting his arm round its neck held it tight till he had choked it; so laying it on his shoulders he carried it to Kleonai. And finding Molorchos on the last of the thirty days about to offer the victim to him as to a dead man, he sacrificed to Saviour Zeus and brought the lion to Mycenae. Amazed at his manhood, Eurystheus forbade him thenceforth to enter the city, but ordered him to exhibit the fruits of his labors before the gates. They say, too, that in his fear he had a bronze jar made for himself to hide in under the earth, and that he sent his commands for the labors through a herald, Kopreus, son of Pelops the Elean. This Kopreus had killed Iphitos and fled to Mycenae, where he was purified by Eurystheus and took up his abode.

(2.5.2) As a second labor he ordered him to kill the Lernaian hydra. That creature, bred in the swamp of Lerna, used to go forth into the plain and ravage both the cattle and the country. Now the hydra had a huge body, with nine heads, eight mortal, but the middle one immortal.[256] So mounting a chariot driven by Iolaos, he came to Lerna, and having halted his horses, he discovered the hydra on a hill

---

[252] Famously dramatized by Euripides in the tragedy *Herakles Insane*.

[253] According to other authors, his name was Alkaios, the name of Amphitryon's father.

[254] In Hesiod (*Th.* 326 ff.) the Nemean lion was begotten by Echidna and Orthos, the hound of Geryon; in Hyginus by the Moon.

[255] Two different words are used in Greek for sacrificing: *thuein* for a god and *anagizein* for a hero. I have substituted the second word with "offering."

[256] Other authors multiply her heads to one hundred or reduce them to one.

beside the springs of the Amymone, where was its den. By pelting it with fiery shafts he forced it to come out, and in the act of doing so he seized and held it fast. But the hydra wound itself about one of his feet and clung to him. Nor could he effect anything by smashing its heads with his club, for as fast as one head was smashed there grew up two. A huge crab also came to the help of the hydra by biting his foot.[257] So he killed it, and in his turn called for help on Iolaos who, by setting fire to a piece of the neighboring wood and burning the roots of the heads with the brands, prevented them from sprouting. Having thus got the better of the sprouting heads, he chopped off the immortal head, and buried it, and put a heavy rock on it, beside the road that leads through Lerna to Elaious. But the body of the hydra he slit up and dipped his arrows in the gall. However, Eurystheus said that this labor should not be reckoned among the ten because he had not got the better of the hydra by himself, but with the help of Iolaos.

(2.5.3) As a third labor he ordered him to bring the Kerynitian hind alive to Mycenae. Now the hind was at Oinoe[258]; it had golden horns and was sacred to Artemis; so wishing neither to kill nor wound it, Herakles hunted it a whole year. But when, weary with the chase, the beast took refuge on the mountain called Artemisios, and thence passed to the river Ladon, Herakles shot it just as it was about to cross the stream, and catching it put it on his shoulders and hastened through Arcadia. But Artemis with Apollo met him, and would have wrested the hind from him, and rebuked him for attempting to kill her sacred animal. Howbeit, by pleading necessity and laying the blame on Eurystheus, he appeased the anger of the goddess and carried the beast alive to Mycenae.

(2.5.4) As a fourth labor he ordered him to bring the Erymanthian boar alive[259]; now that animal ravaged Psophis, sallying from a mountain which they call Erymanthos. So passing through Pholoe he was entertained by the centaur Pholos, a son of Seilenos by a Melian nymph.[260] He set roast meat before Herakles, while he himself ate his meat raw. When Herakles called for wine, he said he feared to open the jar which belonged to the centaurs in common. But Herakles, bidding him be of good courage, opened it, and not long afterwards, scenting the smell, the centaurs arrived at the cave of Pholos, armed with rocks and firs. The first who dared to enter, Anchios and Agrios, were repelled by Herakles with a shower of brands, and the rest of them he shot and pursued as far as Malea. Thence they took refuge with Chiron,[261] who, driven by the Lapiths from Mount Pelion, took up his abode at Malea. As the centaurs cowered about Chiron, Herakles shot an arrow at them, which, passing through the arm of Elatus, stuck in the knee of Chiron. Distressed at this, Herakles ran up to him, drew out the shaft, and applied a medicine which Chiron gave him.

[257] According to tradition, the crab was rewarded by Hera by turning him into a constellation.

[258] In Argolis (the area around Argos).

[259] The boar's tusks were said to be preserved in a sanctuary of Apollo at Cumae in Campania (Paus. 8.24.5).

[260] For these nymphs, see Hesiod, *Th.* 187. The name perhaps means an ash-tree nymph (from *melia*, an ash tree), as Dryad means an oak-tree nymph (from *drus*, an oak tree).

[261] Chiron (Gr. Kheiron, "hand") was an extraordinary centaur famous for his knowledge, especially of healing, and the mentor of heroes such as Asklepios, Achilles, and Aeneas.

But the hurt proving incurable, Chiron retired to the cave and there he wished to die, but he could not, for he was immortal. However, Prometheus offered himself to Zeus to be immortal in his stead, and so Chiron died. The rest of the centaurs fled in different directions, and some came to Mount Malea, and Eurytion to Pholoe, and Nessos to the river Euenos. The rest of them Poseidon received at Eleusis and hid them in a mountain. But Pholos, drawing the arrow from a corpse, wondered that so little a thing could kill such big fellows; howbeit, it slipped from his hand and lighting on his foot killed him on the spot. So when Herakles returned to Pholoe, he beheld Pholos dead; and he buried him and proceeded to the boar hunt. And when he had chased the boar with shouts from a certain thicket, he drove the exhausted animal into deep snow, trapped it, and brought it to Mycenae.

(2.5.5) The fifth labor he laid on him was to carry out the dung of the cattle of Augeas in a single day. Now Augeas was king of Elis; some say that he was a son of the Sun,[262] others that he was a son of Poseidon, and others that he was a son of Phorbas; and he had many herds of cattle. Herakles accosted him, and without revealing the command of Eurystheus, said that he would carry out the dung in one day, if Augeas would give him the tithe of the cattle. Augeas was incredulous, but promised. Having taken Augeas' son Phyleus to witness, Herakles made a breach in the foundations of the cattle-yard, and then, diverting the courses of the Alpheios and Peneios, which flowed near each other, he turned them into the yard, having first made an outlet for the water through another opening.

When Augeas learned that this had been accomplished at the command of Eurystheus, he would not pay the reward; nay more, he denied that he had promised to pay it, and on that point he professed himself ready to submit to arbitration. The arbitrators having taken their seats, Phyleus was called by Herakles and bore witness against his father, affirming that he had agreed to give him a reward. In a rage Augeas, before the voting took place, ordered both Phyleus and Herakles to pack out of Elis. So Phyleus went to Dulichion and dwelt there, and Herakles repaired to Dexamenos at Olenos. He found Dexamenos on the point of betrothing perforce his daughter Mnesimache to the centaur Eurytion, and being called upon by him for help, he slew Eurytion when that centaur came to fetch his bride. But Eurystheus would not admit this labor either among the ten, alleging that it had been performed for hire.

(2.5.6) The sixth labor he enjoined on him was to chase away the Stymphalian birds. Now at the city of Stymphalos in Arcadia was the lake called Stymphalis, embosomed in a deep wood. To it countless birds had flocked for refuge, fearing to be preyed upon by the wolves.[263] So when Herakles was at a loss how to drive the birds from the wood, Athena gave him brazen castanets, which she had received from Hephaistos. By clashing these on a certain mountain that overhung the lake, he scared the birds. They could not abide the sound, but fluttered up in a fright, and in that way Herakles shot them.

(2.5.7) The seventh labor he enjoined on him was to bring the Cretan bull. Akousilaos says that this was the bull that ferried across Europa for Zeus; but some

---

[262] The name of his father, Eleios, was popularly confused with Helios, the Sun.

[263] In some accounts these birds are said to shoot their feathers like arrows.

say it was the bull that Poseidon sent up from the sea when Minos promised to sacrifice to Poseidon what should appear out of the sea. And they say that when he saw the beauty of the bull he sent it away to the herds and sacrificed another to Poseidon; at which the god was angry and made the bull savage.[264] To attack this bull Herakles came to Crete, and when, in reply to his request for aid, Minos told him to fight and catch the bull for himself, he caught it and brought it to Eurystheus, and having shown it to him he let it afterwards go free. But the bull roamed to Sparta and all Arcadia, and traversing the Isthmos arrived at Marathon in Attica and harried the inhabitants.[265]

(2.5.8) The eighth labor he enjoined on him was to bring the mares of Diomedes the Thracian to Mycenae. Now this Diomedes was a son of Ares and Kyrene, and he was king of the Bistones, a very warlike Thracian people, and he owned man-eating mares. So Herakles sailed with a band of volunteers, and having overpowered the grooms who were in charge of the mangers, he drove the mares to the sea. When the Bistones in arms came to the rescue, he committed the mares to the guardianship of Abderos, who was a son of Hermes, a native of Opus in Lokris, and a minion of Herakles; but the mares killed him by dragging him after them. But Herakles fought against the Bistones, slew Diomedes and compelled the rest to flee.[266] And he founded a city Abdera beside the grave of Abderos who had been done to death,[267] and bringing the mares he gave them to Eurystheus. But Eurystheus let them go, and they came to Mount Olympos, as it is called, and there they were destroyed by the wild beasts.

(2.5.9) The ninth labor he enjoined on Herakles was to bring the belt of Hippolyte. She was queen of the Amazons, who dwelt about the river Thermodon, a people great in war; for they cultivated the manly virtues, and if ever they gave birth to children through intercourse with the other sex, they reared the females; and they pinched off the right breasts that they might not be trammeled by them in throwing the javelin, but they kept the left breasts, that they might suckle. Now Hippolyte had the belt of Ares in token of her superiority to all the rest. Herakles was sent to fetch this belt because Admete, daughter of Eurystheus, desired to get it. So taking with him a band of volunteer comrades in a single ship he set sail and put in to the island of Paros, which was inhabited by the sons of Minos, namely, Eurymedon, Chryses, Nephalion, and Philolaos. But it chanced that two of those in the ship landed and were killed by the sons of Minos. Indignant at this, Herakles killed the sons of Minos on the spot and besieged the rest closely, till they sent envoys to request that in place of the murdered men he would take two, whom he pleased. So he raised the siege, and taking on board the sons of Androgeus, son of

---

[264] This would be the bull with whom Pasiphae begot the Minotaur (see Part 5, documents 9.a, 9.b, and 9.c). On the bull that carried Europa away, see Part 4, document 10.

[265] This is the same bull that Theseus will fight in Attica later on.

[266] These were said to be man-eating mares. According to Diodorus Siculus (4.13.4), Herakles killed Thracian king Diomedes by exposing him to his mares, whose breed allegedly existed down to the time of Alexander the Great.

[267] This is Abdera in Thrace. Ancient sources say that games were performed in honor of Abderos, including athletic contests except for horse racing.

Minos, namely, Alkaios and Sthenelos, he came to Mysia, to the court of Lykos, son of Daskylos, and was entertained by him; and in a battle between him and the king of the Bebrykes Herakles sided with Lykos and slew many, amongst others King Mygdon, brother of Amykos. And he took much land from the Bebrykes and gave it to Lykos, who called it all Herakleia.

Having put in at the harbor of Themiskyra, he received a visit from Hippolyte, who inquired why he had come, and promised to give him the belt. But Hera in the likeness of an Amazon went up and down the multitude saying that the strangers who had arrived were carrying off the queen. So the Amazons in arms charged on horseback down on the ship. But when Herakles saw them in arms, he suspected treachery, and killing Hippolyte stripped her of her belt. And after fighting the rest he sailed away and touched at Troy.

But it chanced that the city was then in distress consequently on the wrath of Apollo and Poseidon. For desiring to put the wantonness of Laomedon to the proof, Apollo and Poseidon assumed the likeness of men and undertook to fortify Pergamon for wages.[268] But when they had fortified it, he would not pay them their wages. Therefore Apollo sent a pestilence, and Poseidon a sea monster, which, carried up by a flood, snatched away the people of the plain. But as oracles foretold deliverance from these calamities if Laomedon would expose his daughter Hesione to be devoured by the sea monster, he exposed her by fastening her to the rocks near the sea. Seeing her exposed, Herakles promised to save her on condition of receiving from Laomedon the mares which Zeus had given in compensation for the rape of Ganymede.[269] On Laomedon's saying that he would give them, Herakles killed the monster and saved Hesione. But when Laomedon would not give the stipulated reward, Herakles put to sea after threatening to make war on Troy.

And he touched at Ainos, where he was entertained by Poltys. And as he was sailing away he shot and killed on the Ainian beach a lewd fellow, Sarpedon, son of Poseidon and brother of Poltys. And having come to Thasos and subjugated the Thracians who dwelt in the island, he gave it to the sons of Androgeus to dwell in. From Thasos he proceeded to Torone, and there, being challenged to wrestle by Polygonos and Telegonos, sons of Proteus, son of Poseidon, he killed them in the wrestling match. And having brought the belt to Mycenae he gave it to Eurystheus.

(2.5.10) As a tenth labor he was ordered to fetch the cattle of Geryon from Erytheia. Now Erytheia was an island near the ocean; it is now called Gadeira.[270] This

---

[268] Pergamon (a city south of Troy in the Aiolic coast of Asia Minor) stands here for Troy. For the gods' work as wall builders, see Hom. *Il.* 7.452 ff., according to which the walls of Troy were built by Poseidon and Apollo jointly for king Laomedon. At *Il.* 21.441–457, however, the walls were built by Poseidon alone, while Apollo served as a herdsman, tending the king's cattle in Mount Ida.

[269] This story is mentioned in the *Iliad* when Diomedes takes the mares of Aeneas (*Il.* 5.270 ff. in document 3.8.a); see also *Hymn to Aphrodite* 210 ff. (Part 5, document 5).

[270] See Hesiod's *Theogony* 287–294 and 979–983. Gadeira is the Phoenician colony of Gadir in southern Spain (Roman Gades, modern Cádiz). Around this area flourished the indigenous culture called Tartessos (mentioned below).

island was inhabited by Geryon, son of Chrysaor by Kallirrhoe, daughter of Ocean. He had the body of three men grown together and joined in one at the waist, but parted in three from the flanks and thighs. He owned red cattle, of which Eurytion was the herdsman and Orthos, the two-headed hound, begotten by Typhon on Echidna, was the watchdog. So journeying through Europe to fetch the cattle of Geryon he destroyed many wild beasts and set foot in Libya, and proceeding to Tartessos he erected as tokens of his journey two pillars over against each other at the boundaries of Europe and Libya.[271] But being heated by the Sun on his journey, he bent his bow at the god, who in admiration of his hardihood, gave him a golden goblet in which he crossed the ocean. And having reached Erytheia he lodged on Mount Abas. However, the dog, perceiving him, rushed at him; but he smote it with his club, and when the herdsman Eurytion came to the help of the dog, Herakles killed him also. But Menoetes, who was there pasturing the cattle of Hades, reported to Geryon what had occurred, and he, coming up with Herakles beside the river Anthemus, as he was driving away the cattle, joined battle with him and was shot dead. And Herakles, embarking the cattle in the goblet and sailing across to Tartessos, gave back the goblet to the Sun.

And passing through Abderia[272] he came to Liguria, where Ialebion and Derkynos, sons of Poseidon, attempted to rob him of the cattle, but he killed them and went on his way through Tyrrhenia.[273] But at Rhegion a bull broke away[274] and hastily plunging into the sea swam across to Sicily, and having passed through the neighboring country since called Italy after it, for the Tyrrhenians called the bull *italus*,[275] came to the plain of Eryx,[276] who reigned over the Elymi. Now Eryx was a son of Poseidon, and he mingled the bull with his own herds. So Herakles entrusted the cattle to Hephaistos and hurried away in search of the bull. He found it in the herds of Eryx, and when the king refused to surrender it unless Herakles should beat him in a wrestling bout, Herakles beat him thrice, killed him in the wrestling, and taking the bull drove it with the rest of the herd to the Ionian Sea. But when he came to the creeks of the sea, Hera afflicted the cows with a gadfly, and they dispersed among the skirts of the mountains of Thrace. Herakles went in pursuit, and having caught some, drove them to the Hellespont; but the remainder were thenceforth wild. Having with difficulty collected the cows, Herakles blamed the river Strymon, and whereas it had been navigable before, he made it unnavigable by filling it with rocks; and he conveyed the cattle and gave them to Eurystheus, who sacrificed them to Hera.

---

[271] These are the so-called "Pillars of Herakles," usually identified with rocky mounds on the two sides of the Straits of Gibraltar. Another tradition identified the pillars with the columns at the temple of Herakles-Melqart in Gadir (Cádiz).

[272] This was a Phoenician colony in southern Spain (not Abdera in Thrace).

[273] Other authors write that Zeus made round big stones fall like rain, which Herakles used as missiles and which could be seen in historical times in the area called Stony Plain (between Marseilles and the Rhone).

[274] The author is deriving the name of Rhegion from the Greek verb *apo-rhegnymi* "break away."

[275] Like other ancient authors, Apollodorus implies that *Italia* (Italy) derived from *vitulus* "calf."

[276] In northwestern Sicily.

(2.5.11) When the labors had been performed in eight years and a month, Eurystheus ordered Herakles, as an eleventh labor, to fetch golden apples from the Hesperides,[277] for he did not acknowledge the labor of the cattle of Augeas nor that of the hydra. These apples were not, as some have said, in Libya, but on Atlas among the Hyperboreans.[278] They were presented <by Earth> to Zeus after his marriage with Hera, and guarded by an immortal dragon with a hundred heads, offspring of Typhon and Echidna, which spoke with many and divers sorts of voices. With it the Hesperides also were on guard, namely, Aigle, Erytheia, Hesperia, and Arethousa. So journeying he came to the river Echedoros. And Kyknos, son of Ares and Pyrene, challenged him to single combat. Ares championed the cause of Kyknos and marshaled the combat, but a thunderbolt was hurled between the two and parted the combatants. And going on foot through Illyria and hastening to the river Eridanos he came to the nymphs, the daughters of Zeus and Themis. They revealed Nereus to him, and Herakles seized him while he slept, and though the god turned himself into all kinds of shapes, the hero bound him and did not release him till he had learned from him where were the apples and the Hesperides. Being informed, he traversed Libya. That country was then ruled by Antaios, son of Poseidon, who used to kill strangers by forcing them to wrestle. Being forced to wrestle with him, Herakles hugged him, lifted him aloft, broke and killed him; for when he touched earth so it was that he waxed stronger, wherefore some said that he was a son of Earth.[279]

After Libya he traversed Egypt. That country was then ruled by Bousiris, a son of Poseidon by Lysianassa, daughter of Epaphos. This Bousiris used to sacrifice strangers on an altar of Zeus in accordance with a certain oracle. For Egypt was visited with dearth for nine years, and Phrasios, a learned seer who had come from Cyprus, said that the dearth would cease if they slaughtered a stranger man in honor of Zeus every year. Bousiris began by slaughtering the seer himself and continued to slaughter the strangers who landed. So Herakles also was seized and haled to the altars, but he burst his bonds and slew both Bousiris and his son Amphidamas.[280]

And traversing Asia he put in at Thermydrai, the harbor of the Lindians.[281] And having loosed one of the bullocks from the cart of a cowherd, he sacrificed it and feasted. But the cowherd, unable to protect himself, stood on a certain mountain and cursed. Wherefore to this day, when they sacrifice to Herakles, they do it with curses.[282]

---

[277] See Hes. *Th*. 215 ff.

[278] The gardens of the Hesperides are usually placed in the far west (Italy or the Iberian Peninsula), not the far north (the land of the Hyperboreans).

[279] According to Pindar, the giant roofed the temple of Poseidon with the skulls of his victims. Roman authors (Ovid, Juvenal, Statius) say that he regained strength through contact with his mother Earth. Antaios (Antaeus in Latin) is placed in western Morocco, on the Atlantic coast, where a hillock was pointed out as his tomb.

[280] Herodotos (2.45) reports the same episode but dismisses it as not consistent with Egyptian customs.

[281] From Lindos, an important harbor city on the island of Rhodes.

[282] Cursing was part of rituals at Eleusis and other places.

And passing by Arabia he slew Emathion, son of Tithonos, and journeying through Libya to the outer sea he received the goblet from the Sun. And having crossed to the opposite mainland he shot on the Caucasus the eagle, offspring of Echidna and Typhon, that was devouring the liver of Prometheus, and he released Prometheus, after choosing for himself the bond of olive, and to Zeus he presented Chiron, who, though immortal, consented to die in his stead.[283]

Now Prometheus had told Herakles not to go himself after the apples but to send Atlas, first relieving him of the burden of the sphere; so when he had come to Atlas in the land of the Hyperboreans, he took the advice and relieved Atlas. But when Atlas had received three apples from the Hesperides, he came to Herakles, and not wishing to support the sphere {he said that he would himself carry the apples to Eurystheus, and bade Herakles hold up the sky in his stead. Herakles promised to do so, but succeeded by craft in putting it on Atlas instead. For at the advice of Prometheus he begged Atlas to hold up the sky till he should} put a pad on his head.[284] When Atlas heard that, he laid the apples down on the ground and took the sphere from Herakles. And so Herakles picked up the apples and departed. But some say that he did not get them from Atlas, but that he plucked the apples himself after killing the guardian snake. And having brought the apples he gave them to Eurystheus. But he, on receiving them, bestowed them on Herakles, from whom Athena got them and conveyed them back again; for it was not lawful that they should be laid down anywhere.

(2.5.12) A twelfth labor imposed on Herakles was to bring Kerberos from Hades. Now this Kerberos had three heads of dogs, the tail of a dragon, and on his back the heads of all sorts of snakes.[285] When Herakles was about to depart to fetch him, he went to Eumolpos at Eleusis, wishing to be initiated. However, it was not then lawful for foreigners to be initiated, since he proposed to be initiated as the adoptive son of Pylios. But not being able to see the mysteries because he had not been cleansed of the slaughter of the centaurs, he was cleansed by Eumolpos and then initiated.[286] And having come to Tainaron in Lakonia, where is the mouth of the descent to Hades, he descended through it.[287] But when the souls saw him, they fled, save Meleager and the Gorgon Medusa. And Herakles drew his sword against the Gorgon, as if she were alive, but he learned from Hermes that she was an empty phantom.[288]

And having come near to the gates of Hades he found Theseus and Peirithoos, him who wooed Persephone in wedlock and was therefore bound fast. And when

[283] On Chiron, see Apollod. 2.5.4. This might be an allusion to the branch of olive brought by Herakles from the Hyperboreans, which became the victor's crown at the Olympic games.

[284] The passage in brackets is missing in Apollodorus' manuscripts but restored from a *scholion*. The episode is also represented in a metope of the temple of Zeus at Olympia.

[285] In Homer and Hesiod the dog has fifty heads.

[286] For Eleusis and the Mysteries, see Part 6, document 8.

[287] Others say he descended at Acherusian Chersonese, near Herakleia on the Black Sea. A cave at the tip of Cape Tainaron (southernmost Peloponnese) was one of the legendary entrances to the Underworld, as was a cave at Eleusis and at Lake Avernus at Cumae (Part 6, document 13).

[288] See encounter of Aeneas with the Gorgons in *Aeneid* (6.288 ff. in Part 6, document 13).

they beheld Herakles, they stretched out their hands as if they should be raised from
the dead by his might. And Theseus, indeed, he took by the hand and raised up, but
when he would have brought up Peirithoos, the earth quaked and he let go. And he
rolled away also the stone of Askalaphos. And wishing to provide the souls with
blood, he slaughtered one of the cattle of Hades.[289] But Menoites, son of Keuthony-
mos, who tended the king, challenged Herakles to wrestle, and, being seized round
the middle, had his ribs broken; howbeit, he was let off at the request of Persephone.
When Herakles asked Plouton for Kerberos, Plouton ordered him to take the animal provided he mastered him without the use of the weapons which he carried.
Herakles found him at the gates of Acheron, and, cased in his cuirass and covered
by the lion's skin, he flung his arms round the head of the brute, and though the
dragon in its tail bit him, he never relaxed his grip and pressure till it yielded. So he
carried it off and ascended through Troizen. But Demeter turned Askalaphos into a
short-eared owl, and Herakles, after showing Kerberos to Eurystheus, carried him
back to Hades.

(Wars of Herakles)

(2.6.1) After his labors Herakles went to Thebes and gave Megara to Iolaos, and,
wishing himself to wed, he ascertained that Eurytos, prince of Oichalia, had proposed the hand of his daughter Iole as a prize to him who should vanquish himself
and his sons in archery. So he came to Oichalia, and though he proved himself
better than them at archery, yet he did not get the bride; for while Iphitos, the elder
of Eurytos's sons, said that Iole should be given to Herakles, Eurytos and the others refused, and said they feared that, if he got children, he would again kill his
offspring.

(2.6.2) Not long after, some cattle were stolen from Euboia by Autolykos, and
Eurytos supposed that it was done by Herakles; but Iphitos did not believe it and
went to Herakles. And meeting him, as he came from Pherai after saving the dead
Alkestis for Admetos, he invited him to seek the cattle with him.[290] Herakles promised to do so and entertained him; but going mad again he threw him from the
walls of Tiryns. Wishing to be purified of the murder he repaired to Neleus, who
was prince of the Pylians. And when Neleus rejected his request on the score of his
friendship with Eurytos, he went to Amyklai and was purified by Deiphobos, son
of Hippolytos. But being afflicted with a dire disease on account of the murder of
Iphitos he went to Delphi and inquired how he might be rid of the disease. As the
Pythian priestess answered him not by oracles, he was fain to plunder the temple,
and, carrying off the tripod,[291] to institute an oracle of his own. But Apollo fought
him, and Zeus threw a thunderbolt between them. When they had thus been parted,
Herakles received an oracle, which declared that the remedy for his disease was for

---

[289] See the *Odyssey*, Book 11 (Part 6, document 7), where Odysseus attracts the souls with sacrificial
blood.

[290] The details of the incident vary in different versions, and in all of them except Apollodorus
the animals involved were mares, not cattle.

[291] This scene was often represented in art, as in the preserved reliefs of the Siphnian treasury at
Delphi.

him to be sold, and to serve for three years, and to pay compensation for the murder to Eurytos.

(2.6.3) After the delivery of the oracle, Hermes sold Herakles, and he was bought by Omphale, daughter of Iardanos, queen of Lydia, to whom at his death her husband Tmolos had bequeathed the government. Eurytos did not accept the compensation when it was presented to him, but Herakles served Omphale as a slave, and in the course of his servitude he seized and bound the Kerkopes at Ephesos[292]; and as for Syleus in Aulis, who compelled passing strangers to dig, Herakles killed him with his daughter Xenodoke, after burning the vines with the roots. And having put in to the island of Doliche, he saw the body of Ikaros washed ashore and buried it, and he called the island Ikaria instead of Doliche. In return Daidalos made a portrait statue of Herakles at Pisa, which Herakles mistook at night for living and threw a stone and hit it. And during the time of his servitude with Omphale it is said that the voyage to Colchis and the hunt of the Kalydonian boar took place,[293] and that Theseus on his way from Troizen cleared the Isthmos of malefactors.

(2.6.4) After his servitude, being rid of his disease he mustered an army of noble volunteers and sailed for Ilion (i.e., Troy) with eighteen ships of fifty oars each. And having come to port at Ilion, he left the guard of the ships to Oikles and himself with the rest of the champions set out to attack the city. However, Laomedon marched against the ships with the multitude and slew Oikles in battle, but being repulsed by the troops of Herakles, he was besieged. The siege once laid, Telamon[294] was the first to breach the wall and enter the city, and after him Herakles. But when he saw that Telamon had entered it first, he drew his sword and rushed at him, loath that anybody should be reputed a better man than himself. Perceiving that, Telamon collected stones that lay to hand, and when Herakles asked him what he did, he said he was building an altar to Herakles the Glorious Victor. Herakles thanked him, and when he had taken the city and shot down Laomedon and his sons, except Podarkes, he assigned Laomedon's daughter Hesione as a prize to Telamon and allowed her to take with her whomsoever of the captives she would. When she chose her brother Podarkes, Herakles said that he must first be a slave and then be ransomed by her. So when he was being sold she took the veil from her head and gave it as a ransom; hence Podarkes was called Priam.[295]

(2.7.1) When Herakles was sailing from Troy, Hera sent grievous storms, which so vexed Zeus that he hung her from Olympos. Herakles sailed to Kos, and the Koans, thinking he was leading a piratical squadron, endeavored to prevent his approach by a shower of stones. But he forced his way in and took the city by night,

---

[292] The Kerkopes were two (or more) perhaps "monkey-like"creatures (from Gr. *kerkos*, "tail"); they are portrayed as hanging down from a pole carried by Herakles in a metope of temple C at Selinous (Sicily). Different authors place them in different areas, and their treatment by Herakles varies between killing them, delivering then to Omphale, setting them free after they amused him, and having them transformed into monkeys by Zeus.

[293] The voyage to Colchis is that of the Argonauts; the hunt of the Kalidonian boar is famously narrated in Homer's *Iliad* 9.524–599.

[294] The father of Aiax ("Great Aiax"), one of the principal heroes in the *Iliad* and the Epic Cycle.

[295] Following the traditional etymology that derived the name Priam from the Greek verb *priamai*, "to buy."

and slew the king, Eurypylos, son of Poseidon by Astypalaia. And Herakles was wounded in the battle by Chalkodon; but Zeus snatched him away, so that he took no harm. And having laid waste Kos, he came through Athena's agency to Phlegra, and sided with the gods in their victorious war on the Giants.

(2.7.2) Not long afterwards he collected an Arcadian army, and joined by volunteers from the first men in Greece he marched against Augeias. But Augeias, hearing of the war that Herakles was levying, appointed Eurytos and Kteatos generals of the Eleians. They were two men joined in one, who surpassed all of that generation in strength and were sons of Aktor by Molione, though their father was said to be Poseidon; now Aktor was a brother of Augeias. But it came to pass that on the expedition Herakles fell sick; hence he concluded a truce with the Molionides. But afterwards, being apprized of his illness, they attacked the army and slew many. On that occasion, therefore, Herakles beat a retreat; but afterwards at the celebration of the third Isthmian festival,[296] when the Eleians sent the Molionides to take part in the sacrifices, Herakles waylaid and killed them at Kleonai, and marching on Elis took the city. And having killed Augeias and his sons, he restored Phyleos and bestowed on him the kingdom. He also celebrated the Olympian games and founded an altar of Pelops, and built six altars of the twelve gods.[297]

(2.7.3) After the capture of Elis he marched against Pylos, and having taken the city he slew Periklymenos, the most valiant of the sons of Neleus, who used to change his shape in battle. And he slew Neleus and his sons, except Nestor; for he was a youth and was being brought up among the Gerenians. In the fight he also wounded Hades, who was siding with the Pylians.[298]

Having taken Pylos he marched against Lakedaimon (Sparta), wishing to punish the sons of Hippokoon, for he was angry with them, both because they fought for Neleus, and still angrier because they had killed the son of Likymnios. For when he was looking at the palace of Hippokoon, a hound of the Molossian breed ran out and rushed at him, and he threw a stone and hit the dog, whereupon the Hippokoontids darted out and dispatched him with blows of their cudgels. It was to avenge his death that Herakles mustered an army against the Lakedaimonians. And having come to Arcadia he begged Kepheus to join him with his sons, of whom he had twenty. But fearing lest, if he quitted Tegea, the Argives would march against it, Kepheus refused to join the expedition. But Herakles had received from Athena a lock of the Gorgon's hair in a bronze jar and gave it to Sterope, daughter of Kepheus, saying that if an army advanced against the city, she was to hold up the lock of hair thrice from the walls, and that, provided she did not look before her, the enemy would be turned to flight. That being so, Kepheus and his sons took the field, and in the battle he and his sons perished, and besides them Iphikles, the brother of

---

[296] The Isthmian games were pan-Hellenic (like the Olympic, Nemean, and Pythian), celebrated at Isthmia in the Gulf of Corinth every other year.

[297] The traditional date for the foundation of the Olympic games was 776 BCE (centuries after the legendary time of Herakles' exploits). The Greeks used the first Olympiad as a point of reference for the dating of events.

[298] See Homer's *Iliad* 5.391–394 (400 ff. in III.8.A), where Herakles is said to have wounded Hera with an arrow in the right breast. In the same fight at Pylos, according to Hesiod (*Shield of Herakles* 359 ff.), Herakles gashed the thigh of Ares with his spear and laid the deity in the dust.

Herakles. Having killed Hippokoon and his sons and subjugated the city, Herakles restored Tyndareos[299] and entrusted the kingdom to him.

(2.7.4) Passing by Tegea, Herakles ravaged Auge, not knowing her to be a daughter of Aleos. And she brought forth her babe secretly and deposited it in the precinct of Athena. But the country being wasted by a pestilence, Aleos entered the precinct and on investigation discovered his daughter's motherhood. So he exposed the babe on Mount Parthenios, and by the providence of the gods it was preserved: for a doe that had just cast her fawn gave it suck, and shepherds took up the babe and called it Telephos.[300] And her father gave Auge to Nauplios, son of Poseidon, to sell far away in a foreign land; and Nauplios gave her to Teuthras, the prince of Teuthrania, who made her his wife.

(Deianeira, Iole, and Herakles' death)

(2.7.5) And having come to Kalydon, Herakles wooed Deianeira, daughter of Oineus. He wrestled for her hand with Acheloios, who assumed the likeness of a bull; but Herakles broke off one of his horns. So Herakles married Deianeira, but Acheloios recovered the horn by giving the horn of Amalthea in its stead. Now Amalthea was a daughter of Haimonios, and she had a bull's horn, which, according to Pherekydes, had the power of supplying meat or drink in abundance, whatever one might wish.[301]

(2.7.6) And Herakles marched with the Kalydonians against the Thesprotians, and having taken the city of Ephyra, of which Phylas was king, he had intercourse with the king's daughter Astyoche, and became the father of Tlepolemos. While he stayed among them, he sent word to Thespios to keep seven of his sons, to send three to Thebes and to dispatch the remaining forty to the island of Sardinia to plant a colony.[302] After these events, as he was feasting with Oineus, he killed with a blow of his knuckles Eunomos, son of Architeles, when the lad was pouring water on his hands. (Now the lad was a kinsman of Oineus.) Seeing that it was an accident, the lad's father pardoned Herakles; but Herakles wished, in accordance with the law, to suffer the penalty of exile, and resolved to depart to Keyx at Trachis. And taking Deianeira with him, he came to the river Euenos, at which the centaur Nessos sat and ferried passengers across for hire, alleging that he had received the ferry from the gods for his righteousness. So Herakles crossed the river by himself, but on being asked to pay the fare he entrusted Deianeira to Nessos to carry over. But he, in ferrying her across, attempted to violate her. She cried out, Herakles heard her, and shot Nessos to the heart when he emerged from the river. Being at the point of death, Nessos called Deianeira to him and said that if she wanted to have a

---

[299] He was (with Leda) the mortal father of Helen, Klytaimnestra, Kastor, and Polydeukes (Latin Castor and Pollux) among other children.

[300] The name is understood here to derive from *thele*, "teat, nipple," and *elaphos*, "dear/doe."

[301] According to some, Amalthea was the goat on whose milk the infant Zeus was nourished. From one of its horns flowed ambrosia and from the other flowed nectar, and, according to others, she was only the nymph who owned the goat, which suckled the god.

[302] In other words, of the fifty sons Herakles had begotten with Thespios' daughter (see 2.4.10). Other sources hold that Herakles commissioned the colony in Sardinia to Iolaos instead.

love charm to operate on Herakles she should mix the seed he had dropped on the ground with the blood that flowed from the wound inflicted by the arrow. She did so and kept it by her.

(2.7.7) Going through the country of the Dryopes and being in lack of food, Herakles met Thiodamas driving a pair of bullocks; so he unloosed and slaughtered one of the bullocks and feasted. And when he came to Keyx at Trachis he was received by him and conquered the Dryopes.[303]

And afterwards setting out from there, he fought as an ally of Aigimios, king of the Dorians. For the Lapiths, commanded by Koronos, made war on him in a dispute about the boundaries of the country; and being besieged he called in the help of Herakles, offering him a share of the country. So Herakles came to his help and slew Koronos and others, and handed the whole country over to Aigimios free. He slew also Laogoras, king of the Dryopes, with his children, as he was banqueting in a precinct of Apollo; for the king was a wanton fellow and an ally of the Lapiths. And as he passed by Itonos he was challenged to single combat by Kyknos, a son of Ares and Pelopia[304]; and closing with him Herakles slew him also. But when he came to Ormenion, king Amyntor took arms and forbade him to march through; but when he hindered his passage, Herakles slew him also.

On his arrival at Trachis he mustered an army to attack Oichalia, wishing to punish Eurytos.[305] Joined by Arcadians, Melians from Trachis, and Epiknemidian Lokrians, he slew Eurytos and his sons and took the city. After burying those of his own side who had fallen, namely, Hippasos, son of Keyx, and Argeios and Melas, the sons of Likymnios, he pillaged the city and led Iole captive. And having put in at Kenaion, a headland of Euboia, he built an altar of Kenaian Zeus. Intending to offer a sacrifice, he sent the herald Lichas to Trachis to fetch fine clothes. From him Deianeira learned about Iole, and fearing that Herakles might love that woman more than herself, she supposed that the spilt blood of Nessos was in truth a love-charm, and with it she smeared the tunic.[306] So Herakles put it on and proceeded to offer sacrifice. But no sooner was the tunic warmed than the poison of the hydra began to corrode his skin; and on that he lifted Lichas by the feet, hurled him down from the headland, and tore off the tunic, which clung to his body, so that his flesh was torn away with it. In such a sad plight he was carried on shipboard to Trachis: and Deianeira, on learning what had happened, hanged herself. But Herakles, after charging Hyllos, his elder son by Deianeira, to marry Iole when he came of age, proceeded to Mount Oite, in the Trachinian territory, and there constructed a pyre, mounted it, and gave orders to kindle it. When no one would do so, Poias, passing

---

[303] The Dryopes were a Greek tribe from the area of Mount Parnassos who allegedly dispersed through Thessaly, Euboia, the Peloponnese, and Cyprus with the advance of the Dorians. Down to the second century CE, the descendants of the Dryopes maintained tribal traditions and a sense of autochthonous identity at Asine, on the coast of Messenia (southern Peloponnese).

[304] Not the same as Kyknos in 2.5.11.

[305] Eurytos was the king of Oichalia.

[306] The episode is famously dramatized in Sophocles' *Trachiniai* 755 ff.

NEAR EASTERN, GREEK, AND ROMAN MYTHOLOGY

✦

CA. 2200 BCE–135 CE

VISUAL EVIDENCE HELPS scholars to understand and reconstruct the role of myth in the classical world.

In Egyptian funerary art, Osiris was represented as both a king of the dead and a green-faced (decomposing) corpse himself, having become the first mummy (Fig. 1); every king and later on every deceased person was identified as an Osiris. In the Greek world, the god Dionysos appears interceding between mortals and the king of the dead, Hades, with whom he has cut a deal that favors his initiates (Fig. 11). In turn, in the Gold Tablets (Fig. 12), members of mystery cults inscribed instructions for the afterlife journey, a practice not unlike that in the Egyptian *Book of the Dead*.

In Figure 2 we see a strange variation of the cosmic cyclical struggle between forces of chaos and darkness (Apophis) and of order and light (Re), in which the snaky enemy Apophis is killed by a rabbit-lion demon. The stories of the Canaanites and Hittite Storm Gods, as well as of Zeus, include fights with serpent-dragon monsters (Yam, Hedammu, Illuyanka, Typhon). As Weather Gods, their weapon is the thunderbolt, which they brandish in similar fashion (Figs. 5 and 6).

Famous heroes such as Gilgamesh, Perseus, Herakles, and Theseus were celebrated as "tamers of beasts," both in narratives and in iconography

(Figs. 3, 7, 8, 14, 21). In Figure 4 we see the Old Babylonian monster Humbaba, whose face might have been inspiration for that of Gorgon Medusa (see Fig. 8). Figure 3 is a striking scene in which a bull-like human (Enkidu?) and a hero (Gilgamesh?) fight a lion and a bull, respectively; seals and reliefs showing Gilgamesh and Enkidu slaying Humbaba and other beasts may have inspired reliefs showing Perseus (with Athena) killing Medousa (Fig. 8) and Theseus and the Minotaur (Fig. 21) during the "orientalizing" phase that accompanied the flourishing of the Greek visual arts in the eighth–seventh centuries BCE.

The persistence of religious and mythical ideas is also remarkable in the Kuntillet Ajrud ostracon from the Sinai peninsula (Fig. 9), in which someone invokes "Yahweh of Samaria and his Asherah" above two puzzling painted figures, suggesting that the Canaanite goddess and consort of the principal gods continued in the same role as the consort of Yahweh at an early stage in the development of Israelite religion. In a coin from the Phoenician city Sidon, minted during Roman times (Fig. 10), the myth of the "rape of Europa" is represented alongside the emperor's bust; this image of an east-to-west journey bounced back to the Hellenized east to become an emblem of the bustling entrepôt, where Roman, Phoenician, and Greek cultures merged. The image of Europa carried off by a bull is also represented today on the two-euro coin of modern Greece.

Like other kings before him, Alexander the Great (Fig. 13) explicitly associated himself with divine figures; he claimed to be the son of Zeus and represented himself as Herakles (also a son of Zeus) and as the son of the principal god of Egypt, Amon, who was equated with Zeus by the Greeks. The Carthaginian Barcid leaders (Hannibal and his predecessors) followed in Alexander's footsteps and represented themselves as Herakles (merged with Phoenician Melqart) (Fig. 14), and thus as *the* civilizing force in the western Mediterranean. The Romans, in turn, showcased their own Hellenic connections through the myths that made them the heirs of the Trojans, so that Julius Caesar could choose to represent his alleged ancestor Aeneas on the back of his coins (Fig. 15).

The connection with the goddess of love is also apparent in the enterprise of philhellene emperor Hadrian, who dedicated the largest temple in Rome to Roma Aeterna and Venus Felix (Fig. 16). Two statues of the goddesses, seated back to back, divided the double temple, playfully representing the way in which the letters of the words ROMA-AMOR mirror each other. ✦

FIGURE 1 ✦ Osiris as king of the dead and first mummy. Wall painting in tomb of Pharaoh Horemheb. West Thebes, Egypt (end fourteenth century BCE, Eighteenth Dynasty).

FIGURE 2 ✦ A hare-looking cat or "solar cat," which is a form of Re, killing the sun-enemy Apophis under the persea tree of Heliopolis. Wall painting in tomb of Inherkha. Deir el-Medina, Thebes, Egypt (ca. 1186–1070 BCE, Twentieth Dynasty).

FIGURE 3 ✦ Scene with bull-man fighting a lion and hero fighting a bull, perhaps alluding to the exploits of Gilgamesh and Enkidu. Akkadian cylinder seal of lapis lazuli, from the Royal Cemetery of Ur, Iraq (ca. 2200–2100 BCE).

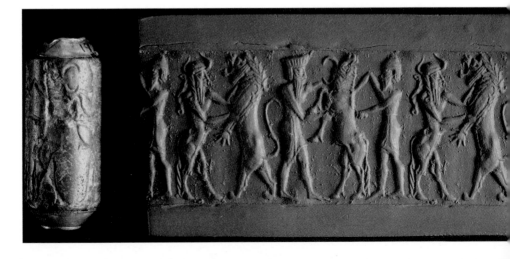

FIGURE 4 ✦ Clay mask of Humbaba (or Huwawa), the monster killed by Gilgamesh and Enkidu. From Sippar, southern Iraq (ca. 1800 to ca. 1600 BCE).

FIGURE 5 ✦ North-West Semitic Storm God Baal brandishing thunderbolt and mace. The sea and mountains appear schematized at the base, and a small figure (the king?) is represented under the god's arm. Limestone stele from the temple of Baal at Ugarit, Syria (Late Bronze Age).

FIGURE 6 ✦ Neo-Hittite Storm God (Tarhun) holding thunderbolt and hammer. Bas-relief in basalt stele from Babylon (ninth century BCE).

FIGURE 7 ✦
Assyrian statue
of a hero taming
a lion, probably
Gilgamesh.
From the palace
of Sargon II
(722–705 BCE)
in Khorsabad
(northern Iraq);
this was one of
several protective
figures flanking
the entrance to
the throne room.

FIGURE 8 ✦ Perseus slaying the Gorgo Medousa with the aid of Athena. Metope from archaic Greek Temple C at Selinous, Sicily (ca. 600–550 BCE).

FIGURE 9 ✦ Early Israelite drawing, perhaps of the figures of Yahweh and Asherah, next to lyre player and suckling calf. Painted on an ostracon from Kuntillet Ajrud (Sinai Peninsula) (ninth to eighth centuries BCE).

FIGURE 10 ✦ *(above)* Coin from Phoenician city of Sidon, with image of Emperor Hadrian (r. 117–138 CE) on one side and scene of "Rape of Europa" on the other; she sits on the bull (Zeus) holding a veil and the bull's horn.

FIGURE 11 ✦ Volute crater from Apulia, southern Italy, used as funerary dedication and depicting an Underworld scene. Hades, seated in his throne and accompanied by Persephone, shakes Dionysos' hand (fourth century BCE).

FIGURE 12 ✦ *(above)* Orphic Gold Tablet from Petelia (modern Strongoli), southern Italy. This is one of many such documents in Greek, buried with their owners and containing instructions for the afterlife journey (fourth century BCE).

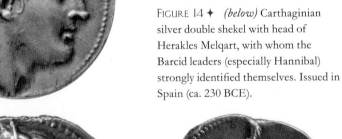

FIGURE 13 ✦ Tetradrachm of Alexander the Great represented with ram's horns as the Egyptian God Amon (ca. 300 BCE).

FIGURE 14 ✦ *(below)* Carthaginian silver double shekel with head of Herakles Melqart, with whom the Barcid leaders (especially Hannibal) strongly identified themselves. Issued in Spain (ca. 230 BCE).

FIGURE 15 ✦ Denarius of Julius Caesar (issued 47–46 BCE) depicting Aeneas carrying his father Anchises and the Palladium out of Troy, on one side, and Aeneas' mother Venus, on the other.

FIGURE 16 ✦ *(below)* Reconstruction of the interior of the temple dedicated to Venus and Roma in Rome, built by Emperor Hadrian in 135 CE. The back-to back statues of the goddesses reflected in art the (unwritten) pun between the words ROMA-AMOR.

LATE ANTIQUITY
TO THE PRESENT

✦

THE FOLLOWING IMAGES exemplify the wide range of contexts in which classical myths persisted in the post-classical and modern worlds, often with unexpected twists.

A mosaic from Syria (Fig. 17), probably from a Christian dwelling, represents the creation of humans. The Soul is carried into a human mould by a Prometheus-like figure (Hermes?), with Zeus, Hera, Athena, and Aion (Eternal Time) as witnesses. In Byzantine mosaics from Jordan, pagan motifs were prominent, in a region where the dominating monotheistic cultures appropriated Hellenic traditions: the floor of a house could show Aphrodite playfully spanking her son Cupid (Fig. 18), just above a scene of the tragic story of Phaedra and Hyppolytus.

Such passionate tales were the subject of mimes and plays in Christian Late Antiquity, as was the theme of Achilles "coming out" as a soldier after years passing for a girl at Skyros (Fig. 19). Classicism was "revived" in the Renaissance, when even churches were decorated with Greek-style naked figures. Michelangelo's downfall of Adam and Eve (Fig. 20), in turn, mirrors Hesiod's Five Races story, where humankind declines into an age of toil and isolation from the divine.

Monster-slaying and cosmic battles persisted in Neoclassical art, when Europe adopted classical symbols to represent rationality over ignorance and primitivism (Figs. 21 and 22). (Already in Archaic Athens, the Peisistratid tyrants used Theseus in their propaganda of progress and reform.) At the same time, the advent of archaeological discovery in Greece and the Near East in the late eighteenth and the nineteenth centuries led to the creation of museums in Europe and to such enterprises as the real-size replica of the Athenian Parthenon in Nashville, Tennessee (Fig. 22). The fight between Poseidon and Athena (Fig. 22) is deeply connected with Athenian identity, as even reflected in the opposite values that these gods represent in Plato's Atlantis Myth.

Classical characters also served as emblems of modern cultural identities: in New York, the rebellious Titan Prometheus was chosen in the 1930s as an icon of the technological progress and resourcefulness of America (Fig. 23). Finally, classical motifs have inspired modern artists, from Pablo Picasso to Cy Twombly. Most recently, Elliott Hundley has merged myth, visual art, and text in his monumental collage about Dionysos and his mother Semele (Fig. 24). ✦

FIGURE 17 ✦ The so-called "Prometheus mosaic" from Edessa, Syria, with scene of creation of humans and labels in Syriac (third century CE).

FIGURE 18 ✦ *(below)* Aphrodite spanks Cupid in a Byzantine mosaic, showing also Adonis, a Grace, and pla Erotes (lit. "Loves"). Floor of the "Hippolytus mansion" in Madaba, Jordan (sixth to seventh centuries CE).

FIGURE 19 ✦ Achilles, who had been hidden and disguised as a maiden at the island of Skyros, reveals himself as a soldier. Sculpted in the central medallion of a late Roman silver plate.

FIGURE 20 ✦ *(below)* Adam and Eve are banned from Eden, in one of the biblical scenes that decorate the Sistine Chapel in Rome. Fresco painted by Renaissance artist Michelangelo (early sixteenth century CE).

FIGURE 21 ✦ *(top left)* Neoclassical sculpture of Theseus slaying the Minotaur, by Étienne-Jules Ramey (1796–1852), in the Jardin des Tuileries, Paris.

FIGURE 22 ✦ *(bottom left)* Contest between Athena and Poseidon. Sculpted on the pediment of the Athenian Parthenon replica in Nashville, Tennessee (1897).

FIGURE 23 ✦ *(top right)* Paul Manship's statue of Prometheus stealing fire away from Zeus, at Rockefeller Center in New York (1934).

Figure 24 ✦ Detail of *The Lightning's Bride*, by Elliott Hundley, featuring Semele stricken by Zeus' lightning, with translations of the play by Euripides in the background (2011).

by to look for his flocks, set a light to it.[307] On him Herakles bestowed his bow. While the pyre was burning, it is said that a cloud passed under Herakles and with a peal of thunder wafted him up to heaven.[308] Thereafter he obtained immortality, and being reconciled to Hera he married her daughter Hebe, by whom he had sons, Alexiares and Aniketos.

(2.7.8, skipped here, lists a long catalogue of the children of Herakles by different women.)

(Sons of Herakles and fate of Eurystheus)

(2.8.1) When Herakles had been transported to the gods, his sons fled from Eurystheus and came to Keyx.[309] But when Eurystheus demanded their surrender and threatened war, they were afraid, and, quitting Trachis, fled through Greece. Being pursued, they came to Athens, and sitting down on the altar of Mercy, claimed protection. Refusing to surrender them, the Athenians bore the brunt of war with Eurystheus, and slew his sons, Alexander, Iphimedon, Eurybios, Mentor, and Perimedes. Eurystheus himself fled in a chariot, but was pursued and slain by Hyllos just as he was driving past the Skironian cliffs; and Hyllos cut off his head and gave it to Alkmene; and she gouged out his eyes with weaving-pins.

(2.8.2–5 account for the deeds of the descendants of Hillos—called Herakleidai—in their "return" and conquest of main cities of the Peloponnese.)

3.11.c. Theseus

Theseus was a legendary king of Athens who can best be defined as the Herakles of Attica. He provides an Ionian counterpart to the tradition by which the Dorians claimed descent from Herakles. Considered a historical figure by the Greeks (as were the Trojan War and most other heroic characters and events), Theseus' exploits fall into two different categories. First, there are the heroic fights with monsters and human adversaries modeled on those of Herakles: besides the general idea of heroic fights, both heroes battle Centaurs and Amazons, they both wrestle with the Marathonian bull (Cretan bull in Herakles, who brought it to Attica), and they both visit the Underworld. Furthermore, advances of a cultural and political nature are attributed to Theseus anachronistically, such as unifying Attica around Athens (*synoikismos*) and establishing a proto-democratic state, as narrated in Plutarch's *Life of Theseus* (Part 4, document 11).

The hero's life runs chronologically parallel to that of Herakles as well as to the saga of the slightly older Argonauts, since Medea appears as the companion of Theseus' father after being separated from Jason. All of these are traditionally situated one generation before the Trojan War. The popularity and

---

[307] According to a less famous version, Herakles was tortured by the poisoned robe and flung himself into a neighboring stream to ease his pain, where he drowned. The waters of the stream have been hot ever since and are called Thermopylae ("Hot Gates").

[308] In Diodorus' account (4.38.4), when Herakles' friends came to collect his bones they could find none and supposed he had been transported to the gods. The notion that fire separates the immortal from the mortal element in man is also present in other stories, especially that of Demeter's attempt to make baby Demophoon immortal (see Part 6, document 8).

[309] The king of Trachis who had given shelter to Herakles.

representation of Theseus in Attica, however, dates to the sixth century BCE, not before (unlike Herakles' earlier preeminence in the area). At that time, he was promoted and used politically as part of the propaganda of the Peisistratid tyrants (Peisistratos and his sons Hippias and Hipparchos), who used him to legitimize their own reforms and building projects in Attica. Later Athenian political figures also exploited the popularity of the Athenian hero, as when Kimon in 475 BCE orchestrated the recovery of Theseus' bones from the island of Skyros, following an oracle and thus linking the newly acquired Athenian dominion over the island to the Athenian heroic past. The bones were brought to Athens and were believed to be located at the fifth-century BCE temple of Hephaistos in the Agora, after some point renamed Theseion. Unlike Herakles, Theseus, Perseus, and other heroes never become gods. However, like other many heroes, Theseus received heroic honors (or "hero cult"), even though the two categories of worship are not always distinct: he was associated with the establishment of various rites and had in fact his own yearly festival (the *Theseia*), besides a specially dedicated day every month (the same dedicated to Poseidon, his father), as well as several shrines around Attica.

The Theseion exemplifies the hero's popularity in art, as a cycle of his exploits was part of the decorative reliefs, which also featured the labors of Herakles and other famous battles. The treasury of the Athenians at Delphi also features Theseus, and the motif of his adventures, especially his fight with the Minotaur, became a favorite artistic theme throughout antiquity, manifested in sculpture, painting, and mosaics (see Figure 21).

(3.15.6) After the death of Pandion[310] his sons marched against Athens, expelled the Metionids, and divided the government in four; but Aigeus had the whole power.[311] The first wife whom he married was Meta, daughter of Hoples, and the second was Chalkiope, daughter of Rhexenor. As no child was born to him (i.e., to Aigeus), he feared his brothers, and went to Pythia (i.e., Delphi) and consulted the oracle concerning the begetting of children. The god answered him:

> The bulging mouth of the wineskin, O best of men, loose not until you have reached the height of Athens.

Not knowing what to make of the oracle, he set out on his return to Athens.

(3.15.7) And journeying by way of Troizen, he lodged with Pittheus, son of Pelops, who, understanding the oracle, made him drunk and caused him to lie with his daughter Aithra. But in the same night Poseidon also had contact with her. Now Aigeus charged Aithra that, if she gave birth to a male child, she should rear it, without telling whose it was; and he left a sword and sandals under a certain rock,

---

[310] This was Pandion II, son of Kekrops II (descendants from the legendary founding kings of Athens). Pandion had been banished by the seditious sons of Metion (called Metionids).

[311] Aigeus was one of the sons of Pandion, begotten at Megara during Pandion's exile, during which he had married the local princess (Pylia) and become king of the city.

saying that when the boy could roll away the rock and take them up, she was then to send him away with them.[312]

But he himself came to Athens and celebrated the games of the Panathenaian festival, in which Androgeus, son of Minos, vanquished all comers. Him Aigeus sent against the bull of Marathon, by which he was destroyed. But some say that, as he journeyed to Thebes to take part in the games in honor of Laios,[313] he was ambushed and murdered by the jealous competitors. But when the tidings of his death were brought to Minos, as he was sacrificing to the Graces in Paros, he threw away the garland from his head and stopped the music of the flute, but nevertheless completed the sacrifice; hence down to this day they sacrifice to the Graces in Paros without flutes and garlands.

(3.15.8) But not long afterwards, being master of the sea, he attacked Athens with a fleet and captured Megara, then ruled by king Nisos, son of Pandion, and he slew Megareos, son of Hippomenes, who had come from Onchestos to the help of Nisos.[314] Now Nisos perished through his daughter's treachery. For he had a purple hair on the middle of his head, and an oracle ran that when it was pulled out he should die; and his daughter Skylla fell in love with Minos and pulled out the hair. But when Minos had made himself master of Megara, he tied the maiden by the feet to the stern of the ship and drowned her.

When the war lingered on and he could not take Athens, he prayed to Zeus that he might be avenged on the Athenians. And the city being visited with a famine and a pestilence, the Athenians at first, in obedience to an ancient oracle, slaughtered the daughters of Hyakinthos, namely, Antheis, Aegleis, Lytaia, and Orthaia, on the grave of Geraistos, the Cyclops; now Hyakinthos, the father of the girls, had come from Lakedaimon and dwelt in Athens. But when this was of no avail, they inquired of the oracle how they could be delivered; and the god answered them that they should give Minos whatever satisfaction he might choose. So they sent to Minos and left it to him to claim satisfaction. And Minos ordered them to send seven youths and the same number of maidens without weapons to be fodder for the Minotaur.[315] Now the Minotaur was confined in a labyrinth, in which he who entered could not find his way out; for many a winding turn shut off the secret outward way. The labyrinth was constructed by Daidalos, whose father was Eupalamos, son of Metion, and whose mother was Alkippe[316]; for he was an excellent architect and the first inventor of images. He had fled from Athens, because he had thrown down from the acropolis Talos, the son of his sister Perdix; for Talos was his pupil, and Daida-

---

[312] To prove his descent from Poseidon, Theseus is said by other sources to have dived into the sea and brought up a golden crown, the gift of Amphitrite, together with a golden ring, which Minos had thrown into the sea in order to test his claim to be a son of the Sea God.

[313] Laios was the father of Oedipus, and the allusion here is to his funerary games, which like all heroic funerals comprised athletic games and other festive events such as music and poetry contests.

[314] Paus. 1.39.5 calls Megareus a son of Poseidon and says that Megara took its name from him.

[315] The Minotaur was born to Minos' wife, Pasiphae, as mentioned later (see Part 5, documents 9.a, 9.b, and 9.c).

[316] Sources generally agree in relating Daidalos to the Metionid royal house of Athens, and some make him a cousin of Theseus.

los feared that with his talents he might surpass himself, seeing that he had sawed a thin stick with a jawbone of a snake which he had found. But the corpse was discovered. Daidalos was tried in the Areopagus,[317] and being condemned fled to Minos. And there Pasiphae having fallen in love with the bull of Poseidon, Daidalos acted as her accomplice by contriving a wooden cow, and he constructed the labyrinth, to which the Athenians every year sent seven youths and as many maidens to be fodder for the Minotaur.

(3.16.1) Aithra bore to Aigeus a son Theseus, and when he was grown up, he pushed away the rock and took up the sandals and the sword,[318] and hastened on foot to Athens. And he cleared the road, which had been beset by evildoers. For first in Epidaurus he slew Periphetes, son of Hephaistos and Antikleia, who was surnamed the Clubman from the club which he carried. For being weak on his legs he carried an iron club, with which he dispatched the passers-by. That club Theseus wrested from him and continued to carry about. [3.16.2] Second, he killed Sinis, son of Polypemon and Sylea, daughter of Korinthos. This Sinis was surnamed the Pine-bender; for inhabiting the Isthmos of Corinth he used to force the passersby to keep bending pine trees; but they were too weak to do so, and being tossed up by the trees they perished miserably. In that way also Theseus killed Sinis.

(Continuation of Theseus' life in Apollodorus' Epitome *1.1–24)*

(E.1.1) Third, he slew at Krommyon the sow that was called Phaia after the old woman who bred it[319]; that sow, some say, was the offspring of Echidna and Typhon.

(E.1.2) Fourth, he slew Skeiron, the Corinthian, son of Pelops, or, as some say, of Poseidon. He in the Megarian territory held the rocks called after him Skeironian, and compelled passers-by to wash his feet, and in the act of washing he kicked them into the deep to be the prey of a huge turtle. (E.1.3) But Theseus seized him by the feet and threw him into the sea.

Fifth, in Eleusis he slew Kerkyon, son of Branchos and a nymph Argiope. This Kerkyon compelled passers-by to wrestle, and in wrestling killed them. But Theseus lifted him up on high and dashed him to the ground.

(E.1.4) Sixth, he slew Damastes, whom some call Polypemon. He had his dwelling beside the road, and made up two beds, one small and the other big; and offering hospitality to the passers-by, he laid the short men on the big bed and hammered them, to make them fit the bed; but the tall men he laid on the little bed and sawed off the portions of the body that projected beyond it.[320]

---

[317] The Areopagus (Gr. Areiopagos) was a special court of eleven judges who tried murder of family members (in this case Daidalos murdered his nephew). Its institution is the theme of Aeschylus' *Eumenides*, when Orestes is judged by the new court after the murder of his mother, Klytaimnestra.

[318] The tokens that Aigeus had left for him, so he could recognize him as his son.

[319] Hyginus (*Fab.* 38) calls the animal a boar. No ancient writer but Apollodorus mentions the old woman Phaia who nursed the sow, but she appears on vase paintings showing the slaughter of the sow by Theseus.

[320] This malefactor was also called Prokroustes (by Ovid, for instance). In another version, he had only one bed, to which length he would adjust each of his victims.

So, having cleared the road, Theseus came to Athens.

(E.1.5) But Medea, then wedded to Aigeus,[321] plotted against him and persuaded Aigeus to beware of him as a traitor. And Aigeus, not knowing his own son, was afraid and sent him against the Marathonian bull. (E.1.6) And when Theseus had killed it, Aigeus presented to him a poison, which he had received the same day from Medea. But just as the drink was about to be administered to him, he gave his father the sword, and on recognizing it Aigeus dashed the cup from his hands. And when Theseus was thus made known to his father and informed of the plot, he expelled Medea. (E.1.7) And he was numbered among those who were to be sent as the third tribute to the Minotaur; or, as some affirm, he offered himself voluntarily. And as the ship had a black sail, Aigeus charged his son, if he returned alive, to spread white sails on the ship.

(E.1.8) And when he came to Crete, Ariadne, daughter of Minos, being amorously disposed to him, offered to help him if he would agree to carry her away to Athens and have her as wife. Theseus having agreed on oath to do so, she besought Daidalos to disclose the way out of the labyrinth. (E.1.9) And at his suggestion she gave Theseus a thread when he went in; Theseus fastened it to the door, and, drawing it after him, went in. And having found the Minotaur in the last part of the labyrinth, he killed him by smiting him with his fists; and drawing the thread after him made his way out again. And by night he arrived with Ariadne and the children[322] at Naxos. There Dionysos fell in love with Ariadne and carried her off[323]; and having brought her to Lemnos he enjoyed her, and begat Thoas, Staphylos, Oinopion,[324] and Peparethos.

(E.1.10) In his grief on account of Ariadne, Theseus forgot to spread white sails on his ship when he stood for port; and Aigeus, seeing from the acropolis the ship with a black sail, supposed that Theseus had perished; so he cast himself down and died.[325] (E.1.11) But Theseus succeeded to the sovereignty of Athens, and killed the sons of Pallas, fifty in number[326]; likewise all who would oppose him were killed by him, and he got the whole government to himself.

(E.1.12) On learning about the flight of Theseus and his company, Minos shut up the guilty Daidalos in the labyrinth, along with his son Ikaros, who had been born to Daidalos by Naukrate, a female slave of Minos. But Daidalos constructed wings for himself and his son, and commanded his son, when he took to flight, neither to fly high, lest the glue should melt in the sun and the wings should drop off, nor to fly near the sea, lest the pinions should be detached by the damp. (E.1.13) But the

---

[321] Medea (Gr. Medeia) had arrived in Greece from Colchis with Jason after the Argonauts' adventure but ended up taking asylum in Athens under Aigeus' protection (see Part 5, document 6).

[322] That is, the boys and girls brought from Athens to be sacrificed.

[323] For Theseus and Ariadne, see also Part 5, documents 10.a and 10.b.

[324] Staphylos and Oinopion are said by others to be sons of Theseus and Ariadne, although their names are related to grapes (*staphyle*) and wine (*oinos*), and hence to Dionysos.

[325] Latin authors thought the Aegean Sea was called after him. He was thought to have jumped from the Akropolis of Athens (though it is not on the sea) or at Cape Sounion.

[326] Pallas was the brother of Aigeus, so a cousin of Theseus, who had a claim to the throne until Theseus appeared.

infatuated Ikaros, disregarding his father's orders, soared ever higher, till, the glue melting, he fell into the sea called after him Ikarian, and perished.[327] But Daidalos made his way safely to Kamikos in Sicily.

(E.1.14) And Minos pursued Daidalos, and in every country that he searched he carried a spiral shell and promised to give a great reward to him who should pass a thread through the shell, believing that by that means he should discover Daidalos. And having come to Kamikos in Sicily, to the court of Kokalos, with whom Daidalos was concealed, he showed the spiral shell. Kokalos took it, and promised to thread it, and gave it to Daidalos; (E.1.15) and Daidalos fastened a thread to an ant, and, having bored a hole in the spiral shell, allowed the ant to pass through it. But when Minos found the thread passed through the shell, he realized that Daidalos was with Kokalos, and at once demanded his surrender. Kokalos promised to surrender him, and made an entertainment for Minos; but after his bath Minos was dissolved by the daughters of Kokalos; some say, however, that he died through being drenched with boiling water.[328]

(E.1.16) Theseus joined Herakles in his expedition against the Amazons and carried off Antiope, or, as some say, Melanippe; but Simonides calls her Hippolyte. Wherefore the Amazons marched against Athens, and having taken up a position about the Areopagus they were vanquished by the Athenians under Theseus.[329] And though he had a son Hippolytos by the Amazon, (E.1.17) Theseus afterwards received from Deukalion[330] in marriage Phaidra, daughter of Minos; and when her marriage was being celebrated, the Amazon that had before been married to him appeared in arms with her Amazons, and threatened to kill the assembled guests. But they hastily closed the doors and killed her. However, some say that she was slain in battle by Theseus.

(E.1.18) And Phaidra, after she had born two children, Akamas and Demophon, to Theseus, fell in love with the son he had by the Amazon, namely, Hippolytos, and besought him to lie with her. However, he fled from her embraces, because he hated all women. But Phaidra, fearing that he might accuse her to his father, cleft open the doors of her bed-chamber, rent her garments, and falsely charged Hippolytos with an assault. (E.1.19) Theseus believed her and prayed to Poseidon that Hippolytos might perish. So, when Hippolytos was riding in his chariot and driving beside the sea, Poseidon sent up a bull from the surf, and the horses were frightened, the chariot dashed in pieces, and Hippolytos, entangled in the reins, was dragged to death. And when her passion was made public, Phaidra hanged herself.[331]

---

[327] See the Pasiphae and Minotaur story in documents included in Part 5, document 9.

[328] Lit. "he became unfastened/undone/unnerved" or the like (Frazer translates "was undone" where I translate "was dissolved").

[329] The battle against the Amazons was a popular artistic motif, famously represented in the metopes of the Parthenon at Athens, alongside other mythical battles between gods and giants, Centaurs and Lapiths, and Greeks and Trojans.

[330] This Deukalion was a son of Minos (brother of Paidra), not the Deukalion of the Flood story.

[331] For this story, see also Part 5, document 11. This tragedy was the subject of Euripides' *Hippolytos* and Seneca's *Phaedra*.

(E.1.20) Ixion[332] fell in love with Hera and attempted to force her; and when Hera reported it, Zeus, wishing to know if the thing were so, made a cloud in the likeness of Hera and laid it beside him; and when Ixion boasted that he had enjoyed the favors of Hera, Zeus bound him to a wheel, on which he is whirled by winds through the air; such is the penalty he pays. And the cloud, impregnated by Ixion, gave birth to Kentauros.[333]

(E.1.21) And Theseus allied himself with Peirithoos, when he engaged in war against the Centaurs. For when Peirithoos wooed Hippodameia,[334] he feasted the Centaurs because they were her kinsmen. But being unaccustomed to wine, they made themselves drunk by swilling it greedily, and when the bride was brought in, they attempted to violate her. But Peirithoos, fully armed, with Theseus, joined battle with them, and Theseus killed many of them.

(E.1.22) Caeneus was formerly a woman, but after Poseidon had intercourse with her, she asked to become an invulnerable man; wherefore in the battle with the Centaurs he thought scorn of wounds and killed many of the Centaurs; but the rest of them surrounded him and by striking him with fir trees buried him in the earth.[335]

(E.1.23) Having planned with Peirithoos that they would marry daughters of Zeus, Theseus, with the help of Peirithoos, carried off Helen from Sparta for himself, when she was twelve years old, and in the endeavor to win Persephone as a bride for Peirithoos he went down to Hades. And the Dioskouroi,[336] with the Lakedaimonians and Arcadians, captured Athens and carried away Helen, and with her Aithra, daughter of Pittheus, into captivity; but Demophon and Akamas fled. And the Dioskouroi also brought back Menestheus from exile, and gave him the sovereignty of Athens.[337]

(E.1.24) But when Theseus arrived with Peirithoos in Hades, he was beguiled; for, on the pretence that they were about to partake of good cheer, Hades bade them first be seated on the Chair of Forgetfulness, into which they grew and were held fast by coils of serpents. Peirithoos, therefore, remained bound forever, but Herakles brought Theseus up and sent him to Athens. Thence he was driven by Menestheus and went to Lykomedes, who threw him down an abyss and killed him.[338]

---

[332] King of the Lapiths, a tribe in Thessaly, and father of Peirithoos, companion of Theseus.

[333] According to Pindar (*Pythian Ode* 2), Kentauros (Centaur) then engendered the Centaurs' race by mating with mares in Mount Pelion. The Centaurs are also called *Ixionidai* after Ixion (Kentauros' father).

[334] Not the Hippodameia whom Pelops married, but another one.

[335] On Caeneus (Gr. *Kaineus*) and his change of gender, see also Part 5, document 18.

[336] In other words, Kastor and Polydeukes (Lat. Castor and Pollux), sons of Leda with Zeus and brothers of Helen.

[337] Menestheus was a descendant of Erechtheus, hence of the Athenian royal family. Other sources also say he was given the throne by the Dioskouroi in the absence of Theseus.

[338] Lykomedes was the king of the island of Skyros, in whose court Achilles was hidden by Thetis, on which see Part 5, document 19.

PART 4 ✦ OF CITIES
AND
PEOPLES

> For it is easier, Timaeus, to seem to speak satisfactorily about the gods to other men, than (to speak) about mortals to us . . . (Plato, *Kritias* 107a–b).

✦

WITH THIS STATEMENT in Plato's dialogue, Kritias hopes to win over the favor of his audience (among whom is Socrates) as he sets out to describe how the ideal state would work in practice (see his account, the Atlantis myth, in Part 7, document 3). Unlike Timaeus before him, Kritias will be speaking about human beings, not gods. As he contends, this is a much more demanding subject to examine because audiences know more about human affairs than about the gods. In this way, the variety, specificity, and disparity of narratives increase as the myths progress from being less about purely divine actions (cosmogonies) and more about human beings (anthropogonies) and the origins of their communities (foundation stories). In the case of foundation stories, there must have been as many stories as there were communities, both big and small, only a few of which have reached us. Of all the thematic strands woven throughout this volume, the "foundation stories" thread is the one that most finely divides myth from history. In this part are stories about the foundations of cities, first leaders of communities, and religious founders. With roots in ahistorical times ("long ago"), and embodying divine and fantastic elements, these stories are still semi-mythical or "legendary," to use a different term. At the same time, in some cases there is no doubt that they are initially based on real events, magnified and adapted into the conventions of mythical narratives with the passing of time (e.g., Cyrus, the foundation of Cyrene).

The stories in this fourth section include narratives that range from physical foundations of cities, such as Thebes by Kadmos and the colony of Cyrene by Battos, to political restructuring of an existing city or state, such as the reforms attributed to Theseus in Attica. In the Hebrew Bible, by contrast, we see the establishment of religious "pacts" with a single God and the restoration of a people to a state of freedom, establishing new religious and territorial expectations. Genealogies occupy a crucial place in these community narratives as well, even though they are not included in this volume. Long passages in the Hebrew Bible focus on the offspring of such main figures as Noah, Abraham, Isaac, and Jacob. In Greek and Roman tradition long genealogies connecting important families with ancestral heroes and even gods were also passed down. In archaic Greece, the division of Greek speakers among three dialectal groups—Ionian, Dorian, and Aiolian—was explained in genealogical terms and associated with cultural differences. The most famous of these lines is the one connecting the Dorians to the "return of the Herakleidai," that is, the descendants of Herakles to the Peloponnese. The connection of the Julian family in Rome with Aeneas and hence Venus herself is another good example.

In contrast to the genealogies that connect families or a whole people to an incoming, migrating, legendary figure are the myths of autochthony (already discussed in the introduction of Part 2). The story of Kadmos and Europa and the foundation of Thebes combines both types of narrative, since Theban elites considered themselves the descendants of the Phoenician prince and in turn the population was born from the Spartoi, the warriors born from the earth itself.

Conflict lies at the heart of numerous narratives that concern the birth of new communities. In the family nucleus, the theme of fratricide (killing of a brother) looms over the foundational periods of the Israelite and the Roman peoples, as the stories of Cain and Abel and Romulus and Remus show. In Greece, the same brotherly conflict stains the early history of Thebes in the mutual fratricide of Eteokles and Polyneikes, sons of Oedipus, most famously evoked in the play of Aeschylus, *Seven Against Thebes*. Even Abraham's near-sacrifice of his son evokes the possibility of family murder, albeit within the framework of human sacrifice and with different motivations.

On a larger scale, war and destruction appear frequently in Genesis. Some examples (not all of which are included here) are the destruction of mankind by the Flood (on which see Part 2), the divine scattering of a prospering civilization in the story of Babel, the targeted destructions of Sodom and Gomorrah (Gen. 19), and the divine attack on the Egyptian oppressors in Exodus. The destruction of other peoples during the Israelite conquest of the land in the historical books of the Bible also fit into a legendary narrative inseparable from the emergence of the Israelite people and their distinct identity among the Canaanites.

The rise and destruction of an entire civilization is also at the center of the Atlantis story by Plato (Part 7, document 3), in which Atlantis and an idealized primitive Athens are pitted against each other as opposite socio-political models.

The Hittite "Song of Release" (document 4.2) and the Greek story of the Trojan War preserve motifs of divinely wrought destruction of historical Bronze Age cities, namely Ebla in Syria and Troy in Asia Minor. In the case of Troy and the stories of the Trojan Cycle, this legendary "international war" turned into a foundational myth for all Greeks as their first common enterprise. Most likely based upon Late Bronze Age historical events, Homer's account was later understood as poetically elaborated and exaggerated by the historians Herodotos and Thucydides, who still never doubted the historicity of the war itself and incorporated it into their narratives about the pre-history of the Greeks. Moreover, the Trojan War story soon traversed Greek cultural boundaries and was adopted by Romans and other peoples in contact with the Hellenic milieu. The heroes returning from Troy (e.g., Aeneas and Diomedes, the part of the cycle called *Nostoi*, "Returns") became useful instruments for the inclusion of other peoples into the heroic world. In a separate and extremely popular group of myths, the figure of Herakles served a similar purpose, as his wanderings allowed peoples around the Mediterranean to connect themselves to the prestigious Hellenic heroic milieu.

Other foundational stories provide an *aition* for particular aspects of civilization and culture. Linguistic diversity (the Babel story) has already been mentioned, and the beginning of professions or guilds is represented in the Bible at different points: Cain and Abel appear as the first farmer and the first shepherd, respectively; the descendants of Lamech (Gen 4.20–22) are connected to the division of labor among husbandry, metal working, and arts/music; and Noah appears as the first vine cultivator ("Noah, a man of the soil, was the first to plant a vineyard"; Gen. 9.20). In Greece, stories that serve as *aitia* of cultural features also abound. The story of Prometheus' double deceit of Zeus (Hesiod's *Theogony* 535–569; see Part 1, document 5) establishes the origins of animal sacrifice and the acquisition (or retention) of fire; the myth of Demeter's search for her daughter (see *Hymn to Demeter* in Part 6, document 8) explains not only the natural phenomenon of the seasons and agriculture but the foundation of the Eleusinian Mysteries. Other professions also have their mythical origins, such as the story of Arachne (preserved in Ovid's elaboration), the Athenian first waver, to mention just one. The story of Adapa (mentioned in Part 2) is a good example of the cultural hero, the first of the seven antediluvian sages of Mesopotamia, to whom their tradition ascribed the arts of civilization. In Philon of Byblos' *Phoenician History* (Part 1, document 7.a) we have also a list of first inventors (in Greek *protoi heuretai*).

Another recurring theme, represented in several stories here, is that of the leader's birth and miraculous survival to fulfill his destiny. Moses, Sargon, Cyrus, Oedipus, Romulus, and Jesus all share this pattern. Independent of the historicity or lack thereof of each character, their childhood narratives follow certain heroic patterns, which were noted in the nineteenth and early twentieth century by scholars such as Thomas Carlyle (*On Heroes, Hero-Worship, and the Heroic in History*, 1841), Otto Rank (*The Myth of the Birth of the Hero*, 1909; in English 1914), and Lord Raglan (*The Hero: A Study in Tradition, Myth, and Drama*, 1936). The role of the early lawgiver is intertwined with these foundational narratives as well. We have only to look to Moses in Israel and, in later times, to Greece to such historical figures as Solon in Athens and Lykourgos in Sparta, whose lives were to a degree "heroized" and mythologized.

Colonization stories, represented in this part by the sources concerning Cyrene, also share a narrative pattern. The main recurring features are the alleged civil/social conflict in the motherland, the instructions and authorization given by the oracle at Delphi, and the initial failed approach to the new land, whereby the colonists use an island as a gateway and later settle on the mainland. Examples not included here are the foundation of Gadir (Cádiz in southern Spain) by Phoenicians (Strabo 3.5.5), that of Taras (Tarentum in southern Italy) by men expelled from Sparta (Strabo 6.3.2), and the foundation of Pithekoussai and Cumae in the Bay of Naples by Euboians (Strabo 5.4.9, 5.4.4), with a strong Semitic presence in its early stages, as shown by archaeological and epigraphical sources. ✦

4.1. THE FOUNDATION OF A HELIOPOLIS TEMPLE BY SENUSERT I

This Egyptian text was written on a leather roll during the mid-Eighteenth Dynasty (ca. 1400 BCE), but, according to several scholars, it could be a copy of an older composition written during the reign of Senusert I (ca. 1956–1911 BCE), from the Twelfth Dynasty. Similar, though less well-preserved, compositions connected to temple foundations were carved during the same reign on the walls of sanctuaries in Karnak, Elephantine, and Tod. Consequently, the Berlin leather roll could be a copy of a similar inscription, currently lost, which would have been carved on a temple at Heliopolis. There is, in fact, abundant evidence of intense building activity by Senusert at Heliopolis (modern el-Matariya district in Cairo).

The text is an example of the so-called *Königsnovelle* (literally "kings-novellas," or royal romance) subgenre. The features of this kind of narrative are very heterogeneous and flexible. Generally speaking, tales of this genre depict the king making an important decision (constructing a building, military actions, etc.) in front of his retinue. He usually expresses his intention through direct speech, including a self-eulogy, which is approved or, in some instances, contested by his officials by means of another speech that, again, is a royal eulogy.[1] Finally, the royal intention—often inspired by a divinity—prevails and is successfully accomplished. Moreover, these compositions were usually intended to be displayed (in the form of inscriptions) at a specific public location.

SOURCE: Berlin Leather Roll (*Pap. Berlin* 3029, I,1–II,19), translated and annotated by A. Diego Espinel.

Year 3, third month of the *ak[het]*-season, day [8], under the majesty of the Dual King Kheperkare, [the son of re] Senwosret (I), justified, may he live for ever eternally. Appearance of the king wearing the double-crown. A sitting happened in the hall; a consultation with his entourage, the companions of the palace, l.i.h., and the officials of the private apartments; a speech after hearing it; a consultation to instruct them: "Look, my majesty is ordering a work, conscious that it will be an example of excellence in the future. I will make a monument and I will establish durable decrees for the sake of Horakhty,[2] because he begot me in order to do what he has done; in order to cause what he has ordered to come into existence. He has created me in order to be the shepherd of this land, because he knew that I would organize it for him. He has offered me what he guards, what the eye which is inside him illuminates. I will act in every respect according to what he wants, as I have acquired (?) what he has ordered to be known.

"I AM a king because of his creation, a sovereign, l.i.h., who was not appointed (initially as king). As a fledgling, I took (it). I was (already) a notable in the egg. I administered as a hereditary prince. He enriched me until I became Yahweh of the

---

[1] The initial setting of the *Book of the Heavenly Cow* (see Part 2, document 2.b) adopts many features from this subgenre.

[2] Horakhty or "Horus of the two horizons" is the form of the sun god Re as morning sun.

two portions of Egypt while I was an uncircumcised boy. [He] appointed me to become Yahweh of plebeians, and a manifestation in front of the sun-people. He raised me in order to be the one inside the palace as a child, when I hadn't come out from the thighs (of my mother). Its length and width [were given to me]. I have been nursed in order to become a conqueror. The land has been given to me, I am its possessor. I have reached the pow[ers] of the highest part of the sky. Why is it excellent to act for the one who has acted? God will appease when he is given [. . .] [I am] his son, his [protec]tor. He has ordered me to conquer what he conquered.

"I COME AS HORUS. I HAVE ASSESSED MY PROPERTY. I have established the offerings for the gods, and I have created works in the Great Domain of my father Atum.[3] He will permit to broaden himself as he has permitted my [achieve]ment. I will provide his offering tables over the land and [I] will erect my domain in his neighborhood. My benevolence will be remembered in his house, an obelisk (*pyramidion*) will be [my] name, a channel will be my monument. Achieving excellence is eternity. A king who is mentioned because of his deeds cannot die. Assistants are not necessary (lit. "known") when he plans for himself, as his name proclaims the discourse(s) and action(s) related to them (i.e., "his deeds"). Matters of eternity won't perish, as what will exist is what is done; effectiveness i[s] what has to be sought. [A name] is an able provision, it is watchful on matters of eter[nity]."

THEN, THESE king's COMPANIONS SAID, and they answered to their god: "Hu is <in> your mouth and Sia is [wi]th you![4] O sovereign, l.i.h., what is happening is your plan: the royal appearance as the unifier of the Two Lands for the stre[tching the cord] in your temple.[5] It is well regarded to look to the future as something effective for (your) lifetime. The crowd cannot accomplish anything without Yahweh, as your majesty, l.i.h., is the eyes of everyone. It is great that you make your monuments in Heliopolis, the shrine of the gods, before your father, Yahweh of the Great Domain, Atum, the bull of the Ennead of gods. Build your domain, and provide the offering stone. It will generate the revenues for the image which is inside, and for your statues through endless time."

THE king HIMSELF SAID: "*bit-s*eal bearer, sole companion, overseer of the Two Houses of [gold] and the Two Houses of silver, privy of the secrets of the Two Crowns! It is your counsel that will allow [all] the works that my majesty desires to be made. You will be their master therein, who will act according to my desire. Skill [is strength] and watchfulness. It will come into being (only) without feebleness. All the tasks belong to the [ac]complished person. He who puts in effectiveness is Yahweh of achievements. Your hour is a time for doing [. . .] according to your needs in orders and matters. Ma[ke] the place, the creation of that which is desired! Order the workers to work according to what you have ordained."

---

[3] The Great Domain is the temple of Atum in Heliopolis, a city that lies principally in the el-Matariya suburb, northeast of Cairo, where Senusert I's obelisk (the al-Masalla obelisk) is still standing.

[4] On Hu and Sia, see note 35 in *Coffin Texts* spell 80 in Part 1, document 3.b.

[5] The stretching of the cord formed part of the Egyptian temple foundation ritual, as can be also observed in the last lines of the text.

Appearance of the king wearing the double crown and all the plebeians around him; the chief lector priest and scribe of the divine book were stretchi[ng] the cord; a rope was loose and put on the ground, tracing the aforementioned domain.[6] Then his majesty covered (it), and the king turned himself back in front of the workers gathered together, Upper and Lower Egypt, who are flourishing on earth. (...) (?)

4.2. THE HURRO-HITTITE *SONG OF RELEASE* (DESTRUCTION OF THE CITY OF EBLA)

The Hurro-Hittite *Song of Release* was discovered during excavations in Hattusa in 1983 and 1985. The text was presented in a bilingual format on the tablets, with the Hurrian version in columns i and iv and the Hittite version in columns ii and iii. The sign forms and the language of the Hittite version show that the tablets were inscribed during the Middle Hittite period, the early fourteenth century BCE. Repetitions and parallels among the fragments suggest that there was more than one version or recension. It does not appear to have been a popular text in scribal circles, however, since it was not recopied in later times. The relationship between the Hurrian and Hittite versions remains under debate, namely, whether the Hittite version is simply a translation of the Hurrian and, if so, whether the translation was done by a scribe or the singer mentioned in the explanatory closing lines (colophons) of two of the tablets. Another possibility is that the two versions are the product of an oral poet who could perform in both Hurrian and Hittite.

The discovery of the *Song of Release* was a momentous event for scholars interested in the history of the epic genre in the eastern Mediterranean, providing another important parallel to Greek epics. The story tells of the destruction of the Syrian town of Ebla (Tell Mardikh), overseen by the Storm God, because its assembly, against the advice of their king, Meki, refuses to release the people of the town Ikinkalis, who are serving the assembly members. Thus, the plot has similarities to that of the *Iliad*, in which Troy is destroyed because of the failure to return Helen. More specifically, we learn from glancing references to events before the start of the war that the Trojan assembly, swayed by bribes from Paris, had refused to return Helen to a Greek embassy (*Il.* 3.204–224, 11.122–142). Moreover, the opening scenes of the *Iliad*, which create the motivation for Achilles' refusal to fight, retell in a nutshell the same plot, with the request to return a female captive (Chryseis), backed by a god (Apollo). When the request is refused, the god sends a plague on the Achaeans. Likewise, the praise of Zazalla, best speaker in the assembly in the *Song of Release*, matches descriptions of excellent speakers in the *Iliad*, such as Thoas (*Il.* 283–4) and Diomedes (*Il.* 9.54–56). There are also parallels between the *Song of Release* and the Hebrew Bible, specifically Leviticus 25.10 and 26 and Jeremiah 34.

There are still major divergences of opinion on the sequence of events and the overall point of the story. Three sections must belong to the sto-

---

[6] These were the initial stages in the erection of a building and formed part of temple foundation rituals.

ryline, because their colophons state they belong to the *Song of Release*: the proem, which mentions the Storm God, the Syrian goddess Ishhara, and a human named Pizikarra; a meeting in the palace of the Underworld Goddess (Hurrian Allani, the Hittite Sun Goddess of the Earth) with the Storm God (Hurrian Teshub, Hittite Tarhun), his brother Suwaliyatt, and the Former Gods; and the story that takes place in Ebla, involving the Storm God, a man named Purra, the Eblaite king Meki, and an important speaker in assembly named Zazalla. Also found with these tablets and parallel fragments are two more tablets and quite a few small fragments containing parables. Many argue that the parables do not belong to the *Song of Release* at all. The parables are included here, however, with further discussion of their possible relationship with the Ebla storyline. The fragments are presented in one possible logical order, which creates one specific overall meaning for the text, but other orders, which would create different messages for the *Song of Release*, are certainly possible.

It is not evident from the text why the Storm God is interested in Purra and the other people of Ikinkalis and steps in to demand their release, threatening to visit destruction on Ebla if the assembly does not comply and promising prosperity and victory for the town if they do. A new interpretation is proposed here, namely, that Purra and the other people of Ikinkalis are meant to be serving the cult of the nine dead kings of Ebla, and it is the task of Meki, the tenth king, to ensure his ancestors receive their due, for the prosperity of his kingdom depends on their goodwill and intercession in the Underworld. Other solutions have been presented to explain why Purra is described as serving nine kings, with Meki as the tenth: for example, they are regional kings all alive at the same time, or Purra has a supernaturally long life span.

We do not know how this text arrived at Hattusa. Many scholars now accept that it could have been recited in Anatolia as far back as the Old Hittite period, when the first great Hittite king, Hattusili I, was fighting the Hurrians to the south and east of Hatti, ca. 1600 BCE. Indeed, either Hattusili or his grandson (adopted son) Mursili appears to have been responsible for the destruction of Ebla (Tell Mardikh stratum IIIb), although there is no strong reason to assume that this event, as opposed to one of the earlier destructions of the town, is the one mythologized in the song.

SOURCE: Hurro-Hittite *Song of Release*, edition of Neu (1996), translated and annotated by M. Bachvarova. Unless otherwise noted, the Hittite version is translated here (CTH 789). All texts come from KBo 32, which stands for *Keilschrifttexte aus Bogazköi*, one of the two main series that publishes hand copies of the tablets (on the numbering system for Hittite texts; see longer explanation in III. Part 3, document 4, page 136).

The First Tablet

(The beginning of column i on the obverse is preserved, along with the end of column iv on the reverse [in Hurrian], with the colophon [in Hittite]. The opening appears to mention the principal antagonists, including one human, Pizikarra. The back side presents a conversation between the Storm God, Teshub, of the city Kummi, and the Syrian goddess Ishhara, apparently setting the stage for the attack on Ebla.)

(KBo 32.11 i 1–3) I shall sing of Teshub, p[owerful] lord of Kummi. I shall exalt the young w[oman], the doorbolt of the earth, Alla[ni].

(i 4–6) And along with them I shall tell of the young woman Ishhara, the word-mak[er,] famous for wisdom, goddess.

(i 7–9) I shall tell of Pizikarra . . . E[bla . . .] who (will) bring [. . .] Pizikarra des[troy . . .] (from?) Nuhashe,[7] and Ebla [. . .]

(i 10–13) *(Mostly incomprehensible. Pizikarra, the Ninevan,[8] is mentioned, and the action of binding, along with "to the gods.")*

(i 14–18) *(Incomprehensible except for "to Teshub.")*

(i 19–20) *(Only a few signs visible.)*

(Column i breaks off before paragraph end. A gap of approximately 50 lines follows. On the reverse, a dialogue between Teshub and Ishhara closes the first tablet. Although little of the beginning of the passage is comprehensible, the pronoun "I" appears, someone is not listening, and the topic is freeing. Ishhara mentions the request of another person, perhaps the request for freedom on the part of the people of Ikinkalis, while Teshub discusses the future destruction of Ebla with her.)

(iv 12'-15') Ish[hara s]ays words to [Te]shub. S/he asks, ask[s . . .] . . . Ishhara asks, ask[. . . " . . .] I shall give [. . . ."]

(iv 16'-21') Tesh[ub says] words to Ishhara, "And [n]ow des[troy] Ebla [. . .] . . . Ishhara [. . .] he will destroy. Who . . . them/it [. . .] Ishhara. Ebla . . . them [. . .]. And, the countries are destroyed, destroy[ed . . . "]

(Colophon)

(iv 22') First tablet of the Song [of] Release o[f . . .]

Messenger Scene

(In the following fragment, in which only the Hittite version is preserved, the Storm God, roused from bed by a messenger, talks with his brother Suwaliyat and sends him to Ebla to discuss something with Ishhara. In the Kumarbi Cycle, *messengers are typically sent to demand that a god make a visit to the messenger's master to discuss a problem, so it is likely that a similar situation occurs here. It is not known where in the narrative this scene belongs, but it could be part of the action that leads to Teshub and Ishhara's meeting in which they have the conversation preserved in column iv of KBo 32.11.)*

(KBo 32.37 4'-7') [. . .] in the night [. . . . E]arly in the morning [. . .] message rep[ort- . . . Tarh]un aro[se] from his bed [. . .]

(8'-11') [sw]iftly he crossed [. . .] And Tarhun [. . .] release (obj.) [. . . " . . . l]et go!" And, Tarhun [began] t[o] speak [words] t[o Suwal]iyat.

(12'-19') "[. . .] loyal Suwaliyat, hold [your ear c]locked! Swiftly go to the city of the throne,[9] and go [to the house] of Ishhara. You go and stress these wo[rds in] front of [Ishhara . . .] I, far away, you be[fore . . .] you . . . I [will] bring [. . .]. Call [. . .] to you!"

---

[7] Nuhashe was an area in north Syria.

[8] Nineveh was the home city of the Hurrian goddess Shawushka, who was syncretized with Ishtar.

[9] Ebla.

Allani's Feast in the Underworld

(The meeting between the Storm God and the Sun Goddess of the Earth [Hurr. Allani] in her underworld palace may come next, again following the trajectory found in other Hurro-Hittite narrative songs, in which one meeting leads to another meeting to continue the discussion of a problem. According to my interpretation, the Storm God goes to the Underworld to discuss the problem of the captivity of the people of Ikinkalis, because the Underworld gods are interested in the fate of the dead kings whom the people of Ikinkalis should be caring for. Indeed, Ishhara, who is connected to the Former Gods, that is, the earlier generation of gods, could have been the one to suggest the meeting. This tablet preserves most of the obverse, but only fragments of the reverse.)

(KBo 32.13 ii 1–8) When Tarhun went, he went inside the palace of the Sun Goddess of the Earth. His throne [was X]. When Tarhun the king went in from outside, Tarhun sat aloft on a throne the size of an field of an IKU,[10] and he raised his feet on a stool of the size of a field of seven *tawalla*s.

(ii 9–14) Tarhun and Suwaliyat went under the dark earth. The Sun Goddess of the Earth girded herself up. She turned before Tarhun. She made a fine feast, the doorbolt of the earth, the Sun Goddess of the Earth.

(ii 15–20) She slaughtered 10,000 oxen before great Tarhun. She slaughtered 10,000 oxen. She slaughtered 30,000 fatty-tailed sheep, and there was no counting for those kids, lambs, and billy goats, she slaughtered so many.

(ii 21–27) The bakers prepared (food) and the cup-bearers came in, [wh]ile the cooks set forth the breast meat. They brought them (the pieces) with bowls [. . .]. The time of eating arrived, and Tarhun sat to eat, while she seated the Former Gods to Tarhun's right.

(ii 28–34) The Sun Goddess of the Earth before Tarhun stepped like a cup-bearer. The fingers of her hand are long, and her four fingers lie below the cup, and the drinking-vessels with which [she gives] to drink, inside them lies goodness.

(The column breaks off before paragraph end. The back side of the tablet is very damaged. We can pick out "they [d]ivide (the food?)," "when it was di[vid]ed," and "in front of Tarhun s/he stood [u]p." The next paragraph opens with the name of the Storm God, then a second singular verb form shows the passage is in direct speech, probably produced by Tarhun, then the Sun Goddess of the Earth appears as the subject and, "b[owing, began] t[o s]peak." The colophon is partially preserved, showing that the song is attributed to a singer: "[. . .] Release [. . .] sing[er] not finished.")

Events in Ebla

According to the interpretation offered here, a discussion among the gods about the plight of the deceased kings of Ebla, who are not receiving the veneration that is their due, leads to the decision to threaten the Eblaite assembly with the destruction of their city. However, it is unknown how the Storm God first made contact with the Eblaite king Meki. Perhaps a negative omen or other sign incites Meki to find out the state of mind of the Storm God. Or perhaps Purra receives a sign and approaches Meki, leading to a meeting between the three of

---

[10] One IKU = 15 meters, but its value as a measurement of area is unknown.

them. According to my interpretation, the Storm God first speaks directly to the king, then the king goes to the assembly to convey his threats, repeating them word for word. Meki, as the representative of the Storm God, is comparable to the Hebrew Bible prophets who utter the word of God but are often ignored. He bears a name that is known to have belonged to a nineteenth-century ruler of Ebla (cf. West Semitic *mlk*, "king," as in Ugaritic *milku*, Hebrew *melekh*).

This section of the *Song of Release* begins in the middle of the conditional threats of the Storm God. KBo 32.20 contains some of the beginning of the god's demand, but unfortunately only the Hurrian side is preserved, leaving the highly repetitious passage nearly incomprehensible. From the scattered words and phrases we can discern in the passage, we know that the god mentions a set of kings, whose names are Hurrian, two of them compounds with "Ebla": Aribibla, "who gave Ebla," and Paibibla, "who built Ebla" (which means they must be kings of Ebla and not regional kings outside Ebla, as some scholars have postulated). In column i on the obverse we can pick out, for example, "for eighteen/eighty years," "they brought as king Paibibla to the throne," and "in the eighteenth/eightieth year," and then the next king is introduced, so it seems that we are hearing about a series of kings' reigns, with comments on Purra interspersed. I suggest that Purra and the others care for the ancestor cult of the dead kings, a duty that would include remembering their names and some facts about each of their reigns. In between, we learn about something "of Purra," "with a gift," "loosing" (a verb), and Teshub, "lord of Kummi," as an agent in the sentence. In column iv on the reverse side, there is mention of "giving to a lord" and of a "female slave," and we learn that "Teshub knows."

Then we segue into the following passage translated from KBo 32.19, with KBo 32.22 used to fill in some *lacunae*. Somehow Purra and other servants are involved with a series of kings of Ebla, and the Storm God has taken notice of the situation.

(KBo 32.19 ii 1–4) "Re[lease in goodwill] the sons of the city Ikinkal, and release [especial]ly [Purra], the o[ne] to be given back, who [give]s to eat [to the nine kin]gs.

(ii 5–10) "[And,] Ikin[kalis in the city of the throne gav]e [to eat] to three kings. B[ut], (in) Ebla, [in the city of the throne he] ga[ve] to eat [t]o six kings. But, now he, T[arhun, gets] u[p] before [y]ou, [Mek]i.[11]

(ii 11–15) "If [you (pl.) make] re[lease] in Ebla, [the city of the throne,] if you [make] r[elease, I will] exalt your weapons like [X].

(ii 16–19) "Your [weapons] alone will begin [t]o [defeat] the enem[y], [while] your plowed fiel[ds will go and thrive for you] in prai[se.]

(ii 20–23) "Bu[t] if y[ou] don't [ma]ke release in [Eb]la, in the city of the throne, then (when it is) the seventh da[y], I will come to you, yo[urse]lves.

(ii 24–26) "I will destroy the ci[ty] of Ebla. As if it had n[ever] been settled, so I will make it! (ii 27–31) "I will smash the [lower] walls of the city of Ebla like a c[up]. And, I will trample the upper wall [li]ke a clay pit!"

---

[11] The Hurrian version specifies that Meki is the tenth king (i 9–10).

(The tablet becomes too fragmentary for continuous translation, but discernable is: "[bef]ore (him) he speaks" (ii 45), marking the end of the speech. Although the speaker of these words is not mentioned in the remains of the tablet, it can be surmised that it is Tarhun arguing on behalf of Purra, who seems to be the leader of the people of Ikinkalis, as Purra stands before Meki, the tenth king of Ebla.

We next pick up the action in Ebla in KBo 32.16, of which only the Hittite side is decipherable. Zazalla, a particularly renowned speaker in assembly, who bears a name known from the third-millennium archives at Ebla, is introduced responding antagonistically to the king.)

(KBo 32.16 ii 1–5, KBo 32.59 1'-4') [. . . there is no one] who speaks against him [. . .] among the elders, there is no one who speaks against him. [There is no] one who makes a response to him. [No] on[e] talks.

(KBo 32.16 ii 6–10, KBo 32.54 6'-10') But [i]f there is one who speaks greatly in [the ci]ty, [whose wo]rds no one turns aside, Zazalla is the one who speaks greatly. In the place of assembly, his words [n]o one overcomes.

(KBo 32.16 ii 11–13) [Zazal]la began [t]o speak to Meki, "Why [do you] speak obeisance, star of Ebla, Me[ki . . .]?"

(The rest of KBo 32.16 is very damaged, but KBo 32.15 runs parallel to KBo 32.16 ii 17–iii 18', which is used here to fill in the lacunae *of KBo 32.15. Here Zazalla [or another member of the anti-release party] rebuts the words of Meki, arguing that if Tarhun were in want, each would contribute whatever he might need; if someone were depriving the god, the Eblaites would mitigate the god's suffering. He acknowledges that even a god can suffer like a human. But under no circumstances will he agree to releasing the people of Ikinkalis. The king then speaks in front of the Storm-god again, the deity possibly represented as a baetyl.)*

(KBo 32.15 ii 4'-6a') "[If Tar]hun is injured by oppression and he [a]sks [for release], if Tarhun is [o]ppressed, each will g[i]ve Tarhun [one shekel of sil]ver.

(ii 7'-9') "[Ea]ch will give half a shekel [of gold], [w]e [will each give] him [one shekel] of silver. But, if he, Tarhun, is hungry, we will each give one measure of barley [to the g]od.

(ii 10'-13') "[Ea]ch will pour a half measure of wheat, [a]nd each will pour for him one measure of barley. But if [Tarhun] is naked, we will each clothe him with a fine garment. The god is (like) a person.

(ii 14'-17') "But, if he, Tarhun, is cursed, each of us will give him one *kupi*-vessel of fine oil, we will (each) pour out for him fuel, and we will free him from deprivation. The god is (like) a person.

(ii 18'-21') "We will rescue him, Tarhun the oppressed. He who harms him, we will not make him a release. Does your mind rejoice inside you, Meki?

(ii 22'-25') "First of all, your heart will not rejoice inside you, Meki, while, secondly, inside Purra, who is to be given back, his mind will <not> rejoice.

(ii 26'-29') "In the case we let those ones go, who will give to us t[o] eat? They are cupbearers for us, and they give out to us. They are cooks for us, and they wash for us.

(iii 1–4) "And, the thread which they spin is [thick] like the hair [of an ox.] But, if for you releasing [is desirable,] re[lease] your male and female servants!

(iii 5–7) "Surrender your son! Send [. . . your] wife! With u[s . . .] on the throne in the city, Me[ki . . .]"

(iii 8–11) When Mek[i] he[ard] the word, he b[eg]an to wail. [He] wai[ls . . .], Meki. He [di]d obeisance a[t] the feet of [T]arhun.

(iii 12–14) Meki, bowing to Tarhun, spoke the words, "[L]isten to me, Tarhun, great ki[n]g of Kummi,

(iii 15–20) "I will g[i]ve it, (i.e.,) compensation, but my [c]ity will not give i[t]. Nor will Zazalla, son of Pazz[anik]arri give, relea[se]." Meki (tried to?) purify his ci[ty] from sin, the [ci]ty of Eb[la]. He (tried to?) throw aside the sins for the sake of his city.

(iii 21–24) [. . .] Because the great king of Kummi [. . .] the great king of Kummi, [. . .]. Before the stone [. . .]

(iii 25'-26') *(Only a few signs remain.)*

(Colophon)

(left edge) Fifth tablet of Release, no[t finished.]

(Another fragment seems to fit into the narrative around this point or a bit later in the action on the human plane. It begins with a direct speech, which could be either by a human or a god, but it is likely that the speaker is human, because he appears to be on a different plane than the Sun God, the all-seeing shepherd and administrator of justice, who [looks?] down from the sky.)

(KBo 32.10 ii 1–3) [" . . . the lan]d of Lulluwa[12] [. . . let] not good, let not [. . .] let him/it not find [X]."

(ii 4–6) [. . .] shepherd of all [. . .] from the sky Istanu [. . .] began [to do X].

(ii 7–10) [. . .] the great king of [Kumm]i [. . .] slay[. . . the land of L]ulluwa [. . .] not [. . .]

(The obverse breaks off before paragraph end.)

(iii 2'-7') [. . .] Piz[ikarra . . .] in pr[ison . . .] bound to the stone. God [X] of Kummi, god [Y] has bound the destruction of Purra to the basalt stone.

(It appears, then, that Purra lost his life in the course of the story. I suggest the stone mentioned here is a baetyl of the Storm God. Pizikarra also appears in another fragment in which destroying in the third person is mentioned: "Pizi- . . . / he destroyed . . . / he injured . . . " (KBo 32.32 right col. 3'–5'). Pizikarra seems to be the human agent of the city's destruction.)

The Parables

Two tablets (KBo 32.12 and KBo 32.14), each containing a series of parables, were found spilled out of the same large jar that contained the fragments of the *Song of Release*. How the parables could fit into the *Song of Release* and even whether they belong to that narrative has been a matter of dispute. Both preserve the end of the tablet, where a colophon could be inscribed, but only one of them (KBo 32.12) contains a mostly lost colophon. It is possible to reconstruct it as follows: "second tablet (of the Song) [o]f R[elease], not finished," although this has been disputed. However, this tablet cannot follow directly on KBo 32.11. Those who wish to include the parables in the *Song of Release* must assume KBo 32.11 and 12 each belong to different versions of the text. Others prefer to simply exclude the parables from the narrative altogether. It is true that if an entire tablet of parables were included in the narrative, it would be a major digression in the action.

---

[12] Lullu(wa) is a semi-mythical land to the north of Mesopotamia.

There is no clear place for the parables in the preserved narrative, nor are we told who is telling these tales, which are described as "wisdom" (Hurr. *madi*, Hitt. *hattatar*). I suggest that Ishhara, described as "the word-mak[er,] famous for wisdom" in the proem, is the speaker, and that she tells the tales to illustrate the consequences of the behavior of the Eblaite assembly, who fail to obey their king and the Storm God. Besides the general thematic parallels between the parables' message and the point of the *Song of Release*, there is one specific link, the fate of the insubordinate cup, which is smashed by the Storm God in KBo 32.14, just as the god threatens to smash Ebla like a cup (KBo 32.19 ii 27–31); these passages have parallels with Isaiah 29.16, 45.9; Jeremiah 18.6. A cup is the protagonist in the last parable of KBo 32.12 as well, but the story (fragmentary and in Hurrian) is different than that in KBo 32.14.

Only one tablet (KBo 32.14), which is well preserved, is translated here. For reasons having to do with the layout of the text in the tablet and the lack of a colophon, it has been considered to be a draft, rather than final copy. The final parable, concerning a woodpile, which represents an ungrateful apprentice, is very fragmentary, so a composite of the Hurrian and Hittite versions is presented here, with words of unknown meaning represented by question marks.

(KBo 32.14 ii 1–16) A mountain expelled a deer fro[m its] own body. The deer we[nt] forth to another mountain, and he got fat. He became rebellious, and he began to curse the mountain in return, "On which mountain I graze, if only fire would burn it up, and Tarhun would strike it! If only fire would burn it up!" And, when the mountain heard, his heart was sickened inside him, and the mountain cursed the deer in return, "The deer whom I fattened, now he curses me in return. Let the hunters also bring him, the deer, down, and let the bird catchers take him! His fat let the hunters take, and his hide let the bird catchers take!"

(ii 17–21) But, it is not a deer. That one is a man, a man who ran away from his city and arrived at another land. When he became rebellious, he began to plot evil in return against the city, so the gods of the city have cursed him.

(ii 23–25) Leave aside that word; I will tell you another word. List[e]n to the message, and I will tell you wisdom.

(ii 26–30) There was a deer – the meadows which were on the side of a river, those ones he grazes, but which meadows are on the far side, he keeps placing his e[yes] on those also. He did not arrive at the meadows on (that) side, nor did he reach anything.

(ii 31–38) But, it is not a deer. That one is a man, a man whom his lord makes a borderland commander. They made him borderland commander in one district, but he keeps placing his eyes on a second district. The gods impressed upon that man wisdom, so he did not arrive at that district, nor did he reach a second district.

(ii 39–41) Leave aside that word; I will tell you another word. Listen to the message, and I will tell you wisdom.

(ii 42–51) A smith cast a cup for glory; he cast it and stood it up. He set it with ornamentation. He engraved it. He made it shine with brilliance. But, the one who cast it, him the foolish copper beg[an] to curse in return, "If only he who cast me, his han[d] would break off, and his right tendon would wither away!" When the smith heard, his heart was sickened inside him.

(ii 52–60) The smith began to speak before his heart, "Why does the copper which I poured curse me in return?" The smith said a curse against the cup, "Let Tarhun also strike it, the cup, <let> him wrench off its ornaments. Let the cup fall into the canal, and let the ornaments fall into the river."

(iii 1–5) It is not a cup. That one is a man, a son who is an enemy before his father. He grew up, and he reached maturity, and he was no longer paying attention to his father, (he is one) whom the gods of his father have cursed.

(iii 6–8) Leave aside that word; I will tell you another word. Listen to the message, and I will tell you wisdom.

(iii 9–12) A dog pulled out a *kugulla*-bread from an oven. He dragged it forth from the oven, and he drenched it in oil. He drenched it in oil, and he sat down, and he began to eat it.

(iii 13–19) It is not a dog. He is a man whom his lord makes district commander. He increased the collecting of taxes in that city afterwards, and he became very rebellious, and he was no longer paying attention to the city. They were able to report him before his lord, and the taxes that he had swallowed he began to pour out before his lord.

(iii 20–22) Leave aside that word; I will tell you another word. Listen to the message, and I will tell you wisdom.

(rev. 28–32) [A p]ig(?) pulls forth a *kugulla*-bread from an oven. He dragged [it] forth from the oven, and he drenched [it] in oil. He drenched it in oil, and he sat down, and he began to eat it. It is [not a p]ig (?). He is a man whom his lord makes the commander of a land. He increased the collecting of taxes in that [city] afterwards, and he became very rebellious, and he was no longer [paying attention] to the city. They were able to report him before his lord, and the taxes that he had swallowed he began to pour out before his lord.

(rev. 34) Leave [as]ide that word; I will tell you another w[or]d. Listen to the message, and I will tell [yo]u wisdom.

(rev. 41–47) [A craftsman] built a tower for glory. Its excavation trenches reached down to the Sun Goddess of the Earth, and [its bat]tle[ments] reached up close to heaven. But, the one who built it, him the fooli[sh wall] began to curse in return, "He who built me, if only his hand would bre[a]k off, [a]nd his [right] tendon would wither away!" The craftsman heard, and his heart f[elt] bad inside him. [The craftsman] says before his mind, "Why does the tower which I built curse me?" The craftsman spoke a curse [against the tower], "Let Tarhun also strike it, the tower, let him pull up its foundations. Let [X] fall down into the canal, and let the brickwork fall down into the river."

(rev. 50–52) [It is not] a tower. That one is a man, a son who is an enemy before his father. He grew up, and [he] reached to (the age of) [s]ense, and he was no longer paying attention to his father, and the gods of his father [ ] have cursed him.

(rev. 54) [L]eave [aside] that [w]ord; I will tell you another word. Listen to the message, and I will tell you wisdom.

(rev. 55–65, lower edge 66–71, left edge 1–7) *(Hurrian version:)* [W]ood [. . .] a saw [. . .] the one who places (it) [. . .] so that [. . .] struck (it) repeatedly, so that a donkey transported (it). The [r]aiser stacked the woodpile near a canal. (Its) base ?-ed the [ea]rth below; (its) ? ?-ed them (to) heave[n] above. The [fo]olish wood cursed the one who erected (it), "If only I could brea[k] the hand of the one who stacked me, and I could [paral]yze his right hand within." The raiser, hearing, w[as] sickened on his inside. The raiser said, he spoke to his [i]nside, "Why does the wood which was raised by me keep cursing me?" The raise[r] said a [curs]e against the wood. *(Combining the Hittite and Hurrian versions:)* "Let [Tarhun] also strike it, [the wood . . .]. Let the roots (?) fall into the canal, and [let] the leaves [be] scattered into the water. It is not wood, it is a man. He is an apprentice (?). He ?-ed. He grew up, and he reached to (the age of) sense, and he ?-es his master. [. . .]. He will die in [. . .]. Lik[e] a dog [. . .] under a [ch]air he will die [. . .].

4.3. CAIN AND ABEL: GENESIS 4

This passage follows the Eden story in Genesis (see Part 2, document 3). It is interesting to note that it belongs to the Jahwistic redaction, but it is followed by an alternate Priestly account of the descendants of Adam until Noah (Gen. 5), which does not include Cain and Abel and which precedes the Flood. The Cain and Abel genealogy, on the contrary, does not lead to Noah and does not anticipate the Flood. Notice, for instance, that in Genesis 4.17 Cain goes on to marry, which presumes the existence of other people, so the brothers' story might not have been initially about the first descendants of Adam and Eve.

SOURCE: The Hebrew Bible, Genesis 4, New Revised Standard Version, with minor modifications.

(1) Now the man knew his wife Eve, and she conceived and bore Cain, saying, "I have produced a man with the help of Yahweh." (2) Next she bore his brother Abel. Now Abel was a keeper of sheep, and Cain a tiller of the ground. (3) In the course of time Cain brought to Yahweh an offering of the fruit of the ground, (4) and Abel for his part brought of the firstlings of his flock, their fat portions. And Yahweh had regard for Abel and his offering, (5) but for Cain and his offering he had no regard. So Cain was very angry, and his countenance fell. (6) Yahweh said to Cain, "Why are you angry, and why has your countenance fallen? (7) If you do well, will you not be accepted? And if you do not do well, sin is lurking at the door; its desire is for you, but you must master it."

(8) Cain said to his brother Abel, "Let us go out to the field." And when they were in the field, Cain rose up against his brother Abel and killed him. Then Yahweh said to Cain, (9) "Where is your brother Abel?" He said, "I do not know; am I my brother's keeper?" (10) And Yahweh said, "What have you done? Listen; your brother's blood is crying out to me from the ground! (11) And now you are cursed from the ground, which has opened its mouth to receive your brother's blood from your hand. (12) When you till the ground, it will no longer yield to you its strength; you will be a fugitive and a wanderer on the earth." (13) Cain said to Yahweh, "My punishment is greater than I can bear! (14) Today you have driven me away from the soil, and I shall be hidden from your face; I shall be a fugitive and a wanderer on the earth, and anyone who meets me may kill me." (15) Then Yahweh said to

him, "Not so! Whoever kills Cain will suffer a sevenfold vengeance." And Yahweh put a mark on Cain, so that no one who came upon him would kill him. (16) Then Cain went away from the presence of Yahweh, and settled in the land of Nod, east of Eden.

(17) Cain knew his wife, and she conceived and bore Enoch; and he built a city, and named it Enoch after his son Enoch. (18) To Enoch was born Irad; and Irad was the father of Mehujael, and Mehujael the father of Methushael, and Methushael the father of Lamech. (19) Lamech took two wives; the name of one was Adah, and the name of the other Zillah. (20) Adah bore Jabal; he was the ancestor of those who live in tents and have livestock. (21) His brother's name was Jubal; he was the ancestor of all those who play the lyre and pipe. (22) Zillah bore Tubal-cain, who made all kinds of bronze and iron tools. The sister of Tubal-cain was Naamah.

(23) Lamech said to his wives: 'Adah and Zillah, hear my voice; you wives of Lamech, listen to what I say: I have killed a man for wounding me, a young man for striking me. (24) If Cain is avenged sevenfold, truly Lamech seventy-sevenfold.'

(25) Adam knew his wife again, and she bore a son and named him Seth, for she said, "God has appointed for me another child instead of Abel, because Cain killed him." (26) To Seth also a son was born, and he named him Enosh. At that time people began to invoke the name of Yahweh.

4.4. THE TOWER OF BABEL: GENESIS 11

The story of the Tower of Babel follows the Flood story and the account of the genealogies of the descendants of Noah and the peoples who populated the earth after the flood (the so-called Table of Nations in Gen. 10). The story explains the dispersion of peoples into groups with different languages, hence undermining their capacity to unite their strength and become too powerful. The theme echoes the previous preoccupation of God and the different solutions he implemented in the Eden and Flood episodes, all connected by the emphasis on the necessary boundaries between human beings and God. As has been noticed, the dispersion of peoples would best fit the narrative preceding the Table of Nations in Genesis 10.

SOURCE: The Hebrew Bible, Genesis 11, New Revised Standard Version, with minor modifications.

(1) Now the whole earth had one language and the same words. (2) And as they migrated from the east, they came upon a plain in the land of Shinar and settled there. (3) And they said to one another, "Come, let us make bricks, and burn them thoroughly." And they had brick for stone, and bitumen for mortar. (4) Then they said, "Come, let us build ourselves a city, and a tower with its top in the heavens, and let us make a name for ourselves; otherwise we shall be scattered abroad upon the face of the whole earth." (5) Yahweh came down to see the city and the tower, which mortals had built. (6) And Yahweh said, "Look, they are one people, and they have all one language; and this is only the beginning of what they will do; nothing that they propose to do will now be impossible for them. (7) Come, let us go down,

and confuse their language there, so that they will not understand one another's speech." (8) So Yahweh scattered them abroad from there over the face of all the earth, and they left off building the city. (9) Therefore it was called Babel, because there Yahweh confused the language of all the earth; and from there Yahweh scattered them abroad over the face of all the earth.

4.5. ABRAHAM'S TEST, FROM GENESIS 22

Yahweh's promises and instructions to Abraham, beginning in Genesis 12.1–3, are the first given to the three major Israelite patriarchs (Abraham, Isaac, and Jacob). In the following passage, Yahweh tests Abraham by asking him to sacrifice his son Isaac to him. Besides being his only son, Isaac had been miraculously born from an aging barren Sarah. The sacrifice of first-born children is generally associated with barbaric Canaanite practices in the Hebrew Bible and in classical sources with Carthaginian culture. The discovery in Punic sites of separate infant cemeteries dedicated to the gods Tanit and Baal Hammon has fueled the debate about the reality of such practices. Be that as it may, in the Abraham story the sacrifice is presented as an exceptional and painful act.

SOURCE: The Hebrew Bible, Genesis 22.1–18, New Revised Standard Version, with minor modifications.

(1) After these things God tested Abraham. He said to him, "Abraham!" And he said, "Here I am." (2) He said, "Take your son, your only son Isaac, whom you love, and go to the land of Moriah, and offer him there as a burnt-offering on one of the mountains that I shall show you."[13] (3) So Abraham rose early in the morning, saddled his donkey, and took two of his young men with him, and his son Isaac; he cut the wood for the burnt-offering, and set out and went to the place in the distance that God had shown him. (4) On the third day Abraham looked up and saw the place far away. (5) Then Abraham said to his young men, "Stay here with the donkey; the boy and I will go over there; we will worship, and then we will come back to you." (6) Abraham took the wood of the burnt-offering and laid it on his son Isaac, and he himself carried the fire and the knife. So the two of them walked on together. (7) Isaac said to his father Abraham, "Father!" And he said, "Here I am, my son." He said, "The fire and the wood are here, but where is the lamb for a burnt-offering?" (8) Abraham said, "God himself will provide the lamb for a burnt-offering, my son." So the two of them walked on together.

(9) When they came to the place that God had shown him, Abraham built an altar there and laid the wood in order. He bound his son Isaac, and laid him on the altar, on top of the wood. (10) Then Abraham reached out his hand and took the knife to kill his son. (11) But the angel of Yahweh called to him from heaven, and said, "Abraham, Abraham!" And he said, "Here I am." (12) He said, "Do not lay your hand on the boy or do anything to him; for now I know that you fear God, since you have not withheld your son, your only son, from me." (13) And Abraham

---

[13] The episode is traditionally situated in Jerusalem.

looked up and saw a ram, caught in a thicket by its horns. Abraham went and took the ram and offered it up as a burnt-offering instead of his son. (14) So Abraham called that place "Yahweh will provide"; as it is said to this day, "On the mount of Yahweh it shall be provided."

(15) The angel of Yahweh called to Abraham a second time from heaven, (16) and said, "By myself I have sworn, says Yahweh: Because you have done this, and have not withheld your son, your only son, (17) I will indeed bless you, and I will make your offspring as numerous as the stars of heaven and as the sand that is on the seashore. And your offspring shall possess the gate of their enemies, (18) and by your offspring shall all the nations of the earth gain blessing for themselves, because you have obeyed my voice."

4.6. THE ISRAELITES' ESCAPE FROM EGYPT, FROM THE BOOK OF EXODUS

Exodus is the second book of the Torah or Pentateuch, following Genesis. Its name comes from the Greek *exodos aigyptou*, "exit from Egypt," but the Hebrew name is *Shemot* ("names"), following the tradition of naming books by their opening words ("These are the names . . . "). The book of Exodus (and by extension the whole Pentateuch) was attributed to Moses, given his central role in the story and some allusions to his writing "the words of Yahweh" (e.g., Ex. 24.4). However, like the other books of the Torah, the book is the result of many traditions woven together into its present form. Elements from all four main sources of the Pentateuch (Jahwistic, Elohistic, Priestly, and Deuteronomistic) are present and intricately merged in Exodus.

Exodus continues the Genesis narrative of the patriarch Jacob (son of Isaac, son of Abraham) and his sons, among whom was Joseph, who had been abandoned by his siblings and had become an officer of Pharaoh in Egypt. After the reunion of the brothers, they and Jacob (also known as Israel) settled in Egypt following God's advice (Gen. 46.3–4, 46.8). Exodus narrates the salvation of the Israelites who lived in Egypt some generations after Joseph. The Israelites' growth and prosperity had turned the new Pharaoh against them, beginning an era of oppression. Through the leadership of Moses, the god of the Israelites frees the enslaved people and leads them into the wilderness, where Yahweh makes a covenant with them (represented in the Ten Commandments) and leads them toward the promised land of Israel. The book of Exodus thus establishes crucial themes in Jewish (and later Christian) religion, such as the redemption of the oppressed and the commitment of God to his chosen people (expressed in a series of covenants with Abraham, Isaac, Jacob, and Moses), and institutes the tradition of the Passover (commemorating the escape from Egypt).

The excerpt here follows the nine "wonders" or plagues sent by God to the Egyptians (bloody waters, frogs, gnats, etc.). The tenth one is a plague that will take the lives of all firstborn animals and children of the Egyptians, after which the Israelites will leave, led by Moses.

SOURCE: The Hebrew Bible, Exodus 1–2.15 and 12.29–14.31, New Revised Standard Version, with minor modifications.

(Oppression of the Israelites and birth of Moses)

Exodus 1. (1) These are the names of the sons of Israel who came to Egypt with Jacob, each with his household: (2) Reuben, Simeon, Levi, and Judah, (3) Issachar, Zebulun, and Benjamin, (4) Dan and Naphtali, Gad and Asher. (5) The total number of people born to Jacob was seventy. Joseph was already in Egypt. (6) Then Joseph died, and all his brothers, and that whole generation. (7) But the Israelites were fruitful and prolific; they multiplied and grew exceedingly strong, so that the land was filled with them.

(8) Now a new king arose over Egypt, who did not know Joseph. (9) He said to his people, "Look, the Israelite people are more numerous and more powerful than we. (10) Come, let us deal shrewdly with them, or they will increase and, in the event of war, join our enemies and fight against us and escape from the land." (11) Therefore they set taskmasters over them to oppress them with forced labor. They built supply cities, Pithom and Rameses, for Pharaoh. (12) But the more they were oppressed, the more they multiplied and spread, so that the Egyptians came to dread the Israelites. (13) The Egyptians became ruthless in imposing tasks on the Israelites, (14) and made their lives bitter with hard service in mortar and brick and in every kind of field labour. They were ruthless in all the tasks that they imposed on them.

(15) The king of Egypt said to the Hebrew midwives, one of whom was named Shiphrah and the other Puah, (16) "When you act as midwives to the Hebrew women, and see them on the birthstool, if it is a boy, kill him; but if it is a girl, she shall live." (17) But the midwives feared God; they did not do as the king of Egypt commanded them, but they let the boys live. (18) So the king of Egypt summoned the midwives and said to them, "Why have you done this, and allowed the boys to live?" (19) The midwives said to Pharaoh, "Because the Hebrew women are not like the Egyptian women; for they are vigorous and give birth before the midwife comes to them." (20) So God dealt well with the midwives; and the people multiplied and became very strong. (21) And because the midwives feared God, he gave them families. (22) Then Pharaoh commanded all his people, "Every boy that is born to the Hebrews you shall throw into the Nile, but you shall let every girl live."

Exodus 2. (1) Now a man from the house of Levi went and married a Levite woman. (2) The woman conceived and bore a son; and when she saw that he was a fine baby, she hid him for three months. (3) When she could hide him no longer she got a papyrus basket for him, and plastered it with bitumen and pitch; she put the child in it and placed it among the reeds on the bank of the river. (4) His sister stood at a distance, to see what would happen to him.

(5) The daughter of Pharaoh came down to bathe at the river, while her attendants walked beside the river. She saw the basket among the reeds and sent her maid to bring it. (6) When she opened it, she saw the child. He was crying, and she took pity on him. "This must be one of the Hebrews' children," she said. (7) Then his sister said to Pharaoh's daughter, "Shall I go and get you a nurse from the Hebrew women to nurse the child for you?" (8) Pharaoh's daughter said to her, "Yes." So the girl went and called the child's mother. (9) Pharaoh's daughter said to her, "Take this child and nurse it for me, and I will give you your wages." So the woman took

the child and nursed it. (10) When the child grew up, she brought him to Pharaoh's daughter, and she took him as her son. She named him Moses, "because," she said, "I drew him out of the water."

(Moses flees to Midian)

(11) One day, after Moses had grown up, he went out to his people and saw their forced labor. He saw an Egyptian beating a Hebrew, one of his kinsfolk. (12) He looked this way and that, and seeing no one he killed the Egyptian and hid him in the sand. (13) When he went out the next day, he saw two Hebrews fighting; and he said to the one who was in the wrong, "Why do you strike your fellow Hebrew?" (14) He answered, "Who made you a ruler and judge over us? Do you mean to kill me as you killed the Egyptian?" Then Moses was afraid and thought, "Surely the thing is known." (15) When Pharaoh heard of it, he sought to kill Moses. But Moses fled from Pharaoh. He settled in the land of Midian, and sat down by a well.

(Exodus 2.16–12.28 skipped)

(The plague strikes Egypt)

Exodus 12. (29) At midnight Yahweh struck down all the firstborn in the land of Egypt, from the firstborn of Pharaoh who sat on his throne to the firstborn of the prisoner who was in the dungeon, and all the firstborn of the livestock.

(30) Pharaoh arose in the night, he and all his officials and all the Egyptians; and there was a loud cry in Egypt, for there was not a house without someone dead. (31) Then he summoned Moses and Aaron in the night, and said, "Rise up, go away from my people, both you and the Israelites! Go, worship Yahweh, as you said. (32) Take your flocks and your herds, as you said, and be gone. And bring a blessing on me too!"

(The Exodus: from Rameses to Succoth)

(33) The Egyptians urged the people to hasten their departure from the land, for they said, "We shall all be dead." (34) So the people took their dough before it was leavened, with their kneading-bowls wrapped up in their cloaks on their shoulders. (35) The Israelites had done as Moses told them; they had asked the Egyptians for jewellery of silver and gold, and for clothing, (36) and Yahweh had given the people favour in the sight of the Egyptians, so that they let them have what they asked. And so they plundered the Egyptians.

(37) The Israelites journeyed from Rameses to Succoth, about six hundred thousand men on foot, besides children. (38) A mixed crowd also went up with them, and livestock in great numbers, both flocks and herds. (39) They baked unleavened cakes of the dough that they had brought out of Egypt; it was not leavened, because they were driven out of Egypt and could not wait, nor had they prepared any provisions for themselves.

(40) The time that the Israelites had lived in Egypt was four hundred and thirty years. (41) At the end of four hundred and thirty years, on that very day, all the companies of Yahweh went out from the land of Egypt. (42) That was for Yahweh a night of vigil, to bring them out of the land of Egypt. That same night is a vigil to be kept for Yahweh by all the Israelites throughout their generations.

(Directions for the Passover)

(43) Yahweh said to Moses and Aaron: This is the ordinance for the passover: no foreigner shall eat of it, (44) but any slave who has been purchased may eat of it after he has been circumcised; (45) no bound or hired servant may eat of it. (46) It shall be eaten in one house; you shall not take any of the animal outside the house, and you shall not break any of its bones. (47) The whole congregation of Israel shall celebrate it. (48) If an alien who resides with you wants to celebrate the passover to Yahweh, all his males shall be circumcised; then he may draw near to celebrate it; he shall be regarded as a native of the land. But no uncircumcised person shall eat of it; (49) there shall be one law for the native and for the alien who resides among you.

(50) All the Israelites did just as Yahweh had commanded Moses and Aaron. (51) That very day Yahweh brought the Israelites out of the land of Egypt, company by company.

Exodus 13. (1) Yahweh said to Moses: (2) Consecrate to me all the firstborn; whatever is the first to open the womb among the Israelites, of human beings and animals, is mine.

(The festival of unleavened bread)

(3) Moses said to the people, "Remember this day on which you came out of Egypt, out of the house of slavery, because Yahweh brought you out from there by strength of hand; no leavened bread shall be eaten. (4) Today, in the month of Abib, you are going out. (5) When Yahweh brings you into the land of the Canaanites, the Hittites, the Amorites, the Hivites, and the Jebusites, which he swore to your ancestors to give you, a land flowing with milk and honey, you shall keep this observance in this month. (6) For seven days you shall eat unleavened bread, and on the seventh day there shall be a festival to Yahweh. (7) Unleavened bread shall be eaten for seven days; no leavened bread shall be seen in your possession, and no leaven shall be seen among you in all your territory. (8) You shall tell your child on that day, 'It is because of what Yahweh did for me when I came out of Egypt.' (9) It shall serve for you as a sign on your hand and as a reminder on your forehead, so that the teaching of Yahweh may be on your lips; for with a strong hand Yahweh brought you out of Egypt. (10) You shall keep this ordinance at its proper time from year to year.

(The consecration of the firstborn)

(11) "When Yahweh has brought you into the land of the Canaanites, as he swore to you and your ancestors, and has given it to you, (12) you shall set apart to Yahweh all that first opens the womb. All the firstborn of your livestock that are males shall be Yahweh's. (13) But every firstborn donkey you shall redeem with a sheep; if you do not redeem it, you must break its neck. Every firstborn male among your children you shall redeem. (14) When in the future your child asks you, 'What does this mean?' you shall answer, 'By strength of hand Yahweh brought us out of Egypt, from the house of slavery. (15) When Pharaoh stubbornly refused to let us go, Yahweh killed all the firstborn in the land of Egypt, from human firstborn to the firstborn of animals. Therefore I sacrifice to Yahweh every male that first opens the womb, but every firstborn of my sons I redeem.' (16) It shall serve as a sign on your

hand and as an emblem on your forehead that by strength of hand Yahweh brought us out of Egypt."

(The pillars of cloud and fire)

(17) When Pharaoh let the people go, God did not lead them by way of the land of the Philistines, although that was nearer; for God thought, "If the people face war, they may change their minds and return to Egypt." (18) So God led the people by the roundabout way of the wilderness towards the Red Sea. The Israelites went up out of the land of Egypt prepared for battle. (19) And Moses took with him the bones of Joseph, who had required a solemn oath of the Israelites, saying, "God will surely take notice of you, and then you must carry my bones with you from here." (20) They set out from Succoth, and camped at Etham, on the edge of the wilderness. (21) Yahweh went in front of them in a pillar of cloud by day, to lead them along the way, and in a pillar of fire by night, to give them light, so that they might travel by day and by night. (22) Neither the pillar of cloud by day nor the pillar of fire by night left its place in front of the people.

(Crossing the Red Sea)

Exodus 14. (1) Then Yahweh said to Moses: (2) "Tell the Israelites to turn back and camp in front of Pi-hahiroth, between Migdol and the sea, in front of Baal-zephon; you shall camp opposite it, by the sea. (3) Pharaoh will say of the Israelites, 'They are wandering aimlessly in the land; the wilderness has closed in on them.' (4) I will harden Pharaoh's heart, and he will pursue them, so that I will gain glory for myself over Pharaoh and all his army; and the Egyptians shall know that I am Yahweh." And they did so.

(5) When the king of Egypt was told that the people had fled, the minds of Pharaoh and his officials were changed towards the people, and they said, "What have we done, letting Israel leave our service?" (6) So he had his chariot made ready, and took his army with him; (7) he took six hundred picked chariots and all the other chariots of Egypt with officers over all of them. (8) Yahweh hardened the heart of Pharaoh king of Egypt and he pursued the Israelites, who were going out boldly. (9) The Egyptians pursued them, all Pharaoh's horses and chariots, his chariot drivers and his army; they overtook them camped by the sea, by Pi-hahiroth, in front of Baal-zephon.

(10) As Pharaoh drew near, the Israelites looked back, and there were the Egyptians advancing on them. In great fear the Israelites cried out to Yahweh. (11) They said to Moses, "Was it because there were no graves in Egypt that you have taken us away to die in the wilderness? What have you done to us, bringing us out of Egypt? (12) Is this not the very thing we told you in Egypt, 'Let us alone and let us serve the Egyptians'? For it would have been better for us to serve the Egyptians than to die in the wilderness." (13) But Moses said to the people, "Do not be afraid, stand firm, and see the deliverance that Yahweh will accomplish for you today; for the Egyptians whom you see today you shall never see again. (14) Yahweh will fight for you, and you have only to keep still."

(15) Then Yahweh said to Moses, "Why do you cry out to me? Tell the Israelites to go forward. (16) But you lift up your staff, and stretch out your hand over the sea

and divide it, that the Israelites may go into the sea on dry ground. (17) Then I will harden the hearts of the Egyptians so that they will go in after them; and so I will gain glory for myself over Pharaoh and all his army, his chariots, and his chariot drivers. (18) And the Egyptians shall know that I am Yahweh, when I have gained glory for myself over Pharaoh, his chariots, and his chariot drivers."

(19) The angel of God who was going before the Israelite army moved and went behind them; and the pillar of cloud moved from in front of them and took its place behind them. (20) It came between the army of Egypt and the army of Israel. And so the cloud was there with the darkness, and it lit up the night; one did not come near the other all night. (21) Then Moses stretched out his hand over the sea. Yahweh drove the sea back by a strong east wind all night, and turned the sea into dry land; and the waters were divided. (22) The Israelites went into the sea on dry ground, the waters forming a wall for them on their right and on their left. (23) The Egyptians pursued, and went into the sea after them, all of Pharaoh's horses, chariots, and chariot drivers. (24) At the morning watch Yahweh in the pillar of fire and cloud looked down upon the Egyptian army, and threw the Egyptian army into panic. (25) He clogged their chariot wheels so that they turned with difficulty. The Egyptians said, "Let us flee from the Israelites, for Yahweh is fighting for them against Egypt."

(The pursuers drowned)
(26) Then Yahweh said to Moses, "Stretch out your hand over the sea, so that the water may come back upon the Egyptians, upon their chariots and chariot drivers." (27) So Moses stretched out his hand over the sea, and at dawn the sea returned to its normal depth. As the Egyptians fled before it, Yahweh tossed the Egyptians into the sea. (28) The waters returned and covered the chariots and the chariot drivers, the entire army of Pharaoh that had followed them into the sea; not one of them remained. (29) But the Israelites walked on dry ground through the sea, the waters forming a wall for them on their right and on their left.

(30) Thus Yahweh saved Israel that day from the Egyptians; and Israel saw the Egyptians dead on the seashore. (31) Israel saw the great work that Yahweh did against the Egyptians. So the people feared Yahweh and believed in Yahweh and in his servant Moses.

4.7. THE SARGON LEGEND

Sargon of Akkad (also called "Sargon the Great") was the founder of the Akkadian Empire, conquering most of Mesopotamia (including today's Iraq and parts of Iran and Syria). He lived around 2334–2279 BCE, and his empire lasted for 150 years. Its capital, Akkad (called Agade in Sumerian) has not yet been identified. The Akkadians inhabited northern Mesopotamia and were speakers of a Semitic language distantly akin to later Hebrew. During this empire of 150 years started by Sargon, they conquered the Sumerian cities to the south and adopted their script, preserving the Sumerian language as part of their literary culture, while Akkadian became the main spoken language of the entire region and continued in use by the cultures of Assyria (northern

Mesopotamian) and Babylonia (southern Mesopotamian) during the second and first millennia BCE. While there is no doubt that Sargon is a historical figure (attested in the Sumerian king lists and other documents), and he indeed usurped the throne of the Sumerian king of Kish, stories about his rise to power and his childhood are imbued with legendary features (divine interventions, impossible threats, and miraculous survival). His grandson, King Naram-Sin, was also the subject of an elaborate literary tradition in later times.

The Sumerian text called the "Sargon Legend" (document 4.7.a) narrates how he became prominent in the court of the king of Kish and how the goddess Inana saved his life. Although the text is incomplete, we know he survives a second murder attempt and then usurps the throne and embarks on his conquest of Mesopotamia. The second text (document 4.7.b) contains the "Sargon Birth Legend," famously similar to that of Moses but of much later date (seventh century BCE?). This is an Akkadian text of unknown authorship in which the story of Sargon's extraordinary birth is put in his own mouth. Since the story of Sargon's early life is not preserved in the Sumerian Sargon Legend (there is a *lacuna* at the beginning of the text), we cannot know whether this version was part of the older myth or a later elaboration. Instead of providing historical information, these texts provide an insight into the mythologizing of early kings' lives (cf. story of Gilgamesh, who also was a historical king).

4.7.a. The Sargon Legend (Sumerian Text)

SOURCE: "The Sargon Legend," J. A. Black et al., *The Electronic Text Corpus of Sumerian Literature* (http://www-etcsl.orient.ox.ac.uk/), Oxford, 1998–2006.

Segment A

(1–9) To . . . the sanctuary like a cargo-ship; to . . . its great furnaces; to see that its canals . . . waters of joy, to see that the hoes till the arable tracts and that . . . the fields; to turn the house of Kic,[14] which was like a haunted town, into a living settlement again – its king, shepherd Ur-Zababa,[15] rose like Utu over the house of Kic. An and Enlil,[16] however, authoritatively (?) decided (?) by their holy command to alter his term of reigning and to remove the prosperity of the palace.

(10–13) Then Sargon – his city was the city of . . . , his father was La'ibum, his mother . . . , Sargon . . . with happy heart. Since he was born . . . *(unknown number of lines missing)*

Segment B

(1–7) One day, after the evening had arrived and Sargon had brought the regular deliveries to the palace, Ur-Zababa was sleeping (and dreaming) in the holy bedchamber, his holy residence. He realized what the dream was about, but did not

---

[14] A city-state founded by Sumerians and later known as Kish (modern Tall al-Uhaymir, 80 kilometers south of Baghdad).

[15] This king is listed as reigning during the Third Dynasty of Kish around 2340 BCE. His theophoric name bears the royal title Ur and the divine name Zababa.

[16] Utu, An (Anu), and Enlil are gods.

put into words, did not discuss it with anyone. After Sargon had received the regular deliveries for the palace, Ur-Zababa appointed him cupbearer, putting him in charge of the drinks cupboard. Holy Inana did not cease to stand by him.

(8–11) After five or ten days had passed, king Ur-Zababa . . . and became frightened in his residence. Like a lion he urinated, sprinkling his legs, and the urine contained blood and pus. He was troubled, he was afraid like a fish floundering in brackish water.

(12–24) It was then that the cupbearer of Ezina's wine-house, Sargon, lay down not to sleep, but lay down to dream. In the dream, holy Inana drowned Ur-Zababa in a river of blood. The sleeping Sargon groaned and gnawed the ground. When king Ur-Zababa heard about this groaning, he was brought into the king's holy presence, Sargon was brought into the presence of Ur-Zababa (who said:) "Cupbearer, was a dream revealed to you in the night?" Sargon answered his king: "My king, this is my dream, which I will tell you about: There was a young woman, who was as high as the heavens and as broad as the earth. She was firmly set as the base of a wall. For me, she drowned you in a great river, a river of blood."

(25–34) Ur-Zababa chewed his lips, he became seriously afraid. He spoke to . . . , his chancellor: "My royal sister, holy Inana, is going to change (?) my finger into a . . . of blood; she will drown Sargon, the cupbearer, in the great river. Belic-tikal,[17] chief smith, man of my choosing, who can write tablets, I will give you orders, let my orders be carried out! Let my advice be followed! Now then, when the cupbearer has delivered my bronze hand-mirror (?) to you, in the E-sikil,[18] the fated house, throw them (the mirror and Sargon) into the mould like statues."

(35–45) Belic-tikal heeded his king's words and prepared the moulds in the E-sikil, the fated house. The king spoke to Sargon: "Go and deliver my bronze hand-mirrors (?) to the chief smith!" Sargon left the palace of Ur-Zababa. Holy Inana, however, did not cease to stand at his right hand side, and before he had come within five or ten *nindan* of the E-sikil, the fated house, holy Inana turned around toward him and blocked his way, (saying:) "The E-sikil is a holy house! No one polluted with blood should enter it!" Thus he met the chief smith of the king only at the gate of the fated house. After he delivered the king's bronze hand-mirror(?) to the chief smith, Belic-tikal, the chief smith, . . . and threw it into the mould like statues.

(46–52) After five or ten days had passed, Sargon came into the presence of Ur-Zababa, his king; he came into the palace, firmly founded like a great mountain. King Ur-Zababa . . . and became frightened in his residence. He realized what was it about, but did not put into words, did not discuss it with anyone. Ur-Zababa became frightened in the bed-chamber, his holy residence. He realized what was it about, but did not put into words, did not discuss it with anyone.

(53–56) In those days, although writing words on tablets existed, putting tablets into envelopes did not yet exist. King Ur-Zababa dispatched Sargon, the creature of the gods, to Lugal-zage-si[19] in Unug with a message written on clay, which was about murdering Sargon.

(Unknown number of lines missing)

---

[17] A personal name (not royal or divine).

[18] A temple name.

[19] Name of a king.

Segment C

(1–7) With the wife of Lugal-zage-si . . . She (?) . . . her feminity as a shelter. Lugal-zage-si did not . . . . . . the envoy. "Come! He directed his steps to brick-built E-ana[20]!" Lugal-zage-si did not grasp it, he did not talk to the envoy. But as soon as he did talk to the envoy . . . Yahweh said "Alas!" and sat in the dust.

(8–12) Lugal-zage-si replied to the envoy: "Envoy, Sargon does not yield." After he has submitted, Sargon . . . Lugal-zage-si . . . Sargon . . . Lugal-zage-si . . . Why . . . Sargon . . . ?

(Rest not preserved)

4.7.b. Sargon Birth Legend (Neo-Assyrian Text)

SOURCE: L. W. King, *Chronicles Concerning Early Babylonian Kings*, II, London, 1907, pp. 87–96.

"My mother was a high priestess, my father I knew not. The brothers of my father loved the hills. My city is Azupiranu, which is situated on the banks of the Euphrates. My high priestess mother conceived me, in secret she bore me. She set me in a basket of rushes, with bitumen she sealed my lid. She cast me into the river which rose over me. The river bore me up and carried me to Akki, the drawer of water. Akki, the drawer of water, took me as his son and reared me. Akki, the drawer of water, appointed me as his gardener. While I was a gardener, Ishtar granted me her love, and for four and . . . years I exercised kingship."

4.8. BIRTH OF CYRUS THE GREAT, FROM HERODOTOS' *HISTORIES*

Herodotos was a historian from Halikarnassos in Asia Minor (today's Bodrum, on the western coast of modern Turkey). He lived in the fifth century BCE (ca. 485–425) and was the first writer to compose a "history," a name that comes precisely from the word he uses to describe his work (Greek *historie*, "observation, research"). Herodotos organized his vast narrative, divided into nine books, around the rise and expansion of the Persian Empire, from Cyrus the Great in the mid-sixth century BCE to the first invasion of Greece by Darius in 490 and the second by Xerxes in 480. Herodotos' masterpiece is much more than a political history. Drawing from the emerging genres of ethnography and geography (e.g., the work of Hekataios of Miletos in the mid-sixth to early fifth centuries), and with a strong element of folklore, Herodotos' work is driven by an exploration of the human experience and by an insatiable curiosity and sensitivity to local traditions and cultural diversity (religious, linguistic, customary). Herotodos himself was born into a multicultural environment, as Halikarnassos was a Greek foundation in a region of Karian (non-Greek) indigenous population, which in turn was under Persian domination during part of Herotodos' lifetime.

---

[20] A temple name.

Cyrus, called "the Great," was the founder of the Persian Empire. Inheriting a small Persian kingdom from his father Cambyses I, around the mid-sixth century BCE Cyrus conquered Media, Sardis, Lydia, to which he later added the neo-Babylonian empire (which included Mesopotamia and Syria-Palestine) and then expanded deep into Central Asia. By the time of Darius' march on Greece in 490 the empire also included Egypt and parts of northern Greece. In Herdotos' version, the child's destiny to become a great king prevails over the murder attempts by his grandfather Astyages. This type of story line also occurs in the legends about other royal or founding figures, such as Romulus and Remus, Moses, Sargon, and Jesus. Herodotos shows his rational line of inquiry by following a version in which the baby was not raised by a dog but by a woman whose name could have led to that confusion (cf. Romulus and Remus story). After the passages about Cyrus' miraculous survival, the story skips the child's early years and resumes when his true identity is revealed, ten years later. The child was spared by Astyages and sent to his father Kambyses the Persian. When Cyrus grows up and becomes king of his small vassal kingdom, he rebels against Astyages and embarks upon his conquests.

SOURCE: Herodotos, *Histories*, Book 1.107–113, translated and annotated by C. López-Ruiz.

(107) After those events, Kyaxares died, having ruled for forty years, including those in which the Skythains ruled. And so Astyages, the son of Kyaxares, inherited the throne. A daughter had been born to him too, whom he had named Mandane, and who seemed to Astyages in a dream to flow with water so much that she filled his own city and overflowed even the whole of Asia.

Submitting the dream vision to the Magi in charge of interpreting dreams, he was terrified as he learned from them every single thing. So when this Mandane was already ripe to take a husband, he would not give her as wife to any of the Medes who would be worthy of himself, fearing the vision, but he gave her to a Persian whose name was Kambyses, whom he found to be of good house and of calm character, while he considered him much below a Mede of medium status.

(108) But, after Mandane lived with Kambyses for the first year, Astyages saw another vision: it seemed to him that from the genitals of this daughter of his, a vine grew, and that the vine extended through the whole of Asia. After he saw this and he submitted it to the interpreters of dreams, he sent to bring his daughter back from the Persians, as she was about to give birth, and when she arrived he watched over her with the plan to kill the child who would be born from her. For those among the Magi who interpret dreams had indicated from the vision that the offspring of his daughter was going to rule in his place. Vigilant about these things, therefore, when Cyrus was born, he called Harpagos, a man of his household (servant) and most trustworthy among the Medes and who took care of all his (Astyages') affairs, and said to him some such words:

"Harpagos, this business that I set upon you, by no means disregard it, nor put me aside lest preferring to follow others you end up tripping on yourself. Take the child whom Mandane has given birth to, and taking him to your place, kill him. After that, bury him in whatever way you want."

And he answered: "Oh king, you have never before observed anything ungrateful in this man, and so I will take care of not offending you also in the coming time. However, if you want this, so it will happen; it is absolutely necessary that I on my part serve you appropriately."

(109) After Harpagos had answered with these words, thus the baby was given to him, adorned in the way for burial, and Harpagos went to his house weeping. When he entered, he told to his wife the whole speech said to him by Astyages. And she told him: "So now, what do you have in mind to do?" And he answered: "Astyages will not have it prescribed in this way; not even if he goes out of his mind and becomes more demented than he is now; I will not put myself forward for this plan nor will I aid him in this kind of crime. For many reasons I will not kill him: not only because the child is my own relative, but also because Astyages is old and lacking a male descendant; so if the monarchy, after he dies, ends up passing on to this daughter whose son now he is killing through me, will I be left in that situation with anything else but the greatest of risks? But for safety reasons it is necessary for me that the child dies; however, one of Astyages' own men should become the murderer, not one of mine."

(110) So he said, and immediately he sent a messenger to one of the cowherds of Astyages, whom he knew pastured in the most adequate fields and in the mountains with most wild animals, and whose name was Mitridates. He lived with a servant like him, and the name of the woman with whom he lived was Kyno in the Greek language, in the Median language Spako: for the Medes call a dog "*spaka*."[21] And the foothills of the mountains where this cowherd had the pastures for his cows are by the north side of Ecbatana and near the Euxine Sea. For in this area the Median territory by the Saspires[22] is extremely mountainous and high and thickly wooded, whereas the rest of the Median territory is completely plain. When the cowherd arrived with great haste, as he had been summoned, Harpagos said the following:

"Astyages orders that you take this baby and place him in the most isolated part of the mountains, so that he might perish as fast as possible. And he also ordered to tell you that, if you do not kill him but in some way you spare him, you will suffer the most terrible doom; and I am in charge to supervise that he is exposed."

(111) After he heard this, taking the baby, the cowherd went back through the same way and arrived to his stables. As it turned out that his own wife had also been about to give birth all day, then, so the gods wanted it, she gave birth while he was away in the city. They had both been in each others' minds, he worried about the labor of his wife, and the wife about why Harpagos would have sent for her husband so unexpectedly. So when he returned and stood there, as she was surprised to see

---

[21] The Greek Kyno is understood as a translation of the Median, as *kyna* is "dog/bitch" in Greek (with both words, in Greek and in Median, rendered in the accusative case).

[22] This northern part of Media is modern Azerbaijan.

him, the woman was the first one to ask why had Harpagos sent for him so urgently. And he said:

"Oh wife, going into the city I have seen and I have heard things that ought not to be seen nor ought to ever happen to our lords. The whole house of Harpagos was overwhelmed by weeping; so, perplexed, I went inside. As soon as I entered, I saw a baby lying there, struggling and wailing, adorned with gold and with a colorful garment. When Harpagos saw me, he commanded me to take the baby immediately and go away carrying him and to set him down where the wildest part of the mountains might be, declaring that this task set upon me came from Astyages, and severely threatening me if I did not do it. And I took him and carried him away, thinking he was of one of the servants; for I could have never imagined where he was from. But I was amazed as I saw him adorned with gold and fine clothing, as well as at the evident lament set upon the house of Harpagos. And indeed right away I learned the whole story on the way, from the servant who escorted me outside the city and who handed me the newborn: that he was the son of Astyages' daughter, Mandane, and of Kambyses, son of Cyrus, and that Astyages had commissioned to kill him. And now here he is."

(112) And just as he was saying these words, the cowherd also uncovered him and showed him. And when she saw the baby, big and good looking, she begged him not to expose him in any way, while crying and grabbing onto her husband's knees.[23] But he said that he could not deal with this in any other way; that spies from Harpagos would come to look into it and he would die horribly if he did not carry this out. Since she did not convince her husband, the wife went on to say this:

"Being as it is that I am not capable of convincing you not to expose him, then do this – if by all means it is necessary that a child is seen exposed. I have also given birth, but I have born a dead baby; take this one and expose him, and let us raise Astyages daughters' child as if he was ours; and in this way, neither you will be caught acting against our masters nor will it be badly planned for ourselves. For the one who is dead will get a royal burial and the one surviving will not lose his life."

(113) It very much seemed to the cowherd that his wife spoke well for the present circumstances, and carried this out right away. He handed to his wife the child whom he had brought with the plan to let him die, and in turn taking his own, the one who was dead, he placed him in the receptacle in which he had brought the other one. Adorning him with all the adornments of the other child, he took him to the most solitary place of the mountains and set him there. When the third day after the baby had been exposed arrived, the cowherd went to the city, leaving one of his herdsmen to guard the body, and so going into Harpagos' house he declared that he was ready to show the corpse of the baby. Sending the most trusted of his spear-bearers,[24] Harpagos saw this through them and had the baby buried. And

---

[23] In Greek culture, touching or holding onto the knees of another person (as well as touching his or her chin) was a formal gesture of supplication.

[24] Personal guards or bodyguards.

while the one was being buried, the cowherd's wife was nourishing the other one, the one later called Cyrus by them, having adopted him and given him some other name and not "Cyrus."

4.9. THE FOUNDATION OF CYRENE

4.9.a. Herodotos on the Foundation of Cyrene

In this passage, the Greek historian Herodotos narrates the foundation of Cyrene (in today's eastern Libya) by people from the island of Thera, following (and contrasting) the versions he has heard from both Therans and Cyrenaeans. (See the introduction to Herodotos in document 4.8.)

Thera, modern Santorini, is one of the Greek Cycladic islands. The island was inhabited in the Bronze Age by an Aegean culture similar to that of the Minoan one of Crete. Its civilization was buried by the cataclysmic eruption of a volcano some time between the seventeenth and the sixteenth centuries BCE, and impressive remains have been excavated from that period. In later times (ca. 850 BCE), Lakonian colonists renamed the island (previously called Kalliste according to Herodotos) after its founder, Theras. The later foundation of Cyrene by people from Thera, who left the island due to a drought, is dated to ca. 631 BCE.

The foundation of this prosperous north African colony is attested in several written sources. Besides Herodotos' narrative, two poems by Pindar composed in 462 BCE (*Pythian Odes* 4 and 5) celebrate a chariot-race victory of the ruler of Cyrene in the Pythian games at Delphi. In his poems Pindar evokes Cyrene's ancestor Battos and the role of the Delphic oracle in the colonial enterprise. As Pindar's *Pythian Ode* 5 exemplifies (see document 4.9.b), the first founder of a colony was typically buried in the agora and transformed into a heroic figure. Gaining the sanction of Apollo at Delphi was therefore "a must" in Greek colonial foundations. Elements that recur in other foundation stories are failed attempts and political strife and exile resulting in colonial enterprises (e.g., Taras in Italy; see introduction to this part). A fourth-century BCE inscription in which Cyrenaeans agree to give lands and rights to new Theran incomers allegedly reproduces the original decree by the Therans, justifying their future rights to be welcomed in the colony and stating that those chosen to sail out were bound by oath to go (threatened by the death penalty and a curse if they broke it) (Meiggs and Lewis 5, *SEG* ix.3+).

SOURCE: Herodotos, *Histories*, Book 4.150–157, translated and annotated by C. López-Ruiz.

(150) Up to this point in the story, the Lacedemonians tell it in the same terms as the Therans, but after this point only the Therans say that it happened thus: Grinnos, son of Aisanios, being the descendant of this same Theras and the king of the island of Thera, arrived at Delphi bringing a hecatomb from his city. Other citizens also accompanied him, in particular Battos, son of Polymnestos, a descendant of Euphemides, of the Minyan family. When this Grinnos, king of the Therans, consulted the

oracle concerning other things, the Pythia[25] prophesized that he should found a city in Libya. And he responded by saying:

"Oh Lord, I am already old and heavy to move around; but you go ahead and command one of these younger ones to do that."

And as he was saying this he pointed at Battos. Nothing else was said then. And when they returned, they disregarded the oracle, since they did not know where on earth Libya was, nor did they dare to send a colony out to an uncertain business.

(151) For seven years after these events it did not rain in Thera, during which all of the trees in the island dried up except for one. When these Therans consulted the oracle, the Pythia brought up the colony in Libya. Since they had no remedy for this, they sent to Crete messengers to find out if anyone of the Cretans or of the foreigners living among them had ever reached Libya. In their many wanderings about the island, they also arrived at the town of Itanos, where they met a man who dealt with purple dye,[26] whose name was Korobios, who told them that, led astray by winds, he had arrived at Libya, concretely to the Libyan island of Platea.[27] Persuading this man with a payment, they brought him to Thera, and from Thera some scouts set sail, at first not many: with Korobios leading the way to this island of Platea, they left Korobios there, leaving food for so many months, while they sailed away as fast as possible to bring news of the island to the Therans.

(In 152 a digression follows about the Samian merchant named Kolaios, who was driven off course in his way to Egypt, arriving at Plataea. He left new provisions for Korobios, which was the beginning of a friendship between Samos, Thera, and Cyrene. Herodotos tells us about the adventure of Kolaios after he left Platea, when he was driven off course toward the far west Mediterranean, arriving at Tartessos.)

(153) So after leaving Korobios in the island, when the Therans and arrived at Thera, they announced that there was an island settled by them in Libya. The Therans decided to send a brother of every two, chosen by lot, and men from every region, there being seven, and that Battos should be their leader and their king. Thus they sent two penteconters[28] to Platea.

(154) This is what the Therans say, and what is for the rest of the story the Therans do agree with the Cyrenaeans. For, regarding Battos, the Cyrenaeans do not agree at all with the Therans, but they say as follows: There is in Crete a town called Oaxos, in which Etearchos became the king, who, for the sake of his motherless daughter, whose name was Phronime, took another wife. But this woman, since she

---

[25] The priestess of Apollo who issued (in hexametric verses) the oracular response she received from Apollo. The questions and responses were in turn handed by male priests who mediated between the Pythia and the visitors.

[26] The word used here, *porphyreus*, indicates that he was involved either in the extraction of purple dye (from the murex shell, *porphyra*) or in some part of its production and trade. This industry was especially associated with the Phoenicians, whose presence is well attested in Crete.

[27] An island now called Bomba, east of Cyrene (modern Libya).

[28] Ships of fifty oarsmen, used both for trade and warfare before specialized warships were developed.

came into the house, judged fair to act also in fact as a stepmother[29] for Phronime, entertaining evil actions and plotting every possible thing against her, and in the end she charged her with the accusation of lust and persuaded her father that this was so. And he, convinced by his wife, plotted against his daughter an impious action. So there was this Themision, a man from Thera trading in Oaxos; taking him in as a guest, Etearchos made him swear that he truly would serve him in whatever was needed. Once he had taken the oath, he brought his own daughter and handed her to him and asked him to take her away and throw her into the ocean. But Themison, aggravated by the deceit of the oath and dissolving the bond of guest-friendship, did the following: taking with him the girl, he sailed away, and when he was in high sea, in order to honor the oath given to Etearchos, tying her with ropes, he lowered her into the sea, and after pulling her back up, they arrived at Thera.

(155) There Polymnestos, who was a notable man among the Therans, kept her as a concubine. With the passing of time, a child of weak and impeded speech was born to him, whom he gave the name of Battos,[30] according to what the Therans and Cyrenaeans say—though, in my opinion, some other name, and he was renamed Battos when he arrived at Libya, making this his nickname following the oracular issue that took place for him at Delphi and the position he took: for the Libyans call their king "battos," and this is why I think the Pythia, when prophesying, called him in the Libyan language, knowing that he would be king in Libya. For when this Battos became a man, he went to Delphi regarding his speech; and when he consulted her, the Pythia gave him the following oracle:

> "Battos, you have come for your speech; but Phoibos Apollo
> sends you to be a founder in Libya, nurse of sheep."

Such as if she had been prophesying in the Greek language: "King, you have come for your speech . . . " And he responded with these words: "Lord, I have come to you in order to inquire about my speech, but you prophesize to me other impossible things, asking me to settle a colony in Libya. With what authority? With what help?" Even saying this, he did not persuade the god to give him another oracle; so when Apollo kept prophesying to him in the same terms as he did before, Battos left in the midst of it and headed for Thera.

(156) But after this things turned sour again not only for him but for the rest of the Therans too. At a loss regarding their misfortunes, the Therans send to Delphi regarding the present difficulties. And the Pythia proclaimed that they would fare better if they helped Battos found the colony of Cyrene in Libya. After this the Therans sent away Battos with two penteconters. These men sailed to Libya, but not knowing what else to do then, they turned back to Thera. But the Therans threw them away as they were disembarking and would not let them approach the land, but instead ordered them to sail back. And they sailed away thus forced and settled an island lying by Libya, which name, as was already said before, is Platea. And this island is said to be the same as the current city of Cyrene.

---

[29] Alluding to the proverbial stereotype of malevolent stepmother.

[30] Meaning "stutterer" in Greek.

(157) After living in this island for two years, since it did not go well for them at all, they left one of them behind and the rest sailed to Delphi, and as soon as they arrived at the sanctuary they inquired, declaring that they were settled in Libya but the settlers were not faring any better. And the Pythia gave them this oracle regarding this matter:

> "If you, who have not been there, know Libya, nurse of sheep,
> better than I do, who have been there, then I am in awe of your wisdom."

After they heard this, those with Battos sailed back; for the god clearly would not set them free from colonizing until they reached Libya itself. Once they arrived to the island and picked up the one they had left there, they settled a territory of Libya itself across the island, named Aziris, which the most beautiful wooded valleys enclose, while a river flows on one of its sides.

4.9.b. Cyrene in Pindar, *Pythian Ode* 5

Pindar was one of the leading lyric poets of ancient Greece. He lived and wrote at the end of the sixth and first half of the fifth centuries BCE (ca. 522–443), a time of complex associations and rivalries between the *poleis* (city-states) of the Greek world. He created his compositions at the request of wealthy patrons and cities who knew that being able to commission a poem from a poet as famous as Pindar was one way of elevating their own status and that of their community. Like the work of many ancient authors, much of his production has been lost, but we retain his *Epinikians* or Victory Odes (from *nike*, "victory"). These were songs performed, like most early Greek poetry, to musical accompaniment and possibly dance. They were written to celebrate the success of victors in a circuit of athletic contests (Pythian, i.e., at Delphi; Olympic), which were considered prestigious throughout the Greek world. These events took place in the context of a festival celebrating a divinity, and, as you can see in the following ode, the threads of religious expression, the victor's pride in himself and his family, and the identity of the victor's community are intricately woven together.

The following ode celebrates Arkesilaos' victory at the Pythian games, celebrated in honor of Apollo. In his ode, Pindar first foregrounds Arkesilaos' exalted position as ruler of Cyrene (lines 1–17), then shifts his focus to the victory itself. After his account of the present-day festival, Pindar uses a reference to Battos, the mythical founder of Cyrene, to transition into an account of Cyrene's mythical past. The story he tells of the colonization of Cyrene by Greeks from Sparta allows him to incorporate the assistance of Apollo into Cyrene's past. As is typical of Pindar's odes, this one presents elements of the mythical past which are present in the city landscape of Pindar's contemporaries: the section containing the myth concludes with the grave of Battos, a physical element of the city that its inhabitants could regularly observe. By collapsing the mythical past into the present reality of the city, Pindar weaves the victor and his contemporaries into the glorious tradition of their community, and their community into the broader network of shared Greek traditions.

SOURCE: Pindar, *Pythian Ode 5*, translated and annotated by Hanne Eisenfeld.

The power of wealth is wide:
when wealth is compounded with excellence
it trails a mortal man as his personal attendant,
fate allowing.
(5) Arkesilaos, man marked out by the gods,
with good repute you obtain this wealth,
already standing on the highest steps
of a renowned life
by the grace of Kastor with his golden chariot
(10) who wafts calm weather to your fortunate hearth
after the stormy rains.
For you know that noble men are better able to wield power,
especially that granted by the gods.
As you approach, and rightly so, great fortune dwells about you:
(15) for one, because you are the ruler of great cities:
your inborn excellence holds this most revered prize,
a glory worked into your nature.
And at this moment, too, you are blessed,
for just now driving your chariot at the renowned Pythian festival
(20) you received what you had prayed for, this revelry of men,
a delight to Apollo.
These two things, do not let them escape you
as, in Cyrene, you are celebrated in the sweet garden of Aphrodite:
to recognize the divine as the cause of everything,
(25) and to love Karrhotos especially of all your companions.
For he, without bringing Excuse with him,
that daughter of Epimetheus who thinks too late,
arrives at the homes of the Battidai
whose rule is ordained by the gods.
(30) Welcomed as a guest by the waters of Kastalia,
he placed the prize for a victorious chariot race
on your hair.

       He traversed the sacred precinct, twelve times round its
           swift track
with reins undamaged.
(35) For no portion of the powerful chariot was smashed;
rather he hangs it entire as a dedication,
elaborate handiwork of craftsmen,
driving it to the Krisaian crest,

bringing it to the nestled valley of the god

(40) where the cypress-wood chamber houses it,

close by the statue

which the bow-bearing Cretans dedicated in a chamber on
Parnassos

carved from a single piece of living wood.

It is fitting then, for you

(45) with a willing mind to welcome

the one who has done you this service.

Son of Alexibias, you also the lovely-haired Graces set ablaze.

How blessed you are,

a man who possesses the memorial of glorious praise

(50) especially after hard labor.

For racing among forty rushing charioteers

you preserved the chariot in its entirety, your mind unshaken

and now you have come from the glorious contests

to the plain of Libya and the city of your fathers.

(55) For there is no one who is – or will be – without a share of toils.

The fortune of ancient Battos follows you

– though its course varies –

towering defense of the city

and a glory shining brightly for its guests.

(60) Deep roaring lions fled him in fear

when he sent abroad to them his voice from beyond the sea.

And Apollo Archagetes gave the beasts over to terrible fear

lest his prophecies to the guardian of Cyrene

prove unfounded.

(65)   He it is[31] who also guides the remedies of grievous illnesses
to men and women,

and bears the kithara and grants the Muse to those he chooses,

escorting good order, unwarlike, to their minds,

and he attends the prophetic glen by whose power

in Lakedaimon and in Argos and in most holy Pylos

(70) he dwells among the mighty descendants of Herakles

and of Aigimios.

But it is my task

to sing the longed-for glory of Sparta

from which place, where they were born, the Aigeidai

---

[31] "He" still refers to Apollo: the enumeration of a god's particular capabilities often appears in hymns and songs of praise.

(75)   arrived at Thera, my fathers,

not without the help of the gods – for some Fate led them.

Receiving there a feast with many sacrifices,

Apollo Karneios, at your banquet we revere

the well-built city of Cyrene.

(80)   The foreigners who delight in their bronze armor possess her,

the Trojan sons of Antenor, for they came with Helen

when they saw the smoke of war enveloping their fatherland.

This horse-driving race the men faithfully received

at their sacrifices, approaching them with gifts,

(85)   the men whom Aristoteles brought in swift ships,

opening the deep path of the sea.

He founded in the midst of the city the grove of the gods

and established, cut straight and level, a road for the procession

of Apollo who grants aid to men, a paved path to ring

(90)   under the feet of horses.

There Aristoteles lies, at the edge of the agora,

set apart also in death.

He lived blessed among men,

and also in later times, revered by his people as a hero.

(95)   The other holy kings who have obtained their portion of Hades

lie separately before the houses

under streams of revelries sprinkled

with the soft dew of great achievements,

even covered by the earth, their spirits hear

(100) their own fortune and a shared glory for their sons,

fitting too for Arkesilaos.

It is appropriate to celebrate in the songs of young men

Phoibos of the golden sword,

he who from Pytho

(105) holds the recompense for labors found in glorious victory,

delightful song.

Those who are wise praise that man[32]

and I shall speak what is said of him:

He nourishes within himself a mind superior to his age

(110) and a tongue too. Bold and wide-winged

is the eagle among birds,

---

[32] Arkesilaos.

such a bulwark too is this man's strength

in athletic contests.

His mother's son, he has wings among the Muses,

(115) and has shown himself to be a skilled charioteer.

However many paths there are of excellence on this earth

he has dared them. The god

at this moment looks upon Arkesilaos with kindness

and consummates his strength.

(120) In the future too, blessed children of Kronos,

grant that he be capable in works and councils,

do not allow the wind that brings destruction to the harvest

to wear away his days with wintry breath.

You know that the great mind of Zeus guides

(125) the fortune of men dear to him.

I boast now that he will grant this prize at Olympia as well

to the race of Battos.

4.10. THE "RAPE OF EUROPA" AND THE FOUNDATION OF THEBES, FROM OVID, *METAMORPHOSES*, BOOKS 2–3

(For Ovid's *Metamorphoses*, see Part 1, document 10.) The myths surrounding the foundation and dynasties of Thebes included stories about Kadmos, Dionysos, Oedipus, and Herakles, among others. This cluster of Theban myths was among the most famous and extensively developed, only second to the Trojan War cycle. The Roman poet Ovid elaborates here a new (Latin) version of the story of Zeus' kidnapping of Europa and the story of the foundation of the Greek city of Thebes (located in Boiotia, the region west of Attica) by Kadmos, her brother, in his search for her. The so-called "rape of Europa," a popular motif in artistic representations in the Greek and Roman world, was one of the innumerable love affairs of Zeus with mortal women, sometimes taking the form of an animal (eagle, swan, bull, etc.). This transformation (Greek *metamorphosis*) is the focus of Ovid's elaboration. (See also Figure 10.)

The story of Kadmos (Lat. Cadmus) and Europa makes Thebes a Phoenician foundation, since Kadmos was a Phoenician prince, the son of Agenor, king of Tyre, and Europa was his sister (in other versions Kadmos and Europa are children of Phoinix, son of Agenor). Notice, however, how Ovid used "Tyrian" and "Sidonian" (i.e., from Sidon) interchangeably. Kadmos' name probably derives from the Semitic root *kdm*, meaning "early, ancient," and hence "easterner," and Europa's from the Semitic root *'rb* (cf. Hebrew *'erev*), "sunset, evening," hence "western." The figure of Kadmos is associated in Greek tradition with the acquisition of the Phoenician alphabet by the Greeks, who called the new writing system (from which ours ultimately derives) "Phoenician letters" and "Kadmeian letters." The Thebans call themselves Kadmeians and their acropolis the Kadmeia. The foundation of Thebes by the Phoenician prince, however, contrasts with the autochthonous birth of the first men in Theban lands, the Spartoi ("sown men"), who spring from the earth. Kadmos was, according to different versions, turned into a snake toward the end of his life. Among the children of Kadmos and Harmonia (daughter of Ares and Aphrodite) are Ino, Agave, and Semele (mother of the god Dionysos), who are famous for their own mythological connections. Europa, in turn, stayed in Crete, where she bore three famous children to Zeus: Minos, Rhadamanthys, and Sarpedon, who became judges in the afterlife.

Again, these stories are alluded to in many sources and summarized in Apollodorus' *Library*, but the poetic elaboration of Ovid is the one best preserved. An archaic epic poem about the Theban saga (attributed by some to Homer), called the *Thebaid*, was lost, and only scattered citations of it survive.

SOURCE: Ovid, *Metamorphoses*, Book 2.836–3.130. F. J. Miller, *Ovid, Metamorphoses* (Loeb Classical Library, Cambridge, MA and London, 1921, 2nd ed.), with minor modifications.

(Zeus and Europa)

Here his father (Jove) calls Mercury aside; and not revealing his love affair as the real reason, he says: "My son, always faithful to perform my bidding, delay not, but swiftly in accustomed flight glide down to earth and seek out the land that looks up at your mother's star from the left. The natives call it the land of Sidon. There you are to drive down to the sea-shore the herd of the king's cattle which you will see grazing at some distance on the mountain-side."

He spoke, and quickly the cattle were driven from the mountain and headed for the shore, as Jove had directed, to a spot where the great king's daughter was accustomed to play in company with her Tyrian maidens. Majesty and love do not go well together, nor tarry long in the same dwelling-place. And so the father and ruler of the gods, who wields in his right hand the three-forked lightning, whose nod shakes the world, laid aside his royal majesty along with his scepter, and took upon him the form of a bull. In this form he mingled with the cattle, lowed like the rest, and wandered around, beautiful to behold, on the young grass. His color was white as the untrodden snow, which has not yet been melted by the rainy south-wind. The muscles stood rounded upon his neck, a long dewlap hung down in front; his horns were small, but perfect in shape as if carved by an artist's hand, cleaner and more clear than pearls. His brow and eyes would inspire no fear, and his whole expression was peaceful.

Agenor's daughter looked at him in wondering admiration, because he was so beautiful and friendly. But, although he seemed so gentle, she was afraid at first to touch him. Presently she drew near, and held out flowers to his snow-white lips. The disguised lover rejoiced and, as a foretaste of future joy, kissed her hands. Even so he could scarce restrain his passion. And now he jumps sportively about on the grass, now lays his snowy body down on the yellow sands; and, when her fear has little by little been allayed, he yields his breast for her maiden hands to pat and his horns to entwine with garlands of fresh flowers. The princess even dares to sit upon his back, little knowing upon whom she rests. The god little by little edges away from the dry land, and sets his borrowed hoofs in the shallow water; then he goes further out and soon is in full flight with his prize on the open ocean. She trembles with fear and looks back at the receding shore, holding fast a horn with one hand and resting the other on the creature's back. And her fluttering garments stream behind her in the wind.

(Cadmus' Foundation of Thebes)

And now the god, having put off disguise of the bull, owned himself for what he was, and reached the fields of Crete. But the maiden's father, ignorant of what had happened, bids his son, Cadmus, go and search for the lost girl, and threatens exile as a punishment if he does not find her—pious and guilty by the same act. After roaming over all the world in vain (for who could search out the secret loves of Jove?), Agenor's son becomes an exile, shunning his father's country and his father's wrath. Then in suppliant wise he consults the oracle of Phoebus, seeking thus to learn in what land he is to settle. Phoebus replies: "A heifer will meet you in the wilderness, one who has never worn the yoke or drawn the crooked plough. Follow where she leads, and where she lies down to rest upon the grass there see that you build your city's walls and call the land Boeotia."[33]

Hardly had Cadmus left the Castalian grotto[34] when he saw a heifer moving slowly along, all unguarded and wearing on her neck no mark of service. He follows in her track with deliberate steps, silently giving thanks the while to Phoebus for showing him the way. And now the heifer had passed the fords of Cephisus and the fields of Panope, when she halted and, lifting towards the heavens her beautiful head with its spreading horns, she filled the air with her lowings; and then, looking back upon those who were following close behind, she kneeled and let her flank sink down upon the fresh young grass. Cadmus gave thanks, reverently pressed his lips upon this stranger land, and greeted the unknown mountains and the plains.

With intent to make sacrifice to Jove, he bade his attendants hunt out a spring of living water for libation. There was a primeval forest there, scarred by no axe; and in its midst a cave thick set about with shrubs and pliant twigs. With well-fitted stones it fashioned a low arch, whence poured a full-welling spring, and deep within dwelt a serpent sacred to Mars. The creature had a wondrous golden crest; fire flashed from his eyes; his body was all swollen with venom; his triple tongue flickered out and in and his teeth were ranged in triple row. When with luckless steps the wayfarers of the Tyrian race had reached this grove, they let down their vessels into the spring, breaking the silence of the place. At this the dark serpent thrust forth his head out of the deep cave, hissing horribly. The urns fell from the men's hands, their blood ran cold, and, horror-struck, they were seized with a sudden trembling. The serpent twines his scaly coils in rolling knots and with a spring curves himself into a huge bow; and, lifted high by more than half his length into the unsubstantial air, he looks down upon the whole wood, as huge, could you see him all, as is that

---

[33] An etymology is assumed here connecting the name Boeotia (Gr. *Boiotia*) with the Greek *bous*, "heifer" (as in "the land of the heifer").

[34] At Delphi the divine oracle was given by the Pythia (priestess of Apollo) from an inner room or cave inside the temple of Apollo.

serpent in the sky that lies outstretched between the twin bears.[35] He makes no tarrying, but seizes on the Phoenicians, whether they are preparing for fighting or for flight or whether very fear holds both in check. Some he slays with his fangs, some he crushes in his constricting folds, and some he stifles with the deadly corruption of his poisoned breath.

The sun had reached the middle heavens and drawn close the shadows. And now Cadmus, wondering what has delayed his companions, starts out to trace them. For shield, he has a lion's skin; for weapon, a spear with glittering iron point and a javelin; and, better than all weapons, a courageous soul. When he enters the wood and sees the corpses of his friends all slain, and victorious above them their huge-bodied foe licking their piteous wounds with bloody tongue, he cries: "Most loyal dead friends, either I shall avenge your death or be your comrade in it." So saying, he heaved up a massive stone with his right hand and with mighty effort hurled its mighty bulk. Under such a blow, high ramparts would have fallen, towers and all; but the serpent went unscathed, protected against that strong stroke by his scales as by an iron doublet and by his hard, dark skin. But that hard skin cannot withstand the javelin too, which now is fixed in the middle fold of his tough back and penetrates with its iron head deep into his flank. The creature, mad with pain, twists back his head, views well his wound, and bites at the spear-shaft fixed therein. Then, when by violent efforts he had loosened this all round, with difficulty he tore it out; but the iron head remained fixed in the backbone. Then indeed fresh fuel was added to his native wrath; his throat swells with full veins, and white foam flecks his horrid jaws. The earth resounds with his scraping scales, and such rank breath as exhales from the Stygian cave befouls the tainted air. Now he coils in huge spiral folds; now shoots up, straight and tall as a tree; now he moves on with huge rush, like a stream in flood, sweeping down with his breast the trees in his path. Cadmus gives way a little, receiving his foe's rushes on the lion's skin, and holds in check the ravening jaws with his spear-point thrust well forward. The serpent is furious, bites vainly at the hard iron and catches the sharp spear-head between his teeth. And now from his venomous throat the blood begins to trickle and stains the green grass with spattered gore. But the wound is slight, because the serpent keeps backing from the thrust, drawing away his wounded neck, and by yielding keeps the stroke from being driven home nor allows it to go deeper. But Cadmus follows him up and presses the planted point into his throat; until at last an oak-tree stays his backward course and neck and tree are pierced together. The oak bends beneath the serpent's weight and the stout trunk groans beneath the lashings of his tail.

While the conqueror stands gazing on the huge bulk of his conquered foe, suddenly a voice sounds in his ears. He cannot tell whence it comes, but he hears it saying: "Why, son of Agenor, do you gaze on the serpent you have slain? You too shall be a serpent for men to gaze on." Long he stands there, with quaking heart and pallid cheeks, and his hair rises up on end with chilling fear. But behold, the hero's helper, Pallas,[36] gliding down through the high air, stands beside him, and she

---

[35] A constellation between the Great and Little Bears (Ursa Major and Minor).

[36] Athena.

bids him plow the earth and plant therein the dragon's teeth, destined to grow into a nation. He obeys and, having opened up the furrows with his deep-sunk plow, he sows in the ground the teeth as he is bid, a man-producing seed. Then, a thing beyond belief, the plowed ground begins to stir; and first there spring up from the furrows the points of spears, then helmets with colored plumes waving; next shoulders of men and breasts and arms laden with weapons come up, and the crops grows with the shields of warriors.[37] So when on festal days the curtain in the theatre is raised, figures of men rise up, showing first their faces, then little by little all the rest; until at last, drawn up with steady motion, the entire forms stand revealed, and plant their feet upon the curtain's edge.[38]

Frightened by this new foe, Cadmus was preparing to take his arms. "Take not your arms," one of the earth-sprung brood cried out, "and take no part in our fratricidal strife." So saying, with his hard sword he clave one of his earth-born brothers, fighting hand to hand; and instantly he himself was felled by a javelin thrown from far. But he also who had slain this last had no longer to live than his victim, and breathed forth the spirit which he had but now received. The same dire madness raged in them all, and in mutual strife by mutual wounds these brothers of an hour perished. And now the youth, who had enjoyed so brief a span of life, lay writhing on their mother earth warm with their blood—all save five.[39] One of these five was Echion,[40] who, at Pallas' bidding, dropped his weapons to the ground and sought and made peace with his surviving brothers. These the Sidonian wanderer had as comrades in his task when he founded the city granted him by Phoebus' oracle.

4.11. THESEUS' UNIFICATION OF ATTICA, FROM PLUTARCH'S *LIFE OF THESEUS*

Plutarch (ca. 46–126 CE) was a prolific Greek writer from Chaironeia, a city of Boiotia. His writings cover historical and philosophical (Platonist) topics, and he was most active as a political figure in his own community as well as a priest at the nearby temple of Apollo at Delphi. His intellectual reputation reached Rome, and he eventually became a Roman citizen. The *Parallel Lives* are his most famous work. It contains the biographies of famous Greek and Roman characters (Theseus, Solon, Perikles, Alexander the Great, Cicero, Julius Caesar, Marc Antony), arranged in pairs so as to draw comparisons between the characters' moral qualities and flaws. The *Life of Theseus* is paired with that of Romulus, both being legendary kings and founders of Athens and Rome, respectively.

Theseus, the son of Poseidon and a mortal woman, is a figure only attested in the realm of legend, although Plutarch treats him as an historical figure, collecting and contrasting various accounts of him. Theseus' life is situated in the

---

[37] These men were called *Spartoi* ("sewn") in Greek tradition, with no relation to Sparta.

[38] Alluding to figures painted in the curtain, which in Roman theaters was raised, not lowered, so the figures would emerge gradually from the bottom up (note after Melville 1986).

[39] These five are the ancestors of the Theban principal families. Notice that the fratricidal theme anticipates the death of Oedipus' sons, Eteokles and Polyneikes, at each others' hands in the later stage of the Theban saga (theme of Sophocles' tragedy *Seven against Thebes*).

[40] His name means "Viperman."

remote past inhabited by figures such as Herakles, Medea, and the Argonauts, hence one generation before the Trojan War. Theseus' birth and exploits before he becomes king are not included below but instead are found in Part 3, document 11.c, as narrated in Apollodorus' *Library* and *Epitome*, the other main source for Theseus besides Plutarch. The passage here narrates how, after he becomes king, he is responsible for a series of political reforms (projected from later historical times), especially the unification of the region of Attica around the city of Athens (a process called *synoikismos*). To Theseus is also ascribed the foundation of rituals and festivals and other crucial components of Athenian culture. (For more on Theseus, see the headnote to Part 3, document 11.c; see also Figure 21.)

SOURCE: Plutarch, *Life of Theseus* 24–25.3. B. Perrin, *Plutarch's Lives,* vol. 1 (Loeb Classical Library, Cambridge, MA and London, 1914), with minor modifications.

(24) After the death of Aigeus, Theseus conceived a wonderful design, and settled all the residents of Attica in one city, thus making one people (*demos*) of one city out of those who up to that time had been scattered about and were not easily called together for the common interests of all; at times they even quarreled and fought with each other. He visited them, then, and tried to win them over to his project township by township and clan by clan. The common folk and the poor quickly answered to his summons; to the powerful he promised government without a king and a democracy,[41] in which he should only be commander in war and guardian of the laws, while in all else everyone should be on an equal footing. Some he readily persuaded to this course, and others, fearing his power, which was already great, and his boldness, chose to be persuaded rather than forced to agree to it. Accordingly, after doing away with the town-halls and council-chambers and magistracies in the several communities, and after building a common town-hall and council-chamber for all on the ground where the upper town of the present day stands, he named the city Athens, and instituted a Panathenaic festival. He instituted also the Metoikia, or "Festival of Settlement," on the sixteenth day of the month Hekatombaion, and this is still celebrated. Then, laying aside the royal power, as he had agreed, he proceeded to arrange the government, and that too with the sanction of the gods. For an oracle came to him from Delphi, in answer to his enquiries about the city, as follows:

> "Theseus, offspring of Aigeus, son of the daughter of Pittheus,
> many indeed the cities to which my father has given
> bounds and future fates within your citadel's confines.
> Therefore be not dismayed, but with firm and confident spirit
> counsel only; the bladder will traverse the sea and its surges."

And this oracle they say the Sibyl afterwards repeated to the city, when she cried:

> "Bladder may be submerged; but its sinking will not be permitted."

---

[41] Meaning literally "the power (*kratos*) of the people (*demos*)."

(25) Desiring still further to enlarge the city, he invited all men thither on equal terms, and the phrase "Come hither all people" they say was a proclamation of Theseus when he established a people, as it were, of all sorts and conditions. However, he did not suffer his democracy to become disordered or confused from an indiscriminate multitude streaming into it, but was the first to separate the people into noblemen and husbandmen and handicraftsmen. To the noblemen he committed the care of religious rites, the supply of magistrates, the teaching of the laws, and the interpretation of the will of Heaven, and for the rest of the citizens he established a balance of privilege, the noblemen being thought to excel in dignity, the husbandmen in usefulness, and the handicraftsmen in numbers. And that he was the first to show a leaning towards the multitude, as Aristotle says, and gave up his absolute rule, seems to be the testimony of Homer also, in the Catalogue of Ships,[42] where he speaks of the Athenians alone as a "people" (*demos*).

He also coined money, and stamped it with the effigy of an ox, either in remembrance of the Marathonian bull, or of Tauros, the general of Minos, or because he would invite the citizens to agriculture. From this coinage, they say, "ten oxen" and "a hundred oxen" came to be used as terms of valuation. Having attached the territory of Megara securely to Attica, he set up that famous pillar on the Isthmos, and carved upon it the inscription giving the territorial boundaries. It consisted of two trimeters, of which the one towards the east declared: "Here is not Peloponnesos, but Ionia;" and the one towards the west: "Here is the Peloponnesos, not Ionia."

4.12. THE FOUNDATION OF CARTHAGE

4.12.a. Foundation Legend, from Justin, *Epitome of Trogus*

Justin (Marcus Iunianus Iustinus) was a Roman historian who wrote an abridged version (known as an "Epitome") of Trogus Pompeius' massive historical work *Philippic Histories* (*Historiae philippicae et totius mundi origines et terrae situs*), which narrated in forty-four books the history of the areas of the world that came under Alexander the Great's domination. His organizing scheme was similar to that of Herodotos, framed around the expansion of the Persian Empire. The date of Justin is uncertain, except that he postdates Trogus, a Celtic-Roman who wrote under Augustus (first century BCE to first century CE, a contemporary of Livy), and who based his work on earlier Greek sources.

Carthage (*Qart-Hadasht* or "New Town" in Phoenician) was a colony founded by Phoenicians from Tyre (in today's Lebanon) on the coast of North Africa, on the outskirts of today's capital of Tunisia, Tunis. According to tradition, Carthage was founded in 814 BCE, and archaeological remains, if about a century later, attest to the Phoenician foundation and rapid development of the city and its surroundings. Since Carthaginian literary texts have not survived, it is difficult to distinguish original Carthaginian elements in the story from the Greek and later Roman versions of it. However, allusions to some of the same facts and characters were recorded in the Annals of Tyre (as transmitted by Josephus), and features such as sacred prostitutes and the inherited system of

[42] A reference to Homer's *Iliad* 2.547.

priesthood are genuinely Near Eastern. In turn, the names Pygmalion, Elissa, and Acerbas are all adaptations of the attested Phoenician names Pumayyaton, Elisha or Alashya, and Zakarbaal. The Cypriot element in the story also points to possible historical links, as Alashya was an ancient name for Cyprus in Near Eastern sources and another legendary king, Pygmalion, is associated with Cyprus and the cult to Aphrodite/Ashtart (see story in Part 5, document 16).

In any event, the exceptional circumstances of this foundation befit a city that would become a great Mediterranean power. The ties with the Phoenician mother city of Tyre are essential to the story, and in fact the Carthaginians maintained a strong sense of descent from Tyre even as they quickly developed their own unique culture and empire. In turn, the story of the first queen of Carthage, Elissa, was the inspiration for Virgil's Dido in the *Aeneid*, and her dramatic death on a pyre in order to avoid an undesired marriage is turned into Dido's similar suicide on a pyre after Aeneas abandons her (on which see Part 5, document 8).

SOURCE: Justin, *Epitome of Trogus' Philippic Histories*, Book 18.4–6. J. S. Watson, *Justin, Cornelius Nepos, and Eutropius* (London, 1876, reprint 2008), with minor modifications.

(4) The Tyrians, being thus settled under the auspices of Alexander, quickly grew powerful by frugality and industry.

Before the massacre of the masters by the slaves, when they abounded in wealth and population, they sent a portion of their youth into Africa, and founded Utica. Meanwhile their king (?) Mutto died at Tyre, appointing his son Pygmalion and his daughter Elissa, a maiden of extraordinary beauty, his heirs. But the people gave the throne to Pygmalion, who was quite a boy. Elissa married Acerbas, her uncle, who was priest of Hercules, a dignity next to that of the king. Acerbas had great but concealed riches, having laid up his gold, for fear of the king, not in his house, but in the earth; a fact of which, though people had no certain knowledge of it, report was not silent. Pygmalion, excited by the account, and forgetful of the laws of humanity, murdered his uncle, who was also his brother-in-law, without the least regard to natural affection. Elissa long entertained a hatred to her brother for his crime, but at last, dissembling her detestation, and assuming mild looks for the time, she secretly contrived a mode of flight, admitting into her confidence some of the leading men of the city, in whom she saw that there was a similar hatred of the king, and an equal desire to escape. She then addressed her brother in such a way as to deceive him; pretending that "she had a desire to move to his house, in order that the home of her husband might no longer revive in her, when she was desirous to forget him, the oppressive recollection of her sorrows, and that the sad remembrances of him might no more present themselves to her eyes." To these words of his sister, Pygmalion was no unwilling listener, thinking that with her the gold of Acerbas would come to him. But Elissa put the attendants, who were sent by the king to assist in her moving, on board some vessels in the early part of the evening, and sailing out into the deep, made them throw some loads of sand, put up in sacks as if it was money, into the sea. Then, with tears and mournful voice, she invoked Acerbas, entreating that "he would favorably receive his wealth which he had left behind him, and accept that as an offering to his shade, which he had found to be the cause of his death."

Next she addressed the attendants, and said that "death had long been desired by her, but as for them, cruel torments and a direful end awaited them, for having disappointed the tyrant's avarice of those treasures, in the hopes of obtaining which he had committed fratricide." Having thus struck terror into them all, she took them with her as companions of her flight. Some senators, too, who were ready against that night, came to join her, and having offered a sacrifice to Hercules, whose priest Acerbas had been, proceeded to seek a settlement in exile.

(5) Their first landing place was the isle of Cyprus, where the priest of Jupiter, with his wife and children, offered himself to Elissa, at the instigation of the gods, as her companion and the sharer of her fortunes, stipulating for the perpetual honor of the priesthood for himself and his descendants. The stipulation was received as a manifest omen of good fortune. It was a custom among the Cyprians to send their daughters, on stated days before their marriage, to the sea-shore, to prostitute themselves, and thus procure money for their marriage portions, and to pay, at the same time, offerings to Venus for the preservation of their chastity in time to come. Of these Elissa ordered about eighty to be seized and taken on board, that her men might have wives, and her city a population. During the course of these transactions, Pygmalion, having heard of his sister's flight, and preparing to pursue her with unfeeling hostility, was scarcely induced by the prayers of his mother and the menaces of the gods to remain quiet; the inspired augurs warned him that "he would not escape with impunity, if he interrupted the founding of a city that was to become the most prosperous in the world." By this means some respite was given to the fugitives; and Elissa, arriving in a gulf of Africa, attached the inhabitants of the coast, who rejoiced at the arrival of foreigners, and the opportunity of bartering commodities with them, to her interest. Having then bargained for a piece of ground, as much as could be covered with an ox-hide, where she might refresh her companions, wearied with their long voyage, until she could conveniently resume her progress, she directed the hide to be cut into the thinnest possible strips, and thus acquired a greater portion of ground than she had apparently demanded; whence the place had afterwards the name of Byrsa. The people of the neighborhood subsequently gathering about her, bringing, in hopes of gain, many articles to the strangers for sale, and gradually fixing their abodes there, some resemblance of a city arose from the concourse. Ambassadors from the people of Utica, too, brought them presents as relatives, and exhorted them "to build a city where they had chanced to obtain a settlement." An inclination to detain the strangers was felt also by the Africans; and, accordingly, with the consent of all, Carthage was founded, an annual tribute being fixed for the ground which it was to occupy. At the commencement of digging the foundations an ox's head was found, which was an omen that the city would be wealthy, indeed, but laborious and always enslaved. It was therefore removed to another place, where the head of a horse was found, which, indicating that the people would be warlike and powerful, portended an auspicious site. In a short time, as the surrounding people came together at the report, the inhabitants became numerous, and the city itself extensive.

(6) When the power of the Carthaginians, from success in their proceedings, had risen to some height, Hiarbas, king of the Maxitani, desiring an interview with ten of the chief men of Carthage, demanded Elissa in marriage, denouncing war in case

of a refusal. The deputies, fearing to report this message to the queen, acted towards her with Carthaginian artifice, saying that "the king asked for some person to teach him and his Africans a more civilized way of life, but who could be found that would leave his relations and go to barbarians, and people that were living like wild beasts?" Being then reproached by the queen, "in case they refused a hard life for the benefit of their country, to which, should circumstances require, their life itself was due," they disclosed the king's message, saying that "she herself, if she wished her city to be secure, must do what she required of others." Being caught by this subtlety, she at last said (after calling for a long time with many tears and mournful lamentations on the name of her husband Acerbas), that "she would go whither the fate of her city called her." Taking three months for the accomplishment of her resolution, and having raised a funeral pile at the extremity of the city, she sacrificed many victims, as if she would appease the shade of her husband, and make her offerings to him before her marriage; and then, taking a sword, she ascended the pile, and, looking towards the people, said, that "she would go to her husband as they had desired her," and put an end to her life with the sword. As long as Carthage remained unconquered, she was worshipped as a goddess. This city was founded seventy-two years before Rome; but while the bravery of its inhabitants made it famous in war, it was internally disturbed with various troubles, arising from civil differences. Being afflicted, among other calamities, with a pestilence, they adopted a cruel religious ceremony, an execrable abomination, as a remedy for it; for they immolated human beings as victims, and brought children (whose age excites pity even in enemies) to the altars, entreating favor of the gods by shedding the blood of those for whose life the gods are generally wont to be entreated.

4.12.b. Aeneas' Arrival at Carthage, from Virgil's *Aeneid*, Book 1

(For Virgil and the *Aeneid*, see headnotes to Part 1, documents 11 and 11.a.) In this passage, Virgil narrates how a shipwrecked Aeneas reaches the shores of North Africa. His mother, Venus, leads him into the city of Carthage, where he will be received by Dido, its founder and queen (for their romance, see Part 5, document 8). In the first passage, Venus, appearing as a hunter to Aeneas, tells him where he is and recounts the story of the foundation of Carthage by Dido (see Elissa's story as reported by Justin, document 4.12.a). Then, as he reaches the city, he sees it under construction. The anachronism is fantastic, as it clearly evokes the building of a Roman city (alluding to the theater and its columns, for instance), pointing the reader to the rebuilding of Carthage as a Roman colony by Augustus in 29 BCE (during Virgil's life time), over a century after its total destruction in 146 BCE in the Third Punic War. The connection between Aeneas and Carthage had been made already by Gnaeus Naevius (third century BCE) in his epic poem about the First Punic War, though he did not mention Dido explicitly. The centrality of Carthage in this poetic masterpiece about the origins of Rome showcases the importance of the Carthage-Rome conflict for Roman identity as a Mediterranean power, especially after the Second Punic War (218–201 BCE). The *Aeneid*, in fact, opens with an Odyssey-like presentation of the main character, Aeneas ("Arms and the man

. . ."), followed by a statement about Carthage: "Once, an old city existed, and Tyrian settlers controlled it, / Carthage, a distant menace to Italy. . . . This was her (Juno's) candidate city to rule as the king of all nations, / If fate allowed, etc." (lines 12–18).

Aeneas, who appears most prominently in the *Iliad* fighting Diomedes (Book 5) and Achilles (Book 20), was protected by the gods (mostly Apollo and Aphrodite), who often rendered him invisible through different means. The invisibility that Venus also bestows upon her son in the *Aeneid* (1.411–413) allows the hero to walk among potential enemies. It also portrays him as displaced in time, cruising through a city founded centuries after the fall of Troy and described as the Roman city refounded many centuries later. The anachronism is even more poignant when Aeneas gazes upon the reliefs just being carved on the temple of Juno, portraying the great battles of the Trojan War.

In this fresh recasting of the *Aeneid*, F. Ahl produces a tightened-up version of the traditional English hexameter. Each line contains between twelve and seventeen syllables, as does Virgil's Latin hexameter, but Ahl's meter is based on both syllabic quantity and English stress. Italics are used to help the reader position stress in cases where there might be ambiguity.

SOURCE: Virgil, *Aeneid*, Book 1. 418–457. F. Ahl, *Virgil, Aeneid* (Oxford World Series, Oxford and New York, 2007), with minor modifications.

(Venus appears to Aeneas dressed as a female hunter after he is shipwrecked on the coast near Carthage)

"What shall I call you, O virgin? For neither your face nor expression

Seems merely human and, further, your voice doesn't sound like a mortal's.

Surely you *must* be a god. Phoebus' sister? Related to some Nymph?

(330) Bring us fulfillment, whoever you are, please lighten our struggle!

Please inform us, at least, where under the sun we are stranded,

Where in the world are these shores? We know neither the place nor the people;

We are just wandering lost, driven here by the winds and the wild seas;

Many a victim will fall by our hands to show thanks at your altars."

(335) Venus said: "I don't think I deserve any honors of that sort.

Wearing the quiver is normal style for us Tyrian virgins,

As are the calf-high costume boots laced tight, and in purple.

Tyrians live here. Phoenician settlements: Agenor's city,[43]

That's what you see, but on Libyan soil among war-toughened peoples.

---

[43] In other words, Tyre, since Agenor was in Greek legend the ancestor of the Tyrians (father of Kadmos, Europa, and Phoenix and others in some versions, in others only father of Phoinix, who fathered Kadmos and the others).

(340) Dido's the ruler in charge. She came here to escape from her brother,
Sailing from Tyre. It's a long tale of wrong and injustice, a long tale:
Twists, turns, full of deceit.[44] But I'll summarize most of the main
points.

Dido had married Sychaeus, the richest of all the Phoenician
Landowners. She, poor girl, loved him deeply. For she was a virgin

(345) Child-bride, betrothed the first time that her father had checked
wedding omens

Ruling Tyre, in those days, was Pygmalion. He was her brother,
And quite a monster of crime, far surpassing all possible rivals.
Conflict arose among in-laws. Pygmalion, secure in his sister's
Love for them both, lusting blindly for gold, killed Sychaeus in
cold blood

(350) Secretly, catching him quite off guard and in front of an altar.
Evil, unrighteous man, he concealed what he'd done for a long
time,
Toyed with the lovesick bride, raised false hopes, crafted illusions.
But in her dreams, the true form of her unburied husband
approached her,
Raising before her a face that was wasted with terrible pallor,

(355) Baring the truth of the brutal crime at the altar, the daggered
Breast, and disclosing each unseen crime concealed in the palace.
Then the dream urges her on to craft speedy escape from her
homeland,
And, as resources for travel, reveals where there's long-buried tre-
asure,
Massive ingots, silver and gold. No one knew they existed.

(360) Dido, moved by all this, made her plans, sought allies in exile.
All those who felt cruel hate for the tyrant, all people who feared
him
Keenly, assembled; then, pirating ships which, by chance, were
already
Outfitted, loaded the gold. So greedy Pygmalion's riches
Take to the open seaways-a bold coup, led by a woman.

(365)   Putting in here, at this very place where you now see enormous
Ramparts, the rising castle of Carthage's new town, they purchased
Land, just as much as one could mark off with the hide of a single
Ox. And they called it Byrsa, 'The Hide,' to recall the transaction.

---

[44] Here as in the lines below (see 350) and in other passages, Virgil stresses the Carthaginian
stereotypes of deceitfulness and untrustworthiness (what the Romans called *Punica fides*), impiety,
and lack of family values, to be contrasted with Roman defense of *fides, pietas,* and family.

What about you? Who are you? What part of the world have you
   come from?

(370) Where are you travelling to?" In response to her various enquiries,

He gave a sigh, reached into his heart, gave a genuine answer:

"Goddess, were I to retrace the whole tale from its very beginning,

If you had free time to hear our chronicles, all of our troubles,

Venus, the Evening Star,[45] would end daylight and close up Olympus.

(375)   Ancient Troy was our home, though I wonder if Troy's name
   has ever

Passed through the ears of you gods.[46] We've been blown over various seaways;

Now, some self-willed tempest has beached us on Libya's coastline.

I am Aeneas the Righteous. I carry with me on my vessel

Household gods that I saved from the foe. My fame reaches heaven.

(380) Seeking a homeland in Italy, I, mighty Jupiter's offspring,

Had, when I launched upon Phrygian seas, two squadrons of ten
   ships.

My goddess mother showed me my course. Fate commanded. I
   followed.

Just seven ships have survived, all damaged by high seas and east
   winds.

Nobody knows me, I've nothing, I'm wandering Libyan deserts.

(385) Europe and Asia reject me."[47]

(385–417 skipped: After Venus gives reassurance and instructions to Aeneas, he and his men,
who had also made it to shore separately, all march into the city veiled by a protective opaque cloud.)

Meanwhile, they've hurried the length of the route pointed out by
   the pathway

And are ascending a hill whose menacing heights offer full views

(420) Over the city and look both across at, and down on, its castle.

Awed by the massive construction, where once there were rickety
   hovels,

Awed by the gates, by the noise, the paved roadways, Aeneas just
   marvels.

---

[45] Note the irony that he is talking to Venus the goddess without knowing it.

[46] The comment must be intended as a reproach, as the Trojan War was stirred by a dispute
between gods, more specifically by Aphrodite as she promised to give Helen to Paris in the
famous Judgment of Paris.

[47] But he has now arrived at Africa.

Fired-up Tyrians work at their tasks; some extend the defense walls,
Strengthen the castle and, with bare hands, lever masonry uphill.
(425) Some decide housing-sites, mark boundary lines with a furrow.
Magistrates, legal codes, and a sacred senate are chosen.
Others excavate ports, still others are laying foundations,
Deep in the ground, for a theatre. Some chisel out from the
     cliff-sides
Tall columns, massive in size: decor for a stage in the future.
(430) Work keeps bees just as busy as this in the sunshine of early
Summer across meadows covered with flowers when they lead out
     the now grown
New generation from hives, as they store up the streams of their
     honey,
Stretching the combs' wax cells to the full with the sweetness of
     nectar,
Or when unloading the incoming swarm, or when, massed like an
     army,
(435) Driving those useless creatures, the drones, from the bounds of
     their compound.
Work seethes; thyme's sweet savor enhances the fragrance of
     honey.
"O, how blessed are people whose ramparts are already rising!"
So Aeneas observes, looking up at the roofs of the city,
Fenced, as he walks, by a fortress of cloud (it's a marvelous story)
(440) Moving along in their midst unseen, yet mingling with people.
Centrally placed in the city a park, most delightfully shaded,
Marked where Phoenicians, battered by waves and by violent storm
     winds,
Landed and dug up the sign pointed out as an omen by ruling
Juno: the head of a spirited horse, foretelling the nation's
(445) Future: distinction in war and in steady traffic of commerce.
Dido of Sidon was here constructing a temple to Juno . . .
Bronze-bound beams, and the doors rasped open on hinges of
     wrought brass.
Here, in this park, something new first touched him now, and it
     gentled
(450) Fears; now Aeneas dared, for the first time, dream of survival,
Dared put greater trust in events, despite his reversals.
For, while awaiting the ruler below the huge temple, he took in
All its details, marveling at how that city had prospered,

(455) Noting the artists' skill, the combined success of their labors.

Awestruck, he saw the whole series of battles at Troy represented,

Wars that were already famed world-wide in rumor and story . . .

4.13. THE FOUNDATION OF ROME

4.13.a. Beginning of Livy's *History of Rome*, Book 1

Titus Livius was a Roman historian who lived during the second half of the first century BCE and into the first century CE (59 BCE–17 CE). He was thus a contemporary of Octavian Caesar (called Augustus as emperor), who ruled from 27 BCE to 14 CE. His most important and only surviving work was a history of Rome, entitled *Ab urbe condita* (*History of Rome*, lit. "From the foundation of the city"), covering the time from Rome's foundation, traditionally set in 753 BCE, to Augustus' reign. Livy was sympathetic to Republican ideals, that is, to the nonmonarchic type of political government before the emperors started ruling Rome, which happened during his lifetime. However, his history, which glorifies the accomplishments of the Roman people and its leaders, includes Augustus, with whose family he was on good terms. Livy's work was acclaimed and hugely influential from the outset not only in Rome but across the empire. The Preface to Livy's work, excerpted below, explains his motivations and goals in contributing to the already existing histories of Rome. In particular, it admits the difficulties inherent in treating the more distant and semi-legendary events as history.

Livy's contemporary Virgil also wrote a glorified work about the origins of the Romans for Augustus, but he did so in the form of an epic poem, the *Aeneid*, centered around the figure of Aeneas and his son Iulus, who were claimed as ancestors by the Julian family (which included Julius Caesar and Augustus; for this propaganda, see Figure 15). Aeneas was the son of Anchises (who belonged to the house of Priam, king of Troy) and Aphrodite (Venus in Latin tradition), thus making the Julian family descended from a goddess. (On Aeneas, see document 4.12.b; Part 5, document 8; and Part 6, document 13; on Anchises and Aphrodite, see Part 5, document 5.)

Traditions about Aeneas are much older, however, and in the *Iliad* Aeneas is saved from death several times by the gods, who make clear his destiny as a survivor and head of a royal lineage (e.g., *Iliad* 20.307–08). The identification of the Romans with the Trojans is also an interesting commentary on how they viewed and represented themselves: as part of the Greek heroic tradition, yet remaining distinctly non-Greeks.

SOURCE: Livy, *History of Rome*, Book 1 (Preface-7.3). B. O. Foster, *Livy*, vol.1 (Loeb Classical Library, Cambridge, MA and London, 1919), with minor modifications.

(Preface) Whether I am likely to accomplish anything worthy of the labor, if I record the achievements of the Roman people from the foundation of the city, I do not really know, nor if I knew would I dare to avouch it – perceiving as I do that the theme is not only old but hackneyed, through the constant succession of new historians, who believe either that in their facts they can produce more authentic information, or that in their style they will prove better than the rude attempts of the ancients. Yet, however this shall be, it will be a satisfaction to have done myself as much as lies in me to commemorate the deeds of the foremost people of the world; and if in so vast a company of writers my own reputation should be obscure, my consolation would be the fame and greatness of those whose renown will throw mine into the shade. Moreover, my subject involves infinite labor, seeing that it must be traced back above seven hundred years, and that proceeding from slender beginnings it has so increased as now to be burdened by its own magnitude; and at the same time I doubt not that to most readers the earliest origins and the period immediately succeeding them will give little pleasure, for they will be in haste to reach these modern times, in which the might of a people which has long been very powerful is working its own undoing. I myself, on the contrary, shall seek in this an additional reward for my toil, that I may avert my gaze from the troubles which our age has been witnessing for so many years, so long at least as I am absorbed in the recollection of the brave days of old, free from every care which, even if it could not divert the historian's mind from the truth, might nevertheless cause it anxiety.

Such traditions as belong to the time before the city was founded, or rather was presently to be founded, and are rather adorned with poetic legends than based upon trustworthy historical proofs, I purpose neither to affirm nor to refute. It is the privilege of antiquity to mingle divine things with human, and so to add dignity to the beginnings of cities; and if any people ought to be allowed to consecrate their origins and refer them to a divine source, so great is the military glory of the Roman People that when they profess that their Father and the Father of their Founder was none other than Mars, the nations of the earth may well submit to this also with as good a grace as they submit to Rome's dominion. But to such legends as these, however they shall be regarded and judged, I shall, for my own part, attach no great importance. Here are the questions to which I would have every reader give his close attention what life and morals were like: through what men and by what policies, in peace and in war, empire was established and enlarged; then let him note how, with the gradual relaxation of discipline, morals first gave way, as it were, then sank lower and lower, and finally began the downward plunge which has brought us to the present time, when we can endure neither our vices nor their cure.

What chiefly makes the study of history wholesome and profitable is this, that you behold the lessons of every kind of experience set forth as on a conspicuous monument.[48] From these you may choose for yourself and for your own state what to imitate, from these mark for avoidance what is shameful in the conception and shameful in the result. For the rest, either love of the task I have set myself deceives me, or no state was ever greater, none more righteous or richer in good examples, none ever was where avarice and luxury came into the social order so late, or where humble means and thrift were so highly esteemed and so long held in honor. For

---

[48] This "monument" is a metaphor for the nation's grand achievements (note the architectural metaphor above as the morals "plunge" as a decaying building).

true it is that the less men's wealth was, the less was their greed. Of late, riches have brought in avarice, and excessive pleasures the longing to carry wantonness and license to the point of ruin for oneself and of universal destruction.

But complaints are sure to be disagreeable, even when they shall perhaps be necessary; let the beginning, at all events, of so great an enterprise have none. With good omens rather would we begin, and, if historians had the same custom which poets have, with prayers and entreaties to the gods and goddesses, that they might grant us to bring to a successful issue the great task we have undertaken.

(1) First of all, then, it is generally agreed that when Troy was taken vengeance was wreaked upon the other Trojans, but that two, Aeneas and Antenor, were spared all the penalties of war by the Achivi,[49] owing to long-standing claims of hospitality, and because they had always advocated peace and the giving back of Helen. They then experienced various vicissitudes. Antenor, with a company of Eneti who had been expelled from Paphlagonia in a revolution and were looking for a home and a leader—for they had lost their king, Pylaemenes, at Troy—came to the inmost bay of the Adriatic. There, driving out the Euganei, who dwelt between the sea and the Alps, the Eneti and Trojans took possession of those lands. And in fact the place where they first landed is called Troy, and the district is therefore known as Trojan, while the people as a whole are called the Veneti.

Aeneas, driven from home by a similar misfortune, but guided by fate to under-takings of greater consequence, came first to Macedonia; thence was carried, in his quest of a place of settlement, to Sicily; and from Sicily laid his course towards the land of Laurenturn. This place too is called Troy. Landing there, the Trojans, as men who, after their all but immeasurable wanderings, had nothing left but their swords and ships, were driving booty from the fields, when King Latinus and the Aborigines, who then occupied that country, rushed down from their city and their fields to repel with arms the violence of the invaders. From this point the tradition follows two lines. Some say that Latinus, having been defeated in the battle, made a peace with Aeneas, and later an alliance of marriage.[50] Others maintain that when the opposing lines had been drawn up, Latinus did not wait for the charge to sound, but advanced amidst his chieftains and summoned the captain of the strangers to a parley. He then inquired what men they were, whence they had come, what mishap had caused them to leave their home, and what they sought in landing on the coast of Laurentum. He was told that the people were Trojans and their leader Aeneas, son of Anchises and Venus; that their city had been burnt, and that, driven from home, they were looking for a dwelling-place and a site where they might build a city. Filled with wonder at the renown of the race and the hero, and at his spirit, prepared alike for war or peace, he gave him his right hand in solemn pledge of lasting friendship. The commanders then made a treaty, and the armies saluted each other. Aeneas became a guest in the house of Latinus; there the latter, in the pres-ence of his household gods, added a domestic treaty to the public one, by giving his daughter in marriage to Aeneas. This event removed any doubt in the minds of the Trojans that they had brought their wanderings to an end at last in a permanent

---

[49] The Achaeans in Homer, one of the names used for the Greek contingents.

[50] This is the version that Virgil follows in the *Aeneid* (books 7–12).

and settled habitation. They founded a town, which Aeneas named Lavinium, after his wife. In a short time, moreover, there was a male scion of the new marriage, to whom his parents gave the name of Ascanius.

(2) War was then made upon Trojans and Aborigines alike. Turnus was king of the Rutulians, and to him Lavinia had been betrothed before the coming of Aeneas. Indignant that a stranger should be preferred before him, he attacked, at the same time, both Aeneas and Latinus. Neither army came off rejoicing from that battle. The Rutulians were beaten: the victorious Aborigines and Trojans lost their leader Latinus. Then Turnus and the Rutulians, discouraged at their situation, fled for succor to the opulent and powerful Etruscans and their king Mezentius, who held sway in Caere, at that time an important town. Mezentius had been, from the very beginning, far from pleased at the birth of the new city; he now felt that the Trojan state was growing much more rapidly than was altogether safe for its neighbors, and readily united his forces with those of the Rutulians. Aeneas, that he might win the goodwill of the Aborigines to confront so formidable an array, and that all might possess not only the same rights but also the same name, called both nations Latins[51]; and from that time on the Aborigines were no less ready and faithful than the Trojans in the service of King Aeneas.

Accordingly, trusting to this friendly spirit of the two peoples, which were growing each day more united, and, despite the power of Etruria, which had filled with the glory of her name not only the lands but the sea as well, along the whole extent of Italy from the Alps to the Sicilian Strait, Aeneas declined to defend himself behind his walls, as he might have done, but led out his troops to battle. The fight which ensued was a victory for the Latins: for Aeneas it was, besides, the last of his mortal labors. He lies buried, whether it is fitting and right to term him god or man, on the banks of the river Numicus; men, however, call him Jupiter Indiges.[52]

(3) Ascanius, Aeneas' son, was not yet ripe for authority; yet the authority was kept for him, unimpaired, until he arrived at manhood. Meanwhile, under a woman's regency, the Latin State and the kingdom of his father and his grandfather stood unshaken—so strong was Lavinia's character—until the boy could claim it. I shall not discuss the question—for who could affirm for certain so ancient a matter?—whether this boy was Ascanius, or an elder brother, born by Creusa while Ilium yet stood, who accompanied his father when he fled from the city, being the same whom the Julian family call Iulus[53] and claim as the author of their name. This Ascanius, no matter where born or of what mother (it is agreed in any case that he was Aeneas' son), left Lavinium to his mother (or stepmother) when its population came to be too large, for it was already a flourishing and wealthy city for those days, and founded a new city himself below the Alban Mount. This was known from its position, as it lay stretched out along the ridge, by the name of Alba Longa.

---

[51] Cf. Virgil's *Aeneid* 12.835.

[52] Meaning "indigenous" ("of/from a place"), equivalent to Greek *chthonios* ("from the land"). He was also called *Pater Chthonios* (a Greek equivalent to *Pater Indiges*), *Deus Indiges,* and *Aeneas Indiges.*

[53] The family of Julius Caesar and the subsequent Julio-Claudian dynasty claimed this descent from Iulus son of Aeneas and thus from Venus (Aphrodite) herself.

From the settlement of Lavinium to the planting of the colony at Alba Longa was an interval of some thirty years. Yet the nation had grown so powerful, in consequence especially of the defeat of the Etruscans, that even when Aeneas died, and even when a woman became its regent and a boy began his apprenticeship as king, neither Mezentius and his Etruscans nor any other neighbors dared to attack them. Peace had been agreed to on these terms, that the River Albula, which men now call the Tiber, should be the boundary between the Etruscans and the Latins. Next Silvius reigned, son of Ascanius, born, as it chanced, in the forest. He begat Aeneas Silvius, and he Latinus Silvius. By him several colonies were planted, and called the Ancient Latins. Thereafter the cognomen Silvius was retained by all who ruled at Alba. From Latinus came Alba, from Alba Atys, from Atys Capys, from Capys Capetus, from Capetus Tiberinus. This last king was drowned in crossing the River Albula, and gave the stream the name which has been current with later generations. Then Agrippa, son of Tiberinus, reigned, and after Agrippa Romulus Silvius was king, having received the power from his father. Upon the death of Romulus by lightning, the kingship passed from him to Aventinus. This king was buried on that hill, which is now a part of the City of Rome, and gave his name to the hill. Proca ruled next. He begat Numitor and Amulius; to Numitor, the elder, he bequeathed the ancient realm of the Silvian family. Yet violence proved more potent than a father's wishes or respect for seniority. Amulius drove out his brother and ruled in his stead. Adding crime to crime, he destroyed Numitor's male issue; and Rhea Silvia, his brother's daughter, he appointed a Vestal under pretence of honoring her, and by consigning her to perpetual virginity, deprived her of the hope of children.

(4) But the Fates were resolved, as I suppose, upon the founding of this great City, and the beginning of the mightiest of empires, next after that of Heaven. The Vestal was ravished, and having given birth to twin sons, named Mars as the father of her doubtful offspring, whether actually so believing, or because it seemed less wrong if a god were the author of her fault. But neither gods nor men protected the mother herself or her babes from the king's cruelty; the priestess he ordered to be manacled and cast into prison, the children to be committed to the river. It happened by singular good fortune that the Tiber having spread beyond its banks into stagnant pools afforded nowhere any access to the regular channel of the river, and the men who brought the twins were led to hope that being infants they might be drowned, no matter how sluggish the stream. So they made shift to discharge the king's command, by exposing the babes at the nearest point of the overflow, where the fig-tree Ruminalis formerly, they say, called Romularis now stands. In those days this was a wild and uninhabited region. The story persists that when the floating basket in which the children had been exposed was left high and dry by the receding water, a she-wolf, coming down out of the surrounding hills to slake her thirst, turned her steps towards the cry of the infants, and with her teats gave them suck so gently, that the keeper of the royal flock found her licking them with her tongue.

Tradition assigns to this man the name of Faustulus, and adds that he carried the twins to his hut and gave them to his wife Larentia to rear. Some think that Larentia, having been free with her favors, had got the name of "she-wolf" among the shepherds, and that this gave rise to this marvelous story.[54] The boys, thus born and reared, had no sooner attained to youth than they began yet without neglecting the farmstead or the flocks to range the glades of the mountains for game. Having in this way gained both strength and resolution, they would now not only face wild beasts, but would attack robbers laden with their spoils, and divide up what they took from them among the shepherds, with whom they shared their toils and pranks, while their band of young men grew larger every day.

(5) They say that the Palatine was even then the scene of the merry festival of the Lupercalia, which we have today, and that the hill was named Pallantium, from Pallanteum, an Arcadian city, and then Palatium.[55] There Evander, an Arcadian of that stock, who had held the place many ages before the time of which I am writing, is said to have established the yearly rite, derived from Arcadia, that youths should run naked about in playful sport, doing honor to Lycaean Pan, whom the Romans afterwards called Inuus. When the young men were occupied in this celebration, the rite being generally known, some robbers who had been angered by the loss of their plunder laid an ambush for them, and although Romulus successfully defended himself, captured Remus and delivered up their prisoner to King Amulius, even lodging a complaint against him. The main charge was that the brothers made raids on the lands of Numitor, and pillaged them, with a band of young fellows, which they had got together, like an invading enemy. So Remus was given up to Numitor to be punished.

From the very beginning Faustulus had entertained the suspicion that they were children of the royal blood that he was bringing up in his house; for he was aware both that infants had been exposed by order of the king, and that the time when he had himself taken up the children exactly coincided with that event. But he had been unwilling that the matter should be disclosed prematurely, until opportunity offered or necessity compelled. Necessity came first; accordingly, driven by fear, he revealed the facts to Romulus. It chanced that Numitor too, having Remus in custody, and hearing that the brothers were twins, had been reminded, upon considering their age and their far from servile nature, of his grandsons. The inquiries he made led him to the same conclusion, so that he was almost ready to acknowledge Remus. Thus on every hand the toils were woven about the king. Romulus did not assemble his company of youths for he was not equal to open violence but commanded his shepherds to come to the palace at an appointed time, some by one way, some by another, and so made his attack upon the king; while from the house of Numitor came Remus, with another party which he had got together, to help his brother. So Romulus slew the king.

(6) At the beginning of the fray Numitor exclaimed that an enemy had invaded the city and attacked the palace, and drew off the active men of the place to serve as an armed garrison for the defense of the citadel; and when he saw the young men approaching, after they had dispatched the king, to congratulate him, he at once

---

[54] The word for she-wolf, *lupa*, could also mean "prostitute," a sense preserved in Romance languages. For instance, in Spanish "lupanar" is a name for brothel.

[55] The etymology of the word is probably simpler, perhaps from *palus* ("pale, stick"), indicating a "fenced precinct." Our word for "palace" (and "palatial") comes from Palatium, since the Roman ruling families build their mansions in this hill.

summoned a council, and laid before it his brother's crimes against himself, the parentage of his grandsons, and how they had been born, reared, and recognized. He then announced the tyrant's death, and declared himself to be responsible for it. The brothers advanced with their band through the midst of the crowd, and hailed their grandfather king, whereupon such a shout of assent arose from the entire throng as confirmed the new monarch's title and authority.

The Alban state being thus made over to Numitor, Romulus and Remus were seized with the desire to found a city in the region where they had been exposed and brought up. And in fact the population of Albans and Latins was too large; besides, there were the shepherds. All together, their numbers might easily lead men to hope that Alba would be small, and Lavinium small, compared with the city which they should build. These considerations were interrupted by the curse of their grand-sires, the greed of kingly power, and by a shameful quarrel which grew out of it, upon an occasion innocent enough. Since the brothers were twins, and respect for their age could not determine between them, it was agreed that the gods who had those places in their protection should choose by augury who should give the new city its name, who should govern it when built. Romulus took the Palatine for his augural quarter, Remus the Aventine.

(7) Remus is said to have been the first to receive an augury, from the flight of six vultures. The omen had been already reported when twice that number appeared to Romulus. Thereupon each was saluted king by his own followers, the one party lay-ing claim to the honor from priority, the other from the number of the birds. They then engaged in a battle of words and, angry taunts leading to bloodshed, Remus was struck down in the affray. The commoner story is that Remus leaped over the new walls in mockery of his brother, whereupon Romulus in great anger slew him, and in menacing wise added these words withal, "So perish whoever else shall leap over my walls!"[56] Thus Romulus acquired sole power, and the city, thus founded, was called by its founder's name.

4.13.b. Romulus and Remus, from Plutarch's *Life of Romulus*

In his *Parallel Lives* (on which see headnote to document 4.11), Plutarch nar-rates the life of Romulus in detail, contrasting different versions and sources in a rather scholarly way. The passage selected below complements nicely Livy's account above, adding some interesting details about the process of founding the new city.

SOURCE: Plutarch, *Life of Romulus* 11–12.1. B. Perrin, *Plutarch's Lives*, vol. 1 (Loeb Classical Library, Cambridge, MA and London, 1914), with minor modifications.

(11) Romulus buried Remus, together with his foster-fathers, in the Remonia,[57] and then set himself to building his city, after summoning from Tuscany men who

---

[56] Another tradition makes Celer (the man in charge of the walls, appointed by Romulus) the killer of Remus.

[57] The fortified precinct that Remus had founded in the Aventine hill, called Remonium after him but later called Rignarium (according to Plutarch in 9.4).

prescribed all the details in accordance with certain sacred ordinances and writings, and taught them to him as in a religious rite. A circular trench was dug around what is now the Comitium,[58] and in this were deposited first-fruits of all things the use of which was sanctioned by custom as good and by nature as necessary; and finally, every man brought a small portion of the soil of his native land, and these were cast in among the first-fruits and mingled with them. They call this trench, as they do the heavens, by the name of *mundus*. Then, taking this as a centre, they marked out the city in a circle round it. And the founder, having shod a plough with a brazen ploughshare, and having yoked to it a bull and a cow, himself drove a deep furrow round the boundary lines, while those who followed after him had to turn the clods, which the plough threw up, inwards towards the city, and suffer no clod to lie turned outwards. With this line they mark out the course of the wall, and it is called, by contraction, *pomerium*, that is *post murum*, behind or next the wall. And where they purposed to put in a gate, there they took the share out of the ground, lifted the plough over, and left a vacant space. And this is the reason why they regard all the wall as sacred except the gates; but if they held the gates sacred, it would not be possible, without religious scruples, to bring into and send out of the city things which are necessary, and yet unclean.

(12) Now it is agreed that the city was founded on the twenty-first of April, and this day the Romans celebrate with a festival, calling it the birthday of their country. And at first, as it is said, they sacrificed no living creature at that festival, but thought they ought to keep it pure and without stain of blood, since it commemorated the birth of their country. However, even before the founding of the city, they had a pastoral festival on that day, and called it Parilia.

At the present time, indeed, there is no agreement between the Roman and Greek months, but they say that the day on which Romulus founded his city was precisely the thirtieth of the month, and that on that day there was a conjunction of the sun and moon, with an eclipse, which they think was the one seen by Antimachos, the epic poet of Teos, in the third year of the sixth Olympiad.[59]

---

[58] A space for popular assembly near the forum. The *mundus* (said below to be in the same place) was really the sacred center of the city in the Palatinum (Palatine).

[59] That is, the year 753 BCE.

PART 5

EROS
AND THE
LABORS
OF LOVE

STORIES OF LOVE, fulfilled and unfulfilled, loom over a great part of ancient literature. Eros (Passionate Love) and Pothos (Desire) represent the human emotions, but also a philosophical principle, an impulse or tendency toward something we lack, which has moved the story of cosmic and human existence since the beginning. In Hesiod's *Theogony*, Eros was among the first four primordial elements (Chaos, Earth, Tartaros, and Eros, in that order, *Th.* 116–120; see Part 1, document 5). Sexual tension is in Hesiod the motor behind the first cosmic struggle, the division between Earth and Sky. An illegitimate love promised by Aphrodite to Paris triggered the greatest war of all, the Trojan War. Even at Troy, it was the quarrel over another captive woman that caused the strife between Achilles and Agamemnon, hence setting in motion the plot of Homer's *Iliad*. In the Hebrew Bible, generations of heroes or superhuman beings were born from the desire of gods for mortal women (Genesis 6.1–4 preceding the Flood; Part 2, document 4), just as in Greek myth (see Hesiod's *Catalogue of Women*, following the *Theogony*). We cannot reproduce here all the love stories in ancient Mediterranean myths. The following is a selection that represents the different cultures and literary genres and showcases some of the most prominent motifs surrounding Love.

One of these motifs is the danger and the often disastrous consequences of an amorous union between a god and a mortal. The relationship is more frequently, but not always, between a male god and a mortal woman (see Cupid and Psyche in document 5.20; Hades and Persephone in Part 6, document 8; Zeus and Semele in Part 3, document 10.b). Many such stories, not included here, feature unions between Zeus and women, such as Semele, Europa, Leda, Io, and others. Hesiod's *Catalogue of Women* lists many of them, and a sort of catalogue is also offered in the *Odyssey,* Book 11 (see Part 6, document 7). Less frequently, a female goddess seduces a mortal hero, which we see in the stories of Gilgamesh and Ishtar, Venus and Anchises in the *Hymn to Aphrodite*, Cybele and Attis, and Aphrodite and Adonis. In yet other cases, a male god seduces a male mortal, usually a young one (here Zeus and Ganymede, Apollo and Hyacinth).

Although most love stories in antiquity represent heterosexual relationships, already in antiquity there are stories of homoerotic love. This is especially true in the Greek and Roman sources, and it is not by coincidence that homosexuality was more widely accepted in Greek culture than in most cultures and periods up to modern times. Aristophanes' speech in Plato's *Symposium* (Part 7, document 4) is an inspiring, if comical, defense of the equality of both homo- and heterosexual orientations, and the stories of Apollo and Hyathinth (document 5.15) and of Zeus and Ganymede (*Hymn to Aphrodite* 203–217; document 5.5) also portray the *erastes-eromenos* ("male lover–male beloved") relationship. The "dispute" between Horus and Seth (Part 3, document 2), involving homosexual intercourse, could have been reproduced in this section, too. In the stories of Caenis-Caeneus (document 5.18), Hermaphroditus (document 5.13), and Achilles at Skyros (document 5.19), we see characters crossing gender boundaries, whether by cross-dressing (Achilles), having their gender physically changed (Caenis-Caeneus), or even physically merging with the person of the opposite sex (Hermaphroditus). A story also circulated about the famous Theban seer Teiresias (who appears most famously in Sophokles' *Oedipus King* and Euripides' *Bacchae*) according to which he was temporarily transformed into a woman (Hesiod, fr. 275 M-W and Apollodorus' *Library*, 3.6.7).

The theme of incest (whether fulfilled or only intended) is also present in the selections here, as in the stories of Phaidra (document 5.11) and Myrrha (document 5.17). Not included in this volume is the interesting biblical story of Lot and his daughters (Genesis 19.30–38), in which, after the fall of Sodom and Gomorrah and the death of their mother, Lot's daughters get him drunk in order to sleep with him and conceive offspring. The dynamics driving other famous love stories include extreme jealousy (Cephalus and Procris, Medea and Jason); the desperation caused by abandonment by the male lover (Theseus and Ariadne, Aeneas and Dido, Achilles at Skyros); the rare exemplary case of perfect fidelity and endurance (Penelope and Odysseus); the workings of unnatural passions (Pasiphae and the bull; Pygmalion and the statue); and powerful women who fail to seduce a man and punish him in some way (wife in the *Story of the Two Brothers*, Potiphar's wife, Ishtar, Phaidra). Some love stories cross the boundaries of life and death: these have been included in Part 7 because of their close connection with the Underworld. These are the stories about Aphrodite and Adonis and Orpheus and Eurydice and the already-mentioned forced marriage between Persephone and Hades in the *Hymn to Demeter*.

The idea, derived from Plato's philosophical writings, that there are two types of Aphrodite or Venus, a higher and a lower one, is not directly represented in this part, although it is perhaps vaguely echoed in Apuleius' portrayals of Cupid and Venus in the *Golden Ass* as they play with Psyche, the soul (document 5.20). This dichotomy between a celestial Aphrodite (on whose Semitic origins see document 5.5) and the lower goddess of sexuality who enslaves the weak human body is articulated in Plato's *Symposium* 180d–181b (Pausanias' speech), *Phaedrus* 248c, and in Apuleius' *Apology*. The goddesses of Love, be they Ishtar, Aphrodite, or Venus, intervene in the following narratives, changing the fates of heroes and even of nations, such as in the case of Carthage and Rome in the story of Aeneas (document 5.8). (The ties of Venus with Rome are also showcased in Figures 15 and 16.)

All in all, the workings of Love are far from romanticized in these ancient myths: the picture is instead rather grim. Desire is often dangerous and the cause of suffering, but then again, these are good components of what makes stories worth telling. ✦

5.1. ISHTAR AND GILGAMESH: *EPIC OF GILGAMESH*, TABLET VI

In this episode from the *Epic of Gilgamesh* (for which see the headnote to Part 3, document 1), the Mesopotamian goddess of Love, Ishtar, makes an advance on the hero Gilgamesh and is shamefully rejected and scorned. In what follows, a resentful Ishtar begs her father (the sky god Anu) to release the Bull of Heaven to attack Gilgamesh and his friend Enkidu. The heroes kill the Bull, which will in turn lead the divine council to decree Enkidu's demise in Tablet VII.

The offense of the love goddess has been compared to the episode in the *Iliad* where the hero Diomedes physically harms Aphrodite, who then goes up to heaven to complain to her parents, Zeus and Dione (not the traditional parents of the goddess but in this episode seemingly parallel to Anu and Antu) (see episode in Part 3, document 8.a and footnote 122 there).

This text comes from the Standard Babylonian Version of the *Epic of Gilgamesh* (SBV), Tablet VI, divided into six columns (i, ii, etc.).

SOURCE: S. Dalley, *Myths from Mesopotamia: Creation, The Flood, Gilgamesh, and Others* (Oxford World's Classics, Oxford and New York, 1989, rev. ed. 2000), with minor modifications.

TABLET VI

(SBV) (i) He washed his filthy hair, he cleaned his gear, shook out his locks over his back, threw away his dirty clothes and put on fresh ones. He clothed himself in robes and tied on a sash. Gilgamesh put his crown on his head and Ishtar the princess raised her eyes to the beauty of Gilgamesh.

"Come to me, Gilgamesh, and be my lover! Bestow on me the gift of your fruit! You can be my husband, and I can be your wife.[1] I shall have a chariot of lapis lazuli and gold harnessed for you, with wheels of gold, and horns of *elmeshu*-stone.[2] You shall harness *umu*-demons as great mules!

"Enter into our house through the fragrance of pine! When you enter our house, the wonderfully-wrought threshold shall kiss your feet! Kings, nobles, princes shall bow down beneath you.

"The verdure (?) of mountain and country shall bring you produce; your goats shall bear triplets, your ewes twins, your loaded donkey shall outpace the mule. Your horses shall run proud at the chariot; [your ox] shall be unrivalled at the yoke."

Gilgamesh made his voice heard and spoke; he said to Ishtar the princess: "What could I give you if I possessed you? I would give you body oil and garments, I would give you food and sustenance. Could I provide you with bread fit for gods? Could I provide you with ale fit for kings? *(one line missing)* Could I heap up [. . .] a robe? [. . . if] I possess you? [You would be . . .] ice, a draughty door that can't keep out winds and gusts, a palace that [rejects (?)] its own warriors (?), (ii) an elephant which [. . .] its covering bitumen which [stains (?)] its carrier, a waterskin which [soaks (?)]

---

[1] Cf. the identical proposal by Ereshkigal to Nergal in the Mesopotamian story of *Nergal and Ereshkigal* (not in this volume).

[2] The "horns" are the yoke terminals of the chariot.

its carrier, a juggernaut (?) which [smashes (?)] a stone wall, a battering ram which destroys [. . .] of war, a shoe which bites into [the foot] of its wearer.

"Which of your lovers [lasted] forever? Which of your masterful paramours went to heaven? Come, let me [describe (?)] your lovers to you! He of the sheep (?) [. . .] knew him: For Dumuzi the lover of your youth you decreed that he should keep weeping year after year. You loved the colorful *allallu*-bird,³ but you hit him and broke his wing. He stays in the woods crying 'My wing!' You loved the lion, whose strength is complete, but you dug seven and seven pits for him. You loved the horse, so trustworthy in battle, but you decreed the whip, goad, and lash for him; you decreed that he should gallop seven leagues (non-stop); you decreed that he should be overwrought and thirsty; you decreed endless weeping for his mother Sililu. You loved the shepherd, herdsman, and chief shepherd, who was always heaping up the glowing ashes for you, and cooked ewe-lambs for you every day. But you hit him and turned him into a wolf; his own herd-boys hunt him down and his dogs tear at his haunches.⁴ You loved Ishullanu, your father's gardener, who was always bringing you baskets of dates. They brightened your table every day; you lifted your eyes to him and went to him: 'My own Ishullanu, let us enjoy your strength, so put out your hand and touch our vulva!'

(iii) "But Ishullanu said to you: 'Me? What do you want of me? Did my mother not bake for me, and did I not eat? What I eat (with you) would be loaves of dishonor and disgrace; rushes would be my only covering against the cold.' You listened as he said this, and you hit him, turned him into a frog (?), left him to stay amid the fruits of his labors. But the pole (?) goes up no more, [his] bucket goes down no more.

"And how about me? You will love me and then [treat me] just like them!"

When Ishtar heard this, Ishtar was furious, and [went up] to heaven. Ishtar went up and wept before her father Anu; her tears flowed before her mother Antu: "Father, Gilgamesh has shamed me again and again! Gilgamesh spelt out to me my dishonor, my dishonor and my disgrace."

Anu made his voice heard and spoke. He said to the princess Ishtar: "Why (?) didn't you accuse Gilgamesh the king for yourself, since Gilgamesh spelt out your dishonor, your dishonor and your disgrace?"

Ishtar made her voice heard and spoke. She said to her father Anu: "Father, please give me the Bull of Heaven, and let me strike Gilgamesh down! Let me [. . .] Gilgamesh in his dwelling! If you don't give me the Bull of Heaven, I shall strike (?) [. . .] I shall set my face towards the infernal regions, I shall raise up the dead, and they will eat the living,⁵ I shall make the dead outnumber the living!"

Anu made his voice heard and spoke. He said to the princess Ishtar: "On no account should you request the Bull of Heaven from me! There would be seven

---

³ Probably a roller. The Akkadian word for "my wing" (*kappi*) is used onomatopoeically for the bird's cry.

⁴ This transformation has been compared to the Greek myth of Aktaion, a hunter who was turned into a stag by Artemis and hunted.

⁵ The same threat is made by Ishtar to the doorkeeper of the Underworld in *Ishtar's Descent* (see Part 6, document 2) and by Ereshkigal in *Nergal and Ereshkigal*. In *Odyssey* 12.377–383 Helios threatens to shed light in the Netherworld.

years of chaff in the land of Uruk; you would gather chalk (?) [instead of gems (?)]; you would raise (?) grass (?) [instead of . . . (?)]."

Ishtar made her voice heard and spoke. She said to her father Anu: "I have heaped up a store [of grain in Uruk (?)], I have ensured the production of [. . .], [. . .] years of chaff. [. . .] has been gathered.[. . .] grass.[. . .] for him.

(gap of 1 or more lines) [. . .] of the Bull of Heaven [. . .]."

(iv) Anu listened to Ishtar speaking, and he put the Bull of Heaven's reins in her hands. Ishtar [took hold] and directed it. When it arrived in the land of Uruk it [. . .] It went down to the river, and seven [. . .] river [. . .].

At the snorting of the Bull of Heaven a chasm opened up, and one hundred young men of Uruk fell into it; two hundred young men, three hundred young men. At its second snorting another chasm opened up, and another hundred young men of Uruk fell into it; two hundred young men, three hundred young men fell into it. At its third snorting a chasm opened up, and Enkidu fell into it. But Enkidu leapt out. He seized the Bull of Heaven by the horns. The Bull of Heaven blew spittle into his face, with its thick tail it whipped up its dung.

Enkidu made his voice heard and spoke. He said to Gilgamesh: "My friend, we were too arrogant [when we killed Humbaba]. How can we give recompense [for our action]? My friend, I have seen [. . .] And my strength [. . .] Let me pull out [. . .] Let me seize [. . .] Let me [. . .] In [. . .] And plunge your sword [. . .] In between the base of the horns and the neck tendons."

Enkidu spun round [to] the Bull of Heaven, and seized it by its thick tail, and [. . .]

(v) Then Gilgamesh, like a but[cher (?)] heroic and [. . .] plunged his sword in between the base of the horns and the neck tendons. When they had struck down the Bull of Heaven they pulled out its innards, set them before Shamash, backed away and prostrated themselves before Shamash. Then the two brothers sat down.

Ishtar went up on to the wall of Uruk the Sheepfold. She was contorted with rage, she hurled down curses: "That man Gilgamesh who reviled me has killed the Bull of Heaven!"

Enkidu listened to Ishtar saying this, and he pulled out the Bull of Heaven's shoulder and slapped it into her face: "If I could only get at you as that does, I would do the same to you myself; I would hang its intestines on your arms!"

Ishtar gathered the crimped courtesans, prostitutes and harlots.[6] She arranged for weeping over the Bull of Heaven's shoulder.

Gilgamesh called craftsmen, all the armorers, and the craftsmen admired the thickness of its horns. Thirty minas of lapis lazuli was (needed for) each of their pouring ends; two minas of gold (?) (was needed for) each of their sheathings. Six kor of oil was the capacity of both.[7] He dedicated (them) for anointing his god Lugalbanda[8]; took them in and hung them on his bed (where he slept) as head of the family. In the Euphrates they washed their hands and held hands and came

---

[6] The cultic servants of the goddess.

[7] Thirty minas is about 15 kilograms, two about 1 kilogram, and six kor about 1,800 liters. Lapis lazuli was one of the most valued stones in Mesopotamia, obtained in northeast Afghanistan.

[8] Lugalbanda was Gilgamesh's father.

riding through the main street of Uruk. The people of Uruk gathered and gazed at them.

(vi) Gilgamesh addressed a word to [his] retainers: "Who is finest among the young men? Who is proudest among the males?"

"Gilgamesh is finest among the young men! Gilgamesh is proudest among the males! [. . .] we knew in our anger. There is nobody like him who can please her [. . .]. [. . .]"

Gilgamesh made merry in his palace. Then they lay down, the young men were lying in bed for the night, and Enkidu lay down and had a dream. Enkidu got up and described the dream. He said to his friend,

(Catchline)

"My friend, why are the great gods consulting together?"

5.2. KING SNEFRU AND THE OARSWOMEN

The following Egyptian tale forms part of the so-called *Tales of King Khufu's Court*. This composition survives only on the *Papyrus Westcar* (*Pap. Berlin* 3033), dated to the Second Intermediate Period (ca. 1600 BCE), or perhaps the early Eighteenth Dynasty (ca. 1550 BCE), although the original text was possibly composed earlier, during the late Middle Kingdom (ca. 1773–1650 BCE). Like the later *Thousand and One Nights* (or *Arabian Nights*), the *Tales of King Khufu's Court* is a group of tales embedded into a framing story where King Khufu (Fourth Dynasty, ca. 2589–2566 BCE) asks his sons to narrate stories from the past for his amusement. The preserved part of the story (its beginning and end are lost) records tales set in the reigns of kings Djeser and Nebka (Third Dynasty) and Snefru (Fourth Dynasty, ca. 2613–2494 BCE), who was Khufu's father and predecessor. The tale of the oarswomen is narrated by prince Baefre, who was considered in later documents to be a Fourth Dynasty king but is not otherwise known in Old Kingdom texts. Toward the end, prince Hordjedef, who was considered a sage in later times, offers to Khufu a different entertainment: he presents to the king a man called Djedi, who predicts the arrival of the Fifth Dynasty kings. Setting aside this last tale, with important religious connotations, the general goal of this compilation of "wonders" is, above all, worldly entertainment, which includes, for instance, stories of infidelity or, in this case, consensual voyeurism.

SOURCE: Excerpt from the *Tales of King Khufu's Court*, *Papyrus Westcar* = *Papyrus Berlin* 3033, 4,17–6,22, translated and annotated by A. Diego Espinel.

(. . .) [THEN] BAEFRE STOOD UP TO SPEAK, AND SAID: "I will [cause that your majesty hears a wonder],[9] which happened in the time of your father Snef[ru, justified,[10]

---

[9] Many *lacunae* in the text have been restored thanks to some reiterations and similar narrative structures in the preserved text.

[10] Lit. "true of voice," an epithet given to the deceased. It served to indicate that its possessor had positively passed the judgment of the dead (or "weighing of the heart"), thus attaining eternal survival.

among the ones made] by the chief lector priest [Dj]adjaem[ankh] [. . .] [. . .] One day of these, the totality [. . .] all the [. . .] of the house of the king, l.i.h., in order to seek for himself [a quiet (lit. "cool") place, but he couldn't find it. Then he said:] 'Go and bring to me the chief [lector priest, the writer of texts. Djadjaemankh].'

"Then [he] was brought [to hi]m [immedia]tely, and [his majesty] said to him: ['I have dragged myself around every chamber of the] house [of the king, l.i.h.], in order to seek for myself a quiet [place] but I have not found it.'

"Then Djadjaemankh said to him: 'O may your majesty go to the pool of the Great House, l.i.h; provide yourself a vessel with every beautiful woman from the interior of your palace, and the heart of your majesty will be quiet while watching them rowing northwards and southwards. You will see the beautiful marshes of your pool, and you will see the fields and their beautiful shores, and your heart will be quiet because of this.'

"'Yes, I will make my rowboat ride. Bring me twenty oars of ebony decorated with gold, with handles of sandal wood decorated with electrum! Bring me twenty women with beautiful bodies, (well) breasted and haired, who have not given birth yet! And bring me twenty nets, and I will give these nets to these women setting aside their clothes.' Then all was done according to what his majesty had ordered.

"THEN THEY ROWED NORTHWARDS AND SOUTHWARDS, and the heart of his majesty was happy watching them row. Then one of them, who was at the steering-oar, got her braid tangled and a fish-pendant of new turquoise fell into the water. Then she stopped and did not row, and her line of rowers stopped and did not row.

"Then his majesty said: 'Why are you not rowing?'

"They said: 'Our steer has stopped and she does not row.'

"Then his majesty said to her: 'Why [are you] not ro[wing]?'

"[Th]en she said: ['(My) fish-pendant o]f ne[w turquoise fell] into the water.'

"[Then] he [. . .] [to her] [. . .] ['If you want] it, [I will give you another as] replacement.'

"[Then she said: 'I prefer] my object [rather than its copy.']

"Then [his majesty] sa[id: 'Go and bring to me the chief] lector priest [Djadjaemankh.']

"[Then he was brought to him immedia]tely, and his majesty said: 'Djadjaemankh, my brother! I have acted according to what you said, and the heart of his majesty was quiet watching them, but a fish-pendant of new turquoise of one steer has fallen into the water, and then she stopped and did not row, and therefore she has upset her line of rowers. Then I said to her 'why are you not rowing?' And she said to me, 'it is because a fish-pendant of new turquoise fell into the water.' Then I said to her: 'Row, it is me who will replace it,' and she told me, 'I prefer my object rather than its copy.'

"Then, the chief lector priest Djadjaemankh said his magical spells, and put one side of the water of the pool over the other one, and he found the fish-pendant lying on a sherd. Then he took it and gave it to its owner. Now, the water was twelve cubits (high) at the middle (of the pool), being twenty four cubits (tall) after being folded.[11] Then he said his magical spells and he brought back the waters of the pool to their

---

[11] Approximately 6 meters and 12 meters, respectively.

place. His majesty spent a nice day together with the whole Great House, l.i.h. There-fore, he rewarded the chief lector priest Djadjaemankh with every good thing.

"Look, the marvel happened in the time of your father, the Dual King Snefru, justified, as a deed by the chief lector priest and writer of texts, Djadjaemankh."

Then the majesty of the Dual King Khufu, justified, said: "Make an offering of a thousand loaves, a hundred jars of beer, an ox, and two pellets of terebinth resin to the majesty of the Dual King Snefru, justified; and make sure that a cake, a jar of beer, and a pellet of terebinth resin are given to the chief lector priest and writer of texts, Djadjaemankh, as I have seen his demonstration of wisdom." Then every thing [was] done according to what [his] majesty ordered. (. . .)

5.3. EGYPT: *STORY OF THE TWO BROTHERS*

This tale is only known through the *Papyrus d'Orbiney* (BM 10183) of the late Nineteenth Dynasty (ca. 1200 BCE). Its grammatical features, as well as the absence of other copies of the text, hint at an oral origin. The tale also resembles folk stories from other parts of the world. Despite these features, the main char-acters in the *Story of the Two Brothers* are divine beings, and, therefore, the story can be regarded as a popular rendition of a mythological narrative: Bata is the city god of Sako (current el-Keis?) in the Seventeenth province of Upper Egypt, and Inpu is the jackal god Anubis.

The present excerpt is part of the beginning of the tale and clearly recalls the story of Joseph and Potiphar's wife in Genesis 39 (document 5.4). The events that follow this excerpt are, however, very different, and rather more complex. After fleeing from his brother, Bata is transformed into different beings (a conifer tree, a bull, and a persea tree), which are successively killed. However, the repentant Inpu manages to revivify Bata in every occasion. Finally, Bata becomes king of Egypt and is succeeded by his eldest brother when he dies after a reign of thirty years.

SOURCE: Excerpts from *Papyrus d'Orbiney* (BM 10183: 1,1–1,4; 2,5–7,2), translated and anno-tated by A. Diego Espinel.

IT IS SAID that there were two brothers of the same mother and the same father: Inpu was the name of the elder, and Bata was the name of the younger. Inpu had a house and had a wife, and his younger brother was to him as if he were <his> son. It was he (i.e., Bata) who made the clothes for him (i.e., Inpu). He was the one who went behind his cattle to the fields. It was he who ploughed, and who harvested for him. It was he who made every task in the marshes. Indeed, his younger brother was an excellent [man]. There was no other like him in the entire land, for a god's strength was in him. (. . .)[12]

(. . .) Now, AFTER DAWN, WHEN A (NEW) DAY HAD COME, they went to the fields with their [seeds], and they started to plough. [Their hearts] were very happy with their achievements from the beginning of their work.

---

[12] For the sake of brevity, some lines have been omitted here because they do not add anything to the plot.

Now, MANY [DAYS] LATER, they were in the fields, and they needed seeds. THEN HE (INPU) sent his younger brother, saying: "Hurry up, and bring us seeds from the village." His younger brother fou[nd the] wife of his elder brother seated and plaiting (her hair), AND HE said to her: "Get up and give me seeds, as I have to hurry to the fields. My elder brother is waiting for me. Do not delay." THEN SHE said to him: "Go, open the barn and take whatever you want. Do not make me leave my hairdo unfinished." AND the youth entered his barn and he took a big vessel, as he wanted to take many seeds. He loaded himself with barley and emmer, and he came out carrying them. THEN SHE said to him: "How much is what is in your shoulder?" He said to her: "It is three sacks of emmer, and two sacks of barley: altogether totalling five, which are on my shoulder." So he said to her, AND SHE [spoke to him] saying: "There is [great] strength in you. I have observed your vigour daily." And she wanted to know him as a [man]. THEN SHE got up, grabbed him, and said to him: "Come, let's spend an [ho]ur lying together. It will be to your advantage. I will make good clothes for you."

THEN the youth became like a panther in [. . .] rage over the immoral proposal she had made to him, and she became very frightened, AND HE <had wo>rds with her, saying: "Look, you are like a mother to me, and your husband is like a father to me. He, who is older than me, is the one who has raised me. What is this great outrage you have said to me? Do not say it to me again! But I am not going to tell anyone, nor will I allow it to come out of my mouth to anybody." He took up his load, and he went to the fields. THEN HE reached his elder brother, and they finished the achievements of their work.

THEN, LATER, AT EVENING TIME, his elder brother returned to [his] house, while his younger brother was taking care of his cattle, and was loading himself with all the products of the fields, and was bringing the cattle back in front of him to let them sleep in the ba[rn, which was] in the village. Indeed, the wife of his elder brother was frightened <because of> the proposal she had made. THEN SHE took some fat and grease,[13] and she falsely pretended to be a battered woman, with the intention of saying to her husband: "It was your young brother who beat (me)." Her husband returned at evening time according to his daily routine, he reached his house, and he found his wife lying down and falsely ill. She did not pour water on his hands as usual, and she did not light up a fire in front of him. His house was in darkness, and she was prostrated, vomiting. Her husband said to her: "Who has had words with you?" Then she said to him: "No one has had words with me except your young brother. When he came to take seeds for you, he found me seated alone and he said to me: 'come, let's spend an hour lying together, loosen (your) braids.' So he said to me, but I did not listen to him. 'Am I not your mother? And is not your elder brother like your father?' So I said to him. Then he became frightened and he beat (me) to prevent me from informing you. If you let him live, I will die. Look, when he comes back, do not [. . .], for I curse the immoral proposal that he was about to make this morning."

---

[13] The precise function of these materials is unknown. Perhaps they could cause vomiting and therefore render the wife sick, or be used to simulate fake bruises.

THEN his elder brother became like a panther. He sharpened his spear, and he took it in his hand, AND his elder <brother> stood behind the door of the barn in order to kill his younger brother when he returned in the evening to let his cattle enter the barn. When the sun set, he loaded himself with all the vegetables of the fields according to his daily custom, and he returned. The lead cow entered into the barn and said to her herdsman: "Look, your elder brother is waiting for you holding a spear in order to kill you. Get away from him!" THEN HE heard what his lead cow had said. Another one entered, and it said the same to him. He looked under the door(leaf) of his barn, and he could see the legs of [his] elder [brother] who was waiting behind the door, with his spear in his hand. He left his load on the ground and he went away, and started to run away in flight. His elder brother went after him holding his spear.

THEN his younger brother invoked Re-Horakhty, saying: "My good lord, you are the one who distinguishes falsehood from truth." Then Re heard all his petitions and created a great body of water separating him from his elder <brother>, and he filled (it) with crocodiles, so one of them would be on one side and the other one on the other <side>. His elder brother struck his hand twice because he had not killed him. THEN his younger brother called him from his side, saying: "Wait here until dawn. When the sun disk has risen, I will litigate with you in front of him (i.e., Re) and he will deliver the guilty to the innocent, for I will not be with you anymore, and I will not be in the same place where you are. I will go to the Valley of the Conifer[14] (. . .)"

5.4. JOSEPH AND POTIPHAR'S WIFE: GENESIS 39

The story of Joseph and his rejection of Potiphar's wife is part of the so-called "ancestral history" in Genesis (Gen. 11.27–50.26), which follows the "primeval history" (Gen. 1.1–11.26) and tells the story of Abraham and his descendants, in this case the descendants of Jacob/Israel. The story of Joseph and his family (Gen. 37.1–50.26) revolves around the complicated relations between Joseph and his father and brothers, who had attempted to murder him. Joseph survives and is taken to Egypt as a slave, but he ends up serving as adviser to the Pharaoh himself. The story of passion and deceit in this passage provides the cause for Joseph to go to jail, from where he will rise to the favor of the Pharaoh thanks to his visions.

The story, whereby a powerful woman fails to seduce a man and then accuses him of being the seducer, has been most frequently compared with the Egyptian *Story of the Two Brothers* (document 5.3). The motif is also present in the story of Hippolytos and Phaidra (document 5.11) and of Bellerophon and Anteia in *Iliad* 6. 150 ff., as well as in the Near East in Gilgamesh's rejection of Ishtar's advances (document 5.1), which she punishes through the bull of heaven, although she does not issue a false accusation of the type found in the other stories.

SOURCE: The Hebrew Bible, Genesis 39, New Revised Standard Version, with minor modifications.

---

[14] An unknown and possibly imaginary place located in Lebanon.

(1) Now Joseph was taken down to Egypt, and Potiphar, an officer of Pharaoh, the captain of the guard, an Egyptian, bought him from the Ishmaelites who had brought him down there. (2) Yahweh was with Joseph, and he became a successful man; he was in the house of his Egyptian master. (3) His master saw that Yahweh was with him, and that Yahweh caused all that he did to prosper in his hands. (4) So Joseph found favor in his sight and attended him; he made him overseer of his house and put him in charge of all that he had. (5) From the time that he made him overseer in his house and over all that he had, Yahweh blessed the Egyptian's house for Joseph's sake; the blessing of Yahweh was on all that he had, in house and field. (6) So he left all that he had in Joseph's charge; and, with him there, he had no concern for anything but the food that he ate.

Now Joseph was handsome and good-looking. (7) And after a time his master's wife cast her eyes on Joseph and said, "Lie with me." (8) But he refused and said to his master's wife, "Look, with me here, my master has no concern about anything in the house, and he has put everything that he has in my hand. (9) He is not greater in this house than I am, nor has he kept back anything from me except yourself, because you are his wife. How then could I do this great wickedness, and sin against God?" (10) And although she spoke to Joseph day after day, he would not consent to lie beside her or to be with her. (11) One day, however, when he went into the house to do his work, and while no one else was in the house, (12) she caught hold of his garment, saying, "Lie with me!" But he left his garment in her hand, and fled and ran outside. (13) When she saw that he had left his garment in her hand and had fled outside, (14) she called out to the members of her household and said to them, "See, my husband has brought among us a Hebrew to insult us! He came in to me to lie with me, and I cried out with a loud voice; (15) and when he heard me raise my voice and cry out, he left his garment beside me, and fled outside." (16) Then she kept his garment by her until his master came home, (17) and she told him the same story, saying, "The Hebrew servant, whom you have brought among us, came in to me to insult me; (18) but as soon as I raised my voice and cried out, he left his garment beside me, and fled outside."

(19) When his master heard the words that his wife spoke to him, saying, "This is the way your servant treated me," he became enraged. (20) And Joseph's master took him and put him into the prison, the place where the king's prisoners were confined; he remained there in prison. (21) But Yahweh was with Joseph and showed him steadfast love; he gave him favor in the sight of the chief jailer. (22) The chief jailer committed to Joseph's care all the prisoners who were in the prison, and whatever was done there, he was the one who did it. (23) The chief jailer paid no heed to anything that was in Joseph's care, because Yahweh was with him; and whatever he did, Yahweh made it prosper.

5.5. APHRODITE AND ANCHISES: THE *HOMERIC HYMN TO APHRODITE*

(For the *Homeric Hymns*, see headnote to Part 3, document 9.) The earliest account of Aphrodite's birth is in Hesiod's *Theogony* (*Th.* 189–206; see Part 1, document 5), where she is born from Ouranos (Sky), more specifically from his severed genitalia and the foam around them, as they drift over the sea toward

Cyprus. The "foam" detail is in all likelihood an *aition* created in order to explain her otherwise obscure name, as if derived from *aphros* "foam." In the Homeric poems, however, she is the daughter of Zeus, specifically of Zeus and Dione (*Iliad* 5.370 ff.; see Part 3, document 8.a). In the *Homeric Hymn to Aphrodite*, as in Hesiod, the Love and Sex goddess is associated with the islands of Cyprus and Kythera, which is why she is frequently called Cypris and Kythereia.

The goddess's mythological roots in Cyprus are intimately connected with the importance of her cult on the island, especially at the sanctuary of Paphos (see line 59 below, also *Od.* 8.362–363), where she was assimilated with Phoenician Ashtart (Gr. Astarte), whose cult was widespread in the Near East, under different variants such as Mesopotamian Ishtar and Ugaritic Athtart. These connections are echoed by Herodotos when he says that the Phoenicians were the ones who introduced her cult into Greece via Kythera (Hdt. 1.105). Her title Kythereia might in fact be originally completely unrelated to the island and instead derived from the Semitic craftsman god Kothar (Ugaritic Kothar-wa-Hasis), whose consort she might have been in her eastern context, just as Aphrodite is Hephaistos' wife in Greek tradition. The title "Heavenly Aphrodite" (*Ourania*) that appears ubiquitously in Greek sources, such as Herodotos, Plato, and Pausanias, also echoes the Semitic Ashtart, who was called "Queen of Heaven." This quality of hers entered philosophical discussions about the different types of love, in which this "heavenly" Aphrodite was understood to represent a more elevated type of love in contrast to an Aphrodite called *Pandemos*, "of all the people," representing "lower" sexual needs and prostitution (e.g., Plato, *Symposium*, 180d).

The long *Homeric Hymn to Aphrodite* (*HH* 5) is regarded as among the earliest hymns (early seventh century BCE) because of its more archaic, Homeric language and its direct connection to the Epic Cycle (Homer echoes the affair between the goddess and Anchises in *Il.* 2.819–821, 5.311–313). The hymn focuses on the love affair between Aphrodite and the Trojan Anchises on Mount Ida, from which union the Trojan hero Aeneas will be born. Aeneas' escape from Troy is of course most celebrated in Virgil's *Aeneid*, but the story is at least as old as the *Iliad*, where he is saved several times against all odds and Poseidon "predicts" the continuation of the hero's line (*Il.* 20.302–308).

The *Hymn to Aphrodite* also contains the longest account of the story of Ganymede, the young son of Tros (eponymous ancestor of the Trojans), who was snatched by Zeus to become his cup-bearer and presumably lover, and it is alluded to briefly in numerous other sources. The myth is found already in Homer: in *Iliad* 5.265–266 it is mentioned in reference to the divine breed of horses given to Tros and inherited by Laomedon, also mentioned in the *Hymn* below. In *Iliad* 20.232–235 Ganymede is listed among the sons of Tros, and it is said that the gods snatched him away to be the cup-bearer of Zeus "on account of his beauty, so that he would live with the immortals." The motif was quite popular in artistic representations, in which Zeus was represented as an eagle, and appears briefly in a number of later literary sources (Apollodorus' *Library* 2.5.9 and 3.12.2, Ovid's *Metamorphoses* 10.152, Virgil's *Aeneid* 1.28 and 5.252, and Pausanias 24.5). The story of Tithonos is used in the *Hymn* as yet another example of how some gods made their mortal lovers immortal, contrary to what Aphrodite intends to do with Anchises.

SOURCE: *Homeric Hymn to Aphrodite* (*HH* 5), translated and annotated by C. López-Ruiz.

Muse, tell me the deeds of very golden Aphrodite of Cyprus, who aroused sweet desire in the gods, and dominated the tribes of mortal people and the birds from the sky and all the wild animals, as many as the dry land and as many as the sea nourish; for they all care for the deeds of well-crowned Kythereia.[15]

But there are three minds she cannot persuade nor deceive: the daughter of Zeus who bears the aegis, bright-eyed Athena, for she did not enjoy the deeds of very golden Aphrodite, (10) but enjoys wars and the works of Ares, and combat and battle and arranging for glorious deeds. She first taught carpenter-men who live on earth to make carts and chariots adorned with bronze; then she taught glorious works to the soft-skinned maidens in the halls, placing them in each one's minds. Nor does smile-loving[16] Aphrodite ever overpower Artemis in love-making, the noisy goddess of the golden bow; for this one also enjoys bows and slaying beasts in the mountains, and lyres and dances and acute cries (20) and shady woods and a city of just men.

Neither does the modest maiden Hestia take pleasure in the works of Aphrodite, she whom crooked-minded Kronos bore first, and who is in turn the youngest,[17] by the plan of Zeus the aegis-bearer; the lady whom both Poseidon and Apollo tried to marry; but she really did not want to, and firmly refused, and swore a great oath, which is most certainly fulfilled, as she touched the head of her father Zeus the aegis-bearer: that she would be a virgin all her days, magnificent among goddesses. But Zeus gave her a noble reward in place of marriage, (30) and so she sits at the heart of the house and takes the richest offerings.[18] In all the temples she is honored among the gods, and she is considered by all mortals the eldest of the gods.

She[19] cannot dominate the mind of these three nor deceive them; but of the others, not a thing escapes Aphrodite, neither among blessed gods nor among mortal people. She even led astray the mind of thunder-loving Zeus, who *is* the greatest and was hence allotted the greatest honor. Deceiving even his heart when she pleases, with ease she involved him with mortal women, (40) keeping the secret from Hera, his sister and wife, who by far is the best in beauty among the immortal goddesses, for she was born most glorious by crooked-minded Kronos and her mother Rhea; and Zeus, who knows eternal counsels, made her his revered and caring wife.[20]

---

[15] One of the main epithets of Aphrodite.

[16] *Philommeides*, "laughter-loving" or "smile-loving" is one of Aphrodite's most common epithets, which plays on the similarity in sound of *meidao* "to laugh" and *medea* "genitals."

[17] She was born first (the oldest) but "re-born" last, when Kronos vomited his children in reverse order than he had swallowed them (Hesiod, *Th.* 495–497).

[18] Hestia was the goddess of the hearth and the house (like Vesta in Roman religion).

[19] Aphrodite.

[20] A pun might be at play between *medea* "counsels" and *medea* "genitals" (both spelled in the same way, with *eta*), as well as with *aidoien* ("revered, modest") and *aidoion/aidoia* also meaning (as an euphemism) "genitals" (see similar pun with *philomedeia*, "smile-loving," epithet above).

But even upon Aphrodite's own heart Zeus cast sweet desire to be joined with a mortal man, so that *she* would not be left out from a human bed either, and one day brag in the midst of all the gods, sweetly smiling, (50) saying how she joined gods with mortal women and they bore mortal children for the gods, and how she also joined goddesses with mortal people.

And so Zeus cast in her heart sweet desire for Anchises, who was then tending cattle on the high peaks of Mount Ida, rich in springs,[21] looking just like the immortals in his build. When she saw him, smile-loving Aphrodite fell in love, and violent desire got hold of her senses. Off she went to Cyprus and entered her fragrant temple, at Paphos—for there she has a sanctuary and a fragrant altar—(60) there she entered and shut the gleaming doors; and there the Graces[22] washed her and anointed her with immortal olive oil, such as is poured onto the ever-lasting gods, aromatic, divine; this one in fact was perfumed just for her. Dressing herself well with all her beautiful clothes around her skin, adorning herself with gold, smile-loving Aphrodite rushed towards Troy, leaving behind fragrant Cyprus, making her way swiftly high up with the clouds. She reached Ida, rich in springs, mother of beasts, and she marched straight to the stable through the mountain; (70) and the gray wolves, light-eyed lions, bears, and swift leopards insatiable for deer were marching along with her, fawning; and when she saw them she rejoiced in her heart and cast desire in their chests, so they all lied together in pairs throughout their shady lairs.[23]

But she herself arrived at the well-built shelters; and she found him left alone in the stables, apart from the others—Anchises, the hero who possessed beauty from the gods. For all the others were following their herds along grassy fields, while he, left alone in the stables, apart from the others, (80) was pacing from here to there playing the lyre with penetrating sound. And she stood right in front of him, the daughter of Zeus, Aphrodite, like an unwed virgin in stature and appearance, lest he would be perturbed when he noticed her with his eyes. But when Anchises noticed her, he perceived and marveled at her appearance and her stature and her gleaming clothes. For she was dressed in a robe more radiant than the flame of fire, and had spiral bracelets and shiny brooches, and the most beautiful necklaces were around her soft neck, very fine works of gold; (90) and she was shining like the moon around her soft breasts, a marvel to see.[24]

Love took hold of Anchises, and he said these words to her: "Greetings, my lady, whoever of the blessed ones you are who arrives at these abodes, Artemis or Leto or golden Aphrodite, or well-born Themis or Athena of the gleaming eyes; or perhaps being one of the Graces you have come here, the ones who accompany all the gods

---

[21] Mt. Ida was southeast of Troy in Asia Minor. In *Iliad* 14.153–360 Hera seduces Zeus in this same mountain, with the help of Aphrodite.

[22] With the Horai ("Seasons") they are attendants (in some versions daughters) of Aphrodite.

[23] Aphrodite here is portrayed as a "mistress of beasts," as her Near Eastern counterparts Ishtar and Ashtart, and in Greek religion more frequently Artemis. See also her characterization in Lucretius' "Hymn to Venus" (document 5.7).

[24] In the Sumerian hymn to Inanna, she appears to her lover "like the light of the moon" and her beauty preparations are described similarly.

and are called immortal, or one of the nymphs who roam the beautiful woods, or one of the nymphs who inhabit this fine mountain, both its river-springs and its grassy meadows. (100) I will build you an altar on a hill-top, on a most visible spot, and I will perform for you fine sacrifices in every season. But you in turn, keeping a benevolent spirit, grant me to be a distinguished man among the Trojans, and make my offspring thrive in the future and that I myself live well for long and see the light of the sun, a happy man among my people, and reach the threshold of old age."

Then Zeus' daughter, Aphrdite, answered to him: "Anchises, most glorious of earth-born people, see, I am not a god; why do you keep comparing me to goddesses? (110) On the contrary, I am a mortal, for a woman was the mother who gave birth to me. Otreus is my father, of famous name, in case you have heard it, who rules over all of well-fortified Phrygia.[25] But your language as well as mine I know well; for a Trojan nurse raised me in the palace, who reared me since I was a small child, taking me from my dear mother's arms. So it is that I also know your language well. But now, the Argos-slayer[26] of the golden staff snatched me away from the dance of noisy Artemis of the golden bow. Many of us were playing, maidens and marriageable virgins, (120) and all around a countless multitude was encircling us. From there the Argos-slayer of the golden staff snatched me, and carried me over many labored fields of mortal people, and over many poor and abandoned lands, through which wild animals, eaters of raw flesh, roam by the shady lairs, and I thought I would not set my feet on the life-giving earth.

"He kept saying that I would be called the lawful wife of Anchises in his bed, and that I would bear you illustrious children. But when he had already indicated and explained this he certainly left, the strong Argos-slayer, to join the tribes of the immortals. (130) Thus I have come to you, and an overpowering anguish is upon me. But I beg you, by Zeus, or by your excellent parents (for base ones would not have born such a son): taking me, unwedded and innocent of love as I am, show me to your father and your caring mother and to your brothers who indeed share with you the same origin; I will not be an unseemly daughter-in-law for them, but a seemly one. But, quickly, send a messenger to the swift-horsed Phrygians, to tell my father and my afflicted mother; and they will surely send you sufficient gold and woven garments, (140) and you, please accept the many and rich presents as dowry. After you do this arrange for a pleasant wedding fitting for human beings and immortal gods."

When she had said this, she cast sweet desire in his heart. And Anchises was seized by love, and he uttered a word and said: "If you are a mortal, and a woman was the mother who gave birth to you, and Otreus is your father, of famous name, as you claim, and it is by the will of the immortal guide, Hermes, that you arrived here, and you are to be called my wife for all our days, then no one of the gods or of mortal people (150) will hold me back before I join you in love making here, right now; not even if the far-shooter Apollo himself should shoot fulminating darts from his silver bow. Then I would be willing, o woman who looks like the goddesses, to go down to the house of Hades, after going up your bed."

---

[25] Phrygia was a region northwest of Troy. King Otreus appears as an ally of Priam in the *Iliad*.

[26] Hermes.

So speaking, he grasped her hand, and smile-loving Aphrodite turned around, casting her beautiful eyes down, and followed towards the well-spread bed, to the place where it was always ready with soft covers for its lord; for upon it lay the hides of bears and deep-roaring lions, (160) whom he had himself killed in the high mountains. And when they had climbed onto the well-built bed, he first removed from her body the gleaming jewelry, the pins and spiral bracelets and the brooches and necklaces. Then he loosened her girdle and took off her radiant clothes and set them on a silver-studded chair, Anchises did. And then he, a mortal man, by the will of the gods and fate, lay with a deathless goddess, not knowing it for sure.

But when the shepherds turn their cattle and robust sheep back to the stable from the blooming pastures, (170) at that time she poured a sweet, deep, sleep over Anchises, while she herself dressed her body with beautiful clothes. When she had completely dressed her body, the radiant goddess stood in the hut, and she reached the roof of the well-made ceiling, and an immortal beauty shone out of her cheeks,[27] of the sort that befits well-crowned Kythereia. Then she woke him up, and she uttered a word and said: "Get up, son of Dardanos! Why are you sleeping so soundly? At least indicate if I seem to you the same as you perceived me with your eyes before!"

(180) So she spoke; and he obeyed very quickly out of his sleep. And as he saw the neck and the beautiful eyes of Aphrodite, he was scared and turned his eyes away, in another direction. At once he also covered his handsome face with a cloak, and addressed to her these winged words as a supplicant: "The moment I saw you with my eyes, goddess, I realized you were a god; but you would not tell me the truth. But I implore you, by Zeus the aegis-bearer, do not let me dwell among human beings, living without strength, but have pity; for the man becomes impotent, (190) who sleeps with immortal goddesses."

Aphrodite, the daughter of Zeus, then answered to him: "Anchises, most glorious among mortal people, have courage, and do not be too afraid in that heart of yours; there is no fear for you to suffer any harm from me, at least, or from the other blessed ones, since you are indeed dear to the gods. For you will have a dear son, who will be lord among the Trojans, and children will be born to his children forever. His name will be Aeneas, since an awful[28] grief got hold of me because I fell into the bed of a mortal man; (200) but among mortal people, those from your race have always been the closest to the gods in both beauty and figure.

"Certainly wise Zeus captured blond Ganymede[29] because of his beauty, so that he would live among the immortals and pour wine for the gods in the halls of Zeus, a marvel to see, honored among all the immortals, as he poured red nectar from a golden bowl. But inconsolable grief took hold of Tros' heart, and he did not know where the god-sent hurricane had snatched away his dear son, and indeed he lamented him continuously day after day. (210) Surely Zeus took pity on him and

---

[27] The same elements of height and radiance appear in the epiphany of Demeter in the *Homeric Hymn to Demeter* 188–189 (see Part 6, document 8).

[28] The poet plays with the name Aeneas (*Aineas* in Greek) and the adjective "awful" (*ainos*).

[29] Son of Tros of Dardania, eponymous ancestor of Troy. In the most common versions, also represented in mosaics and paintings, Ganymede was captured by Zeus in the form of an eagle.

gave him horses who raise their feet high, and who carry the immortals, as ransom for his son. He gave him these to keep as a gift. And the guide, Argos-slayer, told him everything at the orders of Zeus, that he[30] would be immortal and ageless just like the gods. When he heard the tidings from Zeus, then he ceased his lamenting, and instead he rejoiced inside his heart and rode away, joyful, in the hurricane-like horses.

"So, in turn, did golden-throned Eos[31] snatch up Tithonos,[32] one of your race, a man like the immortals. (220) She set out and went to ask the dark-clouded son of Kronos that he become immortal and live for all days; and Zeus nodded to her and fulfilled her desire. How naïve she was, for lady Eos did not realize in her mind she should ask for youth, and so scrape from him painful old age. And indeed, while he kept desirable youth, he lived by the streams of Ocean at the limits of the earth, enjoying himself with Eos of the golden throne, the early-born goddess; but when the first gray hairs flowed down from his fine head and illustrious chin, (230) certainly lady Eos withdrew from his bed, although she still nourished him, keeping him in her palace and giving him food and ambrosia and beautiful clothes. But when hateful old age weighed down on him completely and he had no strength to move or lift his limbs, the following solution seemed best to her in her heart: she placed him in his bedroom and shut the shining doors. There his voice keeps flowing incessantly, and there is no energy at all such as there used to be before in his agile limbs.[33]

"*I* for one would not take you among the immortals in such way, (240) to be deathless and live for all days. Though, if you could live staying as you are in beauty and figure, and you could be called my husband, in that case grief would not engulf my otherwise firm heart. But now the same old age will engulf you; implacable, it stands by human beings later on, something which even the gods abhor. And yet, because of you, I will have great and constant shame for ever more among the immortal gods, who previously used to fear my chatting and my schemes, (250) by means of which at some point I have made every immortal mingle with a mortal woman. For my designs used to overpower them all. But now my mouth will not be able to mention this among the immortals, since I was the victim of infatuation, a miserable thing not to be made light of, for I was driven out of my mind, and after sleeping with a mortal I put a child under my girdle.

"When he first sees the light of the sun, the mountain nymphs of deep bosoms will raise him, those who inhabit this great sacred mountain; as it turns out, they do not fit in with either mortals or immortals; (260) they live long and eat ambrosial food, and even enjoy the fine dance with the immortals. And the Silenoi and

---

[30] Ganymede.

[31] Dawn. Her epithets "golden-throned," "early-born," and "rosy-fingered" all allude to the first light of the morning.

[32] Son of Laomedon and brother of Priam. Eos with Tithonos will father Memnon (who fights in the Trojan War) and Emathion (king of the Ethiopians).

[33] In later versions he was turned into a cicada. A recently discovered poem by Sappho of Lesbos is dedicated to him, and nineteenth-century British poet A. Tennyson also evoked him in "Tithonus."

sharp-eyed Argos-slayer mingle with them in love-making in the depth of coveted caves. Together with them, as they are born, firs or tall oaks grow over the fertile earth, beautiful, sprouting in the lofty mountains. They stand tall and are invoked as sacred groves of the immortals, and mortals do not ever cut them with the axe. But when the lot of death is in sight for them, (270) first the beautiful trees wither on the earth, and their bark decays all around them, and their branches fall off, and then, at the same time [for both trees and nymphs], their soul leaves the light of the sun.

"These ones will raise my son, keeping him with them. When desirable youth first gets hold of him, the goddesses will bring him here to you, and will show you the boy. But to you (so that I explain to you everything in my mind) I will come again towards the fifth year bringing your son.[34] As soon as you see your offspring with your eyes, you will rejoice in the sight; for he will be greatly similar to the gods. (280) Then you shall take him right away to windy Ilion. And if anyone among mortal people asks you which mother placed your dear son under her girdle,[35] remembering to tell it as I order you, you say to him: 'They say he is the offspring of a nymph of blushing face, of those who inhabit this mountain covered in woods.' For if you reveal and boast with insensible mind that you mingled in love-making with well-crowned Kythereia, Zeus will strike you with his smoky thunderbolt, enraged at you.[36] Everything has been said to you. But you, aware of this in your mind, (290) refrain from naming me, and be fearful of the anger of the gods."

After saying so, she rushed towards the windy sky.

Hail, goddess who oversees well-built Cyprus; having started with you, I will now move on to another hymn.

5.6. MEDEA AND JASON, FROM EURIPIDES' *MEDEA*

The Athenian playwright Euripides (see headnote to Part 3, document 10.a) put the tragedy *Medea* on stage in 431 BCE. In this play, he engages with the Argonautic myth but focuses on the sentimental drama after the return of Jason and Medea to Greece, where she had followed him after helping him retrieve the Golden Fleece from Colchis on the Black Sea (in modern Georgia). In Euripides' play, Medea, Jason, and their two children are living in Corinth after Medea had Pelias killed—he was the king of Iolkos who had usurped the throne there and sent Jason on the impossible trip. Betrayed by Jason, who decides to marry the local princess, Medea struggles with jealousy and anger and is sentenced to exile by the king of Corinth, Kreon. After several scenes that explore her pain and psychological stress and dialogues in which her intentions are not exactly clear, Medea punishes Jason by killing the new bride, her father, and, lastly, her own children. Having been offered refuge at Athens by king Aigeus (father of Theseus), she flees Corinth in a chariot of the Sun (Helios was her grandfather), sometimes depicted as pulled by snakes. The horrific ending of Euripides' play seems to have deviated from other traditions whereby Medea

---

[34] The previous lines in which the Nymphs are the ones bringing Aeneas to his father seem contradictory with this last statement, and some critics think they are a later addition.

[35] In other words, had him in her womb, with the same expression used in line 255.

[36] In some versions he was indeed struck (Hyginus, *Fab.* 94).

tried to immortalize her children; she was, after all, a semi-divine sorcerer. The association of the story with Corinth is old, and there was a cult for the children there. We can only guess why Euripides chose (or invented?) this version and whether this was the reason that the playwright came last in the theatrical contest in 431. For Medea and Jason, see also Ovid's *Heroides* 12 and *Metamorphoses* Book 7 (not in this volume).

The play opens with the Nurse's speech, which outlines the current situation and state of mind of Medea. Her view of marriage is one of subordination (lines 14–15), which contrast with the strong-willed character of Medea and with the harmonious ideal expressed in other works, such as in *Odyssey* 6.182–184, where Odysseus says to Nausikaa: "there is nothing stronger and better that this, when a husband and wife keep a household together, being of one mind." Later on, the discussion between Medea and Jason toward the middle of the play underscores their different readings of the situation, of their own history, and ultimately of what love is all about. The discussion takes the form of an ***agon*** or contest of arguments, which mirrors the use of rhetorical skill and **sophistry** in Athenian courts and public life.

SOURCE: Euripides' *Medea* (excerpts), translated and annotated by C. López-Ruiz.

(Opening lines by Nurse, lines 1–45)

   (Setting: in front of Medea's house in Corinth. Out of the house comes the old nurse of Medea.)

NURSE: How I wish the hull of the Argo had never flown through the shady Symplegades[37] and into the land of the Colchians,[38] nor that the pine tree had ever fallen, cut in the valleys of Mount Pelion,[39] and that it had not furnished with oars the hands of excellent men, who went after the golden fleece for Pelias.[40] For then would my mistress Medea not have sailed for the towers of the land of Iolkos, stricken in her heart with love for Jason. Nor would she have settled in this Corinthian land with her husband and children, (10) after having persuaded the daughters of Pelias to kill their father,[41] pleasing the citizens whose land she had come to, like exiles do, and agreeing with Jason himself in everything; which is precisely the greatest salvation: when the wife does not dissent from her husband.

But now everything is hatred and what is most dear to her is sickening. For, betraying his own children and my mistress, Jason is going to bed with a royal wedding, by marrying a child of Kreon, who rules in the land. (20) So wretched Medea, thus wronged, cries out for the vows, invokes the right hands, greatest proof of fidelity, and calls the gods as witnesses of what kind of reply she obtains from Jason.

---

[37] The "Clashing Rocks."

[38] Colchis, at the extreme eastern end of the Black Sea (modern Georgia), was the home of king Aietes, father of Medea. The Argonauts arrived there in search of the Golden Fleece.

[39] Mt. Pelion in Thessaly, the region where Iolkos is (modern Volos), homeland of Jason.

[40] Pelias usurped the throne from Jason's father (Pelias' brother) and sent Jason on this "impossible" mission, promising to return the throne if he succeeded.

[41] Medea had persuaded Pelias to be cut and boiled by his daughters so he could be rejuvenated by sorcery.

And she goes without food, abandoning her body to sufferings, consuming all her time in tears, ever since she realized she had been wronged by her husband; she neither lifts her eyes nor turns her face away from the earth. Like a rock or a sea wave she listens to friends when given advice, (30) if she does not at some point turn her white neck and start lamenting to herself for her own father and her land and her home, betraying whom she arrived here with a husband, who now has dishonored her. The poor woman, she has learned through her misfortune what it would be like not to have left her homeland.

She abhors her children and does not rejoice at their sight. I am afraid she might plan some new thing. Her heart is harsh and will not put up with ill-treatment; I know her, and fear for her, (40) lest she drives a sharp blade through her liver, entering the house in silence where the bed is tended, or that she might kill the king and the groom and so bring upon herself greater misfortune. For she is fearful! No one who becomes her enemy will easily sing victory.

(Exchange between Jason and Medea, lines 446–626)

(Jason enters from the side of the palace, unannounced, and starts criticizing Medea, already on stage.)

JASON: Not just now for the first time but many times before I have seen what a hopeless evil is an abrupt anger attack. Even though it was possible for you to keep this land and this house, taking lightly the decisions of those ruling, (450) because of your foolish words you will be expelled from the land. And this is not a big problem for me; don't ever stop saying what an evil man Jason is; but for the things you have said against the rulers, consider it a total gain that you are punished with exile. In fact I kept trying to diminish the anger of the enraged monarch and I was intending for you to stay; but you would not cease from your foolishness, always speaking badly of the king; and so you will be expelled from the land. Yet, despite all this, I come as one who does not give up on his friends, (460) looking after your interests, woman, so that you don't go into exile with the children without means nor lacking anything; exile itself carries with it many troubles. For even if you hate me, I could never be ill-disposed towards you.

MEDEA: O you utterly wicked man!—for this is the greatest insult I can say with my tongue in face of your cowardice,—you have come *to me*, you have come despite having become my worst enemy! This is not in fact courage or audacity, (470) to look at your friends in the face after harming them, but the greatest of all sicknesses among humans: shamelessness. But you did well in coming, for I will lighten my heart by speaking ill of you, and you will suffer listening.

I will start to speak first from the first things. I saved you, as all the Greeks who boarded with you on the Argos' hull know, when you were sent to master the fire-breathing bulls with yokes and you sawed the lethal field; (480) as for the dragon, who safeguarded the golden fleece surrounding it with its multiple foils, never sleeping, I raised for you the salvation light by killing it. Then, betraying my father and my house, I myself came with you to Iolkos, land of Pelias, with more willingness than good sense; and I killed Pelias, in the most painful way to die, by his own children's hands, and ruined their whole house. But even having experienced these things from me, O most evil of men, you have betrayed us, and you have procured a new marriage, (490) even when you had children; for if you were still without a child, it would be excusable for you to desire this wedding. The faith of your vows is gone, and I have no way of knowing if you think that the gods of back then do not rule anymore or that new laws are in place for people now, since you are surely aware of having broken your oath to me. O right hand of mine, which you would often clasp, as well as these knees,[42] how in vain were we touched by an evil man, for we were mistaken in our hopes.

But come, I will consult with you as though you were a friend (500) (expecting what good outcome from your side exactly?—but nevertheless I'll do it, since you will look worse when you are asked). Tell me, now where should I turn to? Perhaps to my father's house, whom I betrayed, as I did my fatherland, coming here for you? or perhaps to the wretched daughters of Pelias? They would receive me in their house beautifully, after I killed their father! For this is how it is; I have become hateful to my dear ones at home, and while it was not necessary for me to harm them, doing you a favor I have them as enemies. And yet, how blessed in the eyes of many Greek women you have made me in return for all this! (510) An amazing and faithful husband I have in you, poor me, if I am to leave the land and be banned, with no friends, alone, with only my children; a nice dishonor for the new groom, for his sons and for the one who saved you, to wander homeless! O Zeus, why have you provided for human beings a safe proof of false gold, but there is no mark by nature in the bodies of men, by which we might tell a bad one apart?

CHORUS: (520) A terrible anger ensues, and difficult to bear, when loved ones confront each other in anger.

JASON: It is necessary, as it seems, that I show myself not a bad speaker; instead, as a prudent helmsman of the ship, with the very fringes of the sail I run away from your endless chattering, woman. As for me, since you also magnify your favors in excess, I deem Cypris[43] to be, among gods and men, the only savior of my voyage. Even though you have a subtle mind . . . (530) it would be unseemly to relate how Love with his inescapable arrows forced you to save my skin. But I will not push too much for precision in this; in whichever way you helped me it was not bad. But you have surely obtained more out of my salvation than you have given, as I will explain. First, you live in Hellas instead of in a barbaric land and you have become acquainted with our custom to use laws that do not favor violence. Then, all the Hellenes recognize that you are wise, and you have become a celebrity; (540) if you had lived in the furthest limits of the earth, nobody would talk about you. At least for me, I'd rather not have gold in my house or be able to sing a more beautiful song than Orpheus, if my destiny was not a famous one. These many things I have said to you about my labors, since you proposed a contest of arguments. But

[42] Embracing the knees was a gesture of supplication.

[43] Aphrodite.

regarding the reproaches you made about my royal wedding, in this I will show you that first, I have been smart, then, sensible, and finally, a great friend of yours and of my children. (550) *(As Medea shows restlessness)* But keep calm . . . When I arrived here from the land of Iolkos, dragging with me many unsolvable difficulties, what more fortunate event could I have come across than this, to marry the daughter of a king, an exile as I am? Neither do I do it out of spite for your bed (which is what torments you) and smitten by desire of a new bride, nor having any hurry to compete for more children (for those born are enough and I have no reproach), but—this is the main reason—so that we might live well and not lack anything, (560) knowing that every dear thing goes away and escapes the poor; so that I might raise the children in a way worthy of my house and, sowing siblings for your children, I might place them at the same level and be happy as I bind the family together. For what need do you have of children? But is worthwhile for me to benefit the living children by means of those who will come. Is this badly planned? Not even *you* would say so, if the wedding didn't torment you. But you women have reached such a point that, if things in bed are alright, (570) you think you have everything, and in turn if anything wrong comes up in your marriage, you consider the best and most convenient things to be the most hateful. It ought to be that mortals bore children from some other source, and that there would be no female gender; surely in this way there would be no evil for human beings.

CHORUS: Jason, you have put together a very nice speech. However, it seems to me (even if I will speak against your opinion) that you do not act justly when you betray your wife.

MEDEA: I surely disagree with many of the mortals in many respects; (580) for, to me, the one who is unjust but is by nature smart with words deserves the greatest punishment. For, confident in his tongue so as to perfectly cover injustice, he dares to do everything. But he is not really smart, just like you, Jason: do not try to come out as decent towards me while a genius at speaking; for a single word will knock you down; you should have arranged this marriage *after* convincing me, if you were not a bad man, not behind the back of your dear ones.

JASON: Right, you would have helped me beautifully in this plan, I suppose, if I had confessed to you this wedding, you who not even now (590) are capable of putting aside the great anger of your heart.

MEDEA: This is not what kept you silent, but the fact that a foreign marriage would result in a less than honorable old age for you.

JASON: Know this well: that it is not because of a woman that I marry into the royal bed that I now have, but, as I already said before, in my will to save you, and to breed royal children of the same seed as my sons, a sure protection for our house.

MEDEA: May I not have a fortunate life that is painful, nor a prosperity which torments my heart!

JASON: (600) Won't you change your prayer and prove yourself wiser? Wishing that what is good for you may never seem painful, and that you won't consider yourself unfortunate when you are fortunate?

MEDEA: Insult me, since *for you* there is where to turn to, while *I* will leave this land alone.

JASON: You have chosen this yourself. Do not blame anybody else.

MEDEA: And how did I do that? Was it by marrying and betraying you?

JASON: No, by uttering impious curses against the royal family.

MEDEA: Yes, and now I happen to bring curses for your house too . . .

JASON: Kow that I am not going to argue with you anymore. (610) But, if you want to take some of my money as an aid for your exile, for the children or for yourself, just say it, since I am ready to extend an unresentful hand and to send tokens[44] to friends who shall treat you well. You will profit more if you cease from your anger.

MEDEA: I would never deal with your friends nor would I accept anything, so don't give it to me; for the gifts of a base person are of no use.

JASON: Nonetheless I invoke the divinities as witnesses (620) that in every way I wish to assist you and the children. What is good does not suffice for you, but instead you arrogantly reject your friends; therefore you will suffer more.

MEDEA: *(Probably said as Jason is leaving)* Go! You must be full of desire for your virginal bride, since you are wasting time out of sight of the palace. Get married! For all the same (and let it be said with the god's favor) you wed such a marriage as will make you grief.

5.7. "HYMN TO VENUS," FROM LUCRETIUS' *DE RERUM NATURA*

Lucretius was a Roman poet and philosopher active during the first half of the first century BCE. He belonged to a school of philosophy called Epicureanism. Epicureans postulated that everything in the world consisted of atoms. They believed that when a person dies, his soul, like his body, disperses into unrelated atoms and he ceases to exist. Because of this understanding, the goal of the Epicurean life is to seek pleasure, understood as the satisfaction of needs

---

[44] These *symbola* were tokens divided in two parts and kept by families as proof of friendship and bonds of hospitality. The word used here for "friend," *xenos*, can be translated as "host" or as "foreigner" and is related to *xenia*, hospitality.

and the avoidance of pain, including excessive desire. Lucretius presented these ideas in his only work, a long poem in six books called "On the Nature of Things" (*De rerum natura*). In his poem Lucretius argues against the need to fear the gods or to fear death: since man is mortal and will completely cease to exist when he dies, there is no point in suffering anxiety and unhappiness during one's life by worrying about death or the gods. The best way of living is to philosophize.

The excerpt included here is the opening of Lucretius' poem, which draws on a number of different Greek literary traditions: First, it is a didactic poem, that is, it is intended to educate the reader, in this case about the Epicurean worldview. Two Greek philosophers, Empedokles and Parmenides, had already written didactic philosophical poems, and these provided models for Lucretius. Second, it is written in the traditional epic verse, hexameters, linking the author with Homer, Hesiod, and the *Homeric Hymns*, all of which deal with mythology and the gods. In this specific passage, Lucretius looks back to these earlier poets by beginning with what is effectively a hymn to the Love Goddess Venus. At first he represents her as an anthropomorphic figure and the mother of Aeneas, but then he merges her into the generative principle, following Epicurean philosophy, which rejects the idea that the gods interfere in human affairs. The idea of Love (Eros) or Desire (Pothos) as a motor of the universe is also present in the *Theogony* of Hesiod and the Phoenician cosmogonies (see Part 1, documents 5, 7.a, and 7.b).

SOURCE: Lucretius, *De rerum natura*, 1.1–26, translated by H. Eisenfeld.

> You who created Aeneas and his race, delight to men and gods,
> fruitful Venus, you who beneath the turning constellations of the heavens
> cause the ship-carrying sea and fruit-bearing land to teem with life
> —for it is through you that the whole tribe of beings that draw breath
> (5) is conceived, and once sprung into existence perceives the light of the sun:
> you, goddess, you the winds flee, and the clouds of heaven
> flee as you approach, for you the gentle, dappled earth
> sends up its flowers, at you smile the waters of the sea,
> and the heavens, now calm, shine with scattered light.
> (10) For as soon as the springtime appearance of the day stands revealed
> and the fruitful breeze of the west wind blooms, set free,
> the lofty birds, first, mark your arrival, heartstruck by your power;
> then the wild flocks leap among joyful pastures
> and swim across swift rivers: thus captured by charmed desire
> (15) each heart follows where you hasten to lead.
> Through the seas, then, and the mountains and the violent floods
> and the leaf-bearing dwellings of the birds and the verdant fields

driving soft love into every chest you bring it about
that the generations increase with desire, each according to its kind.
(20) Since you alone govern the nature of things, nor without you
would any day rise into the regions of light
nor anything become capable of inspiring joy or love,
I seek you as an ally for these verses that I write
concerning the nature of things, which I am attempting to fix fast
(25) for our Memmias, whom you, goddess, for all time
wished to be eminent, furnished with everything.

5.8. AENEAS AND DIDO, FROM VIRGIL'S *AENEID*, BOOKS 1 AND 4

(For an introduction to Virgil and the *Aeneid*, see Part 1, document 11.) Aeneas' arrival at Dido's court in Carthage after a shipwreck puts an end to his long haz-ardous sea voyage from Troy. The episode, including a love relationship gone sour, evokes Odysseus' relationships with Circe, and even more with Kalypso, both of whom tried to retain him on their islands. It is also at Dido's palace where Aeneas relates his past adventures, just as Odysseus did at the palace of the Phaeacians. The relationship between Dido and Aeneas has important political overtones. First, it served as a backdrop for the historical rivalry and bloodshed between the Carthaginians and the Romans in the third and second centuries BCE (the Punic Wars). Second, the affair also evoked the relationship between Roman leaders (Julius Caesar and Mark Antony) and the last Egyptian queen, Cleopatra VII. Dido's *wish* for a baby from Aeneas (line 328) would have reminded readers of the child that Cleopatra *did* have with Julius Caesar, Caesarion (killed after Cleopatra's defeat by Augustus), and her children with Marc Antony. Finally, the loyalty of Aeneas to his future Italian destiny would contrast with Marc Antony's surrender to the queen's love and his neglect of Roman interests.

The following passages show how Aeneas and Dido were framed by Venus to fall in love and their breakup when Aeneas decides to go on to Italy, leav-ing Dido behind. The rest of Book 4 of the *Aeneid*, following these passages, narrates Dido's desperation and suicide while Aeneas prepares his departure. Only when he is at sea does Aeneas notice the smoke from the pyre where Dido is burning, though he does not know it. The queen's self-immolation follows a long-standing association of Carthaginian-Phoenician culture with death by fire. Dido's death directly follows the tradition of Elissa's self-immolation in Carthage's foundation myth (see Part 4, document 12.a), although modifying the reasons for her suicide. At the same time, the episode might have resonated with the suicide, by same method, of the wife of Carthage's leader Hasdrubal (and their children), who chose that fate before surrendering (like her husband) to Scipio Aemilianus in 146 BCE. Self-immolation more generally alludes to the alleged Carthaginian practice of ritual child sacrifice by fire, about which the classical authors wrote. Even the death of Harakles, who threw himself on a pyre and became immortal, could have been shaped by his long-standing association with Phoenician religion, especially through his identification with the god Melqart.

SOURCE: Virgil, *Aeneid* (Book 1.657–722 and 4.165–174, 281–396). F. Ahl, *Virgil, Aeneid* (Oxford World Series, Oxford and New York, 2007), with minor modifications. (See headnote to document 4.12.b for note on Ahl's English hexameter.)

Book 1: 657–722

Venus, Cythera's goddess, however, was spinning some new tricks,

New plots deep in her heart. Her intent was that Cupid, her own child,

Switch his appearance and face, then come in to replace sweet Ascanius,

(660)   Madden the queen, kindle fire with the gifts, set her bone-marrow blazing.

Moods at the palace, she feared, could shift; double-talk was a Tyrian art-form.[45] Juno was ruthless—that burned in her mind, and at night-time

Anxious cares coursed back. So she said this to Love, winged Amor:

"Son, you're my strength, you alone are the principal source of my power.

(665)   Thunderbolts mighty Jupiter launched at Typhoeus don't worry

You. So it's you that I run to and kneel to, whose grace I'm beseeching.

You're well aware that Aeneas, your brother, is now being harried,

Tossed all over the world by the bitter hatred of Juno.

You've felt my rue and my pain, often sharing that ruefulness with me.

(670)   Now a Phoenician, Dido, controls him, and she, with her smooth talk,

Makes him delay. I'm afraid of the ends to which Juno might channel

This hospitality. She won't stop at this pivotal moment.

My plan is then: Strike first; take the queen by a ruse, with encircling

Fences of fire so she won't change course through divine interference,

(675)   Bind her to me, then, with bonds of a mighty love for Aeneas.

Now, as to how you can manage this task. Just pursue my suggestion. My chief

Concern is the royal prince. He's at this time preparing,

At his dear father's behest, to come into the city of Carthage

Carrying gifts that survived both the burning of Troy and the voyage.

(680)   I, then, will drug him to sleep and I'll tuck him away in my sacred

Shrine in Cythera's heights or within my Idalian temple

---

[45] Deceitfulness, what the Romans called *punica fides* (Punic "faith"), became a stereotypical trait assigned to the Carthaginians during the Punic Wars.

So he has no way to learn, or to hinder, the ruse I'm devising.
Your job is making the ruse work on Dido by feigning his features,
Just for one night, no more. You're a boy. A boy's facial expressions

(685) Are, thus, familiar to you. So, when Bacchic juices[46] are flowing
During the banquet, when Dido takes *you* in her lap, O so blissful,
Hugs you and cuddles you, plants on your forehead a few tender kisses,
You can rouse unseen fire, deceive her with venomous love-draughts."
Amor obeys his dear mother's instructions and now sheds his feathered

(690) Wings, takes Iulus' manner and mien and enjoys what he's doing.
Venus, for her part, drips sleep's calming dew on Ascanius'
Limbs, and then carries him up, nestled close to her breast, to her gardens
High on Idalia, where marjoram softly enfolds him in gently
Shaded embrace as it soothes him with fragrant breath from its flowers.

(695) Cupid, obeying his parent's words, strode on, bringing regal
Gifts for the Tyrians, thrilled that Achates was there to escort him.
When he arrives, Dido's already taken her place in the centre,
Seating herself on a gilded divan, amid sumptuous draperies.
Father Aeneas and Troy's young men are joining the gathering,

(700) Shown to their couches. And now they're reclining on coverings of purple.[47]
Slaves pour water over their hands, serve baskets of Ceres'
Breads, and supply serviettes whose nap has been razored to smoothness.
Fifty storehouse maids inside lay dishes in long lines
Side by side, and keep light in the fires at the shrines of Penates.[48]

(705) Then there's a hundred more, and a hundred boys of the same age,
Loading the tables with fine foods, setting out goblets for drinking.
Tyrians have also been crowding through doors set ringing with laughter;
They too are guided to pre-assigned places on needleworked couches.
All are impressed by Aeneas's presents, impressed by Iulus—

(705) Or, rather, by the god's dazzling face and his staged conversation—
And Helen's mantle and veil embroidered with saffron acanthus.

---

[46] Wine.

[47] The Phoenicians were widely known for the industry of purple dye (from murex shells).

[48] The Penates were Roman household deities (*dii familiares*), worshipped in domestic rituals.

She above all, the descendant of Phoenix,[49] cannot sate her senses,

Unfulfilled and vowed as an offering for future destruction,

Burns as she stares, roused equally both by the gifts and the young boy.

(715) After embracing Aeneas and hugging his neck, satisfying

All the quite genuine love of a father who wasn't his father,

Amor made for the queen. And she, with her eyes and her whole heart

Clung to him, took him, at times, in her lap, poor Dido, not knowing

How great a god set snares for her there to suffuse her with torment.

(720) Amor, recalling his Acidalian[50] mother, now slowly

Starts to erase Sychaeus[51] and tries to surprise, with a living

Passion, a heart where the fire has died and where love is a memory.

(At Dido's request, Aeneas will narrate his voyage up until his arrival to Carthage. This story occupies Books 2 and 3. Book 4 is then dedicated to the love story between the two leaders. The romance ensues when, at a hunting expedition, Dido and Aeneas take refuge from a storm in a cave.)

Book 4: 165–174

(165) Dido and Troy's chief come down together inside the same cavern.

Earth gives the sign that the rites have begun, as does Juno, the nuptial Sponsor.

The torches are lightning, the shrewd sky's brilliance is witness,

Hymns for the wedding are howling moans of the nymphs upon high peaks.

That first day caused death, that first day begun the disasters.[52]

(170) Dido no longer worries about how it looks or what rumor

Says, and no longer thinks of enjoying a secret liaison.

Now she is calling it a marriage; she's veiling her sin with a title.

Out in a flash through Libya's cities Rumor is blazing.

No other evil is swifter than she . . .

---

[49] Phoenix was the eponymous ancestor of the Phoenicians. The Phoenix is also a mythological bird, who burns and is reborn from its own ashes, perhaps a reference to Dido's future self-immolation in the pyre and her prophecy that an avenger will emerge from her burned bones.

[50] Acidalius was a fountain in Boiotia dedicated to the Graces. Virgil plays with the previously mentioned Idalia in Cyprus.

[51] Dido's deceased husband.

[52] This first union is the seed for the future tragedy of Dido but also anticipates the future wars between Carthage and Rome.

(Following this union, in Book 4 Virgil narrates the effects of Rumor: the north African King Iarbas, son of Ammon [Phoenician Hammon], the native god identified by the Romans with Jupiter, who was in love with Dido, begs his father for help. Jupiter at once sends Mercury with a stern message for Aeneas, scolding him for neglecting his mission: "Obsessed with your wife, you're now building a lovely city for her. You've forgotten your obligations and kingdom," 266–267. When Mercury disappears, Aeneas is shocked and ponders what to do.)

Book 4: 281–396

Still, though, he burns to get out, to escape from the lands that delight him,

Stunned by the mighty force of the gods' commandment and warning,

Wondering what he should do, how he'd dare to get round the besotted

Ruler[53] with some explanation, or find ways of broaching the subject.

(285) This way and that, he channeled his swift mind, testing his options,

Every alternative he could conceive. He approached from all angles.

This, as his thoughts vacillated, appeared the most forceful decision:

So he calls Mnestheus, Sergestus as well, and the valiant Serestus[54];

Then, he instructs them to refit the ships, muster crews on the seashore,

(290) Ready their weapons. *No word must get out.* The entire re-equipment

Must be disguised. In the meantime, since excellent Dido knew nothing,

And wouldn't dream that their great love affair was in fact being shattered,

He would himself test out some approaches, and find the most tactful

Times for a talk, and how best he could frame it. Reaction was instant.

(295) Each obeyed orders and followed instructions. They all were delighted.

Still though, the queen detected his ruse. Who *could* fool a lover?

Scared because things seemed safe, she discovered his plans for departure

First. Rumor, ever unrighteous, informed on him, telling the furious

Ruler the navy was being refitted and readied for sailing.

---

[53] Dido.

[54] These three men were Trojan captains accompanying Aeneas.

(300) Mind now out of control, all ablaze, she screams through the city,
Bacchic in fury, resembling a Thyiad[55] frenzied by brandished
Thyrsus and loud Bacchic cries when Thebes' biennial orgies
Madden her soul, when Cithaeron's voice howls shrill in the night-
time.

Finally, *she* broached the subject, addressing Aeneas as follows:

(305)   "Was it your hope to disguise, you perfidious cheat,[56] such a
monstrous
Wrong, to get out, *with no word said*, from this land that I govern?
You are not bound by our union of love, by the hand you once
gave me,
Nor does Dido, doomed to a cruel death, now detain you.
Why so much work on your fleet? Constellations tell us it's winter,

(310) Yet you are rushing to put out to sea, cruel man, while the north
winds
Rule. Why is this? Were you not in pursuit of some other man's
ploughlands,
Unknown homes, and if ancient Troy were still in existence,
Would Troy, then, be the goal for your fleet on the water's expanses?
Could you be running from me? Let me urge you, with tears, by
your right hand

(315) (Thanks to my pitiful conduct that's all I have left now to swear by),
Urge you by love we have shared, by the steps we have taken to
marriage:
If I have ever earned your thanks for services rendered,
Or given you any pleasure, I beg you, if prayer still has meaning,
Pity this falling house, shrug off your present intention.

(320) Libyan tribesmen, nomad sheikhs all loathe me. The Tyrians
Hate me on your account; and on your account I have ruined
My sole claim to a stellar distinction: my chastity's good name,
Once honored, even by Rumor. I'm dying, and yet you desert me,
Houseguest—the lone name left for the man I called 'partner in
marriage.'

(325) What should I wait for? My brother Pygmalion's attack on my city?
Or till I'm captured and wed by Gaetulia's monarch, Iarbas?
If I'd at least, before you ran off, conceived from our closeness

[55] A follower of the rites of Bacchus (Dionysos). These rites, banned in Rome, were
traditionally associated with the women of Thebes (the birth home of Dionysos) and their
Bacchic rituals on Mt. Kithairon, as most famously dramatized by Euripides in his *Bacchae* (see
Part 3, document 10.a).

[56] Dido's use of the adjective "perfidious" for Aeneas is paradoxical in that this attribute was
associated with the Carthaginians, as pointed out above when "double-talk" was mentioned.

Some child fathered by you, if there just were a baby Aeneas
Playing inside my halls, whose face might in some way recall you,
(330) I would not feel so wholly trapped yet wholly deserted."

       That's what she said. He, conscious, however, of Jupiter's
    warning,
Never once blinked, and he struggled to keep his anxiety stifled
Deep in his heart. Yet he briefly replied: "That I owe you, my ruler,
All you could list in your speech I would never deny. You have
    earned it.
(335) Memory will never elicit regret for my missing Elissa[57]
While I remember myself, while my spirit rules in this body!
Now, a few words in defense. This escape: slipping out like a bandit,
That was not what I hoped. Don't *twist* my words. And I never
Formally wed you nor did I endorse any contract as 'husband.'
(340) If fate's orders allowed me to live out the life of my choosing,
Putting my anguish to rest as I myself would have wanted,
Troy is the city where I'd be now, looking after my own folk's
Relics and remnants; the great house of Priam would still stand in
    spirit,
My own hands would have rebuilt Pergamum's shrines for the
    vanquished.
(345) But, great Italy now is the land that Apollo of Grynia
And Lycian oracles tell me to seize, it is Italy's great land.
This is my love and my homeland. If you, since you are a Phoenician,
Focus your gaze on the towers of Carthage, your Libyan city,
Why does the vision of Teucrians settling the land of Ausonia
(350) Evil your eye? We too have the right to seek overseas kingdoms.[58]
Each time night cloaks earth with opaque, dank shadows of
    spectral
Darkness, and fire-born stars rise upwards, my father, Anchises'
Angry face in my dreams chastises me, stalks me with terror,
As does my son, Ascanius. The damage I've done his dear person!
(355) Cheating him out of his destined Hesperian kingdom and
    croplands!
Jupiter now has dispatched his divine intercessor, who bears me
Personal orders, I swear by them both, through the swift-blowing
    breezes.

---

[57] Calling Dido by the usual name in legend of the founder of Carthage, Elissa, Virgil makes a pun between Elissa and *elisa*, which in Latin would mean "forgotten" (in feminine gender).

[58] "We too" since Phoenicians from Tyre and other centers had founded colonies and trading posts throughout the Mediterranean world.

I myself, in clear day's light, saw Mercury enter

These very walls, and my own ears heard each word he was saying.

(360) Stop enraging me, and yourself, with all this complaining.

Going to Italy's not my choice."

Such was his tally of words. For a while, she just watched him obliquely,

Eyes flashing this way and that as he spoke, scrutinizing at random

His whole being with silent looks. Then her anger exploded:

(365) "No goddess gave you birth, no Dardanus authored your bloodline!

Caucasus, jagged with flint, fathered *you*—in Hyrcania![59] Savage

Tigresses stuck their teats in your mouth, you perfidious liar!

Why disguise what I feel, hold back, knowing worse is to follow?

When I wept, did he groan, did he soften his glance or surrender,

(370) Conquered by torrents of tears? Did he pity the woman who loved him?

Which thought shall I express first? It's clear neither mightiest Juno

Nor Saturn's son, the great Father, looks fairly at this situation.

Nowhere can one treat trust as secure. I found you in dire need,

Shipwrecked; and, fool that I was, I gave you a share in my kingdom,

(375) Brought back the fleet you'd lost, at the same time saving your comrades.

O, I am burning with fury! Now: enter Apollo the Augur;

Lycian oracles next; then, in person, Jupiter sending

Gods' intercessor down, bringing hideous commands through the breezes.

Maybe this is a dilemma for powers above, anguish to trouble

(380) *Their* deep inertia. I won't try to keep you, or craft a rebuttal.

Go with the winds! Pursue Italy! Chase across seas for your kingdoms!

My hope, if righteous forces prevail, is that, out on some mid-sea

Reefs, you'll drink retribution in deep draughts, often invoking

Dido's name. When I'm absent, I'll chase you with dark fire! When cold death

(385) Snaps away body from soul, evil man, my dank ghost will haunt you.

My destination is yours. There'll be no impunity. You'll pay.

Tireless Rumor will come to my buried remains. I will hear her."

[59] Hyrcania is the classical name of a vast region on the south shores of the Caspian Sea (called the Hyrkanian Sea by the Greeks), covering regions of today's Iran and Turkmekistan. Known to the Greeks as a Persian satrapy, it was evoked as a remote region full of tigers.

Breaking away before all had been said, she escaped from
the outside

Breezes. She felt quite sick, as she turned and then fled from his vision.

(390) He was left trapped: hesitating through fear to say much, and yet so
much

Wanting to speak. Dido's failing limbs were supported by handmaids

Back to her marbled chamber and there set to rest on her mattress.

Righteous Aeneas, much as he wished he could soften her angry

Pain by consoling her grief and find words to rechannel her
anguish,

(395) Much as he groaned and felt shaken at heart by the great force of
love's power,

Nonetheless followed the gods' commands, and returned to his navy.

5.9. PASIPHAE AND THE CRETAN BULL

The story of Minos and his family forms an important cluster of myths connected with the island of Crete. Minos was the son of Zeus and Europa, the Phoenician princess who had been kidnapped and left in Crete by Zeus in the shape of a bull (though his "official" father was Asterios, king of Crete) (see Figure 10). The story of Minos includes the famous episode of the Minotaur, whose origins are described in the texts below. The Minotaur then leads into the story of Theseus, the Athenian prince who defeated him. Theseus' escape from the island with Ariadne, the Cretan princess, is represented in documents 5.10.a and 5.10.b, while his future marriage with Phaidra (Ariadne's sister) will lead to the tragic story of Phaidra and Hippolytos (document 5.11).

It is worth noting the central role of bulls in myths related to Crete, such as the rape of Europa by a bull, the story of Poseidon's bull sent to Minos, the Minotaur, and Theseus' fight with the Marathonian or Cretan bull in Attica (see Part 3, document 11.c) (see Figures 10 and 21). These motifs reflect the centrality of bulls in Minoan civilization, judging by the preserved artwork, including frescoes of bull-leaping acrobatics, bull-shaped ritual implements, and horned-shaped altars.

5.9.a. Minos, Pasiphae, and the Bull, from Apollodorus' *Library*, Book 3

(For Apollodorus' *Library* [*Bibliotheke*], see Part 3, document 11.) Because of its low literary quality, Apollodorus' *Library* makes few appearances in this volume (here and in Part 3, documents 11.a, 11.b, and 11.c). However, it is a great resource to consult, and this version of the Pasiphae and Minos story has been chosen to exemplify the style and contents of this mythographic work, in sharp contrast to Ovid's poetic rendering of the same episode, which immediately follows.

SOURCE: Apollodorus' *Library*, Book 3. Sir J. G. Frazer. *Apollodorus. The Library* (Loeb Classical Library, Cambridge, MA and London, 1921), with minor modifications.

(3.1.3) Asterios[60] dying childless, Minos wished to reign over Crete, but his claim was opposed. So he alleged that he had received the kingdom from the gods, and in proof of it he said that whatever he prayed for would be done. And in sacrificing to Poseidon he prayed that a bull might appear from the depths, promising to sacrifice it when it appeared. Poseidon did send him up a fine bull, and Minos obtained the kingdom, but he sent the bull to the herds and sacrificed another. [Being the first to obtain the dominion of the sea, he extended his rule over almost all the islands.]

(3.1.4) But angry at him for not sacrificing the bull, Poseidon made the animal savage, and contrived that Pasiphae should conceive a passion for it. In her love for the bull she found an accomplice in Daidalos, an architect, who had been banished from Athens for murder. He constructed a wooden cow on wheels, took it, hollowed it out in the inside, sewed it up in the hide of a cow which he had skinned, and set it in the meadow in which the bull used to graze. Then he introduced Pasiphae into it; and the bull came and coupled with it, as if it were a real cow. And she gave birth to Asterios, who was called the Minotaur. He had the face of a bull, but the rest of him was human; and Minos, in compliance with certain oracles, shut him up and guarded him in the Labyrinth. Now the Labyrinth which Daidalos constructed was a chamber "that with its tangled windings perplexed the outward way." The story of the Minotaur, and Androgeus, and Phaidra, and Ariadne, I will tell hereafter in my account of Theseus.

5.9.b. Pasiphae's Passion, from Ovid, *Ars Amatoria*, Book 1

The *Ars Amatoria* ("The Art of Love"), by the Roman poet Ovid (on whom see headnote to Part 1, document 10), is an elegiac work (i.e., written in elegiac couplets) organized in three books, which contain instructions on how to find, seduce, and keep lovers. Ovid interweaves mythological examples in his didactic poem, anticipating the full-blown mythological elaborations in his later *Metamorphoses* and *Fasti*. In this section of Book 1, Ovid brings in the story of Pasiphae's love for the Cretan bull as one example among many of how all women can be won and how women are subject to passions as much as men, even if they usually let men take the initiative.

SOURCE: Ovid, *Ars Amatoria*, Book 1. Julian L. May, *The Love Books of Ovid, being the Amores, Ars amatoria, Remedia amoris, and Medicamina faciei femineae*. Illustrated by Jean de Bosschère (London, 1925).

First of all, be quite sure that there isn't a woman who cannot be won, and make up your mind that you will win her. Only you must prepare the ground. Sooner would the birds cease their song in the springtime, or the grasshopper be silent in the summer, or the hare turn and give chase to a hound of Maenalus, than a woman resist the tender wooing of a youthful lover. Perhaps you think she doesn't want to yield. You're wrong. She wants to in her heart of hearts. Stolen love is just as sweet to women as it is to us. Man is a poor dissembler; woman is much

---

[60] King of Crete, married to Europa and father of Minos.

more skilful in concealing her desire. If all the men agreed that they would never more make the first advance, the women would soon be fawning at our feet. Out in the springy meadow the heifer lows with longing for the bull; the mare neighs at the approach of the stallion. With men and women love is more restrained, and passion is less fierce. They keep within bounds. Need I mention Byblis, who burned for her brother with an incestuous flame, and hanged herself to expiate her crime? Or Myrrha, who loved her father, but not as a father should be loved, and now her shame is hidden by the bark of the tree that covered her. O sweetly scented tree, the tears which she distils, to us give perfume and recall the ill-fated maid's unhappy name.

One day in wood-crowned Ida's shady vale, a white bull went wandering by. The pride of all the herd was he. Between his horns was just a single spot of black; save for that mark, his body was as white as milk; and all the heifers of Gnossus and of Cydonia sighed for the joy of his caress. Pasiphae conceived a passion for him and viewed with jealous eye the loveliest among the heifers. There's no gainsaying it, Crete with her hundred cities, Crete, liar though she be, cannot deny it. It is said that Pasiphae, with hands unused to undertake such toil, tore from the trees their tenderest shoots, culled from the meadows bunches of sweet grass and hastened to offer them to her beloved bull. Whithersoever he went, she followed him; nothing would stay her. She recked not of her spouse; the bull had conquered Minos: "What avails it, Pasiphae, to deck yourself in costly raiment? How can your lover of such riches judge? Wherefore, mirror in hand, dost thou follow the wandering herd up to the mountain top? Wherefore dost thou for ever range thy hair? Look in thy mirror: it will tell thee thou art no meet mistress for a bull. Ah, what wouldst thou not have given if Nature had but armed thy brow with horns! If Minos still doth hold a corner in thy heart, cease this adulterous love; or if thou must deceive thy spouse, at least deceive him with a man." She hearkens not, but, fleeing from his royal couch, she ranges ever on and on, through forest after forest, like to a Bacchante full of the spirit that unceasingly torments her.

How often, looking with jealous anger on a heifer, did she exclaim: "How then can she find favor in his sight? See how she prances before him on the green. Fool, she doubtless deems that thus she is lovelier in his eyes." Then, at her command, the hapless beast is taken from the herd and sent to bow her head beneath the yoke; or else, pretending to offer sacrifice to the gods, she orders her to be slain; at the altar; and then with joy fingers o'er the entrails of her rival. How often, under the guise of one who offers sacrifice, hath she appeased the alleged displeasure of the gods, and waving the bleeding trophies in her hand exclaimed: "Go, get thee to my lover, please him now!" Now she would be Europa; now she would be Io;[61] the one because she was a heifer, the other because a bull bore her on his back. Howbeit, deceived by the image of a cow of maple wood, the king of the herd performed with her the act of love, and by the offspring[62] was the sire betrayed.

---

[61] Io, who was coveted by Zeus, was transformed into a cow by jealous Hera.

[62] That is, the Minotaur, who would be born from that union.

5.9.c. Minos and the Bull, from Ovid, *Metamorphoses*, Book 8

(On Ovid, see headnote to Part 1, document 10.) Scylla, the daughter of legendary king Nisus of Megara, attacks Minos as he has denied her refuge (she had betrayed her father's city to his enemies). In this passage Ovid returns to the motif of the Cretan bull, which he had explored in his *Ars Amatoria*, and plays with the theme of the connection between bulls and both Minos and Pasiphae.

SOURCE: Ovid, *Metamorphoses*, Book 8.119–137 (excerpt). F. J. Miller, *Ovid, Metamorphoses* (Loeb Classical Library, Cambridge, MA and London, 1921, 2nd ed.), with minor modifications.

" . . . And if you forbid me Crete as well, and, O ungrateful, leave me here, Europa is not your mother, but the inhospitable Syrtis, the Armenian tigress and storm-tossed Charybdis. You are no son of Jove,[63] nor was your mother tricked by the false semblance of a bull. That story of your birth is a lie: it was a real bull that begot you, a fierce, wild thing that loved no heifer." . . . "She is a true mate for you who with unnatural passion deceived the savage bull by that shape of wood and bore a hybrid offspring in her womb. Does my voice reach your ears? Or do the same winds blow away my words to emptiness that fill your sails, you ingrate? Now, now I do not wonder that Pasiphae preferred the bull to you, for you were a more savage beast than he."

5.10. THESEUS AND ARIADNE

Theseus was a legendary king of Athens to whom political reforms as well as fantastic adventures comparable to those of Herakles were attributed (see Part 3, document 11.c and Part 4, document 11). One of Theseus' most celebrated adventures of his youth was the liberation of Athenian boys and maidens who were sent to King Minos of Crete to be sacrificed to the Minotaur as a tribute (see Figure 21). In the story, the Cretan princess, in love with Theseus, helps him escape from the Labyrinth and then departs with him, but he then abandons her on his way back to Athens.

The motif of this love story was very popular and is echoed in other sources (e.g., Catullus' *Carmen* 64, Apollodorus' *Library*) as well as in **iconography**, where Ariadne appears sometimes with Dionysos, who, according to some versions, married her after she was abandoned. Plutarch's account here offers a good example of the author's concern with contrasting literary sources that deal with the same story. In contrast, Ovid's *Heroides* 10 brings the episode to life through the poetic dramatization of Phaidra's feelings.

5.10.a. From Plutarch, *Life of Theseus*

(For Plutarch and his *Parallel Lives*, see headnote to Part 4, document 11.) This passage illustrates the rather scholarly approach to myths that Plutarch takes when confronted with different sources, which he sorts out for the reader in an objective way, not in a new embellished tale of his own. He inserts direct

---

[63] Another form of the name of Jupiter, the Roman equivalent to Greek Zeus (father of Minos).

quotations of those sources in his account, mostly coming from mythographers from Hellenistic and Roman times, whose works have been lost.

SOURCE: Plutarch, *Life of Theseus*, 20. B. Perrin, *Plutarch's Lives*, vol. 1 (Loeb Classical Library, Cambridge, MA and London, 1914), with minor modifications.

There are many other stories about these matters, and also about Ariadne, but they do not agree at all. Some say that she hung herself because she was abandoned by Theseus; others that she was conveyed to Naxos by sailors and there lived with Oenarus the priest of Dionysos, and that she was abandoned by Theseus because he loved another woman:

"Dreadful indeed was his passion for Aigle child of Panopeus."

This verse Peisistratos expunged from the poems of Hesiod, according to Hereas the Megarian, just as, on the other hand, he inserted into the Inferno of Homer the verse:

"Theseus, Peirithoos, illustrious children of Heaven,"[64] and all to gratify the Athenians. Moreover, some say that Ariadne actually had sons by Theseus, Oinopion and Staphylos, and among these is Ion of Chios,[65] who says of his own native city:

"This, once, Theseus's son founded, Oinopion."

Now the most auspicious of these legendary tales are in the mouths of all men, as I may say; but a very peculiar account of these matters is published by Paion the Amathusian. He says that Theseus, driven out of his course by a storm to Cyprus, and having with him Ariadne, who was big with child and in sore sickness and distress from the tossing of the sea, set her on shore alone, but that he himself, while trying to succor the ship, was borne out to sea again. The women of the island, accordingly, took Ariadne into their care, and tried to comfort her in the discouragement caused by her loneliness, brought her forged letters purporting to have been written to her by Theseus, ministered to her aid during the pangs of travail, and gave her burial when she died before her child was born. Paion says further that Theseus came back, and was greatly afflicted, and left a sum of money with the people of the island, enjoining them to sacrifice to Ariadne, and caused two little statuettes to be set up in her honor, one of silver, and one of bronze. He says also that at the sacrifice in her honor on the second day of the month Gorpiaeus, one of their young men lies down and imitates the cries and gestures of women in travail; and that they call the grove in which they show her tomb, the grove of Ariadne Aphrodite.

Some of the Naxians also have a story of their own, that there were two Minoses and two Ariadnes, one of whom, they say, was married to Dionysos in Naxos and

---

[64] Referring to Odysseus' visit to the Underworld. Cf. *Odyssey* 11.631: "Theseus and Peirithoos, the glorious offspring of the gods" (593 in translation in Part 6, document 7).

[65] Ion of Chios was a playwright, philosopher, and lyric poet from the fifth century BCE. We only have titles and quotations from his work in later authors, such as this one by Plutarch (coming from his lyric poems).

bore him Staphylos and his brother, and the other, of a later time, having been carried off by Theseus and then abandoned by him, came to Naxos, accompanied by a nurse named Korkyne, whose tomb they show; and that this Ariadne also died there, and has honors paid her unlike those of the former, for the festival of the first Ariadne is celebrated with mirth and revels, but the sacrifices performed in honor of the second are attended with sorrow and mourning.

5.10.b. Ovid, *Heroides* 10

(For Ovid, see headnote to Part 1, document 10.) The *Heroides* or "Heroines" is a collection of epistolary poems, that is, poems written in the form of letters. The letters are addressed by female mythological figures ("heroines") to their absent husbands or lovers. *Heroides* numbers 1–14 follow this format, while Heroides number 15, perhaps not by Ovid, is put in the mouth of Sappho (a real Greek poet from the Archaic period), and numbers 16–21 contain the so-called "Double Heroides" or paired letters (e.g., Paris to Helen and Helen to Paris) and were probably written at a later stage. As with all other verses by Ovid except the *Metamorphoses*, they are written in elegiac couplets, which here are translated in prose.

SOURCE: G. Showerman, *Ovid, Heroides and Amores* (Loeb Classical Library, Cambridge, MA and London, 1914), with minor modifications.

Ariadne to Theseus

(1) Gentler than you I have found every race of wild beasts; to none of them could I so ill have trusted as to you. The words you now are reading, Theseus, I send you from that shore form which the sails bore off your ship without me, the shore on which my slumber, and you, so wretchedly betrayed me—you, who wickedly plotted against me as I slept.

(7) It was the time when the earth is first sprinkled with crystal rime, and birds hidden in the branch begin their lament. Half waking only, languid from sleep, I turned upon my side and put forth hands to clasp my Theseus—he was not there! I drew back my hands, a second time I tried, and over the whole couch moved my arms—he was not there! Fear struck away my sleep; in terror I arose, and threw myself headlong from my abandoned bed. Straight then my palms resounded upon my breasts, and I tore my hair, all disarrayed as it was from sleep.

(17) The moon was shining; I bend my gaze to see if anything but shore lies there. So far as my eyes can see, nothing do they find but shore. Now this way, and now that, and ever without plan, I course; the deep sand stays my girlish feet. And all the while I cried out "Theseus!" alone the entire shore, and the hollow rocks sent back your name to me; as often as I called out for you, so often did the place itself call out your name. The very place felt the will to aid me in my woe.

(25) There was a mountain, with bushes rising here and there upon its top; a cliff hangs over from it, gnawed into by deep-sounding waves. I climb its slope—my spirit gave me strength—and thus with prospect broad I scan the billowy deep. From there—for I found the winds cruel, too—I beheld your sails stretched full by the headlong southern gale. As I looked on a sight I thought I had not deserved

to see, I grew colder than ice, and life half left my body. Nor does anguish allow me long to lie thus quiet; it rouses me, it stirs me up to call on Theseus with all my voice's might. "Where are you flying?" I cry aloud. "Come back, O wicked Theseus! Turn about your ship! She has not all her crew!"

(37) Thus did I cry, and what my voice could not avail, I filled with beating of my breast; the blows I gave myself were mingled with my words. That you at least might see, if you could not hear, with might and main I sent you signals with my hands; and upon a long tree-branch I fixed my shining veil—yes, to put in mind of me those who had forgotten! And now you had been swept beyond my vision. Then at last I let flow my tears; till then my tender eyeballs had been dulled with pain. What better could my eyes do than weep for me, when I had ceased to see your sails? Alone, with hair loose flying, I have either roamed about, like to a Bacchant roused by the Ogygian god, or, looking out upon the sea, I have sat all chilled upon the rock, as much a stone myself as was the stone I sat upon. Often do I come again to the bed that once received us both, but was fated never to show us together again, and touch the imprint left by you—it is all I can in place of you!—and the sheets that once grew warm beneath your limbs. I lie down upon my face, wet the bed with pouring tears, and cry aloud: "We were two who pressed you—give back two! We came to you both together; why do we not depart the same? Ah, faithless bed—the greater part of my being, O, where is he?

(59) What am I to do? Whither shall I take myself—I am alone, and the isle untilled. Of human traces I see none; of cattle, none. On every side the land is girt by sea; nowhere a sailor, no craft to make its way over the dubious paths. And suppose I did find those to go with me, and winds, and ship—yet where am I to go? My father's realm forbids me to approach. Grant I do glide with fortunate keel over peaceful seas, that Aeolus tempers the winds—I still shall be an exile! It is not for me, O Crete composed of the hundred cities, to look upon thee, land known to the infant Jove! No, for my father and the land ruled by my righteous father—dear names!—were betrayed by my deed[66] when, to keep you, after your victory, from death in the winding halls, I gave into your hand the thread to direct your steps in place of guide—when you said to me: "By these very perils of mine, I swear that, so long as both of us shall live, you shall be mine!"

(75) We both live, Theseus, and I am not yours!—if indeed a woman lives who is buried by the treason of a perjured mate. Me, too, you should have slain, O false one, with the same bludgeon that slew my brother; then would the oath you gave me have been absolved by my death. Now, I ponder over not only what I am doomed to suffer, but all that any woman left behind can suffer. There rush into my thought a thousand forms of perishing, and death is less frightening for me than the delay of death. Each moment, now here, now there, I look to see wolves rush on me, to rend my vitals with their greedy fangs. Who knows but that this shore breeds, too, the tawny lion? Perchance the island harbors the savage tiger as well. They say, too, that the waters of the deep cast up the mighty seal! And who is to keep the swords of men from piercing my side?

---

[66] When she helped Theseus slay the Minotaur and escape from the Labyrinth.

(89) But I care not, if I am but not left captive in hard bonds, and not compelled to spin the long task with servile hand—I, whose father is Minos, whose mother the child of Phoebus, and who—what memory holds more close—was promised bride to you! When I have looked on the sea, and on the land, and on the wide-stretching shore, I know many dangers threaten me on land, and many on the waters. The sky remains—yet there I fear visions of the gods! I am left helpless, a prey to the maws of ravening beasts; and if men dwell in the place and keep it, I put no trust in them—my hurts have taught me fear of stranger-men.

(99) O, that Androgeus were still alive,[67] and that you, O Cecropian land,[68] had not been made to atone for your impious deeds with the doom of your children! and would that you upraised right hand, O Theseus, had not slain with knotty club him that was man in part, and in part bull[69]; and I had not given you the thread to show the way of your return—thread often caught up again and passed through the hands led on by it. I marvel not—ah, no!—if victory was yours, and the monster smote with his length the Cretan earth. His horn could not have pierced that iron heart of yours; your breast was safe, even if you did nothing to shield yourself. There you bore flint, there you bore adamant; there you have a Theseus harder than any flint!

(111) Ah, cruel slumbers, why did you hold me thus inert? Or, better had I been weighed down once for all by everlasting night. You, too, were cruel, O winds, and all too well prepared, and you breezes, eager to start my tears. Cruel the right hand that has brought me and my brother to our death, and cruel the pledge—an empty word—that you gave at my demand! Against me conspiring were slumber, wind, and treacherous pledge—treason three-fold against one maid!

(119) Am I, then, to die, and, dying, not behold my mother's tears; and shall there be no one's finger to close my eyes? Is my unhappy soul to go forth into stranger-air, and no friendly hand compose my limbs and drop them on the unguent due? Are my bones to lie unburied, the prey of hovering birds of the shore? Is this the entombment due to me for my kindnesses? You will go to the haven of Cecrops; but when you have been received back home, and have stood in pride before your thronging followers, gloriously telling the death of the man-and-bull, and of the halls of rock cut out in winding ways, tell, too, of me, abandoned on a solitary shore—for I must not be stolen from the record of your honors! Neither is Aegeus your father, nor are you the son of Pittheus' daughter Aethra; they who begot you were the rocks and the deep!

(133) Ah, I could pray the gods that you had seen me from the high stern; my sad figure had moved your heart! Yet look upon me now—not with eyes, for with them you cannot, but with your mind—clinging to a rock all beaten by the wandering wave. Look upon my locks, let loose like those of one in grief for the dead, and on my robes, heavy with tears as if with rain. My body is a-quiver like standing corn struck by the northern blast, and the letters I am tracing falter beneath my trembling hand. It is not for my kindness—for that has come to nothing—that I

---

[67] Her brother, who had died accidentally in Athens (which was the reason or pretext for Minos to demand the tribute of the young girls and boys to be sacrificed to the Minotaur).

[68] Athens, whose ancestor king was Kekrops.

[69] The Minotaur.

entreat you now; let no favor be due for my service. Yet neither let me suffer for it! If I am not the cause of your deliverance, yet neither is it right that you should cause my death.

(145) These hands, wearied with beating of my sorrowful breast, unhappy I stretch toward you over the long seas; these locks—such as remain—in grief I bid you look upon! By these tears I pray you—tears moved by what you have done—turn about your ship, reverse your sail, glide swiftly back to me! If I have died before you come, it will yet be you who bear away my bones!

5.11. HIPPOLYTUS AND PHAEDRA: OVID, *HEROIDES* 4

(For Ovid, see headnote to Part 1, document 10; for the *Heroides*, see headnote to document 5.10.b.) The love drama behind this letter is complex. Hippolytos (here Lat. Hippolytus) is the offspring of Theseus and an Amazon. He devotes his life to hunting and cultivating his mind and spirit, worshipping Artemis and rejecting marriage and the temptations of Aphrodite. The Love Goddess punishes his disdain by causing Phaidra (here Lat. Phaedra), Theseus' wife, to fall in love with her stepson. Rejected by Hippolytos, Phaidra commits suicide but falsely inculpates innocent Hippolytos first, causing Theseus to cast his son out. Hippolytos dies while fleeing from Troizen, when a bull comes out of the sea and causes his chariot to crash. The beast was sent by Poseidon (who is Theseus' father) in answer to Theseus' request for a punishment. The figure of Hippolytos is connected with hero cult and rituals in honor of Poseidon, which involve the unharnessing of horses in Troizen (in Attica), where this version of the story by Euripides must have originated.

The motif of the love goddess's revenge due to a mortal's rejection appears in the *Epic of Gilgamesh*, when Ishtar tries to seduce the hero (see document 5.1) and more distantly in Book 5 of the *Iliad* (see Part 3, document 8.a), when Aphrodite is wounded and thus humiliated by Diomedes in battle. In both *Gilgamesh* and *Iliad*, the goddess flies up to complain to her heavenly parents about the hero's offense. The story of Hippolytos and Phaidra was immortalized in numerous literary works in antiquity. Two lost tragedies by Sophocles and Euripides dramatized the story, as did the preserved tragedy *Hippolytos* by Euripides and Seneca's tragedy *Phaedra*. The theme remained popular in late antiquity and flourished well into the Christian era, judging by numerous mosaics and other artistic representations. The tragic romance was represented in mimes throughout the Roman Empire, and its popularity might have had to do also with the association of Hippolytos with *virtus* and chastity, as well as the character's love for books and his characterization as an Orphic initiate.

SOURCE: G. Showerman, *Ovid, Heroides and Amores* (Loeb Classical Library, Cambridge, MA and London, 1914), with minor modifications.

Phaedra to Hippolytus

With wishes for the welfare which she herself, unless you give it her, will ever lack, the Cretan maid greets the hero whose mother was an Amazon. Read to the end, whatever is here contained—what shall reading of a letter harm? In this one, too, there may be something to pleasure you; in these characters of mine, secrets are borne over land and sea. Even foe looks into missive written by foe.

(7) Thrice making trial of speech with you, thrice had my tongue vainly stopped, thrice the sound failed at first threshold of my lips. Wherever modesty may attend on love, love should not lack in it; with me, what modesty forbade to say, love has commanded me to write. Whatever Love commands, it is not safe to hold for naught; his throne and law are over even the gods who are lords of all. It was he who spoke to me when first I doubted if to write or no: "Write; the iron-hearted one will yield his hand." Let him aid me, then, and, just as he heats my marrow with his avid flame, so may he transfix your heart that it yield to my prayers!

(17) It will not be through wanton baseness that I shall break my marriage-bond; my name—and you may ask—is free from all reproach. Love has come to me, the deeper for its coming late—I am burning with love within; I am burning, and my breast has an unseen wound. As the first bearing of the yoke galls the tender steer, and as the rein is scarce endured by the colt fresh taken from the drove, so does my untried heart rebel, and scarce submit to the first restraints of love, and the burden I undergo does not sit well upon my soul. Love grows to be but an art, when the fault is well learned from tender years; she who yields her heart when the time for love is past, has a fiercer passion. You will reap the fresh first-offerings of purity long preserved, and both of us will be equal in our guilt. It is something to pluck fruit from the orchard with full-hanging branch, to cull with delicate nail the first rose. If nevertheless the white and blameless purity in which I have lived before was to be marked with unwonted stain, at least the fortune is kind that burns me with a worthy flame; worse than forbidden love is a lover who is base. Should Juno yield me him who is at once her brother and her lord, I should prefer Hippolytus to Jove!

(37) Now too—you will scarce believe it—I am changing to pursuits I did not know; I am stirred to go among wild beasts. The goddess first for me now is the Delian, known above all for her curved bow; it is your choice that I myself now follow. My pleasure leads me to the wood, to drive the deer into the net, and to urge on the fleet hound over the highest ridge, or with arm shot forth to let fly the quivering spear, or to lay my body upon the grassy ground. Often do I delight to whirl the light chariot in the dust of the course, twisting with the rein the mouth of the flying steed; now again I am borne on, like daughters of the Bacchic cry driven by the frenzy of their god, and those who shake the timbrel at the foot of Ida's ridge,[70] or those whom half-divine Dryad creatures and two-horned Fauns have touched with their own spirit and driven distraught. For they tell me of all these things when that madness of mine has passed away; and I keep silence, conscious it is love that tortures me.

(53) It may be this love is a debt I am paying, due to the destiny of my line, and that Venus is exacting tribute of me for all my race. Europa—this is the first beginning of our line—was loved of Jove; a bull's form disguised the god. Pasiphae my

---

[70] The "daughters of the Bacchic cry" are devotees of Dionysos (see Part 3, document 10.a), and those "who shake the timbrel at the foot of Ida" are devotees of Cybele, the Great Mother of the Gods, whose cult was very popular in Asia Minor.

mother, victim of the deluded bull, brought forth in travail her reproach and burden. The faithless son of Aegeus followed the guiding thread, and escaped from the winding house through the aid my sister gave.[71] Behold, now I, lest I be thought too little a child of Minos' line, am the latest of my stock to come under the law that rules us all! This, too, is fateful, that one house has won us both; your beauty has captured my heart, my sister's heart was captured by your father. Theseus' son and Theseus have been the undoing of two sisters—rear you a double trophy at our house's fall!

(67) That time I went to Eleusis, the city of Ceres, would that the Gnosian land had held me back! It was then you pleased me most, and yet you had pleased before; piercing love lodged in my deepest bones. Shining white was your raiment, bound round with flowers your locks, the blush of modesty had tinged your sun-browned cheeks, and, what others call a countenance hard and stern, in Phaedra's eye was strong instead of hard. Away from me with your young men arrayed like women!— beauty in a man would fain be striven for in measure. That hardness of feature suits you well, those locks that fall without art, and the light dust upon your handsome face. Whether you draw rein and curb the resisting neck of your spirited steed, I look with wonder at your turning his feet in circle so slight; whether with strong arm you hurl the pliant shaft, your gallant arm draws my regard upon itself, or whether you grasp the broad-headed cornel hunting-spear. To say no more, my eyes delight in whatsoever you do.

(85) Do you only lay aside your hardness upon the forest ridges; I am no fit spoil for your campaign. What use to you to practice the ways of girded Diana, and to have stolen from Venus her own due? That which lacks its alternations of repose will not endure; this is what repairs the strength and renews the wearied limbs. The bow—and you should imitate the weapons of your Diana—if you never cease to bend it, will grow slack. Renowned in the forest was Cephalus, and many were the wild beasts that had fallen on the sod at the piercing of his stroke; yet he did not ill in yielding himself to Aurora's love. Often did the goddess sagely go to him, leaving her aged spouse.[72] Many a time beneath the ilex did Venus and he[73] that was sprung of Cinyras recline, pressing some chance grassy spot. The son of Oeneus, too, took fire with love for Maenalian Atalanta; she has the spoil of the wild beast as the pledge of his love. Let us, too, be now first numbered in that company! If you take away love, the forest is but a rustic place. I myself will come and be at your side, and neither rocky covert shall make me fear, nor the boar dreadful for the sidestroke of his tusk.

(105) There are two seas that on either side assail an isthmus with their floods, and the slender land hears the waves of both. Here with you will I dwell, in Troezen's land, the realm of Pittheus; that place is dearer to me now than my own native soil. The hero son of Neptune is absent now, in happy hour, and will be absent

---

[71] His sister Ariadne, who helped Theseus defeat the Minotaur. The Minotaur was born from the love between Pasiphae and the bull sent by Poseidon.

[72] Tithonus.

[73] Adonis.

long; he is kept by the shores of his dear Pirithous.[74] Theseus—unless, indeed, we refuse to own what all may see—has come to love Pirithous more than Phaedra, Pirithous more than you. Nor is that the only wrong we suffer at his hand; there are deep injuries we both have had from him. The bones of my brother he crushed with his triple-knotted club and scattered over the ground; my sister he left at the mercy of wild beasts. The first in courage among the women of the battle-axe bore you,[75] a mother worthy of the vigor of her son; if you ask where she is—Theseus pierced her side with the steel, nor did she find safety in the pledge of so great a son. Yes, and she was not even wedded to him and taken to his home with the nuptial torch—why, unless that you, a bastard, should not come to your father's throne? He has bestowed brothers on you too, from me, and the cause of rearing them all as heirs has been not myself, but he. Ah, would that the bosom, which was to work you wrong, fairest of nurses, had been rent in the midst of its agony! Come now, reverence the bed of a father who thus deserves of you—the bed which he neglects and is disowning by his deeds.

(129) And, should you think of me as a stepmother who would mate with her husband's son, let empty names fright not your soul. Such old-fashioned regard for virtue was rustic even in Saturn's reign, and doomed to die in the age to come. Jove fixed that virtue was to be in whatever brought us pleasure; and naught is wrong before the gods since sister was made wife by brother. That bond of kinship only holds close and firm in which Venus herself has forged the chain. Nor need you fear the trouble of concealment—it will be easy; ask the aid of Venus! Through her our fault will be covered under name of kinship. Should someone see us embrace, we both shall meet with praise; I shall be called a faithful stepmother to the son of my lord. No portal of a harsh husband will need unbolting for you in the darkness of night; there will be no guard to be eluded; as the same roof has covered us both, the same will cover us still. Your wont has been to give me kisses unconcealed, your wont will be still to give me kisses unconcealed. You will be safe with me, and will earn praise by your fault, though you be seen upon my very couch. Only, away with tarrying, and make haste to bind our bond—so may Love be merciful to you, who is bitter to me now! I do not disdain to bend my knee and humbly make entreaty. Alas! Where now are my pride, my lofty words, fallen! I was resolved—if there was a thing love could resolve—both to fight long and not to yield to fault; but I am overcome. I pray to you, to clasp your knees I extend my queenly arms. Of what befits, no one who loves takes thought. My modesty has tied, and as it fled it left its standards behind.

(156) Forgive me my confession, and soften your hard heart! That I have for sire Minos, who rules the seas, that from my ancestor's hand comes hurled the lightning-stroke,[76] that the front of my grandsire, he who moves the tepid day with gleaming chariot,[77] is crowned with palisade of pointed rays—what of this, when my noble

---

[74] The son of Neptune is Theseus, and Peirithoos is the king of the Lapiths, whom Theseus helped in the war against the Centaurs and who accompanied Theseus in this trip to Hades.

[75] Here referring to the Amazon Antiope, although generally her sister Hippolyte was regarded as Hippolytos' mother.

[76] Minos was the son of Zeus and Europa.

[77] Helios, the Sun, was the father of Phaedra's mother, Pasiphae.

name is prostrate under love? Have pity on those who have gone before, and, if me you will not spare, O, spare my line! To my dowry belongs the Cretan land, the isle of Jove—let my whole court be slaves to my Hippolytus!

(165) Bend, O cruel one, your spirit ! My mother could pervert the bull; will you be fiercer than a savage beast? Spare me, by Venus I pray, who is chief with me now. So may you never love one who will spurn you; so may the agile goddess wait on you in the solitary glade to keep you safe, and the deep forest yield you wild beasts to slay; so may the Satyrs be your friends, and the mountain deities, the Pans, and may the boar fall pierced in full front by your spear; so may the Nymphs—though you are said to loathe womankind—give you the flowing water to relieve your parching thirst!

(175) I mingle with these prayers my tears as well. The words of her who prays, you are reading; her tears, imagine you behold!

5.12. PENELOPE AND ULYSSES: OVID, *HEROIDES* 1

(For Ovid, see headnote to Part 1, document 10; for the *Heroides*, see headnote to 5.10.b.) The story of loyalty and infinite patience of Penelope as she waited for twenty years for her husband's return is first and most famously narrated in Homer's *Odyssey*, culminating in their recognition scene in Book 23. In Ovid's rendition, the letter from Penelope to Ulysses (Odysseus) is situated chronologically within the story toward the end of the wait, when Ulysses' son, Telemachos, has been sent to Pylos and Sparta to inquire about his father.

SOURCE: G. Showerman, *Ovid, Heroides and Amores* (Loeb Classical Library, Cambridge, MA and London, 1914), with minor modifications.

Penelope to Ulysses

(1) This missive your Penelope sends to you, O Ulysses, slow of return that you are—yet write nothing back to me; yourself come! Troy, to be sure, is fallen, hated of the daughters of Greece; but scarcely were Priam and all Troy worth the price to me. O would that then, when his ship was on the way to Lacedaemon, the adulterous lover[78] had been overwhelmed by raging waters! Then had I not lain cold in my deserted bed, nor would now be left alone complaining of slowly passing days; nor would the hanging web be wearying now my widowed hands as I seek to beguile the hours of spacious night.

(11) When have I not feared dangers graver than the real? Love is a thing ever filled with anxious fear. It was upon you that my fancy ever told me the furious Trojans would rush; at mention of the name of Hector my pallor ever came. Did someone begin the tale of Antilochus laid low by the enemy, Antilochus was cause of my alarm; or, did he tell of how the son of Menoetius fell in armor not his own,[79] I wept that wiles could lack success. Had Tlepolemus' with his blood made warm

---

[78] Referring to Paris, whose abduction of Helen of Sparta triggered the Trojan War (Lacedaemon, Gr. Lakedaimon, stands for Sparta; the region was called Lakedaimonia or Lakonia in Greek).

[79] Patroklos, who was killed by Hektor while wearing Achilles' armor.

the Lycian spear,[80] in Tlepolemus' fate was all my care renewed. In short, whoever it was in the Argive camp that was pierced and fell, colder than ice grew the heart of her who loves you.

(23) But good regard for me had the god who looks with favor upon chaste love. Turned to ashes is Troy, and my lord is safe. The Argolic chieftains have returned, our altars are a-smoke; before the gods of our fathers is laid the barbarian spoil. The young wife comes bearing thank-offering for her husband saved; the husband sings of the fates of Troy that have yielded to his own. Righteous elder and trembling girl admire; the wife hangs on the tale that falls from her husband's lips. And someone about the board[81] shows thereon the fierce combat, and with scant tracing of wine pictures forth all Pergamum: "Here flowed the Simois; this is the Sigeian land; here stood the lofty palace of Priam the ancient. Yonder tented the son of Aeacus; yonder, Ulysses; here, in wild course went the frightened steeds with Hector's mutilated corpse."

(37) For the whole story was told your son, whom I sent to seek you; ancient Nestor told him, and he told me. He told as well of Rhesus' and Dolon's fall by the sword,[82] how the one was betrayed by slumber, the other undone by guile. You had the daring—O too, too forgetful of your own!—to set foot by night in the Thracian camp, and to slay so many men, all at one time, and with only one to aid! Ah yes, you were cautious, indeed, and ever gave me first thought! My heart leaped with fear at every word until I was told of your victorious riding back through the friendly lines of the Greeks with the coursers of Ismarus.[83]

(47) But of what avail to me that Ilion has been scattered in ruin by your arms, and that what once was wall is now level ground—if I am still to remain such as I was while Troy endured, and must live to all time bereft of my lord? For other Pergamum has been brought low; for me alone it still stands, though the victor dwell within and drive there the plow with the ox he took as spoil. Now are fields of corn where Troy once was, and soil made fertile with Phrygian blood waves rich with harvest ready for the sickle; the half-buried bones of her heroes are struck by the curving plough, and herbage hides from sight her ruined palaces. A victor, you are yet not here, nor am I let know what causes your delay, or in what part of the world hard-heartedly you hide.

(59) Whoever turns to these shores of ours, his stranger ship is plied with many a question when he goes away, and into his hand is given the sheet written by these fingers of mine, to render up should he but see you anywhere. We have sent to Pylos, the land of ancient Nestor, Neleus' son; the word brought back from Pylos was nothing sure.[84] We have sent to Sparta, too; Sparta also could tell us nothing

---

[80] Tlepolemos was killed by Sarpedon, king of Lycia.

[81] Reference to the use of wooden boards with maps or drawings by storytellers.

[82] Both Rhesus and Dolon fought on the Trojan side and appear in *Iliad* Book 10 (known as "The Doloneia"), where Dolon is captured by Odysseus and Diomedes and killed and Rhesus' horses are stolen.

[83] Ismaros or Ismara is the city of the Kikones, which Odysseus raided after the fall of Troy.

[84] In the *Odyssey* (2.373) Telemachos goes to Pylos and Sparta accompanied by Athena, but without his mother's knowledge. Ovid's Penelope can be referring to other envoys.

true. In what lands are you abiding, or where do you idly tarry? Better for me, were the walls of Phoebus[85] still standing in their place—ah me inconstant, I am angered by the vows I myself have made! Had they not fallen, I should know where you were fighting, and have only war to fear, and my plaint would be joined with that of many another. But now, what I am to fear I know not—yet none the less I fear all things, distraught, and wide is the field open for my cares. Whatever dangers the deep contains, whatever the land, suspicion tells me are cause of your long delay. While I live on in foolish fear of things like these, you may be captive to a stranger love[86]—such are the hearts of you men! It may be you even tell how rustic[87] a wife you have—one fit only to dress fine the wool. May I be mistaken, and this charge of mine be found slight as the breeze that blows, and may it not be that, free to return, you will to be away!

(81) As for me—my father Icarius enjoins on me to quit my widowed couch, and ever chides me for my measureless delay. Let him chide on—yours I am, yours must I be called; Penelope, the wife of Ulysses, ever shall I be. Yet is he bent by my faithfulness and my chaste prayers, and of himself abates his urgency. The men of Dulichium and Samos, and they whom high Zacynthus bore—a wanton throng—come pressing about me, suing for my hand. In your own hall they are masters, with none to say them nay; my heart is being torn, your substance spoiled. Why tell you of Pisander, and of Polybus, and of Medon the cruel, and of the grasping hands of Eurymachus and Antinous, and of others, all of whom through shameful absence you yourself are feeding fat with store that was won at cost of your blood? Irus the beggar, and Melanthius, who drives in your flocks to be consumed, are the crowning disgrace now added to your ruin.

(97) We number only three, unused to war—a powerless wife; Laertes, an old man; Telemachus, a boy. He was of late almost taken away from me by trickery, while making ready, against the will of all of them, to go to Pylos. The gods grant, I pray, that our fated ends may come in due succession—that he be the one to close my eyes, the one to close yours! To sustain our cause are the guardian of your cattle and the ancient nurse, and, as a third, the faithful ward of the unclean sty; but neither Laertes, unable as he is to wield arms now, can sway the scepter in the midst of our foes—Telemachus, indeed, so he live on, will arrive at years of strength, but now should have his father's aid and guarding—nor have I strength to repel the enemy from our halls. Do you yourself make haste to come, haven and altar of safety for your own! You have a son—and may you have him ever, is my prayer—who in his tender years should have been trained by you in his father's ways. Have regard for Laertes; in the hope that you will come at last to close his eyes, he is withstanding the final day of fate.

(115) As for myself, who when you left my side was but a girl, though you should come straightway, I surely shall seem turned into an aged woman.

---

[85] Troy, since the city was protected by Apollo.

[86] As she fears, Odysseus is probably still caught in Kalypso's island (he also fell under the spell of Circe and was accepted by the Phaeacians as a possible husband for Nausikaa).

[87] The adjective *rustica* appears frequently in the *Heroides* and can mean "simple," "homely," "unsophisticated."

5.13. HERMAPHRODITUS, FROM OVID, *METAMORPHOSES*, BOOK 4

(For Ovid and the *Metamorphoses*, see headnote to Part 1, document 10.) Hermaphroditus was a mythological character, a divinized representation of natural androgynous beings. His name is a composite of Hermes and Aphrodite, who were his parents and at the same time symbolize his composite nature with both male and female sexual organs. Hermaphroditus was in fact worshipped as a deity in fourth-century BCE Athens and became a popular artistic motif in Hellenistic and Roman times, appearing always with female breasts and male genitals.

Physically androgynous-born people were seen as an unnatural phenomenon and in Republican Rome were considered a bad omen and sometimes drowned at birth. In the story told by Aristophanes in Plato's *Symposium* (Part 7, document 4), however, the comedian puts androgynous people on equal footing with males and females, the three "genders" descending from different astral bodies.

SOURCE: Ovid, *Metamorphoses*, Book 4.285–388. F. J. Miller, *Ovid, Metamorphoses* (Loeb Classical Library, Cambridge, MA and London, 1921, 2nd ed.), with minor modifications.

How the fountain of Salmacis is of ill-repute, how it enervates with its enfeebling waters and renders soft and weak all men who bathe therein, you shall now hear. The cause is hidden; but the enfeebling power of the fountain is well known. A little son of Hermes and of the goddess of Cythera[88] the Naiads[89] nursed within Ida's caves. In his fair face mother and father could be clearly seen; his name also he took from them. When fifteen years had passed, he left his native mountains and abandoned his foster mother, Ida, delighting to wander in unknown lands and to see strange rivers, his eagerness making light of toil.

He came even to the Lycian cities and to the Carians, who dwell hard by the land of Lycia. Here he saw a pool of water crystal clear to the very bottom. No marshy reeds grew there, no unfruitful swamp-grass, nor spiky rushes; it is clear water. But the edges of the pool are bordered with fresh grass, and herbage evergreen. A nymph dwells in the pool, one that loves not hunting, nor is wont to bend the bow or strive with speed of foot. She only of the Naiads follows not in swift Diana's train. Often, it is said, her sisters would chide her: "Salmacis, take now either hunting-spear or painted quiver, and vary your ease with the hardships of the hunt." But she takes no hunting-spear, no painted quiver, nor does she vary her ease with the hardships of the hunt; but at times she bathes her shapely limbs in her own pool; often combs her hair with a boxwood comb, often looks in the mirror-like waters to see what best becomes her. Now, wrapped in a transparent robe, she lies down to rest on the soft grass or the soft herbage. Often she gathers flowers; and on this occasion, too,

---

[88] Aphrodite.

[89] Naiads were nymphs of sweet waters, i.e., rivers, springs, wells, etc. (counterparts of the Oceanids or Nereids for sea waters).

she chanced to be gathering flowers when she saw the boy and longed to possess what she saw.

Not yet, however, did she approach him, though she was eager to do so, until she had calmed herself, until she had arranged her robes and composed her countenance, and taken all pains to appear beautiful. Then did she speak:

"O youth, most worthy to be believed a god, if you are indeed a god, you must be Cupid; or if you are mortal, happy are they who gave birth to you, blessed is your brother, fortunate indeed any sister of yours and your nurse who breast-fed you. But far, O, far happier than they all is she, if any is your promised bride, if you shall deem any worthy to be your wife. If there be any such, let mine be stolen joy; if not, may I be your bride, and may we be joined in wedlock."

The maiden said no more. But the boy blushed rosy red; for he knew not what love is. But still the blush became him well. Such color have apples hanging in sunny orchards, or painted ivory; such has the moon, eclipsed, red under white, when brazen vessels clash vainly for her relief. When the nymph begged and prayed for at least a sister's kiss and was in act to throw her arms round his snowy neck, he cried: "Have done, or I must flee and leave this spot—and you." Salmacis trembled at this threat and said: "I yield the place to you, fair stranger," and turning away, pretended to depart. But even so she often looked back, and deep in a neighboring thicket she hid herself, crouching on bended knees.

But the boy, freely as if unmatched and alone, walks up and down on the grass, dips his toes in the lapping waters, and his feet. Then quickly, charmed with the coolness of the soothing stream, he threw aside the thin garments from his slender form. Then was the nymph as one spellbound, and her love kindled as she gazed at the naked form. Her eyes shone bright as when the sun's dazzling face is reflected from the surface of a glass held opposite his rays. Scarce can she endure delay, scarce bear her joy postponed, so eager to hold him in her arms, so madly incontinent. He, clapping his body with hollow palms, dives into the pool, and swimming with alternate strokes flashes with gleaming body through the transparent flood, as if one should encase ivory figures or white lilies in translucent glass.

"I win, and he is mine!" cries the Naiad, and casting off all her garments dives also into the waters: she holds him fast though he strives against her, steals reluctant kisses, fondles him, touches his unwilling breast, clings to him on this side and on that. At length, as he tries his best to break away from her, she wraps him round with her embrace, as a serpent, when the king of birds[90] has caught her and is bearing her on high: which, hanging from his claws, wraps her folds around his head and feet and entangles his flapping wings with her tail; or as the ivy often-times embraces great trunks of trees, or as the sea-polyp holds its enemy caught beneath the sea, its tentacles embracing him on every side. The son of Atlas resists as best he may and denies the nymph the joy she craves; but she holds on, and clings as if grown fast to him: "Strive as you may, wicked boy," she cries, "still shall you not escape me. Grant me this, ye gods, and may no day ever come that shall separate him from me or me from him.'"

---

[90] In other words, an eagle. The eagle carrying a struggling snake appears in classical literature, especially as a portent or omen.

The gods heard her prayer. For their two bodies, joined together as they were, were merged in one, with one face and form for both. As when one grafts a twig on some tree, he sees the branches grow one, and with common life come to maturity, so were these two bodies knit in close embrace: they were no longer two, nor such as to be called, one, woman, and one, man. They seemed neither, and yet both. When now he saw that the waters into which he had plunged had made him but half-man, and that his limbs had become enfeebled there, stretching out his hands and speaking, though not with manly tones, Hermaphroditus cried: "O, grant this boon, my father and my mother, to your son who bears the names of both: whoever comes into this pool as man may he go forth half-man, and may he weaken at touch of the water." His parents heard the prayer of their two-formed son and charged the waters with that uncanny power.

5.14. CEPHALUS AND PROCRIS, FROM OVID, *METAMORPHOSES*, BOOK 7

(For Ovid and the *Metamorphoses*, see headnote to Part 1, document 10.) Cephalus (Greek Kephalos) was a mythical hunter who appears in Hesiod (*Theogony* 985–987) and in the Epic Cycle. He is sometimes associated with the region of Attica, where he was worshipped, as well as with Phokis and Kephallenia. Cephalus' connection with Attica comes from his marriage to Procris (Gr. Prokris), daughter of the founding king of Athens Erechtheus. In this tragic story of love and jealousy, Cephalus accidentally kills his wife Procris, for which, according to tradition, he was tried at the court of the Areopagus and exiled from Athens by his father-in-law Erechtheus. He then became a founding figure at Kephallenia (a large island in the Ionian Sea in western Greece). Cephalus tells his tragic story at the court of king Aeacus (Gr. Aiakos) of Aigina (an island off the coast of Attica), as he leads a group of Athenians to ask for help in the face of the imminent attack on Attica by king Minos of Crete. Aeacus granted Aigina's help, and the worriers drank and told stories all night, and at dawn they woke to prepare for war.

SOURCE: Ovid, *Metamorphoses*, Book 7.665–865. F. J. Miller, *Ovid, Metamorphoses* (Loeb Classical Library, Cambridge, MA and London, 1921, 2nd ed.), with minor modifications.

The sons of Pallas[91] came to Cephalus, who was the older, and Cephalus with the sons of Pallas went together to the king. But deep sleep still held the king.[92] Phocus, son of Aeacus, received them at the threshold; for Telamon and his brother[93] were marshalling the men for war. Into the inner court and beautiful apartments Phocus conducted the Athenians, and there they sat them down together. There Phocus

---

[91] In other words, the Athenians, whose patron goddess is Pallas Athena.

[92] Aeacus (Gr. Aiakos), legendary king of Aigina. He was the father of Peleus (the father of Achilles) and Telamon (father of the great Aiax), as well as of Phocus (Gr. Phokos), who was murdered by his brothers, for which they were exiled. Aiakus (Aeacus) in turn was a son of Zeus (which made Achilles and Aiax great-grandsons of Zeus).

[93] Peleus.

noticed that Cephalus carried in his hand a javelin with a golden head, and a shaft made of some strange wood. After some talk, he said abruptly: "I am devoted to the woods and the hunting of wild beasts. Still, I have for some time been wondering from what wood that weapon you hold is made. Surely if it were of ash it would be of deep yellow hue; if it were of cornel-wood there would be knots upon it. What wood it is made of I cannot tell; but my eyes have never seen a javelin for throwing more beautiful than that." And one of the Athenian brothers replied: "You will admire the weapon's use more than its beauty; it goes straight to any mark, and chance does not guide its flight; and it flies back, all bloody, with no hand to bring it."

(685) Then indeed young Phocus was eager to know why it was so, and whence it came, who was the giver of so wonderful a gift. Cephalus told what the youth asked, but he was ashamed to tell at what price he gained it. He was silent; then, touched with grief for his lost wife, he burst into tears and said: "It is this weapon makes me weep, thou son of a goddess—who could believe it?—and long will it make me weep if the fates shall give me long life. This destroyed me and my dear wife together. And O, that I had never had it! My wife was Procris, or, if by more likely chance the name of Orithyia has come to your ears, the sister of the ravished Orithyia. If you should compare the form and bearing of the two, Procris herself is the more worthy to be ravished away. It is she that her father, Erechtheus, joined to me; it is she that love joined to me. I was called happy, and happy I was. But the gods decreed it otherwise, or, perchance, I should be happy still. It was in the second month after our marriage rites. I was spreading my nets to catch the antlered deer, when from the top of ever-blooming Hymettus the golden goddess of the dawn, having put the shades to flight, beheld me and carried me away, against my will: may the goddess pardon me for telling the simple truth; but as truly as she shines with the blush of roses on her face, as truly as she holds the portals of the day and night, and drinks the juices of nectar, it was Procris I loved; Procris was in my heart, Procris was ever on my lips. I kept talking of my wedding and its fresh joys of love and the first union of my now deserted couch. The goddess was provoked and exclaimed: 'Cease your complaints, ungrateful boy; keep your Procris! but, if my mind can foresee at all, you will come to wish that you had never had her'; and in a rage she sent me back to her.

(714) "As I was going home, and turned over in my mind the goddess' warning, I began to fear that my wife herself had not kept her marriage vows. Her beauty and her youth made me fear unfaithfulness; but her character forbade that fear. Still, I had been absent long, and she from whom I was returning was herself an example of unfaithfulness; and besides, we lovers fear everything. I decided to make a cause for grievance and to tempt her chaste faith by gifts. Aurora helped me in this jealous undertaking and changed my form (I seemed to feel the change). And so, unrecognizable I entered Athens, Pallas' sacred city, and went into my house. The household itself was blameless, showed no sign of aught amiss, was only anxious for its lost lord. With much difficulty and by a thousand wiles I gained the presence of Erechtheus' daughter; and when I looked upon her my heart failed me and I almost abandoned the test of her fidelity which I had planned. I scarce kept from confessing the truth, from kissing her as was her due. She was sad; but no woman could be more beautiful than was she in her sadness. She was all grief with longing for the

husband who had been torn away from her. Imagine, Phocus, how beautiful she was, how that grief itself became her.

(734) "Why should I tell how often her chastity repelled my temptations? To every plea she said: 'I keep myself for one alone. Wherever he is I keep my love for one.' What husband in his senses would not have found that test of her fidelity enough? But I was not content and strove on to my own undoing! By promising to give fortunes for her favor, and at last, by adding to my promised gifts, I forced her to hesitate. Then, victor to my sorrow, I exclaimed: 'False one, he that is here is a feigned adulterer! I was really your husband! By my own witness, betrayer, you are detected!' She, not a word. Only in silence, overwhelmed with shame, she fled her treacherous husband and his house. In hate for me, loathing the whole race of men, she wandered over the mountains, devoted to Diana's pursuits.

(747) "Then in my loneliness the fire of love burned more fiercely, penetrating to the marrow. I craved pardon, owned that I had sinned, confessed that I too might have yielded in the same way under the temptation of gifts, if so great gifts were offered to me. When I had made this confession and she had sufficiently avenged her outraged feelings, she came back to me and we spent sweet years together in harmony. She gave me besides, as though she had given but small gifts in herself, a wonderful hound which her own Cynthia had given, and said as she gave: 'He will surpass all other hounds in speed.' She gave me a javelin also, this one which, as you see, I hold in my hands. Would you know the story of both gifts? Hear the wonderful story: you will be moved by the strangeness of the deed.

(759) "Oedipus, the son of Laius, had solved the riddle which had been inscrutable to the understanding of all before; fallen headlong she lay, the dark prophet, forgetful of her own riddle. Straightway a second monster was sent against Aonian[94] Thebes (and surely kind Themis does not let such things go unpunished!) and many country dwellers were in terror of the fierce creature, fearing both for their own and their flocks' destruction. We, the neighboring youths, came and encircled the broad fields with our hunting nets. But that swift beast leaped over the nets, over the very tops of the toils which we had spread. Then we let slip our hounds from the leash; but she escaped their pursuit and mocked the hundred dogs with speed like any bird. Then all the hunters called upon me for my Laelaps (that is the name of the hound my wife had given me). Long since he had been struggling to get loose from the leash and straining his neck against the strap that held him. Scarce was he well released when we could not tell where he was. The warm dust kept the imprint of his feet, he himself had quite disappeared from sight. No spear is swifter than he, nor leaden bullets thrown by a whirled sling, or the light reed shot from a Gortynian bow.

(779) There was a high hill near by, whose top overlooked the surrounding plain. Thither I climbed and gained a view of that strange chase, in which the beast seemed now to be caught and now to slip from the dog's very teeth. Nor does the cunning creature flee in a straight course off into the distance, but it eludes the pursuer's jaws and wheels sharply round, so that its enemy may lose his spring. The dog presses him hard, follows him step for step, and, while he seems to hold him, does not

---

[94] A mythological name from Aonia, synonymous with Boiotia (the region of Thebes).

hold, and snaps at the empty air. I turned to my javelin's aid. As my right hand was balancing it, while I was fitting my fingers into the loop, I turned my eyes aside for a single moment; and when I turned them back again to the same spot—O, wonderful! I saw two marble images in the plain; the one you would think was fleeing, the other catching at the prey. Doubtless some god must have willed, if there was any god with them, that both should be unconquered in their race." Thus far he spoke and fell silent. "But what charge have you to bring against the javelin itself?" asked Phocus. The other thus told what charge he had against the javelin:

(796) "My joys, Phocus, were the beginning of my woe. These I will describe first. O, what a joy it is, son of Aeacus, to remember the blessed time when during those first years I was happy in my wife, as I should be, and she was happy in her husband. Mutual cares and mutual love bound us together. Not Jove's love would she have preferred to mine; nor was there any woman who could lure me away from her, no, not if Venus herself should come. An equal passion burned in both our two hearts. In the early morning, when the sun's first rays touched the tops of the hills, with a young man's eagerness I used to go hunting in the woods. Nor did I take attendants with me, or horses or keen-scented dogs or knotted nets. I was safe with my javelin. But when my hand had had its fill of slaughter of wild creatures, I would come back to the cool shade and the breeze that came forth from the cool valleys. I wooed the breeze, blowing gently on me in my heat; the breeze I waited for. She was my labor's rest. 'Come, Aura,' I remember I used to cry, 'come soothe me; come into my breast, most welcome one, and, as indeed you do, relieve the heat with which I burn.' Perhaps I would add, for so my fates drew me on, more endearments, and say: 'You are my greatest joy; you refresh and comfort me; you make me to love the woods and solitary places. It is ever my joy to feel your breath upon my face.'

(821) "Someone overhearing these words was deceived by their double meaning; and, thinking that the word 'Aura' so often on my lips was a nymph's name, was convinced that I was in love with some nymph. Straightway the rash tell-tale went to Procris with the story of my supposed unfaithfulness and reported in whispers what he had heard. A credulous thing is love. Smitten with sudden pain (as I heard the story), she fell down in a swoon. Reviving at last, she called herself wretched, victim of cruel fate; complained of my unfaithfulness, and, excited by an empty charge, she feared a mere nothing, feared an empty name and grieved, poor girl, as over a real rival. And yet she would often doubt and hope in her depth of misery that she was mistaken; she refused to believe the story she had heard, and, unless she saw it with her own eyes, would not think her husband guilty of such sin.

(835) "The next morning, when the early dawn had banished night, I left the house and sought the woods; there, successful, as I lay on the grass, I cried: 'Come, Aura, come and soothe my toil' — and suddenly, while I was speaking, I thought I heard a groan. 'Come, dearest one,' I cried again. And as the fallen leaves made a slight rustling sound, I thought it was some beast and hurled my javelin at the place. It was Procris, and, clutching at the wound in her breast, she cried, 'O, woe is me.' When I recognized the voice of my faithful wife, I rushed headlong towards the sound, beside myself with horror. There I found her dying, her disordered garments stained with blood, and, O, the pity! trying to draw the very weapon she had given me from her wounded breast. With loving arms I raised her body, dearer to me than my own,

tore open the garment from her breast and bound up the cruel wound, and tried to staunch the blood, praying that she would not leave me stained with her death.

(851) "She, though strength failed her, with a dying effort forced herself to say these few words: 'By the union of our love, by the gods above and my own gods, by all that I have done for you, and by the love that still I bear you in my dying hour, the cause of my own death, I beg you, do not let this Aura take my place.' And then I knew at last that it was a mistake in the name, and I told her the truth. But what availed then the telling? She fell back in my arms and her last faint strength fled with her blood. So long as she could look at anything she looked at me and breathed out her unhappy spirit on my lips. But she seemed to die content and with a happy look upon her face."

This story the hero told with many tears. And now Aeacus came in with his two sons and his new levied band of soldiers, which Cephalus received with their valiant arms.

5.15. HYACINTH AND APOLLO, FROM OVID, *METAMORPHOSES*, BOOK 10

(For Ovid and the *Metamorphoses*, see headnote to Part 1, document 10.) As we will see in the story of Myrrha, the myth of Hyacinth (Lat. Hyacinthus, Gr. Hyakinthos) is a story of love, death, and transformation associated with a plant, here the iris flower (*hyakinthos*). Hyacinth is in fact a cult figure at Amyklai, near Sparta, where the story is set, and probably in other Dorian cities as well, judging by the use of his name as a month in local calendars. Paired with a sister called Polyboia ("she of abundant cattle"), Hyacinth was probably a pre-Greek nature-god representing the cycle of vegetation (dying and returning), a type of phenomenon represented later in other cults, such as those of Adonis and the two goddesses Demeter and Persephone.

The theme of the young beloved of Apollo and the jealousy of Zephyrus (the wind that caused his death) must have been broadly known, since other authors mention it (e.g., Euripides' *Helen*, 1469 ff., and Apollodorus' *Library* 1.3.3). It also became a popular homoerotic theme in Attic vase painting. The story is narrated by Orpheus, who takes over the narrative voice after his own story is told at the beginning of Book 10 of the *Metamorphoses*.

SOURCE: Ovid, *Metamorphoses*, Book 10.162–219. F. J. Miller, *Ovid, Metamorphoses* (Loeb Classical Library, Cambridge, MA and London, 1921, 2nd ed.), with minor modifications.

You also, youth of Amyclae,[95] Phoebus would have set in the sky,[96] if grim fate had given him time to set you there. Still in what fashion you may you are immortal: as often as spring drives winter out and the Ram succeeds the watery Fish,[97] so often do you come up and blossom on the green turf. Above all others did my father love you,[98] and Delphi, set at the very center of the earth, lacked its presiding deity

[95] In other words, Hyacinth.

[96] "Also" refers to Ganymede, whose story Ovid tells very briefly right before this passage in the *Metamorphoses*.

[97] Refering to the constellations of Aries and Pisces, respectively.

[98] In other words, Apollo, who is Orpheus' father in some versions of his genealogy.

while the god was hunting Eurotas' stream and Sparta, the unwalled.[99] No more has he thought for zither or for bow. Entirely heedless of his usual pursuits, he refuses not to bear the nets, nor hold the dogs in leash, nor go as comrade along the rough mountain ridges. And so with long association he feeds his passion's flame. And now Titan was about midway between the coming and the banished night, standing at equal distance from both extremes; they strip themselves and, gleaming with rich olive oil, they try a contest with the broad discus. This, well poised, Phoebus sent flying through the air and cleft the opposite clouds with the heavy iron. Back to the wonted earth after long time it fell, revealing the hurler's skill and strength combined. Straightaway the Taenarian[100] youth, heedless of danger and moved by eagerness for the game, ran out to take up the discus. But it bounced back into the air from the hard earth beneath full in your face, O Hyacinthus.

The god grows deadly pale even as the boy, and catches up the huddled form; now he seeks to warm you again, now he tries to staunch your dreadful wound, now strives to stay your parting soul with healing herbs. But his arts are of no avail; the wound is past all cure. Just as when in a garden, if someone has broken off violets or brittle poppies or lilies, still hanging from the yellow stems, fainting they suddenly droop their withered heads and can no longer stand erect, but gaze, with tops bowed low, upon the earth, so the dying face lies prone, the neck, its strength all gone, cannot sustain its own weight and falls back upon the shoulders. "You are fallen, defrauded of your youth's prime, Oebalides,"[101] says Phoebus, "and I your wound do I see my guilt; you are my cause of grief and self-reproach; my hand must be proclaimed the cause of your destruction. I am the author of your death. And yet, what is my fault, unless my playing with you can be called a fault, unless my loving you can be called a fault? And O, that I might give up my life for you, so well-deserving, or give it up with you! But since we are held from this by the laws of fate, you shall be always with me, and shall stay on my mindful lips. You shall be my lyre, struck by my hand, you shall my songs proclaim. And as a new flower, by your markings shall you imitate my groans. Also the time will come when a most valiant hero[102] shall be linked with this flower, and by the same markings shall he be known." While Apollo thus spoke with truth-telling lips, behold, the blood, which had poured out on the grounds and stained the glass, ceased to be blood, and in its place there sprang a flower brighter than Tyrian dye.[103] It took the form of a lily, save that the one was of purple hue, while the other was silvery white. Phoebus, not satisfied with this—for it was he who wrought the honoring miracle—himself inscribed this grieving words upon the leaves, and the flower bore the marks, AI AI, letters of lamentation, drawn thereon. Sparta, too, was proud that Hyacinthus was her son, and even to this day his honor still endures; and still, as the anniversary returns, as did their sires, they celebrate the Hyacinthia in solemn festival.

---

[99] Sparta being the home of Hyacinth.

[100] Poetic synonym for Lakonian, same as Lakedaimonian (i.e., Spartan).

[101] Descendant of the Spartan Oibalos.

[102] Aiax (see Ovid, *Met.* 13. 396).

[103] In other words, red like the purple dye, an industry that the Phoenicians (here called Tyrians) were famous for.

5.16. PYGMALION'S STATUE, FROM OVID, *METAMORPHOSES*, BOOK 10

(For Ovid and the *Metamorphoses*, see headnote to Part 1, document 10.) Pygmalion was a legendary king of Cyprus. In Ovid's version, he was the grandfather of Kinyras, the king of Cyprus who appears in Homer and other sources (also the father of Myrrha; see document 5.17). That this character is originally Phoenician is indicated by his name (a Greek adaptation of the Phoenician Pumayyaton), which contains the name of the god Pumay and is attested in Phoenician inscriptions. The other known Pygmalion recorded in legend is the Tyrian brother of Elissa (Virgil's Dido), the founder of Carthage (see foundation story in Part 4, documents 12.a and 12.b).

The Phoenician-Cypriot location of the story fits well with Pygmalion's attachment to the goddess of love and sexuality, Aphrodite (here Latin Venus), whose cult at Paphos in Cyprus was extremely famous and originally was a Phoenician cult to Ashtart (Astarte). The Phoenician background of Pygmalion and Aphrodite/Ashtart suggests a possible connection with the Canaanite ritual of "sacred marriage," whereby the king symbolically mated with the fertility goddess once a year (incarnated by the queen or by a priestess) during the New Year festival. The daughter of Pygmalion and the statue (turned maiden) is thus called Paphos, becoming the **eponymous** ancestor of the city. As for the statue, no ancient author mentions its name, although later traditions called her Galatea.

The passion of Pygmalion also echoes the commotion created by a particular statue: that of Aphrodite at Knidos, a Greek settlement on the coast of Asia Minor. It was sculpted by Praxiteles of Athens in the fourth century BCE and was the first known representation of a full-size naked female body. Its beauty stirred passions among male visitors and copies of it were reproduced throughout the Classical world. The narrator of this episode is Orpheus, as in most of Book 10 of the *Metamorphoses*.

SOURCE: Ovid, *Metamorphoses*, Book 10.243–297. F. J. Miller, *Ovid, Metamorphoses* (Loeb Classical Library, Cambridge, MA and London, 1921, 2nd ed.), with minor modifications.

Pygmalion had seen these women[104] spending their lives in shame, and, disgusted with the faults, which in such full measure nature had given the female mind, he lived unmarried and long was without a partner of his couch. Meanwhile, with wondrous art he successfully carves a figure out of snowy ivory, giving it a beauty more perfect than that of any woman ever born. And with his own work he falls in love. The face is that of a real maiden, whom you would think living and desirous of being moved, if modesty did not prevent. So does his art conceal his art. Pygmalion looks in admiration and is inflamed with love for this semblance of a form. Often he lifts his hands to the work to try whether it be flesh or ivory; nor does he yet confess

---

[104] Referring to the Propetides, a group of women who neglected the correct worship of Venus and were reduced to prostitution by the goddess.

it to be ivory. He kisses it and thinks his kisses are returned. He speaks to it, grasps it and seems to feel his fingers sink into the limbs when he touches them; and then he fears lest he leave marks of bruises on them. Now he addresses it with fond words of love, now brings it gifts pleasing to girls, shells and smooth pebbles, little birds and many-hued flowers, and lilies and colored balls, with tears[105] of the Heliades that drop down from the trees. He drapes its limbs also with robes, puts gemmed rings upon its fingers and a long necklace around its neck; pearls hang from the ears and chains adorn the breast. All these are beautiful; but no less beautiful is the statue unadorned. He lays it on a bed spread with coverlets of Tyrian hue, calls it the consort of his couch, and rests its reclining head upon soft, downy pillows, as if it could enjoy them.

And now the festal day of Venus had come, which all Cyprus thronged to celebrate; heifers with spreading horns covered with gold had fallen beneath the death-stroke on their snowy necks, and the altars smoked with incense. Pygmalion, having brought his gift to the altar, stood and falteringly prayed: "If ye, O gods, can give all things, I pray to have as wife −" he did not dare add "my ivory maid," but said, "one like my ivory maid." But golden Venus (for she herself was present at her feast) knew what that prayer meant; and, as an omen of her favoring deity, thrice did the flame burn brightly and leap high in air. When he returned he sought the image of his maid, and bending over the couch he kissed her. She seemed warm to his touch. Again he kissed her, and with his hands also he touched her breast. The ivory grew soft to his touch and, its hardness vanishing, gave and yielded beneath his fingers, as Hymettian wax grows soft under the sun and, molded by the thumb, is easily shaped to many forms and becomes usable through use itself. The lover stands amazed, rejoices still in doubt, fears he is mistaken, and tries his hopes again and yet again with his hand. Yes, it was real flesh! The veins were pulsing beneath his testing finger. Then did the Paphian hero pour out copious thanks to Venus, and again pressed with his lips real lips at last. The maiden felt the kisses, blushed and, lifting her timid eyes up to the light, she saw the sky and her lover at the same time. The goddess graced with her presence the marriage she had made; and as the ninth moon had brought her crescent to the full, a daughter was born to them, Paphos, from whom the island takes its name.

5.17. MYRRHA AND CINYRAS, FROM OVID, *METAMORPHOSES*, BOOK 10

(For Ovid and the *Metamorphoses*, see headnote to Part 1, document 10.) Ovid places this dramatic story of incest and doom immediately after the story of Pygmalion (see above). Cinyras (Greek Kinyras) was the son of Paphos, and the grandson of Pygmalion, king of Cyprus, according to Ovid. This episode of Myrrha, in turn, continues in Ovid with the story of her offspring Adonis (for which see Part 6, document 11). The tragic transformation of Myrrha offers an *aition* for the bitter aromatic resin that the plant "weeps." In another version she

---

[105] Referring to amber.

is the daughter and lover of Theias of Assyria and called Smyrna or Zmyrna, like the city in the coast of Asia Minor. The narrator of this episode is still Orpheus, as in most of Book 10 of the *Metamorphoses*.

SOURCE: Ovid, *Metamorphoses*, Book 10.298–502. F. J. Miller, *Ovid, Metamorphoses* (Loeb Classical Library, Cambridge, MA and London, 1921, 2nd ed.), with minor modifications.

Cinyras was her son[106] and, had he been without offspring, might have been counted fortunate. A horrible tale I have to tell. Far hence be daughters, far hence, fathers; or, if your minds find pleasure in my songs, do not give credence to this story, and believe that it never happened; or, if you do believe it, believe also in the punishment of the deed. If, however, nature allows a crime like this to show itself, I congratulate the Ismarian[107] people, and this our country; I congratulate this land on being far away from those regions where such iniquity is possible. Let the land of Panchaea be rich in balsam, let it bear its cinnamon, its costum,[108] its frankincense exuding from the trees, its flowers of many sorts, so long as it bears its myrrh-tree, too: a new tree was not worth so great a price. Cupid himself avers that his weapons did not harm you, Myrrha, and clears his torches from that crime of yours. One of the three sisters with firebrand from the Styx and with swollen vipers blasted you. It is a crime to hate one's father, but such love as this is a greater crime than hate. From every side the pick of princes desire you; from the whole Orient young men are here vying for your couch; out of them all choose one for your husband, Myrrha, only let not one[109] be among them all.

   She, indeed, is fully aware of her vile passion and fights against it and says within herself: "To what is my purpose tending? What am I planning? O gods, I pray you, and piety and the sacred rights of parents, keep this sin from me and fight off my crime, if indeed it is a crime. But I am not sure, for piety refuses to condemn such love as this. Other animals mate as they will, nor is it thought base for a heifer to endure her sire, nor for his own offspring to be a horse's mate; the goat goes in among the flocks which he has fathered, and the very birds conceive from those from whom they were conceived. Happy they who have such privilege! Human civilization has made spiteful laws, and what nature allows, the jealous laws forbid. And yet they say that there are tribes among whom mother with son, daughter with father mates, so that natural love is increased by the double bond. O, wretched me, that it was not my lot to be born there, and that I am thwarted by the mere accident of place! Why do I dwell on such things ? Avaunt, lawless desires! Worthy to be loved is he, but as a father. — Well, if I were not the daughter of great Cinyras, to Cinyras could I be joined. But as it is, because he is mine, he is not mine; and, while my very propinquity is my loss, would I as a stranger be better off? It is well to go far away, to leave the borders of my native land, if only I may flee from crime; but unhappy passion keeps the lover here, that I may see Cinyras face to face, may touch him, speak with him and

---

[106] Of Paphos, daughter of Pygmalion.

[107] A way of referring to the Trojans, as forefathers of the Romans via Aeneas (Ismaros was the city of the Kikones near Troy, whom Odysseus attacked after the fall of Troy).

[108] An oriental aromatic plant without English equivalent.

[109] In other words, her father.

kiss him, if nothing else is granted. But can you hope for anything else, you unnatural girl? Think how many ties, how many names you are confusing! Will you be the rival of your mother, the mistress of your father? Will you be called the sister of your son, the mother of your brother? And have you no fear of the sisters with black snakes in their hair, whom guilty souls see brandishing cruel torches before their eyes and faces? But you, while you have not yet sinned in body, do not conceive sin in your heart, and defile not great nature's law with unlawful union. Grant that you wish it: facts themselves forbid. He is a righteous man and heedful of moral law— and O how I wish a like passion were in him!"

She spoke; but Cinyras, whom a throng of worthy suitors caused to doubt what he should do, inquired of her herself, naming them over, whom she wished for husband. She is silent at first and, with gaze fixed on her father's face, wavers in doubt, while the warm tears fill her eyes. Cinyras, attributing this to maidenly alarm, bids her not to weep, dries her cheeks and kisses her on the lips. Myrrha is too rejoiced at this and, being asked what kind of husband she desires, says: "One like you." But he approves her word, not understanding it, and says: "May you always be so filial." At the word "filial" the girl, conscious of her guilt, casts down her eyes.

It was midnight, and sleep had set free men's bodies from their cares; but the daughter of Cinyras, sleepless through the night, is consumed by ungoverned passion, renews her mad prayers, is filled now with despair, now with lust to try, feels now shame and now desire, and finds no plan of action; and, just as a great tree, smitten by the axe, when all but the last blow has been struck, wavers which way to fall and threatens every side, so her mind, weakened by many blows, leans unsteadily now this way and now that, and falteringly turns in both directions; and no end nor rest for her passion can she find save death. She decides on death. She rises from her couch, resolved to hang herself, and, tying her girdle to a ceiling-beam, she says: "Farewell, dear Cinyras, and know why I die," and is in the act of fitting the rope about her death-pale neck.

They say that the confused sound of her words came to the ears of the faithful nurse who watched outside her darling's door. The old woman rises and opens the door; and when she sees the preparations for death, all in the same moment she screams, beats her breasts and rends her garments, and seizes and snatches off the rope from the girl's neck. Then at last she has time to weep, time to embrace her and ask the reason for the noose. The girl is stubbornly silent, gazes fixedly on the ground, and grieves that her attempt at death, all too slow, has been detected. The old woman insists, bares her white hair and thin breasts, and begs by the girl's cradle and her first nourishment that she trust to her nurse her cause of grief. The girl turns away from her pleadings with a groan. The nurse is determined to find out, and promises more than confidence.

"Tell me," she says, "and let me help you; my old age is not without resources. If it be madness, I know one who has healing-charms and herbs; or if someone has worked an evil spell on you, you shall be purified with magic rites; or if the gods are wroth with you, wrath may be appeased by sacrifice. What further can I think? Surely your household fortunes are prosperous as usual; your mother and your father are alive and well." At the name of father Myrrha sighed deeply from the bottom of her heart. Even now the nurse had no conception of any evil in the girl's soul, and yet she had a presentiment that it was some love affair, and with persistent purpose she begged her to tell her whatever it was. She took the weeping girl on her aged bosom, and so holding her in her feeble arms she said: "I know, you are in love! and in this affair I shall be entirely devoted to your service, have no fear; nor shall your father ever know." With a bound the mad girl leaped from her bosom and, burying her face in her couch, she said: "Go away, I pray you, and spare my unhappy shame." Still pressed: "Go away," she said again, "or cease asking why I grieve. It is a crime, what you want so much to know."

The old woman is horrified and, stretching out her hands trembling with age and fear, she falls pleadingly at her nursling's feet, now coaxing and now frightening her if she does not tell; she both threatens to report the affair of the noose and attempt at death, and promises her help if she will confess her love. The girl lifts her head and fills her nurse's bosom with her rising tears; often she tries to confess, and often checks her words and hides her shamed face in her robes. Then she says: "O mother, blest in your husband!" — only so much, and groans. Cold horror stole through the nurse's frame (for she understood), and her white hair stood up stiffly over all her head, and she said many things to banish, if she might, the mad passion. The girl knew that she was truly warned; still she was resolved on death if she could not have her desire. "Live then," said the other, "have your"—she did not dare say "father"; she said no more, calling on Heaven to confirm her promises.

It was the time when married women were celebrating that annual festival of Ceres at which with bodies robed in white raiment they bring garlands of wheaten ears as the first offerings of their fruits, and for nine nights they count love and the touch of man among things forbidden. In that throng was Cenchreis, wife of the king, in constant attendance on the secret rites. And so since the king's bed was deprived of his lawful wife, the over-officious nurse, finding Cinyras drunk with wine, told him of one who loved him truly, giving a false name, and praised her beauty. When he asked the maiden's age, she said: "The same as Myrrha's." Bidden to fetch her, when she had reached home she cried: "Rejoice, my child, we win!" Not with all her heart did the unhappy girl feel joy, and her mind was filled with sad forebodings; but still she did also rejoice; so inconsistent were her feelings.

It was the time when all things are at rest, and between the Bears Bootes had turned his wain with down-pointing pole.[110] She came to her guilty deed. The golden moon fled from the sky; black clouds hid the skulking stars; night was without her usual fires. You were the first, Icarus, to cover your face, and you, Erigone, deified for your pious love of your father. Thrice was Myrrha stopped by the omen of the stumbling foot; thrice did the funereal screech-owl warn her by his uncanny cry; still on she went, her shame lessened by the black shadows of the night. With her left hand she holds fast to her nurse, and with the other she gropes her way through the dark. Now she reaches the threshold of the chamber, now she opens the door, now is led within. But her knees tremble and sink beneath her; color and blood flee from her face, and her senses desert her as she goes. The nearer she is to her crime, the more she shudders at it, repents her of her boldness, would gladly turn back unrecognized. As she holds back, the aged crone leads her by the hand to the side

---

[110] Midnight, when these constellations reach the highest point in the firmament and start their descent.

of the high bed and, delivering her over, says: "Take her, Cinyras, she is yours"; and leaves the doomed pair together. The father receives his own flesh in his incestuous bed, strives to calm her girlish fears, and speaks encouragingly to the shrinking girl. It chanced, by a name appropriate to her age, he called her "daughter" and she called him "father," that names might not be lacking to their guilt.

Forth from the chamber she went, full of her father, with crime conceived within her womb. The next night repeated their guilt, nor was that the end. At length Cinyras, eager to recognize his mistress after so many meetings, brought in a light and beheld his crime and his daughter. Speechless with woe, he snatched his bright sword from the sheath which hung near by. Myrrha fled and escaped death by grace of the shades of the dark night. Groping her way through the broad fields, she left palm-bearing Arabia and the Panchaean country; then, after nine months of wandering, in utter weariness she rested at last in the Sabaean land. And now she could scarce bear the burden of her womb. Not knowing what to pray for, and in a strait between fear of death and weariness of life, she summed up her wishes in this prayer: "O gods, if any there be who will listen to my prayer, I do not refuse the dire punishment I have deserved; but lest, surviving, I offend the living, and, dying, I offend the dead, drive me from both realms; change me and refuse me both life and death!" Some god did listen to her prayer; her last petition had its answering gods. For even as she spoke the earth closed over her legs; roots burst forth from her toes and stretched out on either side the supports of the high trunk; her bones gained strength, and, while the central pith remained the same, her blood changed to sap, her arms to long branches, her fingers to twigs, her skin to hard bark. And now the growing tree had closely bound her heavy womb, had buried her breast and was just covering her neck; but she could not endure the delay and, meeting the rising wood, she sank down and plunged her face in the bark. Though she has lost her old-time feelings with her body, still she weeps, and the warm drops trickle down from the tree. Even the tears have fame, and the myrrh which distils from the tree-trunk keeps the name of its mistress and will be remembered through all the ages.

(The birth of Adonis from the tree follows; his story is included in Part 6, document 11.)

5.18. CAENIS-CAENEUS, FROM OVID, *METAMORPHOSES*, BOOK 12

(For Ovid and the *Metamorphoses*, see headnote to Part 1, document 10.) This story of Caeneus' (Gr. Kaineus) change of sex is told by wise old Nestor to a group of Achaeans (Greeks) during their entertainment time at night, immediately after the victory of Achilles over near-invincible Cycnus, which Ovid has just narrated in the previous passage. Caeneus appears in Homer, and he is found in other archaic sources. He was known as a leader of the Lapiths, a Thessalian clan most famous for its legendary war with the Centaurs. According to Apollodorus (*Epitome* 1.23, see Part 3, document 11.c), Caeneus was invulnerable, but he was buried by the Centaurs under a pile of logs. Ovid (*Met.* 12.524 ff.) suggests that he was transformed into a bird with yellow wings, who flew out of the heap. In yet another tradition Caeneus set up his spear in the middle of the marketplace and ordered people to worship it as a god and to swear by it, which he himself did, bringing about the wrath of Zeus, who instigated the Centaurs to overwhelm him.

SOURCE: Ovid, *Metamorphoses*, Book 12.169–209. F. J. Miller, *Ovid, Metamorphoses* (Loeb Classical Library, Cambridge, MA and London, 1921, 2nd ed.), with minor modifications.

(Nestor speaking) "In this your generation there has been one only, Cycnus, who could scorn the sword, whom no stroke could pierce; but I myself long ago saw one who could bear a thousand strokes with body unharmed, Thessalian Caeneus: Caeneus of Thessaly, I say, who once dwelt on Mount Othrys, famed for his mighty deeds; and to enhance the marvel of him, he had been born a woman." All who heared were struck with wonder at this marvel and begged him to tell the tale. Among the rest Achilles said: "Tell on, old man, eloquent wisdom of our age, for all of us alike desire to hear who was this Caeneus, why was he changed in sex, in what campaign did you know him and fighting against whom; by whom he was conquered if he was conquered by anyone." Then said the old man: "Though time has blurred my memory, though many things which I saw in my young years have quite gone from me, still can I remember much; nor is there anything, amidst so many deeds of war and peace, that clings more firmly in my memory than this. And, if long-extended age could have made anyone an observer of many deeds, I have lived for two centuries and now am living my third.

"Famous for beauty was Elatus' daughter, Caenis, most lovely of all the maids of Thessaly, both throughout the neighboring cities and your own (for she was of your city, Achilles), and she was the longed-for hope of many suitors. Peleus, too, perchance, would have tried to win her; but he had either already wed your mother or she was promised to him. And Caenis would not consent to any marriage; but, so report had it, while walking along a lonely shore she was ravished by the god of the sea. When Neptune had tasted the joys of his new love, he said: 'Make now your prayers without fear of refusal. Choose what you most desire.' This, also, was a part of the same report. Then Caenis said: 'The wrong that you have done me calls for a mighty prayer, the prayer that I may never again be able to suffer so. Grant me that I be not a woman: so grant all my prayers.' She spoke the last words with a deeper tone, which could well seem to be uttered by a man. And so it was; for already the god of the deep ocean had assented to her prayer, and had granted her besides that she should be proof against any wounds and should never fall to any sword. The Atracides[111] went away rejoicing in his gift, spent his years in manly exercises, and ranged the fields of Thessaly."

5.19. ACHILLES AT SKYROS, FROM STATIUS, *ACHILLEID*, BOOKS 1–2

Publius Papinius Statius was a Roman poet from Naples, who wrote in the late first century CE during the reign of Domitian. Besides the unfinished *Achilleid*, he is the author of a collection of dedicatory poems entitled the *Silva*, and the epic poem *Thebaid* in twelve books, which relates the story of the Seven

---

[111] An adjective for the Thessalians (referring to Caenis, now Caeneus).

against Thebes. The *Achilleid* focuses on the youth of Achilles, with the Homeric poems and the Epic Cycle as Statius' main sources.

The lines preceding this excerpt describe how Thetis tries to keep her son Achilles from going to the Trojan War, which, according to the chief gods, is fated to happen. Thetis hides Achilles at the court of King Lykomedes of Skyros, dressing him up as a girl and making him pass for Achilles' sister. While the Greeks, led by Ulysses (Greek Odysseus), learn from a prophet where Achilles is hidden (they need him in order to win the war), Achilles and Deidamia, the king's daughter, fall in love. Achilles' son Neoptolemos would be born from this union. The culminating point of the story is Achilles' struggle to keep his identity hidden when he meets the Greek warriors. The theme of Achilles' cross-dressing and revelation is mentioned in other sources (e.g., Apollodorus *Library* 3.13.8 and Ovid's *Metamorphoses* Book 13) and became very popular in Roman art (see Figure 19).

SOURCE: Statius, *Achilleid*, Books 1B–2.49. J. H. Mozley, *Statius, Thebaid, Achilleid* (Loeb Classical Library, Cambridge, MA and London, 1928), with minor modifications.

Book 1B

(560) But far away Deidamia—and she alone—had learnt in stolen secrecy the manhood of Aeacides,[112] that lay hidden beneath the show of a feigned sex; conscious of guilt concealed there is nothing she does not fear, and thinks that her sisters know, but hold their peace. For when Achilles, rough as he was, stood amid the maiden company, and the departure of his mother rid him of his artless shyness, straightway although the whole band gathers round him, he chose her as his comrade and assails with new and winning wiles her unsuspecting innocence. He follows, and persistently besets her, toward her he directs his gaze again and again. Now too zealously he clings to her side, nor does she avoid him, now he pelts her with light garlands, now with baskets that let their burden fall, now with the thyrsus that harms her not, or again he shows her the sweet strings of the lyre he knows so well, and the gentle measures and songs of Chiron's teaching, and guides her hand and makes her fingers strike the sounding harp, now as she sings he makes a conquest of her lips, and binds her in his embrace, and praises her amid a thousand kisses. With pleasure does she learn of Pelion's summit and of Aeacides, and hearing the name and exploits of the youth is spellbound in constant wonder, and sings of Achilles in his very presence.

(580) She in her turn teaches him to move his strong limbs with more modest grace and to spin out the unwrought wool by rubbing with his thumb, and repairs the distaff and the skeins that his rough hand has damaged; she marvels at the deep tones of his voice, how he shuns all her fellows and pierces her with too-attentive gaze and at all times hangs breathless on her words; and now he prepares to reveal the fraud, but she like a fickle girl avoids him, and will not allow him to confess. In this same way, when his mother Rhea ruled, the young prince of Olympus gave treacherous kisses to his sister; he was still her brother and she thought no harm,

---

[112] Achilles' epithet from his grandfather Aiakos, father of Peleus and son of Zeus himself.

until the reverence for their common blood gave way, and the sister feared a lover's passion.[113]

(592) At length the timorous Nereid's cunning was laid bare. There stood a lofty grove, scene of the rites of Agenorean Bacchus,[114] a grove that reached to heaven; within its shade the pious matrons used to renew the recurrent three-yearly festival, and to bring torn animals of the herd and uprooted saplings, and to offer to the god the frenzy in which he delights. The law required males to keep far away; the reverend monarch repeats the command, and makes proclamation that no man may draw near the sacred haunt. Nor is that enough; a venerable priestess stands at the appointed limit and scans the approaches, lest any defiler come near in the train of women; Achilles laughed silently to himself. His comrades wonder at him as he leads the band of virgins and moves his mighty arms with awkward motion—his own sex and his mother's counterfeit alike become him. No more is Deidamia the fairest of her company, and as she surpasses her own sisters, so is she herself defeated compared to proud Aeacides. But when he let the fawn-skin hang from his shapely neck, and with ivy gathered up its flowing folds, and bound the purple fillet high upon his flaxen temples, and with powerful hand made the enwreathed missile[115] quiver, the crowd stood awestruck, and leaving the sacred rites preferred to throng about him, uplifting their bowed heads to gaze. Thus Euhius, when he has relaxed at Thebes his martial spirit and frowning brow, and sated his soul with the luxury of his native land, takes chaplet and mitre from his locks, and arms the green thyrsus for the fray, and in more martial guise sets out to meet his Indian foes.[116]

(619) The Moon in her rosy chariot was clinging to the height of mid-heaven, when drowsy Sleep glided down with a full sweep of his wings to earth and gathered a silent world to his embrace: the choirs slumbered, the stricken bronze was mute for a while, when Achilles, alone, away from the virgin train, thus spoke with himself: "How long will you endure the precepts of your anxious mother, and waste the first flower of your manhood in this soft imprisonment? No weapons of war may you brandish, no beasts may you pursue. O! for the plains and valleys of Haemonia! Do you look in vain, Spercheus,[117] for my swimming, and for my promised tresses? Or have you no regard for the foster-child that has deserted you? Am I already spoken of as borne to the Stygian shades afar, and does Chiron in solitude bewail my death? You, O Patroclus, now aim my darts, you bend my bow and mount the team that was nourished for me; but I have learnt to fling wide my arms as I grasp the vine-wands, and to spin the distaff-thread—ah! shame and vexation to confess it! No more, night and day should you disguise the love that seizes you, and your passion for the maid of equal years. How long will you conceal the wound that galls your heart? Will you not—even in love—for shame!—prove your own manhood?"

---

[113] A reference to the courting of Hera (Juno) by Zeus (Jupiter), her brother.

[114] Bacchus (Dionysos) is called Agenorean because his mother, Semele, was the grandaughter of Agenor, king of Tyre (Phoenicia).

[115] The thyrsus, which the Bacchants hold.

[116] Note how Achilles putting on Bacchic attire is compared with Bacchus (called Euhius) preparing for battle (in his travels he was believed to have reached India).

[117] A river in Phthiotis, the homeland of Achilles (Gr. Spercheios).

(640) So he speaks; and in the thick darkness of the night, rejoicing that the unstirring silence gives timely aid to his secret deeds, he gains by force his desire, and with all his vigor strains her in a real embrace; the whole choir of stars beheld from on high, and the horns of the young moon blushed red. She indeed filled the grove and mountain with her cries, but the train of Bacchus, dispelling slumber's cloud, deemed it the signal for the dance; on every side the familiar shout arises, and Achilles once more brandishes the thyrsus; yet first with friendly speech he solaces the anxious maid: "I am he—why should you fear?—whom my cerulean mother bore almost to Jove,[118] and sent to find my nurture in the woods and snows of Thessaly. I would not have endured this dress and shameful garb, had I not seen you on the seashore; it was for you that I submitted, for you I carry skins and bear the womanly timbrel. Why do you weep who have become the daughter-in-law of mighty ocean? Why do you moan, who shall bear valiant grandsons to Olympus?[119] But your father—Scyros shall be destroyed by fire and sword and these walls shall be in ruins and the sport of wanton winds, before you pay with cruel death for my embraces: not so utterly am I subject to my mother."

(662) Horror-struck was the princess at such dark happenings, although long since she had suspected his good faith, and shuddered at his presence, and his countenance was changed as he made confession. What is she to do? Shall she bear the tale of her misfortune to her father, and ruin both herself and her lover, who would perhaps suffer untimely death? And still there remained within her breast the love so long deceived. Silent is she in her grief, and conceals the crime that both now share alike; her nurse alone she resolves to make a partner in deceit, and she, yielding to the prayers of both, assents. With secret cunning she conceals the rape and the swelling womb and the burden of the months of ailing, till Lucina the informer brought the appointed season, her course now fully run, and gave deliverance of her child.

(Skipped: Ulysses and Diomedes cruise the Aegean and arrive at Skyros, where they are received by the king.)

(750) Long since has a rumor been whispered throughout the secret chamber where the maidens had their safe abode, that Pelasgian chiefs have come, and a Grecian ship and its mariners have been made welcome. With good reason are the rest afraid; but Pelides scarcely conceals his sudden joy, and eagerly desires even as he is to see the newly-arrived heroes and their arms. Already the noise of princely trains fills the palace, and the guests are reclining on gold-embroidered couches, when at their sire's command his daughters and their chaste companions join the banquet; they approach, like Amazons on the Maeotid shore, when, after plundering Scythian homesteads and capturing strongholds of the Getae, they lay aside their arms and feast. Then indeed does Ulysses with intent gaze ponder carefully both forms and features, but night and the lamps that are brought in deceive him, and their stature is hidden as soon as they recline. One nevertheless with head erect and wander-

---

[118] Referring to Thetis, his sea nymph mother (hence "cerulean"). He says "almost" because she was destined to bear a son to Zeus who would surpass him; thus, Zeus married Thetis to Peleus instead.

[119] Achilles was the great-grandchild of Zeus (Peleus' father, Aiakos, was Zeus' son).

ing gaze, one who preserves no sign of virgin modesty, he marks, and with sidelong glance points out to his companion. But if Deidamia, to warn the hasty youth, had not clasped him to her soft bosom, and ever covered with her own robe his bare breast and naked arms and shoulders, and many a time forbidden him to start up from the couch and ask for wine, and replaced the golden hair-band on his brow, Achilles would have even then been revealed to the Argive chieftains.

(773) When hunger was assuaged and the banquet had twice and three times been renewed, the monarch first addresses the Achaeans, and pledges them with the wine-cup: "You famous heroes of the Argolic race, I envy, I confess, your enterprise; would that I too were of more valiant years, as when I utterly subdued the Dolopes who attacked the shores of Scyros, and shattered on the sea those keels that you beheld on the forefront of my lofty walls, tokens of my triumph! At least if I had offspring that I would send to war,—but now see for yourselves my feeble strength and my dear children: ah, when will these numerous daughters give me grandsons?"

(784) He spoke, and seizing the moment crafty Ulysses made reply: "Worthy indeed is the object of thy desire; for who would not burn to see the countless peoples of the world and various chieftains and princes with their trains? All the might and glory of powerful Europe has sworn together willing allegiance to our righteous arms. Cities and fields alike are empty, we have spoiled the lofty mountains, the whole sea lies hidden beneath the far-spread shadow of our sails; fathers give weapons, youths snatch them and are gone beyond recall. Never was offered to the brave such an opportunity for high renown, never had valor so wide a field of exercise."

(794) He sees him all attentive and drinking in his words with vigilant ear, though the rest are alarmed and turn aside their downcast eyes, and he repeats: "Whoever has pride of race and ancestry, whoever has sure javelin and valiant steed, or skill of bow, all honor there awaits him, there is the strife of mighty names: scarcely do timorous mothers hold back or troops of maids; ah! doomed to barren years and hated of the gods is he whom this new chance of glory passes by in idle sloth."

(802) Up from the couches he would have leaped, had not Deidamia, watchfully giving the sign to summon all her sisters, left the banquet clasping him in her arms; yet still he lingers looking back at the Ithacan, and goes out from the company the last of all. Ulysses indeed leaves unsaid part of his intended speech, yet adds a few words: "But do you abide in deep and tranquil peace, and find husbands for your beloved daughters, whom fortune has given to you, goddess-like in their starry countenances. What awe touched me once and holds me silent? Such charm and beauty joined to manliness of form!"

(812) The sire replies: "What if you could see them performing the rites of Bacchus, or about the altars of Pallas? Yes, and you shall if perchance the rising south wind provides delay." They eagerly accept his promise, and hope inspires their silent prayers. All the others in Lycomedes' palace are at rest in peaceful quiet, their troubles laid aside, but to the cunning Ithacan the night is long; he yearns for the day and rejects slumber.

(819) Scarcely had day dawned, and already the son of Tydeus accompanied by Agyrtes was present bringing the appointed gifts. The maids of Scyros too went forth from their chamber and advanced to display their dances and promised rites

to the honored strangers. Brilliant before the rest is the princess with Pelides her companion: even as beneath the rocks of Aetna in Sicily Diana and bold Pallas and the consort of the Elysian monarch shine forth among the nymphs of Enna. Already they begin to move, and the Ismenian[120] pipe gives signal to the dancers; four times they beat the cymbals of Rhea,[121] four times the maddening drums, four times they trace their manifold windings. Then together they raise and lower their wands, and complicate their steps, now in such fashion as the Curetes and devout Samothracians use,[122] now turning to face each other in the Amazonian comb, now in the ring where the Delian sets the Laconian girls dancing, and whirls them shouting her praises into her own Amyclae.[123] Then indeed, then above all is Achilles manifest, caring neither to keep his turn nor to join arms; then more than ever does he scorn the delicate step, the womanly attire, and breaks the dance and mightily disturbs the scene. Even so did Thebes already sorrowing behold Pentheus spurning the wands and the timbrels that his mother welcomed.[124]

(841) The troop disperses amid applause, and they seek again their father's threshold, where in the central chamber of the palace the son of Tydeus had long since set out gifts that should attract maidens' eyes, the mark of kindly welcome and the reward for their toil; he bids them choose, and the peaceful monarch allows it. Alas! how simple and untaught, who knew not the cunning of the gifts nor Grecian fraud nor Ulysses' many wiles! Thereupon the others, prompted by nature and their ease-loving sex, try the shapely wands or the timbrels that answer to the blow, and fasten jewelled band around their temples; the weapons they observe but think them a gift to their mighty father. But the bold son of Aeacus no sooner saw before him the gleaming shield enchased with battle-scenes—by chance too it shone red with the fierce stains of war—and leaning against the spear, than he shouted loud and rolled his eyes, and his hair rose up from his brow; forgotten were his mother's words, forgotten his secret love, and Troy fills all his breast. As a lion torn from his mother's teats submits to be tamed and lets his mane be combed, and learns to have awe of man and not to fly into a rage save when bidden, yet if but once the steel has glittered in his sight, his fealty is forsworn, and his tamer becomes his foe: against him he first rages, and feels shame to have served a timid lord. But when he came nearer, and the emulous brightness gave back his features and he saw himself mirrored in the reflecting gold, he thrilled and blushed together.

(866) Then quickly went Ulysses to his side and whispered: "Why do you hesitate? We know you, you are the pupil of the half-beast Chiron, you are the grandson of the sky and sea; the Dorian fleet awaits you, your own Greece awaits you with standards uplifted for the march, and the very walls of Pergamum totter and

---

[120] In other words, Theban (from the river Ismenos), here standing for Bacchic (Bacchus was from Thebes).

[121] Rhea here stands for Cybele, the Mother of the Gods, whose worshippers used cymbals.

[122] The Curetes (Gr. Kouretes) were priests of Zeus in Crete; the Samothracians celebrated mysteries in honor of the Cabiri (Gr. Kabeiroi).

[123] Apollo was worshipped at Amyclae (Gr. Amyklai), near Sparta, but Artemis (Apollo's twin sister, born on Delos like him) is evoked here.

[124] Pentheus, king of Thebes, cousin of Dionysos (see Part 3, document 10.a).

sway for you to overturn. Up! delay no more! Let perfidious Ida grow pale, let your father delight to hear these tidings, and guileful Thetis feel shame to have so feared for you."

(874) Already was he stripping his body of the robes, when Agyrtes, so commanded, blew a great blast upon the trumpet: the gifts are scattered, and they flee and fall with prayers before their father and believe that battle is joined. But from his breast the raiment fell without his touching, already the shield and puny spear are lost in the grasp of his hand—marvelous to believe!—and he seemed to surpass by head and shoulders the Ithacan and the Aetolian chief: with a sheen so awful does the sudden blaze of arms and the martial fire dazzle the palace-hall. Mighty of limb, as though immediately summoning Hector to the fray, he stands in the midst of the panic-stricken house: and the daughter of Peleus is sought in vain.

(885) But Deidamia in another chamber wept over the discovery of the fraud, and as soon as he heard her loud lament and recognized the voice that he knew so well, he quailed and his spirit was broken by his hidden passion. He dropped the shield, and turning to the monarch's face, while Lycomedes is dazed by the scene and distraught by the strange portent, just as he was, in naked panoply of arms, he addresses him: "It was I, dear father, I whom bounteous Thetis gave you— dismiss you anxious fears!—long since did this high renown await you; it is you who will send Achilles, long sought for, to the Greeks, more welcome to me than my mighty sire—if it is right to say it—and than beloved Chiron. But, if you will, give me your mind for a moment, and hear these words: Peleus and Thetis, your guest, make you the father-in-law of their son, and recount their kindred deities on either side; they demand one of your train of virgin daughters: do you give her? Or do we seem a mean and coward race? You do not refuse. Join then our hands, and make the treaty, and pardon your own kin. Already Deidamia has been known to me in stolen secrecy; for how could she have resisted these arms of mine, how once in my embrace repel my might? Bid me atone that deed: I lay down these weapons and restore them to the Pelasgians, and I remain here. Why these angry cries? Why is your aspect changed? You are already my father-in-law"—he placed the child before his feet, and added: "and already a grandfather! How often shall the pitiless sword be plied! We are a multitude!"

(910) Then the Greeks too and Ulysses with his persuasive prayer entreat by the holy rites and the sworn word of hospitality. He, though moved by the discovery of his dear daughter's wrong and the command of Thetis, though seeming to betray the goddess and so grave a trust, yet fears to oppose so many destinies and delay the Argive war—even were he wanted to do so, Achilles had spurned even his mother then. Nor is he unwilling to take unto himself so great a son-in-law: he is won. Deidamia comes full of shame from her dark privacy, in her despair she does not at first believe his pardon, and puts forward Achilles to appease her father.

(921) A messenger is sent to Haemonia to give Peleus full tidings of these great events, and to demand ships and comrades for the war. Moreover, the Scyrian prince launches two vessels for his son-in-law, and makes excuse to the Achaeans for so poor a show of strength. Then the day was brought to its end with feasting, and at last the bond was made known to all, and conscious night joined the now fearless lovers.

(927) Before her eyes new wars and Xanthus and Ida pass, and the Argolis fleet, and she imagines the very waves and fears the coming of the dawn; she flings herself about her new lord's beloved neck, and at last clasping his limbs gives way to tears: "Shall I see you again, and lay myself on your breast, O son of Aeacus? Will you care once more to look upon your offspring? Or will you proudly bring back spoils of captured Pergamum and Teucrian homes and wish to forget where you hid as a maid? What should I entreat, or alas! what rather fear? How can I in my anxiety lay a request on you, who have scarcely time to weep? One single night has given and grudged you to me! Is this the season for our espousals? Is this free wedlock? Ah! those stolen sweets! that cunning fraud! Ah! how I fear! Achilles is given to me only to be torn away. Go! for I would not dare to delay such mighty preparations; go, and be cautious, and remember that the fears of Thetis were not vain; go, and good luck be with you, and come back mine!

(944) "Yes too bold is my request: soon the fair Trojan maidens will sigh for you with tears and beat their breasts, and pray that they may offer their necks to your fetters, and weigh your couch against their homes, or Tyndaris herself[125] will please thee, too much praised for her incestuous rape. But I shall be a story for your henchmen, the tale of a lad's first fault, or I shall be disowned and forgotten. No, come, take me as your comrade; why should I not carry the standards of Mars with you? You carried with me the wands and holy things of Bacchus, though ill-fated Troy does not believe it. Yet this babe, whom you leave as my sad solace—keep him at least within your heart, and grant this one request, that no foreign wife bear you a child, that no captive woman give unworthy grandsons to Thetis."

(956) As thus she speaks, Achilles, moved to compassion himself, comforts her, and gives her his sworn oath, and pledges it with tears, and promises her on his return tall handmaidens and spoils of Ilium and gifts of Phrygian treasure. The fickle breezes swept his words unfulfilled away.

Book 2

(1) Day arising from Ocean set free the world from dank enfolding shades, and the father of the flashing light upraised his torch still dimmed by the neighboring gloom and moist with sea-water not yet shaken off. And now all behold Aeacides, his shoulders stripped of the scarlet robe, and glorious in those very arms he first had seized—for the wind is calling and his kindred seas are urging him—and quake before the youthful chieftain, not daring to remember a thing; so wholly changed to the sight had he come back, as though he had never experienced the shores of Scyros, but were embarking from the Pelian cave. Then duly—for so Ulysses counseled—he does sacrifice to the gods and the waters and south winds, and venerates with a bull the cerulean king below the waves and Nereus his grandfather: his mother is appeased with a garlanded heifer. Thereupon casting the swollen entrails on the salt foam he addresses her: "Mother, I have obeyed you, though your commands were hard to bear; too obedient have I been: now they demand me, and I go to the Trojan war and the Argolic fleet." So speaking he leapt into the ship, and was swept away far from the vicinity of land by the whistling south wind; already

---

[125] Helen, daughter of Tyndareus (her divine father was Zeus).

lofty Scyros begins to gather mist about her, and to fade from sight over the long expanse of sea.

(23) Far away on the summit of a tower, with weeping sisters round her, his wife leaned forth, holding her precious charge, who bore the name of Pyrrhus, and with her eyes fixed on the canvas sailed herself upon the sea, and all alone still saw the vessel. He too turned his gaze aside to the walls he held dear, he thinks upon the widowed home and the sobs of her he had left: the hidden passion glows again within his heart, and martial wrath gives place. The Laertian hero[126] perceives him sorrowing, and draws near to influence him with gentle words: "Was it you, O destined destroyer of great Troy, whom Danaan fleets and divine oracles are demanding, and War aroused is awaiting with unbarred portals—was it you whom a crafty mother profaned with feminine robes, and trusted a far-away hiding-place with so great a secret, and hoped the trust was sure? O too anxious, O too true a mother! Could such valor lie inert and hidden, that barely hearing the trumpet-blast fled from Thetis and companions and the heart's unspoken passion? Nor is it due to us that you come to the war, and comply with our prayers; you would have come . . ."

(42) He spoke, and thus the Aeacian hero takes up the word: "Leave aside the causes of my tarrying and my mother's crime; this sword shall make excuse for Scyros and my dishonorable garb, the reproach of destiny. Do you rather, while the sea is peaceful and the sails enjoy the zephyr, tell how the Danaans began so great a war: I would rather draw straightway from your words a righteous anger."

(49) Then the Ithacan, tracing far back the beginning of the tale: . . .

5.20. CUPID AND PSYCHE, FROM APULEIUS, *THE GOLDEN ASS*, BOOKS 4–6

Apuleius was a writer and orator from the Roman city of Madaurus in North Africa (modern M'Daourouch, Algeria), who lived in the second century CE (born in 125). Raised among the elite, he was educated at Carthage, Rome, and Athens, becoming a Platonist philosopher. His works (in Latin) include the *Apology*, a speech of defense against charges of magic after he married a friend's mother in order to protect her patrimony from her extended family; the *Florida*, a collection of very elaborate speeches given at Carthage; and the novel called *The Golden Ass* or the *Metamorphoses*, besides a number of lost and dubiously attributed works.

The Golden Ass (the exact date of which is uncertain) is the only complete Latin novel preserved and is Apuleius' own elaboration on a previous novel in Greek, called *Lucius or the Ass*, by an unknown author (attributed to Lucian of Samosata), of which we only have an abridged version. Apuleius' long novel in eleven books tells the fantastic story of a young man, Lucius, whose curiosity for the world of magic leads him into an adventure full of surprise, eroticism, and humor, the highlight of which is his transformation into an ass. When the goddess Isis returns him to his human state, the character finds a new religious

[126] Ulysses (Odysseus), son of Laertes.

meaning in this redemption. The relationship between the story and Apuleius' own experiences and philosophical ideas is still hotly debated.

The story of Cupid and Psyche (Love/Desire and the Soul) is the most famous and most elaborate of a number of stories and anecdotes inserted into the novel. Regardless of its connection with Lucius' adventures and Apuleius' religious and philosophical ideas, the story is placed at the center of the novel (Books 4–6 out of 11 books), and the tale somehow projects into myth "the sin, sufferings, and redemption of Lucius" (Walsh, p. xxv). Stemming from Platonic influence, the relationship between Cupid and Psyche had become a popular theme in Hellenistic art and literature (see also Venus and Cupid in Figure 18). Statues of Cupid embracing a winged maiden were reproduced throughout the Mediterranean. The original source of this specific story, however, is unclear, and North African tales from Apuleius' native land might have contributed some elements to his narrative. Apuleius' novel indeed masterfully merges folktale elements (the two jealous sisters, the vindictive stepmother who inflicts impossible tests on the bride) with philosophical allegory (the soul's aspiration to reach the divine) and other theological and philosophical speculation, including the different kinds of Venus, celestial and mundane, and the power of Eros, as already explored in Plato's works, especially the *Phaedrus* and the *Symposium*.

SOURCE: Apuleius, *The Golden Ass*, excerpts from Books 4–6. P. G. Walsh, *Apuleius, The Golden Ass* (Oxford World's Classics, Oxford and New York, 1994), with minor modifications.

Book 4

(28) In a certain city there lived a king and queen with three notably beautiful daughters. The two elder ones were very attractive, yet praise appropriate to humans was thought sufficient for their fame. But the beauty of the youngest girl was so special and distinguished that our poverty of human language could not describe or even adequately praise it. In consequence, many of her fellow-citizens and hordes of foreigners, on hearing the report of this matchless prodigy, gathered in ecstatic crowds. They were dumbstruck with admiration at her peerless beauty. They would press their hands to their lips with the forefinger resting on the upright thumb, and revere her with devoted worship as if she were none other than Venus herself. Rumor had already spread through the nearest cities and bordering territories that the goddess who was sprung from the dark-blue depths of the sea and was nurtured by the foam from the frothing waves was now bestowing the favor of her divinity among random gatherings of common folk; or at any rate, that the earth rather than the sea was newly impregnated by heavenly seed, and had sprouted forth a second Venus invested with the bloom of virginity.

(29) This belief grew every day beyond measure. The story now became widespread; it swept through the neighboring islands, through tracts of the mainland and numerous provinces. Many made long overland journeys and travelled over the deepest courses of the sea as they flocked to set eyes on this famed cynosure of their age. No one took ship for Paphos, Cnidos, or even Cythera to catch sight of the goddess Venus. Sacrifices in those places were postponed, shrines grew unsightly, couches become threadbare, rites went unperformed; the statues were not garlanded, and the altars were bare and grimy with cold ashes. It was the girl who was

entreated in prayer. People gazed on that girl's human countenance when appeasing the divine will of the mighty goddess. When the maiden emerged in the mornings, they sought from her the favor of the absent Venus with sacrificial victims and sacred feasts. The people crowded round her with wreaths and flowers to address their prayers, as she made her way through the streets. Since divine honors were being diverted in this excessive way to the worship of a mortal girl, the anger of the true Venus was fiercely kindled. She could not control her irritation. She tossed her head, let out a deep growl, and spoke in soliloquy:

(30) "Here am I, the ancient mother of the universe, the founding creator of the elements, the Venus that tends the entire world, compelled to share the glory of my majesty with a mortal maiden, so that my name which has its niche in heaven is degraded by the foulness of the earth below! Am I then to share with another the supplications to my divine power, am I to endure vague adoration by proxy, allowing a mortal girl to strut around posing as my double? What a waste of effort it was for the shepherd whose justice and honesty won the approval of the great Jupiter to reckon my matchless beauty superior to that of those great goddesses! But this girl, whoever she is, is not going to enjoy appropriating the honors that are mine; I shall soon ensure that she rues the beauty which is not hers by rights!"

She at once summoned her son, that winged, most indiscreet youth whose own bad habits show his disregard for public morality. He goes rampaging through people's houses at night armed with his torch and arrows, undermining the marriages of all. He gets away scot-free with this disgraceful behavior, and nothing that he does is worthwhile. His own nature made him excessively wanton, but he was further roused by his mother's words. She took him along to that city, and showed him Psyche in the flesh (that was the girl's name). She told him the whole story of their rivalry in beauty, and grumbling and growling with displeasure she added:

(31) "I beg you by the bond of a mother's affection, by the sweet wounds which your darts inflict and the honeyed blisters left by this torch of yours: ensure that your mother gets her full revenge, and punish harshly this girl's arrogant beauty. Be willing to perform this single service which will compensate for all that has gone before. See that the girl is seized with consuming passion for the lowest possible specimen of humanity, for one who as the victim of Fortune has lost status, inheritance and security, a man so disreputable that nowhere in the world can he find an equal in wretchedness."

With these words she kissed her son long and hungrily with parted lips. Then she made for the nearest shore lapped by the waves. With rosy feet she mounted the surface of the rippling waters, and lo and behold, the bright surface of the sea-depths, was becalmed. At her first intimation, her retinue in the deep performed her wishes, so promptly indeed that she seemed to have issued instructions long before. Nereus' daughters appeared in singing chorus, and shaggy Portunus sporting his blue-green beard, and Salacia, the folds of her garment sagging with fish, and Palaemon, the elf-charioteer on his dolphin. Bands of Tritons sported here and there on the waters, one softly blowing on his echoing shell, another fending off with silk parasol the heat of the hostile sun, a third holding a mirror before his mistress's face, while others, yoked in pairs to her chariot, swam below. This was the host of Venus' companions as she made for the Ocean.

(32) Meanwhile, Psyche for all her striking beauty gained no reward for her ravishing looks. She was the object of all eyes, and her praise was on everyone's lips, but no king or prince or even commoner courted her to seek her hand. All admired her godlike appearance, but the admiration was such as is accorded to an exquisitely carved statue. For some time now her two elder sisters had been betrothed to royal suitors and had contracted splendid marriages, though their more modest beauty had won no widespread acclaim. But Psyche remained at home unattached, lamenting her isolated loneliness. Sick in body and wounded at heart, she loathed her beauty which the whole world admired. For this reason the father of that ill-starred girl was a picture of misery, for he suspected that the gods were hostile; and he feared their anger. He sought the advice of the most ancient oracle of the Milesian god, and with prayers and sacrificial victims begged from that mighty deity a marriage and a husband for that slighted maiden.

Apollo, an Ionian Greek, framed his response in Latin to accommodate the author of this Milesian tale:

(33)   Adorn this girl, O king, for wedlock dread,
       And set her on a lofty mountain-rock.
       Renounce all hope that one of mortal stock
       Can be your son-in-law, for she shall wed
       A fierce, barbaric, snake-like monster. He,
       Flitting on wings aloft, makes all things smart,
       Plaguing each moving thing with torch and dart.
       Why, Jupiter himself must fearful be.
       The other gods for him their terror show,
       And rivers shudder, and the dark realms below.

The king had formerly enjoyed a happy life, but on hearing this venerable prophecy he returned home reluctant and mournful. He unfolded to his wife the injunctions of that ominous oracle, and grief, tears and lamentation prevailed for several days. But now the grim fulfillment of the dread oracle loomed over them. Now they laid out the trappings for the marriage of that ill-starred girl with death; now the flames of the nuptial torch flickered dimly beneath the sooty ashes, the high note of the wedding-flute sank into the plaintive Lydian mode, and the joyous marriage-hymn tailed away into mournful wailing. That bride-to-be dried her tears on her very bridal-veil. Lamentation for the harsh fate of that anguished household spread throughout the city, and a cessation of business was announced which reflected the public grief.

(34) But the warnings of heaven were to be obeyed, and unhappy Psyche's presence was demanded for her appointed punishment. So amidst intense grief the ritual of that marriage with death was solemnized, and the entire populace escorted her living corpse as Psyche tearfully attended not her marriage but her funeral. But when her sad parents, prostrated by their monstrous misfortune, drew back from the performance of their monstrous task, their daughter herself admonished them with these words:

"Why do you rack your sad old age with protracted weeping? Or why do you weary your life's breath, which is dearer to me than to yourselves, with repeated lamentations? Why do you disfigure those features, which I adore, with ineffectual tears? Why do you grieve my eyes by torturing your own? Why do you tear at your gray locks? Why do you beat those breasts so sacred to me? What fine rewards my peerless beauty will bring you! All too late you experience the mortal wounds inflicted by impious envy. That grief, those tears, that lamentation for me as one already lost should have been awakened when nations and communities brought me fame with divine honors, when with one voice they greeted me as the new Venus. Only now do I realize and see that my one undoing has been the title of Venus bestowed on me. Escort me and set me on the rock to which fate has consigned me. I hasten to embark on this blessed marriage, I hasten to behold this noble husband of mine. Why should I postpone or shrink from the arrival of the person born for the destruction of the whole world?"

(35) After this utterance the maiden fell silent, and with resolute step she now attached herself to the escorting procession of citizens. They made their way to the appointed rock set on a lofty mountain, and when they had installed the girl on its peak, they all abandoned her there. They left behind the marriage-torches, which had lighted their way but were now doused with their tears, and with bent heads made their way homeward. The girl's unhappy parents, worn out by this signal calamity, enclosed themselves in the gloom of their shuttered house, and surrendered themselves to a life of perpetual darkness.

But as Psyche wept in fear and trembling on that rocky eminence, the Zephyr's kindly breeze with its soft stirring wafted the hem of her dress this way and that, and made its folds billow out. He gradually drew her aloft, and with tranquil breath bore her slowly downward. She glided down over the sloping side of that high cliff, and he laid her down in the bosom of the flower-decked turf in the valley below.

Book 5

(Skipped: Psyche lands in a grove with a palace, where she is lavishly attended by a host of invisible servants whose voices and cares surround her. After a banquet she goes to sleep, waiting for her groom's visit.)

(4) The pleasant entertainment came to an end, and the advent of darkness induced Psyche to retire to bed. When the night was well advanced, a genial sound met her ears. Since she was utterly alone, she trembled and shuddered in fear for her virginity, and she dreaded the unknown presence more than any other menace. But now her unknown bridegroom arrived and climbed into the bed. He made Psyche his wife, and swiftly departed before dawn broke. At once the voices in attendance at her bed-chamber tended the new bride's violated virginity. These visits continued over a long period, and this new life in the course of nature became delightful to Psyche as she grew accustomed to it. Hearing that unidentified voice consoled her loneliness.

Meanwhile her parents were aging in unceasing grief and melancholy. As the news spread wider, her elder sisters learnt the whole story. In their sadness and grief they vied with each other in hastily leaving home and making straight for their parents, to see them and discuss the matter with them.

(5) That night Psyche's husband (he was invisible to her, but she could touch and hear him) said to her: "Sweetest Psyche, fond wife that you are, Fortune grows more savage, and threatens you with mortal danger. I charge you: show greater circumspection. Your sisters are worried at the rumor that you are dead, and presently they will come to this rock to search for traces of you. Should you chance to hear their cries of grief, you are not to respond, or even to set eyes on them. Otherwise you will cause me the most painful affliction, and bring utter destruction on yourself."

Psyche consented and promised to follow her husband's guidance. But when he had vanished in company with the darkness, the poor girl spent the whole day crying and beating her breast. She kept repeating that now all was up with her, for here she was, confined and enclosed in that blessed prison, bereft of conversation with human beings for company, unable even to offer consoling relief to her sisters as they grieved for her, and not allowed even to catch a glimpse of them. No ablutions, food, or other relaxation made her feel better, and she retired to sleep in floods of tears.

(6) At that moment her husband came to bed somewhat earlier than usual. She was still weeping, and as he embraced her, he remonstrated with her: "Is this how the promise you made to me has turned out, Psyche my dear? What is your husband to expect or to hope from you? You never stop torturing yourself night and day, even when we embrace each other as husband and wife. Very well, have it your own way, follow your own hell-bound inclination. But when you begin to repent at leisure, remember the sober warning which I gave you."

Then Psyche with prayers and threats of her impending death forced her husband to yield to her longing to see her sisters, to relieve their grief, and he also allowed her to present them with whatever pieces of gold or jewelry she chose. But he kept deterring her with repeated warnings from being ever induced by the baleful prompting of her sisters to discover her husband's appearance. She must not through sacrilegious curiosity tumble headlong from the lofty height of her happy fortune, and forfeit thereafter his embrace.

(7) She thanked her husband, and with spirits soaring she said: "But I would rather die a hundred times than forgo the supreme joy of my marriage with you. For I love and cherish you passionately, whoever you are, as much as my own life, and I value you higher than Cupid himself. But one further concession I beg for my prayers: bid your servant the Zephyr spirit my sisters down to me, as he earlier wafted me down." She pressed seductive kisses on him, whispered honeyed words, and snuggled close to soften him. She added endearments to her charms: "O my honey-sweet, darling husband, light of your Psyche's life!" Her husband unwillingly gave way before the forceful pressure of these impassioned whispers, and promised to do all she asked. Then, as dawn drew near, he vanished from his wife's embrace.

(Skipped: Psyche's sisters go the cliff where Psyche had been abandoned, and Zephyrus carries them safely to Psyche's palace, where they admire the luxury in which Psyche lives. In this first visit, following her husband's advice, Psyche does not reveal the mystery of her husband's visits but tells her sisters that she is married to a young handsome hunter. The sisters return to their homes, envious of Psyche, and start plotting against her. Despite her husband's repeated warnings, Psyche asks him to grant her sisters a second visit. Cupid has by now revealed to Psyche that she is pregnant with their

child. The sisters return, and Psyche carelessly tells them a different story about who her husband is. The sisters notice the inconsistency and realize that Psyche has no idea what her husband looks like. They think he must be a god. In their third visit, they convince Psyche that she is married to a monstrous dragon-like creature, just like the prophecy predicted. Trusting them, Psyche accepts their advice to kill her mate with a razor during his next visit.)

(21) Their sister was already quite feverish with agitation, but these fiery words set her heart ablaze. At once they[127] left her, for their proximity to this most wicked crime made them fear greatly for themselves. So the customary thrust of the winged breeze bore them up to the rock, and they at once fled in precipitate haste. Without delay they embarked on their ships and cast off.

But Psyche, now left alone, except that being harried by the hostile Furies was no solitude, tossed in her grief like the waves of the sea. Though her plan was formed and her determination fixed, she still faltered in uncertainty of purpose as she set her hands to action, and was torn between the many impulses of her unhappy plight. She made haste, she temporized; her daring turned to fear, her diffidence to anger, and to cap everything she loathed the beast but loved the husband, though they were one and the same. But now evening brought on darkness, so with headlong haste she prepared the instruments for the heinous crime. Night fell, and her husband arrived, and having first skirmished in the warfare of love, he fell into a heavy sleep.

(22) Then Psyche, though enfeebled in both body and mind, gained the strength lent her by fate's harsh decree. She uncovered the lamp, seized the razor, and showed a boldness that belied her sex. But as soon as the lamp was brought near, and the secrets of the couch were revealed, she beheld of all beasts the gentlest and sweetest, Cupid himself, a handsome god lying in a handsome posture. Even the lamplight was cheered and brightened on sighting him, and the razor felt suitably abashed at its sacrilegious sharpness. As for Psyche, she was awe-struck at this wonderful vision, and she lost all her self-control. She swooned and paled with enervation; her knees buckled, and she sought to hide the steel by plunging it into her own breast. Indeed, she would have perpetrated this, but the steel showed its fear of committing so serious a crime by plunging out of her rash grasp. But as in her weariness and giddiness she gazed repeatedly on the beauty of that divine countenance, her mental balance was restored. She beheld on his golden head his luxuriant hair steeped in ambrosia; his neatly pinned ringlets strayed over his milk-white neck and rosy cheeks, some dangling in front and some behind, and their surpassing sheen made even the lamplight flicker. On the winged god's shoulders his dewy wings gleamed white with flashing brilliance; though they lay motionless, the soft and fragile feathers at their tips fluttered in quivering motion and sported restlessly. The rest of his body, hairless and rosy, was such that Venus would not have been ashamed to acknowledge him as her son. At the foot of the bed lay his bow, quiver, and arrows, the kindly weapons of that great god.

(23) As Psyche trained her gaze insatiably and with no little curiosity on these her husband's weapons, in the course of handling and admiring them she drew out

---

[127] Psyche's sisters.

an arrow from the quiver, and tested its point on the tip of her thumb. But because her arm was still trembling she pressed too hard, with the result that it pricked too deeply, and tiny drops of rose-red blood bedewed the surface of the skin. So all unknowing and without prompting Psyche fell in love with Love, being fired more and more with desire for the god of desire. She gazed down on him in distraction, and as she passionately smothered him with wanton kisses from parted lips, she feared that he might stir in his sleep. But while her wounded heart pounded on being roused by such striking beauty, the lamp disgorged a drop of burning oil from the tip of its flame upon the god's right shoulder; it could have been nefarious treachery, or malicious jealousy, or the desire, so to say, to touch and kiss that glorious body. O, you rash, reckless lamp, Love's worthless servant, do you burn the very god who possesses all fire, though doubtless you were invented by some lover to ensure that he might possess for longer and even at night the object of his desire? The god started up on being burnt; he saw that he was exposed, and that his trust was defiled. Without a word he at once flew away from the kisses and embrace of his most unhappy wife.

(24) But Psyche seized his right leg with both hands just as he rose above her. She made a pitiable appendage as he soared aloft, following in his wake and dangling in company with him as they flew through the clouds. But finally she slipped down to earth exhausted. As she lay there on the ground, her divine lover did not leave her, but flew to the nearest cypress-tree, and from its summit spoke in considerable indignation to her:

"Poor, ingenuous Psyche, I disregarded my mother Venus' instructions when she commanded that you be yoked in passionate desire to the meanest of men, and that you be then subjected to the most degrading of marriages. Instead, I preferred to swoop down to become your lover. I admit that my behavior was not judicious; I, the famed archer, wounded myself with my own weapon, and made you my wife—and all so that you should regard me as a wild beast, and cut off my head with the steel, and with it the eyes that dote on you! I urged you repeatedly, I warned you devotedly always to be on your guard against what has now happened. But before long those fine counselors of yours will make satisfaction to me for their heinous instructions, whereas for you the punishment will be merely my departure." As he finished speaking, he soared aloft on his wings.

(Skipped: Psyche tries to kill herself by jumping into a river, but the river puts her back ashore. The god Pan advises her to not risk her life again, but to direct her efforts toward reconquering Cupid. She sets off and arrives at the city where one of her sisters lives. She fools her into believing that her husband, whom she had discovered was the god Cupid, had repudiated her, and had asked for her sister in marriage. The sister hurries and jumps off the cliff, this time to her death. Psyche proceeds in the same way with her other sister.)

(28) While Psyche was at this time visiting one community after another in her concentrated search for Cupid, he was lying groaning in his mother's chamber, racked by the pain of the wound from the lamp. But then the tern, the white bird which wings her way over the sea-waves, plunged swiftly into the deep bosom of ocean. She came upon Venus conveniently there as the goddess bathed and swam;

she perched beside her, and told her that her son had suffered burning, and was lying in considerable pain from the wound, with his life in danger. As a result the entire household of Venus was in bad odor, the object of gossip and rebuke on the lips of people everywhere. They were claiming that Cupid was relaxing with a lady of easy virtue in the mountains, and that Venus herself was idly swimming in the ocean, with the result that pleasure and favor and elegance had departed from the world; all was unkempt, rustic, uncouth. There were no weddings, no camaraderie between friends, none of the love which children inspire; all was a scene of boundless squalor, of unsavory tedium in sordid alliances. Such was the gossip which that garrulous and prying bird whispered in Venus' ear, tearing her son's reputation to shreds.

Venus was absolutely livid. She burst out: "So now that fine son of mine has a girl-friend, has he? Come on, then, tell me her name, since you are the only one who serves me with affection. Who is it who has tempted my innocent, beardless boy? Is it one of that crowd of nymphs, or one of the Hours, or one of the band of Muses, or one of my servant-Graces?" The garrulous bird did not withhold a reply. She said: "I do not know, mistress; I think the story goes that he is head over heels in love with a girl by the name of Psyche, if my memory serves me rightly." Then Venus in a rage bawled out at the top of her voice: "Can it really be true that he is in love with that Psyche who lays claim to my beauty and pretends to my name? That son of mine must surely have regarded me as a procuress, when I pointed the girl out to him so that he could win her acquaintance."

(29) As she grumbled she made haste to quit the sea, and at once made for her golden chamber. There she found her son lying ill as she had heard, and from the doorway she bellowed out as loudly as she could: "This is a fine state of affairs, just what one would expect from a child of mine, from a decent man like you! First of all you trampled underfoot the instructions of your mother—or I should say your employer—and you refused to humble my personal enemy with a vile love-liaison; and then, mark you, a mere boy of tender years, you hugged her close in your wanton, stunted embraces! You wanted me to have to cope with my enemy as a daughter-in-law! You take too much for granted, you good-for-nothing, loathsome seducer! You think of yourself as my only noble heir, and you imagine that I'm now too old to bear another. Just realize that I'll get another son, one far better than you. In fact I'll rub your nose in it further. I'll adopt one of my young slaves, and make him a present of these wings and torches of yours, the bow and arrows, and all the rest of my paraphernalia which I did not entrust to you to be misused like this. None of the cost of kitting you out came from your father's estate.

(30) "Ever since you were a baby you have been badly brought up, too ready with your hands. You show no respect to your elders, pounding them time after time. Even me your own mother you strip naked every day, and many's the time you've cuffed me. You show me total contempt as though I were a widow, and you haven't an ounce of fear for your stepfather,[128] the bravest and greatest of warriors. And why

---

[128] Here assumed to be Mars (Greek Ares), with whom Venus had a famous love affair (*Od.* 8.266–366). The paternity of Cupid is rarely mentioned in any works. In Hesiod's *Theogony*, Eros is a primordial element (along side Gaia and Tartaros), self-generated and "motor" for the world's subsequent sexual generation (see Part 1, document 5).

should you? You are in the habit of supplying him with girls, to cause me the pain of having to compete with rivals. But now I'll make you sorry for this sport of yours. I'll ensure that you find your marriage sour and bitter.

"But what am I to do, now that I'm becoming a laughingstock? Where shall I go, how shall I curb in this scoundrel? Should I beg the assistance of my enemy Sobriety, so often alienated from me through this fellow's loose living? The prospect of having to talk with that unsophisticated, hideous female gives me the creeps. Still I must not despise the consolation of gaining revenge from any quarter. She is absolutely the only one to be given the job of imposing the harshest discipline on this rascal. She must empty his quiver, immobilize his arrows, unstring his bow, extinguish his torch, and restrain his person with sharper correction. Only when she has sheared off his locks—how often I have brushed them, shining like gold with my own hands!—and clipped those wings, which I have steeped in my own breast's liquid nectar, shall I regard the insult dealt to me as expiated."

(Skipped: At the end of Book 5, Ceres and Juno try to persuade Venus to be more lenient toward her son, whom the goddesses want to keep on their side, but Venus does not yield.)

Book 6

(Skipped: Book 6 begins with Psyche's encounter with Ceres and Juno and her failure to obtain their aid, for they also do not want to incur Venus' anger. Left to her own devices, Psyche decides to try to win over Venus in person. Venus in the meantime asks Jupiter to let her use Mercury to find Psyche. When Psyche arrives at Venus' house, the goddess has her tortured and then addresses her harshly, calling her unborn son a bastard and declaring the union between Psyche and Cupid illegal, since "it took place in a country house, without witnesses and without a father's consent." What follows is a series of trials set by Venus upon Psyche, all of which the girl successfully overcomes with the aid of talking animals and elements of nature. Enraged by her success, and considering Psyche as "a witch with great and lofty powers," Venus sets out for her a final task: going down to Hades, where she is required to ask Proserpina herself [Gr. Persephone] to fill a box with divine makeup for Venus. After successfully fulfilling her mission, Psyche cannot resist her curiosity and opens the box. A deadly sleep creeps up on her and holds her in Hades. Cupid, now recovered from his wound, comes to her rescue, brushing off the sleep that binds her, so she can bring the box to Venus [see this Underworld episode in Part 6, document 15].)

(22) Meanwhile Cupid, devoured by overpowering desire and with lovelorn face, feared the sudden arrival of his mother's sobering presence, so he reverted to his former role and rose to heaven's peak on swift wings. With suppliant posture he laid his case before the great Jupiter, who took Cupid's little cheek between his finger and thumb, raised the boy's hand to his lips and kissed it, and then said to him: "Honored son, you have never shown me the deference granted me by the gods' decree. You keep piercing this heart of mine, which regulates the elements and orders the changing motion of the stars, with countless wounds. You have blackened it with repeated impulses of earthly lust, damaging my prestige and reputation by involving me in despicable adulteries which contravene the laws—the *lex Julia* itself—and public order. You have transformed my smiling countenance into grisly shapes of snakes, fires, beasts, birds, and cattle. Yet in spite of all this, I shall observe my usual moderation, recalling that you were reared in these arms of mine. So I will

comply with all that you ask, as long as you know how to cope with your rivals in love; and if at this moment there is on earth any girl of outstanding beauty, as long as you can recompense me with her."

(23) After saying this, he ordered Mercury to summon all the gods at once to an assembly, and to declare that any absentee from the convocation of heavenly citizens would be liable to a fine of ten thousand sesterces. The theatre of heaven at once filled up through fear of this sanction. Towering Jupiter, seated on his lofty throne, made this proclamation: "You gods whose names are inscribed on the register of the Muses, you all surely know this young fellow who was reared by my own hands. I have decided that the hot-headed impulses of his early youth need to be reined in; he has been the subject of enough notoriety in day-to-day gossip on account of his adulteries and all manner of improprieties. We must deprive him of all opportunities; his juvenile behavior must be shackled with the chains of marriage. He has chosen the girl, and robbed her of her virginity, so he must have and hold her. Let him take Psyche in his embrace and enjoy his dear one ever after."

Then he turned to address Venus. "My daughter," he said, "do not harbor any resentment. Have no fear for your high lineage and distinction in this marriage to a mortal, for I shall declare the union lawful and in keeping with the civil law, and not one between persons of differing social status." There and then he ordered that Psyche be detained and brought to heaven through Mercury's agency. He gave her a cup of ambrosia, and said: "Take this, Psyche, and become immortal. Cupid will never part from your embrace; this marriage of yours will be eternal."

(24) At once a lavish wedding-feast was laid. The bridegroom reclined on the couch of honor, with Psyche in his lap. Jupiter likewise was paired with Juno, and all the other deities sat in order of precedence. Then a cup of nectar, the gods' wine, was served to Jupiter by his personal cup-bearer, that well-known country lad, and to the others by Bacchus. Vulcan cooked the dinner, the Hours brightened the scene with roses and the other flowers, the Graces diffused balsam, and the Muses, also present, sang in harmony. Apollo sang to the lyre, and Venus took to the floor to the strains of sweet music, and danced prettily. She had organized the performance so that the Muses sang in chorus, a Satyr played the flute, and one of Pan's people sang to the shepherd's pipes. This was how with due ceremony Psyche was wed to Cupid, and at full term a daughter was born to them. We call her Pleasure.

DEATH
AND THE
AFTERLIFE
JOURNEY

A S WITH MANY other stories and narrative tropes whose scope goes beyond the confines of one genre, tales about death also explore passion and love, loss and adventure, and other themes that are examined elsewhere in this volume. I have thus included in this part texts that deal specifically with ideas about the afterlife and journeys by the living into the Beyond.

The oldest surviving texts that include voyages to the Underworld come from the Near East: in Mesopotamia and Egypt, and a bit later from the Hittite world in Anatolia. For reasons of space, only a few paradigmatic texts from this tradition are included here. Especially in Egypt, funerary culture provides a vast literary corpus, in which ritual and mythology are inseparable, including the famous collection known as the *Book of the Dead* as well as *Pyramid* and *Coffin Texts*, hymns, magical spells, mummy labels, etc. Despite this richness, Egyptian tradition did not embrace mythical narratives proper, whether in verse or prose, of the sort we find in Mesopotamian and Greco-Roman culture.

Mesopotamian myths relating to the Underworld can be found in the earliest Sumerian texts, laying out the foundations for later stories written in Akkadian, some of which are reproduced in this part. For instance, the Sumerian story of the *Descent of Inanna* (not included here) serves as background to the *Ishtar's Descent* (document 6.2). For lack of space, the story of *Nergal and Ereshkigal* is also not included. This tale, attested in Late Bronze Age and Neo-Assyrian texts of the seventh century BCE, recounts the descent of Nergal to the Underworld and his position there as consort of Ereshkigal, the queen of that realm. The figure of Nergal, the chief Mesopotamian god of the Underworld, was at some point partly assimilated to that of Gilgamesh, who was considered a judge of the dead. The name Nergal (also Erakal or "Lord of Erkalla," the "Great City") may have been the basis for the name of Herakles (Hercules), which in Greek tradition was re-interpreted as "famous because of Hera." The Greek superhero, in fact, is among the few in Greek myth who travel (several times) into the realm of Hades.

In the Hittite and Canaanite worlds, the theme of a dying or disappearing god was also important, as reflected in the *Telipinu* story (document 6.6) and the fight between Baal (Storm God) and Mot (Death) in the Ugaritic *Baal Cycle* (Part 3, document 5.a). Baal's temporary death causes a terrible drought, and his return symbolizes the return of fertility. The Phoenicians might have inherited some of this tradition, as there are indications that the god Melqart ("King of the City") was also a "returning" god, although the details of his story and cult are still obscure. The parallels with the Demeter and Persephone story are obvious, with Demeter's withdrawal causing a terrible drought and her reunion with her daughter marking the fertile season (document 6.8).

Regarding the afterlife journey, in Greek literature and myth very few characters are granted that forbidden voyage. Orpheus successfully enchanted Hades and Persephone and *almost* brought his wife back to the upper world (document 6.12). Odysseus and Aeneas present heroic cases of Underworld exploration (documents 6.7 and 6.13). Herakles, in turn, crosses the boundaries during his "labors" in order to capture Cerberus (the watch-dog of Hades). He is even supposed to have gone to Hades on two other occasions: once to rescue Alkestis, who had gone voluntarily in exchange for her husband (cf. Euripides' tragedy *Alkestis*), and yet again to rescue Theseus (see Herakles' exploits in Part 3, document 11.b). The famed Athenian king, in turn, had gone down to help his companion Peirithoos abduct Persephone; they both became stuck in stone chairs, and only Herakles succeeded in bringing up Theseus (see Theseus' exploits in Part 3, document 11.c). Like Herakles, the Dioskouroi ("Zeus' lads") also inhabited the liminal zone between mortal and immortal existence, and they trespassed these limits daily, as Polydeukes (Pollux) was allowed by Zeus to share immortality with his dead brother Kastor, so that both alternated between the realms of the living and the dead. In the Roman world there are no preserved indigenous myths of this sort except for Greek ones that were re-elaborated in Roman ways. Thus, the descent or **katabasis** of Aeneas in the *Aeneid* is modeled on Odysseus' encounter with the dead, though vastly transformed to suit Roman views. Cults related to some of these myths (Cybele and Attis, Hercules, the Dioscuri) were in fact very popular in the Roman world.

Stories about the Underworld were written in many different literary genres, from epic poetry (*Gilgamesh, Odyssey, Aeneid*) to ritual texts (Egyptian texts, the Gold Tablets), texts partly connected with rites (*Ishtar's Descent, Hymn to Demeter*), and tragedies (Euripides' *Alkestis*, but also Aeschylus' *Eumenides* and *Persians*). Sometimes they are preserved by mythographers (Apollodorus' *Library*) or written as novels (such as the Psyche story in Apuleius' *Golden Ass*) and even embedded into philosophical dialogues ("Myth of Er" in Plato's *Republic*; *Dream of Scipio* in Cicero's *De re publica*), a tradition also exemplified in Lucian of Samosata's *Dialogues with the Dead* (not included here), in which the second-century CE author treated the theme of death and the vanity of human beings in a satiric fashion.

The texts in this part reveal essential differences between ancient and modern ideas about death. In monotheistic belief systems (Judaism, Christianity, Islam), death is a state of the soul, situated in a realm of punishment (Purgatory, Hell) or reward (Paradise, Heaven). In the ancient Near East and the Classical world, generally polytheistic, Death is also a god, a personified concept and anthropomorphic character. He thus plays a role in many narratives. Hades, Thanatos (literally "Death"), Persephone, Ereshkigal and Nergal, Osiris, Mot (also "Death")—all represent the realm of death itself, depicted as a kingdom, just as Olympos is the seat of the upper god's kingdom. Sometimes the god and the place are interchangeable (e.g., Hades); at other times they are clearly distinguished (the Greek Tartaros is more often than not a space, not a character). The geography of the realm varies widely, and the way in which it is accessed is sometimes obscure. It may be clearly represented as an *Under*-world, situated on a vertical axis, deep under the earth (as in Hesiod, *Th.* 722–725, Part 1, document 5, and in the *Odyssey*, document 6.7), or it may be perceived as a place "at the edge of the world," set on a horizontal axis, as in *Gilgamesh* or the story of Baal's death (Part 3, document 5.a), although there is some merging of the two concepts in some texts. For instance, the river Ocean, which encircles the earth, hence at its limits, is the place of access to the Underworld in the *Odyssey*, while in the Ugaritic *Baal Cycle* Mot lives both at the end of the world and in a pit under the earth. While in *Gilgamesh* the crossing of a river is an important motif, in other Mesopotamian texts the idea is absent. The term **eschatology** itself comes from *eschaton*, "limit" in Greek, mostly understood as that which comes at the end of life or the end of the world, but also reflecting the physical notion of the unknown realms beyond the ultimate frontiers.

Regarding the geography of the Beyond, there are several rivers in Hades, the most famous being Styx, over which the gods themselves make their oaths. The figure of the ferryman, who crosses the souls to the shore where they will find final rest (or different rivers, depending on the tradition), appears in *Gilgamesh* (Ur-shanabi) and was known in Egyptian eschatology as well. In Greek tradition he is Charon (not present in the *Odyssey* but in the Psyche story; document 6.15 and others), who is given an important role in the *Aeneid* and became an important figure in later Greek culture and into the medieval (Byzantine) period, where he was equated with Death itself. Gloom and darkness pervade these Underworlds. They are sometimes represented explicitly as a prison, impregnably fortified and guarded, as in Hesiod's *Theogony*, where it has bronze gates and a surrounding moat (*Th.* 729–733; see description of Tartaros in Part 1, document 5) and in the *Baal Cycle* (Part 3, document 5.a), when Baal is Mot's prisoner in the euphemistically labeled "house of freedom."

In addition, an alternative type of Underworld also appears in the Greek world, which deeply influenced Roman authors. Stemming from Pythagorean philosophy, ideas of rebirth (reincarnation) appear in Orphic eschatology (see the Gold Tablet in document 6.9) as well as in Plato's "Myth of Er" (document 6.5) and Virgil's *Aeneid* (document 6.13). In these texts the topography of the Underworld becomes more complex. There is a path for the privileged souls of initates in the Gold Tablets, and in Plato's and Virgil's portrayal there is a process whereby different groups of souls receive various treatments of punishment or purification. The *Dream of Scipio* (document 6.14) was also influenced by Platonic ideas and outlines a philosophical-moral view of the soul's destiny. Even in such an early writer as Hesiod, the myth of the "Five Races of Men" (Part 2, document 5) imagines an alternative afterlife for the purer and superior souls of some of the races.

In the end, all the texts included in this section grapple with the anxiety of not knowing what it feels like to be dead, where souls go if they go anywhere, and whether the living can learn anything from the dead. In ancient texts, we can also find the tendency by philosophers to demythologize the Afterlife and the Underworld. In Plato's *Apology*, Socrates, who was facing the death penalty, says death is not to be feared, since he thinks it might be like a long sleep without dreams. Epicurean philosophers, in turn, postulated that death and the gods should not be feared, because the divine world is completely separate from and oblivious of ours, and there is nothing we can do to change our fate. The best way of spending life is to enjoy it and exercise our minds and souls through philosophy. Even further back in time, already in the Old Babylonian version of *Gilgamesh*, the female tavernkeeper Siduri gives the tormented hero this important lesson, the earliest attestation of the *carpe diem* motif and one of the main messages of the whole epic:

"Gilgamesh, where do you roam? You will not find the eternal life that you seek.

When the gods created mankind, they appointed death for mankind, kept eternal

life in their own hands.

So, Gilgamesh, let your stomach be full, day and night enjoy yourself in every

way, every day arrange for pleasures.

Day and night, dance and play, wear fresh clothes. Keep your head washed, bathe

in water, appreciate the child who holds your hand, let your wife enjoy herself in

your lap."[1] ✦

---

[1] Translation from Dalley (2000), 150.

6.1. GILGAMESH AND THE UNDERWORLD: *EPIC OF GILGAMESH*, TABLETS X–XI

(For a general introduction to the *Epic of Gilgamesh*, see Part 3, document 1.) In Tablet IX (not included here) Gilgamesh mourns his friend bitterly and decides to "take the road and go quickly to see Ut-napishtim," the survivor of the great flood. He crosses a mountain pass and travels through the Underworld passage which the sun traverses during the night. The passage is guarded by the Scorpion men, who interrogate Gilgamesh and try to dissuade him from completing his journey. Gilgamesh passes through the darkness and emerges "in front of the sun." Amidst a heavenly landscape he sees the tavern of Siduri, an alewife or tavernkeeper, who will give him instructions as to how to proceed further to the Underworld in Tablet X.

When Gilgamesh reaches the "other side," he is received by Ut-napishtim ("He who found life") and his wife. They are the only survivors of the flood sent by the gods to wipe out humanity, an episode comparable in detail with the Noah story in Genesis (see Part 2, documents 1.a and 4). This version of the epic ends in Tablet XI with Gilgamesh's return to Uruk with Ur-shanabi, the boatman, who never ferries anybody to the Underworld again. The ending, as Ur-shanabi contemplates the well-built city, is a sort of epilogue that closes the epic in a ring structure.

There is yet another tablet, added later to this version and labeled Tablet XII (not included here), which is partly based on a Sumerian story called "Gilgamesh and the *halub*-tree" or "Gilgamesh, Enkidu, and the Netherworld." In this text Gilgamesh sends Enkidu down to the Netherworld with instructions to recover some objects that Gilgamesh made for himself out of the *halub*-tree (sacred to Inana). But the Earth traps Enkidu and the gods do not allow him to go back up, despite Gilgamesh's pleas. Gilgamesh, however, manages to open a hole in the Underworld in order to let the spirit of Enkidu come out of the earth "like a gust of wind." In their brief encounter, "they hugged and kissed (?), they discussed, they agonized," and Gilgamesh asked Enkidu: "Tell me, my friend, tell me, my friend, tell me Earth's conditions that you found!" Enkidu then tells Gilgamesh about the pitiful state of the spirits down there, especially those not buried or not tended to, in contrast with those who die in battle and are honored and cried over (cf. description of the Underworld by Enkidu from a dream he had before he died, in Tablet VII, in Part 3, document 1). The episode has been compared with the visit of Patroklos to Achilles in *Iliad* 23, where, however, they fail to hug each other.

The texts below come from the Standard Babylonian Version (SBV). The tablets are divided into six columns each, numbered i, ii, etc. (For more information see headnote to document 1 in Part 3.)

SOURCE: S. Dalley, *Myths from Mesopotamia: Creation, The Flood, Gilgamesh, and Others* (Oxford World's Classics, Oxford and New York, 1989, rev. ed. 2000), with minor modifications.

TABLET X

(SBV) (i) Siduri the alewife,[2] who lives down by the sea, lives and [. . .]. Vat-stands are made for her, [fermentation-vats] are made for her, covered by a covering and [. . .]. Gilgamesh was pacing around and [. . .], clad only in a (lion)skin [. . .] He had the flesh of gods upon [his body], but grief was in [his innermost being]. His face was like that of a long-distance traveler.

The alewife looked at him from a distance. She pondered in her heart, and [spoke] a word to herself, and she [advised herself]: "Perhaps this man is an assassin. Is he going somewhere in [. . .] ?"

The alewife looked at him and locked [her door]; she locked her door, locked it [with a bolt]. Then he, Gilgamesh, noticed [. . .] Raised his chin and [. . .] Gilgamesh spoke to her, to the alewife: "Alewife, why did you look at me [and lock] your door, lock your door, [lock it] with a bolt? I will smash the door, I will shatter [the bolt]!"[3]

(10 very fragmentary lines)

"[We destroyed Humbaba, who lived in the] Pine Forest. [We killed] lions at the mountain passes."

[The alewife] spoke to him, to Gilgamesh: "[If you are truly Gilgamesh], that struck down the Guardian, [destroyed] Humbaba, who lived in the Pine Forest, killed lions at the mountain [passes], [seized the Bull of Heaven who came down from the sky, struck him down], [why are your cheeks wasted], your face dejected, [your heart so wretched, your appearance worn] out, [and grief] in your innermost being? Your face is like that of a long-distance traveler, your face is weathered by [cold and heat . . .], [clad only in a lionskin] you roam open country."

[Gilgamesh spoke to her, to Siduri the alewife:] "[How could my cheeks not be wasted, nor my face dejected, nor my heart wretched, nor my appearance worn out, nor grief in my innermost being, (ii) nor my face like that of a long-distance traveler, nor my face weathered by cold and heat [. . .], nor roaming open country, clad only in a lionskin? My friend whom I love so much, who experienced every hardship with me, Enkidu, whom I love so much, who experienced every hardship with me— the fate of mortals conquered him!]

"Six days [and seven nights I wept over him, I did not allow him to] be buried, [until a worm fell out of his nose. I was frightened and . . .]. I am afraid of Death, [and so I roam open country]. The words of my friend [weigh upon me. I roam open country] for long distances; the words of my friend Enkidu weigh upon me.[4] I roam open country on long journeys. [How, O how] could I stay silent, how, O how could I keep quiet [. . .]? My friend whom I love has turned to clay: Enkidu my friend

---

[2] Literally a "server of beer," this profession is attested for independent women already in the second millennium BCE (Code of Hammurabi and other legal texts). The episode is in some ways comparable to those of Kalypso and Circe in the *Odyssey*.

[3] Same threat as the one made by Ishtar in *Ishtar's Descent* (document 6.2).

[4] It is unclear which words exactly. Some suggest these are the reproach or curse that Enkidu pronounced in a previous lost episode alluded to in Tablet VIII, in which they were killing lions and Gilgamesh acted cowardly.

whom I love [has turned to clay]. Am I not like him? Must I lie down too, never to rise, ever again?"

Gilgamesh spoke to her, to the alewife: "Now, alewife, which is the way to Ut-napishtim?[5] Give me directions (?), [whatever they are]; give me directions (?). If it is possible, I shall cross the sea; if it is impossible I shall roam open country again."

The alewife spoke to him, to Gilgamesh: "There has never been a ferry of any kind, Gilgamesh, and nobody from time immemorial has crossed the sea. Shamash the warrior is the only one who has crossed the sea: apart from Shamash, nobody has crossed the sea. The crossing is difficult, the way of it very difficult, and in between are lethal waters which bar the way ahead.[6] Wherever, then, could you cross the sea, Gilgamesh? And once you reached the lethal waters, what would you do? (Yet) there is, Gilgamesh, a boatman of Ut-napishtim, Ur-shanabi, he—the "things of stone"[7] identify him (?)—will be trimming a young pine in the forest. Go, and let him see your face. If it is possible, cross with him. If it is impossible, retreat back."

When Gilgamesh heard this he took up an axe to his side, drew the sword from his belt, stole up and drove them off,[8] like an arrow he fell among them. In the midst of the forest the noise resounded (?). Ur-shanabi looked and drew (?) his sword (?), took up an axe and [crept up on (?)] him. Then he, Gilgamesh, hit him on the head; seized his arms and [. . .] of his chest. And the "things of stone" [. . .] the boat, which do not [. . .] lethal [waters . . .] broad [sea (?)] In the waters [. . .] held back. He smashed [them and . . .] to the river. [. . .] the boat and [. . .] on the bank.

[Gilgamesh spoke to him, to Ur-shanabi] the boatman: "[. . .] I shall enter [. . .] to you." (iii) Ur-shanabi spoke to him, to Gilgamesh: "Why are your cheeks wasted, your face dejected, your heart so wretched, your appearance worn out, and grief in your innermost being? Your face is like that of a long-distance traveler. Your face is weathered by cold and heat [. . .], clad only in a lionskin, you roam open country."

Gilgamesh spoke to him, to Ur-shanabi the boatman: "How could my cheeks not be wasted, nor my face dejected, nor my heart wretched, nor my appearance worn out, nor grief in my innermost being, nor my face like that of a long-distance traveler, nor my face weathered by wind and heat [. . .] nor roaming open country clad only in a lionskin?

"My friend was the hunted mule, wild ass of the mountain, leopard of open country, Enkidu my friend was the hunted mule, wild ass of the mountain, leopard of open country. We who met, and scaled the mountain, seized the Bull of Heaven and slew it, demolished Humbaba who dwelt in the Pine Forest, killed lions in the passes of the mountains; my friend whom I love so much, who experienced every

---

[5] The only mortal who became immortal: in the Hittite version Ulluya and in Hurrian Ullush.

[6] Lit. "waters of death," an idea similar to that of the Greek's River Ocean encircling the earth, beyond which is the Underworld (as in the *Odyssey*; see document 6.7). However, Gilgamesh then travels to the mouth of the rivers, reflecting a different tradition.

[7] The boatman is akin to Charon in Greek tradition. The meaning of the "things of stone" is uncertain ("anchors" and "stone stern-poles" have been suggested). They help Ur-shanabi cross safely.

[8] Unclear whom, the "things of stone"?

hardship with me, Enkidu my friend whom I love so much, who experienced every hardship with me— The fate of mortals conquered him!

"For six days and seven nights I wept over him: I did not allow him to be buried until a worm fell out of his nose. I was frightened and [. . .]. I am afraid of Death, and so I roam open country. The words of my friend weigh upon me. I roam open country for long distances; the words of Enkidu my friend weigh upon me. I roam open country on long journeys. How, O how could I stay silent, how, O how could I keep quiet? My friend whom I love has turned to clay: Enkidu my friend whom I love has turned to clay. Am I not like him? Must I lie down too, never to rise, ever again?"

Gilgamesh spoke to him, to Ur-shanabi the boatman: "Now, Ur-shanabi, which is the way to Ut-napishtim? Give me directions (?), if it is impossible, I shall roam open country again."

Ur-shanabi spoke to him, to Gilgamesh: "Your own hands, Gilgamesh, have hindered [. . .], you have smashed the "things of stone," you have [. . .]. The "things of stone" are smashed, and their strings (?) are pulled out. Take up an axe, Gilgamesh, to your side, go down to the forest, [cut] three hundred poles each thirty meters (long). Trim (them) and put "knobs" (on them); then bring them to me (?) [at the boat (?)]."⁹

When Gilgamesh heard this, he took up an axe to his side, drew a sword from his belt, went down to the forest and [cut] three hundred poles each thirty metres (long). He trimmed (them) and put "knobs" (on them): he brought them [to Ur-shanabi at the boat (?)]. And Gilgamesh and Ur-shanabi embarked [in the boat(s)]; they cast off the *magillu*-boat and sailed away.¹⁰ (After) a journey of a new moon and a full moon, on the third day [. . .] Ur-shanabi reached the lethal waters.

(iv) Ur-shanabi spoke to him, to Gilgamesh: "Stay clear, Gilgamesh, take one pole at a time, don't let the lethal water wet your hand! [Hold (?)] the knob! Take a second, a third, then a fourth pole, Gilgamesh. Take a fifth, a sixth, then a seventh pole, Gilgamesh. Take an eighth, a ninth, then a tenth pole, Gilgamesh. Take an eleventh, a twelfth pole, Gilgamesh."

Within seven hundred and twenty metres (?) Gilgamesh had used up the poles. Then he undid his belt, [. . .] Gilgamesh stripped himself; [. . .] with his arms he lifted up (?) the thwart (?). Ut-napishtim was looking on from a distance, pondered and spoke to himself, took counsel with himself: "Why are the [things of stone(?)] broken, and the wrong gear aboard [. . .]? Surely it can't be my man coming on? And on the right [. . .]. I am looking, but I can't make [it out], I am looking, but [. . .] I am looking, [. . .]

(gap of about 20 lines)

[Ut-napishtim spoke to him, to Gilgamesh]: ["Why are your cheeks wasted, your face dejected, your heart so wretched, your appearance worn out, and grief in your innermost being? Your face is like that of a long-distance traveler. Your

---

⁹ The poles and the knobs seem to be replacing the "things of stone" in their function of not letting the waters touch Gilgamesh.

¹⁰ The *magillu* was a mythical boat and fantastic creature, which the god Ninurta conquered and displayed among his many trophies.

face is weathered by cold and heat . . . Clad only in a lionskin you roam open country]."

[Gilgamesh spoke to him, to Ut-napishtim]: ["How would my cheeks not be wasted, nor my face dejected, (v) nor my heart wretched, nor] my appearance [worn out, nor grief in] my innermost being, [nor] my face like [that of a long-distance traveler, nor] my face [weathered by cold and heat . . . nor] roaming open country [clad only in a lionskin]?

"My friend was the hunted mule, wild ass of the mountain, leopard of open country, Enkidu my friend was the hunted mule, wild ass of the mountain, leopard of open country. We who met and scaled the mountain, seized the Bull of Heaven and slew it, demolished Humbaba who dwelt in the Pine Forest, killed lions in the passes of the mountains; my friend whom I love so much, who experienced every hardship with me, Enkidu my friend whom I love so much, who experienced every hardship with me—The fate of mortals conquered him!

"For six days and seven nights I wept over him, I did not allow him to be buried until a worm fell out of his nose. I was frightened [. . .]. I am afraid of Death, [and so I roam open country]. I roam open country for long distances; the words of my friend weigh upon me. The words of Enkidu my friend weigh upon me. I roam the open country on long journeys. How, O how could I stay silent, how, O how could I keep quiet? My friend whom I love has turned to clay: Enkidu my friend whom I love has turned to clay. Am I not like him? Must I lie down too, never to rise, ever again?"

Gilgamesh spoke to him, to Ut-napishtim: "So I thought I would go to see Ut-napishtim the far-distant, of whom people speak. I searched, went through all countries, passed through and through difficult lands, and crossed to and fro all seas. My face never had enough of sweet sleep, my fibre was filled with grief. I made myself over-anxious by lack of sleep. What did I gain from my toils? I did not make a good impression (?) on the alewife, for my clothes were finished. I killed a bear, hyena, lion, leopard, tiger, deer, mountain goat, cattle, and other wild beasts of open country. I ate meat from them, I spread out their skins. Let her door be bolted against grief with pitch and bitumen! Because of me, games are spoiled [. . .], my own misfortunes (?) have reduced me to misery (?)."

Ut-napishtim spoke to him, to Gilgamesh: "Why do you prolong grief, Gilgamesh? Since [the gods made you] from the flesh of gods and mankind, since [the gods] made you like your father and mother, [death is inevitable (?)] at some time, both for Gilgamesh and for a fool, but a throne is set down [for you (?)] in the assembly [. . .]. To a fool is given dregs instead of butter, rubbish and sweepings which like [. . .] Clothed in a loincloth (?) like [. . .] Like a belt [. . .] Because he has no [sense (?)] Has no word of advice [. . .]."

(after 18 very damaged lines, Ut-napishtim continues:)

(vi) "(. . .) [Why (?)] have you exerted yourself? What have you achieved (?)? You have made yourself weary for lack of sleep, you only fill your flesh with grief, you only bring the distant days (of reckoning) closer. Mankind's fame is cut down like reeds in a reed-bed. A fine young man, a fine girl, [. . .] of Death.

"Nobody sees Death, nobody sees the face of Death, nobody hears the voice of Death. Savage Death just cuts mankind down. Sometimes we build a house, sometimes we make a nest, but then brothers divide it upon inheritance. Sometimes there is hostility in [the land], but then the river rises and brings flood-water. Dragonflies drift on the river, their faces look upon the face of the Sun, (but then) suddenly there is nothing.

"The sleeping (?) and the dead are just like each other, Death's picture cannot be drawn. The primitive man (is as any) young man (?). When they blessed me, the Anunnaki,[11] the great gods, assembled; Mammitum who creates fate decreed destinies with them. They appointed death and life. They did not mark out days for death, but they did so for life."

TABLET XI

(SBV) (i) Gilgamesh spoke to him, to Ut-napishtim the far-distant: "I look at you, Ut-napishtim and your limbs are no different—you are just like me. Indeed, you are not at all different—you are just like me. I feel the urge to prove myself against you (?), to pick a fight (?) [. . .] you lie on your back. [. . .] how you came to stand in the gods' assembly and sought eternal life ?"

Ut-napishtim spoke to him, to Gilgamesh: "Let me reveal to you a closely guarded matter, Gilgamesh, and let me tell you the secret of the gods. Shuruppak[12] is a city that you yourself know, situated [on the bank of] the Euphrates. That city was already old when the gods within it decided that the great gods should make a flood . . . "

(Now for almost half of the tablet, Ut-napishtim tells Gilgamesh the story of the flood, included separately in Part 2, document 1.b. We resume in the middle of column iv: after Ut-napishtim survived the flood with the aid of the god Ea, the supreme god Ellil [=Enlil], made him and his wife immortals:)

(iv) "(. . .) They took me and made me dwell far off, at the mouth of the rivers. So now, who can gather the gods on your behalf, (Gilgamesh,) that you too may find eternal life which you seek? For a start, you must not sleep for six days and seven nights."

As soon as he was sitting, (his head?) between his knees, sleep breathed over him like a fog. Ut-napishtim spoke to her, to his wife: "Look at the young man who wants eternal life! Sleep breathes over him like a fog!"

His wife spoke to him, to Ut-napishtim the far-distant: "Touch him, and let the man wake up. Let him go back in peace the way he came, go back to his country through the great gate, through which he once left."

Ut-napishtim spoke to her, to his wife: "Man behaves badly: he will behave badly towards you. (v) For a start, bake a daily portion for him, put it each time by his head, and mark on the wall the days that he sleeps."

She baked a daily portion for him, put it each time by his head, and marked on the wall for him the days that he slept. His first day's portion was dried out, the second was going bad, the third was soggy, the fourth had white mould on (?), the

---

[11] The Anunaki (also called Anunna, Anukki, and Enunaki) are old Sumerian deities of fertility and the Underworld, associated with Anu (Sky God). They became judges of the Underworld. They are often paired with the Igigi, a Sumerian group of younger sky gods, headed by Enlil.

[12] Not far from Uruk, the city of Gilgamesh.

fifth had discolored, the sixth was stinking (?), the seventh—at that moment he touched him and the man woke up. Gilgamesh spoke to him, to Ut-napishtim the far-distant: "No sooner had sleep come upon me than you touched me, straight away, and roused me!"

Ut-napishtim spoke to him, to Gilgamesh: "[Look (?), Gil]gamesh, count your daily portions, [that the number of days you slept] may be proved to you. Your [first] day's ration [is dried out], the second is going bad, the third is soggy, the fourth has white mould on (?), the fifth has discolored, the sixth is stinking (?), [the seventh—] at that moment you woke up."

Gilgamesh spoke to him, to Ut-napishtim the far-distant: "How, O how could I have done it, Ut-napishtim? Wherever can I go? The Snatchers have blocked my [routes (?)]: Death is waiting in my bedroom, and wherever I set my foot, Death is there too."

Ut-napishtim spoke to him, to Ur-shanabi the boatman: "Ur-shanabi, the quay will cast you out, the ferry will reject you. Be deprived of her side, at whose side you once went.[13] The man whom you led: filthy hair fetters his body, skins have ruined the beauty of his flesh. Take him, Ur-shanabi, bring him to a wash-bowl, and let him wash in water his filthy hair, as clean as possible (?). Let him throw away his skins, and let the sea carry them off. Let his body be soaked (until it is) fresh. Put a new headband on his head. Have him wear a robe as a proud garment until he comes to his city, until he reaches his journey's end. The garment shall not discolor, but stay absolutely new."

Ur-shanabi took him and brought him to a wash-bowl, and he washed in water his filthy hair, as clean as possible (?). He threw away his skins, and the sea carried them off. His body was soaked (until it was) fresh. He put a new headband on his head. He wore a robe as a proud garment until he came to his city, until he reached his journey's end. The garment would not discolor, and stayed absolutely new.

Gilgamesh and Ur-shanabi embarked on the boat. They cast off the *magillu*-boat and sailed away. His wife spoke to him, to Ut-napishtim the far-distant: "Gilgamesh came, weary, striving, what will you give him to take back to his country?"

And Gilgamesh out there raised the pole, he brought the boat near the shore. Ut-napishtim spoke to him, to Gilgamesh: (vi) "Gilgamesh, you came, weary, striving, what can I give you to take back to your country? Let me reveal a closely guarded matter, Gilgamesh, and let me tell you the secret of the gods. There is a plant whose root is like camel-thorn, whose thorn, like a rose's, will spike [your hands]. If you yourself can win that plant, you will find [rejuvenation (?)]."

When Gilgamesh heard this, he opened the pipe, he tied heavy stones to his feet. They dragged him down into the Apsu, and [he saw the plant]. He took the plant himself: it spiked [his hands]. He cut the heavy stones from his feet. The sea threw him up on to its shore. Gilgamesh spoke to him, to Ur-shanabi the boatman: "Ur-shanabi, this plant is a plant to cure a crisis! With it a man may win the breath of life. I shall take it back to Uruk the Sheepfold; I shall give it to an elder to eat, and so tryout the plant. Its name (shall be): 'An old man grows into a young man.' I too shall eat (it) and turn into the young man that I once was."

---

[13] Perhaps referring to Ur-shanabi's boat.

At twenty leagues they ate their ration. At thirty leagues they stopped for the night. Gilgamesh saw a pool whose water was cool, and went down into the water and washed. A snake smelt the fragrance of the plant. It came up silently and carried off the plant. As it took it away, it shed its scaly skin.[14] Thereupon Gilgamesh sat down and wept. His tears flowed over his cheeks. [He spoke to (?)] Ur-shanabi the boatman: "For what purpose (?), Ur-shanabi, have my arms grown weary? For what purpose (?) was the blood inside me so red (?)? I did not gain an advantage for myself, I have given the advantage to the 'lion of the ground.'[15] Now the current will carry (?) twenty leagues away. While I was opening the pipe, [arranging (?)] the gear (?), I found (?) a door-thong (?) which must have been set there as an omen for me. I shall give up. And I have left the boat on the shore."

At twenty leagues they ate their ration. At thirty leagues they stopped for the night. They reached Uruk the Sheepfold. Gilgamesh spoke to him, to Ur-shanabi the boatman: "Go up on to the wall of Uruk, Ur-shanabi, and walk around, inspect the foundation platform and scrutinize the brickwork! Testify that its bricks are baked bricks, and that the Seven Counselors must have laid its foundations! One square mile is city, one square mile is orchards, one square mile is clay-pits, as well as the open ground of Ishtar's temple. Three square miles and the open ground comprise Uruk."

(Catchline)
"If only I had left the *pukku* in the carpenter's house today!"

6.2. *ISHTAR'S DESCENT TO THE UNDERWORLD*

Written in Akkadian, this story is attested in texts from both Late Bronze Age Babylonia and Assyria, as well as in later Neo-Assyrian sources, such as those found in the library of Nineveh. The story is based on an older Sumerian version, called *The Descent of Inanna.* Sumerian Inanna is Ishtar in Babylonia and Assyria, the goddess of sexual love, fertility, and war (cognate with Astarte/Ashtart in the North-West Semitic world). The Sumerian version is in fact much longer and provides a more complete background, although neither story is explicit about the goddess's motivations for going into the Underworld. Once there, she is retained (i.e., dead) and apparently only let free (back to life) once she sends a substitute to the Underworld. That substitute will be her husband/lover Dumuzi (whose name means "faithful son"). In the Sumerian version, she sends him down out of anger because he has not mourned her "death" properly. He will then spend half of the year in the Underworld and return to Earth for the other half. His alternation between the two realms brings on the fertile and unfertile seasons, since during his time in the Underworld Ishtar/Inanna's powers, and hence the Earth's fertility, are diminished.

---

[14] This provides an *aition* for why serpents shed their skin, which is a sign of rejuvenation, and why they are associated with medicine and magic in many cultures.

[15] Referring to the snake. Curiously, "lion of the ground" is exactly the meaning of the Greek word *chamaleon.*

These stories seem to be linked with a ritual journey of the statue of Ishtar/ Inanna from Uruk (her principal city) to Kutha (city of Underworld god Nergal). In turn, the ending lines of this Akkadian version seem to give instructions for a ritual bathing, anointing, and setting up of the statue of Dumuzi, such as was done in the *taklimtu* ("lying-in-state") festival in honor of the god at Nineveh, carried out annually in the month of Dumuzi (Tammuz) in June/July.

The text shares some motifs and even identical lines with the *Epic of Gilgamesh* and with the Underworld-related myth of *Nergal and Ereshkigal*. More generally speaking, the theme of this story also closely resembles other stories of "dying and rising gods" (e.g., Adonis, Baal), but especially that of Persephone's forced marriage to Hades and her seasonal return to her mother (document 6.8).

SOURCE: S. Dalley, *Myths from Mesopotamia: Creation, The Flood, Gilgamesh, and Others* (Oxford World's Classics, Oxford and New York, 1989, rev. ed. 2000), with minor modifications.

To Kurnugi, land of [no return], Ishtar daughter of Sin was [determined] to go[16]; the daughter of Sin was determined to go to the dark house, dwelling of Erkalla's god, to the house which those who enter cannot leave, on the road where travelling is one-way only, to the house where those who enter are deprived of light, where dust is their food, clay their bread. They see no light, they dwell in darkness, they are clothed like birds, with feathers.[17] Over the door and the bolt, dust has settled. Ishtar, when she arrived at the gate of Kurnugi, addressed her words to the keeper of the gate:

"Here gatekeeper, open your gate for me, open your gate for me to come in! If you do not open the gate for me to come in, I shall smash the door and shatter the bolt, I shall smash the doorpost and overturn the doors, I shall raise up the dead and they shall eat the living: The dead shall outnumber the living!"[18]

The gatekeeper made his voice heard and spoke, he said to great Ishtar:

"Stop, lady, do not break it down! Let me go and report your words to queen Ereshkigal."

The gatekeeper went in and spoke to [Ereshkigal]: "Here she is, your sister Ishtar [. . .] Who holds the great *keppu*-toy, stirs up the Apsu in Ea's presence [. . .]?"

When Ereshkigal heard this, her face grew livid as cut tamarisk, her lips grew dark as the rim of a *kuninu*-vessel.[19]

"What brings her to me? What has incited her against me? Surely not because I drink water with the Anunnaki, I eat clay for bread, I drink muddy water for beer? I have to weep for young men forced to abandon sweethearts. I have to weep for girls wrenched from their lovers' laps. For the infant child I have to weep, expelled before its time. Go, gatekeeper, open your gate to her. Treat her according to the ancient rites."

---

[16] In the *Epic of Gilgamesh* she is named the daughter of Anu instead.

[17] Underworld creatures appear with feathers in Mesopotamian artistic representations.

[18] The same threat is made by Ishtar in *Gilgamesh*, Tablet V (document 5.1), and by Ereshkigal in *Nergal and Ereshkigal*.

[19] A type of boat made of reeds, the rims of which were coated with (black) bitumen.

The gatekeeper went. He opened the gate to her: "Enter, my lady: may Kutha give you joy, may the palace of Kurnugi be glad to see you."[20]

He let her in through the first door, but stripped off (and) took away the great crown on her head.

"Gatekeeper, why have you taken away the great crown on my head?"

"Go in, my lady. Such are the rites of the Mistress of Earth."[21]

He let her in through the second door, but stripped off (and) took away the rings in her ears.

"Gatekeeper, why have you taken away the rings in my ears?"

"Go in, my lady. Such are the rites of the Mistress of Earth."

He let her in through the third door, but stripped off (and) took away the beads around her neck.

"Gatekeeper, why have you taken away the beads around my neck?"

"Go in, my lady. Such are the rites of the Mistress of Earth."

He let her in through the fourth door, but stripped off (and) took away the toggle-pins at her breast.

"Gatekeeper, why have you taken away the toggle-pins at my breast?"

"Go in, my lady. Such are the rites of the Mistress of Earth."

He let her in through the fifth door, but stripped off (and) took away the girdle of birth-stones around her waist.

"Gatekeeper, why have you taken away the girdle of birthstones around my waist?"

"Go in, my lady. Such are the rites of the Mistress of Earth."

He let her in through the sixth door, but stripped off (and) took away the bangles on her wrists and ankles.

"Gatekeeper, why have you taken away the bangles from my wrists and ankles?"

"Go in, my lady. Such are the rites of the Mistress of Earth."

He let her in through the seventh door, but stripped off (and) took away the proud garment of her body.

"Gatekeeper, why have you taken away the proud garment of my body?"

"Go in, my lady. Such are the rites of the Mistress of Earth."

As soon as Ishtar went down to Kurnugi,[22] Ereshkigal looked at her and trembled before her. Ishtar did not deliberate (?), but leant over (?) her. Ereshkigal made her voice heard and spoke, addressed her words to Namtar[23] her vizier:

"Go, Namtar [. . .] of my [. . .] Send out against her sixty diseases [. . .] Ishtar: Disease of the eyes to her [eyes], disease of the arms to her [arms], disease of the feet

---

[20] Kutha is a city in Babylon, center of the cult of Nergal, consort of Ereshkigal, and lord of the Underworld. Kurnagi ("land of no return") is an old Sumerian term for the Underworld. This is the passage in which Ishtar is treated as a statue to be received at Kutha.

[21] The "Mistress of Earth" is Ereshkigal.

[22] The transition between the two realms is not described, e.g., with the crossing of a river or the like (as in *Gilgamesh*). This feature is absent also in the story of *Nergal and Ereshkigal*.

[23] The vizier of Ereshkigal was a demonic Sumerian god of the Underworld, whose name means "decider of fate."

to her [feet], disease of the heart to her [heart], disease of the head [to her head], to every part of her and to [. . .]."

After Ishtar the mistress of (?) [. . . had gone down to Kurnugi], no bull mounted a cow, [no donkey impregnated a jenny]; no young man impregnated a girl in [the street (?)]; the young man slept in his private room, the girl slept in the company of her friends.

Then Papsukkal, vizier of the great gods, hung his head, his face [became gloomy]; he wore mourning clothes, his hair was unkempt. Dejected (?), he went and wept before Sin his father, his tears flowed freely before king Ea:

"Ishtar has gone down to the Earth and has not come up again. As soon as Ishtar went down to Kurnugi no bull mounted a cow, no donkey impregnated a jenny; no young man impregnated a girl in the street; the young man slept in his private room, the girl slept in the company of her friends."

Ea, in the wisdom of his heart, created a person. He created Good-looks the playboy:[24] "Come, Good-looks, set your face towards the gate of Kurnugi. The seven gates of Kurnugi shall be opened before you. Ereshkigal shall look at you and be glad to see you. When she is relaxed, her mood will lighten. Get her to swear the oath by the great gods. Raise your head, pay attention to the waterskin,[25] saying: 'Hey, my lady, let them give me the waterskin, that I may drink water from it.'"

(And so it happened. But)

When Ereshkigal heard this, she struck her thigh and bit her finger: "You have made a request of me that should not have been made! Come, Good-looks, I shall curse you with a great curse. I shall decree for you a fate that shall never be forgotten. Bread (gleaned (?)) from the city's ploughs shall be your food,[26] the city drains shall be your only drinking place, the shade of a city wall your only standing place, threshold steps your only sitting place, the drunkard and the thirsty shall slap your cheek."

Ereshkigal made her voice heard and spoke, she addressed her words to Namtar her vizier: "Go, Namtar, knock (?) at Egalgina,[27] decorate the threshold steps with coral (?), bring the Anunnaki out and seat (them) on golden thrones,[28] sprinkle Ishtar with the waters of life and conduct her into my presence."

Namtar went, knocked at Egalgina, decorated the threshold steps with coral, brought out the Anunnaki, seated (them) on golden thrones, sprinkled Ishtar with the waters of life and brought her to her (sister). He let her out through the first door, and gave back to her the proud garment of her body. He let her out through the second door, and gave back to her the bangles for her wrists and ankles. He let her out through the third door, and gave back to her the girdle of birth-stones around her waist. He let her out through the fourth door, and gave back to her the toggle

---

[24] Literally "his appearance is bright." Possibly a castrated youth is meant here, as castrated boys might have been connected with Ishtar's cult and appear in the Sumerian version.

[25] Unclear what the "waterskin" means here, probably some pun having to do with Ishtar.

[26] Same phrasing used for the curse of Enkidu to Shamhat in Gilgamesh VII.

[27] A place in the Underworld, meaning "The everlasting palace."

[28] In the Sumerian *Descent of Inanna*, the Anunnaki seize the goddess and send her out of the Netherworld with demons who will bring her back if she does not find a substitute.

pins at her breast. He let her out through the fifth door, and gave back to her the beads around her neck. He let her out through the sixth door, and gave back to her the rings for her ears. He let her out through the seventh door, and gave back to her the great crown for her head.

"Swear that (?) she has paid you her ransom, and give her back (in exchange) for him, for Dumuzi, the lover of her youth. Wash (him) with pure water, anoint him with sweet oil, clothe him in a red robe, let the lapis lazuli pipe play (?). Let party-girls raise a loud lament (?)"[29]

Then Belili[30] tore off (?) her jewelry, her lap was filled with eyestones. Belili heard the lament for her brother, she struck the jewelry [from her body], the eyestones with which the front of the wild cow was filled: "You shall not rob me (forever) of my only brother! On the day when Dumuzi comes back up, (and) the lapis lazuli pipe and the carnelian ring come up with him.[31] (When) male and female mourners come up with him, the dead shall come up and smell the smoke offering."

(3 lines missing)

6.3. GREAT HYMN TO OSIRIS

This Egyptian hymn was carved on a stele (or stela) commissioned by Amenmes, the "overseer of the cattle of Amun," and his wife, Nefertari. The stele is currently in the Louvre Museum, Paris. Its provenance is unknown, but it is safely dated to the mid-Eighteenth Dynasty (ca. 1450 BCE). Through numerous epithets and juxtaposed sentences, the hymn records a series of mythological notions roughly ordered in a chronological sequence, which offers an almost complete Egyptian "version" of the Osirian Myth. The only episode the hymn omits is the killing and dismemberment of Osiris by his brother Seth. Some scholars consider the whole hymn a variant of *Book of the Dead* spell 185 (Spell 185A).

Many of the epithets of Osiris mentioned in the first part of this hymn appear also in a Twenty-second Dynasty stele of a priest of Amun called Ameneminet. The stele probably comes from the area of Thebes and is currently in the British Museum in London (BM 645, ca. 800 BCE). This other stele includes a wider catalogue of Osirian names and attributions than the one reproduced below, but many of their epithets overlap, which means they might have drawn from a common source now lost. The shared epithets are set in italics in the translation here.

SOURCE: Great Hymn to Osiris (Stela Louvre C 286, 1–25), translated and annotated by A. Diego Espinel.

Praise to Osiris by the overseer of the cattle of [Amun, Amenm]es, and the lady of the house, Nefertari. He says:

---

[29] In Mesopotamia corpses were wrapped in red garments, of which traces have been found. The "party girls" were Ishtar's cultic personnel, which included sacred prostitutes.

[30] "She who always weeps," sister of Dumuzi, in Sumerian named Geshtin-anna.

[31] Perhaps referring to royal emblems that Ishtar (Inanna) takes down to the Underworld.

(*Names, forms, and epithets of Osiris*)³² "Hail to you, Osiris, *lord of eternity, king of the gods, rich in names, of sacred manifestations and secret forms in the temples. He is the august soul who presides over Busiris, the rich in possessions in Letopolis,* the lord of the acclamations in the ninth province of Lower Egypt. *The one who presides over the provisions in Heliopolis,*³³ the lord of remembrance in the room of the two Maats, *the secret soul, the lord of the cavern, the sacred one in Memphis, the soul of Re and his very body. The one who rests in Herakleopolis; the one who excels in the acclamations in Naret*³⁴; the one who has come into existence in order to bear his (own) soul. The lord of the great domain in Hermopolis, the very dreaded one in Shashetep.*³⁵* The lord of eternity who presides over Abydos in his distant place of the sacred land (i.e., the necropolis). *Whose name is enduring in the mouth of human beings.*

(*Osiris as primeval god, universal lord and king of Egypt*) "The primeval god of the whole Two Lands, provision and food in front of the Ennead of gods, *excellent spirit among the spirits. To whom Nun has given his waters, for whom the northern wind blows southward. The sky has conceived the wind for his nose so his heart can be satisfied.*³⁶ *Plants grow because of his desire and the horizon conceived the provisions for him.* The sky and its stars obey him, and the great doors are opened for him, the lord of acclamations in the southern sky, the praised one in the northern sky. The imperishable stars are under his command, and the unwearying (stars) are his thrones.

"The offering has come out for him, according to the command of Geb, and the Ennead of gods adores him. The ones who are in the Duat³⁷ kiss the ground, and the ones in the necropolis bow down. The ones from ancient times (?) are in joy when they see him, and the yonder ones (i.e., the dead) are in terror because of him. The united Two Lands adore him when his majesty approaches, the noble spirit who presides the nobles, the firm of rank, who establishes government, the good leader of the Ennead of gods, gracious of face. The one who loves those who see him, the one who puts the terror he inspires in all the lands, so they place his name in a foremost position. Everyone makes offerings to him, the lord of remembrance in the sky and the earth, rich in acclamations during the *Wag*-festival. Joy is created for him by the Two Lands in unison.

"First senior of his brothers and senior of the Ennead of gods. The one who has established Maat along the Two Banks, when the son was placed on the throne of the father. Praised by his father Geb and beloved of his mother Nut. Great in strength when he throws the rebel, powerful of arm when he kills his enemy. He

---

³² Italics in parentheses do not form part of the text. These epigraphs follow roughly the titles and divisions of the text made by Alexandre Moret in one of the first studies of the hymn in 1931.

³³ Variant in BM 645, line 6: "the provisions in the domain of the *ben-ben*-pyramidion in Heliopolis."

³⁴ Probably a reference to the Herakleopolitan province (nineteenth province of Upper Egypt) or to a place close to Herakleopolis.

³⁵ Probably current ash-Shateb, a village south of Asyut, Upper Egypt.

³⁶ Variant in BM 645, line 11: "*The sky has conceived the wind for his nose so his ka can be satisfied.*"

³⁷ The Beyond or, in other words, the realm of Osiris and realm of the dead.

places the terror he inspires in his rival. The one who brings away the far limits of evil, whose heart is firm when he tramples the insurgents.

"The heir of Geb (in) the kingship of the Two Lands, as he (Geb) has seen his abilities. He (Geb) has ordered him to guide the lands to successful times. He has placed this land in his hand: its waters, its winds, its plants, all its cattle, every thing which flies and every thing which alights, its reptiles and its desert animals were given to Nut's son. The Two Lands are happy because of it. The one appearing over the throne of his father like Re when he rises from the horizon. He places the light over the darkness. He has turned the shade into light with his two plumes. He floods the Two Lands like the sun-disk at dawn. It is his white crown which has pierced the sky, which has fraternized with the stars. He is the one who guides every god, the one who is excellent in his commands; praised by the Great Ennead of gods and beloved by the Small Ennead of gods.

(Isis' search for Osiris' corpse)[38] "His sister acts as his guard, repelling the rivals, and cutting out the disturber(s) by her able mouth. The capable tongue whose words do not fail, excellent in commands. Effective is Isis, the protectress of her brother, the one who looked for him without being weary, who walked this land weeping, without rest until she discovered him. The one who created a shade with her plumage, who created air with her wings, who made acclamations when she saved his brother.

(Isis as mother of Osiris' son, Horus) "The one who raised the inertness of the tired heart, the one who received his semen conceiving the heir (Horus), who raised the child in solitude, no one knowing the place in which they were.

(Horus' legitimacy is recognized by the Ennead of gods; coronation of Horus) "The one who introduced him (Horus) into the great domain of Geb, when his arm was strong. The Ennead of gods was happy: 'Come, come, Osiris' son, Horus, firm of heart, justified, Isis' son, the heir of Osiris!' The council of Maat gathered together: the Ennead of gods and the lord of the totality himself [39]; the lords of Maat, assembled together with her (i.e., Isis)—who turned their back on disorder, were seated in the domain of Geb in order to give the office to its lord, the kingship to its legitimate owner. Horus and his speech were found innocent, and the office of his father was given to him. He came out crowned according to Geb's command. He took the government of the Two Banks, and the white crown was firm in his head. He reckoned the land as his possession. Sky and earth are under his throne. Human beings are entrusted to you: plebeians, aristocracy and sun-folk. Egypt and the totality which is beyond, which the sun-disk encircles, are under his control: the northern wind, the river-channel, the waters, the trees of life (?), and every plant. Nepri is the one who has given every plant to him, the provisions from the soil. He gives it to all the lands. Every body is in joy, their hearts are happy, their breasts are glad. Every face rejoices, everyone is praising his beauty, how sweet is his love for us! His grace surrounds the hearts and his love is great in every body.

---

[38] The hymn omits the killing and dismemberment of Osiris by his brother Seth, for which see Plutarch's *Isis and Osiris* in document 6.5.

[39] This is an allusion to an independent deity, probably a demiurge (creator deity such as Atum or Re).

(*Seth's defeat and punishment*) "They brought to Isis' son his enemy (Seth), who fell because of his (Horus') courage. Evil is done to the disturber (Seth), since the one who attacks the courageous one encounters the proof of his courage. Isis' son has protected his father. His name has become sacred and excellent. It is the charisma which has been restored to its place. Magnificence is established according to its (own) laws. The path is clear and the roads are open. How prosperous are the Two Banks! Evil has gone away, the plaintiff (Seth) is gone. The land is in peace under his lord (Horus), and Maat has been established for her lord. Their back has been turned on disorder. May your heart be happy, Wennefer![40] Isis' son has taken the white crown, and the rank of his father has been given to him inside Geb's domain. It is Re who spoke. Thot was his scribe, and the council assented. Your father Geb has given you the order that it is to be done according to what he said. (. . .)"

6.4. THE FIGHT BETWEEN RE AND APEP, FROM THE *BOOK OF THE DEAD*

The Egyptian *Book of the Dead* is first attested with certainty in the Theban area at the beginning of the Second Intermediate Period (ca. 1650 BCE). Initially, this collection of funerary compositions was the exclusive prerogative of members of the royal family, who had these texts painted on coffins and shrouds, although spells are also found on tomb walls, heart scarabs, and ushabtis (i.e., little statuettes deposited in tombs). However, some time during the joint reign of Tutmosis III and Hatshepsut (Eighteenth Dynasty, ca. 1473–1458 BCE), copies of the *Book of the Dead* became available to laypeople, usually on papyrus rolls. The latest examples date to the first century BCE. Unlike the *Pyramid* and *Coffin Texts*, the *Book of the Dead* contains fewer spells (fewer than 200), with more canonized texts in a great number of vignettes. Above all, the function of these texts was to protect their owner and magically assure his continued existence in the afterlife.

Spell 108 of the *Book of the Dead* forms part of a set of chapters (ns. 108–109 and 112–116) devoted to equip the deceased with knowledge about different places and the *bau* ("souls" or "powers") in them. The text offers an unusually precise description of a religious landscape and a serpent, called Apep. The text also alludes to the fight between Seth and the malignant serpent Apep (also called Apophis) during the nocturnal trip of the solar boat in the Netherworld (see also *Coffin Texts* Spell 80 in Part 1, document 3.b; see Figure 2). Seth is depicted in a different way than in the Osirian myth (see Part 3, document 2), being an effective protector of the sun boat. The entire spell, particularly Seth's speech and the serpent's name, served as a magical protection for the deceased in the Beyond.

---

[40] An epithet of Osiris that means "the one who is continually young/good" and in later times adapted into Greek as the name Onuphrios.

Below is a translation of an early version of the spell, preserved in the *Book of the Dead* of Nebseny, a mid-Eighteenth Dynasty scribe from Memphis (ca. 1400 BCE). Later variants and minor changes are indicated in the footnotes.

SOURCE: *Book of the Dead*, Spell 108 (*Pap. of Nebseni*, BM 9900), translated and annotated by A. Diego Espinel.

SPELL FOR KNOWING THE WESTERN SOULS. IT IS X (name of the deceased) WHO SAYS: "Regarding that mountain of Bakhu,[41] on which the sky is supported, there are walls (whose) cubit(s) are of seven palms and a half of the 'Scale of the land' (Memphis).[42] It is three hundred cubits long and two hundred cubits broad.[43] Sebek, lord of Bakhu is east of that mountain. His temple is of *het*-material.[44] There is a serpent on the top of that mountain: it is fifty cubits long and its initial three cubits are of flint.[45] I know the name of the aforementioned serpent, which is over its mountain: 'the one which is in his fire' is his name.

"Now, after midday, he (Apep) will turn his eye against Re and an interruption will happen in the (solar) boat, a great astonishment (will happen) among the ship crew, as he (Apep) will swallow one cubit and three palms of the great waters.[46] Seth will throw a spear of iron/copper against him, and he will make him vomit everything he swallowed. Then Seth will place himself as his enclosing wall saying with magic: 'Retreat before my sharpened iron/copper, which is in my hand! I stand as your enclosing wall, while the voyage of the (solar) boat is re-established. (You), farsighted one (i.e., Apep), close your eye, and veil your head, that I may sail! Retreat before me as I am a male! Veil your face and keep your upper lip cool; as I am intact you will be intact, as I am great at magic! <Magical effectiveness> has been given to me against <you>.'

"What is this? 'This is a noble spirit![47] (O you, Apep,) who goes on his belly, his hinder parts and his vertebrae. Look, I am going against him, your strength is in me, as I display strength.[48] I have come to look after the earth Gods of Re, so he may be gracious to me in the evening. He (Re)[49] has encircled the sky, while you are in fetters, as it was ordered against you previously. Then Re will rest in life in his horizon. I know the guidelines of the ones who know why APEP[50] is punished. I know the western souls. They are Atum, Sebek, lord of Bakhu, and Hathor, mistress of the evening.'"

---

[41] The eastern mountain, which holds the sky. The western one was called Manu.

[42] Egyptian royal cubits were divided into 7 palms (ca. 52 centimeters). Bakhu's walls would have been built using a slightly larger unit.

[43] Approximately 150 meters × 100 meters (in a frequent variant approximately 150 × 25 meters).

[44] Other versions mention carnelian as material of the shrine.

[45] Approximately 25 meters long × 1.5 meters of flint. Other versions have different measures.

[46] Approximately 67 cm. Other versions have "7 cubits" (approximately 3.5 meters).

[47] Seth and/or the deceased.

[48] These sentences are possibly said by the deceased, referring to Seth's strength.

[49] Other versions have "I have encircled . . . "

[50] The name of Apep was written in red as a prophylactic (i.e., protective) measure.

6.5. ISIS AND OSIRIS, FROM PLUTARCH'S *DE ISIDE ET OSIRIDE*

This mythical narrative about Isis and Osiris is part of a much longer treatise on the two gods (usually known by the Latin title *De Iside et Osiride*, "Concerning Isis and Osiris"), written in Greek by Plutarch of Chaeronea (46–126 CE) (for whom see Part 4, document 11). In turn, the treatise is part of the voluminous collection of essays and speeches known as the *Moralia* (original Greek title *Ethika*, i.e., "matters relating to custom").

Despite the Hellenized character and late date of this account, this *interpretatio graeca* ("Greek interpretation") of the Egyptian story provides one of the most important sources for Egyptian religion and myth. This is in part because Plutarch put together a mythological narrative of the sort that is practically absent in Egyptian texts. Moreover, scattered references show that some of the elements in Plutarch's account existed already in the Old Kingdom (2686–2160 BCE), with others appearing in the Middle Kingdom (2040–1640 BCE). Therefore, it seems that Plutarch's source (unknown to us) was at least partly informed by Egyptian traditions. Among the previously attested elements are Osiris' death by drowning, Isis' discovery of his body, and the attribution of his death to Seth. Although the dismemberment is not mentioned in the older testimonies, stories about Osiris' death are connected with the funerary practice of mummification, which entailed a process of partial dismemberment and reassembling. Osiris, after all, became the first mummy (see Figure 1). Furthermore, in some traditions the *ba* (soul) of the dead Osiris is said to have emerged from a sacred tree, and the crocodile-Nile god Sobek was said to have searched the Great Green (Mediterranean) for Osiris. Isis is also abundantly represented experiencing the loneliness and suffering of a woman in mourning.

As has long been noticed, the parallel with the story in the *Hymn to Demeter* is remarkable (see document 6.8): both women wandered the earth in search of their beloved dead (Osiris, Persephone), and both goddesses landed among mortals and nursed infants at royal houses. However, it is difficult to trace when and how both narratives came into contact.

SOURCE: Plutarch, *Isis and Osiris* 12–19. F. Cole Babbit, *Moralia V: Isis and Osiris. The E at Delphi. The Oracles at Delphi No Longer Given in Verse. The Obsolescence of Oracles* (Loeb Classical Library, Cambridge, MA and London, 1936), with minor modifications.

(12) Here follows the story related in the briefest possible words with the omission of everything that is merely unprofitable or superfluous:

They say that the Sun, when he became aware of Rhea's intercourse with Kronos, invoked a curse upon her that she should not give birth to a child in any month or year; but Hermes, being enamored of the goddess, consorted with her. Later, playing at draughts with the moon, he won from her the seventieth part of each of her periods of illumination, and from all the winnings he composed five days, and intercalated them as an addition to the three hundred and sixty days.

The Egyptians even now call these five days intercalated and celebrate them as the birthdays of the gods. They relate that on the first of these days Osiris was born, and at the hour of his birth a voice issued forth saying, "The Lord of All advances to the light." But some relate that a certain Pamyle, while he was drawing water in Thebes, heard a voice issuing from the shrine of Zeus, which bade him proclaim with a loud voice that a mighty and beneficent king, Osiris, had been born; and for this Kronos entrusted to him the child Osiris, which he brought up. It is in his honor that the festival of Pamylia is celebrated, a festival which resembles the phallic processions.

On the second of these days Arueris was born whom they call Apollo, and some call him also the elder Horus. On the third day Typhon was born, but not in due season or manner, but with a blow he broke through his mother's side and leapt forth. On the fourth day Isis was born in the regions that are ever moist; and on the fifth Nephthys, to whom they give the name of Teleute (Finality) and the name of Aphrodite, and some also the name of Nike (Victory). There is also a tradition that Osiris and Aroueris were sprung from the Sun, Isis from Hermes, and Typhon and Nephthys from Kronos. For this reason the kings considered the third of the intercalated days as inauspicious, and transacted no business on that day, nor did they give any attention to their bodies until nightfall. They relate, moreover, that Nephthys became the wife of Typhon[51]; but Isis and Osiris were enamored of each other and consorted together in the darkness of the womb before their birth. Some say that Arueris came from this union and was called the elder Horus by the Egyptians, but Apollo by the Greeks.

(13) One of the first acts related of Osiris in his reign was to deliver the Egyptians from their destitute and brutish manner of living. This he did by showing them the fruits of cultivation, by giving them laws, and by teaching them to honor the gods. Later he travelled over the whole earth civilizing it without the slightest need of arms, but most of the peoples he won over to his way by the charm of his persuasive discourse combined with song and all manner of music. Hence the Greeks came to identify him with Dionysos.

During his absence the tradition is that Typhon attempted nothing revolutionary because Isis, who was in control, was vigilant and alert; but when he returned home Typhon contrived a treacherous plot against him and formed a group of conspirators seventy-two in number. He had also the co-operation of a queen from Ethiopia who was there at the time and whose name they report as Aso. Typhon, having secretly measured Osiris's body and having made ready a beautiful chest of corresponding size artistically ornamented, caused it to be brought into the room where the festivity was in progress. The company was much pleased at the sight of it and admired it greatly, whereupon Typhon jestingly promised to present it to the man who should find the chest to be exactly his length when he lay down in it. They all tried it in turn, but no one fitted it; then Osiris got into it and lay down, and those who were in the plot ran to it and slammed down the lid, which they fastened by nails from the outside and also by using molten lead. Then they carried the chest to the river and sent it on its way to the sea through the Tanitic Mouth. Wherefore the Egyptians even to this day name this mouth the hateful and execrable. Such is the tradition. They say also that the date on which this deed was done was the seventeenth day of Athyr,

---

[51] Typhon stands for Seth, brother of Osiris.

when the sun passes through Scorpion, and in the twenty-eighth year of the reign of Osiris; but some say that these are the years of his life and not of his reign.

(14) The first to learn of the deed and to bring to men's knowledge an account of what had been done were the Pans and Satyrs who lived in the region around Chemmis, and so, even to this day, the sudden confusion and consternation of a crowd is called a panic. Isis, when the tidings reached her, at once cut off one of her tresses and put on a garment of mourning in a place where the city still bears the name of Kopto. Others think that the name means deprivation, for they also express "deprive" by means of "koptein."[52] But Isis wandered everywhere at her wits' end; no one whom she approached did she fail to address, and even when she met some little children she asked them about the chest. As it happened, they had seen it, and they told her the mouth of the river through which the friends of Typhon had launched the coffin into the sea. Wherefore the Egyptians think that little children possess the power of prophecy, and they try to divine the future from the portents which they find in children's words, especially when children are playing about in holy places and crying out whatever chances to come into their minds.

They relate also that Isis, learning that Osiris in his love had consorted with her sister through ignorance, in the belief that she was Isis, and seeing the proof of this in the garland of melilote which he had left with Nephthys, sought to find the child; for the mother, immediately after its birth, had exposed it because of her fear of Typhon. And when the child had been found, after great toil and trouble, with the help of dogs, which led Isis to it, it was brought up and became her guardian and attendant, receiving the name of Anubis, and it is said to protect the gods just as dogs protect men.

(15) Thereafter Isis, as they relate, learned that the chest had been cast up by the sea near the land of Byblos[53] and that the waves had gently set it down in the midst of a clump of heather. The heather in a short time ran up into a very beautiful and massive stock, and enfolded and embraced the chest with its growth and concealed it within its trunk. The king of the country admired the great size of the plant, and cut off the portion that enfolded the chest (which was now hidden from sight), and used it as a pillar to support the roof of his house. These facts, they say, Isis ascertained by the divine inspiration of Rumor, and came to Byblos and sat down by a spring, all dejection and tears; she exchanged no word with anybody, save only that she welcomed the queen's maidservants and treated them with great amiability, plaiting their hair for them and imparting to their persons a wondrous fragrance from her own body. But when the queen observed her maidservants, a longing came upon her for the unknown woman and for such hairdressing and for a body fragrant with ambrosia. Thus it happened that Isis was sent for and became so intimate with the queen that the queen made her the nurse of her baby. They say that the king's name was Malkathros; the queen's name some say was Astarte, others Saosis, and still others Nemanous, which the Greeks would call Athenais.

(16) They relate that Isis nursed the child by giving it her finger to suck instead of her breast, and in the night she would burn away the mortal portions of its body.

---

[52] Cf. Greek *kopto*, "to cut."

[53] Byblos, one of the oldest (Canaanite, later Phoenician) cities in the coast of modern Lebanon.

She herself would turn into a swallow and flit about the pillar with a wailing lament, until the queen who had been watching, when she saw her babe on fire, gave forth a loud cry and thus deprived it of immortality. Then the goddess disclosed herself and asked for the pillar which served to support the roof. She removed it with the greatest ease and cut away the wood of the heather which surrounded the chest; then, when she had wrapped up the wood in a linen cloth and had poured perfume upon it, she entrusted it to the care of the kings; and even to this day the people of Byblos venerate this wood which is preserved in the shrine of Isis.

Then the goddess threw herself down upon the coffin with such a dreadful wailing that the younger of the king's sons expired on the spot. The elder son she kept with her, and, having placed the coffin on board a boat, she put out from land. Since the Phaidros river toward the early morning fostered a rather boisterous wind, the goddess grew angry and dried up its stream.

(17) In the first place where she found seclusion, when she was quite by herself, they relate that she opened the chest and laid her face upon the face within and caressed it and wept. The child came quietly up behind her and saw what was there, and when the goddess became aware of his presence, she turned about and gave him one awful look of anger. The child could not endure the fright, and died. Others will not have it so, but assert that he fell overboard into the sea from the boat that was mentioned above. He also is the recipient of honors because of the goddess; for they say that the Maneros of whom the Egyptians sing at their convivial gatherings is this very child. Some say, however, that his name was Palaistinos or Pelousios, and that the city founded by the goddess was named (Pelousion) in his honor. They also recount that this Maneros who is the theme of their songs was the first to invent music. But some say that the word is not the name of any person, but an expression belonging to the vocabulary of drinking and feasting: "Good luck be ours in things like this!", and that this is really the idea expressed by the exclamation "maneros" whenever the Egyptians use it. In the same way we may be sure that the likeness of a corpse which, as it is exhibited to them, is carried around in a chest, is not a reminder of what happened to Osiris, as some assume; but it is to urge them, as they contemplate it, to use and to enjoy the present, since all very soon must be what it is now and this is their purpose in introducing it into the midst of merry-making.

(18) As they relate, Isis proceeded to her son Horus, who was being reared in Buto, and bestowed the chest in a place well out of the way; but Typhon, who was hunting by night in the light of the moon, happened upon it. Recognizing the body he divided it into fourteen parts and scattered them, each in a different place. Isis learned of this and sought for them again, sailing through the swamps in a boat of papyrus. This is the reason why people sailing in such boats are not harmed by the crocodiles, since these creatures in their own way show either their fear or their reverence for the goddess.

The traditional result of Osiris's dismemberment is that there are many so-called tombs of Osiris in Egypt; for Isis held a funeral for each part when she had found it. Others deny this and assert that she caused effigies of him to be made and these she distributed among the several cities, pretending that she was giving them his body, in order that he might receive divine honors in a greater number of cities, and also that, if Typhon should succeed in overpowering Horus, he might despair of ever finding the true tomb when so many were pointed out to him, all of them called the tomb of Osiris.

Of the parts of Osiris's body the only one which Isis did not find was the male member, for the reason that this had been at once tossed into the river, and the lepidotus, the sea-bream, and the pike had fed upon it; and it is from these very fishes the Egyptians are most scrupulous in abstaining. But Isis made a replica of the member to take its place, and consecrated the phallus, in honor of which the Egyptians even at the present day celebrate a festival.

(19) Later, as they relate, Osiris came to Horus from the other world and exercised and trained him for the battle. After a time Osiris asked Horus what he held to be the most noble of all things. When Horus replied, "To avenge one's father and mother for evil done to them," Osiris then asked him what animal he considered the most useful for them who go forth to battle; and when Horus said, "A horse," Osiris was surprised and raised the question why it was that he had not rather said a lion than a horse. Horus answered that a lion was a useful thing for a man in need of assistance, but that a horse served best for cutting off the flight of an enemy and annihilating him. When Osiris heard this, he was much pleased, since he felt that Horus had now an adequate preparation. It is said that, as many were continually transferring their allegiance to Horus, Typhon's concubine, Thoueris, also came over to him; and a serpent which pursued her was cut to pieces by Horus's men, and now, in memory of this, the people throw down a rope in their midst and chop it up.

Now the battle, as they relate, lasted many days and Horus prevailed. Isis, however, to whom Typhon was delivered in chains, did not cause him to be put to death, but released him and let him go. Horus could not endure this with equanimity, but laid hands upon his mother and wrested the royal diadem from her head; but Hermes put upon her a helmet like unto the head of a cow. Typhon formally accused Horus of being an illegitimate child, but with the help of Hermes to plead his cause it was decided by the gods that he also was legitimate. Typhon was then overcome in two other battles. Osiris consorted with Isis after his death, and she became the mother of Harpokrates,[54] untimely born and weak in his lower limbs.

6.6. *TELIPINU*: AN ANATOLIAN MYTH ABOUT A DEPARTED GOD

(For Hittite civilization and literature, see headnote to Part 3, document 4.) The Hittite "invocation ritual," called *mugawar,* tells the myth of the departure and return of an angry deity. The best known of these invocations tells of the disappearance of the Hattic (pre-Hittite, non–Indo-European Anatolian) Vegetation God Telipinu ("Great Son"), but *mugawars* are applied to other gods, including the Sun God and Hannahanna ("Grandmother," also written dMAH "Great Goddess," and dNIN.TU) and various local and personal Storm Gods.

---

[54] Harpokrates was the Greek adaptation in Hellenistic times of Egyptian Baby Horus.

Furthermore, *mugawars* are embedded in prayers, bringing the deity close so the worshipper's request may be heard.

This is an important example of the ritual of lament for a disappeared or departed god, followed by rejoicing, a practice widespread in the eastern Mediterranean. The similarities of the *mugawar*'s plot with other eastern Mediterranean seasonal myths have long been recognized, especially the Mesopotamian *Descent of Inanna/Ishtar* (Dumuzi's name "strong son" even matches the meaning of the Hattic name, Telipinu; see document 6.2), and the story of Demeter withdrawing from her duties when her daughter Persephone disappeared (document 6.8). Also, we must not forget the search for the dismembered Osiris; the death of Baal, searched for by his sister Anat (Part 3, document 5.a); the search and resurrection of the dismembered Dionysus in Orphic myth; and the advent of the angry Dionysus as told in Euripides' *Bacchae*, which appears to have been the etiology for the Athenian Dionysia (see Part 3, document 10).

The performer's telling of the myth was framed by a description of the ritual actions, but the *mugawar* as a whole is characterized by a collapsing of the separation between the mythic world and the actions of the practitioner. The text here provides a translation of the Telipinu myth with its accompanying ritual. There are some nine extant versions of the Telipinu myth, some in multiple copies. I draw on a total of nine different texts coming from four different versions (no single version is complete), so as to include as many details as possible. Thus, the translation is not meant to represent a specific version as it was actually performed.

First, the performer, probably an "Old Woman," a respected practitioner of Hittite magic, gathers the supplies and makes offerings "before the god," that is, before a statue or other representation of the god, for example, an *eya* tree, perhaps an evergreen oak or yew. Then, the performer begins to tell the story of the soothing of Telipinu's anger. The better-preserved version picks up with Telipinu already angry, leaving unclear for us exactly what has angered him. Smoke seizes the house, perhaps an allusion to burning the fields before sowing in the fall, and he departs in such haste that he puts his shoes on the wrong feet. Because he has abandoned his customary haunts, all fertility comes to an end. Telipinu then disappears into the steppe in a mysterious manner. While in the *mugawar* translated here Telipinu is described as becoming part of the Earth, there is no evidence that any of the other gods for whom *mugawars* were performed do so, although they may hide themselves in a pit. Next, famine and drought take over the land, and the gods cannot be sated at the feast. The Storm God, Telipinu's father, sends out search parties but they cannot find him. The only one who is able to find Telipinu is a lowly bee, who stings him awake, further infuriating the god. The bee is unable to soothe him, having run out of honey and wax. Thus, it is left to the practitioner to placate the god with all manner of soothing things and analogic magic, as if she were Kamrusepa, the goddess of magic. In this aspect the figure of Telipinu is similar to that of Demeter, whose withdrawal causes a terrible famine and whose favor has to be sought by her initiates and worshippers for the renewal of fertility each year.

The translation opens with the "first version" of the myth, that is, the best-preserved version. No version is clearly the "original" version; rather, the multiformity is a by-product of the oral-derived nature of the myth. The tablet is of Middle Hittite date (ca. 1400 BCE), but linguistic evidence shows that it must have had Old Hittite predecessors (ca. 1500 BCE). Because there are multiple versions, each with different paragraph numbering, the version number comes before the paragraph number (e.g., 1, §3', etc.; on the numbering system for Hittite texts, see longer explanation in Part 3, document 4).

SOURCE: Hittite texts in the electronic editions of CTH 324 by E. Rieken et al. (2009), on the Konkordanz der hethitischen Texte, translated and annotated by M. Bachvarova.

(The first two paragraphs preserved from this tablet are too fragmentary for translation, but an angry Telipinu seems to be implicated in destructive activities involving a city.)

(1, §3', A₂ i 10'-15' + A₁ i 1'-4') [. . .] nothing [. . .] august Telipinu [bega]n [to speak], "Drive [. . . !] Don't be frighten[ed!" And, he w]as sullen, and he pulled the right with the left, [while] he pulled the lef[t with the right]. He w[en]t from the house.

(1, §4', A₂ i 16' + A₁ i 5'-9') Smolder seized the windows. Smoke smothere[d] the house, and on the hearth the logs were smothere[d, within the altar] the gods were smothered. In the fold the sheep likewise, in the cow pen the cattle were smothered. The sheep rejected her lamb, while the cow rejected her calf.

(1, §5', A i 10'-15') Meanwhile, Telipinu went away. He carried away barley, Immarni,[55] abundance, growth, and satiety into the steppe, the meadow, the moors. Meanwhile, Telipinu went and disappeared into the moor, while on top of him *halenzu*-grass grew, so barley (and) wheat were no longer thriving, and cattle, sheep, humans were no longer becoming pregnant, nor were those who were pregnant giving birth.

(1, §6', A i 16'-20', B i 1'-5') The [mou]ntains dried up, the forest dried up, so the leaves were not coming out. The pastures dried up, the springs dried up, so that in the land [f]amine occurred. Humans and gods were dying from hunger. The great Istanu[56] made a feast, and he invited the thousand gods. They ate, but they were not sated, and they drank, but they were not sl[a]ked.

(1, §7', A i 21'-25', B i 6'-10') Tarhun[57] noticed (that) his son Telipinu (was not there). "Telipinu, my [s]on, is not here. He has become sullen, so he has taken away everything good." The great [go]ds, the small gods began to search for Telipinu. The Sun God sent the swift eagle. "Go! Search the high mountains!

(1, §8', A i 26'-31', B i 11'-16') "Search the deep valleys! Search the dark blue wave!" The eagle went, but he did not find him, and he brought back a message to the Sun God. "I did not find Telipinu, the august god." Tarhun said to Hannahanna, "How shall we act? We are dying of hunger." Hannahanna said to Tarhun, "Do something, Tarhun! Go and search for Telipinu yourself!"

---

[55] A fertility god.
[56] The Sun God.
[57] The Storm God.

(1, §9', A i 32'-35', B i 17'-20') Tarhun went and began to search for Telipinu. He [go]es to the city gate of his town, but he is not able to open it, and he broke his hammer and peg. [. . .] Tarhun (subj.). He covered himself up in (his cloak), and he sat down. Hannahanna [sen]t [the bee]. "You go and look for Telipinu!"

(Version 2 presents a more detailed version of the goddess's directions:)

(2, §5', D ii 5'-9', B ii 12'-15') . . . "When you [find him], sting him on his hands (and) feet. Make him stand up, and take your wax, and wipe him off and purify him and cleanse him and bring him [b]ack to me."

(The "first" version continues with the gods' reaction to Hannahanna's proposal.)

(1, §10', A i 36'-39') [Tarhun sai]d [to Hannahanna], "The great gods, the small gods searched for him, but [they did not find] him, so will this [bee] go and [find] him? His [w]ings are small, that one is also small, [the bee!] Furthermore, he is pinched into parts!"[58]

(The first column of the obverse of exemplar A of the "first" version ends here, and column ii is missing a considerable part of the top half. We turn, therefore, to exemplars of the "second" and "third" versions of the myth.)

(2, §7', D ii 15'-20') [Hannahann]a spoke to Tarhun, "Let (him go). T[hat one wi]ll [go] and find [him]." The bee [went and] began to [sea]rch [for Telipinu. He searche]d the hig[h mountains], and [he searche]d the [. . .] rivers. The springs, *silm[a . . .]*

(3, §3', B ii 1–5, A ii 7'-12') [He went], the bee. He searche[d the high mountains, he sea[r]ched the [deep valle]ys, [he searched the dark blue] wav[e]. He use[d] up the honey in [his heart], he [us]ed up [the wax.] And [he found] him in a meadow in the ci[ty Lihz]ina,[59] [in] a grov[e], and he stung [him] on his hands (and) his feet, so he go[t up.]

(3, §4', B ii 6–12, A ii 13'-14') On his part, [thus] Telipinu: "I was sulki[ng . . .], I was doing [X, why] then [did] you (pl.) [rouse] me, who was sleeping, and why did you (pl.) make [me,] who was sulking, speak? [Telipinu] became [wrath]ful, and he [X]-ed the spring, the *silma* [. . .], and he dragg[ed] the flowing rivers. [. . .] he [X]-ed. He tore them down, the banks [. . .]. He overturned [citi]es, [he] over[threw] houses.

(3, §5', B ii 13–16) He destroyed [manki]nd, he destro[yed the cat]tle (and) the sheep. [. . .] he [get]s [up]. The god[s fl]ed from him. [. . . "T]elipinu h[as] become [wr]athful. [Ho]w [shall] w[e] act? [What] sha[ll] we do?"

(We return to the "first" version here. The previous paragraph corresponds to 1, §12'.')

(1, §13", A₂ ii 9'-15') "Call mankind! Let t[hat one t]ake out the [st]inger, [X *wooden thing*], for him on Mount Ammuna. Let the eagle approach, and [let him/her] b[urn] it. [. . . " . . .] s/he burned, but the eagle [with] his win[g . . .], and they extinguished it, and s/he [. . .]. They took his fury, they took [his anger, they] to[ok] his sin, [they took sullenness.]

(1, §14"-16" are mostly unintelligible.)

---

[58] This describes the bee's segmented body.

[59] A city that appears in Hattic-derived myths.

(1, §17", A ii 3'-8') Telipin[u . . .]. S/he groun[d] the malt (and) beer bread[60] [. . .] . . . [. . .]. The good[. . .] s/he cut the gate. Telipinu [. . .] the fine scent (subj.) [. . .]. But, smothered, in return [. . .]

(1, §18", A ii 9'-11') Here now the water of striking [. . .]. Your mind, (that) of Telipinu [. . . Turn] to the king i[n] well-being [. . .]

(1, §19", A ii 12'-14') Here now *galaktar*[61] lies. [. . .] Let [X] be appeased. Here now *parh*[*uena*-nut lies]. L[et] its inside pull him.

(1, §20", A ii 15'-18') Here now the *samamma*-nut lies. [As the *samamma* is oily,] let [your mind likewise] be drenched (in oil). Here now figs [lie,] as [the fig] is sweet, let [your mind] also, (that) of T[elipinu], likewise be sweet.

(1, §21", A ii 19'-21', B ii 1'-2') And, as the olive [holds] its oil with its heart, [as the raisin] holds wine with its heart, you also, Telipinu, [. . .] likewise hol[d] goodness with your mind (and) with your heart.

(1, §22", A ii 24'-27', B ii 3'-9', C 1'-3') Here now *liti*[62] lies. Let it anoint [your mind,] (that) of Telipinu [. . .]. As malt (and) beer bread are joined together with their mind, [let] your mind [also], (that) of Telipinu, likewise b[e] joined together with the words of humans. [A]s [wheat] is pure, let Telipinu, his mind, likewise be pure. [As] hone[y] is sweet, as fine oil is soft, let [his] mi[nd] also, (that) of Telipinu, likewise be sweet, and let it likewise be soft.

(*Different versions of the* mugawar *offer different soothing substances, reminding the god that he should be sweet and soothing like them:*)

(2, §15''', D iii 8'-16', C iii 8'-17') [Here no]w for you [m]alt (and) beer bread li[kewise] lie. [As] malt and beer bread join together with their m[i]nd, and their mind (and) inside become one, [. . .]. They intoxicate an angry [ma]n with beer, and his anger [vanish]es, while they [intoxic]ate a fearful man, and his fear [vanish]es [away, likewise may the malt and beer bread] intoxicate you also, [Telipinu. . . . a]nger (obj.) [. . . let it a]ll vanish.

(*The "first" version of the Telipinu* mugawar *incorporates elements of "drawing paths" rituals, which mark a way for the deity with appealing items, such as scattered and dripped food or a length of cloth:*)

(1, §23", A ii 28'-32', C 4'-9") Here now your paths, (those) of Telipinu, I have sprinkled with fine oil. Telipinu, set out on the paths sprinkled with fine oil. Let *sahi* (and) *happuriyasa* (boughs) be in the fore. Just as fragrant reed is fitting, may you also, Telipinu, likewise be fitting.

(*Another version suggests that Telipinu sleep on the* sahi *and* happuriyasa:)

(7, §9", A iii 15'-22') Eat your fill of fine thing(s), and drink fine thing(s). Here now let the path of Telipinu be sprinkled with fine oil, and go on (it). Your bed is *sahi* and *happ*[*uriyasa* (boughs)], so sleep on it. Just as fragrant reed is fitting, may yo[u also] b[e] fitting likewi[se w]ith the king (and) que[en] for the land of Hatti.

---

[60] Malt and beer bread, used to make beer, often appear in incantations to symbolize a change of state, because they cause a change of state by the fermentation process (malt is sprouted and roasted barley, and beer bread is probably dried-out bread used to seed the yeast in the beer mash) and a change of state in the person who drinks the beer.

[61] The soothing substance *galaktar* may be opium.

[62] A plant-based substance.

(The "first" version returns to the mythical plane, although the actions of the goddess Kamrusepa are enacted by the human practitioner.)

(1, §24", A ii 33'-36') Telipinu came, wrathful. He th[un]dered wi[th] lightning, he was smiting the dark earth below. Kamrusepa saw him, and she waved [. . .] the win[g] of an eagle, and she s[topped] him.

(1, §25", A iii 1–2) The fury, she stopped it. The ange[r, she stopped it]. She stopped [sin]. She stopped the sullenness.

(1, §26", A iii 3–7) Kamrusepa speaks in return to the gods, "G[o], gods, here and now put to p[asture] his rams, (those) of Istanu, for Hapantali, and separate out twelve rams, and I will treat his w[ra]ths, (those) of Telipinu. I took for myself a basket (of) a thousand eyes,[63] and on (it) I poured the wheat-grains, (which are) her sheep, (those) of Kamrusepa."

(1, §27", A iii 8–12) "I burnt away on one side above Telipinu, and on the other I burnt. I took from Telipinu, from his body his evil, I took his sin, I took his fury, I took his anger, [I] too[k] his wrath, I took his sullenness."

(1, §28", A iii 13–20) "Telipinu is angered. His mind, [his] inside was smothered in the logs. As they burned these lo[gs], bur[n] likewise the fury, anger, sin, sullenness of Telipinu also. As [malt] is dry—[they do] not carry it to the steppe, and they do not treat it as seed, nor do t[hey] make it (into) bread, (and) set it in the store house—likewise [let] the fury, [anger,] sin, sullenness of Telipinu also be dried up.

(1, §29", A iii 21–23) Telipinu is angered. His mind, [his] i[nside] is burning fire, and a[s] this fire [is extinguished], likewis[e let] rage, sullenness also [be extinguished].

(1, §30", A iii 24–26, B iii 1') Telipinu, release fury, [release] ang[er], release sullenness, and as (that) of the reed does not flow i[n reverse], likewise [let] the r[age, fury], sullenness of Telipinu also not g[o] back.

(1, §31", A iii 28–34, B iii 2'-8') The gods are under the hawthorn tree [in the place of] assem[bly], while under the hawthorn long [. . .]. All the gods also sit, [Papaya, Ist]ustaya, the Fate Goddesses, the Great Goddesses, Halki,[64] the Genius of Prosperity, Telipinu, the Tutelary Deity, Hapantal[iya, X], and wit[h] the gods I have trea[t]ed the images of long years. I have purified Telipinu.

(1, §32", B iii 9'-12', A iii 35) [. . . I took] evil from Telipinu, [from his] b[ody . . .], I took [hi]s [fury, I took his] an[ger], I too[k h]is [sin, I took] sullenne[ss . . .]. I took the [evil] tongue, [I took] the e[vil way of life.]

(We can only make out one more word in column iii of exemplar B: "name." The text then resumes after a break with exemplar A, which alludes to a ritual action well known from Hittite and Luwian incantations, the purificatory plucking of evil or pollution from a client as if s/he is a sheep passing under a thorny hawthorn tree.)

(1, §34'", A iv 1–3) *(Speaking to the hawthorn tree:)* You pulled a tuft of hair [from i]t. The sheep [goe]s past underneath you, so you pulled a tuft of wool from it. Pull also [fu]ry, rage, sin, sullenness from Telipinu.

---

[63] A sieve.

[64] The goddess of grain.

(1, §35''', A iv 4–7) Tarhun comes, wrathful, and the Man of the Storm God[65] stops him, while the pot comes, and the spoon stops it.[66] [Theref]ore, let my words also, (those) of humans, likewise stop for Telipinu [f]ury, rage, sullenness.

(1, §36''', A iv 8–13, B iv 1'-5') Let the fury, rage, sin, sullenness of Telipinu go. Let the house release it, let the inner pillar [r]elease it, let the window release it. The hinge—let the inner courtyard release it. Let the city gate release it. Let the gate complex release it. Let the royal road release it. Let it not go into the fruitful field, garden, grove. Let it go by the path of the Sun Goddess of the Earth.

(1, §37''', A iv 14–19, B iv 6') The gatekeeper opened the seven doors, he pulled back the seven bolts. Under the dark earth stand bronze vessels. Their lids (are) of lead, their latches of iron. What goes in, does not come up again; it perishes inside. Let it also confine the fury, anger, sin, sullenness of Telipinu inside, and let it not come up again.

(The "third" version, although lacunose, offers a few more details:)

(3, §9'', A iii 9'-11', E iii 8'-12') [. . .] s/he brought forth [fr]om [the oven] grain, Immarni, the Genius of Prospe[rity], (and) Teli[pinu . . .] good rains, good winds, [X] of the land, blooming [. . . , and] s/he brought forth everything.

(3, §10'', A iii 12'-14') [. . .] let him/her make powerful the apple (tree) of the deity [*name lost in gap* . . .] the *marsigga* (tree) o[f . . .] his mind [. . .].[67]

(The "third" version then continues in parallel with the "first," to which we return:)

(1, §38''', A iv 20–26, B iv 13'-14') Telipinu came back to his house, and he took notice of his country. The smolder released the window, the smoke released the house. On the altar the gods were lined up. He released the log (on) the hearth. I[nt]o the fold he released the sheep, into the cow pen he released the cattle. So, the mother drew her child near, the sheep drew her lamb near, the cow drew her calf near. For his part, Telipinu <drew> the king (and) queen <near>, and he took notice of them, for life, for vigor, for future days.

(1, §39''', A iv 27–31) Telipinu took notice of the king. In front of Telipinu an *eya* tree stands. From the *eya* is hanging a hunting bag of sheep(-skin),[68] and therein lies fat of a sheep, and therein lie (that) of grain, Shakkan,[69] (and) wine, and therein lie cattle (and) sheep, and [th]erein lie long years (and) descendants.

(1, §40''', A iv 32–34) And, therein lie the mild bleats[70] of the lamb, and therein lie [content]ment (and) obedience, and therein the god [X] likewise, and therein lies the right thigh,[71] and [there]in [lie abund]a[nc]e, g[rowth, and satiety.]

---

[65] In other words, the god's priest.

[66] The spoon stirs the pot and keeps it from boiling over.

[67] It is unclear what type of tree the *marsigga* is and what its connotations were. Apples were known for their sourness, and in incantations apples appeared because they could extract teeth, as a sorceress wanted to extract evil.

[68] The *kursa* or hunting bag made from the fleece of a sheep or goat was a cult symbol of prosperity, sometimes divinized. It has been compared to Jason's golden fleece and Zeus' aegis.

[69] Shakkan is an equid god symbolizing the flourishing of wild spaces.

[70] Literally, "messages."

[71] The right thigh is a sacrificial portion.

(Text 1.A breaks off here. Texts 3.C and D, although only in fragments, show that the remainder of the text focuses on Telipinu, who interacts with the king. A city is involved, and purificatory substances are used to remove the god's anger.)

6.7. ODYSSEUS' *NEKYIA* IN HOMER, *ODYSSEY*, BOOK 11

(For Homer, see headnote to Part 3, document 8.) Odysseus' incursion in the Underworld is one of the many trials he experiences during the course of his journey back from Troy to his home in Ithaca. After his adventure on the island of the sorceress Circe, he is instructed by her to consult the dead, more specifically the spirit of Teiresias, the legendary Theban seer, in order to receive instructions for his homeward journey. Acting as a necromancer, Odysseus follows a special ritual to invoke the dead, whose spirits come to him, thirsty for sacrificial blood, which they drink in order to gain strength. Those who drink it speak to him and he to them. In this sense, the *katabasis* ("descent") is more of a *nekyia* (consultation to the dead or necromancy) and less of a "descent," although at a certain point it seems like Odysseus is in fact inside and touring the Underworld. This Underworld episode also provides the framework for cataloguing dead heroes and famous women whom Odysseus sees while there. In general, the eschatology presented in the episode is simple and "egalitarian," since all the spirits seem to end up in the same place, a rather "flat" Hades (in contrast with the complex Underworld of the *Aeneid*; document 6.13). The theme is repeated later on in the *Odyssey*, where the suitors' souls follow Hermes down to Hades, as they flutter and squeak around him like bats, and they speak with other heroes who are already there (*Od.* 24.1–205). Only some special punishments are described for specific characters, and the Isles of the Blessed or the Elysean Fields are not mentioned, which first appear as especial destiny of the heroes' souls in Hesiod (see myth of the Five Races, Part 2, document 5).

The narrative is in the first person, since it is told by Odysseus himself, who is entertaining the court of the Phaeacians with his adventures. He had reached their island (Scheria) after spending a long time on the island of Kalypso, where he had arrived already alone (all his comrades had died along the way). At this point of the story, he and his companions have followed Circe's directions and have sailed to the river Ocean, where they will invoke the dead.

SOURCE: Homer, *Odyssey*, Book 11, translated and annotated by B. B. Powell. (Powell's full translation of the *Odyssey* is forthcoming from Oxford University Press. Notes have been selected from Powell's by the editor, with some changes and additions.)

> "But when we came down to the ship and the sea, we dragged
> the ship first of all into the shining sea, and we set up
> the mast and the sail on the black ship. We took on
> the flocks and embarked. We went off mourning and shedding
> 5   warm tears. Circe, with the lovely tresses,

dread goddess of human speech,[72] sent a wind that came
behind the ship with its dark prow and filled
the sails, a noble companion. Once we made
secure all the tackle in the ship, we took our seats.

10 Wind favored us and the helmsman kept her on a straight course.
    "All day long the ship's sail was stretched
as she sped across the sea. The sun went down
and the ways grew dark. We came to the limits
of deep-flowing Ocean.[73] We came to the people and the city

15 of the Kimmerians,[74] hidden in mist and cloud, nor does
the shining sun look down upon them with its rays,
not when he mounts toward the starry heaven, nor when
he turns again to the earth from the heaven, but total
night is stretched over wretched mortals.
                "We came there

20 and dragged up our ship on the shore and off-loaded the sheep.
We walked along the stream of Ocean until we came to the place
that Circe had described. There Perimedes and Eurylochos held
the sacrificial animals. I drew my sharp sword from my thigh
and dug a trench two feet wide in both directions.

25 Around it I poured an offering to all the dead,
first with honeyed milk, then with sweet wine, and then
with water. I sprinkled white barley. Powerfully I entreated
the strengthless heads of the dead, saying that when
I came to Ithaca I would sacrifice a barren cow to them

30 in my halls, the best I had, and that I would pile
the altar with excellent gifts, and that to Teiresias[75]
I would sacrifice a ram, all black, to him alone,
an outstanding one from our flocks.
             "When with vows and prayers
I had supplicated the tribes of the dead, I took the sheep

---

[72] The meaning of this mysterious phrase is unclear.

[73] Ocean is a river that runs around the world. The word is probably Semitic in origin. Ocean is the husband of Tethys (perhaps derived from Mesopotamian Tiamat; see *Ennuma Elish* in Part 1, document 1). Ocean is the "origin of gods" (*Od.* 14.201) and also the origins of all "rivers, springs, the sea, and wells" (*Od.* 21.194–197).

[74] A historical people who descended over the Caucasus Mountains in the eighth century BCE and for a hundred years terrorized Asia Minor.

[75] The Theban prophet, prominent in later tragedy.

35 and slit their throats over the pit, and the black blood
   flowed. Then the breath-souls of the dead who had passed away
   gathered from Erebos[76]—brides, and unwed youths
   and miserable old men, and tender virgins with hearts
   new to sorrow, many others wounded by bronze spears
40 and men killed by Ares[77]wearing armor spattered with blood.
   These came thronging around the pit, coming from here
   and there, making a wondrous cry.

                                   "A pale fear
   gripped me. I ordered my companions to flay and burn
   the sheep that lay there, their throats cut with the pitiless
45 bronze, and that they pray to the gods, and to powerful Hades
   and terrible Persephone. I myself drew my sharp sword
   from my thigh and sat, not allowing the strengthless heads
   of the dead to come close to the blood before I had interrogated
   Teiresias.

                     "First came the breath-soul of my companion Elpenor,
50 for we did not bury him beneath the earth with its broad ways,
   but left his corpse in the hall of Circe unwept
   and unburied because another task drove us on. I wept
   when I saw him and took pity in my heart, and spoke to him
   words that flew like arrows: 'Elpenor, how did you come
55 beneath the misty darkness? You've gotten here faster
   on foot than I in my black ship!'

                                   "So I spoke, and he answered me[78]
   with a groan: 'Son of Laertes, from the line of Zeus, resourceful
   Odysseus, the evil decree of some spirit, plus endless wine
   has killed me. When I lay down to sleep in the hall of Circe
60 I did not think to go back down the long ladder
   but fell headlong from the roof, and my neck was torn
   away from the spine—my breath-soul went down to the house
   of Hades. Now I beg you by those we left behind,
   those not present, by your wife and father who reared you
65 when you were a tyke, and by Telemachos, whom you left
   as an only son in your halls! For I know that when

---

[76] "Darkness," that is, the Underworld. In Hesiod's *Theogony* it is the fifth primordial element mentioned, which came out of Chaos and with Nyx (Night) fathered Aither (upper air) and Hemera (Day) (see Part 1, document 5).

[77] That is, killed in war.

[78] Elpenor can talk without drinking the blood because he is still unburied.

you leave the house of Hades and go back, you will put
in to the island of Aiaia[79] in your well-built ship.
There—I beg of you, O king!—I urge you to remember me.
70 Do no go off home and leave me unwept and unburied.
Do not turn away from me, or I may become a cause
of the gods' anger! Burn me together with my armor,
all that is mine, and heap up a tomb on the shore
of the gray sea, in memory of a wretched man,
75 so that men yet to be born may learn of me. Do these things
for me and fix on the tomb the oar that I rowed
when I was alive among my companions.'

      "So he spoke,
and I answered: 'I shall accomplish these things for you, my wretched
friend, and bring them to pass.' Then the two of us sat,
80 exchanging melancholy words, I on one side holding
the sword over the blood, the phantom of my companion
on the other, who spoke at length.

      "Then there came the breath-soul
of my dead mother, Antikleia, the daughter of great-hearted
Autolykos,[80] whom I left alive when I went to sacred Ilion.
85 I wept when I saw her and, took pity in my heart, but I would not
let her come close to the blood, though I was deeply
sorrowful, before I had made inquiry of Teiresias.

      "Then the breath-soul
of Theban Teiresias came to the pit, holding
a golden scepter. He recognized me and spoke[81]: 'Son
90 of Laertes, from the line of Zeus, resourceful Odysseus,
why, you wretch! have you left the light of the sun
and come down here—so that you could see the dead
and this joyless land? But stand back from the pit, put up
your sharp sword so that I may drink of the blood and speak
95 the truth.'

    "So he spoke, and I drew back and thrust my silver-studded
sword into its scabbard. When he had drunk

---

[79] The island of Circe.

[80] His name means "True-wolf." He gave Odysseus his name and entertained him as a youth on Mount Parnassos, where in a boar hunt Odysseus received the scar by which he is later identified.

[81] Only Teiresias (because of his prophetic powers) can speak without first drinking from the blood (except for the unburied Elpenor).

the black blood, then the faultless seer said:
'You seek to know about your honey-sweet homecoming,
    O glorious
100 Odysseus. Well, the god will make it harsh for you.
    For I do not think you will escape Poseidon, the earth shaker,
    who has laid up anger in his heart, enraged because you blinded
    his son. Still, you might arrive home after suffering
    many evils, if you are willing to restrain your spirit
105 and that of your companions when you put your well-built ship
    ashore on the island of Thrinakia,[82] escaping the violet-colored sea,
    and you find the cattle and good flocks of Helios, who sees
    all things and hears all things, grazing. If you leave them
    unharmed and remember your return journey, then you might
110 arrive at Ithaca, though suffering many evils. But if
    you harm them, then I predict the destruction of your ship and your
        companions.
    If you yourself escape, you will arrive home late,
    on someone else's ship, in a bad way, having lost all your
        companions.
    You will suffer trouble in your house from arrogant men
115 who consume your substance and try to seduce your godlike
    wife with gifts. Surely you will take vengeance on their violence
    when you arrive. But when you have killed the suitors in your halls
    either by trickery or openly with the sharp bronze,
    then take a well-fitted oar in your hand and travel
120 until you come where they know nothing of the sea, nor do
    they eat food mixed with salt. They do not know
    about ships with purple cheeks or well-shaped oars,
    which are the wings of a boat. I will tell you a sign
    that is very clear and cannot escape you: When another
125 wayfarer who meets you says that is a winnowing-fan[83]
    on your strong shoulder, right there fix your well-shaped oar
    in the ground. Make a generous sacrifice to Poseidon the king—
    a lamb and a bull and a pig and a boar that mates with sows—
    then go home and offer great sacrifice to the deathless

---

[82] Of unknown meaning, the mythical island of Helios was at an early time identified with "Trinakria," or "three-cornered island," another name for Sicily. Even today Sicily is called the Island of the Sun.

[83] A wooden implement used to throw the harvested grain into the air so that the wind blows away the chaff (inedible seed casings) from the heavier grain, which falls to the ground.

130 gods who hold the broad sky, to each of them in turn.
For you a very gentle death will come from the sea.
It will kill you when you are overcome with spruce old age.
Your people shall live in happiness around you. Now I have
told you the truth.'

"So he spoke, and so I answered: 'Teiresias, the gods
135 themselves have spun the thread of all this. But come,
tell me, and tell me truly—I see the breath-soul
of my dead mother. She sits there in silence near the blood in the pit,
nor does she dare to look on her son just opposite,
or to speak to him. Tell me, O master, how
140 can she recognize who I am?'

"So I spoke, and he
at once answered: 'I shall tell you an easy word.
Do fix it in your mind. Whomever of the dead and gone
you allow to come close to the black blood, that one will speak
and tell you the truth. Whomever you refuse,
145 he will surely withdraw from the pit.'

"So saying, the breath-soul
of lord Teiresias went to the house of Hades. He had spoken
his prophecies, but I remained steadfast where I was until
my mother came and drank the dark blood. Immediately
she knew who I was, and moaning she spoke words that went
150 like arrows: 'My child, how have you come beneath the shadowy
dark, being still alive? It is hard for the living to see these things.
For there are great rivers between the living and dead, and mighty
floods—first of all Ocean, which no one can cross on foot,
but only with a well-built ship. Have you come here after
155 long wanderings from Troy with your ship and companions? Have
        you not
yet come to Ithaca, nor seen your wife in your halls?'

"So she spoke, and I said in reply: 'O mother,
my urgent need has been to go down to the house of Hades
to seek an oracle from the breath-soul of Theban Teiresias.
160 So I have not yet come close to Achaia, nor have I walked
on my own land, but always I wander in misery,
ever since I first followed the good Agamemnon to Troy
with its fine horses, that I might help fight the Trojans.

        "'But come,
tell me and report it truly—what fate of grievous death

165 overcame you? Was it a long illness, or did Artemis, the shooter
of arrows, come and with her gentle shafts bring you down?
Tell me too of my father and my son that I left behind—
do they still hold power, or does some other man have it, and do
they say that I shall never return? Tell me of the plans
170 and intentions of my wedded wife—does she stay beside
her child and keep all things steady? Or has someone already
married her, whoever is best of the Achaeans?'

"Thus I spoke,
and at once my revered mother answered: 'Yes, yes,
your wife remains with a steady heart in your halls. Miserable
175 do the nights and days wane for her, weeping tears.
No one else yet holds your power, but Telemachos
rules over your domains without harassment, and he hosts
the equal feast as is fitting for one who gives judgments.
And all men invite him.[84] Your father lives in the country
180 and does not come to the city. For bedding he has no bed,
no cloaks nor bright covers, and in the winter he sleeps with the
   slaves
in the house, in the dust near the fire, and the clothes on his flesh
are filthy. But when summer comes and the rich autumn, then
   everywhere
across the slope of his vineyard leaves are scattered on the ground
185 as a bed. There he lies sorrowing, nursing great sorrow
in his heart and longing for your return. A harsh
old age has come upon him. Even so did I perish
and follow my fate. For Artemis, who sees from a long
way off, who showers arrows, did not strike me down
190 in my halls with her gentle shafts,[85] nor did a sickness come
upon me, which often takes away the spirit from the limbs with
   grievous
wasting, but it was my longing for you and your counsels
   and gentleness,

---

[84] Antikleia seems to be speaking about the current situation, when Odysseus has been away
from home, say, eleven or twelve years. He does not return home until the twentieth year, and we
learn elsewhere that the suitors arrived in the house three or four years before his return, which
is why Antikleia does not mention them (though Teiresias does). If Telemachos was an infant
when Odysseus went to Troy, he must be too young now to receive such respect and to "give
judgments," but Homer is fairly casual about chronology.

[85] When a woman died "of natural causes" in Homer's day, she was said to have fallen to the
shafts of Artemis.

glorious Odysseus, that took away my honey-sweet life.'

  "So she spoke, but I pondered in my heart and wanted
195 to take in my arms my mother's breath-soul, which had passed
away. Three times I leaped toward her, for my heart
urged me to hold her. Three times she flew away, out
of my arms, like a shadow or a dream.

        "A still sharper pain
came to my heart, and I spoke to her words that went
200 like arrows: 'My mother, why do you not await me, eager
to hold you, so that even in the house of Hades we may take
delight in icy wailing, throwing our arms about one another?
Or are you just a phantom that the illustrious Persephone
has sent up, so that I may groan and lament all the more?'

          "So I spoke,
205 and at once my revered mother answered: 'Ah me,
my child, most ill-fated of all mortals: Persephone
the daughter of Zeus does not deceive you, but this
is the way of mortals when someone dies. The tendons
no longer hold together the flesh and the bones, but the mighty
210 force of fire destroys all that, when the spirit
first leaves the white bones and the breath-soul flies off
like a dream, hovering here and there.

        " 'But hasten
to the light as quickly as you can. Remember all these things
so that hereafter you might tell them to your wife.'

        "So we conversed
215 with one other, but other women came to the blood,
for illustrious Persephone sent them, whoever were the wives
and daughters of the chiefs. They gathered in a crowd
around the dark blood, and now I took thought how I might
 question
each one. This seemed the best plan to my mind: Drawing
220 my long sword from my strong thigh, I did not permit
all of them to drink together from the dark blood.
One after another they came, and each told me of her lineage.
I questioned them all.[86]

---

[86] Now follows a "Catalog of Women," a genre of oral poetry in the days of Homer (e.g., Hesiod's *Catalogue of Women*). Book 11 is a series of catalogues: first of women; then of heroes; then of the denizens of the Underworld.

"First I saw Tyro of high birth,
who said she was the offspring of excellent Salmoneus, and she said
225 she was the wife of Kretheus, the son of Aiolos. She fell
in love with the divine river Enipeus,[87] by far
the most beautiful of the rivers that go upon the earth. She went often
to the beautiful waters of the Enipeus. Taking on the likeness
of the river god, Poseidon, the earth-holder, the shaker of the earth,
230 lay with Tyro at the mouth of the swirling river.
A dark wave stood around them, like a mountain, arched over,
and it hid Poseidon and the mortal woman. Poseidon
loosed the virgin belt, and he poured out sleep
upon her. But when the god had finished his work
235 of love, he took her by the hand, and he spoke and addressed her:
'Rejoice, woman, in our love making! As the year rolls around,
you will bear glorious children, because the embraces of a god
are not without effect. You will attend and rear them. Now go
to your house. Be quiet. Tell no man. Know that I am Poseidon,
240 the shaker of the earth.'

"So speaking he descended beneath the waves
of the sea. Thus Tyro conceived and bore Pelias and Neleus,
who both became powerful servants of great Zeus.
Pelias lived in spacious Iolkos and had many flocks.
245 Neleus lived in sandy Pylos. And the queen of women
bore other men to Kretheus—Aison and Pheres and Amythaon,
who rejoiced in chariot-fighting.[88]

"And after Tyro I saw
Antiope, the daughter of Asopos, who boasted that she had slept
in the arms of Zeus, and she bore two children—Amphion
250 and Zethos, who first founded the seat of seven-gated Thebes,
and they built its walls, for without walls they could not live
in spacious Thebes, though the twins were strong.[89]

"After her

---

[87] A river in Thessaly.

[88] Pelias ruled in Iolkos (southeastern Thessaly). He sent Jason and the Argonauts on their quest. Neleus ruled in Pylos in the southwestern Peloponnese and had many sons, all except for Nestor killed by Herakles. Aison was the father of Jason, whose throne Pelias usurped. Pheres was the father of Admetos, who married Alkestis, a daughter of Pelias (cf. play *Alkestis* by Euripides, in which she dies for her husband). Amythaon was the father of the prophet Melampous.

[89] In post-Homeric accounts, Zethos used brute force to move the stones of the walls of Thebes into place, but Amphion played his lyre and enchanted them into place.

I saw Alkmene, the wife of Amphitryon, who gave birth
to Herakles, staunch in the fight, with a heart like a lion,
255 mixing in love in the arms of great Zeus.[90]

                              "And I saw
Megara, the daughter of proud Kreon, whom Herakles married,
the son of Amphitryon, always stubborn in his strength.[91]

                                                "I saw
the mother of Oedipus, beautiful Epikaste, who committed
great evil when in ignorance she married her own son.
260 And Oedipus married her after killing his own father.
The gods made all these things known to men right away.
Oedipus remained as king in lovely Thebes, though
suffering agonies through the destructive designs of the gods.
But Epikaste went down to the house of Hades, the powerful
265 warden of the gate. She fitted a noose on high
from a lofty beam, overcome by her pain. She left
behind many sorrows for him, as many as the Furies
of a mother can bring to pass.[92]

                    "And I saw the most beautiful
Chloris, whom Neleus once married because of her beauty,
270 after he gave her innumerable bridal gifts—Chloris, the youngest
daughter of Amphion, the son of Iasos,[93] who once ruled
with power in Orchomenos of the Minyans. Chloris was queen
of Pylos, and she bore splendid sons, Nestor
and Chromios and lordly Periklymenos. In addition she bore Pero,
275 a marvel to men. All those men who lived nearby
sought Chloris' hand in marriage. But Neleus would give her
only to the man who rustled from Phylake the obstinate
cattle with curly horns and broad faces
of powerful Iphikles. Only the prophet Melampous undertook
280 to drive them off, but a cruel decree of the gods ensnared him—
herdsmen carted him off in grievous chains. But when
the months and days were complete as the year rolled onward

---

[90] See story of Herakles in Part 3, document 11.b.

[91] According to later tradition, Herakles killed Megara and all of their children (see Part 3, document 11.b).

[92] This is the oldest version of the myth of Oedipus, with all the essential elements: incest, the son's murder of his father, the suicide of the mother (later named Iokasta). However, here Oedipus remains as king, nothing is said of his self-blinding (cf. Sophocles' play *Oedipus the King*), Epikaste and Oedipus have no children, and she curses Oedipus when she dies.

[93] As opposed to the Amphion (son of Antiope and Zeus) just mentioned.

and the seasons came around, then the powerful Iphikles freed
　　Melampous

after he told of all the oracles.[94] Thus was the will

285　of Zeus fulfilled.

　　　　　　　　"And I saw Leda, the wife of Tyndareus,

who gave birth to two children, strong of heart, by Tyndareus—

horse-taming Kastor and Polydeukes,[95] good at boxing.

These two the earth, giver of life, covers over,

but beneath the earth they have honor from Zeus, living one day

290　in turn, then dead the next. They have won honor like

to that of the gods.

　　　　　　　　"After Leda, I saw Iphimedeia,

the wife of Aloeus, who they say lay in love with Poseidon

and bore him two children, but to a short life—godlike

Otos and far-famed Ephialtes, whom the earth that brings

295　forth grain raised up as the tallest and much the most beautiful

beings after the celebrated Orion.[96] When only nine,

they were fourteen feet wide and fifty-four feet high, yes,

and they threatened to bring the din of furious war

to Olympos. They were eager to pile Ossa on Olympos, and Pelion

300　with its waving forests on Ossa, so they would have a way

to heaven. And they would have done it, had they reached their
　　maturity.

But Apollo, the son of Zeus, whom Leto had borne,

laid waste to them both before down blossomed

on their cheeks and covered their chins with blooming beards.

305　　　　　　"I saw Phaidra and Prokris and beautiful Ariadne, the
　　daughter

of cruel Minos, whom once Theseus bore

from Crete to the hill of sacred Athens, but he had

no pleasure from her. Before that Artemis killed her on
　　wave-swept

---

[94] Homer clearly assumes his audience already knows the details of the story. The seer Melampous from Pylos (who ended up as king of Argos) wanted to get the cattle on behalf of his brother, but Iphikles caught him and imprisoned him for one year. When Melampous solved the mystery of Iphikles' sexual impotence, he allowed the seer to return to Pylos with the cattle.

[95] Also known as the Dioskouroi (Lat. *Dioscuri*), meaning "children of Zeus."

[96] The hunter Orion was a lover of the goddess Dawn, until Artemis killed him with her arrows. Kalypso (*Od.* Book 5) uses him as an example of the gods' hostility toward goddesses who take on mortal lovers.

Dia, on the testimony of Dionysos.[97]

"I saw Maira and Klymene

310 and hateful Eriphyle, who took gold as the price of her own
husband.[98] I could never tell all the women I saw, nor give
all their names, so many wives of the heroes, and their daughters,
did I see before that immortal night would be gone.

"But it is time that we slept, either with the crew of your
swift

315 ship or here in your own house. My voyage home will rest with the
gods,
and with you."

So he spoke. All were hushed in silence,
and were held enchanted throughout the shadowy halls.
Then white-armed Arete[99] began to speak: "Phaeacians,
how does this man seem to you in comeliness

320 and stature and in his well-balanced mind? Moreover
he is my guest, though each of you has a share
in this honor. So don't be in a hurry to send him off,
and don't cut short your gifts to one in such need.
For you have much treasure in your houses,

325 thanks to the favor of the gods."

The old warrior Echeneos,
one of the Phaeacian elders, then spoke to them:
"My friends, not wide of the mark or of our own thought
are the words of our wise queen! Do act on them,
though it is on Alkinoos that the word and deed depend."

330 Alkinoos answered and said: "This word shall come
to pass, as surely as I am alive and rule over the oar-loving
Phaeacians. Let our guest, who longs so for his return,
remain until tomorrow, so that we may make
our gift-giving complete. His safe passage will be the concern

---

[97] Homer mentions three women connected with Crete: Phaidra (Latin Phaedra), who fell in love with her stepson Hippolytos (see Part 5, document 11); Prokris, who had an affair with Minos and was killed by her husband; and Ariadne, whose story here differs from the later version (see Part 5, documents 10.a and 10.b). This is one of the very few places where Homer mentions Dionysos.

[98] Maira was the daughter of Proitos, king of Tiryns (cured by Melampous of her madness); Anteia propositioned Bellerophon, and when he refused, she said she had been raped; Klymene was the wife of Phylakos and mother of Iphikles (who imprisoned Melampous). Eriphyle accepted a bribe to persuade her husband Amphiaraos to participate in the campaign of the Seven against Thebes, in which his death was certain.

[99] The queen of the Phaeacians.

335 of all men, but especially mine, for I hold the power
among the people here."
Resourceful Odysseus answered him:
"King Alkinoos, most excellent of all people, even if
you encouraged me to stay here a whole year, and would arrange
my escort, and would give wonderful gifts—why, I would do it!
340 Much better to return to the land of one's fathers with a full hand.
I will receive more respect from men and be dearer to all
of them, when they see me returning to Ithaca."
Alkinoos
answered and spoke to him: "O Odysseus, when we look
upon you, we would never liken you to an imposter
345 or a cheat, such men as the black earth nourishes in great numbers
scattered far and wide, making up lies from things that no man
can even see. But you understand the charm of words,
and your mind is noble. You speak as when a singer
speaks with knowledge, telling the sorrows of all the Argives
350 and of you yourself.
"But come, tell me this
and do so truly: whether you saw any of your godlike
companions, who followed you to Ilion and there met their fate?
The night is very long, endless really. It is not time
for you to go to sleep in the hall. Tell me, please,
355 more of your wondrous deeds! I could hold out until
the bright dawn, if you were willing to sit here in our hall
and tell of your many woes."
Resourceful Odysseus said in reply:
"King Alkinoos, most excellent of all people, there is a time
for talk and a time for sleep. If you want to hear
360 still more, I will not hold back from telling
you things still more pitiful than these—the sorrow
of my companions, who perished after we escaped from the shrill
war cry of the Trojans, and those who were destroyed on return
through the will of an evil woman.[100]
"When the holy Persephone
365 had scattered the breath-souls of the women here and there,
up came that of Agamemnon, the son of Atreus, groaning.

---

[100] Referring to Klytaimnestra, who murdered her husband Agamemnon when he returned home.

The breath-souls of all those who died and met
their fate in the house of Aigisthos were gathered around him.
Agamemnon right away knew who I was, after
370 he had drunk of the black blood. He complained shrilly,
pouring down hot tears, throwing out his hands toward me,
longing to embrace me. But there was no lasting strength
or vitality, such as once dwelled in his supple limbs.
    "I wept when I saw him and took pity in my heart,
375 and spoke to him words that went like arrows:
'Most glorious son of Atreus, king of men, Agamemnon, what fate
of grievous death overcame you? Did Poseidon overcome you,
raising up the dreadful blast of savage winds
among your ships? Or did enemy men do you harm
380 on the dry land as you cut out their cattle or their beautiful
flocks of sheep, or fought for a city, or for women?'
    "So I spoke, and he answered me at once: 'O son
of Laertes, of the line of Zeus, resourceful Odysseus—
it was not Poseidon who overcame me, raising up the dreadful
385 blast of savage winds among my ships, nor enemy
men who harmed me on the dry land, but Aigisthos[101]
contrived my death and fate and killed me with the help
of my accursed wife! He invited me to his house and gave
me a meal, as you kill an ox at the manger! So I died
390 a wretched death. And my companions died in numbers
around me, like pigs with white teeth who are slaughtered in the house
of a rich and powerful man at a wedding feast,
or a potluck, or a thriving symposium. You've witnessed the death
of many men, either in single combat or in the strong press
395 of battle, but in your heart you would have pitied the sight of those
    things—
how we lay in the hall across the mixing-bowl and the tables
filled with food, and the whole floor drenched in blood.
But the most pitiful cry I heard came from Kassandra,
the daughter of Priam, whom the treacherous Klytaimnestra killed
400 next to me. I raised my hands, then beat them on the ground,
dying with a sword through my chest. But the bitch turned away,

---

[101] Agamemnon's cousin and the lover of Klytaimnestra. He is the son of Thyestes, the brother of Atreus, Agamemnon's father. In other versions (most famously Aeschylus' play *Agamemnon*), he is killed in the bathtub, not during a banquet.

and although I was headed to the house of Hades she would not
stoop to close my eyes nor to close my mouth!
There is nothing more shameless, more bitchlike, than a woman
405 who takes into her heart acts such as that woman devised—
a monstrous deed, she who murdered her wedded husband.
I thought I'd return welcomed by my children and slaves,
but she, knowing extraordinary wickedness, poured shame
on herself and on all women who shall come later, even on those
410 who do good deeds!'

               "So he spoke, but I answered: 'Yes, yes,
certainly Zeus with the loud voice has cursed the seed
of Atreus from the beginning, through the plots of women.
Many of us perished for Helen's sake, and Klytaimnestra fashioned
a plot against you when you were away.'

                    "So I spoke,
415 and he answered at once: 'And for this reason, be not
too trusting of even *your* wife! Don't tell her everything
that you know! Tell her some things and leave the rest unsaid.
But I don't think you will be murdered by your wife—she is too
discreet and carries only good thoughts in her heart,
420 this daughter of Ikarios, the wise Penelope. We left
her just a young bride when we went to war. She had
a babe at her breasts, just a little tyke, who now must be
counted among the number of men. How happy he will be
when his father, coming home, sees him, and he will greet
425 his father as is the custom. My own wife did not
allow me to feast my eyes on my son! She killed me
before that.

         "'And I will tell you something else,
and please consider it: Secretly, and not in the open, put
your boat ashore in the land of your fathers, for you can no longer
430 trust any woman. But come, tell me this and report it
accurately, whether you have heard my son Orestes is alive
in Orchomenos or in sandy Pylos, or even with Menelaos
in broad Sparta. For Orestes has not yet died
on the earth.'

            "So he spoke, but I answered: 'Son of Atreus,
435 why do you ask me these things? I don't know the truth of it,
whether he is alive or dead. It is an ill thing to speak words
as empty as the wind.'

"And so the two of us stood there
exchanging lamentations and pouring down warm tears.
Then came the breath-soul of Achilles, the son of Peleus,
440 and of the good Patroklos, and of Antilochos, and of Aiax,[102] the best
in form and stature of all the Danaans after Achilles, the good son
of Peleus.

      "The breath-soul of Achilles, the fast runner,
recognized me,
and groaning he spoke words that went like arrows: 'Son of Laertes,
of the line of Zeus, resourceful Odysseus—you wretch!
445 How will you top this plan for audacity? How have you dared
to come down to the house of Hades, where the speechless
dead live,
phantoms of men whose labors are done?'[103]

      "So he spoke,
but I answered him: 'O Achilles, son of Peleus, by far
the mightiest of the Achaeans, I came here out of need
450 for Teiresias, to see if he had advice about how I might come
home again to craggy Ithaca. I have not yet come to Achaia,
nor walked on my own land, but always I'm surrounded
by misfortune. But Achilles, no man in earlier times
or in those that came later is more fortunate than you. When you
were alive
455 we honored you like the gods, and now that you are here
you rule among the dead. Therefore do not be sad that you are dead,
O Achilles.'

      "So I spoke, and he answered me at once:
'Don't sing praise to me about death, my fine Odysseus! If I could live
on the earth, I would be happy to serve as a hired hand
460 to some other, even to some man without a plot of land,
one who has little to live on, than to be king among all the dead
who have perished! But come, tell me of my good son,
whether he followed to the war and became a leader or not.
Tell me of my father Peleus, if you know anything,

---

[102] Antilochos was a son of Nestor; this Aiax was the son of Telamon (not Aiax, son of Oileus). In the *Iliad*, Patroklos died trying to help the Achaeans; in the post-Iliadic tradition, Antilochos fell to Memnon, a Trojan ally from the East; in the *Odyssey* (following the Epic Cycle tradition), Telamonian Aiax killed himself for shame (see just below), as dramatized famously in Sophokles' play *Aiax*.

[103] Although Odysseus is standing beside a pit of blood on the shore of Ocean, the ghosts speak as if he is actually in the Underworld, and soon this will be Odysseus' own point of view.

465　whether he still holds honor among the many Myrmidons,
　　　or whether men deprive him of honor throughout Hellas
　　　and Phthia,[104] because old age has taken possession
　　　of his hands and feet. For I am not there to bear him aid
　　　beneath the rays of the sun, in such strength as I had
470　when at broad Troy I killed the best of their people
　　　defending the Argives. If in such strength I might come
　　　even for a short time to the house of my father,
　　　I would give pain to those who do him violence and deny him
　　　honor, cause to hate my strength and invincible hands!'
475　　　　"So he spoke, and I answered: 'Yes, I know nothing of Peleus,
　　　but I'll tell you everything I know about Neoptolemos, your son,
　　　just as you ask. I brought him in a hollow well-balanced
　　　ship from Skyros to the Achaeans who wear fancy shin guards.
　　　Whenever we took council about the city of Troy, he always
480　spoke first. His words were on the mark—only godlike Nestor
　　　and I surpassed him. But when we fought with bronze
　　　on the plain of the Trojans, he did not remain in the mass
　　　of men, not in the throng, but he ran forth to the front,
　　　yielding to none in his power. He killed many men
485　in dread battle, I could never tell all of them nor give them names,
　　　so many of the people did he kill defending the Argives.
　　　But what a warrior was that son of Telephos whom he slew
　　　with the bronze, I mean Eurypylos! And many of that man's
　　　　companions,
　　　the Keteians, were killed because of gifts desired by a woman![105]
490　Eurypylos was the best-looking man I ever saw, after the good
　　　　Memnon.[106]
　　　　　　　" 'When we, the captains of the Argives, were about
　　　to go down into the horse that Epeios made,[107] and I was given
　　　command over all, both to open and close the door
　　　of our strongly built ambush, then the other leaders and rulers

---

[104]　The Myrmidons ("ants," for unknown reasons) are the followers of the house of Peleus. Hellas is a territory in southern Thessaly near Phthia, Achilles' homeland. By the Classical Period, *Hellas* had come to designate all of Greece, but no one is sure why.

[105]　Priam bribed Eurypylos' mother with a golden vine made by Hephaistos to get Eurypylos to join the Trojan side. The Keteians, mentioned only here, are plausibly the "Hittites" of central Asia Minor, a great power in the Aegean Bronze Age.

[106]　A son of the goddess Dawn and Tithonos, brother of Priam. He was king of the Aithiopians (in Homer someplace east) and was killed by Achilles (outside the *Iliad*'s narrative).

[107]　He built the Trojan horse at Athena's instruction (though Odysseus later takes credit for it).

495 of the Danaans wiped away their tears and their limbs trembled
    beneath them. I never saw your son with my own eyes
    either turning pale in his beautiful skin nor wiping
    away a tear from his cheeks. He constantly begged
    me to let him go out of the horse. He kept handling the hilt
500 of his sword and his spear heavy with bronze. He wanted
    to lay waste the Trojans. And when we sacked the steep city
    of Priam, after taking his share, a noble reward, he went up
    into his ship unharmed, not struck with the sharp spear
    nor wounded in the hand-to-hand, such as often happens in war.
505 For Ares rages in confusion.'

            "So I spoke, and the breath-soul
    of Achilles, grandson of Aiakos, the fast runner, went off,
    taking long strides across the field of asphodel,[108] thrilled
    because I said his son was preeminent. Other breath-souls
    of the dead and gone now stood in a crowd. Each asked
510 about what was important to them. Only the breath-soul of Aiax,
    son of Telamon, stood apart, angry on account
    of the victory that I won over him in the contest for the arms
    of Achilles. Thetis, his revered mother, had set them
    as a prize.[109] The sons of the Trojans were the judges, also Pallas
515 Athena. I wish that I had never won in that contest
    for such a prize! On account of this armor the earth
    covered over so great a head, Aiax, who in comeliness
    and in the deeds of war was superior to the other Danaans,
    except for Achilles.

            "I spoke to him with honeyed words:
520 'Aiax, son of excellent Telamon, even in death
    you won't give up your anger on account of those accursed
    arms? The gods placed them as a calamity to the Argives.
    We lost such a tower of strength in you. The Achaeans
    lament your death ceaselessly, like that of Achilles,
525 son of Peleus. There is no other cause but Zeus, who thoroughly
    hated the army of the Danaan spearmen, who set on you
    your doom. But come now, king, so that you might hear

---

[108] A plant associated with the dead, planted on graves, and worn by Persephone as a crown.

[109] For whomever helped the most in recovering the body of her son, Achilles. Although Aiax deserved the armor, Odysseus somehow won the contest. Aiax then went mad and attacked a herd of sheep, thinking they were the Trojan captains. When he recovered his senses, he threw himself on his sword in shame.

my honest speech. Conquer your anger and your proud spirit!'

"So I spoke, but he did not answer me. He went

530 his way to Erebos, among the other breath-souls of men
who are dead and gone. He might have spoken to me
even though he was angry, or I to him,
but the spirit in my breast wanted to see the breath-souls
of others who had died.

"I saw Minos, the glorious son of Zeus,

535 holding his golden scepter, giving laws to the dead
from his seat, while they sat and stood around the king throughout
the house of Hades with its wide gates, asking for his judgments.[110]

"I saw huge Orion driving wild animals together
across the plain of asphodel, ones that he had himself

540 killed on the lonely mountains. He held in his hands
a club all of bronze, forever unbreakable.

"And I saw
Tityos, the son of Gaia, lying on the ground, sprawled
over nine acres. Two vultures sitting on either side
gnawed at his liver, plunging their heads into his intestines,

545 for he could not ward them off with his hands. For Tityos
tried to carry off Leto, the glorious wife of Zeus,
as she went toward Pytho, through Panopeus with its beautiful
places.[111]

"And I saw powerful Tantalos, suffering agony,
standing in a pool. The water came up to his chin.

550 He stood as if thirsty, but he could not take a drink.
Every time the old man stooped over, eager to drink,
the water would be guzzled up and disappear, and the dark earth
would appear around his feet all dry, as if as some god had made it so.
High leafy trees poured down fruit above his head—

555 pear trees and berry trees and apple trees with their shining fruit,
and sweet figs and luxuriant olive trees. But whenever the old man
would reach out to snare them with his hands, a wind would hurl
them to the shadowy clouds.[112]

---

[110] Odysseus seems to be inside the Underworld itself now. A catalogue of the "Denizens of the Underworld" follows. Minos was a legendary king of Crete and a judge in the Underworld.

[111] Tityos, a giant son of Gaia, was killed by Apollo and Artemis after he attempted to rape their mother, Leto—here called the wife of Zeus (who is usually Hera).

[112] Tantalos chopped up his son Pelops and served him to the gods to test their omniscience. He was reassembled and fled to southern Greece, giving his name to the Peloponnesos ("island of Pelops").

"And I saw Sisyphos suffering

terrible agonies, trying to raise a huge stone

560 with both his hands. Propping himself with hands

and feet, he tried to thrust the stone toward the crest

of a hill. But when he was about to push it over the top,

its mighty weight would turn it back, and the brutish stone

would roll down again to the plain. Then straining

565 he would thrust it back, as sweat flowed down from his limbs

and dust rose from his head.[113]

"Afterward I saw

the mighty Herakles, or a phantom of him—he who

takes his pleasure with the deathless gods at the banquet,

and has Hebe to wife, whose ankles are beautiful, the child

570 of great Zeus and Hera of the golden sandals.[114] About him

arose a clanging of the dead, like birds driven everywhere in terror.

Herakles was like the dark night, holding his bare bow

and an arrow on the string, glaring dreadfully, a man

about to shoot. The baldric around his chest was awesome—

575 a golden strap in which were worked wondrous things,

bears and wild boars and lions with flashing eyes,

and combats and battles and the murders of men. I would wish

that the artist did not make another one like it! He knew

who I was, and weeping he spoke words that went like arrows:

580 'Son of Laertes, of the line of Zeus, resourceful

Odysseus—Ah wretch, do you too lead an evil life,

such as I bore beneath the rays of the sun? Though I was the son

of Zeus, I had pain without limit. For I was bound to a man

far worse than I, who lay upon me difficult tasks.

585 Once he sent me to bring back the hound of Hades,

for he could think of no contest mightier than this. I carried

off the hound and led him out of the house of Hades.

Hermes was my guide, and Athena with the blue-gray eyes.'

"So speaking, Herakles went again to the house of Hades,

---

[113] It is not clear why dust should rise from Sisyphos' head. As with Tantalos, Homer does not mention the crime of Sisyphos (one tradition says he bound Death himself so that for a while no one died). He was the real father of Odysseus (not Laertes) according to a post-Homeric tradition, having seduced Odysseus' mother on her wedding night.

[114] Homer wants to show Herakles in the underworld but must deal with the tradition that he became a god and lives on Olympos, where he married Hebe ("youth"). Homer reconciles the two traditions by saying that the Herakles in the underworld was only a "phantom."

590 but I held my ground where I was, to see if another
   of the warriors who had died in the days of old might come.
      "I would have seen men of earlier times—and I wanted
   to see them, Theseus and Peirithoos, the glorious offspring of the gods,
   but before that the tribes of ten thousand dead gathered
595 around with a wondrous cry. Pale fear seized me—
   maybe the illustrious Persephone would send the Gorgon's head
   upon me, that great monster out of the house of Hades![115]
      "I went at once to the ship and I ordered my companions
   to embark, to loosen the stern cables. Quickly
600 they got on board and sat down on the benches. The wave
   of the stream bore the ship down the river Ocean. At first
   we rowed, then we ran before a fair breeze."

6.8. THE *HOMERIC HYMN TO DEMETER*

One of the major *Homeric Hymns* (for which see headnote to Part 3, document 9), the long *Hymn to Demeter* (*HH* 2)was composed some time in the mid-seventh century BCE. Demeter is the goddess of agriculture and a top-tier Olympian god, being the daughter of Rhea and Kronos and sibling of Hestia, Hera, Poseidon, Hades, and Zeus.

The hymn presents a complex set of themes combined into one single narrative. The abduction of Persephone, representing marriage as a kind of death and highlighting the painful separation of mother and daughter, is also an *aition* for the cycle of the seasons (tied to her absence and return); at the same time, the story focuses on Demeter's encounter with mortals at Eleusis and the establishment of her rites there. Hence, we have themes connected with natural phenomena and cosmic tensions (the boundaries between the realms of life and death, Demeter's challenge of Zeus' authority, her dominion over the land's fertility) tied with historical points of reference, such as Demeter's temple and cult at Eleusis and the famous Mysteries, which were carried out there throughout antiquity. These very popular initiation rites were, however, secretive, and their precise relationship with the hymn is not clear or agreed upon by scholars. Was the hymn itself created for or recited at the Eleusinian Mysteries? Does it also (or mainly) allude to the Athenian women's festival of the Thesmophoria, as suggested by some? What are the precise correlations between details in the text and specific rituals at the festival(s)? Some of the main allusions are briefly explained in the footnotes below, but the extensive discussion about all these issues cannot be summarized here (see Bibliography at the end of the volume).

[115] According to the familiar legend, there were three Gorgons, but only Medusa was mortal. The hero Perseus cut off Medusa's head, and anyone who looked at it was turned to stone. But Homer does not seem to connect the Gorgon with the legend of Perseus.

In other versions of the story (most importantly the Orphic one), the themes of seasonal changes and agriculture dominate, and in them Demeter kills the child in the fire and reveals to Triptolemos (represented as a boy) the gift of agriculture. In no other version, however, does she cause a famine. This theme in the hymn reminds one of the drought and famine inflicted on human beings by the gods in the Mesopotamian epic *Atrahasis* (see Part 2, document 1.a). The motif of the wandering goddess in search for her beloved daughter and her arrival at a nobleman's house is paralleled in the story of Isis and Osiris as narrated in Plutarch's work *On Isis and Osiris*, in which the goddess, searching for her dead brother and husband's casket, arrives at the home of the king of Byblos and acts in a very similar way, trying to make immortal the infant son of the queen (see document 6.5). The motif also famously appears in the story of Achilles, whose mother Thetis tried to immortalize him in various ways, depending on the version.

SOURCE: *Homeric Hymn to Demeter* (*HH 2*), translated and annotated by C. López-Ruiz.

Of Demeter, revered fair-haired goddess, I begin to sing, and of her slim-ankled daughter,[116] whom Aidoneus[117] snatched. For loud-thundering, far-sounding[118] Zeus gave her to him, when she was playing with the deep-bossomed daughters of Ocean, far from Demeter, the one of the golden sword and the splendid fruits, as she was picking flowers, roses and crocuses and beautiful violets, through a soft meadow, and also irises, and hyacinth and narcissus, which Gaia grew as a trap for the blossoming girl, by the will of Zeus, to please the host of many[119]; a marvelous and delightful flower, (10) an honor then for immortal gods and mortal people alike to see. Even from its roots a hundred buds had grown and produced the sweetest smell, so that the wide heaven above and the whole earth laughed, and the salty swell of the sea. And so she, amazed, reached out with both hands to grab the beautiful plaything; and the wide-pathed earth opened up by the plain of Nysa, and the lord, the host of many, jumped on her with his immortal horses, the one who has many names, son of Kronos.

Taking her against her will on his golden chariot, he led her away as she wailed; (20) she screamed with high pitched voice, calling out for her father, the highest and best son of Kronos. But no one either among immortals or mortal people heard her voice, not even the splendid fruit of the olives, except for the daughter of Persaios who perceived it from her cave, kind-minded Hekate of the bright veil, as well as Helios, the bright son of Hyperion, as the girl called for her father the son of Kronos; but he was far away, sitting apart from the gods, in his temple of many suppliants, receiving fine sacrifices from mortal people. (30) So he, the brother of her

---

[116] Persephone, also called Kore, "The Girl."

[117] Another name for Hades.

[118] The epithet used can mean either far (or wide) sounding or seeing. I translate them as two epithets related to thundering.

[119] A euphemistic epithet for Hades (he is also called Plouton, Latinized as Pluto, "the rich one").

father, ruler of many, host of many, carried her against her will, at the suggestion of Zeus, with his immortal horses; the son of Kronos of the many names.

As long as she could look upon the earth and the starry heaven and the sea of strong currents, rich in fish, and the rays of the sun, and she still hoped to see her revered mother and the tribes of ever-existing gods, so long hope calmed her great mind, distressed as she was . . . And the mountain heights and depths of the sea echoed with the voice of the goddess, and her mother, the Lady,[120] heard her.[121] (40) An acute pain took hold of her, deep in her heart, and she tore the head-dress around her divine hair with her own hands, she cast a dark veil upon both shoulders,[122] and rushed like a bird searching over both dry and wet land. But no one wanted to tell the truth to her, neither among gods nor among mortal people, not even one of the birds came to her as a truthful messenger. For nine days afterwards Lady Deo[123] went around the earth holding burning torches in her hands, and in her grief she did not taste ambrosia or the sweet drink of nectar, (50) neither did she wash her skin with water. But when the tenth light-giving Dawn came, Hekate came to meet her, holding a torch in her hands, in order give her the news, so she told the story and said:

"Lady Demeter, who brings the seasons, who grants splendid gifts: Which one of the celestial gods or of mortal people snatched Persephone and afflicted your dear heart? For I heard her voice, but I did not see with my eyes who it was; I am swiftly telling you absolutely everything."

So spoke Hekate; but to this she did not respond with a word, the daughter of fair-haired Rhea; (60) instead she quickly darted with her, bearing burning torches in her hands. They came to Helios, watcher of gods and men, and they stood in front of his horses and the bright one among goddesses said:

"Helios, respect me as a deity, you who are one, if indeed I ever warmed your heart and spirit by word or deed.[124] The child that I bore, sweet bloom of mine, of glorious beauty, her vehement voice I heard through the barren air, as of one being forced, but I did not see it with my eyes. But since you look down on the whole earth and over the sea from the radiant upper air with your rays, (70) tell me truly of my dear child, if you have seen her anywhere, who is it among gods or mortal people that took off after seizing her by force against her will, when she was away from me."

So she spoke, and the son of Hyperion[125] gave her an answer:

---

[120] The epithet *potnia* is a feminine rough equivalent of "lord" and is usually translated in English as "mistress," "lady," or "queenly" (I also translate it as "venerable"). I capitalize Lady to reflect its use as a title.

[121] Her second cry must have happened as she was entering the Underworld, which presumably was made explicit in some missing lines.

[122] A dark veil or cloak was used for mourning.

[123] A shortened name for Demeter.

[124] Note the intended use of a language of heating (instead of "cheering" or the like), corresponding to what Helios does (heating).

[125] Helios.

"Lady Demeter, daughter of Rhea of the noble mane, know you will; for indeed I revere you and also pity you in your grief for your slim-ankled child: no one other than cloud-gatherer Zeus is responsible among the immortals, who gave her to his own brother Hades to be called his robust wife. (80) So that one snatched her with his horses and led her with much wailing under the murky gloom. But put and end to your great wailing, goddess; neither should you bear such immense grief in vain at all; he is not an unseemly groom among the immortals, the lord of many, Aidoneus, your own brother and of the same seed; as for honor, he received his share when the triple division was drawn[126]: he dwells with those whom he was allotted to rule."

So speaking, he called to his horses and, under his taunt, they lightly carried off the swift chariot, like long-winged birds. (90) But a more dreadful and rabid pain reached her heart. Then, enraged at the dark-clouded son of Kronos, she abandoned the gathering of the gods and high Olympos, and went to the cities of people and their rich fields, blurring her divine appearance for a long time. And no one among men or deep-girded women recognized her as they looked at her, at least before she arrived at the house of sensible Keleos, who was at the time a lord of fragrant Eleusis.[127] And she sat near the road, full of sorrow in her heart, by the Maiden's Well, where the town's people would draw water in the shade; (100) for an olive shrub grew above it, resembling an old crone, who has been cut off from childbearing and the gifts of garland-loving Aphrodite, the sort who are nurses of law-giving kings' children and stewards of their echoing homes. The daughters of Keleos, son of Eleusinos saw her, as they came for the easily drawn water, so that they would carry it in bronze pitchers to the dear house of their father; four they were, like goddesses, in the flower of their youth: Kallidike and Kelisidike, and lovely Demo and Kallithoe, (110) who was born before them all. But they did not know her; for gods are not easily perceived by mortal beings. Standing next to her, they addressed to her winged words:

"Who and from where among people of old are you, old woman? Why on earth did you wander away from the city and do you not approach the houses? There, by the shady halls are women just of your age and younger ones, and they would befriend you both in word and deed."

So they said, and she, a queen among goddesses, gave them an answer:

"Dear children, whoever you are of the female-kind, greetings! (120) I will tell you about myself; for it is not unseemly to tell you the truth, since you are asking. Doso[128] is my name; for my venerable mother gave it to me; now I have come from Crete over the broad back of the sea, not wishing to, but pirate men carried me away

---

[126] Namely, the sea (Poseidon), the sky (Zeus), and the underworld (Hades).

[127] In other lines (155, 174–175) Keleos appears to be one among other rulers of the city. He is the son of Eleusinos, eponymous ancestor of the city of Eleusis, where there was a cult to him and his daughters.

[128] The reading of the name is uncertain, but most reconstruct a name having to do with "giving" (Doso, Dos, Doris, etc.).

against my will, by violent force. Then they put in with their swift ship at Thorikos,[129] and there the women landed on the shore all together, and even the men themselves started preparing a meal by the stern of the ship; but my heart was not longing for the soothing evening meal, (130) but instead, rushing secretly through the dark mainland, I escaped my arrogant masters, so that they would not carry me for sale (not having bought me) and enjoy the ransom. This is how I arrived here, wandering, and I do not know at all which land this is and who inhabits it. As for you, may all those who hold Olympian homes give you men as husbands and children to bear, just as parents desire; but have pity upon me, girls, . . . *(lacuna of 1 line)* (tell me) in all seriousness, dear children, whose house do I approach of a man or a woman, (140) so that I may work for them putting my mind to the kinds of things an aged woman can do? Holding a new-born child in my arms I would be a good nurse, and I would take care of the house too, and make the master's bed in the corner of the well-built chamber as well as help with the tasks of the wife."

So spoke the goddess; and at once the unwedded maiden replied to her, Kallidike, the most beautiful of the daughters of Keleos:

"Good mother, we humans endure the gifts of the gods by force, even if we suffer; for they are indeed much stronger. This information I will certainly offer to you (150) and name the men who have the great power of honor here and are first among the people, and who protect the veil of the city with their counsels and straight judgments.[130] They are shrewd Triptolemos, Dioklos, and Polyxeinos, as well as blameless Eumolpos and Dolichos and our own valiant father, and the wives of them all have tasks to manage in their houses; not one of them would keep you away from her house, without respect for your appearance at first sight; rather they will welcome you! For you are certainly godlike. (160) But if you wish, wait here, so we may go to the house of our father and tell our deep-girded mother Metaneira all this from beginning to end, in case she might bid you to come into our house and not look into any others. Her pampered son is being raised in the well-built palace, a late child welcomed with much joy. If you should raise him and he reaches the time of his youth, anyone of the female kind would easily envy you; so much would she pay you for your nursing."

So she spoke. And the goddess nodded with her head, (170) and so they filled with water the shinning vessels and carried them walking tall and proud. Swiftly they reached the great house of their father, and quickly they told their mother what they had seen and heard. And she bid them to go even more quickly and summon her for an enormous salary. And so, just like deer or calves in the spring season jump along the meadow after sating their hearts with pasture, they darted down the hollow road picking up the folds of their lovely robes; and their manes rushed around their shoulders like a crocus flower. And they found the illustrious goddess there, near the way, just where they had left her; (180) and right away they

---

[129] In northeast Attica. The distance between Thorikos and Eleusis could be reasonably covered by foot in a couple of days. Remains of a cult place dedicated to Demeter and Kore have been found at Thorikos.

[130] The veil or headdress stands metaphorically for the city's battlements (the city as a protected woman), as the ruling ability replaces military force.

led her to the dear house of their father, and she marched behind them, mourning in her heart, with her head covered, and the dark robe swirled around the goddess's delicate feet.

Soon they reached the house of Zeus' scion, Keleos, and they walked through the patio, where their venerable mother sat by a pillar that held the solid-made roof, holding a child under her bosom, her new offspring. The girls run to her, but the goddess as it happens stepped on the threshold and her head hit the roof-beam, and she filled the doorway with a divine radiance. (190) Awe and reverence and pale fear took hold of Metaneira. And she yielded her couch and bade her to take a seat. But Demeter, who brings the seasons, who grants splendid gifts, did not want to sit on the silky couch, but rather she remained silent, casting her beautiful eyes down, until diligent Iambe pitched for her a folding chair, and threw over it a purely white fleece. Sitting there, she held the veil in front of her face with her hands. For a long while she sat on the stool, speechless in her grief, and she did not acknowledge anyone, either by word or gesture, (200) but sat without laughing, without tasting food or drink, consumed by longing for her deep-girded daughter, until diligent Iambe, with jokes and making many funny gestures, caused the chaste lady to smile and laugh and have a happy spirit.[131] Indeed, she also improved her mood in later occasions. Then Metaneira offered her a cup filled with honey-sweet wine,[132] but she threw her head back; for she kept saying that it was not allowed for her to drink red wine, but instead she asked for barley and water to drink, mixed with tender pennyroyal. (210) And she, preparing the concoction,[133] provided it to the goddess, just as she had requested; accepting it out of respect, the great Lady . . . *(lacuna)*

Among them, well-girded Metaneira was the first to speak:

"Greetings, lady, for I have guessed you are surely not of base parents but noble ones; respect and grace are evident in your eyes, as though you were born from lawgiving kings. But we humans endure the gifts of the gods by force, even if we suffer; for their yoke lies on our neck. But now that you have come here, you shall partake in all I have. Nurse this child of mine, whom the gods granted to me late-born and unexpected, (220) but who is greatly loved by me. If you should raise him and he reaches the time of his youth, anyone of the female kind would easily envy you; so much would I pay you for your nursing."

And well-crowned Demeter in turn said to her:

"Many greetings to you too, lady, and may the gods provide you with great things. I will very gladly take your child in my arms as you are asking. I will raise him, and I do not expect any spell or the under-cutter to harm him because of his nurse's folly.

---

[131] Iambe is the personification (and eponym) of *iambos*, a verse used in invective or mocking poetry. Iambe's intervention probably included obscene gestures.

[132] The Greeks sweetened their wine with honey and mixed it with water and spices.

[133] A restoring drink with barley and spices was offered to welcome guests in Homeric scenes of *xenia*. She refused wine not so much because gods do not drink and eat what mortals do (she asks for another drink) but as a sign of humility. Drinking a beverage of this sort, called *kykeon*, was part of the rituals at Eleusis.

For I know an antidote much stronger than the wood-cutter,[134] (230) and I know a great safeguard against harmful spells."

After she spoke so, she received him in her fragrant bosom and her immortal arms; and his mother rejoiced in her heart. So she raised in the palace the glorious son of wise Keleos, Demophoon,[135] whom well-girded Metaneira had given birth to. And he thrived like a divine being, neither eating bread nor sucking (*lacuna of 1 line: the milk of his mother . . . by day?*) Demeter used to anoint him with ambrosia, as if he had been born from a god, breathing on him softly and holding him in her lap; during the night, however, she would hide him in the rage of the fire, just like a fire-brand, in secret from the child's parents; (240) and it caused great wonder how pre-cocious he kept showing himself, and how he resembled the gods. She would even have made him ageless and immortal, if it was not that well-girded Metaneira, in her foolishness, spying at night from the fragrant chamber, observed it; she shrieked and struck both thighs, terrified for her son, and was deeply distraught in her heart, so she wailed and uttered flying words:

"Son of mine, Demophoon, the stranger buries you in much fire, and she afflicts on me sorrow and horrible pain!"

(250) So she said wailing; and the brilliant among goddesses heard her. Enraged at her, beautifully-crowned Demeter, with her immortal hands cast Metaneira's dear child (whom she had born in the palace) away from her and onto the floor, after withdrawing him from the fire, terribly irritated in her heart, all the while she addressed well-girded Metaneira:

"You humans are ignorant and brainless when it comes to foreseeing the destiny of good or evil coming your way; so you too have been highly damaged by your own foolishness. For may the bitter water of the Styx, the oath of the gods, (260) know that I would have made your dear son deathless and ageless for all days and would have granted him imperishable honor. But now there is no way for him to avoid death and human fate. Yet his imperishable honor will survive forever, because he climbed up on my lap and slept in my arms. And then, each season, as the years revolve around him, the children of the Eleusinians will wage war and dire battle among each other forever more.[136] For I am always-revered Demeter, who provides immortals and mortals with benefits and joy. (270) But now come, let all the people provide *me* with a great temple and an altar below it, under the city and its steep walls but above Kallichoron on a protruding hill.[137] I will myself institute rites so that later on, performing them impeccably, you may appease my heart."

After saying so, the goddess changed in stature and appearance, shedding old age. Waves of beauty floated round and about her, a pleasant smell scattered from

---

[134] It is uncertain what the meaning of the "under-cutter" and the "wood-cutter" (or "herb-cutter") is.

[135] His name means "shinning for the people." He does not appear in other traditions or iconography connected with Eleusis, and in other stories he is replaced by Triptolemos, who appears here at the end of the poem among the leaders to whom she reveals her mysteries.

[136] Probably referring to a ritual battle enacted at a recurring festival in honor of Demophoon.

[137] The Telesterion or main building for the Eleusinian mysteries has been excavated precisely on a slope below the acropolis of Eleusis.

her fragrant robe, a light shone at a distance from the immortal skin of the goddess, and her blond mane spread over her shoulders. (280) So the sturdy home was filled with brightness, as if by lightning. Then she walked across and out of the palace, and Metaneira's knees gave out at once, and she remained speechless for a long while, and did not even remember to pick up from the floor her late-born child. But his sisters heard the miserable cry and sprung from each of their well-made beds: then one, picking the child up in her arms, placed him in her embrace, another one stirred up the fire, and yet another rushed with her delicate feet to get her mother up from the fragrant chamber. Gathering around him, they washed him as he gasped in agony, while they surrounded him with love; (290) but his mood was not soothed, for surely lesser nannies and nurses were holding him.

All night long, the women, trembling with fear, propitiated the glorious deity[138]; but as soon as dawn appeared, they told everything truthfully to mighty Keleos, just as beautifully-crowned Demeter had instructed. After that, summoning people from many areas into the agora,[139] he ordered that they build a rich temple and an altar to Demeter of the noble mane, on a protruding hill. And they obeyed right away and paid attention to what he said, so they built it just as he instructed; (300) and it grew according to the will of the deity. After they had finished and withdrawn from their toil, they naturally walked to go each to his home; but blond Demeter, sitting there, far away from all the blessed ones, remained consuming herself with longing for her deep-girded daughter. And so she inflicted on mankind the most horrible and miserable year on the bountiful earth; and the earth did not even produce seed, for well-crowned Demeter hid it. Many times the oxen dragged in vain the crooked plough through the furrows, and many times white barley fell upon the earth to no purpose. (310) And she might have also at that point destroyed the race of mortal people, and deprived those who hold Olympian homes of the glorious honor of offerings and sacrifices, had Zeus not realized and deliberated in his heart. First he hurried golden-winged Iris[140] to summon Demeter, the one of the noble mane and lovely appearance. So he said, and she obeyed Zeus, the dark-clouded son of Kronos, and she ran swiftly with her feet across the two realms. So she arrived at the citadel of fragrant Eleusis and found Demeter in the temple with her dark cloak, (320) and addressed her issuing winged words:

"Demeter, father Zeus is calling you, he who has eternal knowledge, to come with the tribe of gods who are born forever. But come, lest my word from Zeus be unfulfilled."

So she said supplicating; but her heart was not convinced. So after that the father put in front of her all the blessed gods who are forever; and, going one after the other, they kept summoning her and they offered her many and gorgeous gifts, and whichever honors she might want to choose among the immortals; but not one of them managed to bend her feelings and her thoughts, (330) as she was angry in

---

[138] An all-night ritual conducted by women only took place at both Eleusis and the Athenian festival of the Thesmophoria, also in honor of Demeter.

[139] The commercial and civic center of the city.

[140] A daughter of Ocean, about whom see note 120 on page 203.

her heart and firmly disregarded their speeches. For she kept saying that she would never set foot on fragrant Olympos, nor allow seed to spring from the earth, until she saw her beautiful-faced daughter with her own eyes.

But at last when loud-thundering, far-sounding Zeus heard it, he sent the Argos-slayer[141] of the golden staff to Erebos,[142] so that he, persuading Hades with smooth words, might bring back pure Persephone out of the foggy gloom, into the light, to join the divine beings, so that her mother, seeing her with her own eyes, might put a stop to her wrath. (340) And Hermes did not disobey, but immediately rushed down precipitously under the caverns of the earth, leaving his seat on Olympos. And he found the lord inside his home, sitting on a couch with his modest wife, very unwilling though she was, out of longing for her mother (but she, far away, . . . [143]). Standing close by, powerful Argos-slayer spoke out:

"Dark-haired Hades, you who rule over those who have perished, father Zeus commanded that you let noble Persephone out of Erebos to join them, (350) so that her mother, seeing her with her own eyes will cease from her wrath and her terrible anger towards the immortals, since she is contriving a huge plan, to destroy the fragile human race, born from the earth, by hiding the seed under the earth, and so to completely do away with the honors due to the gods. For she is throwing a horrible fit, and does not mingle with the gods, instead sitting apart inside her fragrant temple, after she took hold of the rocky citadel of Eleusis."

So he said; and the lord of those under the earth, Aidoneus, smiled with his eyebrows and did not disobey the ordinance of king Zeus. For right away he bid sensible Persephone:

(360) "Go, Persephone, by your mother of the dark robe; go keeping a friendly temper and spirit in your chest, and don't be somehow too upset (no more than the others). Surely among the immortals I will not be an unfitting husband, father Zeus' own brother! As long as you are with me,[144] you will be mistress over all that lives and moves, and you will hold the greatest honors among immortals, and forever more there will be a punishment for those who offend you, who might not propitiate your temper with sacrifices, performing the rites impeccably and delivering fitting gifts."

(370) So he said; and sensible Persephone rejoiced, immediately jumping out of happiness; but he in turn gave her gave her a sweet pomegranate seed to eat, in secret, after peering around him, so that she would not remain all her days there, with revered Demeter of the dark robe.[145] Then in front of them Aidoneus, the lord of many, harnessed his immortal horses to the golden chariot. She mounted on the vehicle and the mighty Argos-slayer by her, grabbing the reins and whip between his

[141] Hermes.

[142] "Darkness," standing for Hades.

[143] The text is corrupted in this line and has not been satisfactorily reconstructed.

[144] The adverb in Greek here can mean "here" (in Hades), "there" (on earth), or more generally "in this/that situation" (with me, being my wife).

[145] The pomegranate fruit was associated with blood and mortality and marriage, with virginity (and loss of it), and with fertility, all of which are pertinent here. The idea that eating in the Underworld binds you to it is popular in folktale also in other cultures.

own hands, zoomed through the halls, and the two horses did not fly unwillingly. (380) Swiftly they completed the long way, and not even the sea, nor the water of the rivers, nor the grassy valleys held back the course of the immortal horses, not even the mountain-peaks, but above them they cut through the deep air as they went. And he stopped them as he led them where well-crowned Demeter remained, in front of her fragrant temple. And when she saw them she rushed like a Maenad[146] through a mountain shaded with woods.[147] And Persephone, for her part, when she saw the beautiful eyes of her mother, jumped down to run, leaving chariot and horses, and fell on her neck wrapped in an embrace. (390) But even as she was holding her dear child in her arms, at once her heart suspected some trick, and she naturally feared terribly, interrupting their hugging, and immediately questioned her:

"My child, surely you haven't eaten any food while you were below, have you? Speak up, don't hide it, so that both of us may know. For, if so, you may dwell with me and your father, the dark-clouded son of Kronos, coming up from hateful Hades and honored by all the immortals. But if you have eaten any, going back under the caverns of the earth you will live there for a third part of the seasons in a year, (400) and the other two with me and the other immortals. Every time the earth blooms with well-scented spring flowers of all sorts, then you come up again, a great marvel for gods and mortal people. Also, with what trick did the powerful host of many deceive you?"

And most beautiful Persephone responded to her in turn:

"Then I will tell you everything in all truth, mother: when Hermes came to me, as a helper, as a swift messenger from my father the son of Kronos and the other celestial ones (saying) that I come out of Erebos, so that you, seeing me with your own eyes (410) might cease from your wrath and your terrible anger towards the immortals, I jumped out of happiness, but then he threw at me a seed of pomegranate, sweet food, and though I was unwilling he made me eat it by force. But I will tell you how, snatching me by the astute design of the son of Kronos, my father, he set out, taking me under the caverns of the earth, and I will show everything as you ask: We are all together in a lovely meadow,[148] Leukippe, Phaino and Elektra, Ianthe, Melite, Iache, Rhodeia, Kalirhoe, (420) Melobosis, Tyche and also beautiful-faced Okyrhoe, Chryseis, Ianeira, Akaste, Admete and Rhodope, Plouto and lovely Kalypso, also Styx, Ourania, charming Galaxaure, battle-stirring Pallas and arrow-pouring Artemis. We are playing and picking delightful flowers with our hands: delicate crocus mixed with irises and hyacinth, and also blooms of roses and lilies, a marvel to see, and a narcissus, which the broad earth grew just like a crocus. So I was cutting it with joy, when the earth opened up under me, (430) and from it rushed out the mighty lord, host of many. Then he left, carrying me in a golden chariot,

---

[146] A female worshipper of Dionysos, whose cult was famous for causing a state of frenzy and wild behavior (see Part 3, document 10).

[147] The following lines, up to line 400, are partly damaged, and translation is based on a hypothetical restoration (following the Oxford edition).

[148] The list that follows corresponds in part with the longer list of daughters of Ocean in Hesiod's *Theogony*, 349 ff. (see Part 1, document 5).

greatly unwilling, and I naturally screamed with a loud voice. I am declaring all this truthfully to you, filled with sorrow though I am."

Then all day long, with harmonious spirit, they spent warming each other's hearts with many hugs, and their spirits gradually put the anger away; and so they kept receiving and giving joy to one another. And Hekate of the bright veil came near them and embraced many times the daughter of holy Demeter; (440) and from that day, the lady became her companion and comrade. Then loud-thundering, far-sounding Zeus sent fair-haired Rhea, Demeter's own mother, as a messenger to them, so that she would take the dark-robed one to join the tribes of gods, for he promised to grant her whichever honors she might choose among the immortal gods; and he gave his consent that the girl be under the foggy gloom one third of the year-cycle and two with her mother and the other immortals. So he said, and the goddess[149] did not disobey the messages from Zeus. Quickly she hurried down the peaks of Olympos (450) and arrived directly at Rharion,[150] a fertile, rich arable land before, but now not at all fertile. Instead it lay undisturbed, all leafless; for the white barley was hidden, due to the designs of beautiful-ankled Demeter. But later on it would rapidly wave with tall ears of corn, as spring advanced, and in the plain the rich furrows would be heavy with grain-stalks, and they would be bound in sheaves. It was there she first set foot from the barren ether; and joyfully they saw each other, and they were thrilled in their heart. And thus spoke to her Rhea of the bright veil:

(460) "Come here my daughter; loud-thundering, far-sounding Zeus summons you to join the tribes of gods, for he promised to grant you whichever honors you might want among the immortal gods, and he gave his consent that the girl be under the foggy gloom one third of the year-cycle and two with you and the other immortals. He assured it would be thus accomplished, and nodded with his head. But come, my daughter, and pay heed to me, and do not be excessively, stubbornly mad at the dark-clouded son of Kronos, but at once make life-giving grain grow for mankind."

(470) So she said, and well-crowned Demeter did not disobey, but at once she made the grain come up from the arable soil. And the whole wide earth was heavy with leaves and flowers. Then, going to the law-giving chiefs, Triptolemos, horse-driving Diokles, mighty Eumolpos and Keleos the people's leader, she showed them the performance of her rites and instructed her mysteries to all (to Triptolemos and Polyxeinos and besides to Diokles[151]), her sacred rites, which are not to be transgressed in any way, or inquired into or spread by rumor; for a kind of great awe for the gods restrains the tongue.[152] (480) Blessed is the one who has seen these rites among earthly people; but the uninitiated in the mysteries, the one with no part

---

[149] Rhea.

[150] A rich plain near Eleusis, the grain products of which are mentioned by the sources in connection with Eleusinian rituals and games.

[151] This line might be a later addition as it is redundant.

[152] In other traditions Demeter gave agriculture to men (in some versions specifically to Triptolemos, who appears as a child in iconography), though that theme would have posed logical problems (how did they then lose agriculture if they did not have it yet?) and presupposes a different stage of human development previous to the one depicted in this hymn.

in them, never has a share of the same things when he perishes under the foggy gloom.

After the radiant among goddesses had instructed all this, they set out to go to Olympos, to join the assembly of the other gods. There they dwell by Zeus, who loves thunder, as holy and revered goddesses. Greatly blessed is the one among earthly people whom those two are disposed to love; for quickly they send Wealth, a god of the hearth, to his great house, who grants abundance to mortal people.

(490) But come now, you two who hold the land of fragrant Eleusis and Paros, surrounded by sea-currents, and rocky Antron[153]; you mistress of glorious gifts, bringer of seasons, Queen Deo, you yourself and your daughter, gorgeous Persephone, in return for my song, benevolently grant me some heart-pleasing goods. For I shall remember both you and another song.

6.9. INSTRUCTIONS FOR THE HEREAFTER: AN ORPHIC GOLD TABLET

Together with the Derveni Papyrus (Part 1, document 6), the so-called Gold Tablets are the most important discovery in the field of Greek religion in modern times. These Greek texts are engraved on thin gold plates or leaves that were buried with men and women who presumably were initiates in one or several mystery cults, such as those of Dionysos, Demeter-Persephone (of the Eleusinian type), and possibly others. An important group of the tablets originated in Greek communities in Italy (Magna Graecia), with five tablets from Thurii, one from Hipponium, one from Petelia, as well as one from Rome and one from Sicily. Other tablets have been found in Crete, as well as in the northern Peloponnese and in northern Greece (Thessaly and Macedonia). There are thirty-nine published tablets so far.

The first tablet surfaced in Naples in 1834 on the "black market" and is thought to come from Petelia (Figure 12). Soon other tablets, often found in excavations, provided the funerary context for the enigmatic texts, and the first comprehensive studies appeared during the early twentieth century. The addition of more tablets and our better understanding of Greek mystery cults and Orphism (including the Derveni Papyrus) have resulted in a recent boom of new editions and publications on the subject.

The details of what function they served still elude us. There is, for instance, no literary source that mentions these tablets, much less explains how they worked. Some seem to be mnemonic devices, specifically the longer ones, offering "short-cuts," as it were, to help the soul find the right path in the hereafter. Others are very brief, bearing a name and a few words (e.g., "To Persephone, Poseidippos, pious initiate"), and these are categorized as "proxies" and are "intended to speak on behalf of the soul."[154] Whatever their type, they were aids

---

[153] These are presumably important places of cult to the two goddesses, although this is only attested for Paros.

[154] Johnston in Graf and Johnston (2007: 95).

for the soul in its journey to the afterlife. Though the ones that have survived are made of gold, and therefore belonged to individuals of rank, similar devices may have been made of leather, papyrus, wood, or other more affordable perishable materials.

These texts for the afterlife journey have been compared with the *Book of the Dead*, and similar mortuary practices might have been widespread in other areas of the Mediterranean. The Derveni Papyrus itself, with a commentary on an Orphic theogony, was thrown in the funerary pyre that consumed its presumed owner. In turn, the eschatology reflected in the Gold Tablets is well rooted in Greek ideas: Their connection with Bacchic rites is explicit (see the mention of *bakkhoi* in the tablet here), as well as with Persephone and her "special" treatment of the initiated in her rites. Other ideas and allusions point to Orphism (on which see Part 1, document 6), in itself a theological-philosophical movement connected with the Eleusinian and Dionysiac rites (see Figure 11). This connection is more obvious in the set of bone plaques from Olbia (on the northern shore of the Black Sea, today's Ukraine) dated to the fifth century BCE, where the names of Dionysos and "Orphic" or "Orphics" appear among other scattered words ("life," "death," "truth"). Similarities with Pythagorean and Platonic ideas about the soul's destiny after life, such as those represented in the "Myth of Er" (Part 7, document 5), are also evident. The precise connection between the tablets and these religious and intellectual movements, however, is still far from clear, not least because mystery cults and initiation groups were by definition secretive and exclusive.

The following tablet, one of the long type, is the oldest so far, coming from Hipponion (Calabria, southern Italy) and dating to ca. 400 BCE. Now in the Archaeological Museum of Vibo, the gold leaf was folded and placed on the upper chest of the skeleton. Probably it originally hung from the deceased's neck by a string (in the way in which amulets were worn).

SOURCE: Gold Tablet from Hipponium (based on the Greek text in Graf and Johnston 2007, tablet n.2), translated and annotated by C. López-Ruiz.

1. This is the task of Memory,[155] when you are about to die,
    (going) to the well-built house of Hades. To the right, there is a spring,
    and next to it stands a white cypress.
4. Going down there, the souls of the dead refresh themselves.[156]
    Do not come close to this spring, not even near!
    Further ahead you will find, from the Lake of Memory,
    cold water pouring forth; but there are guards in front of it.
8. And they will ask you with subtle mind,

---

[155] Mnemosyne. Cf. her role in Hesiod's *Thegony* (Ch.1, section 5), as mother of the Muses and underlying aid for the epic poet.

[156] The words for souls (*psychai, psykai* in the local dilect) and the verb "cool/refresh themselves" (*psychontai*, from the verb *psycho*) not only sound similar but are etymologically related (the soul is conveyed as a breeze of air).

what exactly you are seeking in the darkness of gloomy Hades.

Say: "I am the son of Earth, and of starry Sky.[157]

I am dry[158] with thirst and am perishing; but quickly give me

12. cold water to drink, from the Lake of Memory."

And surely they will announce you to the underground King[159];

and surely they will give you to drink from the Lake of Memory.

And surely you too, having drunk, will walk the way, the sacred one
on which

16. also other initiates and *bakkhoi* march, illustrious ones.

6.10. CYBELE AND ATTIS, FROM ARNOBIUS, *ADVERSUS NATIONES*, BOOK 5

Arnobius was a teacher of Latin rhetoric from Sicca Veneria in Numidia (then in the Roman province of Africa Proconsularis, modern El-Kef in today's Tunisia). He converted to Christianity from paganism around 295 CE, which led him to write the work entitled *Adversus Nationes* ("against the Nations," that is, against the pagans) in seven books, also known as *Adversus Gentes*. In this apologetic work, more influenced by Platonic and Stoic ideas than by Christian theology proper, Arnobius defends the Christian faith against those blaming it for the wrath of the gods and the demise of the Roman world. While he assumes the (pagan) gods exist, he subordinates them to the higher Christian God. Intertwined with his religious debate are multiple references to pagan beliefs and cults, such as this one of Attis, which he traces to specific sources and to which he then adds his interpretation and commentaries. Even though this is an anti-pagan and late source, it contains the longest account of the myth and seems to preserve at least some elements from the older Phrygian version, which Pausanias (7.17.10–12) seems to follow as well (although with Agdistis standing in place of Cybele). In other variants (especially in Ovid's *Fasti* and *Metamorphoses*, Book 10.86–105) there are allusions to Attis' transformation into a tree and to his death due to the attack of a boar. They all contain the motif of self-mutilation.

The cult of Attis can be traced to the Phrygian city of Pessinos in Asia Minor, where the figure is linked with the local and divinized Mount Agdistis, in turn identified at some point with the goddess Cybele, an Anatolian mother goddess, also called in antiquity the Great Goddess and the Mother of the Gods. The castration of Attis in the story is an *aition* for the castrated devotees of Cybele

---

[157] Ge/Gaia (in this dialect Ga) and Ouranos.

[158] The adjective here (*auos*) is masculine, even though the tablet was interred with the body of a woman.

[159] That is, Hades. The text reads "king" (*besilei*) but some scholars think it should be corrected to "queen" (*basileia*) since she (Persephone) is the one mentioned in the other texts and it would fit the meter better. This detail supports the idea of a textual tradition for the tablets.

called *korybantes*, in Rome called *galli* ("Gauls"). The cult to Cybele, with her companion Attis, extended to Lydia early on, and by the fifth century BCE it was introduced in Greece, where she was received as a combination of a mother earth goddess (like Gaia/Rhea) and an agriculture goddess (like Demeter). She was brought to Rome in 205–204 BCE, in the form of a baityl (an uncarved cultic stone) that represented her. There she became the Magna Mater, though her cult only became widely popular from the first century CE onward.

SOURCE: Arnobius, *Adversus Nationes*, Book 5.5–7. A. H. Bryce and H. Campbell, *The Seven Books of Arnobius' Adversus Gentes* (Edinburgh, 1871), with minor modifications.

(5) In Timotheus, who was no mean mythologist, and also in others equally well informed, the birth of the Great Mother of the Gods, and the origin of her rites, are thus detailed, being derived (as he himself writes and suggests) from learned books of antiquities, and from [his acquaintance with] the most secret mysteries: — Within the confines of Phrygia, he says, there is a rock of unheard-of wildness in every respect, the name of which is Agdus, so named by the natives of that district. Stones taken from it, as Themis by her oracle had enjoined,[160] Deucalion and Pyrrha threw upon the earth, at that time emptied of men; from which this Great Mother, too, as she is called, was fashioned along with the others, and animated by the Deity. Her, given over to rest and sleep on the very summit of the rock, Jupiter assailed with lewdest desires. But when, after long strife, he could not accomplish what he had proposed to himself, he, baffled, spent his lust on the stone. This the rock received, and with many groanings Acdestis[161] is born in the tenth month, being named from his mother rock. In him there had been resistless might, and a fierceness of disposition beyond control, a lust made furious, and [derived] from both sexes. He violently plundered and laid waste; he scattered destruction wherever the ferocity of his disposition had led him; he regarded not gods or men, nor did he think anything more powerful than himself; he had contempt for earth, heaven, and the stars.

(6) Now, when it had been often considered in the councils of the gods, by what means it might be possible either to weaken or to curb his audacity, Liber, the rest hanging back, takes upon himself this task. With the strongest wine he drugs a spring much resorted to by Acdestis, where he had been wont to assuage the heat and burning thirst roused [in him] by sport and hunting. Hither runs Acdestis to drink when he felt the need; he gulps down the draught too greedily into his gaping veins. Overcome by what he is quite unaccustomed to, he is in consequence sent fast asleep. Liber is near the snare [which he had set]; over his foot he throws one end of a halter formed of hairs, woven together very skillfully; with the other end he lays hold of his privy members. When the fumes of the wine passed off, Acdestis starts up furiously, and his foot dragging the noose, by his own strength he robs himself of his sex; with the tearing asunder of [these] parts there is an

---

[160] Also, Ovid (*Met.* 1. 321) and others speak of Themis as the first to give oracular responses.

[161] In the Greek versions (e.g., Pausanias), Agdistis.

immense flow of blood; both[162] are carried off and swallowed up by the earth; from them there suddenly springs up, covered with fruit, a pomegranate tree, seeing the beauty of which, with admiration, Nana,[163] daughter of the king or river Sangarius, gathers and places in her bosom [some of the fruit]. By this she becomes pregnant; her father shuts her up, supposing that she had been debauched, and seeks to have her starved to death; she is kept alive by the Mother of the Gods with apples, and other food,[164] [and] brings forth a child, but Sangarius[165] orders it to be exposed. One Phorbas having found the child, takes it home, brings it up on goats' milk; and as handsome fellows are so named in Lydia, or because the Phrygians in their own way of speaking call their goats *attagi*, it happened in consequence that [the boy] obtained the name Attis. Him the Mother of the Gods loved exceedingly, because he was of most surpassing beauty; and (so did) Acdestis, [who was] his companion, as he grew up fondling him, and bound [to him] by wicked compliance with his lust in the only way now possible, leading him through the wooded glades, and presenting him with the spoils of many wild beasts, which the boy Attis at first said boastfully were won by his own toil and labor. Afterwards, under the influence of wine, he admits that he is both loved by Acdestis, and honored by him with the gifts brought from the forest; whence it is unlawful for those polluted by [drinking] wine to enter into his sanctuary, because it discovered his secret.

(7) Then Midas, king of Pessinus, wishing to withdraw the youth from so disgraceful an intimacy, resolves to give him his own daughter in marriage, and caused the [gates of the] town to be closed, that no one of evil omen might disturb their marriage joys. But the Mother of the Gods, knowing the fate of the youth, and that he would live among men in safety [only] so long as he was free from the ties of marriage, that no disaster might occur, enters the closed city, raising its walls with her head, which began to be crowned with towers in consequence. Acdestis, bursting with rage because of the boy's being torn from himself, and brought to seek a wife, fills all the guests with frenzied madness: the Phrygians shriek aloud, panic-stricken at the appearance of the gods; a daughter of adulterous Gallus[166] cuts off her breasts; Attis snatches the pipe borne by him who was goading them to frenzy; and he, too, now filled with furious passion, raving franticly [and] tossed about, throws himself down at last, and under a pine tree mutilates himself, saying, "Take these[167] Acdestis, for which you have stirred up so great and terribly perilous commotions." With the streaming blood his life flies; but the Great Mother of the Gods gathers the parts which had been cut off, and throws earth on them, having first covered them, and wrapped them in the garment of the dead. From the blood which had flowed springs a flower, the violet, and with this the (pine) tree is girt.

---

[162] The genital parts and the blood.

[163] Nata in the manuscript, but in another passage and other writers the name is Nana.

[164] Some editors read "berries" here.

[165] The manuscript reads "sanguinarius" ("blood-thirsty") but the traditional name, restored by most editors, is Sangarius.

[166] Probably part of this chapter has been lost, as the epithet "adulterous" is not explained and this Gallus appears later as if previously introduced.

[167] Referring to his genitalia.

Thence the custom began and arose, whereby you even now veil and wreath with flowers the sacred pine. The virgin who had been the bride (whose name, as Valerius the pontifex relates, was Ia) veils the breast of the lifeless [youth] with soft wool, sheds tears with Acdestis, and slays herself. After her death her blood is changed into purple violets. The Mother of the Gods shed tears also, from which springs an almond tree, signifying the bitterness of death. Then she bears away to her cave the pine tree, beneath which Attis had unmanned himself; and with Acdestis joining in her wailings, she beats and wounds her breast, [pacing] round the trunk of the tree now at rest. Jupiter is begged by Acdestis that Attis may be restored to life: he does not permit it. What, however, fate allowed, he readily grants, that his body should not decay, that his hairs should always grow, that the least of his fingers should live, and should be kept ever in motion; content with which favors, [it is said] that Acdestis consecrated the body in Pessinus, [and] honored it with yearly rites and priestly services.

6.11. ADONIS, FROM OVID, *METAMORPHOSES*, BOOK 10

In the following passage, Ovid (see headnote to Part 1, document 10) narrates the birth of Adonis from the tree into which pregnant Myrrha had been transformed after her incestuous relationship with her father Cinyras (see Part 5, document 17). Ovid's version also tells us about the love of Venus for Adonis and his untimely death by a boar's attack.

There are multiple surviving stories about the origins, life, and death of Adonis. In Apollodorus' version (*Library* 3.14.4), he is the son of Theias and Smyrna, and Aphrodite (Venus) entrusts the child in a box to Persephone, who also falls in love with him and refuses to give him back. Zeus decides to divide him among the rivals, allowing him to stay one third of the year by himself, one third with Aphrodite, and one third with Persephone (though the youth chooses to share his one third with Aphrodite).

Although his precise origin is uncertain, the god seems to be of North-West Semitic origin, probably Phoenician, as his name can be understood as "Lord" (*'adon*; cf. Adonai in the Hebrew Bible) and a cult to Adonis flourished in Byblos (Phoenicia) and Cyprus, from where it was adopted in Athens and Alexandria. He was worshipped by women, who mourned his death and celebrated his return to life annually in different ways and at different times of the year, depending on each city's tradition. His story and nature is very similar to that of the Babylonian Dumuzi/Tammuz (see document 6.2), and he is clearly a god of vegetation who falls into the group of "dying and rising gods" especially popular in (though not restricted to) the eastern Mediterranean, such as Tammuz, Baal (Canaanite), Melqart (Phoenician), Osiris (Egyptian), Attis (Phrygian), Persephone and Dionysos (Greek), and even Odin in Norse mythology.

The narrator of this episode is Orpheus, as in most of Book 10 of the *Metamorphoses*.

SOURCE: Ovid, *Metamorphoses*, Book 10.503–739. F. J. Miller, *Ovid, Metamorphoses* (Loeb Classical Library, Cambridge, MA and London, 1921, 2nd ed.), with minor modifications.

But the misbegotten child had grown within the wood, and was now seeking a way by which it might leave its mother and come forth. The pregnant tree swells in mid-trunk, the weight within straining on its mother. The birth-pangs cannot voice themselves, nor can Lucina be called upon in the words of one in travail. Still, like a woman in agony, the tree bends itself, groans repeatedly, and is wet with falling tears. Pitying Lucina stood near the groaning branches, laid her hands on them, and uttered charms to aid the birth. Then the tree cracked open, the bark was rent asunder, and it gave forth its living burden, a wailing baby-boy. The Naiads laid him on soft leaves and anointed him with his mother's tears. Even Envy would praise his beauty, for he looked like one of the naked loves portrayed on canvas. But, that dress may make no distinction, you should either give the one a light quiver or take it from the other.

Time glides by imperceptibly and cheats us in its flight, and nothing is swifter than the years. That son of his sister and his grandfather,[168] who was but lately concealed within his parent tree, but lately born, then a most lovely baby-boy, is now a youth, now man, now more beautiful than his former self; now he excites even Venus' love, and avenges his mother's passion. For while the goddess' son,[169] with quiver on shoulder, was kissing his mother, he chanced unwittingly to graze her breast with a projecting arrow. The wounded goddess pushed her son away with her hand; but the scratch had gone deeper than she thought, and she herself was at first deceived. Now, smitten with the beauty of a mortal, she cares no more for the borders of Cythera, nor does she seek Paphos, girt by the deep sea, nor fish-haunted Cnidos, nor Amathus, rich in precious ores. She stays away even from the skies; Adonis is preferred to heaven. She holds him fast, she is his companion, and though her wont has always been to take her ease in the shade, and to enhance her beauty by fostering it, now, over mountain ridges, through the woods, over rocky places set with thorns, she ranges with her garments girt up to her knees after the manner of Diana. She also cheers on the hounds and pursues those creatures which are safe to hunt, such as the headlong hares, or the stag with high-branching horns, or the timid doe; but from strong wild boars she keeps away, and from ravenous wolves, and she avoids bears, armed with claws, and lions reeking with the slaughter of cattle.

She (Venus) warns you, too, Adonis, to fear these beasts, if only it were of any avail to warn. "Be brave against timorous creatures," she says; "but against bold creatures boldness is not safe. Do not be rash, dear boy, at my risk; and do not provoke those beasts which nature has well armed, lest your glory be at great cost to me. Neither youth nor beauty, nor the things which have moved Venus, move lions and bristling boars and the eyes and minds of wild beasts. Boars have the force of a lightning stroke in their curving tusks, and the impetuous wrath of tawny lions is irresistible. I fear and hate them all." When he asks her why, she says: "I will tell, and you shall marvel at the monstrous outcome of an ancient crime. But now I am weary with my unaccustomed toil; and see, a poplar, happily at hand, invites us with

---

[168] Adonis was the son of Myrrha and her father Cinyras, hence the double family relations (she is his sister and mother, his father is his grandfather).

[169] Cupid.

its shade, and here is grassy turf for couch. I would fain rest here on the grass with you." So saying, she reclined upon the ground and, pillowing her head against his breast and mingling kisses with her words she told the following tale . . .

(559–708 skipped; Venus tells Adonis the tale of Atalanta and Hippomenes, who were transformed into lions by the goddess Cybele.)

(Continuation in 708–739, end of Book 10:)

Thus the goddess warned and through the air, drawn by her swans, she took her way; but the boy's manly courage would not brook advice. It chanced his hounds, following a well-marked trail, roused up a wild boar from his hiding-place; and, as he was rushing from the wood, the young grandson of Cinyras pierced him with a glancing blow. Straightway the fierce boar with his curved snout rooted out the spear wet with his blood, and pursued the youth, now full of fear and running for his life; deep in the groin he sank his long tusks, and stretched the dying boy upon the yellow sand. Borne through the middle air by flying swans on her light car, Cytherea had not yet come to Cyprus, when she heard afar the groans of the dying youth and turned her white swans to go to him. And when from the high air she saw him lying lifeless and weltering in his blood, she leaped down, tore both her garments and her hair and beat her breasts with cruel hands. Reproaching fate, she said: "But all shall not be in your power. My grief, Adonis, shall have an enduring monument, and each passing year in memory of your death shall give an imitation of my grief. But your blood shall be changed to a flower. Or was it once allowed to you, Persephone, to change a maiden's form to fragrant mint,[170] and shall the change of my hero, offspring of Cinyras, be grudged to me?" So saying, with sweet-scented nectar she sprinkled the blood; and this, touched by the nectar, swelled as when clear bubbles rise up from yellow mud. With no longer than an hour's delay a flower sprang up of blood-red hue such as pomegranates bear, which hide their seeds beneath the tenacious rind. But short-lived is their flower; for the winds from which it takes its name[171] shake off the flower so delicately clinging and doomed too easily to fall.

6.12. ORPHEUS AND EURYDICE, FROM VIRGIL, *GEORGICS*, BOOK 4

(For Virgil, see headnote to document 1.11.) Drawing from different ancient traditions of didactic poetry (from Hesiod to the Hellenistic poets), the four books of Virgil's *Georgics* ("Husbandry") treat different aspects of farming (crops, fruit trees, especially vines, animals, and bees). He intertwines these themes with some mythical narratives, such as the one excerpted here. The *Georgics*, in fact, close with this dramatic account of Orpheus' loss of his bride Eurydice, told by the sea-prophet Proteus to Aristaeus, the very beekeeper who caused Eurydice's death, as she was running away from him when she was bitten by a snake. During his trip to Hades to recover Eurydice, Orpheus, the mythical

---

[170] Alluding to the nymph Menthe.

[171] Referring to the anemone, taking its name to mean "daughter of the wind," from the Greek *anemos*, "wind," and the feminine ending of the sort in Persephone, Antigone, etc., although this is probably a popular etymology of a non-Greek (perhaps Semitic) name.

Thracian poet with magical and prophetic qualities, gains a unique connection with the hereafter, which is exploited by the philosophical-religious movement called Orphism after the singer (on Orphism, see headnote to Part 1, document 6). The story of Orpheus and his dramatic separation from Eurydice is briefly related, for instance, in Apollodorus' *Library* 1.3.2, and his death at the hands of enraged Thracian women (Maenads) is elaborated in Ovid's *Metamorphoses*, Book 11.1–66. According to tradition, his head floated to the island of Lesbos, where it was the source of an oracle, while his soul was finally reunited with Eurydice in the Underworld.

SOURCE: Virgil, *Georgics*, Book 4.453–end. H. R. Fairclough, Virgil. *Eclogues, Georgics, Aeneid* (Loeb Classical Library, Cambridge, MA and London, 1916), with minor modifications.

"It is a god, no other, whose anger pursues you: Great is the crime you are paying for; this punishment, far less than you deserve, unhappy Orpheus arouses against you—did not Fate interpose—and rages implacably for the loss of his bride. She, in headlong flight along the river, if only she might escape you, saw not, doomed maiden, amid the deep grass the monstrous serpent at her feet that guarded the banks. But her sister band of Dryads filled the mountaintops with their cries; the towers of Rhodope wept, and the Pangaean heights, and the martial land (i.e., Thracia) or Rhesus, the Getae and Hebrus and Orithyia, Acte's child.[172] But he, solacing an arching heart with music from his hollow shell, sang of you, dear wife, sang of you to himself on the lonely shore, of you as day drew nigh, of you as day departed.

"He even passed through the jaws of Taenarum, the lofty portals of Dis, the grove that is murky with black terror, and made his way to the land of the dead with its fearful king and hearts no human prayers can soften. Stirred by his song, up from the lowest realms of Erebeus came the unsubstantial shades, the phantoms of those who lie in darkness, as many as the myriads of birds that shelter among the leaves when evening or a wintry shower drives them from the hills – women and men, and figures of great-souled heroes, their life now done, boys and girls unwed, and sons placed on the pyre before their fathers' eyes. But round them are the black ooze and unsightly reeds of Cocytus, the unlovely mere enchaining them with its sluggish water, and Styx holding them fast within this nine-fold circles. Still more: the very house of Death and deepest abysses of Hell were spellbound, and the Furies with livid snakes entwined in their hair; Cerberus stood agape and his triple jaws forgot to bark; the wind subsided, and Ixion's wheel came to a stop.

"And now, as he retraced his steps, he had avoided all mischance, and the regained Eurydice was nearing the upper world, following behind—for that condition had Proserpine imposed—when a sudden frenzy seized Orpheus, unwary in his love, a frenzy meet for pardon, did Hell know how to pardon! He halted, and on the very verge of light, unmindful, alas, and vanquished in purpose, on Eurydice, now regained looked back! In that instant all his toil was split like water, the ruthless tyrant's pact was broken and thrice a peal of thunder was heard amid the pools of Avernus. She cried: 'What madness, Orpheus, what dreadful madness has brought

---

[172] All these are references to landmarks of Thracia, the northern region of Greece where Orpheus hailed from.

disaster alike upon you and me, pour soul? See, again the cruel Fates call me back, and sleep seals my swimming eyes. And now farewell! I am borne away, covered in night's vast pall, and stretching towards you powerless hands, regained, alas! no more.' She spoke, and straightway from his sight, like smoke mingling with thin air, vanished afar and saw him not again, as he vainly clutched at the shadows with so much left unsaid; nor did the ferryman of Orcus suffer him again to pass the barrier of the marsh. What could he do? Whither turn, twice robbed of his wife? With what tears move Hell? To what deities address his prayers? She indeed, already death-cold, was afloat in the Stygian vessel.

"Of him they tell that for seven whole months day after day beneath a lofty crag beside lonely Strymon's stream he wept, and in the shelter of cool dales unfolded his tale, charming tigers and drawing oaks with his song: even as a nightingale, mourning beneath a poplar's shade, bewails her young ones' loss, when a heartless ploughman, watching their resting place, has plucked them unfledged from the nest: the mother weeps all night long, as, perched on a branch, she repeats her piteous song and fills all around with plaintive lamentation. No thought of love or wedding song could bend his soul. Alone he roamed the frozen North, along the icy Tanais, and the fields ever wedded to Riphaean snows, mourning his lost Eurydice and Pluto's cancelled boon; till the Ciconian women, resenting such devotion, in the midst of their sacred rites and their midnight Bacchic orgies, tore the youth limb from limb and flung him over the far-spread plains. And even when Oeagrian Hebrus rolled in mid-current that head, severed from its marble neck, the disembodied voice and the tongue, now cold for ever, called with departing breath on Eurydice—ah, poor Eurydice! 'Eurydice' the banks re-echoed, all along the stream."

6.13. AENEAS' *KATABASIS*, FROM VIRGIL, *AENEID*, BOOK 6

(For Virgil and the *Aeneid*, see headnote to Part 1, document 11.) Aeneas' visit to the Underworld takes place immediately after he first enters Italy, following his long voyage and stops in Carthage and Sicily, where his father Anchises was buried in heroic fashion. Book 6 of the *Aeneid* offers a transition between the "Odyssean" books (1–6), which narrate his exit from Troy and his wanderings until his arrival in Italy, and the "Iliadic" books (7–12), focused on the wars waged afterward in Italy. Aeneas' trip to the Underworld is the most Odyssean of all the *Aeneid*'s passages, directly modeled on Odysseus' *katabasis* (document 6.7), although set in an Italian context and presenting a more complex and different picture of the hereafter.

The setting for this episode is in Cumae, north of Naples, which was the earliest Greek colony in mainland Italy, founded by Euboians (with the Greek name Kyme or Kymai) in the second half of the eighth century BCE. Virgil followed existing traditions that situated the entrance to the Underworld there or at the nearby volcanic crater forming Lake Avernus. Other entrances were traditionally placed in Epirus (western Greece) and Eleusis. At Cumae, Aeneas finds a shrine of Apollo and Hekate (called the "Goddess at Crossroads"), at which the Sibyl, a prophetess, grants him entry to the Underworld and guides his visit. While Sibylline shrines did exist at Cumae and Avernus, by the fourth century BCE they had fallen out of use. The temple of Apollo and its connection with the Sibyl had contemporary resonances, since Augustus did build a temple to the god in Rome after his victory at Actium in 31 BCE, and he placed there the collection of prophecies known as the "Sibylline Books," consulted at crucial moments by the Romans (e.g., during the Second Punic War).

A lengthy comparison between the *Aeneid* and the *Odyssey*'s *katabasis* or *nekya* cannot be made here, but it is worth highlighting some of the main differences: notice that Aeneas *enters* the Underworld and is enmeshed in its complex geography, while Odysseus summons the souls to *come* to him so he can talk to them. Aeneas' trip, in that sense, is more similar to that of Er in the "Myth of Er" (Part 7, document 5), and even to that of Gilgamesh (document 6.1). Also, Odysseus' mission to receive logistical information about his trip from dead seer Teiresias contrasts with Aeneas' search for his dead father. Moreover, the eschatology (afterlife beliefs) presented by Virgil here, with a strict hierarchy of destinies and punishments for the souls depending on their previous lives and the system of reincarnation outlined by Anchises, breaks away from the simpler Homeric and Hesiodic Underworld. Anchises' (if not necessarily Virgil's) view of the afterlife is imbued with philosophical ideas that prevailed in Virgil's time: the idea of reincarnation is mainly Platonic-Pythagorean (see "Myth of Er" Part 7, document 5), and the set of virtues that govern the whole *Aeneid* as well as the centrality of Fate are essentially Stoic.

SOURCE: Virgil, *Aeneid*, Book 6.103–759. F. Ahl, *Virgil, Aeneid* (Oxford World Series, Oxford and New York, 2007), with minor modifications. (See Part 4, document 12.b, for note on Ahl's English hexameter.)

(In the opening of Book 6, lines 1–102, Aeneas and his companions arrive at Cumae where they come across a sanctuary dedicated to Apollo and to Hekate, where the Sibyl exercises her prophetic duties. While they are contemplating the reliefs that decorate it, made by legendary artist Daidalos, they are summoned by the Sibyl. She enters a trance, and Aeneas prays to the god Apollo for help, asking that he allow them to settle in Latium and offering to build him a temple in exchange. The Sibyl then predicts Aeneas' forthcoming struggles in Italy. She comes out of the trance and Aeneas addresses her:)

> "Maiden," Aeneas, the hero, begins, "no struggle you mention
> Comes unexpected by me, or as news. I have pondered these issues
> (105) Well in advance of your words, I've gone over them all in my own mind.
> One thing I ask. Since the gate to the king of the underworld regions
> Is, they say, here, and since here is the place where the Acheron[173]
>   surges
> Up to a dark lake, grant me the chance for a glimpse of my dearest
> Father's face. Could you teach me the route, could you open the
>   sacred

[173] The actual river Acheron is in the region of Epirus (Gr. Epeiros) in western Greece. In eschatological myth it is one of the rivers of the Underworld: in Homer one of five rivers of Hades and in Virgil the principal one, which receives the waters of Styx and which he has flowing into the Avernus Lake. This is the river that Charon will cross with the dead souls.

(110) Gates? For I snatched him away through the flames, through a thou-
       sand pursuing

Javelins, safe on my shoulders, from out of the midst of our foemen.

He was my journey's companion, he sailed every seaway beside me,

Constantly bore every menace the deep and the heavens inflicted.

He wasn't strong—yet his vigor surpassed what is normal in old age.

(115) He himself urged me, implored me to find you, to seek your assistance

Here and to come to your shrine, Holy woman, I beg you to pity

Father and son. It is all in your power. Hecate, with good reason

Put full command of the woodland groves of Avernus in your hands!

Orpheus found, in the resonant strings of his Thracian lyre,

(120) Power to conjure his dead wife's ghost back into existence;

Pollux bought back his brother by sharing his death and so often

Treading, retreading this path—one could also add Theseus and
       mighty

Hercules. Why not me? I too claim descent from Almighty
       Jupiter."

                    While he was praying his prayers and was
                    gripping the altar

(125) Tightly, the seer interrupted: "O Trojan child of Anchises,

Born from the blood of the gods, going down to Avernus[174]
       is easy.

All nights, all days too, dark Dis's[175] portals lie open.

But to recall those steps, to escape to the fresh air above you,

There lies the challenge, the labor! A few have succeeded, those
       people

(130) Fair-minded Jupiter loved or whom blazing manliness wafted

High to the heavens, men born of the gods. The whole centre is
       forest.

Deep-channelled Cocytus'[176] serpentine waters encircle it darkly.

Yet, if there's love so strong in your mind, so mighty a passion

Twice to float over the Stygian lakes, twice gaze upon deep black

(135) Tartarus, if it's your pleasure to wanton in labors of madness,

Grasp what you must do first. On a dense dark tree lurks a hidden

Bough, and its leaves and its pliable, willowy stem are all golden,

---

[174] Avernus stands here for the Underworld in general.

[175] Dis is short for *dis pater*, "rich father," which is how Romans called the god of the Underworld (as Plouton "Rich" was used by the Greeks for Hades). The idea is euphemistic (to avoid the real name) and alludes to his unfailing business of receiving souls.

[176] Another river of the Underworld. Kokytos ("Lamentation") in Homer.

Sacred, they say, to the underworld's Juno.[177] It's masked by the forest,
Dank shadows lock it inside hollow coombs of protective
concealment.

(140) No one's permitted descent beneath earth's deep mantle without first
Harvesting this gold-tressed live growth from the tree where it's
nurtured.
This is the gift you must steal, fair Proserpina rules, as her tribute.
When the first bough's wrenched off, it's replaced, without fail, by
another
Growing identically golden; its branch leafs just the same metal.

(145) So, track it down, but with eyes looking up. When you've found it
in due course
Harvest it, but, with your hand. It will come away, easy and willing,
Only if fate calls *you*. If not, you'll be powerless to wrench it
No matter what force you use, or to hack it away with a steel blade.
One more thing. I'm afraid you don't know, but a friend of yours
now lies

(150) Lost to you, dead, and defiling the fleet with his lifeless cadaver,
Now, while you're hunting for oracles, hanging around at our entrance.
Find him first, bring him back to a tomb of his own and inter him.
Round up some black cattle. Use them in your first rites of appea-
sement.
After this you'll see the groves of the Styx, the terrain through
whose defiles

(155) Life cannot pass." She had spoken. Her mouth was now muted and
silent.

Downcast, Aeneas departs from the cave, eyes lowered,
expression
Sombre as he moves along, as his mind turns over and over
What, in his blindness, he's failed to observe. His faithful Achates
Keeps pace, step by step, at his side. He too was in mourning.

(160) Many ideas they scatter like seed in exchanges of chatter:
Who was the dead friend the priestess meant, what body was needing
Burial? Then, while approaching Misenum, they saw, on the dry
beach,
Cut off by death without honor, a corpse that, in fact, was
Misenus,[178]
Offspring of Aeolus. None could surpass him in raising men's spirits

---

[177] Proserpina (equivalent to Greek Persephone). The golden bough does not appear outside Virgil.
[178] He appears in *Aen.* 3.239–240 alerting of the Harpies' attack. Aeolus is the god of the winds.

(165) High with the bugle's brass. He set Mars all ablaze with its blaring.
Hector the Great's companion in war, he'd served with distinction,
Fighting in Hector's entourage with his lance and his bugle.
He, when Achilles, in triumph, had stripped away Hector's existence,
Joined up with Dardan Aeneas' friends, this bravest of heroes,

(170) Following what was a cause and a destiny no whit the lesser.
Then, as it chanced, one day, as he echoed the seas with his
conch-call,
Losing his senses, he challenged the gods to a contest in bugling.
Triton, his rival, at once took him up—if the story's worth credit—
Only to plunge the man down into rock-strewn sea-spray, and
drown him.

(175) Everyone now gathered round him with cries of intense lamentation,
Notably righteous Aeneas. They hastened, unslowed by the flowing
Tears,
to do just what the Sibyl had ordered. They vied in constructing,
Tree upon tree, sky high, a cremation fire for his last rites.
Into an ancient forest they go, tall lairs for the wild beasts.

(180) Spruces crash to the ground and the ilex and trunks of the rowan
Ring under axe-strokes; fracturing oak splits, sundered by wedges;
Down from the mountains they trundle enormous flowering ashes.
Up amid all of the work is Aeneas himself, as a foreman
Urging his crews on, equipped with a lumberjack's tools like the
others.

(185)   As he surveys the extent of the woodlands, his gloomy
depression
Makes him turn over these thoughts, which, it chances, he voices
as prayers:
"What a huge forest! If only that golden bough would just reach out
All by itself, right in front of us now! Why not? For the priestess
Was, alas, all too truthful a prophet in your case, Misenus!"

(190) Just as he says this, in front of his eyes, twin doves, by convenient
Chance, manage somehow to swoop from the skies and to land on
the green-turfed
Soil. The divinely born hero supreme recognizes his mother's
Own special birds[179] and expresses delight in a prayer that he offers:
"O! Be my guides, if there *is* any pathway, and set a direct course

---

[179] The doves or pigeons are traditionally birds associated with Venus/Aphrodite and her messengers, sometimes depicted (in poetry as in iconography) as carrying her chariot through the skies.

(195) Through the Gold air to the groves where that rich bough darkens the fertile
Earth. O divine mother, don't you fail me in this time of crisis!"
Once he has spoken these fateful words, he stops in his traces,
Noting such ominous signs as the birds make, and where they're proceeding.
Since they keep stopping to scavenge, the birds fly ahead in their passage
(200) Only as far as the eyes of their trackers can follow their progress.
Nearing the venue assigned, they've arrived at Avernus's reeking
Jaws. They ascend in a flash, and then glide on the currents of breezes
Down to a perch on the hybrid tree, where he's hoped they would settle,
Just where the glittering contrast of gold gleams coldly through branches,
(205) Growing as mistletoe grows. For it's not a real shoot of its host tree.
Mistletoe loves bearing green leaves fresh in the frosts of the solstice,
Looping the woods' smooth trunks with its berries, yellow as crocus:
That's how the leafing gold met his eye on the dark of the ilex,
That's how its thin foil crackled insistently under the light wind.
(210) Instantly grabbing the bough from its seat, though it struggles, Aeneas,
Greedily snaps it and takes it home to his seer, the Sibyl.
　　　　Meanwhile, back on the shore, the laments for Misenus continue.
Teucrians give last rites to his unappreciative ashes.
First, they've constructed a massive pyre, rich in resinous pitch-pine,
(215) Split oak too, whose sides they've been weaving with garlands of dark leaves.
Cypresses, symbols of death, they arrange in an upright position
Fronting it; and, on top, they set out all his glittering armor.
Some set water to boil—bronze cauldrons with wavelets of liquid
Seething on flames—and they wash and anoint the now ice-cold cadaver.
(220) Groans echo round. They layout on a couch limbs duly lamented,
Casting upon them his O so familiar vestment: his mantle
Crimson as fire. Other men—it's a grim, sad service to render—
Shoulder the massive bier and they, as their parents before them,
Turn away faces while kindling the pyre with their torches. The heaped gifts

(225) Burn: there is incense and food, olive oil that they've poured into
large bowls.

After the embers collapse and the searing flames have subsided,

Men lave ashes with wine: the remains are still glowing and thirsty.

Bones are collected; and these Corynaeus seals in a bronze urn.

This same man thrice circles his comrades with pure, holy water,

(230) And, with the bough of a fruit-bearing olive, he sprinkles a light dew,

Ritually cleansing the men, then pronounces the last benediction.

Righteous Aeneas constructs him a tomb in a huge mound, enclosing

Arms for the man, and his bugle and oar, at the foot of a towering

Mountain that up to this day bears a name in his honour: Misenus.

(235) Such is the name it retains for eternity, all through the ages.

This done, he's quickly completed the rites that the Sibyl has ordered.

Shaped by an outcrop of rock was a high cavern,[180] opening a
monstrous,

Gaping mouth, guarded well by a black lake and woodland's
tenacious

Shadows. Above it no creature that flies could, without severe peril,

(240) Pass upon fluttering wings, so appalling the breath that came
spewing

Out of its blackened jaws to the vaulted dome of the heavens.

That's why the Greeks named Avernus *Aornos*, "The Place that is
Birdless"[181]:

Here's where the priestess prepares four black-skinned bullocks for
slaughter,

Trickles their foreheads with wine, crops tips of the tough bristle
growing

(245) Midway between the two horn tips, and sets them as ritual first fruits

Over the sacred fires. She next prays aloud, while invoking

Hecate, goddess with power both in Erebus and in the bright sky.

Others press ritual knives to the throats, catch the warm blood in
vessels

Held underneath. And Aeneas, to show his respect for the Furies'[182]
Mother

---

[180] The Sibyl's Grotto (still identified as such today) on the southern shores of Lake Avernus.

[181] As if from *ornis* in Greek. This etymological explanation has been taken by many as an interpolation (later insertion) in the text.

[182] The Furies (Latin Dirae and Gr. Erinyes) are crime-avenging chthonic deities. In the Latin text they are called Eumenides ("Benevolent Ones"), the euphemistic name they received when they were appeased (cf. *Oresteia* by Aeschylus), turning into protecting deities. In Hesiod's *Theogony* they are born from the blood of castrated Ouranos, received by the earth, and in other sources they are daughters of Earth or of Night (see Part 1, document 5). For Virgil (e.g., *Aen.* 7.331) their mother is Night and their sister Earth.

(250) and powerful sister, now kills with his own sword a dark-fleeced
She-lamb. For you then, Proserpina, he kills an unmated heifer.
Next he establishes altars, at night, for the Stygian ruler,
Places unsundered bulls on the flames, and drenches the blazing
Innards with fresh-pressed oil.

                                   Look now: as the sun at its rising
(255) Starts to emerge from beneath its solar threshhold, the solid
Earth bellows under men's feet. Forests yoking the hilltops together
Start into motion and hounds seem to loom up, howling through
   shadows,
Hailing the deity's advent. "Away, clear away, those who must stand
Outside the shrine!" Thus the god's seer cries. "Clear out of the
   whole grove!
(260) You, set forth on your path, pull your blade from its sheath now,
   Aeneas!
Now you need resolute courage and stout-hearted firmness of spirit."
Thus, in her frenzy she spoke, plunging into the cave which had
   opened.
Matching his leader's steps as she strode, he followed her, fearless.

         Gods, under whose command are the breeze-like souls,
         and you silent
(265) Ghost-shadows, Chaos[183] and Phlegethon, speechless spaces,
   extending
Deep into night, say it's right to give voice to the things I have
   heard of,
Grant your assent to disclose what's submerged in the earth's pit of
   darkness.
         Moving, blocked from sight under night's isolation, through
         shadows,
Through Dis's empty homes they strode, through realms that are
   nothing,
(270) As one would travel through moonlight's shimmering vagueness,
   beneath lights
Treasonous dimness, in forests when Jupiter buries the sky's vaults
Deep beneath ghost shadows, when black night robs substance of
   color.
Facing the entrance hall, just past the gate, in the gullet of Orcus,[184]

---

[183] Chaos was the first opening space that existed in the cosmos (see Hesiod's *Theogony*, 123).
Phlegethon or Pyriphlegethon, "Flaming," was another one of the rivers of the Underworld.

[184] A Roman Underworld deity, here standing for the narrow entrance of the Underworld.

Sorrows have set up their quarters, and Heartaches crying for
   vengeance.

(275) Here pale Diseases reside, grim Senility, Terror, and Hunger

Powering evil and crime, and Poverty, vile and degrading:

Shapes terrifying the eyes that behold. Then there's Death and
   Hard Labor.

Next lurks listless Sleep, Death's blood-relation, and nearby

Evil Pleasures of Mind and, across, in the opposite threshold,

(280) War, who is bearer of Death, steeled bedrooms of Family Vengeance,

Mad Civil Strife, viper hair interlaced by her gore-clotted ribbons.

Centrally set: a dark elm with extending branches, its forearms,

Centuries old, peopled strangely. It's here that what men deem
   elusive

Dreams wreathe nests, it is said, clinging tightly beneath all its
   foliage.

(285) Many additional monsters lurk here, bestial hybrids:

Centaurs have stables adjoining the gates, as do Scyllas—part
   human,

Part beast-Briareus, too, with his hundred arms, and the Hydra

Hissing out terror; Chimaera, whose weapons are flames; then the
   Gorgons,

Harpies, and Cerberus' shape with its three-bodied shadow. Aeneas,

(290) Trembling, fear welling up at the sight of them, grabs for his steel
   sword's

Edge as a line of defense as they surge at him. He would be lunging,

Uselessly slashing the menacing shadows apart with his steel blade,

Did not his scholarly escort explain that they're bodiless, flimsy,

No more than flickers of life in the hollow illusion of shaped form.

(295)   Here's where the pathway to Acheron, Tartarus' river,
   commences.

Here, in a riot of mud and a suctioning vortex, a whirlpool

Seethes before vomiting up into Cocytus all of its thick silt.

Charon, repulsive in frightening filth, is the ferryman, plying

Passage across these turbulent waters. A matted and wolf-grey

(300) Beard clings thick to his chin and his eyes glare flame in their
   bright gaze.

Dirt-soiled clothes hang dangling down from a knot at his shoulders.

He works alone. He's propelling his skiff with a pole, trimming
   canvas

Sails as he ferries the bodies across in his iron-girt vessel,

Elderly now—but there's fresh green sap in his elderly godhood.

(305) Pouring his way, all the seething crowd spills down to the stream's
         banks:

Mothers and full-grown men and the bodies of great-hearted heroes

Finished with life, young boys, young girls who have never been
         married,

Youths in their prime set on funeral pyres while their parents are
         watching:

Countless as leaves, during autumn's first frost, falling in forests,

(310) Countless, as clustered birds escaping the turbulent deep sea,

Flocking towards dry land when the freezing cold of the season

Routs them across great seas, propels them to lands that are sun-
         warmed.

Each soul that stands there begs to be first to accomplish the
         crossing,

Stretches out hands in a yearning love for the shore on the far side.

(315) Now the grim sailor lets some come aboard, now decides upon
         others,

Others he just drives off and keeps far away from the bankside.

Moved and amazed by the crowds and the uproar, Aeneas says:
         "Tell me,

Maiden, what does it mean, this gathering down at the waters?

What are the spirits attempting to get? What determines selection?

(320) Why is it some go away, others sweep dark waters with oar strokes?"

Brief in her answer, the long-lived priestess responded in this way:

"Child of Anchises, beyond any doubt you're an offshoot of gods'
         stock,

You're seeing Cocytus' still, deep pools and the Stygian marshes

By whose power gods dread to make oaths. For they dread not to
         keep them.

(325) All this mob you observe is the helpless folk, the unburied.

Charon's the ferryman; those who have tombs are conveyed on the
         waters.

Statutes forbid transportation of souls beyond these banks of horror,

Over these torrents of groans, till their bones receive proper inter-
         ment.

Lost, they must pass a full century wandering, haunting this sho-
         reline,

(330) Then, at long last, they may pass, and revisit the waters they've
         yearned for."

         Stopped in his tracks, Anchises' son stands motionless,
         thinking

Deeply, and pitying deep in his soul the injustice they suffer.

Here, in this group, he observes Leucaspis along with Orontes,

Admiral, once, of the Lycian fleet, sad souls lacking death's dues.

(335) Southerly gales had submerged and engulfed both the men and their vessel

While they were sailing from Troy over wind-swept seaways together.

Look, Palinurus the helmsman is guiding his footsteps among them.

He, while observing the stars on the recent voyage from Carthage,[185]

Fell from the aft-deck and spilled overboard in the water at mid-course.

(340) Scarcely aware who this sad being was, so intense was the shrouding

Darkness, Aeneas spoke first: "Which one of the gods, Palinurus,

Tore you from us in mid-voyage and plunged you beneath the sea's surface?

Tell me, come on. Though Apollo has never before proved deceitful,

He, in this one response, had my mind completely deluded.

(345) *You'd* be unharmed on the seas, so his oracles always insisted,

You'd reach Ausonian land. Well, so much for the worth of that promise!"

"Son of Anchises, commander," he answered, "the cauldron of Phoebus[186]

Didn't deceive you; no god plunged *me*[187] underneath the sea's surface.

Violent but random force ripped our steering away. I, as captain,

(350) Charged with both plotting and holding our course, clung fast to the tiller

Which, as I hurtled down, I dragged with me, and, by the rough seas,

I felt no fear for myself, I swear, near as strong as my terror

That, stripped of steerage, its helmsman ejected, our vessel might founder,

Sunk in the swelling surge that seethed so wildly around us.

(355) Three tempestuous nights I spent in the water, as violent

Southerlies drove me across vast seas. On the fourth day, I just glimpsed

---

[185] Though in *Aen.* 5.827 ff. he is said to drown during the voyage from Sicily.

[186] Greek tripods were valued artifacts (usually of bronze) composed of a three-foot stand holding a cauldron or large bowl. Here it stands for "Apollo's oracle" (nowhere else mentioned in the *Aeneid*).

[187] The narrative in Book 5 makes clear the gods have singled out Palinurus to be sacrificed so the rest of the fleet make it safely to Italy but the helmsman does not know it. At the Sibyl's orders, a mound will be built for him in the future (6.378–381), giving its name to Cape Palinuro in Italy.

Italy's coastline ahead as I rose up high on a wave-crest.
Slowly but surely I swam towards land, I was grasping at safety,
Hooking my hands round the crags of the cliff-top. And I would have made it
(360) Had cruel people, ignorant men, not attacked me with cold steel,
Thinking I was fair game, weighed down as I was by my wet clothes;
Now I belong to the waves; winds roll me about on the seashore.
So, by the wonderful daylight and breezes of heaven, I pray you,
And by your father, by dreams that you cherish for growing Iulus,
(365) Save me from this vile doom! You're a man who is never defeated.
Throw earth upon me! You can! Go about, head for Velia's harbor!
Or—since you're not, I believe, now preparing to cross such a might
Torrent and sail on the waters of Styx without some god's approval—
Give a poor fellow your hand, take me with you over the waters
(370) If there's a way you can find, if the goddess who bore you reveals one,
So I can rest, at least now that I'm dead, in a place that is tranquil."
　　　Such were his prayers and such was the prophet's immediate reaction:
"What brings this terrible urge that sweeps over you now, Palinurus?
You, an unburied soul, plan to gaze upon Stygian waters,
(375) Pitiless Furies' streams? You'll cross to those banks uninvited?
Cease to hope fate, once spoken by gods, can be altered by prayer!
Grasp and remember these words to console you in bitter misfortune.
Those living near—driven far, driven wide, by celestial omens,
City to city—will offer your bones last ritual appeasement;
(380) Build you a mound. And they'll send to that mound solemn, annual tributes.
Through the remainder of time that site will be named Palinurus."
All of his sorrows are driven away. From his heart, sad and aching,
Pain is, for just a brief moment, expelled; he delights in the land's name.
　　　Then they continued the journey begun and moved close to the river.
(385) When, from his boat on the water, the sailor observed them approaching
Down through the silent grove and directing their steps to the bankside,
He, with a verbal assault, challenged them before they could address him:

"Tell me, come on, whoever you are, who now march on our river
Armed to the teeth—Halt—Why are you here? Speak where you
are standing!

(390) This is a land for the shades, and for sleep, and for night that
brings numbness.

It's an offence to convey *live* bodies on Stygian vessels.

I wasn't happy at all to take Hercules, when he came this way,

Onto the lake, or, for that matter, Theseus, Pirithous either,

Though they were born of the gods and invincibly powerful
heroes.

(395) Hercules came into Tartarus planning to chain up its watchdog,

Actually dragged the beast trembling with fear from the king's
throne. The others

Came with intent to abduct Dis' mistress out of his bedroom."

Briefly the seer of the god who himself had defied death,[188]
responded:

"No such treachery here! So stop getting angry! These weapons

(400) Don't threaten force. Your great big doorman can bark on for ever

Inside his cave, let him terrify ghosts that have no blood to drain out,

And let Proserpina stay unabused in her own uncle's household.

Trojan Aeneas, renowned for his righteousness—and martial valor—

Goes to the deepest shadows of Erebus seeking his father.

(405) But, if no icon of righteousness on such a scale can impress you,

Still, you'd acknowledge this bough"—disclosing the bough that
lay hidden

Under her robe. Wrath gone, his surging emotions subsided.

No more was said. As he gazes, in awe, at the marvelous offering,

Destiny's fateful branch, seen now after long years of waiting,

(410) Charon reverses his dark vessel's course and approaches the bankside,

Hurls out other souls already seated across the boat's long thwarts,

Frees up the gangways and, as he does, takes massive Aeneas

Into his reed-woven hull. But when *his* weight is added, the twine-
sewn

Skiff gives a groan, shipping gallons of water through gaps in its
fabric.

(415) Still, it gets seer and hero across, and deposits them safely,

Over the waters, in shifting mud, amid gray river grasses.

---

[188] In reference to the time when Apollo allowed Admetus of Thessaly to become immortal if someone died in his place (which his wife Alkestis did, who was in turn rescued by Herakles), as famously dramatized in Euripides' *Alkestis*.

Cerberus, monstrous, massively stretching out in a cavern

Facing them, sets this whole realm booming with three-throated barking.

Seeing his snake-spiked collar erect now, the seer distracts him,

(420) Tossing him sleep-bringing drug-drenched cakes with a coating of honey.

Opening three throats wide, that dog, quite rabid with hunger,

Snaps up the treats he is tossed; then, his monstrous shoulders relaxing,

Slumps to the ground, sprawled massively over the whole of the cave floor.

Now that its guardian's entombed, Aeneas leaps for the entrance,

(425) Swiftly escaping the banks of the river that knows no re-crossing.

Instantly voices are heard: massed wailing, the weeping of children:

Souls never able to speak, just over the boundary's threshhold,

Stolen by death's dark day, ripped away from the breasts of their mothers,

Plunged in the grave's bitter sourness without any share of the sweetness

(430) Life brings; next are those sentenced to death upon false accusations.

Placement here's not assigned without lot or a process of judgment.

Minos presides[189] in a court, shakes lots in an urn, summons silent

Crowds for a hearing, investigates lives and the charges against them.

Innocent folk who despaired are their neighbors: people whose own hands

(435) Birthed their own deaths in disgust at the world's light, cast away living

Souls. How they'd *long* to get back now beneath sky's limitless, open

Brightness, and suffer in poverty, tolerate grueling labors![190]

Heaven forbids it; and that grim lake's unlovable waters

Bind them; the spiraling Styx loops nine-fold moats of constriction.

(440)   Not far from here, their attention is drawn to what men call the Grieving

Meadows that sprawl their tremendous expanses in every direction.

Here reside people that hardhearted Love, with his cruel corrosion,

---

[189] King Minos of Crete was traditionally considered a judge in the Underworld. Interestingly, Crete was famous for its early law codes.

[190] Cf. similar thoughts by Achilles in *Odyssey* 11 (see document 6.7)

Wholly consumed. Tracks, traceless and secret, conceal them, and myrtle

Forests enclose them. For, even in death, anxiety's heartaches

(445) Fail to desert them. Aeneas discerns here Phaedra and Procris,

And Eriphyle displaying the wounds that her pitiless son dealt.

There is Evadne, Pasiphae too; at their side Laodamia

Walks. And there's Caeneus,[191] a man for a while, now, again, she's a woman:

Fate has reversed its account; she's returned to her former appearance.

(450) Wandering the vast forest, lost, among women of Greece, was Phoenician

Dido, fresh from her wound. Troy's hero, as soon as he neared her,

Knew who she was, in the dark of her heartache, there among shadows,

Dimly, the way one sees, or imagines one *has* seen, the wandering

Moon on the first of the month rise up through a veil of enshrouding Clouds.

(455) As he let tears fall, he addressed her with love in its sweetness:

"Dido unfulfilled, then it really was true, news that reached me,

News that your life had been quenched, that you'd ended it all with a sword point?

Have I, alas, been the cause of your death? O, I swear by the heavens'

Powers above, by the stars, by whatever one trusts in the earth's depths:

(460) It was no choice of my will, good queen, to withdraw from your country.

Rather, commands of the gods, which now compel me to pass through

Ghost-shadows, regions vile with decay, night's oceans of darkness,

Drove me with power supreme. And I couldn't believe I was bringing

Grief so intense, so painful to you, when I made my departure.

(465) Don't walk away, don't draw yourself back from my eyes as I watch you.

Who are you running from? Fate gives me this last chance to address you."

That's how Aeneas attempted to quiet a soul that was blazing,

---

[191] For Phaedra, Pasiphae, and Caeneus, see appropriate sections in Part 5, documents 9.a, 9.b, 9.c, 11, and 18.

Glaring in anger: with words such as these. And he set his eyes
 weeping.

She turned her back on him, stared at the ground, eyes fixed, her
 expression

(470) No more moved by these efforts at conversation than hard flint

Slabs, or the marble face on the crags of Marpessus in Paros.

She, in the end, made the break herself, full of hate, and took
 refuge

Deep in the ghost-shadowed grove where her earlier husband,
 Sychaeus,

Matches her cares with his own and whose love equals hers very
 fairly.

(475) Stunned by her unfair doom, and despite her reaction, Aeneas,

Follows her far with his tears; he feels pity for her as she leaves
 him.

     Travelling onwards as planned needed effort, but soon they
 were reaching

Distant secluded fields, where the heroes of battle assemble.

Tydeus encounters him here and, famed for his prowess in combat,

(480) Parthenopaeus, along with the ghost of the pallid Adrastus.[192]

Here too were Dardanus' sons, those fallen in battle and deeply

Wept to the heavens. Aeneas, on seeing them all in formation,

Gave out a groan: there was Glaucus, and Medon, Thersilochus
 also,

Three sons of Antenor, Ceres' votary too, Polyboetes,

(485) And, still holding fast to his weapons and chariot, Idaeus.[193]

Round him to left and to right these spirits crowd in a circle.

It's not enough just to glance at him once; for they love to delay
 him,

Stroll at his side as he walks, and discover his reasons for coming.

But, when Danaan commanders, and infantry lines Agamemnon

(490) Led, see the man and his arms flash lightning-bright through the
 shadows,

They all tremble in fear. Some turn tail, as in the old days

When they ran off to their ships. Others, trying to raise a thin
 war-cry

---

[192] These three heroes were among the "Seven against Thebes" group. Tydeus was also the father of Diomedes (Aeneas' Greek opponent in the *Iliad*).

[193] The heroes mentioned in lines 483–485 are minor Trojan warriors in the *Iliad*. Besides Agamemnon and Deiphobus, Virgil does not mention an encounter with main Homeric Greek or Trojan soldiers (e.g., Achilles, Hektor), or famous Roman ones for that matter.

Find that the shouts don't emerge from their mouths, though they
open them widely.

Here he sees Priam's son, every part of whose body is mangled:

(495) This is Deiphobus, all of whose face is completely disfigured,
Face, yes, and both of his hands: ears ripped from dehumanized
temples,
Nose lopped off as a common criminal's mark of dishonor.
Just, only just, recognizing the man as he cowered and covered
Punishment's terrible scars, he exclaims in a voice still familiar:

(500) "Master of weapons, Deiphobus, prince of the bloodline of noble
Teucer! What judge in his ruling imposed such a barbarous sen-
tence?
Who had the license to do this to you? I heard rumors, that final
Night: people said you'd collapsed on a mountain of intertwined
corpses,
Worn out by killing Pelasgians during an orgy of slaughter.

(505) I myself built an empty tomb for you, down at Rhoeteum's
Harbour, and cried out the Call for the Dead three times in a loud
voice.
Guarding the spot are your name and your arms. But I couldn't
distinguish
You, my dear friend, and set you, as I left, in the earth of our
homeland."

Priam's son answered: "My friend, for your part, you have overlooked nothing,

(510) You've done the rites due Deiphobus, and to his ghost, at the
graveside.
My own fate and the deadly crime of that bitch of a Spartan[194]
Sank me in all of these evils: she left me these scars as mementoes.
That last night: how we squandered its hours in our false celebrations,
You well know. One is forced to recall it too hideously clearly.

(515) Up from the plain came the fateful horse, leaping over our towering
Pergamum, pregnant with infantry, heavily armed, in its belly.
She staged what seemed like a chorus, and led, in a circle around it,
Phrygian women who screamed in a wild celebration of Bacchus.
She, in their midst, was brandishing fires that would ruin a nation,

(520) Calling Danaans forth from the citadel's crest. I, exhausted,

---

[194] Referring to Helen, to whom Deiphobos was married for a brief time after Paris (his brother)
was killed and before Troy was finally taken and Menelaos recovered her.

Heavy with sleep and with cares, lay trapped in the bed of our
    marriage,
Unfulfilled and accursed, as a sweet, deep slumber like tranquil
Death pressed down on my stillness. My wife, royal pick of the
    whole flock,
Strips, meanwhile, all arms from the house, even eases my trusty
(525) Sword out from under my head, opens doors, calls in Menelaus,
Hoping, I'm sure, this would make a grand gift for her lover and
    stamp out
Rumours based on her past that had made her a byword for evil.
Why draw it out? They burst into my bedroom along with Ulysses,
Aeolus' spawn, always ready to prompt an atrocity. O gods!
(530) Pay the Greeks back in kind, if my prayer for justice is righteous.
Now it is your turn. Explain what occurred that has brought you
Here while you're still alive? Were you lost, washed in by the
    wayward
Seas or did gods so advise? Or were *you* so wearied by Fortune's
Blows as to seek out the land of unrest, grim homes without sun-
    light?"
(535) While they exchanged conversation, Dawn had already completed
Half of her arching course through the skies in her roseate chariot.
Chances were good they'd consume all allotted time on such mat-
    ters.
But his companion, the Sibyl, advised him of this, and said briefly:
"Night is upon us, Aeneas. We're squandering hours in weeping.
(540) Here is the place where the road subdivides into two distinct
    pathways:
This one, the right, leads up past the fortress of Great Dis: it's our
    route
Straight to Elysium[195] now. But the left marches those who are evil
Off to their torments, to Tartarus, dungeon for all the unrighteous."
"Don't get so angry and harsh, great priestess," Deiphobus counters.
(545) "I'll go away, I'll be there for the count, I'll surrender to darkness.
March on, glory of Troy, march on! May *your* fate be kinder!"
That's all he said, and he turned on his heels while his voice was
    still speaking.
      Suddenly, under a cliff to his left, as he glances, Aeneas
Sees an extensive fortress, encircled by triple defense walls.

---

[195] Elysium or the Elysian Fields are mentioned since early Greek sources (Homer, Hesiod, later Plato) as the destination of the blessed souls of heroes (also as the Isles of the Blessed).

(550) Round them Phlegethon roars. Grim Tartarus' river of lava
       Blazes with white-hot flame, spits rocks out hissing and clashing.
       Blocking the entrance, a huge gate stands set in uprights of solid
       Adamant, such as defy any force that a human or even
       Heaven could bring to attack and uproot them, encased in a soaring
(555) Turret of iron. Tisiphone,[196] swathed in a blood-dripping mantle,
       Sleeplessly, day and night, stands permanent guard at the entrance.
       Screams can be heard from within, and the crackle of merciless
          floggings;
       Followed by rasping of iron and chains as they're cranked under
          torsion.
       Halted and frozen with terror, Aeneas absorbs all the bedlam.
(560) "Maiden, can you put a face on the crimes or describe me what
          torments
       Punish them? What is provoking the torrent of screams that I'm
          hearing?"
       So then, the prophet began: "Famous chief of the Teucrian nation,
       Innocent people may never set foot on that criminal threshold.
       Hecate, though, when she put me in charge of the groves of Avernus,
(565) Taught me herself how the gods punish wrongs, took me through
          the whole system.
       This is hell's toughest regime: Rhadamanthus,[197] its warden from
          Knossos,
       Punishes, hears accusations of treachery, forces confession
       When someone smugly delights in illusory flight from detection
       While still alive, and defers his atonement till death, when it's too
          late.
(570) Vengeance is swift on the guilty: Tisiphone, armed with her lashes,
       Leaps up to whip them herself, thrusts her left hand, teeming with
          angry
       Snakes, at their faces, then calls in her armies of merciless sisters.
       That's when the hinges scream and the hideously rasping, accursed
       Gates yawn wide. You can see what manner of jailer is posted
(575) Here at the entrance, what kind of a face watches over the threshold.
       Inside is stationed an even more pitiless monster, with fifty
       Raven and gaping throats. It's the Hydra. Then Tartarus proper

---

[196] One of the three *Dirae* (Furies), with Allecto and Megaera.

[197] Another legendary king of Crete and, like his brother Minos, judge in the Underworld.

Opens a chasm extending on down twice as far[198] into darkness
As the eye's view of Olympus extends up high into brightness.

(580) Here's where the ancient offspring of Earth, great warrior Titans,
Toppled by lightning bolts, now squirm on the floor of her bedrock.
Here I have seen Aloeus's twins.[199] Their bodies are monstrous.
They, bare-handed, attacked and attempted to tear down the vast sky's
Vault, to cast Jupiter down from his realms up above in the heavens.

(585) I've seen Salmoneus[200] too as he suffers in cruel retribution:
He used to ride in a four-horse chariot, parading in triumph,
Brandishing torches of fire, among peoples of Greece, through Olympia
Right in the heartland of Elis. He mimicked the really Olympian
Jupiter's thunder and fire and demanded men grant him official

(590) Status as god. How insane! To use bronze and the clatter of hard-hoofed
Horses to simulate storms and their unreproducible lightning.
But the omnipotent father, within thick and genuine storm clouds,
Torqued up a thunderbolt—no simple torches in his case, no smoky
Pinewood brands—and he blasted him down with a monster tornado.

(595) Tityos,[201] stepchild of Earth who is mother of all, with his body
Stretched over nine full acres, was there to be seen. And a monstrous
Vulture was trimming his liver that can't die, snipping with curving
Beak as it probed through his guts that regenerate tissue and raw pain,
Plucking out food for its feast, tucked under his tall ribs and nesting:

(600) Flesh reborn is not granted a respite for even an instant.
Need I remind you of Lapiths: Pirithous, Ixion[202] also?
Over them looms a black boulder of flint that will fall any moment,

---

[198] A variation on the Greek epic tradition, where the same distance separates earth from sky and earth from Hades. In Hesiod (*Th.* 722–725, in Part 1, document 5), the distance a bronze anvil would cover in a nine-day free fall.

[199] Aeolus' stepchildren Otus and Ephialtes, who attempted a coup on Olympos.

[200] Not much is known about him outside this passage.

[201] A giant who tried to kill Letona (Gr. Leto), the mother of Apollo and Diana (Artemis). His punishment resembles closely that of Prometheus.

[202] Legendary kings of the Lapiths, a tribe from Thessaly (who fought the Centaurs). The punishment assigned here to these two characters is traditionally assigned to Tantalos. Ixion was bound to a fiery, spinning wheel; Pirithous (Gr. Peirithoos) was bound to a stone throne in Hades with Theseus (Herakles freed Theseus, but failed to free Peirithoos).

Seems to be falling now. Gold gleams in the frames elevating
Couches for feasts; and in front of their eyes are set banquets
   of regal

(605) Splendor. But right at their elbows reclines that direst of Demons[203]
Blocking their ghostly hands from touching the food on the tables,
Rearing up, raising her fiery torch while her mouth bellows thunder.
Here are the men who, during their lives, earned hate from their
   brothers,
Lashed out at parents and beat them, or tricked and defrauded
   dependants,

(610) Men who acquired great wealth then roosted alone on their nest-eggs,
Setting no portion aside for their families (this group is largest!).
Then those killed for adultery, those who fought wars for unrighteous
Causes, and those unafraid to betray oaths sworn to their masters.
They're locked up, pending punishment. Please don't ask me to
   teach you

(615) Details of punishment, forms it assumes, individual cases.
Some move large rocks, some stretched taut, lashed tight onto
   wheel spokes,
Hang. There is one who just sits; he'll continue to sit there forever
Unfulfilled: Theseus. Then Phlegyas,[204] misery's symbol,
Cries out his warning, his booming voice bears witness among
   ghosts:

(620) 'Learn what justice means! Be warned! Don't underrate gods'
   power!'
He sold his country for gold, set upon it a powerful tyrant:
He fixed laws in bronze, for a price; for a price he unfixed them.
This one invaded his daughter's room for incestuous marriage.
All of them dared some atrocious wrong and accomplished that
   daring.

(625) Had I a hundred tongues and a hundred mouths[205] and an iron
Voice, I would still fall short of the power I would need to encompass
Every species of crime or name all those judgments inflicted."

     Phoebus's long-lived priestess, her overview finished, adds
   these words:

"Now reap the fruits of your journey. You started an offering; complete it!

---

[203] Her name is not given, but Harpy Calaeno is called "direst of Demons" in *Aeneid*, Book 3.

[204] Ixion's father, only here punished together to sit forever at a banquet.

[205] In 6.43–44 she does have a hundred mouths.

(630) But we must hurry. I see walls wrought upon Cyclopes' anvils,
Also the gates whose arches we're facing. That's where our
instructions
Tell us we must now deposit these gifts." As soon as she's spoken,
Both race, side by side, down the path's last stretches of darkness,
Hurtling along as they're closing the gap and approaching the
gateway.
(635) Gaining the entrance, Aeneas besprinkles his body with fresh-drawn
Water, then fixes the bough on the castle entrance before him.
Once this rite was performed and the goddess's offering
completed,
Down they went to the zone of joy, the green of idyllic
Fortune's groves: the Estates of the Blest. A more generously lustrous
(640) Brightness of sky dresses meadows here with a colorful brilliance.
They know a sun shining only for them and the stars are their own
stars.
Some keep their bodies in shape on the open-air lawns of gymnasi-
ums,
Hold competitions in sport, even wrestle each other on blond sand.
Some beat feet to the rhythms of dance, recite poetry, music.
(645) And there is also a Thracian priest in his long, flowing vestments,
Bridging the seven distinctive notes of his lyre, which he's plucking
Now with his fingers, now with a shuttling ivory plectrum.
Here resides Teucer's family of old, such a handsome assemblage,
Great-hearted heroes they are, who were born in an age that was
better:
(650) Ilus, Assaracus, Dardanus[206] too, Troy's father and founder.
Arms, in the distance, and chariots of men catch his gaze: hollow,
empty.
Spears stand fixed, points down in the earth, while untethered
horses
Wander at random and graze all over the plain. For the pleasure
Men, when alive, took in chariots and arms, and in raising their
well-groomed
(655) Horses, remains, and it follows them under the earth when they're
buried.
Look, he sees others spread out to the left and the right in a meadow,

---

[206] Ilus was father of Laomedon, father of Priam; Dardanus the grandfather of Ilus (after whom Ilion, i.e., Troy, was called), Assaracus, and Ganymede.

Feasting, and singing a paean of joy as they dance through the fragrant

Clusters of laurels in groves from whose springs the Eridanus surges

Up to the surface and rolls in its ample flow through the forest.

(660) Here there are clusters of men who were wounded defending their country,

Priests who kept chastity's vows intact through the course of their lifetimes,

Poets and seers who were righteous and spoke words worthy of Phoebus,[207]

All who enriched human life with the arts and the skills they discovered,

All whose noble deeds earned life in the memory of others.

(665) Every forehead is ringed with a ribbon as white as the pure snow.

As they encircled Aeneas, the Sibyl addressed them, with special

Thought for Musaeus,[208] the focal point of the largest escorting

Throng, and regarded with awe as he stood head and shoulders above them:

"Souls who have found your fulfillment, and you, supreme poet and prophet,

(670) Tell me what district[209] is housing Anchises and at what location?

He's why we've come here and crossed the large span of the Erebus river."

In just a few words, the hero supplied his response to her question:

"Nobody here has a home you can point to. Our dwellings are dark groves,

River-banks serve as our bedding and meadows freshened by brooklets.

(675) That's where we live. Still, if this is your wish, and the choice that your heart prompts,

Climb up this ridge over here. I will plot you a path you can manage."

This said, he strode out in front and he showed them, from up on the summit,

Well-tended grasslands below. So they left the high hill and descended.

Father Anchises, deep in a hollow valley of greenness,

---

[207] Main epithet of Apollo, often standing for his name.

[208] Legendary poet, like Orpheus, in Greek tradition.

[209] The Sibyl wrongly assumes there are here districts or quarters as those in the city of Rome, and in line 681 Anchises is portrayed acting as a Roman censor (an elected office), selecting for the future which souls qualify as Romans.

(680)   Was, as it chanced, making careful review of the souls in confinement

Who, in time, would ascend to the light. He was holding a census,

Counting up all his descendants, the grandsons he doted on, weighing

Fates and fortunes of men, strength of character, power of body.

But, when he noticed Aeneas approach, reaching out across meadows,

(685)   He too opened his arms, reached both hands eagerly forward.

Tears were now flooding his cheeks, words poured from his mouth in a torrent:

"Have you at last really come? Did righteous love for your father

Conquer the rough road here as I thought it would! Son, can I really

Gaze at your face, hear the voice that I know, and be able to answer?

(690)   This thought I nurtured live in my mind, I was sure it would happen,

While I was counting the days. And my anxious hopes didn't fool me!

I have you now! I've heard of the lands, the extent of the seaways

You, dear son, have traversed. What a beating you've taken from danger!

O, how I worried that Libya's powers might harm you in some way!"

(695)   He, in reply, said: "Father, your sad image, rising before me

Time and again compelled me to push to this boundary's threshold.

Anchors are down in Etruscan waters. We've made it! So, father,

Give me your hand! Give it, don't pull away as I hug and embrace you!"

Waves of tears washed over his cheeks as he spoke in frustration:

(700)   Three attempts made to encircle his father's neck with his outstretched

Arms yielded three utter failures.[210] The image eluded his grasping

Hands like the puff of a breeze, as a dream flits away from a dreamer.

Through this, Aeneas observes in a nearby vale, a secluded

Grove with its green-leafed canopy rustling over the woodlands,

(705)   And river Lethe[211] too, flowing on past dwellings of calmness.

Peoples and nations, too many to count, seethe all around, swarming

---

[210] The ghost of Creusa (his wife) also eluded him at Troy. Cf. Achilles' failed attempt to embrace Patroklos' ghost (*Iliad* 23.99) and Odysseus' attempt to embrace his mother's ghost three times (*Odyssey* 11.196; see document 6.7). In the Sumerian version of *Gilgamesh* the hero does embrace Enkidu's spirit (see headnote to document 6.1).

[211] *Lethe* means "Forgetfulness" in Greek, with the added pun of *letum*, "death," in Latin. See the "River of Lethe" in Plato's "Myth of Er" (Part 7, document 5) and the Lake of Memory in the Orphic Gold Tablets (document 6.9).

Much as, on summer's serene, warm days, honey bees in the meadows
Settle on so many species of flowers, pour over the lilies'
Whiteness. The countryside's live with the hum of their buzzing.

(710) Shocked by this sudden sight, unaware of its meaning, Aeneas
Asks for some answers: what river might this be which flows over yonder,
Who are the people who've crowded the banks in a giant formation.
Father Anchises replies: "They're souls that are due second bodies:
So Fate rules, and they're drinking now from the waters of Lethe,

(715) Draughts that will free them of care and ensure long years of oblivion.
These are the souls, my family's line I've been wanting for ages
Just to parade in your presence, to set in your mind, name and number,
So you can, now you've found Italy, share my delight more pro-foundly."

"Father, must I then suppose some souls of ineffable lightness

(720) Soar, once again, to the sky just for reincarnation in clumsy
Bodies? What terrible passion for daylight possesses the poor things?"

"Son, I will not hold *you* in suspense," Anchises commences.
"*I'll* tell you now." He proceeds to reveal every detail in order:
"First, you must grasp that the heaven and earth and the sea's liquid flatness,

(725) Also the gleaming sphere of the moon, constellations, the huge sun
Feed on internal Energy. Mind, which suffuses these cosmic
Limbs, pervades the vast body and keeps the mass vital. This mixture
Generates life within humans and beasts, flying creatures, and also
Monsters Ocean spawns below marbled plains on its surface.

(730) Fire endows them with force, and the source of the seeds for that fire
Is, though it's slowed and restricted by noxious bodies, the heavens.
Earth-made flesh, limbs slouching to death, dull much of its vital
Force, causing people to fear and desire, suffer pain, and feel pleasure,
Fail to see open skies in their prisons of darkness and blindness.

(735) Even when life has departed, along with their last glimpse of daylight,
Not all traces of evil are gone from these pitiful creatures,
Not all bodily maladies leave. Of necessity, many
Harden and grow, become deeply ingrained in mysterious manners.
Therefore the souls are both punished and cleansed, and they pay off the hanging

(740)   Balance of crimes in the past. Some are stretched, hung up to the
empty

Breezes, while others are cleansed of their ingrained crime by
immersion

Deep in a giant whirlpool, or burned from within by a fire.

Each of us suffers his ghostly pain. When it's over, we're sent out,

All through Elysium's breadth. Just a few of us stay in the Blessed
Fields.

(745)   When the circle of time is complete, some day in the future,

Purged of the last trace of crime ingrained, they are left with ethereal

Power of perception, the fire of its clear breath, pure and untainted.

God summons all these souls, when they've rolled time's wheel for
a thousand

Years,[212] to convene in a mass at the Lethe, Oblivion's waters,

(750)   So, with their memories wholly erased, they can walk beneath
heaven's

Dome yet again and begin to desire to go back into bodies."

Finished, Anchises propelled both Aeneas and, with him,
the Sibyl

Into the midst of the seething and noisy assemblage, and clambered

High on a mound from whose top he could plainly distinguish the
faces

(755)   Passing in long lines before him and note their identities clearly.

"Come now: I'll set out in words the whole sequence of glory that
follows

Dardan sons in the future: illustrious spirits, descendants,

Souls that remain to be born of Italian peoples and go forth

Bearing your name. And I'll teach you what *your* fateful destiny
offers . . . "

(Anchises' speech continues until the end of the book, centered in the future of Aeneas in Italy and the glorious future of Rome, culminating in the figure of Octavian, called Caesar, later Augustus, including a passage in praise of Octavian's deceased nephew Marcellus.)

6.14. THE *DREAM OF SCIPIO*, FROM CICERO, *DE RE PUBLICA*, BOOK 6

Cicero (Marcus Tullius Cicero), from Arpinum, south of Rome, is the most highly acclaimed rhetorician (both as orator and writer of speeches) and one of the most influential writers of prose in all of Latin literature. Cicero was also a prominent political figure of his time (106–43 BCE), holding several

---

[212] Same time mentioned in the "Myth of Er" (see Part 7, document 5) and in Aeschylus' tragedy *Prometheus Bound*.

offices, including a consulship (63 BCE), in the midst of the turbulent end of the Republic. His voluminous preserved writings include letters and literary works, as well as famous speeches (e.g., *Against Catiline*, *Phillipics*) and treatises on oratory (*On the Orator*), religion (*On the Nature of the Gods*, *On Divination*), law (*On the Laws*), and philosophical and political thought, such as *De re publica*. The impact of his works on the Renaissance and Enlightenment recovery of Classical culture cannot be overstated.

Cicero wrote *De re publica* ("On the Republic" or more accurately "On the Commonwealth") during a time of retirement from public life, between 54 and 51 BCE, before the civil war between Pompey and Caesar broke out. Inspired by Plato's *Republic*, his treatise is also written in the form of a dialogue (in the Socratic manner). The interlocutors are Scipio Aemilianus (P. Cornelius Scipio Aemilianus Africanus Numantinus, 185–129 BCE) and a group of his close friends, who spend some days together at his country villa discussing matters of forms of government, political leadership, justice, and education.

Like the "Myth of Er" closes Plato's *Republic* with a tale about the soul in the afterlife (Part 7, document 5), at the end of this treatise, Scipio tells his guests of the strange and illuminating dream that also gave him a "view" of the afterlife. This was a dream he had twenty years before, in which his grandfather (through adoption), Publius Cornelius Scipio Africanus (also known as The Elder, 236–183 BE), appears to him. Scipio Africanus was the grandfather of Scipio (father of his adoptive father), most famous for his role during the Second Punic War (218–201 BCE), especially his final victory over Hannibal at Zama in 202. The dream, as Scipio (Aemilianus) tells his friends, happened during his visit to King Massinisa of the Numidians (Libyan tribes west of Carthage) in 149 BCE. The young Scipio had been sent to Africa as military tribune, just at the beginning of hostilities between Rome and Carthage known as the Third Punic War (150–146 BCE). Massinissa knew his grandfather Scipio Africanus personally. The Numidian king in fact died in 148 BCE, which means Scipio sets his narration the year before Massinissa's death, since he says his dream took place twenty years before the gathering at his villa in 129 BCE. The two Scipios, in the dream, look upon the cosmos and the minuscule earth from what we would call "space," while Scipio's ancestor talks about the configuration of the universe around the earth, the fate of the soul after death, the relative nature of all human things, especially fame, and even the future, predicting the military and political success of Scipio and his death at the age of 56. He has now reached this age, just when the scene of this meeting is set (129 BCE), in the same year in which he would be found dead, probably murdered by opposing political factions.

The *Dream of Scipio* (*Somnium Scipionis*) was so popular in antiquity that it maintained a manuscript tradition separate from the rest of the *De re pubica*, which was only partially and more fragmentarily preserved.

SOURCE: Cicero, *De re publica*, Book 6. 9–26. O. J. Thatcher, ed., *The Library of Original Sources*, *Vol. III: The Roman World*, pp. 216–241 (Milwaukee, 1907), with minor modifications.

(9) When I had arrived in Africa, where I was, as you are aware, military tribune of the fourth legion under the consul Manilius, there was nothing of which I was more earnestly desirous than to see King Massinissa, who, for very just reasons, had been always the especial friend of our family. When I was introduced to him, the old man embraced me, shed tears, and then, looking up to heaven, exclaimed: "I thank thee, O supreme Sun, and you also, you other celestial beings, that before I departed from this life I behold in my kingdom, and in my palace, Publius Cornelius Scipio, by whose mere name I seem to be reanimated; so complete and indelibly is the recollection of that best and most invincible of men, Africanus,[213] imprinted in my mind." After this, I inquired of him concerning the affairs of his kingdom. He, on the other hand, questioned me about the condition of our commonwealth, and in this mutual interchange of conversation we passed the whole of that day.

(10) In the evening, we were entertained in a manner worthy the magnificence of a king, and carried on our discourse for a considerable part of the night. And during all this time the old man spoke of nothing but Africanus, all whose actions, and even remarkable sayings, he remembered distinctly. At last, when we retired to bed, I fell in a more profound sleep than usual, both because I was fatigued with my journey, and because I had sat up the greatest part of the night.

Here I had the following dream, occasioned, as I verily believe, by our preceding conversation—for it frequently happens that the thoughts and discourses which have employed us in the daytime, produce in our sleep an effect somewhat similar to that which Ennius writes happened to him about Homer, of whom, in his waking hours, he used frequently to think and speak.

Africanus, I thought, appeared to me in that shape, with which I was better acquainted from his picture, than from any personal knowledge of him. When I perceived it was he, I confess I trembled with consternation; but he addressed me, saying, "Take courage, my Scipio, be not afraid, and carefully remember what I am saying to you.

(11) "Do you see that city Carthage, which, though brought under the Roman yoke by me, is now renewing former wars, and cannot live in peace? (and he pointed to Carthage from a lofty spot, full of stars, and brilliant and glittering.) To attack it you have this day arrived, almost a private soldier. Before two years, however, are elapsed, you shall be consul, and complete its overthrow; and you shall obtain, by your own merit, the surname of Africanus, which, as yet, belongs to you no otherwise than as derived from me. And when you have destroyed Carthage, and received the honor of a triumph, and been made censor, and, in quality of ambassador, visited Egypt, Syria, Asia, and Greece, you shall be elected a second time consul in your absence, and by utterly destroying Numantia, put an end to a most dangerous war.[214] But when you have entered the Capitol in your triumphal car, you shall find

---

[213] Publius Cornelius Scipio, called Africanus for his success against Carthage in North Africa.

[214] In 146 BCE, two years after his arrival in Africa, Scipio was elected consul (under the required age) and led the long siege of the city and its utter destruction. He also had a sucessful military career in Spain, where he took the resisting city of Numantia in 134 BCE, when he was consul for a second time.

the Roman commonwealth all in a ferment, through the intrigues of my grandson Tiberius Gracchus.[215]

(12) "It is on this occasion, my dear Africanus, that you show your country the greatness of your understanding, capacity and prudence. But I see that the destiny, however, of that time is, as it were, uncertain; for when your age shall have accomplished seven times eight revolutions of the sun, and your fatal hours shall be marked out by the natural product of these two numbers, each of which is esteemed a perfect one, but for different reasons,—then shall the whole city have recourse to you alone, and place its hopes in your auspicious name. On you the senate, all good citizens, the allies, the people of Latium, shall cast their eyes; on you the preservation of the state shall entirely depend. In a word, if you escape the impious machinations of your relatives, you will, in the quality of dictator, establish order and tranquility in the commonwealth."

When on this Laelius made an exclamation, and the rest of the company groaned loudly, Scipio, with a gentle smile, said, "I entreat you, do not wake me out of my dream, but have patience, and hear the rest."

(13) "Now, in order to encourage you, my dear Africanus," continued the shade of my ancestor, "to defend the state with the greater cheerfulness, be assured that for all those who have in any way conduced to the preservation, defense, and enlargement of their native country, there is a certain place in heaven, where they shall enjoy an eternity of happiness. For nothing on earth is more agreeable to God, the Supreme Governor of the universe, than the assemblies and societies of men united together by laws, which are called States. It is from heaven their rulers and preservers came, and there they return."

(14) Though at these words I was extremely troubled, not so much at the fear of death, as at the perfidy of my own relations, yet I recollected myself enough to inquire, whether he himself, my father Paulus, and others whom we look upon as dead, were really living. "Yes, truly, replied he, they all enjoy life who have escaped from the chains of the body as from a prison. But as to what you call life on earth, that is no more than one form of death. But see, here comes your father Paulus towards you!" And as soon as I observed him, my eyes burst out into a flood of tears; but he took me in his arms, and bade me not weep.

(15) When my first transports subsided, and I regained the liberty of speech, I addressed my father thus: "You, best and most venerable of parents, since this, as I am informed by Africanus, is the only substantial life, why do I linger on earth, and not rather hasten to come hither where you are?" "That," replied he, "is impossible; unless that God, whose temples is all that vast expanse you behold, shall free you from the fetters of the body, you can have no admission into this place. Mankind have received their being on this very condition, that they should labor for the preservation of that globe, which is situated, as you see, in the midst of this temple, and is called earth. Men are likewise endowed with a soul, which is a portion of the eternal fires, which you call stars and constellations, and which, being round, spheri-

---

[215] The faction of the Gracchi was rumored to have had a role in Scipio's murder, since he had sided with the aristocratic party (*Optimates*) and opposed their popular party (*Populares*), even though they had family ties.

cal bodies, animated by divine intelligence, perform their cycles and revolutions with amazing rapidity. It is your duty, therefore, my Publius, and that of all who have any veneration for the gods, to preserve this wonderful union of soul and body; nor without the express command of him who gave you a soul, should the least thought be entertained of quitting human life, lest you seem to desert the post assigned to you by God himself. But rather follow the example of your grandfather here, and of me, your father, in paying a strict regard to justice and piety; which is due in a great degree to parents and relations, but most of all to our country. Such a life as this is the true way to heaven, and to the company of those, who, after having lived on earth and escaped from the body, inhabit the place, which you now behold."

(16) This was the shining circle, or zone, whose remarkable brightness distinguishes it among the constellations, and which, after the Greeks, you call the Milky Way. From thence, as I took a view of the universe, everything appeared beautiful and admirable; for there, those stars are to be seen that are never visible from our globe, and everything appears of such magnitude as we could not have imagined. The least of all the stars was that removed furthest from heaven, and situated next to earth; I mean our moon, which shines with a borrowed light. Now the globes of the stars far surpass the magnitude of our earth, which at that distance appeared so exceedingly small, that I could not but be sensibly affected on seeing our whole empire no larger than if we touched the earth with a point.

(17) And as long as I continued to observe the earth with great attention, "How long, I pray you," said Africanus, "will your mind be fixed on that object? why don't you rather take a view of the magnificent temples among which you have arrived? The universe is composed of nine circles, or rather spheres, one of which is the heavenly one, and is exterior to all the rest, which it embraces, being itself the Supreme God, and bounding and containing the whole. In it are fixed those stars, which revolve with never-varying courses. Below this are seven other spheres, which revolve in a contrary direction to that of the heavens. One of these is occupied by the globe, which on earth they call Saturn. Next to that is the star of Jupiter, so benign and salutary to mankind. The third in order is that fiery and terrible planet called Mars. Below this again, almost in the middle region, is the Sun—the leader, governor, the prince of the other luminaries; the soul of the world, which it regulates and illumines, being of such vast size that it pervades and gives light to all places. Then follow Venus and Mercury, which attend, as it were, on the Sun. Lastly, the Moon, which shines only in the reflected beams of the Sun, moves in the lowest sphere of all. Below this, every thing is mortal, and tends to dissolution, except for that gift of the gods, the soul, which has been given by the liberality of the gods to the human race; but above the Moon all is eternal. For the Earth, which is in the ninth globe, and occupies the center, is immoveable, and being the lowest, all others gravitate towards it."

(18) When I had recovered myself from the astonishment occasioned by such a wonderful prospect, I thus addressed Africanus, "Pray, what is this sound that strikes my ears in so loud and agreeable a manner?" To which he replied, "It is that which is called the music of the spheres, being produced by their motion and impulse; and being formed by unequal intervals, but such as are divided according to the most just proportion, it produces, by duly tempering acute with grave sounds,

various concerts of harmony. For it is impossible that motions so great should be performed without any noise; and it is agreeable to nature that the extremes on one side should produce sharp, and on the other flat sounds. For which reason the sphere of the fixed stars, being the highest, and being carried with a more rapid velocity, moves with a shrill and acute sound; whereas that of the moon, being the lowest, moves with a very flat one. As to the Earth, which makes the ninth sphere, it remains immovably fixed in the middle or lowest part of the universe. But those eight revolving circles, in which both Mercury and Venus are moved with the same celerity, give out sounds that are divided by seven distinct intervals, which is generally the regulating number of all things.

"This celestial harmony has been imitated by learned musicians, both on stringed instruments and with the voice, whereby they have opened to themselves a way to return to the celestial regions, as have likewise many others who have employed their sublime genius while on earth in cultivating the divine sciences. By the amazing noise of this sound, the ears of mankind have been in some degree deafened, and indeed, hearing is the dullest of all the human senses. Thus, the people who dwell near the cataracts of the Nile, which are called Catadupa, are, by the excessive roar, which that river makes in precipitating itself from those lofty mountains, entirely deprived of the sense of hearing. And so inconceivably great is this sound, which is produced by the rapid motion of the whole universe, that the human ear is no more capable of receiving it, than the eye is able to look steadfastly and directly on the sun, whose beams easily dazzle the strongest sight."

While I was busied in admiring the scene of wonders, I could not help casting my eyes every now and then on the earth.

(19) On which Africanus said, "I perceive that you are still employed in contemplating the seat and residence of mankind. But if it appears to you so small, as in fact it really is, despise its vanities, and fix your attention forever on these heavenly objects. Is it possible that you should attain any human applause or glory that is worth the contending for? The earth, you see, is peopled but in a very few places, and those too of small extent; and they appear like so many little spots of green scattered through vast uncultivated deserts. And those who inhabit the earth are not only so remote from each other as to be cut off from all mutual correspondence, but their situation being in oblique or contrary parts of the globe, or perhaps in those diametrically opposite to yours, all expectation of universal fame must fall to the ground.

(20) "You may likewise observe that the same globe of the earth is girt and surrounded with certain zones, whereof those two that are most remote from each other, and lie under the opposite poles of heaven, are congealed with frost; but that one in the middle, which is far the largest, is scorched with the intense heat of the sun. The other two are habitable, one towards the south—the inhabitants of which are your Antipodes, with whom you have no connection—the other, towards the north, is that which you inhabit, whereof a very small part, as you may see, falls to your share. For the whole extent of what you see is, as it were, but a little island, narrow at both ends and wide in the middle, which is surrounded by the sea which on earth you call the great Atlantic ocean, and which, notwithstanding this magnificent name, you see is very insignificant. And even in these cultivated

and well-known countries, has yours, or any of our names, ever passed the heights of the Caucasus, or the currents of the Ganges? In what other parts to the north or the south, or where the sun rises and sets, will your names ever be heard? And if we leave these out of the question, how small a space is there left for your glory to spread itself abroad? and how long will it remain in the memory of those whose minds are now full of it?

(21) "Besides all this, if the progeny of any future generation should wish to transmit to their posterity the praises of any one of us, which they have heard from their forefathers, yet the deluges and combustions of the earth which must necessarily happen at their destined periods will prevent our obtaining, not only an eternal, but even a durable glory. And after all, what does it signify, whether those who shall hereafter be born talk of you, when those who have lived before you, whose number was perhaps not less, and whose merit certainly greater, were not so much as acquainted with your name?

(22) "Especially since not one of those who shall hear of us is able to retain in his memory the transactions of a single year. The bulk of mankind, indeed, measure their year by the return of the sun, which is only one star. But, when all the stars shall have returned to the place whence they set out, and after long periods shall again exhibit the same aspect of the whole heavens, that is what ought properly to be called the revolution of a year, though I scarcely dare attempt to enumerate the vast multitude of ages contained in it. For as the sun in old time was eclipsed, and seemed to be extinguished, at the time when the soul of Romulus penetrated into these eternal mansions, so, when all the constellations and stars shall revert to their primary position, and the sun shall at the same point and time be again eclipsed, then you may consider that the grand year is completed. Be assured, however, that the twentieth part of it is not yet elapsed.

(23) "Why, if you have no hopes of returning to this place, where great and good men enjoy all that their souls can wish for, of what value, pray, is all that human glory, which can hardly endure for a small portion of one year? If, then, you wish to elevate your views to the contemplation of this eternal seat of splendor, you will not be satisfied with the praises of your fellow-mortals, nor with any human rewards that your exploits can obtain; but Virtue herself must point out to you the true and only object worthy of your pursuit. Leave to others to speak of you as they may, for speak they will. Their discourses will be confined to the narrow limits of the countries you see, nor will their duration be very extensive, for they will perish like those who utter them, and will be no more remembered by their posterity."

(24) When he had ceased to speak in this manner, I said "O, Africanus, if indeed the door of heaven is open to those who have deserved well of their country, although, indeed, from my childhood, I have always followed yours and my father's steps, and have not neglected to imitate your glory, still I will from henceforth strive to follow them more closely." "Follow them, then," said he, "and consider your body only, not yourself, as mortal. For it is not your outward form which constitutes your being, but your mind; not that substance which is palpable to the senses, but your spiritual nature. Know, then, that you are a god—for a god it must be which flourishes, and feels, and recollects, and foresees, and governs, regulates and moves

the body over which it is set, as the Supreme Ruler does the world, which is subject to him. For as that Eternal Being moves whatever is mortal in this world, so the immortal mind of man moves the frail body with which it is connected.

(25) "For whatever is always moving must be eternal, but that which derives its motion from a power, which is foreign to itself, when that motion ceases must itself lose its animation. That alone, then, which moves itself can never cease to be moved, because it can never desert itself. Moreover, it must be the source, and origin, and principle of motion in all the rest. There can be nothing prior to a principle, for all things must originate from it, and it cannot itself derive its existence from any other source, for if it did it would no longer be a principle. And if it had no beginning it can have no end, for a beginning that is put an end to will neither be renewed by any other cause, nor will it produce anything else of itself. All things, therefore, must originate from one source. Thus it follows, that motion must have its source in something which is moved by itself, and which can neither have a beginning nor an end. Otherwise all the heavens and all nature must perish, for it is impossible that they can of themselves acquire any power of producing motion in themselves.

(26) "As, therefore, it is plain that what is moved by itself must be eternal; who will deny that this is the general condition and nature of minds? For, as everything is inanimate which is moved by an impulse exterior to itself, so what is animated is moved by an interior impulse of its own; for this is the peculiar nature and power of mind. And if that alone has the power of self-motion it can neither have had a beginning, nor can it have an end. Do you, therefore, exercise this mind of yours in the best pursuits! And the best pursuits are those, which consist in promoting the good of your country. Such employments will speed the flight of your mind to this its proper abode; and its flight will be still more rapid, if, even while it is enclosed in the body, it will look abroad, and disengage itself as much as possible from its bodily dwelling, by the contemplation of things which are external to itself.

"This it should do to the utmost of its power. For the minds of those who have given themselves up to the pleasures of the body, paying as it were a servile obedience to their lustful impulses, have violated the laws of God and man; and therefore, when they are separated from their bodies, flutter continually round the earth on which they lived, and are not allowed to return to this celestial region, till they have been purified by the revolution of many ages."

Thus saying he vanished, and I awoke from my dream.

6.15. PSYCHE'S DESCENT TO THE UNDERWORLD, FROM APULEIUS, *THE GOLDEN ASS*, BOOK 6

This passage is excerpted from the Cupid and Psyche story in Apuleius' novel *The Golden Ass* (or *Metamorphoses*). The rest of the story is reproduced in Part 5, document 20 (see headnote to that document for further information about Apuleius and his work). Following the events that lead to the union and sudden separation of Cupid ("Love," Venus' son) and Psyche ("The Soul," represented as a young woman), Venus puts Psyche, her undesired daughter-in-law, through impossible trials in order to humiliate her and demoralize her, all of which she accomplishes. Finally, she adds a final test, a journey to the Underworld (the end of the story is in Part 5, document 20).

SOURCE: Apuleius, *The Golden Ass*, Book 6.16–21. P. G. Walsh, *Apuleius, The Golden Ass* (Oxford World's Classics, Oxford and New York, 1994), with minor modifications.

(16) (. . .) Venus flashed a menacing smile as she addressed her with threats of yet more monstrous ill-treatment: "Now indeed I regard you as a witch with great and lofty powers, for you have carried out so efficiently commands of mine such as these. But you will have to undertake one further task for me, my girl. Take this box" (she handed it over) "and make straight for Hades, for the funereal dwelling of Orcus[216] himself. Give the box to Proserpina, and say: 'Venus asks you to send her a small supply of your beauty-preparation, enough for just one day, because she has been tending her sick son, and has used hers all up by rubbing it on him.' Make your way back with it as early as you can, because I need it to doll myself up so as to attend the Deities' Theatre."

(17) Then Psyche came to the full realization that this was the end of the road for her. All pretence was at an end; she saw clearly that she was being driven to her immediate doom. It could not be otherwise, for she was being forced to journey on foot of her own accord to Tartarus and the shades below. She lingered no longer, but made for a very high tower, intending to throw herself headlong from it, for she thought that this was the direct and most glorious possible route down to the world below. But the tower suddenly burst into speech, and said: "Poor girl, why do you seek to put an end to yourself by throwing yourself down? What is the point of rash surrender before this, your final hazardous labor? Once your spirit is sundered from your body, you will certainly descend to the depths of Tartarus without the possibility of a return journey.

(18) "Listen to me. Sparta, the famed Achaean city, lies not far from here. On its borders you must look for Taenarus, which lies hidden in a trackless region. Dis[217] has his breathing-vent there, and a sign-post points through open gates to a track which none should tread. Once you have crossed the threshold and committed yourself to that path, the track will lead you directly to Orcus' very palace. But you are not to advance through that dark region altogether empty-handed, but carry in both hands barley-cakes baked in sweet wine, and have between your lips twin coins. When you are well advanced on your infernal journey, you will meet a lame ass carrying a load of logs, with a driver likewise lame; he will ask you to hand him some sticks which have slipped from his load, but you must pass by in silence without uttering a word. Immediately after that you will reach the lifeless river over which Charon presides. He peremptorily demands the fare, and when he receives it he transports travelers on his stitched-up craft over to the further shore. (So even among the dead, greed enjoys its life; even that great god Charon, who gathers taxes for Dis, does not do anything for nothing. A poor man on the point of death must

---

[216] Latin and Roman god of the Underworld and of oaths. His name (like that of Hades) is often used as equivalent to the Underworld itself.

[217] The Roman god of the Underworld.

find his fare, and no one will let him breathe his last until he has his copper ready.) You must allow this squalid elder to take for your fare one of the coins you are to carry, but he must remove it from your mouth with his own hand. Then again, as you cross the sluggish stream, an old man now dead will float up to you, and raising his decaying hands will beg you to drag him into the boat; but you must not be moved by a sense of pity, for that is not permitted.

(19) "When you have crossed the river and have advanced a little further, some aged women weaving at the loom will beg you to lend a hand for a short time. But you are not permitted to touch that either, for all these and many other distractions are part of the ambush which Venus will set to induce you to release one of the cakes from your hands. Do not imagine that the loss of a mere barley-cake is a trivial matter, for if you relinquish either of them, the daylight of this world above will be totally denied you. Posted there is a massive hound with a huge, triple-formed head. This monstrous, fearsome brute confronts the dead with thunderous barking, though his menaces are futile since he can do them no harm. He keeps constant guard before the very threshold and the dark hall of Proserpina, protecting that deserted abode of Dis. You must disarm him by offering him a cake as his spoils. Then you can easily pass him, and gain immediate access to Proserpina herself. She will welcome you in genial and kindly fashion, and she will try to induce you to sit on a cushioned seat beside her and enjoy a rich repast. But you must settle on the ground, ask for coarse bread, and eat it. Then you must tell her why you have come. When you have obtained what she gives you, you must make your way back, using the remaining cake to neutralize the dog's savagery. Then you must give the greedy mariner the one coin which you have held back; and once across the river you must retrace your earlier steps and return to the harmony of heaven's stars. Of all these injunctions I urge you particularly to observe this: do not seek to open or to pry into the box that you will carry, nor be in any way inquisitive about the treasure of divine beauty hidden within it."

(20) This was how that far-sighted tower performed its prophetic role. Psyche immediately sped to Taenarus, and having duly obtained the coins and cakes she hastened down the path to Hades. She passed the lame ass-driver without a word, handed the fare to the ferryman for the river crossing, ignored the entreaty of the dead man floating on the surface, disregarded the crafty pleas of the weavers, fed the cake to the dog to quell his fearsome rage, and gained access to the house of Proserpina. Psyche declined the soft cushion and the rich food offered by her hostess; she perched on the ground at her feet, and was content with plain bread. She then reported her mission from Venus. The box was at once filled and closed out of her sight, and Psyche took it. She quieted the dog's barking by disarming it with the second cake, offered her remaining coin to the ferryman, and quite animatedly hastened out of Hades. But once she was back in the light of this world and had reverently hailed it; her mind was dominated by rash curiosity, in spite of her eagerness to see the end of her service. She said: "How stupid I am to be carrying this beauty-lotion fit for deities, and not to take a single drop of it for myself, for with this at any rate I can be pleasing to my beautiful lover."

(21) The words were scarcely out of her mouth when she opened the box. But inside there was no beauty-lotion or anything other than the sleep of Hades, a truly

Stygian sleep. As soon as the lid was removed and it was laid bare, it attacked her and pervaded all her limbs in a thick cloud. It laid hold of her, so that she fell prostrate on the path where she had stood. She lay there motionless, no more animate than a corpse at rest.

But Cupid was now recovering, for his wound had healed. He could no longer bear Psyche's long separation from him, so he glided out of the high-set window of the chamber which was his prison. His wings were refreshed after their period of rest, so he progressed much more swiftly to reach his Psyche. Carefully wiping the sleep from her, he restored it to its former lodging in the box. Then he roused Psyche with an innocuous prick of his arrow. "Poor, dear Psyche," he exclaimed, "see how as before your curiosity might have been your undoing! But now hurry to complete the task imposed on you by my mother's command; I shall see to the rest." After saying this, her lover rose lightly on his wings, while Psyche hurried to bear Proserpina's gift back to Venus.

(For the end of the Cupid and Psyche story, see Part 5, document 20.)

PART 7 ✦ # PLATO'S MYTHS

THE ORIGINS OF our culture's foundational myths are buried deep in what historians and anthropologists increasingly call "deep history." This is true even of those myths that have come down to us in association with the names of specific individuals: no one believes that Homer or Hesiod "made up" their accounts of the gods and heroes. The ancient bards were conduits of a sort, channels through which the gods' or the muses' or their ancestors' wisdom flowed down through the ages; these men transmitted traditional tales inherited from a past that appeared ancient even from their own archaic perspective. No doubt they elaborated these tales, embellishing them with the adornments of their own personal genius; yet we can acknowledge and admire the best of the poets' distinct contributions without making the mistake of attributing to them an original act of creation *ex nihilo*.

But what of Plato? Must we insist that those sections of the dialogues commonly referred to as "Plato's myths" are, likewise, independent of and much older than the man most closely identified with them? Or is it not rather the case that here at last we have before us myths whose author we can name? Plato was born to a noble Athenian family sometime near the beginning of the Peloponnesian War (431–404 BCE), probably around 424–423 BCE, and died in 348–347 BCE. As a young man he made the acquaintance of Socrates (470–399 BCE), under whose influence he developed an abiding love for the philosophical life. Not long after Socrates' execution, Plato began to compose philosophical dialogues, a practice he continued until his own death some fifty years later. Working from a plot of land in a grove beyond the city walls, where a shrine to a hero called Akademos stood, he founded and supervised a philosophical school known to us as the "Academy." This school became the first institution of "higher education," from where Plato conceived and disseminated ideas of such astonishing depth and beauty that their influence upon the development of Western civilization is hardly calculable. Strictly speaking, we can classify Plato's literary output as philosophy, but his dialogues are also much more than philosophy— and into many of these dialogues Plato wove his famous myths.

All introductions, headnotes, translations, and notes for this section are by Mark Anderson.

It would be comforting if we had only to name Plato as author of the myths and to produce a brief, general biography of the man. Unfortunately, however, nothing with Plato is ever straightforward or simple. The problem is that, despite our possessing so many of Plato's works (and we may very well be fortunate enough to have his entire oeuvre), his mind remains elusive. We know nothing of his motivations and intentions as an author, for neither he nor any one of his intimates or associates left reliable information directly pertaining to these matters. Nothing prevents us from drawing inferences from the texts themselves, of course, but this procedure has its limitations: it yields no certain truths, and perhaps not even probabilities. Plato's dialectical mode of composition ensures that his readers will glean from his texts only intimations of his intentions. We are left, then, with the most tenuous of possibilities—infinite and tantalizing possibilities, to be sure, but nevertheless something much less than certainty.

Plato famously makes no appearance in the world of his dialogues (he is mentioned by name in three places, but he never speaks). Within this world, the philosophy is articulated by others—most often, of course, by Socrates. Yet in the telling of the myths even Socrates is frequently displaced: although he narrates the *Republic*'s "Myth of Er," he attributes this description of the underworld to an eyewitness who had died and come back to life (*Republic* 614b; see document 7.5); he implies that the poet Stesichoros is in some way responsible for the myth in his second speech in the *Phaedrus* (244a); Protagoras the sophist delivers the myth in the dialogue bearing his name (document 7.2); Aristophanes relates the *Symposium*'s great myth of Eros (document 7.4); and the history and description of Atlantis as told by Kritias comes from Egyptian priests by way of Solon (document 7.3). It has even been argued that far from inventing the image about the soul in the *Phaedo* (not included below), Plato borrowed it from the Pythagorean tradition of Sicily and southern Italy. Who, then, is the author of these myths? This question may have no definite answer.

Even if we could unambiguously identify Plato as the original author of his myths, we would still encounter questions concerning their nature and purpose. Today we are inclined to contrast the terms *mythos* and *logos*, employing a distinction between "fictitious tale" and "rational account" that some trace back to Plato himself. But Plato's presentation of his myths tends to subvert this distinction. Consider, for example, the description of the underworld with which the *Gorgias* concludes: Socrates insists that this description is not a *mythos* but rather a *logos*; he offers it as being true and claims to be persuaded by it (523a, 526d–527a). Similarly, Protagoras calls his discourse a *logos* (324c). Aristophanes refers to his speech as a *logos* (193d), as does his interlocutor Eryximachos (189a–b). The story of Atlantis is repeatedly denominated a *logos* and is even affirmed to be "altogether true" (*Timaeus*: 20d–21d; *Kritias*: 109a, 113a, 120d). Moreover, as we have seen, Kritias attributes this *logos*, by way of Solon—one of the Seven Sages and, therefore, presumably a trustworthy source—to Egyptian priests in possession of actual historical records, presumably even more reliable informants. It is true that in some of these contexts "logos" may properly imply nothing more than "speech" or "discourse," but the point is that we cannot say for sure, and besides, this possibility does not hold for all of these examples. It is also true that we should never simplistically identify the opinions expressed by Plato's characters with Plato's own thoughts and beliefs, but this is not our intention: we mean only to demonstrate that Plato's use of the terms *mythos* and *logos* is so varied that when reading his myths we cannot confidently distinguish what he takes to be fact from what he considers mere fantasy. What are we to say then? Are Plato's myths false stories, or are they instead reasoned expositions of the truth? If they are the latter—and Plato's designating some of them *logoi* at least suggests that they could be—then they can hardly be "myths."

It might be objected that since myths are never passed down explicitly *as* myths, especially if by "myth" one understands an acknowledged falsehood, Plato's tendency to envelop his stories in the rhetoric of truth and reason does not provide the basis for not calling them "myths." This is a serious consideration, yet its impact is somewhat diminished when we reflect that myths are traditionally regarded as true by peoples who have yet to draw clear lines between what we would call historical facts and fictions, whereas Plato seems to be quite aware of the difference. Indeed, his presentation of what seem to us evident *mythoi* as *logoi* is baffling precisely because we are inclined to believe that he understood their substantive dissimilarities. Having noted this, however, we should acknowledge that Plato does not *always* upset the conceptual markers that separate *mythoi* from *logoi*, for he occasionally employs the standard distinction himself. Yet rather than settle our doubts and confusions, Plato's inconsistency here, and the surprising ways he exploits the distinction, only deepen our uncertainty. To take a most striking example: in the *Republic* Socrates explicitly characterizes *mythoi* as false (377d). Even so, he argues that some of these falsehoods may be useful and noble, particularly when, "in the telling of myths," the founders and rulers of a city who do not know the truth about ancient matters construct a falsehood similar to the truth, especially one that will prevent or cure a friend and fellow citizen from bad actions (382c–d, 389b). Nor does Socrates merely argue this case theoretically: he enacts it himself by explicitly advocating the dissemination of his own noble falsehood, which he refers to more than once as a myth, among the rulers and citizens of an ideal city in order to promote internal harmony and friendship (this is the famous "noble lie": 414b–415d). He even calls the "Myth of Er" a *mythos*—despite its substantive similarities to the myth in the *Gorgias*, which, as we have noted, he makes a point of classifying as a *logos*— while in the same breath declaring that if we believe it, it will save us (621b–c). All this is to say that by playing as he does with the categories of *mythos* and *logos* Plato constantly frustrates our expectations and thereby eludes our every endeavor to guess what he thought, and what he hoped his readers would think, of those mystifying passages that we call his "myths."

As for the purpose of Plato's myths, one popular account suggests that Plato employs *mythoi* to communicate truths that transcend the reach of human *logos*, as one turns to poetry to express insights that strain against the limits of prosaic language. But quite apart from the problem of Plato's often overleaping the divide between *mythos* and *logos*, there is the further problem that many of the myths seem to be little more than imaginative restatements of the arguments of the dialogues in which they appear, or at most elaborations of these arguments by way of the introduction of supernatural landscapes and divine beings. The "Myth of Er" may be the best example of this, for the *Republic* is, very specifically and explicitly, an argument that the just life is superior to the unjust life *without any reference whatever to the supernatural*. Socrates relates Er's story only *after* the conclusion of the *logos*, which in and of itself is self-contained—the *mythos* adds no substance to the *logos*, for the *logos* is complete as it is. We may also consider Protagoras' story of Prometheus' gift to humanity or Aristophanes' story of original human nature: these men speak of the gods indeed, but not because their claims exceed human expression or understanding. Their tales, in fact, are straightforward and clear, and one can imagine their making their philosophical points with no reference to the gods at all, though perhaps they would then be less entertaining or moving. This is not to say that by means of his myths Plato intended merely to manipulate our pleasures and emotions, for it would be foolish to deny that any part of any one of Plato's works is without philosophical substance. And this is precisely the point: whatever Plato intended to accomplish by including these myths in his dialogues, his aim no doubt was richer, deeper, and far more varied than any single explanation can account for.

Pursuing the trail of Plato's myths, we are led into an intellectual thicket from which we cannot disentangle ourselves. We know so little about these myths—about their pre-Platonic history, about Plato's understanding of their truth-status and existential value, about their purpose or purposes in the dialogues—that we cannot think our way through the many questions they put to us. Plato had a word for this condition: *aporia*, which literally means "a lack of passage," "an inability to proceed." Many of Plato's dialogues conclude with the characters experiencing the perplexity of *aporia*, so perhaps it is fitting that we reach this point as well.

The followings sections correspond thematically to five of the parts of this *Anthology*. Only the part on epic stories about gods, heroes, and monsters (Part 3) finds no match in the mythical repertoire imbedded in Plato's writings works. The order below, therefore, follows the order of the *Anthology*'s parts, not the internal order in Plato's works. ✦

7.1. THE DEMIURGE, FROM THE *TIMAEUS*

In the following excerpt from Plato's great cosmological dialogue *Timaeus*, the character Timaeus (Gr. *Timaios*), a philosopher from southern Italy (unknown outside the dialogues of Plato), describes for Socrates the nature and composition of the universe. In the course of his account Timaeus discusses the motives of the craftsman deity who constructed the cosmos, the demiurge (*demiourgos*), as well as the materials with which he worked, his mode of construction, and the appearance of his final product.

SOURCE: Plato, *Timaeus* 29d–34b, translated by M. Anderson.

(29) Let us state the reason why he who constructed Becoming and the All constructed it. He was good, and in the good no envy about anything ever comes to be; being free of this he wanted all things as much as possible to be like himself. (30) This is the most fundamental principle of Becoming and of the cosmos, and whoever accepts this from the testimony of wise men would certainly act most correctly. Wanting everything to be good and nothing bad, to the degree that this is possible, the god took hold of as much of the All as was visible and not still but moving inharmoniously and disorderly, and he brought it into order from disorder, judging the former altogether better than the latter. For it neither was nor is right for that which is best to do any other than the most beautiful deed. So, thinking the matter over he found that among those things visible by nature, no mindless whole could ever be more beautiful than an intelligent whole and that, moreover, it is impossible for intellect to be present in something apart from soul. Reasoning thus, he constructed the All by setting intellect in soul and soul in body so that through his working upon it it might be as beautiful and good a work as possible. Thus, according to the likely account, we must say that this cosmos in truth has come into being an ensouled and intelligent living thing through the foresight of god.

Having made this beginning, we must state what comes after these things. In the likeness of which of the living things did the one who constructed this All construct it? Let us not think it appropriate to say that he constructed it in the likeness of any of those that have been born in the form of a part—for nothing like that which is incomplete could ever become beautiful—but rather let us affirm that it is of all things most similar to that of which the other living things individually and by kinds are components. For this comprehends within itself all the intelligible living things, just as this cosmos comprehends us and all the other visible living things that have been made. Particularly wanting to make this All like the most beautiful and altogether most complete of intelligible things, (31) he made it a single visible living thing having within itself all kinds related to itself by nature.

Have we spoken correctly of one heaven or would it have been more correct to say that there are many and countless heavens? There is one, if really this heaven was crafted according to the model. For that which comprehends all intelligible living things could never be second alongside another, for there would have to be yet another living thing around that one, of which those two would be part, and we would more correctly say that our heaven was similar not to the first two but to this comprehensive one. Therefore, in order that our heaven might be as unique as the altogether complete living thing, the maker made neither two nor countless cosmoses, but this heaven has come to be and will remain one of a kind.

That which has come into being is necessarily bodily and visible and tangible, but nothing could ever be visible apart from fire, nor tangible apart from some solidity, nor solid apart from earth. For this reason, when he began to compose the body of the All, he made it from fire and earth. But it is not possible properly to join only two things without a third, for there must be some bond between to bring them together. The best of bonds is that which makes itself and the things it is bonding as unified as possible, and proportion naturally effects this most beautifully. For whenever of three numbers, either solids (32) or squares, the middle term is of the sort that whatever the first is to it, it itself is to the last and, again, whatever the last is to the middle, the middle is to the first, then the middle becomes the first and the last, and the last and the first both become middle terms, and thus necessarily they all are the same and, having come to be the same, they will all be one. If it had been necessary that the body of the All be a plane, having no depth, then one middle term would have sufficed to bind its associated terms with itself, but as it is, it is fitting that it be solid, and solid things are never joined together by one, but always by two middle terms. Therefore, the god placed both water and air between fire and earth, and having related them to one another as proportionally as possible, such that as fire is to air, air is to water, and as air is to water, water is to earth, he bound them together and composed a visible and tangible heaven. For these reasons, and from four things of this sort, the body of the cosmos came to be, harmonized by proportionality. Thus it had friendship and entered into sameness with itself, and so became indissoluble by any other than by him who bound it together.

The composition of the cosmos took the whole of each of the four elements, for he who composed it composed it from all of the fire and water and air and earth, leaving outside of it no part or power of any element, for he reasoned as follows: first, in order that it might be as much as possible a complete whole composed (33) of complete parts; in addition, that it might be one, with none of the elements left out from which another such might come to be; also in order that it might not suffer old age and disease, realizing that heat and cold and all other such extreme conditions, externally surrounding and falling upon a composite body, destroy it before its natural time and, bringing upon it illness and old age, cause it to decay. For this calculated reason he made it a single whole from all wholes, complete, free of old age and illness. He gave to it a shape fitting and kin. The shape befitting that living thing intended to encompass in itself all living things would be a shape embracing in itself all shapes; hence he fashioned it into a spherical, circular form, equidistant in every direction from the middle to the extremities, of all shapes the most complete and the most like itself, for he thought the like to be more beautiful by far than the unlike. He finished it off to be all over externally a smooth circle for many reasons: it had no need of eyes, for nothing visible had been left outside of it; nor of ears, for there was nothing audible; nor had it need of surrounding air for respiration; nor was there need of any organ by which it might receive nourishment into itself or expel that which had been filtered through it, for nothing went out from it, nor did anything from anywhere enter it—for there was nothing—for it had come to be by design to provide its own nourishment from its waste and to suffer and do all things in itself and by itself, for he who composed it judged that it would be better self-sufficient than dependent upon others. He did not think it necessary senselessly to outfit it with hands, with which there was no need to receive anything or to defend itself from anything; nor was there need of feet or any assistance toward walking. (34) He bestowed upon it the natural motion of its body, of the seven motions that which especially involves understanding and wisdom. Hence, spinning it around upon itself in the same place, he made it to revolve in a circle, and he removed the six other motions and finished it off unaffected by their displacements. Since it had no need of feet upon this orbit, he brought it into being legless and footless.

Thinking through this whole chain of reasoning regarding the god that would come to be, the eternally existing god made it smooth and level and equal in every direction from the center and whole and a complete body from all complete bodies. Having placed a soul in the middle of it, he stretched it throughout the whole and cloaked the body in it on the outside, and he founded it a circle turning in a circle, one single solitary heaven, its excellence enabling it to associate with itself, needful of no other, sufficiently known to and friendly with itself. In all these ways it came into being a *eudaimon* god.

7.2. ANTHROPOGONY, FROM THE *PROTAGORAS*

In the following excerpt, the famous sophist Protagoras has come to Athens, and Socrates' friend Hippokrates is eager to study with him. Accompanying Hippokrates to the house of Kallias, where Protagoras is staying, Socrates asks Protagoras to state the substance of his teaching. To Protagoras' declaration that he teaches the art of politics and thereby makes men better citizens, Socrates responds that the Athenians appear not to recognize this as an expertise, for they allow anyone indiscriminately to offer advice on political matters, and he proceeds to doubt whether virtue in general can be taught. Protagoras defends his position in part with the following myth, which includes a version of the story of Prometheus' stealing fire from the gods.

SOURCE: Plato, *Protagoras* 320c–324d, translated by M. Anderson.

(320) Once there was a time when gods existed but mortal kinds did not exist. When the time ordained for their genesis arrived for them too, the gods formed them within the earth, compounding them from earth and fire and all those things mixed of earth and fire. And when they were about to bring them to light, they appointed Prometheus and Epimetheus to adorn them and to distribute to each of them the appropriate powers, but Epimetheus obtained permission from Prometheus to perform the distributions himself.

"After I have made the distributions you inspect them," he said.

And having persuaded his brother in this way, Epimetheus made the distributions, in the course of which to some he gave strength without swiftness, and the weaker ones he adorned with speed. Some he armed, and giving to others a different unarmed nature he devised for them a power toward their preservation: to those he invested with smallness he distributed winged escape or an underground refuge;

others he increased in size, and by this (321) very fact he preserved them; and he distributed the other powers in this way, balancing them out. These matters he worked out with circumspection, lest any species be destroyed. And having assisted them in their escapes from mutual destruction, he devised for them comfort against Zeus' seasons, outfitting them with thick hair and firm hides, sufficiently strong to defend against winter and heat as well, and in order that they might also suffice for their personal and natural bedding upon their entering their dwellings. On the feet of some he placed armor, on others he placed hair and firm and bloodless skins. Then he supplied various foods to the various species, to some the grass of the earth, to others the fruits of the trees, and roots to others. And some he made to be the fleshly food of other animals. Upon some he bestowed limited reproductive possibilities, and to their prey he gave high rates of reproduction, providing for the preservation of their species.

Since Epimetheus was not at all very wise, it did not occur to him that he was lavishing the powers on the non-rational animals. The species of human beings was left over for him still unadorned, and he was at a loss what it needed. Then Prometheus came to his perplexed brother in order to inspect his distributions, and he saw the other animals agreeably in possession of everything while the human being was naked, barefoot, without provision of bedding, and unarmed. But it was already the day ordained for the human being too to go out from the earth into the light. So Prometheus, at a loss what preservation he might discover for mankind, stole from Hephaistos and Athena wisdom in the arts and crafts along with fire—for it was impossible without fire for this possession either to exist or to be of service to anyone—and at that very moment he presented them to humanity. This is how the human being acquired wisdom concerning life, but he lacked political wisdom, for this was with Zeus. Prometheus was no longer permitted to enter the acropolis dwelling of Zeus—and besides, the attendants of Zeus were fearsome—but he sneaked into the common dwelling of Athena and Hephaistos, in which these two practiced their arts, and stealing the fiery craft of Hephaistos and Athena's as well, he gave them to humanity, and it is from this that mankind obtained provision for (322) life. Later Prometheus, because of Epimetheus—so it is said—was prosecuted on a charge of theft.

So the human being received a share of the divine lot, and, in the first place, because of his kinship with god he alone among animals believed in gods, and he set to work constructing altars and statues of the gods. Then very soon he articulated sound and words by skill, and he discovered dwellings, garments, shoes, beds, and foods from the earth. Thus provided for, in the beginning human beings lived scattered about, and there were no cities. They were killed by wild animals because in every way they were weaker than them, and although the craftsman's skill facilitated their acquisition of sufficient food, in their war with wild animals it was inadequate—for they did not yet possess the political art, a part of which is the art of war—so they sought to gather together and preserve themselves by founding cities. But when they had gathered together they were unjust to one another because they did not have the political art. As a result they scattered again and perished. Therefore Zeus, fearing lest our whole species be destroyed, sent Hermes to bring respect and justice to human beings, so that cities might have regulatory rules and uniting bonds of friendship. Hermes then asked Zeus how he should give justice and respect to human beings:

"Shall I distribute respect and justice as the arts have been distributed? One man with the medical art suffices for many private men, and the same holds for the other craftsmen. Shall I set justice and respect among people in this way, or shall I distribute them to all?"

"To all," said Zeus. "Let them all have a share, for cities would not come to be if only a few should have a share of them as of the other arts. And establish a law from me that he who is unable to partake of respect and justice be killed as a disease of the city."

Thus, Socrates, for these reasons other men and Athenians too think that whenever there is reasoning regarding the excellence of the carpenter's art or of some other of the crafts, only a few are qualified to deliberate, and if someone beyond the few should offer advice, they do not endure it, as you say—and with reason, I say. But whenever they enter into counsel concerning (323) political excellence, which must be conducted altogether with justice and temperance, they reasonably admit every man, thinking it belongs to everyone to have a share of this virtue, since otherwise cities would not exist. This, Socrates, is the reason for that.

But in order that you not consider yourself deceived in thinking that all human beings really do believe that every man has a share of justice and the rest of political virtue, take this as evidence: with respect to the other excellences, as you say, if someone claims to be a good flute-player or good at any other art whatever at which he is not, they either laugh at him or give him a hard time, and even his relatives come forward to chastise him as though he were crazy. But in the matter of justice and the rest of political virtue, even if they know that someone is unjust, if this very person speaks the truth about himself in public, then that which in another circumstance they judge to be temperance, namely telling the truth, in this case they judge madness, and they say that everyone must claim to be just, whether they are or not, or they say that he is mad who does not affect to be just—since necessarily there is no one who has no share at all of justice, lest he not be classed among human beings.

So, in support of my assertion that they reasonably accept every man as an advisor concerning this virtue, since they think that everyone has a share of it, I say what I have said. But that they do not think this virtue to be natural or spontaneous, but rather to be teachable and to come to be from practice in the one in whom it comes to be—this I shall now try to reveal to you. For however many faults human beings judge one another to have by nature or by chance, no one gets angry or chastises or lectures or punishes those who have them in order that they not be as they are; rather, they feel sorry for them. Who is so unintelligent that he would try to do any of these things to those who are for example ugly, small, or weak? For I think they know that these flaws come to be in human beings by nature or by chance, the noble characteristics as well as their opposites. But respecting those goods that they think come to be in people by practice, discipline, and teaching, if someone does not have these, but rather the bad things opposed to them, against these men surely there come to be rages, punishments, and chastisements. One of these is injustice, and there is impiety and (324) collectively everything opposed to political virtue. In this case everyone is angry with and chastises everyone, evidently because they consider this possession to result from practice and learning. For if you want to understand punishment, Socrates, what it is capable of with respect to the unjust, it will teach you itself that human beings judge virtue to be something for which one can make provision, for no one punishes those who are unjust simply and solely because of his being unjust, not unless he irrationally exacts vengeance like a wild animal. He who tries to punish rationally does not exact vengeance for the sake of past injustice—for he cannot make what has been done not to have existed—but for the sake of the future, in order that he who is punished not be unjust again, neither this one himself nor another who witnesses his punishment. Having such an understanding, he understands that virtue is acquired through education, and he punishes for the sake of prevention. So this is the opinion of all those who punish others in private as well as in public life. Other people seek to punish and chastise those whom they think to be unjust, and not least the Athenians, your citizens. According to this account, then, the Athenians are among those who consider virtue to be something for which one can make provision and teachable. Therefore, that your citizens reasonably accept the blacksmith and the cobbler as an advisor about political affairs, and that they judge virtue to be teachable and something for which one can make provision—these things have been demonstrated to you, Socrates, sufficiently, or so it seems to me.

7.3. THE ATLANTIS MYTH, FROM *TIMAEUS* AND *KRITIAS*

Plato's account of Atlantis appears in two works, the *Timaeus* (Gr. *Timaios*) and the *Kritias*. In both dialogues the narrator of the story is Kritias, who claims to have the details from his grandfather, who heard them from his father, who learned them from the famous Athenian poet and legislator Solon, who received the history from priests in Egypt. The excerpt from the *Timaeus* relates Solon's initial contact with the priests and their informing him of the ancient Athenians' defense of the Mediterranean peoples against the military aggression of the Atlantids; the second excerpt (*Kritias*) provides details of the foundation of Atlantis, the island's geography, and its social and political arrangements. The narration in the second passage is abruptly interrupted, most likely intentionally (by the author) and not due to textual problems. The *Kritias*, moreover, seems to be written in Plato's so-called late style, which scholars have characterized as rhetorically weighty and syntactically tortuous. Whether or not the work is in fact late, it is most definitely written in a style more complex than that of the other pieces included in this part. I have tried to preserve the unusual qualities of this style in my translation.

The following excepts from Plato's two dialogues are our sole sources for the story of Atlantis; there is no independent evidence that Solon wrote or said anything about the matter, nor do we have reason to believe that records concerning Atlantis ever existed in Egypt. The context of these narratives by Kritias is a gathering at which Socrates asks Kritias, Timaeus, and another (silent) friend to give an account of how the ideal city they have discussed on another occasion would work in reality. Their responses and their relationship with Socrates' proposal still puzzle scholars. (For Timaeus' speech, see document 7.1.)

Note how Athens and Atlantis are represented by the gods Athena and Poseidon, respectively, who symbolize different essential qualities. According to tradition, these two gods had competed for sovereignty over Athens, a contest which Athena won (see Figure 22).

SOURCE: Plato, *Timaeus* 20d–25d and *Kritias* 108e–121c, translated by M. Anderson.

Timaeus

(20) KRITIAS: Listen, Socrates, to an account exceedingly strange but altogether true, as the wisest of the Seven, Solon, once said. He was related and very dear to our great-grandfather Dropides, as he himself notes often in his poems. And to Kritias our grandfather he said, as the old man recounted from memory in turn to us, that the ancient deeds of our city were wondrously great, but they have been obscured by time and the destruction of humanity. One deed in particular was the greatest of them all, (21) and it would be fitting for us to recall it now and present it to you as thanks, and in doing so we shall also be chanting justly and truly something like a hymn of praise to the goddess during her festival.

SOCRATES: Well said! But what sort of unreported deed was this that Kritias narrated as really having been done by this city long ago according the report of Solon?

KRITIAS: I will tell you. I heard the ancient account from no young man, for Kritias was then, as he said, already very nearly ninety years old, and I was somewhere around ten. It happened to be the Koureotis of the Apaturian festival, and what we know as the festival's customary event for children was in place even then: our fathers set up for us prizes for recitation. Many poems of many poets were recited, but since at that time Solon's poems were new, many of us children sang them. Some one of our clansmen said—whether it seemed so to him or it may be he wanted to compliment Kritias—he said that Solon seemed to him to have been the wisest man with respect to other matters and in his poems the most nobly-free of all the poets. The old man—as I well recall—was very pleased, and he smiled and said:

"Amynander, if only Solon had engaged in poetry not merely as a casual pastime, but had been as serious as the other poets; if only he had completed the account he brought here from Egypt and had not been compelled to abandon it because of factional strife and all the other troubles he encountered upon returning here—well then, in my opinion neither Hesiod nor Homer nor any other poet would ever have been more renowned than him."

"What was this account, Kritias?" said Amynander.

"One might most justly have said," said Kritias, "that it concerned the greatest and most famous of all deeds, which deed this very city performed, but the account did not endure unto the present because of time and the destruction of those who accomplished the deed."

"Tell from the beginning," Amynander said, "what and how and from whom having heard it as true, Solon told it."

"There is in Egypt," said Kritias, "in the Delta, around which the flow of the Nile divides at the head, a district called the Saitic, and the greatest city of this district is Sais, of which Amasis was the king. A certain goddess founded this city, whose name among the Egyptians is Neith, but among the Greeks, according to the Egyptians' account, she is Athena. The Egyptians love Athenians dearly and they claim in some way to be related to us. Solon said that when he arrived the Egyptians honored him greatly, (22) and when once he inquired about ancient matters among those of their priests with particular knowledge of these things, he discovered that neither he himself nor any other Greek knew much at all about any of this. And once, when he wanted to draw the priests into a discussion about ancient times, he attempted to tell them about the most ancient of things here—about Phoroneus, for example, who was said to be the first human being, and about Niobe; and he recounted the myth of Deukalion's and Pyrrha's survival following the cataclysmic flood, and he spoke as well of their descendants; and he recalled the number of years of the things he mentioned and tried to reckon the ages—and then some one of the priests who was very old said:

"'O Solon, Solon, you Greeks are eternal children, and there is no old Greek.'

"And Solon, when he heard this, asked: 'How so? What do you mean?'

"'You are young in soul,' replied the priest, 'all of you, for in your souls you have no archaic opinion descended from ancient tradition, nor any learning aged by time. The cause of these facts is this: There have been and there will be many and various destructions of human beings, the greatest caused by fire and water, and lesser destructions caused by countless other phenomena. Indeed, the story told among you that Phaethon, the child of Helios, once yoked his father's chariot and, being unable to drive along his father's road, scorched the things on the earth and was himself struck by lightning and destroyed—this is told in the form of a myth. The truth is there is a deviation in the motions of the bodies moving around the earth through the heavens, and at great intervals of time the things upon the earth are destroyed by intense fire. When this happens, more of those who dwell on mountains and high and dry places are obliterated than those who dwell by rivers and the sea. The Nile, which is our savior in general, floods on these occasions and so protects us from this difficulty. And whenever the gods inundate the earth and purge it with waters, the herdsmen and shepherds upon the mountains are preserved, but those in the cities round about you are borne by rivers into the sea. Here in Egypt, neither on these occasions nor at any other time does water flow down from above upon our fields, but just the opposite—it all rises up naturally from below. For these reasons the things here are said to be the most ancient: the truth is that in all places where extraordinary cold or heat does not prevent it, (23) the human race always exists, at one time more at another time less populous. And if anywhere anything has happened that is noble or great or in some other way distinguished, either among your people or here or in any other place we know of by report, then all these things since ancient times have been written in our temples and preserved; but among yourselves and others, only just after you have become literate and have secured all else of which cities have need, once again after the usual number of years the heavenly stream like a plague comes bearing down and leaves behind only the illiterate and uncultivated of your people, with the result that you start all over again as if you were young, knowing nothing of ancient matters either here or among yourselves. Solon, the genealogies of your people that you just went through are little else than children's myths, for in the first place you people remember only one global cataclysm, although many have previously occurred, and you don't know that the noblest and best race among men existed in your land, from which both you and your whole city and all that pertains to your people descend, from a small seed that was once left behind—this escapes you because for many generations the survivors died illiterate. Indeed, Solon, in the days before the greatest watery destruction, the city that now is Athens was the best in war and exceptionally well governed in every way—its deeds and its civil institutions are said to have been the noblest of those under heaven of which we have received report.'

"Upon hearing this Solon expressed his amazement and pronounced himself utterly desirous that the priests narrate accurately and in order everything related to the ancient Athenians. So the priest said: 'Solon, I have nothing against speaking for your sake and for your city, and especially for the sake of the goddess who chose to nourish and educate both your city and this one, your city first by one thousand years when she received your seed from Earth and Hephaistos, and this city later. As for the founding of Egypt, in our sacred writings the number of eight thousand years has been written; but concerning the citizens who came to be nine thousand years ago, I shall in short order reveal to you their laws, and also their noblest deed. (24) Later we shall go through all these matters meticulously and in order at our leisure, with the writings themselves in hand. For now, compare their laws to ours: you will discover in present-day Egypt many imitations of the laws that existed previously among your people. First of all, the priestly class has been marked off and is separate from the others; then, each class of craftsmen works on its own without mixing with any other class, and the same applies to each of the classes of shepherds and hunters and farmers. And moreover, surely you have observed that our military class is separate from all other classes, for the law prescribes that its members care for nothing other than matters of war; and then there is the nature of their equipment—shields and spears—with which we were the first of the peoples in Asia to arm ourselves, precisely as the goddess revealed them to you in your land first of all. And moreover, regarding wisdom, surely you see how seriously the law attended right from the beginning to the cosmos, discovering all those things, including the prophetic and the medical craft that promotes health, that proceed from those divine beings and bear upon human concerns, and attended as well to all the other categories of knowledge that follow upon these. In those days, then, the goddess arranged and established this entire organization and order among you first, after selecting the place in which you came into being upon observing that the temperance of its seasons would produce the wisest men. So, since the goddess is both a lover of war and a lover of wisdom, she selected that place which would produce men most similar to herself and founded it first. These were the laws according to which you lived, and you were even still better governed and surpassed all men in every virtue, as befits the ancestry and education of men descended from gods.

"'Men marvel at the many great deeds of your city as they are here recorded, but one in particular surpasses them all in magnitude and excellence. The writings relate that your city once successfully resisted a great power's hubristic advance against all of Europe and Asia, a power that bestirred itself from out of the Atlantic sea. At that time the sea there was navigable, for there was an island before the mouth that your people call the Pillars of Herakles, an island larger than Libya and Asia combined, which provided contemporary voyagers access to other (25) islands which in turn provided access to the entire facing continent that surrounds that true sea. All these things inside the mouth of which we speak appear to be a harbor with a narrow entryway, but the land completely surrounding that real sea would truly most correctly be called a continent. Now, on this Atlantic island a great and wondrous power of kings was formed by alliance, which dominated the entire island as well as many other islands and regions on the mainland; and in addition to these, of the places within the straits they ruled Libya as far as Egypt and Europe as far as Tyrrhenia. This power, having been all united into one, once tried by assault to enslave the area encompassing your land and ours and every place within the strait. Then, Solon, the power of your city's virtue and might became evident to everyone; outstripping all others in courage and every art of war, at one time leading the efforts of the Greeks, at another acting alone from necessity as the others revolted from her, she met the extremities of danger, mastered the invaders, and erected a trophy. She prevented the enslavement of those not yet enslaved, and those others of us who dwelt within the boundaries of Herakles she ungrudgingly liberated. But at a later time with the outbreak of intense earthquakes and cataclysmic floods, and under the assault of a harsh day and night, the whole of your military body sank beneath the earth. The island Atlantis likewise sank beneath the sea and vanished, wherefore even now the sea in that area is unnavigable and unexplored, for there is an impediment of mud just beneath the water produced by the settling of the island.'"

Kritias

(108) KRITIAS: First of all, let us recall that the sum was nine thousand years from the time when the war is recorded as having occurred between those living beyond the Pillars of Herakles and all those within, which war it is necessary now to relate. This city is said to have led those within the straits and battled through the whole war, whereas the leaders of their opponents were the kings of the Atlantic island, which island we said was larger than Libya and Asia at one time, but now, having sunk from earthquakes, it has produced a muddy unnavigable impediment to those sailing from there (109) toward the total sea, with the result that they cannot proceed beyond it. As for the many barbarian tribes and all the various Greek peoples there were at that time, the unfolding narrative of our account will disclose each as they everywhere happen to appear; but the Athenian people of that time and the enemy against whom they waged war, we must from the beginning describe these first, the power of each and their social-political arrangements. But we must prefer to begin to speak of the ancient conditions among the Athenians.

The gods once divided the whole earth into regions by lot—not by strife, for it would be incorrect to say that the gods are ignorant of that which is proper to each of them, nor should we say that although they know this they would attempt to acquire for themselves through strife that which more properly belongs to others. So, having obtained their own regions by a just lottery, they laid the foundations of their lands, and having founded them, like shepherds with their flocks they reared us human beings as their property and livestock, not by inflicting physical force upon our bodies, like shepherds managing their flocks with the whip, but rather by the manner according to which the animal is particularly manageable—directing us from the stern, taking hold of the soul by persuasion as if by a rudder according to their own understanding, they lead us and thereby captain the whole human race. As the other gods had obtained other regions by lot and organized their possessions, Hephaistos and Athena—who have a common nature (she being his sister from the same father) and who from the love of wisdom and love of craft engaged in the same activities—these two obtained this land by a single lot as their own, it being naturally fit for virtue and wisdom, and they produced good men from the earth and established in their mind the order of a constitution. The names of these men have been preserved, but their deeds because of the destructions of their successors and the spans of years have vanished.

The type of men that regularly survived these repeated destructions, as was previously mentioned, were mountain dwelling illiterates who had heard only the names of the royalty in the land and knew next to nothing of their deeds. They revered these names and so gave them to their descendants, but they knew nothing about the virtues and traditions of their predecessors excepting a few obscure reports concerning them; and since they themselves (110) and their children were at a loss for necessities through many generations, they directed their minds and dedicated their oratory to these matters exclusively and so neglected those things that once had occurred in earlier archaic eras. Mythology and the investigation of antiquity enter into cities together with leisure, when the citizens see that the necessities of life have already been provided for some, but not before this. In this way the names of the ancients have been preserved but not their deeds. I say these things providing as evidence the fact, reported by Solon, that while narrating the war at that time the priests for the most part named Kekrops and Erechtheus and Erichthonios and Erysichthon, as well as each of the others of those before Theseus who are remembered, and they recounted matters pertaining to women in the same way. And moreover, regarding the form and ornamentation of the goddess Athena, since at that time the pursuits of the women and the men in matters of war were common, and so in accord with that custom the armed goddess was an object of delight to them—this is proof that it is natural for the male and the female of all gregarious animals to pursue as completely in common as possible the virtue proper to each class.

There lived at that time in this land not only other classes of citizens concerned with craftsmanship and the cultivation of the land, but also the military class, which from the beginning had been separated from the others by divine men and so lived apart, and they had all that befitted their nourishment and education; none of them had private possessions, for they considered all of their possessions common and thought it inappropriate to receive excessive sustenance from the store of the other citizens; and they engaged in all those pursuits we noted and spoke of yesterday regarding the proposed guardians. Moreover, that which was said of our region was plausible and true, namely that it had at that time boundaries marked off by the Isthmus and along the northern stretch of the mainland up to the summits of Kithairon and Parnes, and then that the boundaries went down with Oropia on the right, and on the left by the sea it marked off Asopos—also that in agricultural production the entire earth was surpassed by our land, wherefore the land then was able to nourish an army so thoroughly exempt from working the earth. Great is the evidence of its excellence: that which presently remains of the land is equal to any in being all-productively fruitful (111) and having good pasture for every sort of animal. At that time, in addition to its beauty our land bore these things in their multitudes. But how is this credible, and on what grounds might we correctly call this our present land the remnant of that former land? The entire land stretches out from the rest of the mainland far into the sea and is situated like a headland, and the whole basin of the sea around it happens to be deep near the shore. And so, although many great cataclysmic floods have occurred in nine thousand years—for there have been so many years between that time and now—in all these years and through all these events the earth that ran off from the heights did not as in other places form significant deposits, but rather it whirled and whirled around into the depths and vanished. As is the case with the land on small islands, our land today, compared with its former condition, is like the bones of a sick body: the rich and soft parts of the earth have washed away until only a slight body of land remains. At that time the land was pure and there were mountains and high hills; those plains we call "the rocky ground" were full of rich earth; and a vast forestland covered the mountains, of which even now there is still clear evidence, for there exist today some mountains that have sustenance only for bees, but which not long ago were full of trees, and the rafters of roofing-wood cut from there for the greatest build-ings are still sound. There were many other cultivated tall trees, and the land bore endless pasture for feeding animals. And at that time Zeus' annual rain generated produce—it was not, as it is now, lost by flowing from the bare earth into the sea, but instead the deep earth received the water into itself, absorbed and stored it in impervious clay, and then discharged it from the heights into the hollows all around and so provided plentiful water for springs and rivers, and even now there are sacred markers upon these early springs that declare all that we are now saying to be true.

So the rural lands were naturally in this condition, and they had likely been set in order by true farmers who practiced only farming, but who also loved what is noble and were well-born, who possessed the best land and abundant water and overhead the most temperate of seasons. The city, on the other hand, was founded at that time in the following way: first, the acropolis (112) then was not as it is now. For at present it is exceptionally bare, having been melted away in one extraordinarily rainy night, in the course of which earthquakes accompanied this third inundation of water prior to the destruction in Deukalion's time. In a previous age the acropolis was of such a size that it ran down to the Eridanos and the Ilisos and encompassed the Pnyx, with Lykabettos as its boundary on the opposite side from the Pnyx, and it was earthy all over except for a small section of the surface on top. Some parts beyond it were inhabited, those under its slopes, and farmed by the craftsmen and farmers nearby; but the upper part the military class alone occupied exclusively, settling around the temple of Athena and Hephaistos as if surrounding in a circuit the garden of a single family. They lived on the northern parts of the acropolis, having provided for themselves common homes, winter mess-halls, and all the buildings befitting a communal polity of themselves and their priests. They had no gold or silver, for no one used these; rather they pursued the proper mean between ostentation and slavish dullness and built orderly dwellings in which they and their children's children grew old and which they continually handed down unaltered to descendants similar to themselves. And as for the southern parts, when they abandoned the gardens and gymnasia and mess-halls in the summers, they put them to these uses. There was one spring at the site of the present acropolis, which, having been blocked up by the earthquakes, remains today only as little rivulets here and there, but which provided for the people then plentiful waters temperate in both winter and summer. They founded the city according to this scheme, protecting their own citizens and leading the other Greeks by their consent, maintaining as they could their number of men and women—those already able to wage war as well as those who could wage war still—right about twenty thousand.

Since these men were of such a character and in some such manner continuously governed their own land as well as Greece with justice, they were famous throughout the whole of Europe and Asia and were the most notable people of the age for the beauty of their bodies and the polymorphous excellence of their souls. But as for the condition and origins of those who waged war against them, if we have not lost the memory of those things we heard when we were still children, we shall now publically reveal them as common to you our friends.

(113) But it is still necessary to clarify a small point prior to my account, lest you marvel at often hearing Greek names for barbarian people. You will learn the reason for this: Since Solon intended in his poem to make use of the account, he inquired about the meaning of the names and discovered that those early Egyptians had written them out after translating them into their language. Therefore, he recovered the sense of each name himself and recorded them as translated into our language. These very writings were in the possession of my grandfather and are even now in my possession, and I studied them thoroughly when I was a child. Therefore, if you hear such names as are common here, do not wonder at it, for you have the reason. Of the long account something like this was the beginning then:

As was said previously concerning the gods' distribution, namely that they divided the entire earth into larger and smaller lots and established for themselves temples and sacred rites, even so did Poseidon, having received by lot the Atlantic island, settle his descendants born of a mortal woman in some such place on the island as this: by the sea and along the middle of the whole island was a plain, which of all plains is said to have been the most beautiful and abundantly fertile, and by the plain along the middle about fifty stades away was a low mountain. On this mountain lived one of those men who in the beginning came into being from the earth there, Euenor by name, who lived with his wife Leukippe. Kleito was their only daughter. When this maiden was ripe for a husband, her mother and her father both died, and Poseidon desired her and slept with her, and he secured the hill on which she lived by breaking it up all around circularly, forming alternating circuits of sea and earth of increasing size, two of earth and three of sea, rounding them as on a lathe outward from the middle of the island, situating them at equal distances on every side, so as to be impassible for people—for at that time there were no ships and no sailing. Poseidon himself set the central island into order, as easily as a god can, conducting the two streams of water under the earth into above-ground springs, one warm and the other cold, each flowing from its own fountain, and he produced from the earth various and generous forms of sustenance. Having fathered and reared five pairs of twin male children, he divided the whole Atlantic island into ten parts, and to the first born of the oldest pair (114) he gave the maternal dwelling and its circular allotment, which was the largest and the best, and he appointed him king over the others. His other sons he made rulers as well, and to each he gave sovereignty over many human beings and a vast area of land. He gave names to them all, to the eldest and king the name from which the whole island and the sea took its name: it was called Atlantic because the name of the first to reign as king at that time was Atlas; and to the twin born after him, who received the lot of the headland of the island by the Pillars of Herakles over against the region now named Gadeira after that place he gave the name Eumelos in Greek, Gadeiros in the native language, which may have given the place its name. Of the second born twins he called the one Ampheres and the other Euaimon; to the first-born of the pair born third he gave the name Mneseas and to the one born after this one Autochthon; of those born fourth he called the first one Elasippos and the later one Mestor; and to the fifth he gave the name Azaes to the prior and Diaprepes to the later.

All these men, both themselves and their descendants unto many generations, lived and ruled over many other islands throughout the sea, and besides, as was mentioned earlier, they dominated the peoples within the Mediterranean up to Egypt and Tyrrhenia. The family of Atlas multiplied and was honored, and the eldest son as king always passed down to the eldest of his sons the rule, which thereby they preserved for many generations; and they possessed an abundance of wealth as never before had been in the possession of any previous sovereignty of kings, nor will it readily be so again in the future, and all those things were provided for them, in the city as well as in the rest of the land, that are difficult to acquire for oneself. Many resources because of their dominion came to them from beyond their territory, but the island itself provided most of life's necessities, in particular all the solid matter dug up by mining and all that is molten, and as for that which exists only in name in our day—well at that time the substance of "mountain-copper" was more than a name: extracted from the earth in many places of the island, it was the most valuable of all metals in those days except for gold. And the island provided all the wood necessary for the labors of carpenters, bearing all these in abundance, and moreover it provided sufficient nourishment for tame and wild animals alike. There was even a great race of elephants, for there was pasture for all those animals that feed along marshes, harbors, and rivers, (115) also for those that feed on mountains and in the plains—there was enough for all these, and among them even this animal, the largest by nature and the most voracious. In addition to these things, all the fragrances the earth produces now from roots or foliage or trees, or from the oozing juices of either flowers or fruits, it bore these things even then and nourished them well. It produced as well the cultivated fruit, and the dry fruit too, which exists for our nourishment, and all else that we are provided for food—we call the sum of the parts of this class "vegetables"—and all that trees generate of drink and food and oil, and the hard-to-store produce of fruit trees which has come to be for our enjoyment and pleasure, and all the pleasant after-supper reliefs that we give to one suffering from having eaten too much—all these sacred, beautiful, wondrous, and boundlessly numerous things the then sun-drenched island bore. Taking, therefore, all these things from the earth, they constructed temples and royal dwellings and harbors and dock-yards, and all the rest of the land they arranged in the following order:

The circuits of the sea, which surrounded the ancient metropolis, they bridged, making a road out from and up to the palace. And right at the beginning they made a palace in this dwelling of the god and the ancestors, and one king received it from another, adorned it with ornamentations, and always surpassed his predecessor to the extent he was able to do so, until they made their residence bewilderingly awesome to behold from the magnitude and beauty of their works. For beginning from the sea they dug a trench three plethra wide, one hundred feet deep, and fifty stades in length, up to the outermost circle, and they made a canal running this way from the sea to that circle as into a harbor, excavating the mouth sufficiently for the greatest ships to sail into. And then the circuits of earth, which divided those of the sea, they dug out alongside the bridges so that one trireme could sail back and forth between them, and they covered these canals from above so as to be underpassable from beneath, for the rims of the circuits of earth had a height sufficiently raised over the sea. The greatest of the circles, into which the sea had been opened, was three stades wide, and the next circuit of earth was equal to that; of the next two circuits, the water was two stades wide and the dry land was equal again to the preceding water; the circuit running around the island in the middle itself was one stade. And the island (116) on which the palace was situated had a diameter of five stades. This island and the circuits and the bridge, which was one plethron wide, they surrounded on this side and that with a stone wall, setting towers and gates upon each side of the bridges along the passages of the sea. The stone they cut round about from under the island in the middle as well as from the outer and inner circuits, some of it white, some black, and some red, and simultaneous with these excavations they fashioned two internal hollow ship-sheds roofed with this very rock. Some of their buildings were simple, but by intermixing stones they made others variously colored for their enjoyment, imparting to them a natural pleasure. The entire course of the wall around the outermost circuit they faced with bronze as if with varnish, and the wall around the inner circuit they covered with a coating of tin, and the wall around the acropolis itself they coated with mountain-copper of a fiery gleaming.

The palace within the acropolis was outfitted as follows. In the middle a temple sacred to Kleito and Poseidon was designated off-limits and encompassed by a golden enclosure on the spot where in the beginning they had sown and begotten the race of the ten princes. Here every year from all the ten allotments they made first-fruit offerings to each of them. Of Poseidon himself there was a temple, one stade long, three plethra wide, and its height proportional to these to estimate by sight, and he had something of a barbarian form. The whole outside of the temple was overlaid with silver, except for the acroteria, but the acroteria were overlaid with gold; and regarding the parts inside, the whole ceiling was ivory to see, varied by gold, silver, and mountain-copper, and all the other parts of the walls and columns and floors were overlaid with mountain-copper. Golden statues they erected, the god standing upon a chariot, the driver of six winged horses, of such a size that its head touched the ceiling, and one hundred Nereids upon dolphins surrounded him—for of such a number the people then thought them to be—and inside there were many other votive statues from private citizens. Around the outside of the temple stood images of gold depicting the wives and the men themselves who had descended from the ten kings, and there were many other large votive offerings from both the kings and the private citizens, from both the city itself and from all those external cities they ruled. And the altar (117) in its size and the magnitude of its craftsmanship was in accordance with this equipage, and the palace in the same way befitted not only the magnitude of its rule but it befitted as well the adornment of the temples.

They made use of springs, one of cold and one of hot water, whose store was abundant, and by the pleasure and virtue of their waters the usefulness engendered by each was marvelous; and around these they situated buildings and plantings of trees befitting the waters, and reservoirs as well they placed all around, some in the open sky, others for hot baths in winter under cover of a roof. The royal reservoirs were separate from those used by private citizens, and there were others for women and still others for horses and the other yoked animals, each provided with appropriate adornment. The water that flowed off they directed to the grove of Poseidon, whose various trees were daimonically beautiful and tall from the fertility of the earth, and they brought the water by canals to the external circuits alongside the bridges. Here they had built many temples for many gods, many gardens, and many gymnasia, some for men and separate ones for horses, on each island of the circuits; there were other features as well, including along the center of the larger of the islands a racecourse set apart for the horses, one stade wide, and the length around the whole circle was dedicated to the horse-race. There were guardhouses around it here and there for the mass of spearmen; and on the smaller circuit really very close to the acropolis was stationed a guard of the more trustworthy men; but to those excelling everyone in reliability dwellings within the acropolis around the kings themselves were given. The dock-yards were full of triremes and of all the gear belonging to triremes, everything being sufficiently equipped. Thus was the site around the dwelling of the kings constructed.

He who passed through the three external harbors encountered a circular wall taking off from the sea, set back in every place fifty stades from the largest circuit and its harbor, which linked up in the same place near the mouth of the canal against the sea. This entire area was occupied by many densely-packed houses, and the entry-canal and the largest harbor was full of ships and merchants arriving from all over, the crowd of them producing a clamor and every sort of din and noise all day and night.

So the city and that part around the ancient dwelling, pretty nearly as it was then reported, has now been recalled; but how it was with the nature of the rest of the land (118) and the form of its organization we must try to recall. First, the whole place was said to rise very high and precipitously from the sea; and the entire plain around the city, which encompassed the city and was itself encompassed all around by mountains stretching up to the sea, was flat and level and wholly rectangular, measuring upon each side three thousand stades and across the middle up from the sea, two thousand. This part of the whole island was turned to the south and sheltered from the north. The mountains around it were praised in those days for their number, height, and beauty, beyond all those that presently exist, for they had many wealthy villages of local inhabitants in them, and rivers and marshes and meadows of sufficient nourishment for all tame and wild creatures, and woodlands varied in size and kind providing abundantly for the sum total of each of their occupations.

The plain, its natural state having been modified by the work of many kings over many years, was as follows: It was four-sided from the beginning, for the most part straight and elongated, and whatever it lacked they corrected with a trench dug around it; but regarding its depth and width and length, it is unbelievable, considering it was a handcrafted work, that, as it was said, they constructed it on a scale so much greater than that of their other works, yet we must mention what we heard: it had been dug one plethron deep, and its width on all sides was a stade, and the trench having been dug around the whole plain, the length came to ten thousand stades. Receiving the waters that flowed down from the mountains, circulated around the plain, and arrived at various places by the city, at this very spot it released them to flow out to the sea. Inland from the city, straight canals in width about one hundred feet dug across the plain set themselves loose again into the trench near the sea, at a distance from one another of one hundred stades. By this route they brought wood down from the mountains into the city, and the other produce they carried down on sailing vessels, for they had cut cross-channels from one canal into another and also up to the city. Twice annually they harvested the land, in winter employing Zeus' rains and in the summer diverting from the canals all the waters the earth itself brings forth.

Regarding the population, of the men in the plain of service in war (119) each allotment had been assigned to provide one man as leader, and the size of the allotment was about ten times ten stades, and the number of allotments was sixty thousand. The number of the people from the mountains and other parts of the land was said to be limitless, and everyone was assigned to leaders according to the places and the villages in these allotments. It was prescribed that the leader provide for the war a sixth part of a war chariot as contribution to the ten thousand chariots, two horses and horsemen, and also a pair of horses without a chariot but with a man to dismount carrying a small shield and a fighting charioteer for both horses, also two hoplites and archers and slingers, two of each, and light-armed stone-throwers and javelin-throwers, three of each, and four sailors as contribution to the crew of twelve hundred ships. Thus had military matters been severally arranged in the royal city, but the nine other cities had nine different arrangements, which would be a long time in the telling.

Matters concerning positions of authority and honors, having been organized in the beginning, were as follows: Each one of the ten kings in his own region governed his own city's men and most of the laws, punishing and putting to death whomever he wished; but the rule and associations among themselves were conducted according to the commissions of Poseidon as passed down to them in the law and the writings inscribed by the first kings upon a stele of mountain-copper, which was situated in the center of the island in the temple of Poseidon, where they assembled every fifth year and every other sixth year, thereby distributing an equal proportion to the even and to the odd, and when they gathered together they attended to general concerns and examined whether anyone had committed any transgression, and they rendered their judgments. But when they were going to announce their judgments they first gave to one another pledges such as these: there being bulls wandering freely in the sacred enclosure of Poseidon, the ten came together there alone, prayed to the god that they might seize a sacrificial victim pleasing to him, and employing no iron they hunted with sticks and nets, and that one of the bulls which they captured they led up to the stele and slaughtered over the top of it upon the inscriptions. On the stele besides the laws there was an oath invoking great curses against the unfaithful. So, when (120) they had sacrificed according to their laws and were roasting all the parts of the bull, they mixed a large jug of water and wine and tossed inside a clot of blood on behalf of each of them, and the rest they took to the fire after thoroughly purifying the stele. And after this, while drawing liquid from the jug with golden bowls and pouring their libations upon the fire, they swore to judge according to the laws on the stele, to punish whomever had previously committed any transgression, and, moreover, never after this to transgress any one of the inscriptions willingly, and neither to rule nor to obey a ruler except one issuing orders in accordance with the laws of the father. After each of them had prayed these things for themselves and their descendants, and had drunk and dedicated his bowl in the temple of the god, they lingered over dinner and necessary matters; and when it became dark and the sacrificial fire had gone out, all of them donned the most beautiful dark-blue robes, sat in the night on the ground by the embers of the sacrifice, and after extinguishing all the fire around the sacred enclosure they were judged and they passed judgment if anyone of them accused another of having committed any transgression. Having rendered their judgments, when the light came on they wrote their decrees upon a golden registry and dedicated it with their robes as memorials. There were many various laws pertaining particularly to the privileges of each of the kings, but respecting the greatest matters were laws that they would never bear arms against one another and that everyone would help if ever anyone in any city should attempt to dissolve the royal line; also that they would, like their ancestors, formulate opinions about war and other actions in common but would yield hegemony to Atlas' line. And of the death of anyone of his royal relatives no king would be master, unless it seemed right to more than half of the ten.

This power, so great and such as I have described its being in those regions at that time, the god arrayed and conducted into battle against these regions, as the account has it, on some such pretext as the following: for many generations, so long as the nature of the god assisted them, they were subjects of the laws and friendly to their divine relations, for their thoughts were true and thoroughly high-minded; and since they deployed gentleness with wisdom against eternally occurring fortunes as well as toward each other, they disdained everything except virtue, considered (121) their present circumstances trivial, and effortlessly bore as a burden their store of gold and other possessions; nor did their wealth cause them to lose control of themselves and stumble from being drunk on wantonness, but being sober they acutely perceived that all these things are amplified by common friendship accompanied by virtue, whereas by serious regard and reverence these very things waste away and those other goods perish with them. From this sort of reasoning and so long as their divine nature endured, all their possessions were augmented as we previously discussed. But when the portion of the god in them attenuated from often being mixed with much mortality, and their human character was prevailing, then they were powerless to endure present circumstances and they behaved disgracefully, and to those able to see they appeared shameful, for they had lost the most beautiful of their most honorable possessions, whereas to those unable to look upon the true life of *eudaimonia* they seemed just then to be particularly all-beautiful and blessed, although they were full of unjust greed and power. And the god of gods, Zeus, ruling as king according to the laws, since he was able to see such things, considering this good race wretchedly disposed and wanting to impose justice upon them that they might become more harmonious after having been corrected, he summoned all the gods into the most honored of their dwellings, which standing on the middle of the whole heaven looks down upon all that partakes of becoming, and having gathered them together, he said . . .

7.4. ARISTOPHANES' SPEECH ON LOVE, FROM THE *SYMPOSIUM*

The occasion of the following myth is a *symposium* (Gr. *symposion*, literally, a drinking party) in honor of Agathon, who has won first prize in the competition among tragic poets held during the Lenaia, a winter festival of Dionysus. Eryximachos suggests that rather than drink heavily as they had done the previous evening, each of the celebrants should deliver a speech about Eros, the god of love. Aristophanes the comic poet in his speech explains the origin of erotic desire by means of an account of original human nature and the causes and consequences of our separation from our primordial condition.

SOURCE: Plato, *Symposium* 189c–193d, translated and annotated by M. Anderson.

(189) Men seem to me entirely to overlook the power of Eros, for otherwise they would erect for him the greatest temples and altars, and offer him the greatest sacrifices, not like now when none of these things are done for him although they ought most certainly to be. Of the gods Eros is the most kindly disposed toward people; he is their ally and a physician of all those ills whose cure would be the

highest *eudaimonia*[1] for the human race. Therefore, I shall try to reveal to you his power and you will be the teachers of others.

First you must learn about human nature and all that has happened to it. Long ago our nature was not as it is now; it was different. For, first of all, there were three varieties of human beings, not two, as now—male and female—but there was a third as well with characteristics of both of these, of which now only the name remains; it itself has disappeared. At that time there was one androgynous type, taking both its form and its name from commonalities with both male and female. Today it exists only as a term of derision. Secondly, the form of each person was wholly round, its back and ribs making a circle, and it had four hands and as many legs and (190) two faces upon a circular neck, identical in every way; and it had one head for these two faces set in opposite directions, and four ears, two sets of genitalia, and all its other features were as one might infer from what we have said. It walked straight ahead, as we do now, in whichever direction it wished. And when it set out to run quickly, like tumblers who toss their legs straight up and around in a circle, wheeling over in a circle supported by its eight limbs it hurried about wheelingly.

The types were three, and they were such as they were, because the male was originally born of the sun, the female of the earth, and the type that partook of both was born of the moon, which itself partakes of both the sun and earth. They were spherical, both the things themselves and their mode of walking, because they resembled these their ancestors.

Their strength and their power were awful, and since their arrogance was great they assaulted the gods. Indeed, that which Homer tells of Ephialtes and Otos is meant about them, namely that they tried to ascend to heaven to attack the gods. So Zeus and the other gods considered what they should do, but they were at a loss. They could not kill them, as they had struck the giants with thunderbolts and obliterated the race—for then the honors and temples they received from mankind would disappear—but neither could they permit their outrageous behavior. Finally, having thought the matter over, Zeus said:

"I think I have a plan according to which human beings might exist and yet cease their indulgent excess by becoming weaker. For now I will cut each one in half, and thus they will become weaker, and at the same time they will be of more service to us by increasing in number. They will walk slowly straight ahead on two legs. And if they seem still to behave outrageously and are unwilling to keep their peace, then I will cut them in half again, so that they will walk on one leg like dancers upon greasy wineskins."

Having spoken thus, Zeus cut people in half, as those do who slice sorb-apples to preserve them, or like those who slice eggs with a hair.

---

[1] There is no simple English equivalent for the Greek noun *eudaimonia* (*eudaimon* as an adjective). The word is usually translated as "happiness," but this is misleading. We moderns typically understand happiness in terms of pleasure, contentment, self-satisfaction. Happiness for us is a subjective state of mind. For the ancient Platonists, however, *eudaimonia* indicated an objective state of being that encompassed one's character (one's virtues and vices) and the circumstances of one's life. The word, therefore, may be understood to designate "the good life" (and the adjective, *eudaimon*, "one who lives the good life").

Zeus bid Apollo to turn the face and half-neck of whomever he cut toward the cutting, so that from observing the wound the human being might be more orderly; and he bid him to heal the other parts. And so Apollo turned around the face and, drawing together the skin from all sides toward what is now called the stomach, just like a drawstring pouch, he made one opening and tied it up in the middle of the stomach, which now they call the navel. (191) He smoothed out the many other wrinkles and completely joined the chest, employing some such tool as cobblers use to smooth out the wrinkles of hides upon a last. Some he left, those around the stomach itself and the navel, to be a reminder of our former sufferings.

So when the nature of human beings had been cut in half, each half missed and went around with its own half; and throwing their hands around and entwining with each other, desiring to be united, they died from hunger and other forms of idleness because they did not wish to separate from one another. And when some one of the halves died and one remained, the one that remained sought another and entwined with it, whether it met with the half of a whole woman—what *now* we call a woman—or whether with the half of a man. And thus both halves died.

But Zeus pitied them, and he developed another plan and moved their genitals around onto the front—for up to that time they had these on the outside, and they begat and gave birth not in each other but in the earth, like cicadas—so he placed them on their front and thereby made them reproduce in one another, from the male in the female, in order that in their entwining if a male should have intercourse with a female, there might be a conception and propagation of the species, and if a male should have intercourse with a male, satisfaction and rest might come from their being together and they might turn to work and take care of the other aspects of life. From long ago, then, erotic desire for another is implanted in people, and it is a unifier of our original nature, and it tries to make one from two and to heal human nature.

Each of us is a token of a human being, seeing that we have been cut like a flatfish, one from two; and each of us always seeks his own token. Those men who are sections of the common type, which then was called androgynous, are lovers of women, and many adulterers have come from this class; and the women are lovers of men, and adulteresses have come from this class. But those women who are sections of woman, these do not think much of men, but are attracted to women, and lesbians have come from this class. Those who are sections of the male pursue males, and while they are children, since they are little slices of the male, they love men and take delight in lying and (192) intertwining with men, and these are the best of boys and young men because they are the most manly by nature. Some say that these types are shameless, but they lie. They behave this way, not from shamelessness, but from courage and bravery and manliness, clinging to that which is like them. There is great evidence for this: only these types, when they grow up, enter into politics like men. And when they have become men they love boys, and of marriage and reproduction they think nothing by nature, but only from the force of custom. It suffices to them to live their lives with each other, unmarried. Such a man, therefore, is a lover of boys and of lovers, clinging always to his type.

When a boy-lover and every other type encounters a half of his own kind, then they are wondrously struck dumb by friendship, intimacy, and erotic desire, and they are unwilling, so to speak, to spend even a short time apart from each other. And those who go through life together are unable to say what they want from each other. For no one would think it is sexual intercourse, as if anyone is so excessively thrilled to lie with another. But it is clear that the soul wants something else from its partner, which it is unable to say, but it indicates what it wants in a prophetic and riddling way. And if Hephaistos, with tools in hand, should stand over them lying together and say:

"What is it that you want, you human beings, from one another?"

And if after they answered he should speak again:

"Do you desire to be together as much as possible, so that night and day you might not leave one another's side? For if you desire this, I am willing to join and fuse you together into one, so that from two you will become one and, so long as you live, since you are one, you will live together in common, and when you die you will be dead together there in Hades, one instead of two. Consider whether you desire and will be content with this."

We know that no one would reject these things, nor would he want anything else, but he would absolutely think that he had heard the very thing he had desired for so long, namely to come together and be fused with his beloved, one from two. The reason for this is that our original nature was the same and we were whole. For desire of the whole, therefore, (193) and the pursuit of it, the name is Eros.

Previously, as I say, we were one, but now because of injustice god has forced us to live apart, as the Spartans have done to the Arcadians. We fear, therefore, that if we are not orderly toward the gods, we will be split in two and go around like the figures formed in low relief on grave markers, sawn in half through the nose, winding up like half-dice. Therefore, every man must take every precaution to be pious to the gods so that he might avoid the bad consequences and meet with the good, with Eros as our leader and general. Let no one do the opposite— and he who does the opposite is hated by the gods—for if we are friendly and reconciled with god, we will discover and meet with our own beloveds, which few do these days . . . Therefore I insist respecting all of us, men and women, that our race will be *eudaimon* if we attain to the condition of Eros and each of us meets with his beloved and so reverts to our original nature. And if this is best, then of necessity the present state nearest this is best, and this is to meet with the most suitable beloved. For this reason we shall hymn the gods justly if we hymn Eros, who in the present benefits us most by leading us to our own and gives us the greatest hopes that in the future, if we conduct ourselves piously toward the gods, he will resettle us in our original nature and by healing us make us blessed and *eudaimon*.

7.5. THE MYTH OF ER, FROM THE *REPUBLIC*

In the *Republic* Socrates explains to Plato's half-brothers, Glaukon and Adeimantos, why justice is good and injustice is bad, independently of rewards and punishments distributed by either human beings or gods. At the end of the dialogue he insists that the gods do in fact monitor human activities and reward the just and punish the unjust after death. In the "Myth of Er" Socrates recounts the testimony of a man, Er, who died in battle and later came back to life to relate the details of all he witnessed of reward and punishment in the afterlife.

SOURCE: Plato, *Republic* 614b–621d, translated and annotated by M. Anderson.

(614) I will not, I said, tell you a tale for Alkinoos, but rather the tale of a brave man, Er, the son of Armenios, a Pamphylian by race. He once died in battle, and when the corpses were gathered up on the tenth day, already decomposed, he was removed in good condition. Having been carried home and being about to be buried on the twelfth day, he came to life lying on the pyre, and having come to life he related the things he had seen in the Underworld. He said that when his soul left him, it journeyed with many and arrived in some daimonic place in which there were two chasms close together in the earth and two in the heaven above and opposite them. Between them sat judges who, when they rendered judgment, ordered the just to proceed to the right and up into the heaven, affixing signs of their judgments in front of them, and they ordered the unjust to proceed to the left and down bearing signs in their rear of all they had done. When Er himself arrived, they said that he must be a messenger to human beings of all the things in the Underworld, and they ordered him to listen and observe everything in the place.

At one of the pairs of chasms of heaven and earth Er witnessed souls departing after judgments had been rendered them, and at the other pair he saw souls come up from the chasm in the earth covered with dust and ash and from the other chasm other souls come down pure from heaven. The souls, constantly arriving, appeared to have come as if from long journeys, and they went off happily into the meadow as if making camp at a festival, and those who knew one another exchanged greetings. Those who had come from the earth listened to those who had come from the sky and learned of their experiences there, and those from the sky listened to and learned of the experiences of those who had come from the earth. As they shared their experiences, some lamented (615) and cried at recalling the magnitude and nature of their sufferings and all they had seen in their subterranean journey, which journey lasts one thousand years, and those from the sky related the beauty of their good experiences and impossible visions.

The several things would take much time to relate, Glaukon, but the main point was this: however many their unjust deeds, and toward however many men each of them behaved unjustly, they paid the penalty for everything in turn, ten times over for each, one time each century, since this is considered the length of a human life, in order that they may pay a ten-fold penalty for each injustice. If, for example, some were responsible for multiple deaths, either by betraying cities or armies and reducing them to slavery or by assisting in the commission of other base deeds, they received ten-fold pains for all these things for each man wronged, and also, if they had done good deeds and become just and pious, they received their due in accordance with the same procedure. He said other things about those who were born and lived a short time, but they were not worthy of mention.

Er related still greater wages for impiety and piety toward the gods and parents, and for murder. He said he was present when someone sought the whereabouts of Ardiaios the Great. This Ardiaios had been a tyrant in a city of Pamphylia one thousand years earlier and was said to have murdered his old father and elder brother and to have done many other unholy things. According to Er, the man answered: "He has not come and he will not come here, for even this was among the terrible spectacles we saw: when we were near the mouth about to go up and had endured all other sufferings, we suddenly spied that man and others, almost all of them tyrants, but some were private individuals guilty of great offenses. They thought that they would soon go up, but the mouth did not receive them, rather it groaned whenever one who was incorrigibly wicked or who had not sufficiently paid his penalty tried to ascend. There were wild men there, fiery to behold, standing by and attending to the sound, who took some men and led them away, but who bound Ardiaios and others (616) by the hands, feet, and head, threw them down and flayed them, and then dragged them along the outer road, tearing them upon thorns while signifying to those present why this was being done and that they were leading them away to be cast into Tartarus." A great variety of fearful things happened to them, he said, but surpassing them all was the fear that one would hear the sound when he approached, and each man ascended most happily when it was silent. Such were the penalties and punishments and the rewards corresponding to them.

After spending seven days in the meadow, on the eighth day they had to stand up and move on, arriving four days later at a place whence they spied above them a straight light extended through the whole of heaven and earth, like a column, particularly resembling the rainbow, but brighter and more pure. After travelling a day's journey they arrived at this light and saw at its middle the extremities of its bonds stretching from heaven, for this light is the belt of heaven, similar to the bands that undergird triremes, and it holds together the whole revolving circuit. Extending from the extremities was the spindle of Necessity, through which all the revolutions turn. The stalk and the hook of the spindle are made of adamant; its whorl is mixed of adamant and other substances.

The nature of the whorl is like this: its shape is of the nature of our contemporary whorls, but from what he said we must understand it to be like a large, hollow, scooped out whorl with another similar but smaller one fitted inside and encased throughout its length, like boxes fitted into one another, and likewise a third whorl and a fourth and four others. For there are eight whorls altogether, encased within one another, their rims appearing as circles from above and the whole assembly finished off so as to appear from behind as one continuous whorl around the spindle, which was driven through the center of the eighth whorl.

The first and external whorl had the widest circular rim, the rim of the sixth was second widest, the rim of the fourth was third, the rim of the eighth was fourth, the rim of the seventh was fifth, the rim of the fifth was sixth, the rim of the third was seventh, and the rim of the second was eighth. The rim of the largest whorl showed designs, the rim of the seventh was brightest, the rim of the eighth had color taken from the seventh's (617) shining on it, the rims of the second and fifth resembled each other and were lighter than the others, the third had the whitest color, the fourth was reddish, and the sixth was second in whiteness. The whole spindle when turning circled with the same motion, but the seven circles within the rotating whole turned slowly in opposition to the whole. Of these the eighth went the fastest, second fastest and the same as one another were the seventh, sixth, and fifth; the fourth, as it seemed to them, revolved in its motion third fastest, and fourth was the third and the second fifth. And the spindle turned on the knees of Necessity.

Above, upon each of the rims of the spindle's circles, were Sirens, revolving around with them, emitting one sound, one note; from all eight together one harmony resounded. Three others were there, sitting around at equal distances, each upon a throne, daughters of necessity, the Fates, dressed in white with wreaths upon their heads, Lachesis, Klotho, and Atropos, singing with the Sirens' harmony, Lachesis singing what has been, Klotho what is, and Atropos what will be. Klotho with her right hand took hold of and helped to turn the outer circumference of the spindle, ceasing at times; Atropos with her left hand did likewise with the inner circumferences; and Lachesis in turn took hold of each in each hand.

Upon arrival the souls had immediately to approach Lachesis. A certain prophet first set them into divisions, then taking lots and patterns of lives from the knees of Lachesis, he mounted a high platform and said: "The logos of Lachesis, the maiden daughter of necessity: Ephemeral souls, this is the beginning of another death-bearing cycle for the mortal race. A daimon will not choose you, but you will choose a daimon. Whoever obtains the first lot shall select first the life to which he will be bound by necessity. Virtue has no master, but each man will have more or less of virtue according to his honoring or dishonoring her. He who chooses is to blame; god is blameless." And having said these things, he tossed the lots before them all, and each man took up the lot that fell beside him, all except Er, who was not allowed. To the one who (618) took up his lot it was clear what number he had drawn. After this the prophet placed the patterns of lives on the ground before them, many more than the number of those present. There were patterns of every kind: lives of all the animals and particularly of all types of human life. There were tyrannies among them, some permanent, some cut short and ending up in poverty, exile, and beggary. There were lives of famous men, some famous for the beauty, strength, and athleticism of their bodies, some for their birth and the virtues of their ancestors; and there were those of no reputation for these things; and all this applied to women as well. It was not possible to specify the arrangement of the soul because necessarily it was altered by choosing this or that life. Other things were mixed all together and mixed as well with wealth and poverty, sickness and health, and also the intermediate conditions.

It is likely that here, dear Glaukon, there is every danger for a person, and especially for these reasons each of us must be sure to ignore other types of knowledge and be seekers and students of *this* knowledge, namely whether it is possible to learn and discover who will give one the competence and knowledge to distinguish the good life from the wicked and always and everywhere to choose the best life from among the available options; to reflect upon all the things we have just said and how their being combined or divided contributes to a virtuous life, and thereby to know what good or bad thing beauty will affect when mixed with poverty or wealth and combined with the various habits of soul; and regarding noble or ignoble births, private and public lives, strength and weakness, swiftness and sluggishness of mind, and all such natural and acquired states of the soul, to know what they will affect when combined together—the result of all this being the competence to calculate and choose, looking toward the nature of the soul, the worse and the better life, calling worse the life that will lead the soul to be more unjust and better whichever life will lead it to be more just. All other things he will dismiss, for we have seen that in life as well as in death this is the most significant (619) choice. One must go to Hades adamantly holding to this opinion so that even there he may be undaunted by wealth and other such base things and not, by falling into tyranny and other such practices, do many irremediable bad things and suffer still worse himself, but know always to choose the life in the mean with respect to such things and, to the best of one's ability, to flee the excesses on the extremes in both the present and the future life; for thus does a person become most *eudaimon*.

And then the messenger from there, Er, reported that the prophet spoke as follows: "Even to him who comes last, if he makes a rational choice and lives earnestly, a desirable life is available, not a bad one. Let whoever chooses first not be careless, nor he who chooses last be disheartened."

Er said that after the prophet said these things the man who drew the first lot immediately came forward and selected the greatest tyranny, and from thoughtlessness and greed he made his selection without sufficient consideration, and he did not realize that his fate included eating his own children and other evils. After considering the matter at his leisure he struck himself and lamented his choice, but he did not abide by the admonitions of the prophet, for he did not blame himself for the evils, but rather he blamed chance and his daimon and everything other than himself. He was one of those who had come down from heaven after having passed his former life under an orderly constitution, having partaken of virtue by habit without philosophy. And on the whole not a few of those entangled in such things were those who had come from heaven, for they had not trained for labors. And many of those who came from the earth, since they had trained and observed the others, did not make their selections rashly. In this way many of the souls exchanged evils and goods, and this occurred also through the chance of the lot. For whenever someone enters into his life here, if he always philosophizes soundly and if the lot governing his selection does not fall to him last, we may conclude from the reports brought from there not only that a man may be *eudaimon* here, but also that his journey from here to there and back again will not be subterranean and rough but smooth and heavenly.

It was, said Er, a sight worthy to behold, how each (620) of the souls chose their lives, for it is pitiable, laughable, and wondrous to see. For the most part they chose according to the habits formed in their previous life. He said that he saw Orpheus's soul choose the life of a swan: motivated by hatred of the female race because of his death at their hands, his soul did not want to manifest as a woman. He saw the soul of Thamyras choose the life of a nightingale. He saw a swan transform into the choice of a human life, and other musical animals did likewise. The soul with the twentieth lot chose the life of a lion—this was the soul of Aiax, the son of Telamon, which fled human form recalling the distribution of Achilles's arms. The soul of Agamemnon was next: this soul too hated the human race due to his many sufferings and changed for the life of an eagle. The soul of Atalanta received one of the middle lots and, noting the great honors awarded to athletic men, was unable to resist and so took one. After this soul Er saw the soul of Epeios, the son of Pano-peus, enter the nature of a craftswoman. Far among the last he saw the soul of buf-foonish Thersites donning the guise of a monkey. The soul of Odysseus happened to receive the final lot of all and came forward to make its selection: mindful of its former labors and having recovered from the love of honor, it looked around a long time in search of the life of a private apolitical man, which it finally discovered lying around somewhere neglected by the others, and seeing this it said that it would have made the same selection even if it had drawn the first lot, and it chose this life gladly. And similarly the souls of the other animals went into human beings and into each other, the unjust transforming into wild animals, the just into tame animals, and all combinations were mixed together.

When all the souls had chosen lives, they proceeded in the order of their lots toward Lachesis, who sent with each soul the daimon it had chosen as guardian of its life and fulfiller of the selections. The daimon first led the soul to Klotho, under her hand and the turning of the rotation of the spindle, to authorize the fate it had chosen according to the lot. Having met with her, the daimon led the soul to the spinning of Atropos, who rendered the destinies unalterable. From there it went straight forward and came under (621) the throne of Necessity, and after he passed through this, and the others passed through, they all proceeded to the plain of Lethe[2] through a scorching and terrible heat, for the place was bereft of trees and all that earth produces. There, as evening came on, they camped beside the river of Lethe, whose water no vessel holds. Every soul had to drink a certain measure of the water, but those who failed to restrain themselves by prudence drank excessively, and whoever drank continuously forgot everything. When they fell asleep and mid-night came, there were thunder and earthquakes, and suddenly they were borne here and there into becoming, shooting like stars. Er himself was prevented from drink-ing the water, yet by what way and how he came into his body he did not know, but suddenly opening his eyes, he saw himself at dawn lying on the pyre.

And thus, Glaukon, a myth was saved and not lost, and it will save us too if we believe it, and we shall cross well the river of Lethe and our soul will not be defiled.

---

[2] Lethe means "forgetfulness": see the river of Lethe two lines below. For a similar idea in other underworld landscapes, see *Aeneid* 6.705 (Part 6, document 13) and the Orphic Gold Tablets (Part 6, document 9).

GLOSSARY OF TECHNICAL TERMS

✦

agon: (Greek) literally a "contest"; in the context of Greek and Latin drama, the term is used for a rhetorical discussion or argument between two characters.

aition: (Gr. pl. *aitia*, cf. derived English "etiology," also spelled "aetiology") literally "cause"; a mythological narrative that serves as the explanation of a real phenomenon in the author's time (a political institution, a festival, the name of a god, etc.).

anthropogony: (from Gr. *anthropos*, "human being," "person," and *gonia*, "birth") narrative about the birth or creation of human beings.

anthropomorphic: displaying "human-like" characteristics of nonhuman beings, such as gods or personified natural phenomena.

autochthonous: (from Gr. *autos*, "same," "own," and *chthon*, "land") something or someone having originated "in the land," in some stories literally coming out of the ground. The term is normally used to describe a people that claims to belong to its land since time immemorial (e.g., the Athenians).

baetyl: (from Gr. *baitylos*, Lat. *baetulus*, in turn from a Semitic word, cf. Hebrew *beit-el* or Bethel, "house of God") nonanthropomorphic and often uncarved stone used in cults, believed to represent a deity or some sacred entity.

colophon: one or more written lines appended at the end of a text, usually containing information about the author or scribe, content, and other such explanatory matters about the text. Colophons are frequent in Near Eastern texts (tablets).

corpus: (Lat. pl. *corpora*) literally "body," used in scholarship for a group of texts that belong together according to some broad criterion (e.g., Hittite texts, Roman literature, Greek inscriptions, etc.).

cosmogony: (from Gr. *kosmos*, "universe," and *gonia*, "birth") narrative about the origins or creation of the universe.

chthonic: (from Gr. *chthon*, "earth") used to refer to entities that belong in the Underworld realm, normally divinities and heroes.

dactylic hexameters: type of verse used in Greek and Latin epic poetry (e.g., Homer, Hesiod, Virgil) and also used to write magical spells and epigrams. It consists of six "feet" or segments, each containing one long syllable and two short syllables or two long syllables. They are called dactylic from the Greek *daktylos*, "finger," because fingers also have one long and two short "sections."

demiurge: (from Gr. *demiourgos*, "public servant," "artisan," "creator") used in the context of cosmogony to refer to the creator of the universe and/or humankind and the creator's task as an "artisan."

epic: (from Gr. *epos*, "word," "story," "message") used for the genre of epic poetry, that is, long narrative poems that recount the exploits of gods and heroes, such as Homer's *Iliad* and the Ugaritic *Baal Cycle*, but also cosmogonic poems (e.g., *Enuma Elish*, Hesiod's *Theogony*).

epigraphy: (adj. epigraphical; from Gr. *epi*, "on," and *graphe*, "writing") the study of inscriptions, that is, texts written on stone or other materials, such as clay tablets in the Near East, etc. Subcategories of epigraphy include the study of papyri (Papyrology), the study of manuscripts (Paleography), and the study of texts written in coins (part of Numismatics) (see Figs. 10, 13, 14, and 15).

epithet: adjective or adjectival phrase attached to the names of heroes and gods (cloud-rider, Atreid [son of Atreus], son of Kronos, etc.) as well as to other entities (e.g., the wine-dark sea). Epithets are often compound words (*rododaktylos eos*, "rosy-fingered dawn") or include two words (*podas okys Achilleus*, "swift-footed Achilles," *theois epieikelos*, "similar to the gods"). Like the longer formulae (see below), epithets appear frequently in epic poetry.

eponymous: (from Gr. *eponomazo*, "to name;" cf. *onoma*, "name") adjective used for a hero or ancestor who gives its name to a family, a people, or some other entity (e.g., Aiolos for the Aiolian Greeks, Iambe for iambic poetry).

eschatology: (from Gr. *eschaton*, "end," "limit") narratives and beliefs about death and the afterlife, as well as about the end of humanity or the world.

etiology (or aetiology): see *aition*.

Epicureanism: philosophical school established in Athens by moral and natural philosopher Epicurus (341–270 BCE), built upon the earlier atomist principles laid out by Democritus (whose works are lost), according to which the world is the result of accident, not of divine intervention. See more about Epicurean ideas in Part 5, document 7.

epiphany: when a god appears to a mortal, whether in his "real" form (e.g., Dionysos and Demeter at the end of their respective *Homeric Hymns*) or in some other form (Apollo as a Dolphin, Aphrodite as a mortal woman, in the same *Hymns*).

Euhemerism: (adj. Euhemeristic) approach that follows the theory advanced by Euhemerus of Messene (late fourth to early third centuries BCE), according to which myths should be reread as the idealization and distortion of historical events. For instance, gods were really kings who excelled in their deeds and were later divinized (Philon of Byblos' account, in Part 1, document 7.a follows this idea).

formula: (Lat. pl. *formulae*) phrase used repeatedly in epic poetry, usually in recurrent situations (e.g., "Then in turn, the son of Atreus answered him," "When early-born dawn appeared, whose fingers were like roses . . . ") or attached to a character, working as extended epithets (e.g., "the blessed gods who hold Olympos"). The fixed metrical structure of formulae and epithets facilitated the poet's composition process.

genealogy: (adj. "genealogical," from Gr. *genos*, "family," "race") the recording of family trees and ancestry lines, often in long lists embedded in traditional and mythological narratives. Through this mechanism, kings, illustrious families, and whole populations traced their ancestry to heroes and gods.

genre: (French) category or type of art, including literature (thus often "literary genre"), such as epic, drama (with the subgenres of tragedy, comedy), historiography, and philosophical writing.

hexameters: see **dactylic hexameters**.

hybris: Greek word used in the context of myths to refer to the excessive pride and arrogance of a hero or of a god's enemy. In other contexts, it can mean more simply "offense," "crime," "outrage."

iconography: (from Gr. *eikon*, "image," "likeness") the study of images as represented in the visual arts, e.g., vase painting, statues, and reliefs.

interpretatio: (Lat. for "interpretation") term used in the study of myth and religion to describe the process by which one culture identifies a god or some other religious concept or institution with that of another culture (e.g., Herakles as Phoenician Melqart, Demeter as Egyptian Isis, etc.).

katabasis: (Gr. from *kata*, "down," and *baino*, "to walk") literally "descent," "going down," referring to narratives about journeys into the Underworld.

lacuna: (Lat. for "lagoon," "gap") term used in epigraphy and text edition for an "empty" space left in a text by a damaged or otherwise lost section.

Maenads: one of the names given by the Greeks to the female followers of Dionysos. The word is connected to the altered state of mind that Dionysos induced in them (from Gr. *maino/mainomai*, "to be furious or ecstatic," "to be out of your mind").

metope: architectural element used as part of the decoration of the entablature in Greek and Roman buildings. (The entablature is the entire horizontal structure above the columns.) The square space of the metopes was left for relief decoration; they often run all around the temple and represent series of mythological scenes (e.g., the labors of Theseus, the fights between Centaurs and Lapiths) (see Fig. 8).

monotheism: the belief in only one god (as in Judaism, Islam, Christianity), in contrast with polytheism, which is the belief in multiple gods who are often related, forming among them a loose family system (as in Greek, Roman, and most ancient Near Eastern religions).

Mythography: type of literature written by ancient mythographers, especially during the Hellenistic and Roman periods, which consisted of the collection and synthesis of mythical narratives from previous sources (e.g., Apollodorus' *Library*, Hyginus' *Fabulae*).

Neoplatonism: modern term that designates the revival of Platonic philosophy initiated by Plotinus (third century CE), which became the main philosophical trend in late Antiquity up to the sixth century CE. Other famous Neoplatonic authors are Porphyry, Iamblichus, and Proclus.

Orphism: (adj. Orphic) loosely defined philosophical, literary, and religious trend named after the legendary musician and poet Orpheus, to whom the "Orphic" authors attributed their texts. Orphic texts are especially linked with cosmogony and theogony (though also with magic, astrology, and other subjects) and are somehow connected with the Eleusinian and Bacchic mysteries.

ostracon: (Gr. for "shard," pl. *ostraca*) broken piece of clay or (less frequently) stone, used to scribble short texts, often for daily purposes, for instance school exercises, accounting texts, and voting ballots (see Fig. 9).

pantheon: (Gr. for "all gods") the group of gods worshiped by a specific group of people, be it a whole culture, a city, or a smaller group (the Olympian gods, the Ugaritic pantheon, etc.).

pediment: architectural element in Greek and Roman (and later on Neoclassical) buildings, most frequently temples. The pediment is the triangular space in the front and back of the building, created by the roof's triangular angle. Sitting on top of the entablature, the pediment's space was used for decoration, especially sculptural groups alluding to Greek and Roman mythology (see Fig. 22).

polytheism: see **monotheism.**

Presocratic philosophers: (or Pre-Socratic) conventional name given to early Greek thinkers of the sixth and fifth centuries BCE, who were active before Socrates, although also contemporary with him. This category includes, among others, Anaxagoras, Anaximander, Haraclitus, and Thales. They are also called "natural philosophers" (Gr. *physiologoi*).

Satyr: male creature with goat legs and ears, who inhabited the woods and worshiped and escorted the god Dionysos.

scholion: (Gr. for "commentary," interpretation," pl. *scholia*) text written by an ancient scribe or scholar (referred to as the scholiast) in the margins of a manuscript containing an authoritative text, as a way of clarification of or commentary to specific passages. These glosses could be original or copied from earlier commentaries.

shamanism: religious phenomenon associated with the figure of the shaman, a healer and intercessor between the world of the living and that of the dead. The term was originally used for a phenomenon among Turkic and north Asian peoples (from Russia, Mongolia, part of China) but is sometimes applied to ecstatic figures in other cultures, including Greek mythical and charismatic figures, such as Orpheus, Abaris, Zalmoxis, Pythagoras, and Empedokles.

Sophists: (from Gr. *sofistes*, "skilled," "sage," "expert," cf. Gr. *sophos*) professional teachers of rhetoric and philosophy (including mathematics and natural sciences) in the fifth century BCE, such as Protagoras, Gorgias, Hippias, and many others. These itinerant teachers of "higher education" were often criticized (especially by Plato) as greedy and opportunist charlatans.

spell: magical utterance, such as those preserved in the Greek and Latin magical texts; the term is also used for the utterances contained in the Egyptian *Book of the Dead*.

stele: (Gr. pl. *stelai*; Lat. *stela*, pl. *stelae*) stone slab set up for monumental purposes (funerary, commemorative, or other), containing reliefs, inscriptions, or both (see Figs. 5, 6, and 7).

theophoric: (Gr. from *theos*, "god," and *phero*, "to carry") adjective used for a proper name that "carries" the name of a god in it (e.g., Artemidoros, "gift of Artemis," Ilimilku, "king Il/El," Raphael, "God healed").

theogony: (from Gr. *theos*, "god," and *gonia*, birth") narrative about the birth and origins of the gods.

xenia: (Gr. for "hospitality," cf. *xenos*, "foreigner," "guest") the act of hospitality, which rules were sacred in Greek culture and were protected by Zeus himself.

BIBLIOGRAPHY

✦

THIS bibliographical section is arranged as follows: suggestions for further readings are arranged by thematic section, including only the last name of the author and date of the work; full references to each cited work are then listed in the References section below.

Introduction

Greek and Roman Mythology and Religion

For an introduction to the modern theories of myth, see Segal (2004) and Csapo (2005); for classical mythology and its modern reception, see also short introduction by Morales (2007); for the various approaches to the study of Greek mythology, see Graf (1993) and essays in Edmunds (1990, with a revised edition forthcoming). See also overview by J. Bremmer in Dowden and Livingstone (2011), ch.28. The recent "companions" to Greek myth edited by Woodard (2007) and Dowden and Livingstone (2011) cover a variety of topics and approaches (references to specific chapters in them are included below). An overview of artistic representations of archaic myths can be found in Gantz's two volumes (1993), while the most complete source for iconography is *LIMC* (*Lexicon Iconographicum Mythologiae Classicae*, Zurich and Munich, 1981–2009); see also study of the interpretation of Greek mythical images in Junker (2012).

For Greek religion, see Burkert (1985) and Parker (2011); for the intersection between Greek myth and religion, see Calame's contribution in Woodard (2007), ch.8. For Roman religion, see overview and sourcebook in Bear, North, and Price (1998); see also Feeney (1999). For the reception and use of the Homeric tradition in Rome, see Erskine (2001). A guide to ancient religion topics (classical and Near Eastern) is in Johnston (2004).

For general consultation, see the *OCD* (*The Oxford Classical Dictionary*, S. Hornblower, A. Spawforth, and E. Eidinow, eds., London, and New York, 2012, 4th ed.) and *Brill's New Pauly, Encyclopaedia of the Ancient World* (H. Cancik, H. Schneider, and M. Landfester, M., eds., Leiden, 1996).

Greek and Roman History

For a history of Archaic Greece, see Hall (2007); for Classical Greece, Rhodes (2010); and for the Hellenistic period, see Errington (2008). For early Roman history, down to the Punic Wars, see Cornell (1995); see Nicolet (1980) and Bispham (2012) for Republican Rome, and Goodman (2012) for the Empire up to 180 CE. For the use of myth in iconography as part of imperial propaganda in Augustus' time, see Zanker (1988).

Near Eastern History, Literature, and Mythology

For a general history of the ancient Near Eastern civilizations from 3000 to Hellenistic times (330 BCE), see Kuhrt (1995), Van De Mieroop (2007) (not including Egypt), and essays in Snell (2005). For an introduction to the different Near Eastern literatures, see Ehrlich (2009). For ancient Near Eastern mythology, consult dictionary by Leick (1991).

For the history of Mesopotamian divine figures and symbols (with ample illustrations), see Black and Green (1992). For Mesopotamian religion, see classical work by Jacobsen (1976). Collections of Mesopotamian texts in translations can be found in Foster (1995) and Dalley (2000). For different aspects of Babylonian culture, see essays in Leick (2007), and for the scribal world of Babylon, see Charpin (2010). For an account of the discovery of Mesopotamian civilizations and the decipherment of Akkadian, see Larsen (1996).

For Egyptian history, see Hornung (1999) and Shaw (2000). For Egyptian mythology in general, see Pinch (2002) and Pinch (2004). For a selection of Egyptian literature, see Simpson (2003). See also resources in Dieleman and Wendrich (2008–).

For Hittite history and society, see Bryce (2002, 2005). For the city of Hattusha, see Seeher (2011). For Troy and the Homeric epics in the Anatolian context, see Bryce (2006) and Latacz (2004). For Anatolian religions, see Popko (1995) and Taracha (2009).

For Ugaritic history and culture, see studies in Watson and Wyatt (1999); for the city of Ugarit, see Yon (2006); for Ugaritic religious and ritual texts, see de Moor (1987), del Olmo Lete (1999), Wyatt (2002), and Pardee (2002); for the mythical texts, see Parker (1997) and updated collection by Coogan and Smith (2012). For a study of the Hebrew Bible as a literary creation, see Alter (1981) and, for Genesis specifically, Carr (1996).

For early Israelite religion and its Canaanite background, see Smith (2001, 2002). For the history and archaeology of early Israel and Judah, see surveys in Finkelstein and Na'aman (1994) and Soggin (1999), and for the approaches and controversies surrounding Biblical Archaeology, see synthesis in Cline (2009). For the Phoenicians in general, see Markoe (2000). For a history of Carthage, see Miles (2010) and Hoyos (2010).

Greek and Near Eastern Compartive Studies

Comparative works on Greek (to a lesser degree Roman) and Near Eastern myths and literatures have been on the rise, especially since the 1990s. The works of Michael Astour (1967) and Walter Burkert (1979) already paved the ground for this field. Since then, comparison has been explored in numerous articles, book chapters, and encyclopedia entries. Some essential monographs in English, fully focused on comparative issues, are Burkert (1992 and 2004), especially focused on religion; West's monumental compendium of comparable motifs (1997); and Bremmer's collection of specific studies (2008). Studies more narrowly focused on particular areas are Penglase (1994) on archaic Greek and Mesopotamian literature, Brown (1995, 2000, 2001), with three volumes on Greek and Israelite literary parallels, López-Ruiz (2010) on Greek cosmogonies and North-West Semitic sources, Louden (2011) on the *Odyssey* and Near Eastern (especially biblical) parallels, Moyer (2011) on Greek and Egyptian cultures, and Bachvarova (forthcoming) on archaic Greek and Anatolian literatures (Hittite primarily). Dowden and Livingstone (2011) contain three essays on comparative evidence (ch. 19 by A. Livingstone and B. Haskamp, ch.20 by N. Marinatos and N. Wyatt, and ch.24 by I. Rutherford). The guide to religions across the ancient Mediterranean cultures by Johnston (2004) also exemplifies this trend and is a great resource for comparative work.

Part One. And So It Began: Cosmogonies and Theogonies

For translation and notes on *Enuma Elish*, the *Theogony of Dunnu*, and other Mesopotamian myths, see Dalley (2000). See also Foster (1995).

For the Memphite theology, see the most recent study in el-Hawary (2010), Lichtheim (1973), 51–57, with complete translation of the text into English, and Allen (1988), 43–44. For "A Hymn to Life," see Allen (1988), 21–27, and Willems (1996) 293–297, 469–473. For the *Teachings for Merikare*, see Parkinson (1997), 212–234; Simpson (2003), 152–165 (translation by V. A. Tobin). The main general source for the *Coffin Texts* in English is still Faulkner (1973–1978).

See translation and commentary on Genesis by Alter (1996). For the creation stories of Genesis, see also Carr (1996); for Genesis 1, see Smith (2010). For other ancient texts (Jewish and Christian) that deal with creation, see Barnstone (1984), especially ch.1 (Creation Myths).

For Hesiod's complete works, see Most (2006). See study on Hesiod's poems by Clay (2003). For Hesiod's myths and their Near Eastern parallels, see West (1997), ch.6, and López-Ruiz (2010). See also R. Woodard's essay on Hesiod in Woodard (2007), ch.3. For the Orphic cosmogonies, see West (1983); Bernabé (2003) and latest edition of the Orphic Fragments in Bernabé (2004); overview of Orphic myth by R. Edmonds in Dowden and Livingstone (2011), ch.4. See also Athanassakis (2013) for the Orphic Hymns. For the Derveni Papyrus, see Laks and Most (1997) and Betegh (2004). For Presocratic cosmogonic ideas, see McKirahan (1994), and for the connection between Greek early philosophical traditions and Near Eastern sources, see West (1971).

For Philon of Byblos' *Phoenician History*, see Baumgarten (1981), Attridge and Oden (1981), and latest edition, translation, and commentary by Kaldellis and López-Ruiz (2009). For other Phoenician cosmogonies and their connections with

Orphism, see López-Ruiz (2010), especially ch.4; for Greek cosmogonies (including Orphic) and Near Eastern parallels, see also Burkert (2004).

For Aristophanes' *Birds*, see Dunbar's edition (1995) and thorough commentary. On the intersection of philosophy and comedy generally, see Freydberg (2008). For the figure of Socrates in Aristophanes' comedies, see Strauss (1996). For myth in Aristophanes, see also A. Bowie's essay in Woodard (2007), ch.5.

For Apollonios' *Argonautika*, see translation with introduction by Green (1997), and, for the iconography of the Argonauts, Ganz (1993), ch.12.

For Ovid's *Metamorphoses*, see full translations (with introduction and notes) by Melville (1986) and Ambrose (2004). See studies by Brooks (1970), Solodow (1988), Hardie (2002), and Fantham (2004). For the theme of metamorphosis in Greek myths, see Forbes Irving (1990), and for metamorphoses in Ovid and in later cultures and contexts, see Warner (2002). For Ovid and Greek myth, see ch.12 in Woodard (2007) by A. J. Boyle.

For the full translation of Virgil's *Aeneid* and extensive notes, see Ahl (2007). For Virgil's *Aeneid*, see Hardie (1986), Bloom (1986), Cairns (1989), and Reed (2007).

For Virgil's *Eclogues*, see Breed (2006).

Part Two. Mankind Created, Mankind Destroyed

For a translation and more extensive notes on *Atrahasis* and other Mesopotamian myths, see Dalley (2000). See also Foster (1995).

For the Egyptian myth of the destruction of mankind (from the *Book of the Heavenly Cow*), see introduction by Guilhou in Dielman and Wendrich (*UEE*, 2008–) and translation by E. F. Wente in Simpson (2003), 289–298. For the Coffin Texts in general, consult Faulkner (1973–1978).

For the book of Genesis, see translation and commentary by Alter (1996). For the creation stories of Genesis, see also Carr (1996). For other ancient texts (Jewish and Christian) that deal with creation, see Barnstone (1984), especially ch.1 (Creation Myths).

For Hesiod's complete works, see translation by Most (2006). A study of Hesiod's poems and their interrelated themes (especially Prometheus) can be found in Clay (2003). On Hesiod's myths and their Near Eastern parallels, see West (1997), ch.6, and López-Ruiz (2010). For the figure of Prometheus, see comprehensive study by Dougherty (2005). For a study of the myth of Pandora and Prometheus in connection with Mesopotamian myths, see Penglase (1994), ch.9.

For Ovid's *Metamorphoses*, see full translations (with introduction and notes) by Melville (1986) and Ambrose (2004). See studies by Brooks (1970), Solodow (1988), Hardie (2002), and Fantham (2004). For the theme of metamorphosis in Greek myths, see Forbes Irving (1990), and for metamorphoses in Ovid and in later cultures and contexts, see Warner (2002). For Ovid and Greek myth, see ch.12 in Woodard (2007) by A. J. Boyle.

For the Orphic myths about Dionysos and the origin of humans, see Graf and Johnston (2007), especially ch.3. For Orphism, the main points of reference are still the comprehensive studies by Guthrie (1952) and West (1983); for Orphism and Christianity, see Herrero de Jáuregui (2010). (See also references on Gold Tablets and Orpheus in References section.)

Part Three. Epic Struggles: Gods, Heroes, and Monsters

For the *Epic of Gilgamesh*, see full translation, introductions, and notes by Dalley (2000) and George (2003a); George (2003b) is the latest edition of the cuneiform with extensive commentary. For a comparison between the epic of Gilgamesh and Homer's epics, see essay by Currie in Montanari et al. (2010), 543–580. For the genre of epic in the Near East, see overview by Sasson in Foley (2005), 215–231.

For the *Pyramid Texts*, see translation in English by Allen (2005), and for the fights between Horus and Seth, Allen (2005), 146, no. 396. A translation of *Pap. London UCL* 32158, with hieroglyphic text, can be found in Collier and Quirke (2004), 20–21. For a full translation and study (in French) of the so-called "adventures" or "contendings" of Horus and Seth in the *Papyrus Chester Beatty* I, see Broze (1996), 90–100, also translated into English by E. F. Wente in Simpson (2003), 91–103.

For the *Tale of the Shipwrecked Sailor*, see English study and translation by Galán (2005), 17–48. See also Parkinson (1997), 89–101, and translation by W. K. Simpson in Simpson (2003), 45–53.

For the Hittite myths, see introduction and translations by Hoffner (1998). For a comparative discussion of cosmogonic stories, see López-Ruiz (2010), especially ch.3, and for Greek and Hittite epic traditions, Bachvarova (forthcoming). For translations and discussion of Caucasian mythology, see Colarusso (2002).

The latest edition, translation, and study of the *Baal Cycle* can be found in the two volumes by Smith (1994) and Smith and Pitard (2009). Accessible and comprehensive treatments of the *Baal Cycle* and *Aqhat* as well as other Ugaritic literature can be found in Parker (1997), Wyatt (2002), and Coogan and Smith (2012); see also translation and commentary by D. Pardee in Hallo and Younger (1997), (*Baal*) 241–273 and (*Aqhat*) 343–355.

For Hebrew literature and its Canaanite background, see Cross (1998); about Yahweh and the other gods and goddesses of Canaan, see Smith (2001, 2002) and Day (2000); for the Storm God figure in the Ancient Near East, see study by Green (2003). A monograph on biblical giants, including the story of David and Goliath, can be found in Doak (2013); for Goliath and the Philistines, see Bierling (1992).

For Homer's *Iliad*, see overview of the "Homeric question" in West (2011), Part I. Louden (2006) studies the narrative patterns in the *Iliad* and compares them with Ugaritic literature, and Louden (2011) points at common narratives in the *Odyssey* the Hebrew Bible and other Near Eastern sources (see the Cyclops and Humbaba in ch.8). An accessible study of motifs in the *Odyssey* is in Saïd (2011). Lane Fox (2008) offers a study of heroic motifs and their transmission by traveling Greeks during the "Dark Ages" and archaic period. A classical study of the Homeric hero's place in Greek religion and poetics is that by Nagy (1998); see also Nagy's essay in Foley

(2005) 71–89; see also essays on myth in Homer by G. Nagy in Woodard (2007), ch.2, and by F. Létoublon in Dowden and Livingstone (2011), ch.2.

For the *Homeric Hymns*, see translations and notes by Shelmerdine (1995) and Athanassakis (2004) and interpretive essays in Faulkner (2011). For the comparison of Mesopotamian myths with the *Homeric Hymns* and Hesiod, see Penglase (1994), especially ch.5 on Apollo. For the god Apollo in general, see the concise and comprehensive study by Graf (2009) and a similar one on Dionysos in the same series by Seaford (2006). A commentary on Euripides' *Bacchae* can be found in Seaford (1996), accounting for the role of Dionysos in Greek drama and religion.

For Herakles, see the comprehensive study by Stafford (2011); for the pre-historic qualities of his figure, see Burkert (1979), ch.4; for the Near Eastern connections of the Herakles cycle, see West (1997), 458–472; and for the extensive iconography of Herakles, see Gantz (1993), ch.13. For Theseus, see studies by Calame (1990) and Walker (1995) and archaic iconography in Ganz (1993), chs. 8–9. For Perseus, see comprehensive study by Ogden (2008) and iconography in Gantz (1993), ch.10. For the work of Hellenistic mythographers, including Apollodorus' *Library*, see essay by C. Higbie in Woodard (2007), ch.7, and essay by F. Graf in Dowden and Livingstone (2011), ch.11.

Part Four. Of Early Cities and Peoples

For the foundation of a Heliopolis temple by Senusert I, see English translation by Parkinson (1991), 40–43, no. 5, and study by Gundlach in Gundlach and Spence (2011), 103–114.

For the *Song of Release*, see Hoffner (1998) and for further analysis of the poem and its connections with Greek epic, see Bachvarova (forthcoming).

A study of Israel's conquest and settlement traditions can be found in Weinfeld (1993), including comparison with Greek and Roman foundation stories. For the Book of Genesis, see translation and commentary by Alter (1996). For the evidence and debates regarding the reconstruction of early Israelite history, including discussion of the exodus, see Dever (2006) and Finkelstein and Mazar (2007).

For the legends surrounding Sargon of Akkad, see Foster (1995), 165–170, and Van De Mieroop (2007), ch.4.

For Cyrus the Great and the Persian Empire, see the monumental study by Briant (2002). For Herodotos' *Histories*, see study by Thomas (2000) and essays in Derow and Parker (2002), including ch.9 by I. Malkin on Cyrene. The classical commentary on Herodotos' work and its historical context is contained in the two volumes by How and Wells (1989–1990, first published in 1912), but the first volume of a new updated commentary has appeared by Asheri, Lloyd, and Corcella (2007).

For Cyrene and other Greek colonies founded by the Greeks, see general overview in Boardman (1999) and Osborne (1996), 8–17. For the complex relationship between myth and history in the narratives about the foundation of Cyrene, see Calame (2003). A study of the motif of colonization in Archaic Greek poetry can be found in Dougherty (1993), with ch.6 on Pindar's *Pythian Ode*

5 and Cyrene. For myth in Pindar, see also I. Rutherford's essay in Dowden and Livingstone (2011), ch.5. For Greek myth in lyric poetry more generally (including Pindar), see also ch.1 by G. Nagy in Woodard (2007).

For Kadmos and his family and their Near Eastern connections, see West (1997), 448–457; treatment of the archaic iconography of the Theban saga can be found in Gantz (1993), ch.14. For Ovid's *Metamorphoses*, see full translation (with introduction and notes) by Melville (1986) and Ambrose (2004). See further studies by Brooks (1970), Solodow (1988), Hardie (2002), and Fantham (2004).

For Plutarch's *Parallel Lives*, see translation and commentary by Romm and Mensch (2012) and study by Duff (2000). For Theseus, see studies by Calame (1990) and Walker (1995) and archaic iconography in Ganz (1993), chs. 8–9. See also Morris (1992), ch. 12, for the creation of Theseus as an "Athenian Herakles" and national hero.

For the history of Carthage, see Miles (2010), especially 58–62 for its foundation. For Justin's *Epitome*, see translation and commentary in Yardley (1997, 2012). For the full translation of Virgil's *Aeneid* and extensive notes, see Ahl (2007). For the use of the figure of Aeneas and the Trojan Cycle in Rome, see Erskine (2001). See further studies of Virgil's *Aeneid* by Hardie (1986), Bloom (1986), Cairns (1989), and Reed (2007).

For Livy's work on Roman history since its foundation, see Miles (1995). For the history of early Rome, see Cornell (1995).

A broader study of foundation stories (especially of conquest) in the ancient Near East, the Greco-Roman, and the Islamic worlds can be found in McCants (2012).

Part Five. Eros and the Labors of Love

For the *Epic of Gilgamesh*, see translation, introduction, and notes by Dalley (2000) and George (2003a); George (2003b) is the latest critical edition of the cuneiform text with extensive commentary.

For "King Snefru and the Oarswomen," see Blackman (1988), with a hieroglyphic transcription of the hieratic text, and English translations by Parkinson (1997), 102–127, and by W. K. Simpson in Simpson (2003), 16–24. See German study and translation of the text in Lepper (2008), especially 36–40.

For the *Story of the Two Brothers*, see Gardiner (1932), ix–x, 9–30, with a brief presentation of the text and hieroglyphic transcription of the hieratic; see also translation and comprehensive study by Hollis (1990) and translation by E. F. Wente in Simpson (2003), 80–90.

For the book of Genesis, see translation and commentary by Alter (1996). For the creation stories of Genesis, see also Carr (1996).

For the goddess Aphrodite, see comprehensive studies by Budin (2003) and Cyrino (2010). Olson (2012) provides a translation and commentary of the *Hymn to Aphrodite*. For the connections between Aphrodite's myths and Mesopotamian traditions, see Penglase (1994), ch.7.

About the character of Medea, see comprehensive study by Griffiths (2005). For tragedy and myth, see essays by R. Buxton in Woodard (2007), ch.4, and J. Alaux in Dowden and Livingstone (2011), ch.7.

For Lucretius' poem *De rerum natura*, see Gale (1994).

For the full translation of Virgil's *Aeneid* and extensive notes, see Ahl (2007). For Virgil's *Aeneid*, see also studies by Hardie (1986), Bloom (1986), Cairns (1989), and Reed (2007). On Virgil's *Eclogues*, see Breed (2006).

For Apollodoros' *Library*, see new translation with introduction and notes by Hard (1997).

For Ovid's *Ars Amatoria*, see study by Sharrock (1994) and essays in Gibson, Green, and Sharrock (2006). For Ovid's *Metamorphoses*, see translations (with introduction and notes) by Melville (1986) and Ambrose (2004). See studies by Brooks (1970), Solodow (1988), Hardie (2002), and Fantham (2004). For the theme of metamorphosis in Greek myths, see Forbes Irving (1990), and for metamorphoses in Ovid and in later cultures and contexts, see Warner (2002). For Ovid's *Heroides*, see Spentzou (2003) and Lindheim (2003).

For Plutarch's *Parallel Lives*, see translation and commentary by Romm and Mensch (2012) and study by Duff (2000). For Theseus, see studies by Calame (1990) and Walker (1995) and archaic iconography in Ganz (1993) chs. 8–9.

For Statius' *Achilleid*, see new translation by Shackleton Bailey (2004). About the gender of Achilles in Statius' work, see Heslin (2005).

For a full translation and notes on the *Golden Ass*, see Walsh (1994). See also study by Graverini (2012), especially ch.4 on some Carthaginian features of Apuleius' story. For the Psyche and Cupid story in the *Golden Ass*, see Kenny (1990) and essays in Binder and Merkelbach (1968).

A study of the poetics of love in ancient Greece can be found in Calame (1999). An anthology of Greek and Roman erotic poetry, with introductions and notes, is contained in Bing (1991). For a survey of sexuality in the Greek and Roman world and its study, consult Skinner (2005) and different positions represented in the works of Dover (1989) and Davidson (2007). Hubbard (2003) offers a collection of texts related to Greek and Roman homosexuality in English translation. For women in Greek myth, see essay by S. Lewis in Dowden and Livinsgtone (2011), ch.23.

Part Six. Death and the Afterlife Journey

For the *Epic of Gilgamesh*, see translation, introduction, and notes by Dalley (2000) and George (2003a); see George (2003b) for the latest edition of the cuneiform text with extensive commentary. For the *Descent of Ishtar*, see translations and introductions in Dalley (2000) and Foster (1995), 78–84; for the descents of Inanna and Ishtar, see also Penglase (1994), ch.2.

For the "Great Hymn to Osiris," see complete English translation by Lichtheim (1976), 81–86; see also Allen (1974), 203–204 (who classifies it as *Book of the Dead* spell 185A). More recent translations are by Barucq and Daumas (1980), 91–97, no. 11 (in French), and Assmann (1999), 477–482, no. 213 (in German). For Osiris and mortuary practices, see Shaw (2004), ch.7, and for the myth of Isis and Osiris, Pinch (2004), ch.10.

For the *Book of the Dead*, see Allen (1974); for the hieroglyphic text of the papyrus of Nebseni, see Lapp (2004), pl. 21, and for the papyrus of Nu, Lapp (1996), pls. 22–23. Translations can be found in Barguet (1967), 142, a French translation of the variant in the papyrus of Nebseni, and Allen (1974), 85, an English translation of the variant in the papyrus of Nu.

For Plutarch's *Isis and Osiris*, the basic tool is still the text, translation, and commentary by Griffiths (1970); see also comments in Pinch (2004), 115–116, and Shaw (2004), 115–118.

For the Hittite *Telipinu* story, see other *mugawar* myths translated by Hoffner (1998). For the Mediterranean practice of lamenting for a departed god, see Alexiou (2002), 55–82, and Suter (2002), 229–236. For a comparative view of Greek myth and ritual and Hittite *mugawars*, see Burkert (1979), 123–142, and Bremmer (2008), 303–338.

For Odysseus' *katabasis* and its comparison with other myths, see Louden (2011), ch.9. See also comparison with other Near Eastern ideas of the "Beyond" by N. Marinatos and N. Wyatt in Dowden and Livingstone (2011), ch.20.

For the *Hymn to Demeter*, see translations and notes by Shelmerdine (1995) and Athanassakis (2004), comprehensive study by Suter (2002), and translation, commentary, and interpretive essays in Foley (1994); see also the collection of interpretive essays on the *Hymns* in Faulkner (2011). For a comparative study of the *Homeric Hymns* and Mesopotamian myths, see Panglase (1994), especially ch.6 on Demeter. For the connection between initiation and myth, see essay by Dowden in Dowden and Livingstone (2011), ch.26.

For the Orphic Gold Tablets and their eschatology, see Graf and Johnston (2007) and essays by world specialists in Edmonds (2011), including a chapter on their similarity to the Egyptian *Book of the Dead* by T. Dousa. A broader study about afterlife ideas in the Gold Tablets, Plato, and Aristophanes can be found in Edmonds (2004). See also collection of short essays on Orphism, many of them about the Tablets, in Herrero de Jáuregui et al. (2011).

For a comprehensive study of the mythological figure of Cybele and her cult, see Borgeaud (2004). For Arnobius' work, see study by Simmons (1996).

For Ovid's *Metamorphoses*, see full translation (with introduction and notes) in Melville (1986) and Ambrose (2004). See studies by Brooks (1970), Solodow (1988), Hardie (2002), and Fantham (2004). For the theme of metamorphosis in Greek myths, see Forbes Irving (1990), and for metamorphoses in Ovid and in later cultures and contexts, see Warner (2002). Detienne (1994) offers a structuralist interpretation of the myth of Adonis.

For the myth about Orpheus and Eurydice, see Graf and Johnston (2007), 172–174. A general study of the figure of Orpheus and its myths can be found in Segal (1989); see more recent German collection of papers in Maurer Zenck (2004) and short papers about all kinds of aspects of the Orphic tradition in Herrero de Jáuregui et al. (2011). For Virgil's *Georgics*, see Morgan (1999).

For the full translation of Virgil's *Aeneid* and extensive notes, see Ahl (2007). For further studies, see Hardie (1986), Bloom (1986), Cairns (1989), and Reed (2007).

For Cicero's *Dream of Scipio*, see Powell (1990). A student guide of the text is contained in Davis and Lawall (1988).

For a full translation and notes on the *Golden Ass*, see Walsh (1994). See also study by Graverini (2012). For the Psyche and Cupid story in the *Golden Ass*, see Kenny (1990) and essays in Binder and Merkelbach (1968).

For the recurrent motif of the "dying and rising gods" in the Ancient Near East, see Mettinger (2001), and for the representation of death in early Greek art and literature, see Vermeule (1979). A collection of articles (in Spanish) on the Afterlife in different cultures of the Mediterranean can be found in Martín Hernández and Torallas Tovar (2011); for Greek and Near Eastern ideas about the "Beyond," see Dowden and Livingstone (2011), ch.20, by N. Marinatos and N. Wyatt. Johnston (1999) offers a study of the interaction between the worlds of the living and the dead (as ghosts) in ancient Greek sources, and Bremmer (2002) explores ancient ideas about the immortal soul and other beliefs and practices connected with the afterlife.

Part Seven. Plato's Myths

There is no consensus on how to read Plato's dialogues, and interpretations of individual passages and works are the subject of ongoing debate, especially in terms of philosophy. For his use of myths, good starting points are Clay (2000), a good general introduction to the dialogues, Morgan (2000) for the study of the use of myth by Greek philosophers, and essays on Plato and myth in Collobert, Destrée, and Gonzalez (2012). See also ch.6 by D. Clay in Woodard (2007) and ch.9 by P. Murray in Dowden and Livingstone (2011). Another line of study of myth-making in Plato can be found in Brisson (1998) and Brisson (2004), ch.2.

The Atlantis myth and the Myth of Er have received special attention by myth and religion specialists. See, for instance, the structuralist reading of the Atlantis myth by Vidal-Naquet (1986), 263–284. A good translation and commentary of the Atlantis story alongside other utopias can be found in Clay and Purvis (1999). For the "Myth of Er" and its connections with Orphic and Pythagorean movements, see Kingsley (1995), Edmonds (2004), and essays in Edmonds (2011).

REFERENCES

✦

Ahl, F. (2007) *Virgil, Aeneid* (Oxford World's Classics). Oxford.

Alexiou, M. (2002, 2nd ed., revised by D. Yatromanolakis and P. Roilos) *The Ritual Lament in Greek Tradition*. Lanham, Boulder, New York, Oxford.

Allen, J. P. (1988) *Genesis in Egypt: The Philosophy of Ancient Egyptian Creation Accounts* (Yale Egyptological Studies 2). New Haven, CT.

Allen, J. P. (2005) *The Ancient Egyptian Pyramid Texts* (SBL Writings from the Ancient World 23). Atlanta.

Allen, Th. G. (1974) *The Book of the Dead or Going Forth by the Day: Ideas of the Ancient Egyptians Concerning the Hereafter as Expressed in Their Own Terms* (Studies in Ancient Oriental Civilization 37). Chicago.

Alter, R. (1981) *The Art of Biblical Narrative*. New York.

Alter, R. (1996) *Genesis: Translation and Commentary*. New York and London.

Ambrose, Z. Ph. (2004) *Ovid, Metamorphoses (Translation, Introduction, and Notes)*. Newburyport, MA.

Asheri, D., A. Lloyd, and A. Corcella (edited by O. Murray and A. Moreno) (2007) *A Commentary on Herodotus Books I–IV*. Oxford.

Assmann, J. (1999, 2nd ed.) *Ägyptischen Hymnen und Gebete* (Orbis Biblicus et Orientalis). Freiburg and Göttingen.

Astour, M. C. (1967, 2nd ed.) *Hellenosemitica: An Ethnic and Cultural Study in West Semitic Impact on Mycenaean Greece*. Leiden.

Athanassakis, A. (2004, 2nd ed.) *The Homeric Hymns: Translation, Introduction, and Notes*. Baltimore.

Athanassakis, A. (2013) *The Orphic Hymns: Translation, Introduction, and Notes*. Baltimore.

Attridge, H. W., and R. A. Oden (1981) *Philon of Byblos: The Phoenician History. Introduction, Critical Text, Translation, Notes* (Catholic Biblical Quarterly Monographs 9). Washington, DC.

Bachvarova, M. (forthcoming) *From Hittite to Homer: The Anatolian Background of Greek Epic*. Cambridge, UK.

Barguet, P. (1967) *Le livre des morts des anciens égyptiens* (Littératures anciennes du Proche-Orient 1). Paris.

Barnstone, W., ed. (1984) *The Other Bible: Ancient Esoteric Texts Including: Jewish Pseudoepigrapha, Christian Apocrypha, Gnostic Scriptures, Kabbalah, Dead Sea Scrolls*. San Francisco.

Barucq, A., and Fr. Daumas (1980) *Hymnes et prières de l'Égypte ancienne* (Littératures anciennes du Proche-Orient 10). Paris.

Baumgarten, A. I. (1981) *The Phoenician History of Philon of Byblos: A Commentary*. Leiden.

Beard, M., North, J., and Price, S. (1998) *Religions of Rome. (Vol. 1: A History. Vol. 2: A Sourcebook)*. Cambridge, UK.

Bernabé, A. (2003) *Hieros logos: poesía órfica sobre los dioses, el alma y el más allá.* Madrid.

Bernabé, A. (2004) *Poetae Epici Graeci Testimonia et Fragmenta* Pars II: Fasc. 1. *Orphicorum et Orphicis similium testimonia* (Bibliotheca scriptorum Graecorum et Romanorum Teubneriana). Munich and Leipzig.

Betegh, G. (2004) *The Derveni Papyrus: Cosmology, Theology, and Interpretation.* Cambridge, UK.

Bierling, N. (1992) *Giving Goliath His Due: New Archaeological Light on the Philistines.* Grand Rapids, MI.

Binder, G., and R. Merkelbach, eds. (1968) *Amor and Psyche.* Darmstadt.

Bing, P. (1991) *Games of Venus: An Anthology of Greek and Roman Erotic Verse from Sappho to Ovid* (The New Ancient World). New York.

Bispham, E. (2012) *The Roman Republic, 264–44 BC.* London and New York.

Black, J. and Green, A. (1992) *Gods, Demons and Symbols of Ancient Mesopotamia (An Illustrated Dictionary).* Austin, TX.

Blackman, A. M. (ed. by W. V. Davies) (1988) *The Story of King Kheops and the Magicians. Transcribed from Papyrus Westcar (Berlin Papyrus 3033).* Reading, UK.

Bloom, H., ed. (1986) *Virgil* (Modern Critical Views). New York.

Boardman, J. (1999, 4th ed.) *The Greeks Overseas: Their Early Colonies and Trade.* London.

Borgeaud, Ph. (2004; French 1996) *Mother of the Gods: From Cybele to the Virgin Mary.* Baltimore and London.

Breed, B. W. (2006) *Pastoral Inscriptions: Reading and Writing Virgil's Eclogues.* London.

Bremmer, J. N. (2002) *The Rise and Fall of the Afterlife.* New York.

Bremmer, J. N. (2008) *Greek Religion and Culture, the Bible, and the Ancient Near East.* Leiden.

Briant, P. (2002) *From Cyrus to Alexander: A History of the Persian Empire.* Winona Lake, IN.

Brisson, L. (1998; French 1994) *Plato the Myth Maker.* Chicago.

Brisson, L. (2004; German 1996) *How Philosophers Saved Myths: Allegorical Interpretation and Classical Mythology.* Chicago.

Brooks, O. (1970, 2nd ed.) *Ovid as an Epic Poet.* Cambridge, UK.

Brown, J. P. (1995, 2000, 2001) *Israel and Hellas* (3 vols.) (Beihefte zur Wissenschaft vom Alten und Neuen Testament 231, 276, 299). Berlin and New York.

Broze, M. (1996) *Les aventures d'Horus et Seth dans le Papyrus Chester Beatty I: mythe et roman en Égypte ancienne* (Orientalia Lovaniensia Analecta 76). Leuven.

Bryce, T. (2002) *Life and Society in the Hittite World.* Oxford.

Bryce, T. (2005, 2nd ed.) *The Kingdom of the Hittites.* Oxford.

Bryce, T. (2006) *The Trojans and Their Neighbors: An Introduction.* New York.

Budin, S. (2003) *The Origins of Aphrodite.* Bethesda, MD.

Burkert, W. (1979) *Structure and History in Greek Mythology and Ritual* (Sather Classical Lectures 47). Berkeley, CA.

Burkert, W. (1985) *Greek Religion.* Cambridge, MA.

Burkert, W. (1992; German 1984) *The Orientalizing Revolution: Near Eastern Influence on Greek Culture in the Early Archaic Age.* Cambridge, MA.

Burkert, W. (2004) *Babylon, Memphis, Persepolis.* Cambridge, MA.

Cairns, F. (1989) *Virgil's Augustan Epic.* Cambridge, UK.

Calame, C. (1990) *Thesee et l'imaginaire athenien: Legende et culte en Grece antique.* Lausanne.

Calame, C. (1999; Italian 1992) *The Poetics of Eros in Ancient Greece.* Princeton, NJ.

Calame, C. (2003; French 1996) *Myth and History in Ancient Greece: The Symbolic Creation of a Colony.* Princeton and Oxford.

Carr, D. M. (1996) *Reading the Fractures of Genesis: Historical and Literary Approaches.* Louisville, KY.

Charpin, D. (2010; French 2008) *Reading and Writing in Babylon.* Cambridge, MA and London.

Clay, D. (2000) *Platonic Questions: Dialogues with the Silent Philosopher.* University Park, PA.

Clay, D., and A. Purvis (1999) *Four Island Utopias: Plato's Atlantis, Euhemeros of Messene's Panchaia, Iamboulos' Island of the Sun, Sir Francis Bacon's New Atlantis.* Newburyport, MA.

Clay, J. S. (2003) *Hesiod's Cosmos.* Cambridge, UK.

Cline, E. (2009) *Biblical Archaeology: A Very Short Introduction.* Oxford.

Colarusso, J. (2002) *Nart Sagas from the Caucasus: Myths and Legends from the Circassians, Abazas, Abkhaz, and Ubykhs.* Princeton, NJ.

Collier, M., and S. Quirke, eds. (2004) *The UCL Lahun Papyri: Religious, Literary, Legal, Mathematical and Medical* (BAR International Series 1209). Oxford.

Collobert, C., P. Destrée, and F. J. Gonzalez, eds. (2012) *Plato and Myth: Studies on the Use and Status of Platonic Myths* (Mnemosyne Supplements 337). Leiden and Boston.

Coogan, M. D., and M. S. Smith (2012, 2nd ed.) *Stories from Ancient Canaan.* Louisville, KY.

Cornell, T. J. (1995) *The Beginnings of Rome: Italy and Rome from the Bronze Age to the Punic Wars (c.1000–264 BC).* London and New York.

Cross, F. M. (1998) *From Epic to Canon: History and Literature in Ancient Israel.* Baltimore.

Csapo, E. (2005) *Theories of Mythology* (Ancient Cultures). Malden, MA.

Cyrino, M. S. (2010) *Aphrodite* (Gods and Heroes of the Ancient World). London and New York.

Dalley, S. (2000, 2nd rev. ed.) *Myths from Mesopotamia: Creation, The Flood, Gilgamesh, and Others.* Oxford.

Davidson, J. N. (2007) *The Greeks and Greek Love: A Radical Reappraisal of Homosexuality in Ancient Greece.* London.

Davis, S., and G. Lawall (1988) *Cicero's Somnium Scipionis (The Dream of Scipio)* (A Longman Latin Reader). White Plains, NY.

Day, J. (2000) *Yahweh and the Gods and Goddesses of Canaan* (Journal for the Study of the Old Testament Supplement). London and New York.

Derow, P., and R. Parker, eds. (2002) *Herodotus and His World: Essays from a Conference in Memory of George Forrest.* Oxford and New York.

Detienne, M. (1986; French 1981) *Creation of Mythology.* Chicago.

Detienne, M. (1994) *The Gardens of Adonis.* Princeton, NJ.

Dever, W. G. (2006) *Who Were the Early Israelites and Where Did They Come From?* Grand Rapids, MI.

Dieleman, J., and W. Wendrich, eds. (2008-) *UCLA Encyclopedia of Egyptology* (http://escholarship.org/uc/nelc_uee). Los Angeles.

Doak, B. R. (2013) *The Last of the Rephaim: Conquest and Cataclysm in the Heroic Ages of Ancient Israel* (Ilex Series 7). Cambridge, MA.

Dougherty, C. (1993) *The Poetics of Colonization: From City to Text in Archaic Greece.* Oxford.

Dougherty, C. (2005) *Prometheus* (Gods and Heroes of the Ancient World). London and New York.

Dover, K. J. (1989) *Greek Homosexuality.* Cambridge, MA.

Dowden, K., and N. Livingstone, eds. (2011) *A Companion to Greek Mythology.* Malden, MA.

Duff, T. (2000) *Plutarch's Lives: Exploring Virtue and Vice.* Oxford.

Dunbar, N., ed. (1995) *Aristophanes: Birds.* Oxford.

Edmonds, R. III, (2004) *Myths of the Underworld Journey in Plato, Aristophanes, and the 'Orphic' Gold Tablets: A Path Neither Simple Nor Single.* Cambridge, UK.

Edmonds, R., III, ed. (2011) *The Orphic Gold Tablets and Greek Religion: Further Along the Path.* Cambridge, UK.

Edmunds, L., ed. (1990, 2nd rev. ed. forthcoming) *Approaches to Greek Myth.* Baltimore.

Ehrlich, C. S., ed. (2009) *From an Antique Land: An Introduction to Ancient Near Eastern Literature.* Lanham, MD.

el-Hawary, A. (2010) *Worschöpfung: Die Memphitisch Theologie und die Siegesstele des Pije— zwei Zeugen kultureller Repräsentation in der 25. Dynastie* (Orbis Biblicus et Orientalis 243). Freiburg and Göttingen.

Errington, R. M. (2008) *A History of the Hellenistic World: 323–30 BC.* Malden, MA.

Erskine, A. (2001) *Troy between Greece and Rome: Local Tradition and Imperial Power.* Oxford.

Fantham, E. (2004) *Ovid's Metamorphoses.* Oxford.

Faulkner, A., ed. (2011) *The Homeric Hymns: Interpretative Essays.* Oxford.

Faulkner, R. O. (1973–1978) *The Ancient Egyptian Coffin Texts* (three vols.). Warminster, UK.

Feeney, D. (1999) *Literature and Religion at Rome: Cultures, Contexts and Beliefs.* Cambridge, UK.

Finkelstein, I., and A. Mazar, (2007) *The Quest for the Historical Israel: Debating Archaeology and the History of Early Israel* (Archaeology and Biblical Studies 17). Atlanta.

Finkelstein, I., and N. Na'aman, eds. (1994) *From Nomadism to Monarchy: Archaeological and Historical Aspects of Early Israel.* Jerusalem.

Foley, H. P., ed. (1994) *The Homeric Hymn to Demeter: Translation, Commentary, and Interpretive Essays.* Princeton, NJ.

Foley, J. M., ed. (2005) *Companion to Ancient Epic.* Malden, MA.

Forbes Irving, P. M. C. (1990) *Metamorphoses in Greek Myths.* Oxford.

Foster, B. (1995) *From Distant Days: Myths, Tales, and Poetry of Ancient Mesopotamia.* Bethesda, MD.

Freydberg, B. (2008) *Philosophy and Comedy: Aristophanes, Logos, and Eros* (Studies in Continental Thought). Bloomington, IN.

Galán, J. M. (2005) *Four Journeys in Ancient Egyptian Literature* (Lingua Aegyptia. Studia Monographica 5). Göttingen.

Gale, M. R. (1994) *Myth and Poetry in Lucretius.* Cambridge, UK.

Gantz, T. (1993) *Early Greek Myth: A Guide to Literary and Artistic Sources* (2 vols.). Baltimore and London.

Gardiner, A. H. (1932) *Late-Egyptian Stories* (Bibliotheca Aegyptiaca 1). Brussels.

George, A. R. (2003a, 2nd rev. ed.) *The Epic of Gilgamesh.* London.

George, A. R. (2003b) *The Babylonian Gilgamesh Epic: Introduction, Critical Edition, and Cuneiform Texts* (2 vols.). Oxford and New York.

Gibson, R., S. Green, and S. Sharrock (2006) *The Art of Love: Bimillennial Essays on Ovid's Ars Amatoria and Remedia Amoris.* Oxford.

Goodman, M. (2012, 2nd ed.) *The Roman World 44 BC–AD 180.* London and New York.

Graf, F. (1993) *Greek Mythology: An Introduction.* Baltimore.

Graf, F. (2009) *Apollo* (Gods and Heroes of the Ancient World). London and New York.

Graf, F., and S. I. Johnston (2007, 2nd rev. ed. 2013) *Ritual Texts for the Afterlife: Orpheus and the Bacchic Gold Tablets.* London and New York.

Graverini, L. (2012; Italian 2007) *Literature and Identity in The Golden Ass of Apuleius.* Columbus, OH.

Green, A. R. W. (2003) *The Storm-God in the Ancient Near East* (Biblical and Judaic Studies 8). Winona Lake, IN.

Green, P. (1997) *Apollonios Rhodios, The Argonautika: The Story of Jason and the Quest for the Golden Fleece (Translation with Introduction and Notes).* Berkeley, CA.

Griffiths, E. (2005) *Medea* (Gods and Heroes of the Ancient World). London and New York.

Griffiths, J. G. (1970) *Plutarch's De Iside et Osiride (Edited with an Introduction and Translation).* Cambridge, UK.

Gundlach, R., and K. Spence, eds. (2011) *Fifth Symposium on Egyptian Royal Ideology. Palace and Temple. Architecture—Decoration—Ritual* (Königtum, Staat und Gesellschaft früher Hochkulturen 4, 2). Wiesbaden.

Guthrie, W. K. C. (1952) *Orpheus and Greek Religion.* Princeton, NJ.

Hall, J. (2007) *A History of the Archaic Greek World, ca. 1200–479 BCE.* Malden, MA.

Hallo, W. W., and K. L. Younger, eds. (1997) *The Context of Scripture. Volume 1: Canonical Compositions from the Biblical World.* Leiden.

Hard, R. (1997) *Apollodorus. The Library of Greek Mythology* (Oxford Worlds' Classics). Oxford.

Hardie, Ph. (1986) *Virgil's Aeneid: Cosmos and Imperium.* Oxford.

Hardie, Ph. (2002) *Ovid's Poetics of Illusion.* Cambridge, UK.

Herrero de Jáuregui, M. (2010) *Orphism and Christianity in Late Antiquity.* Berlin and New York.

Herrero de Jáuregui, M., et al., eds. (2011) *Tracing Orpheus: Studies of Orphic Fragments (In Honor of Alberto Bernabé)* (Sozomena: Studies in the Recovery of Ancient Texts 10). Berlin and Boston.

Heslin, P. J. (2005) *The Transvestite Achilles: Gender and Genre in Statius' Achilleid.* Cambridge, UK.

Hoffner, H. A., Jr. (1998, 2nd ed.) *Hittite Myths* (SBL Writings from the Ancient World 2). Atlanta.

Hollis, S. T. (1990) *The Ancient Egyptian "Tale of Two Brothers":* The Oldest Fairy Tale in the World (Oklahoma Series in Classical Culture 7). London.

Hornung, E. (1999) *History of Ancient Egypt: An Introduction.* Ithaca, NY.

How, W. W., and J. Wells (1989–1990, 2nd ed.) *A Commentary on Herodotus: With Introduction and Appendices.* Vol. 1 (Books 1–4), Vol. 2 (Books 5–9). Oxford.

Hoyos, D. (2010) *The Carthaginians.* Oxon and New York.

Hubbard, T. K., ed. (2003) *Homosexuality in Greece and Rome: A Sourcebook of Basic Documents.* Berkeley, CA.

Jacobsen, T. (1976) *The Treasures of Darkness: A History of Mesopotamian Religion.* New Haven and London.

Johnston, S. I. (1999) *Restless Dead: Encounters between the Living and the Dead in Ancient Greece.* Berkeley, CA.

Johnston, S. I., ed. (2004) *Religions of the Ancient World: A Guide.* Cambridge, MA and London.

Junker, K. (2012) *Interpreting the Images of Greek Myths: An Introduction.* Cambridge, UK.

Kaldellis, A., and C. López-Ruiz (2009) *BNJ* 790, "Philon of Byblos" (*Brill's New Jacoby,* I. Worthington, ed., online edition).

Kenny, E. J. (1990) *Cupid and Psyche.* Cambridge, UK.

Kingsley, P. (1995) *Ancient Philosophy, Mystery, and Magic.* Oxford.

Kuhrt, A. (1995) *The Ancient Near East, c. 3000–300 BC* (2 vols.). London and New York.

Laks, A., and G. Most, eds. (1997) *Studies on the Derveni Papyrus.* Oxford.

Lane Fox, R. (2008) *Traveling Heroes: Greeks and Their Myths in the Epic Age of Homer.* London.

Lapp, G. (1996) *The Papyrus of Nu (BM EA 10477)* (Catalogues of the Books of the Dead in the British Museum 1). London.

Lapp, G. (2004) *The Papyrus of Nebseni (BM EA 9900)* (Catalogues of the Books of the Dead in the British Museum 3). London.

Larsen, M. T. (1996) *The Conquest of Assyria: Excavations in an Antique Land.* London and New York.

Latacz, J. (2004) *Troy and Homer: Towards a Solution of an Old Mystery.* Oxford.

Leick, G. (1991) *A Dictionary of Ancient Near Eastern Mythology.* London and New York.

Leick, G., ed. (2007) *The Babylonian World.* Abingdon and New York.

Lepper, V. M. (2008) *Untersuchungen zu pWestcar. Eine philologische und literaturwissenschaftliche (Neu-)Analyse* (Ägyptologische Abhandlungen 70). Wiesbaden.

Lichtheim, M. E. (1973) *Ancient Egyptian Literature. Volume I: The Old and Middle Kingdoms.* Berkeley, CA.

Lichtheim, M. E. (1976) *Ancient Egyptian Literature. Volume II: The New Kingdom.* Berkeley, CA.

Lindheim, S. H. (2003) *Mail and Female: Epistolary Narrative and Desire in Ovid's Heroides.* Madison, WI.

López-Ruiz, C. (2009) *BNJ* 784, "Laitos (Mochos)" (*Brill's New Jacoby*, I. Worthington, ed., online edition).

López-Ruiz, C. (2010) *When the Gods Were Born: Greek Cosmogonies and the Near East.* Cambridge, MA.

Louden, B. (2006) *The Iliad. Structure, Myth, and Meaning.* Baltimore.

Louden, B. (2011) *Homer's Odyssey and the Near East.* Cambridge, UK.

Markoe, G. E. (2000) *Phoenicians* (Peoples of the Past). London.

Martín Hernández, R., and S. Torallas Tovar, eds. (2011) *Conversaciones con la muerte: Diálogos del hombre con el Más Allá desde la Antigüedad hasta la Edad Media.* Madrid.

Maurer Zenck, C., ed. (2004) *Der Orpheus-Mythos von der Antike bis zur Gegenwart: Die Vorträge der interdisziplinären Ringvorlesung an der Universität Hamburg, Sommersemester 2003.* Frankfurt and Berlin.

McCants, W. F. (2012) *Founding Gods, Inventing Nations: Conquest and Culture Myths from Antiquity to Islam.* Princeton, NJ.

McKirahan, R. D., Jr. (1994) *Philosophy before Socrates: An Introduction with Texts and Commentary.* Indianapolis, IN.

Meiggs, R., and D. Lewis, eds. (1969) *A Selection of Greek Historical Inscriptions: To the End of the Fifth Century BC.* Oxford.

Melville, A. D. (1986) *Ovid, Metamorphoses* (Oxford World's Classics). Oxford.

Mettinger, T. N. D. (2001) *The Riddle of the Ressurection: Dying and Rising Gods in the Ancient Near East* (Coniectanea Biblica, Old Testament 50). Stockholm.

Miles, G. B. (1995) *Livy: Reconstructing Early Rome.* Ithaca, NY.

Miles, R. (2010) *Carthage Must Be Destroyed: The Rise and Fall of an Ancient Civilization.* London.

Montanari, F., A. Rengakos, and C. Tsagalis, eds. (2012) *Homeric Contexts: Neoanalysis and the Interpretation of Oral Poetry.* Berlin and Boston.

Moor, J. de (1987) *An Anthology of Religious Texts from Ugarit* (Nisaba 16). Leiden and New York.

Morales, H. (2007) *Classical Mythology: A Very Short Introduction.* Oxford.

Morgan, C. (2000) *Myth and Philosophy: From the Presocratics to Plato.* Cambridge, UK.

Morgan, L. (1999) *Patterns of Redemption in Virgil's Georgics.* Cambridge, UK.

Morris, S. P. (1992) *Daidalos and the Origin of Greek Art.* Princeton, NJ.

Most, G. (2006) *Hesiod* (Loeb Classical Library). Cambridge, MA.

Moyer, I. S. (2011) *Egypt and the Limits of Hellenism.* Cambridge, UK.

Nagy, G. (1998) *The Best of the Achaeans: Concepts of the Hero in Archaic Greek Poetry.* Baltimore.

Nicolet, C. (1980) *The World of the Citizen in Republican Rome.* Berkeley, CA.

Ogden, D. (2008) *Perseus* (Gods and Heroes of the Ancient World). London and New York.

Olmo Lete, G. del (1999) *Canaanite Religion According to the Liturgical Texts of Ugarit.* Bethesda, Md.

Olson, B. D. (2012) *The Homeric Hymn to Aphrodite and Related Texts: Text, Translation and Commentary* (Texte und Kommentare 39). Berlin and Boston.

Osborne, R. (1996) *Greece in the Making, 1200–479.* London and New York.

Pardee, D. (2002) *Ritual and Cult at Ugarit* (SBL Writings from the Ancient World 10). Atlanta.

Parker, S. B., ed. (1997) *Ugaritic Narrative Poetry* (SBL Writings from the Ancient World 9). Atlanta.

Parker, R. (2011) *On Greek Religion.* Ithaca, NY and London.

Parkinson, R. (1991) *Voices from Ancient Egypt: An Anthology of Middle Kingdom Writings.* London and Norman.

Parkinson, R. (1997) *The Tale of Sinuhe and Other Ancient Egyptian Poems: 1940–1640 BC.* Oxford.

Penglase, C. (1994) *Greek Myths and Mesopotamia: Parallels and Influence in the Homeric Hymns and Hesiod.* London and New York.

Pinch, G. (2002) *Egyptian Mythology: A Guide to Gods, Goddesses, and Traditions of Ancient Egypt.* Oxford.

Pinch, G. (2004) *Egyptian Myth: A Very Short Introduction.* Oxford.

Popko, M. (1995) *Religions of Asia Minor.* Warsaw.

Powell, J. (1990) *Cicero: On Friendship and The Dream of Scipio.* Wiltshire, UK.

Reed, J. D. (2007) *Virgil's Gaze: Nation and Poetry in the 'Aeneid.'* Princeton, NJ.

Rhodes, P. J. (2010, 2nd ed.) *A History of the Classical Greek World: 478–323 BC.* Malden, MA.

Romm, J., and P. Mensch (ed., comm., trans.) (2012) *Plutarch: Lives that Made Greek History.* Indianapolis and Cambridge, UK.

Saïd, S. (2011) *Homer and the Odyssey.* Oxford.

Seaford, R. (1996) *Euripides: Bacchae, with an Introduction, Translation and Commentary.* Warminster, UK.

Seaford, R. (2006) *Dionysos* (Gods and Heroes of the Ancient World). London and New York.

Seeher, J. (2011) *Hattusha—Guide: A Day in the Hittite Capital.* Istanbul.

Segal, C. (1989) *Orpheus. The Myth of the Poet.* Baltimore.

Segal, R. (2004) *Myth: A Very Short Introduction.* Oxford.

Simmons, M. B. (1996) *Arnobius of Sicca: Religious Conflict and Competition in the Age of Diocletian.* Oxford.

Simpson, W. K., ed. (2003, 3rd ed.) *The Literature of Ancient Egypt: An Anthology of Stories, Instructions, Stelae, Autobiographies, and Poetry.* New Haven, CT.

Shackleton Bailey, D. R. (2004) *Thebaid, Books 8–12. Achilleid* (Loeb Classical Library). Cambridge, MA.

Sharrock, A. (1994) *Seduction and Repetition in Ovid's Ars Amatoria 2.* Oxford.

Shaw, I., ed. (2000) *The Oxford History of Ancient Egypt.* Oxford.

Shaw, I. (2004) *Ancient Egypt: A Very Short Introduction.* Oxford.

Shelmerdine, S. (1995) *The Homeric Hymns.* London.

Skinner, M. B. (2005) *Sexuality in Greek and Roman Culture* (Ancient Cultures). Malden, MA.

Smith, M. S. (1994) *The Ugaritic Baal Cycle (Vol.1): Introduction with Text, Translation and Commentary of KTU 1.1–1.2* (Supplements to Vetus Testamentum 55). Leiden.

Smith, M. S. (2001) *The Origins of Biblical Monotheism: Israel's Polytheistic Background and the Ugaritic Texts.* Oxford.

Smith, M. S. (2002, 2nd rev. ed.) *The Early History of God: Yahweh and Other Deities of Ancient Israel.* San Francisco.

Smith, M. S. (2010) *The Priestly Vision of Genesis 1.* Minneapolis, MN.

Smith, M. S., and W. T. Pitard (2009) *The Ugaritic Baal Cycle (Vol. 2): Introduction with Text, Translation and Commentary of KTU/CAT 1.3–1.4* (Supplements to Vetus Testamentum 114). Leiden.

Snell, D. C., ed. (2005) *A Companion to the Ancient Near East.* Malden, MA and Oxford.

Soggin, J. A. (1999) *An Introduction to the History of Israel and Judah.* Philadelphia.

Solodow, J. B. (1988) *The World of Ovid's Metamorphoses.* Chapel Hill, NC.

Spentzou, E. (2003) *Readers and Writers in Ovid's Heroides: Transgressions of Genre and Gender.* Oxford.

Stafford, E. (2011) *Herakles* (Gods and Heroes of the Ancient World). London and New York.

Strauss, L. (1996) *Socrates and Aristophanes.* Chicago.

Suter, A. (2002) *The Narcissus and the Pomegranate: An Archaeology of the Homeric Hymn to Demeter.* Ann Arbor, MI.

Taracha, P. (2009) *Religions of Second Millennium Anatolia* (Dresdner Beiträge zur Hethitologie 27). Wiesbaden.

Thomas, R. (2000) *Herodotus in Context: Ethnography, Science and the Art of Persuasion.* Cambridge, UK.

Van De Mieroop, M. (2007, 2nd ed.) *A History of the Ancient Near East: ca. 3000–323 BC.* Malden, MA.

Vermeule, E. (1979) *Aspects of Death in Early Greek Art and Poetry.* Berkeley,CA.

Vidal-Naquet, P. (1986; French 1981) *The Black Hunter: Forms of Thought and Forms of Society in the Greek World.* Baltimore.

Walker, H. J. (1995) *Theseus and Athens.* Oxford and New York.

Walsh, P. G. (1994) *Apuleius, the Golden Ass* (Oxford World's Classics). Oxford.

Warner, W. (2002) *Fantastic Metamorphoses, Other Worlds: Ways of Telling the Self.* Oxford.

Watson, W. G. E., and N. Wyatt, eds. (1999) *Handbook of Ugaritic Studies* (Handbuch der Orientalistik 39). Boston.

Weinfeld, M. (1993) *The Promise of the Land: The Inheritance of the Land of Canaan by the Israelites* (Taubman Lectures in Jewish Studies). Berkeley, CA.

West, M. L. (1971) *Early Greek Philosophy and the Orient.* Oxford.

West, M. L. (1983) *The Orphic Poems.* Oxford.

West, M. L. (1997) *East Face of Helicon: West Asiatic Eements in Greek Poetry and Myth.* Oxford.

West, M. L. (2011) *The Making of the Iliad: Disquisition and Analytical Commentary.* Oxford.

Willems, H. (1996) *The Coffin of Heqata (Cairo JdE 36418): A Case Study of Egyptian Funerary Culture of the Early Middle Kingdom* (Orientalia Lovaniensia Analecta 70). Leuven.

Woodard, R. D., ed. (2007) *The Cambridge Companion to Greek Mythology.* Cambridge, UK.

Wyatt, N. (2002, 2nd ed.) *Religious Texts from Ugarit: The Words of Ilimilku and His Colleagues* (Biblical Seminar 53). Sheffield, UK.

Yardley, J. C. (1997, 2012) *Epitome of the Philippic History of Pompeius Trogus/Justin; Translation and Appendices* (2 vols., commentary by W. Heckel). Oxford and New York.

Yon, M. (2006; French 1997) *The City of Ugarit at Tell Ras Shamra.* Winona Lake, IN.

Zanker, P. (1988) *The Power of Images in the Age of Augustus.* Ann Arbor, MI.

CREDITS

✦

Fig. 1 Borromeo / Art Resource, NY; Fig. 2 Borromeo / Art Resource, NY; Fig. 3 © The Trustees of the British Museum / Art Resource, NY; Fig. 4 © The Trustees of the British Museum / Art Resource, NY; Fig. 5 Erich Lessing / Art Resource, NY; Fig. 6 Universal Images Group / Art Resource, NY; Fig. 7 Erich Lessing / Art Resource, NY; Fig. 8 Scala / Art Resource, NY; Fig. 9 Courtesy of Dr. Zev Meshel, the excavator of the site; Fig. 10 Courtesy of Classical Numismatic Group, Inc.; Fig. 11 The Darius Painter (Greek, South Italian, Apulian), Volute Krater, detail, main scene, Side A, about 335–325 B.C., wheel-thrown, slip-decorated earthenware with incised inscriptions, height to top of volutes 36 5/16 in. (92.2 cm); width across volutes 21 7/8 in. (55.5 cm), Toledo Museum of Art, Gift of Edward Drummond Libbey, Florence Scott Libbey, and the Egypt Exploration Society, by exchange, 1994.19; Fig. 12 © The Trustees of the British Museum; Fig. 13 © SuperStock / SuperStock; Fig. 14 © The Trustees of the British Museum / Art Resource, NY; Fig. 15 bpk, Berlin / Muenzkabinett, Staatliche Museen / Art Resource, NY; Fig. 16 drawing from Josef Bühlmann, Die Architektur des klassischen Altertums und der Renaissance, published 1913, Paul Neff Verlag, Munich; Fig. 17 Private NYC Collection; Fig. 18 © Robert Harding Picture Library / SuperStock; Fig. 19 Augusta Raurica, Foto Susanne Schenker; Fig. 20 Erich Lessing / Art Resource, NY; Fig. 21 Archive Timothy McCarthy / Art Resource, NY; Fig. 22 © James Becker; Fig. 23 © Sheldan Collins/CORBIS; Fig. 24 Courtesy Regen Projects, Los Angeles, and Andrea Rosen Gallery, New York © Elliott Hundley.

INDEX OF PLACES AND CHARACTERS

✦

Editor's note about the index

— This index includes materials from translations, introductions, and footnotes. For reasons of economy it does not include *all* character and place names in the volume.

— "Passim" indicates that there are one or two pages in a sequence where the name does not appear. The broad geographical regions represented in this volume are not indexed (Greece, Egypt, Anatolia, Mesopotamia, Phoenicia, Roman world), nor are names in work titles (e.g., *Hymn to Demeter*) or in authors' names (e.g., Herodotos of Halikarnassos). Names in recurring epithets (e.g., "Kronos" in "Zeus, the son of Kronos") are also not included.

— Ethnonyms are embedded in place-names (e.g., Thebans under Thebes), unless they appear *only* as ethnonyms. Other names under which the character appears are specified in the general entry: for example, "Apollo (Phoibos)," "Achilles (son of Peleus)"; less obvious allusions or variants are specified by page.